TERPSICHORE AMIDST THE FORTY HILLS

A Historical Novel
of Wide Scope . . . . .

by

Erwin Gerald Swett

Robert D. Reed Publishers
San Francisco

ISBN 1-885003-23-4

Library of Congress Catalog Card No. TXu 766-813

First Edition

Robert D. Reed Publishers
San Francisco • 2000

DEDICATION

This book is dedicated to American veterans who were disabled while fighting for their country.

The dedication goes beyond words. Royalties the author receives will be donated to Disabled American Veterans for their health care.

>─┤◆►─O─◄►┤─◄

A glimpse at the plot

War destroys cities and disrupts lives. Nobody escapes the disasters of war. The victors in a battle rejoice with tears in their eyes. Victory is bitter-sweet. The victors cry over the loss of their dead comrades in arms. Victory is bitter-sweet. Tears flow as images of the battlefield flash before the victors' eyes. Such ghastly images! bloody body parts severed by shrapnel.

Vincent Armstrong, the protagonist in the story, is a World War II American veteran. A combat casualty, he is hospitalized for months in France. Eventually he is shipped home to the United States where he was discharged from a military hospital. But he is still in a state of shock. Haunted by the deadly memories of war, his movements are almost lifeless.

Someone once said that dance is the lifeblood of movement. Vincent Armstrong seeks peace of mind and renewed life as he joins a national dance studio and works to master the art of social dancing.

Margaret Duffus, M.A.

Contents

It should be noted that "Terpsichore Amidst the Forty Hills"* is unusual in two ways: It is a historical novel combining fiction with nonfiction. And the format does not lend itself to a usual 'table of contents.'

The novel consists of eight books; each contains a complete and authentic history of a traditional social dance: European, American, and Latin-American. By an innovative format the histories were spun into a fictitious story like threads woven into whole cloth. The themes vary, war and peace...satire and sex...and elements of crime.

Because of the complex nature of the various themes, the contents are limited to the page numbers of the Books and the dances, which are listed below for quick reference to the histories.

---

* Terpsichore symbolizes the Grecian mythical goddess of Dance.
  Forty Hills represents hilly San Francisco where many of the scenes occur.

Prologue

Come back here to the year 1950. You are just in time to sit in on a meeting between two men. A personnel director is about to interview someone who has applied for a position. Make yourself comfortable, but sit still—listen.

Interviewer: Give me your full name.
Applicant: Vincent Armstrong.
Interviewer: You have no middle initial?
Applicant: None.
Interviewer: What is your telephone number?
Applicant: Evergreen 6-0020
Interviewer: Your address is?
Applicant: 409 Arguello Boulevard.
Interviewer: Is that an apartment house?
Applicant: No; it's a residence. I live with my parents.
Interviewer: Hmm, I see. Then you must be single, or are you married?
Applicant: I'm single.
Interviewer: When were you born?
Applicant: February 22, 1924.
Interviewer: Well, well, you were born on the same day and month as George Washington. Now let me see, this is 1950 . . . (He does some quick arithmetic in his head.)
If I subtracted correctly, you are twenty-six and a half years old, give or take a few weeks.
Applicant: Correct.
Interviewer: I bet your friends never forget to wish you a happy birthday.

Applicant:	Don't bet on it. You'd lose. They frequently forget.
Interviewer:	That is surprising. One would expect them to be reminded by Washington's birth date.
	(With indelicate abruptness he breaks off the small talk.)
	Where were you born?
Applicant:	Right here in San Francisco.
Interviewer:	A native son! You certainly are a rare specimen these days.
Applicant:	There are still a few natives to be found among the forty hills.
Interviewer:	(Again he is abrupt.)
	Did you go to college?
Applicant:	Two years at Cal.
	(His ego forced an untruth. He had attended the University of California only one year.)
Interviewer:	What did you intend to be?
Applicant:	A teacher.
	(He really had had hopes of becoming a lawyer, but he felt it was simpler not to say so.)
Interviewer:	Did you receive an Associate in Arts degree?
Applicant:	(The prevaricating continues.)
	Oh, yes; I fulfilled all of U.C.'s requirements for an A.A.
Interviewer:	Then why didn't you go on and complete your education?
Applicant:	It's the same old story—money. Bethlehem Steel Corporation hired workers by the droves after World War II broke out. Few were experienced in shipbuilding. The high wages unskilled men were getting paid for defense work led me away from Cal into the shipyard.
	(To himself he says: "I can dream up phony answers just as fast as this character can ask personal questions. I wonder if Nosy would like to know how many times a week I pop my nuts.")
Interviewer:	Were you with Bethlehem Steel long?
Applicant:	No.
Interviewer:	Most likely you went into the service.
Applicant:	Tell me who didn't.
Interviewer:	The ones who were physically unfit.
Applicant:	You mean fellows classified 4-F by the draft boards.

Interviewer: That's right, 4-Fs. Once in a while they apply for a position with us; it never fails, they don't pan out. A person must be in first-rate physical condition to do the job we are offering. You look fit as a fiddle. Were you ever in actual combat?

Applicant: Yes.

Interviewer: By any chance did you get a medical discharge?

Applicant: (Perturbed by the question, he lies awkwardly.)
I was unlucky. I mean I was lucky. No!

Interviewer: You were fortunate, indeed, not to have been injured. Incidentally, are you working at present?

Applicant: No. I've been unemployed since last Thursday.

Interviewer: Before last Thursday where were you employed?

Applicant: (Now he is able to reply without stumbling, as this question was anticipated.)
I worked at the Crystal Palace Market.

Interviewer: For whom did you work?

Applicant: Melvin Torly. He operates a produce concession in the market.
(The truth is Melvin is not a former employer but a distant cousin, who had no objection to being used as a false reference.)

Interviewer: Why did you quit? Or were you laid off?

Applicant: I left of my own accord. I couldn't waste my life hawking fruits and vegetables.
(He volunteers a sincere comment.)
The opening your ad in the newspaper referred to sounds great. It really appealed to me.

Interviewer: Good.
(Subduing his elation with an air or importance, he thinks: "That man has a pleasant personality. He ought to be a money-maker. I hope he doesn't turn down the situation. Yet I better not seem too eager to employ him. He must be sold on the idea that it is a genuine opportunity.")
What other kind of work have you done?

Applicant: (To be consistent he brings up cousin Melvin again.)
None. I started working for Torly not long after I was discharged from the army.

Interviewer: Have you ever had ballroom dancing lessons in a studio or in a school?

Applicant:	(Wondering about the difference between the two terms, he is hesitant.) In a school or . . . studio—neither. But I do dance.
Interviewer:	Oh? You have had private ballroom dancing lessons.
Applicant:	Actually not.
Interviewer:	How did you learn to dance?
Applicant:	By watching others at dances. Also girl friends showed me some steps.
Interviewer:	So you really know how to dance.
Applicant:	Naturally. That is the reason I applied. (His answer leads to a baited question.)
Interviewer:	Do you consider yourself a pretty good dancer?
Applicant:	(Inwardly he cautions himself, "Watch it." He sees the bait but not the hook. "Modesty may spoil your chance.") My friends say that I have yet to be outclassed on a dance floor.
Interviewer:	(The reply is not so unexpected as it is irritating. He seeks relief in his thoughts, "Untrained amateurs give me a pain in my ear. The floor-scrapers pick up a few steps at a dance or at a party; then overnight they fancy themselves to be in the same league with Fred Astaire.") Mr. Armstrong, if you will recall, our ad said we were looking for trainees. It is standard procedure at National that new employees undergo a training program before they can qualify as teachers.
Applicant:	Just how long is the training program?
Interviewer:	Only six weeks, during which time you are simply a trainee. You will not be considered officially on the teaching staff until completion of the program. Does this arrangement meet with your approval?
Applicant:	It depends upon the salary.
Interviewer:	Salary! Trainees are not paid a salary. You will receive thousands of dollars' worth of free instruction and, as a bonus, an invaluable course in salesmanship. However, we do give you a food allowance.
Applicant:	I don't understand. Why?
Interviewer:	Because you will have to eat downtown, around here someplace. You'll be required to train evenings as well as afternoons. There won't be time to go home for

dinner, particularly in your case, since you live way out in the Richmond District.

Applicant: How much will I be allowed for meals?

Interviewer: The food allowance is fifteen dollars a week. You will receive a check every week for the duration of the training program. The management believes in fair play.

(Oddly when he mentioned the fifteen dollars, his voice sounded tight. One wonders if the money might be coming out of his own pocket instead of the studio managers'.)

As soon as you qualify as a teacher, you will be paid a dollar and a half for each hour you actually teach. The studio is open to students Monday through Saturday from two in the afternoon till ten at night. Excluding the dinner hour, you should be teaching seven hours a day. On a six-day basis you'll earn a weekly minimum of sixty-three dollars.

Applicant: I'll get at least that amount?

Interviewer: Provided you don't miss any teaching hours.

(Since much of the director's time was occupied with personnel, how could he be expected to know that students rarely can be supplied every hour of the day, that some often call up to cancel lessons or fail to arrive, and that teachers are not compensated for cancellations even though they must remain on the premises at all times?)

Applicant: Sixty-three dollars a week is something, I suppose. But I certainly want to earn a lot more.

Interviewer: Of course you do. The hourly rate paid for teaching is not the extent of your earnings. You can earn more from commissions.

Applicant: Commissions?

Interviewer: Let me explain. Every time you sell a dance course to somebody, or persuade a student of yours to buy more lessons, you receive a commission. Why only last month Jack Jones, a teacher with less than a year's experience, made almost four hundred dollars in commissions.

(The director omits to say, an oversight no doubt, that Jones had had a stroke of good luck. Never before had he earned a penny in commissions.)

By the way, by the time you are ready to teach advanced students, your hourly rate will probably be increased.

Applicant: By how much?

Interviewer: The first increase is fifty cents an hour. The next increase is . . . I'm not sure. I'll have to check the rate schedule. Whatever it is, the money you earn teaching is not to be sneezed at, but it is just the tip of the iceberg. There is potential for high earnings from the commissions one can make selling dance lessons, especially lifetime courses.

Applicant: Do many people buy dance courses for life?

Interviewer: You would be surprised.

Applicant: Are they expensive?

Interviewer: (With the smoothness of an experienced fisherman, he casts his few remaining lines.)

Lifetime courses are very expensive; they run into the thousands. That is what's great about it. The more you sell, the more you make. The sky is the limit. Believe me, in the long run you'll be well repaid for the time spent in the training program.

Applicant: How many times a week would I be attending classes?

Interviewer: Every day except Sunday. If your references don't take too long to check out, you stand a good chance of being enrolled in time for the next Training Class. It isn't too crowded; so they may try to squeeze you in with the new crop of trainees. What do you say? Shall we give it a whirl?

Applicant: (Boyishly he draws in his stomach and tightens his belt a notch.)

Okay. If I economize, I guess I'll have enough rations to survive six weeks.

(He accepts purely out of frustration over unfulfilled needs—rewarding work and exciting women. The prospect of fulfilling both needs, while engaged in such a pleasurable occupation as teaching women ballroom dancing, was thrilling to anticipate. Not to show the intensity of his feelings, he reaches for a cover.)

I'm curious about something. Before you asked me a question in which you implied that the words "school" and "studio" have different meanings. How do you define the two?

Interviewer: Frankly I haven't looked up the definitions in the dictionary. In the modern dance world, to my knowledge, one thinks of a "school" as a place where stage dancing such as ballet is taught, and of a "studio" as a place where social dancing such as ballroom is taught. The question is what should a place be called that teaches all forms of dancing.

Applicant: Maybe someone ought to invent a name for such a place.

(Still clinging to his cover, he poses another question.) In private and public school, rooms are called "classrooms." What do you call the rooms in a dance studio?

Interviewer: They also are referred to as "studios." I can see how that can be confusing in speaking of studios within a studio.

Applicant: That sounds almost as confusing as the color "red" and the past tense of the verb "read." Like in this sentence: The red book (color, communist, or what?) was read all over.

Interviewer: And for the present tense of "read" there is the same sounding word "reed," which not only is a bamboo-like grass but also is a musical instrument, such as an oboe or clarinet, fitted with a reed. English isn't all that cut and dried, is it?

Applicant: I agree.

Interviewer: Before I forget, I should inform you that we do not allow teachers to date students. Also, beyond professional courtesy, it is against the policy of National for a teacher or a trainee to become familiar with a student.

Applicant: How come? I'm afraid I don't follow you.

Interviewer: It's bad business to get cozy with the clientele. To say the least, familiarity breeds contempt. Besides, not all our students are single. Playing around with a married person inevitably leads to trouble. That's bad for business, too.

Applicant: (He attempts to sidetrack the point.) Where in the school are students taught to dance? Is there a separate place for the trainees?

Interviewer: Eventually all students receive instruction in the open ballroom across the hall. New students, especially the shy ones, are taught in the privacy of the small studios on the first and second floors. A large studio on the second floor is reserved for the Training Class. While on the subject, all studio doors have peepholes . . .

Applicant: Peepholes!

Interviewer: That's right, book-size, like the one over there at the entrance.

(A little oblong pane of clear glass, vertically inserted, can be seen within a frame on the door to his studio.)

Supervisors walking along the hallways occasionally look through the peepholes to see how the lessons are progressing. If any hanky-panky is going on, the teacher, man or woman, is ousted on the spot. After you've been here a while, you will undoubtedly hear from others about horny teachers who were fired for screwing around with their students. And you'll realize I gave you fair warning. Is my point clear?

Applicant: Uh-huh, clear as crystal.

Interviewer: Fine. Take this application form, fill it out, and leave it with the receptionist at the desk in the lobby. Don't forget to write in your Social Security number. Sorry, I must rush off. I'm due to give a dance analysis at two o'clock; it's already one minute past two. Come back next Monday morning.

Applicant: What time?

Interviewer: Around ten o'clock. I shall go into a little more detail regarding increases in hourly rates, your percentage of commissions, the possibilities of advancement, et cetera. Also, I shall answer any additional questions you may wish to ask. If no complications arise, I'll try to convince the management that you are qualified to become a trainee at National Dance Studios.

Amazingly there were no complications. What was even more amazing, the managers were convinced the applicant had special qualities. It took a considerable amount of convincing; nevertheless they were convinced, or so the personnel director told Vincent Armstrong.

BOOK ONE

Chapter 1

Elusively time had glided by at National Dance Studios. The fifth week of a training program for promising ballroom dancing teachers was in progress. Trainees had paired off to work on the tango. Practicing along with the other couples were Vincent Armstrong and his partner.

She was tiny, barely sixty inches high in her stockinged feet. A pair of delicate combs inlaid with artificial gems adorned her flowing honey-hued hair. The mixture of resin and green coloring in the paste tastefully matched the shade of her eyes, two nicely shaped almonds.

In silhouette she appeared to be a mere girl. But flat, toneless lines are misleading. Beyond a shadow of a doubt her birth certificate proved she was twenty-two, of nubile age—a woman.

Alice Scott was beginning to dance with professional grace. Aware of imperfections in her movements she exercised great care. Like a cautious forest nymph, her graceful figure moved around the waxed hardwood to the exotic strains of *La Cumparsita*, while on the record player at one corner of the studio a minute yet powerful needle tormented a writhing disc into releasing from its mass of swirls the voluptuous Latin-American music.

As she tangoed with her partner, she frowned unbecomingly—a habit she had whenever displeased. She kept silent several measures. Finally, unable to restrain herself, she expressed her feelings to her partner:

"Vincent! I'm having trouble following you. Come closer. I feel as if I were a dangling marionette with no human hands on her strings to guide her movements. Are you afraid you will crush me?

I won't break. It seems all the times it's our turn to dance together, you hold me too far away for a proper lead from your diaphragm.

"You should know by now in the tango and in the waltz and in the fox trot the man should stand close enough to his partner so that his diaphragm is tangent to her. It is hard for me to follow you. However slight, I need some pressure near or above my midriff. The pressure you apply to my back with the palm of your right hand is good, but it only helps me to follow when I move to the side or forward. In my backward movements all I'm doing is backing up against your hand. Each time you avoid body contact you weaken your lead.

"On top of that, I've noticed you keep staring at the ceiling instead of focusing your attention on me. See; you are looking up there again. What in heaven is so attractive about acoustical tile! You know how romantic, how expressive our dance director says the tango is supposed to be. The effect of the romantic feeling is lost when you're off in never-never land, and we continually tango miles apart. It simply ruins the mood. I never pictured you as the stand-offish type. For goodness' sake, what's bothering you?"

Alice looked so amusingly fierce with her eyebrows drawn together in a frown, Vincent had an urge to laugh. But he neither laughed nor answered. At the moment he was too absorbed with the intricacies of tangoing. He had just braced himself to lead her in the *media cortéz vuelta*, a tricky tango step new to him. It required all his concentration. Unsure of his footwork, he was having a hard enough time coordinating his movements without adding to the difficulty by attempting to converse as well.

"Nuts!" he ejaculated in annoyance. "I messed it up. My clumsy feet won't stay untangled. If it's the last thing I do, I'll master that step." With mannish determination he tightened his hold on his partner and said, "This time we will get it right."

"Never mind. I still am waiting for an explanation," demanded Miss Scott, frowning now so intensely a hidden defect in her almost perfect Grecian nose showed up.

Again Vincent was evasive: "In a minute," he said, "in a minute. Let's try it once more."

"No, uh-uh, not another step. Answer me first," Alice insisted. Not to be moved, she pulled her arms away, dug her hands into her hips, and planted her feet on the floor.

Her partner, convinced she would not budge unless he replied, spoke up without further delay: "Alice, ordinarily I dislike discussing my idiosyncrasies with others. But I guess I should make an exception in your case. After all, you and Bert are my buddies now; I felt close to the two of you from the first day we met in the Training Class. And last week, when you and he became engaged, neither of you had any qualms about discussing your personal affairs in front of me.

"You even asked my advice on how to deal with Bert's immature family. It was laughable to hear that they objected to their 'one and only child' wanting to marry you, 'a poor girl with runs in her stockings.' Since you confided in me, the sporting thing for me to do is to reciprocate.

"If you'll recall in our heart-to-heart talk, Bert, to your embarrassment, hinted how hot-blooded he is. You thought the little devil was kidding. Maybe he was and maybe he wasn't. Well, I am hot-blooded, and I kid you not. The reason I avoid diaphragm lead while dancing in closed position with you is that in bringing my body squarely up against yours, I get excited as hell. Need I tell you that you're not flat-chested in any shape, manner, or form."

At the man's reference to her anatomy, the woman clutched her jersey dress where her bosom could be exposed. She lowered her hand as soon as she felt assured the clasp she wore at the V of the low-cut neckline was not unfastened. If aware of Alice's modest interplay, Vincent discreetly gave no indication.

"Don't forget, Alice, I was also present in the Training Class the day our dance director showed us how an exhibition team styles the tango by exchanging intimate glances in steps like the Argentine walk. I find just doing the step exciting. But looking at you face to face romantically as I crouch and walk you backward in right parallel position is something else. When our eyes meet, I relive an unforgettable experience I had with a gal several years ago.

"Every time I bent over to kiss her, she'd tilt her head back eagerly and glare wild-eyed at me. Awe-stricken by her look, as I pressed my lips to her lips I would fix my eyes on hers and stare down into the depth of her pupils, deeper and deeper until I had the feeling I was rapidly being drawn into the cavity of a breath-taking whirlpool. It was the most thrilling sensation—almost as thrilling as penetrating a female's . . ."

"Hush!" Miss Scott exclaimed before her partner could utter another word. "I believe I have heard enough. Please, spare me the lurid details." Embarrassment caused her pale cheeks to redden.

"For cryin' out loud, Alice, I didn't mean to embarrass you. You asked me a question, and I was trying my level best to give you a straight answer. I got carried away; that's all. Understand one thing: in my candy store you are the sweetest thing there is. Still that doesn't alter the fact that you are a bit of a prude."

"How can you say that? Explain yourself, Mr. Armstrong, if you dare." Words came to her from a book she once had read: "'I am an incurable romantic,' not a prude."

"Very well, you have the notions of a romantic schoolgirl. But in the grown-up world it is a different story. From what I have perceived, you are too prudish to accept sex as a reality—of life or of romance. Bert, I hate to tell you, shares my opinion, too. Chatting with me over a highball the other night, he loosened up and expressed concern about your eventual honeymoon. He fears you may be so restrained it will be unpleasantly painful."

Alice recoiled, frowning more than ever. "What are you insinuating! Oh my, don't tell me. I don't think I want to hear (?)" She feigned a gesture as if to place her hands over her ears.

"Sorry you take offense at my bluntness," Armstrong said to soothe her. His tone, however, seemed more defensive than apologetic. Don't go jumping to the wrong conclusion. Fellows often talk openly to each other about gals without meaning to be disrespectful toward them." Vincent hoped he had convinced her nothing offensive was intended.

Her pride wounded, Miss Scott lashed out with a cutting remark: "The two of you have a nerve talking about me like that. I'm going to give Bert a piece of my mind. You just wait and see."

"Honest, Alice, he didn't mean anything. Promise me you won't mention it to him. He is liable to think I let him down, or lose trust in me. Why, oh why, did I open my big mouth!"

Vincent looked so abashed, Alice had to smile. "Well, I suppose I asked for it," she admitted, although the straightforward reply he had given her was an unexpected blow. "Don't worry; I won't say anything to Bert. I wouldn't want to spoil your friendship. I know he sometimes says foolish things. Anyway I love the little devil."

"I'm glad—very glad. . . . Speaking of diaphragm lead, Alice, I heard it isn't used at all dance studios. Some seem to place greater importance on the way the woman rests her right arm along the left of the man's. The pressure is supposed to be more constant, or something like that. Maybe we ought to ask our dance director about it."

"That's a good idea. Let's corner him the first chance we get. It should be interesting to hear his explanation. Just the same, Vincent,

I still can't see how you expect to lead your partner if you hold her at arms' length."

In better humor Alice now addressed Armstrong in the same patronizing manner an older sister would use in scolding a naughty brother: "Young man, you'd better stop thinking about that Jezebel who gave you the goofy stares. It won't be long before you'll be teaching women to dance. Leading your students in most of the dances will be awkward if you don't hold them fairly close. Besides, they'll probably be yakking a lot. You're a big boy and should realize it's impolite not to look ladies right in the eyes when they speak to you. How are you planning to get around that, my pet?"

To counteract Alice's address of sisterly belittlement, Vincent addressed her formally: "Miss Scott, I'll admit the predicament has crossed my mind. A consolation to me is that not all women attract me physically, and if one or two of my students should happen to arouse me . . ." As he swallowed his words, he glanced up at the ceiling awkwardly avoiding Alice's eyes. "Hell," he blurted out, "I'll—hell, I wil'—I shall fight each battle as I encounter it. At the moment I'm concerned with conquering the *media cortéz vuelta*."

Before the woman had an opportunity to challenge the man's procrastination, he stepped up to her in closed position, secured his hold on her, steered her out of the way of other trainees dancing nearby, and proceeded to tango. In his rush he barely missed bumping into two men who were dancing together. As they completed a delightful tango step, the *paseo ocho*, the short one of the pair, upon releasing his male partner, called to Alice and Vincent in a loud voice to be heard above the music:

"Now, now, kids, break it up. The buzzer is gonna go off any second." Bert Craig, Miss Scott's fiancé, loved to joke. "I smell smoke. You arsonists are burning holes in your shoes. Help! Fire! Save the shoe leather."

No sooner had Bert spoken when an electric device buzzed, signaling the end of the practice period. "Thar she buzzes," he cried out in fun. Imitating a sailor dancing a jig, Bert swung his arms alternately across his belly and back as he shifted from foot to foot. He stopped jigging to catch his breath yet continued his joking: "Cease and desist! Captain Craig's orders.

"We don't want to over-practice again. Save a little energy for later. It's time for our oral session. We don't want to be the last ones to arrive again. How many days have we been late?" He counted on his fingers: "Three days in a row, that's inexcusable. Enough is enough. Come on, you two. Let's be early for a change. If we don't show up on time today, Mr. Normand is gonna blow a fuse."

Perhaps most uninformed persons looking in on the Training Class before the end of the last scene would have thought it strange indeed to see stocky, bushy-haired Bert Craig dancing arms entwined with a member of his own sex. However, he had no choice; there were more males than females in the recent group of trainees; it was required the men take turns practicing with one another.

Finding women interested in becoming ballroom dancing teachers was difficult. The remuneration was uncertain if not inadequate. And the long hours called for were demanding: training in the mornings, teaching in the afternoons and evenings, attending Sunday sessions. Few women could be talked into being bogged down by such a confining routine purely for the love of dancing. Thus it was small wonder a shortage of female trainees existed.

Although the sight of grown men practicing like couples on a studio dance floor might appear ridiculous or even pointless to the laymen, to the professional this is a serious, meaningful business. When a woman spends exorbitant sums of money on ballroom dancing lessons, in return she should be given the best instruction possible. She would receive what she paid for only if her teacher could meet minimum qualifications: have the ability to follow as well as to lead, have good command of all dance steps offered in a course, and be informed of subtle differences between the footwork executed by the man and the woman.

To amplify, as a rule in ballroom dancing the woman's steps are performed with the opposite foot to the man's: beginning with the <u>left</u> foot, he takes alternate, forward steps (<u>left</u>-right-<u>left</u>-right and so on); beginning with the <u>right</u> foot, she takes alternate backward steps (<u>right</u>-left-<u>right</u>-left and so on). They step in opposition yet they move toward the same destination. The fantasy of the couple dance in the ballroom is that a man and a woman moving in different directions always reach an identical goal—joyfully. Were it only so in real life.

In spite of the fact that the woman follows the man's same patterns (into which he leads her), she executes some differently from him. To enable her to perform the exceptions in a distinctive feminine style, it is essential she be taught unique variants of certain dance steps.

Furthermore, a dance instructor who knows how to lead but not how to follow is limited in his teaching ability, because he lacks the skill to help a student solve the problems encountered in responding to lead. In other words, he is unable to call attention to errors she makes in following improperly, let alone explain how to correct them. Without question much of the value of her expensive lessons is lost in this case.

Obviously in the art of ballroom dancing, the preceding conclusions, or observations if you will, apply in reverse to a male student under the wing of a dance instructress.

Chapter 2

The buzzer having sounded, enthusiastic class members, anxious to be on time for the next phase of the training program, quickly departed. In their hurry, as they stepped out into a hallway, they left swinging behind them the solid doors at both exits of the spacious studio. The momenta of the double-swing doors were stopped and restarted by less spirited individuals slower to exit. Stamping suede oxfords and clicking calf pumps against battleship linoleum, young men and women marched down an L-shaped corridor to a smaller studio.

Here they were greeted by Ralph Normand, one of the supervisors. It was his job to familiarize trainees with standard studio procedures, to give trainees a working knowledge of jargon used by professional ballroom dancers, to instruct trainees in non-technical teaching principles (to make dances appear easy to learn), to teach trainees artful ways to handle students and prospects—and, last but not least, to expose the trainees to shrewd selling techniques.

Slumped in a chair beside his desk, Normand sat thumbing through a loose-leaf binder, his long legs stretched out with his feet resting on the heels of his shoes. To the front of him were rows of folding chairs, eighteen to be exact, as yet unoccupied. To his rear, set in a large wooden easel, was a blackboard on which was neatly chalked in plain print a topic outline of historical data pertaining to the up-to-date dances taught at National Dance Studios.

"Something new has been added," an arrival remarked as he nudged a companion to observe. Other arrivals entering the studio observed also.

In that the arrivals were crowding around the easel, Normand, balancing the open binder in the palm of his left hand, stood up and pulled his chair out of the way. Lazily arms were laid to rest upon sturdy shoulders like football players enclosed in a huddle. One by one positions were shifted until all the trainees had an unobstructed view.

Their scanning of the heads and subheads in the outline was soon cut short by the supervisor when he sent the trainees scurrying to their seats with the warning they were wasting precious time. After they settled down in their seats, he explained that the limited space on the blackboard had enabled him to put there no more than a schematic statement of the material to be covered. The outline, he suggested, might serve later as a mental crutch to help them remember the more complete facts to be presented now and in the future.

A frog formed in his throat; Normand cleared it, swallowing hard. He took a final glance at one of the pages before snapping shut the loose-leaf binder, which contained material he had prepared. For emphasis he tapped the blackboard with an edge of his binder.

"As the outline indicates, the subject matter we are about to deal with is the origin and development of today's social dances. It isn't normal practice for dance studios to concern trainees or teachers about such things. The story behind the dances is strictly a pet project of my own, which I am relating to you voluntarily. How much you absorb of what I relate is your business.

"But let's get something straight. At times certain confidences could be divulged to you. Also, my personal opinions may be expressed. Kindly don't carry any tales out of school. They have a way of getting back to me. If this happens, I will discontinue my lectures without the slightest hesitancy. Rest assured you shall be the losers, not I by a long shot."

The supervisor gave the group a challenging look and casually went on speaking. So nonchalant was his manner one never would have imagined he had just delivered an exhortation. Chairs creaked as interested occupants leaned forward to listen attentively.

"More than most people realize, the 'wheres and whens' and 'whys and ways' of the evolvement of the social dances is a tremendously large subject. Furthermore, it is not reduced an ounce of a pound by the fact that we won't be delving into roundelays and squares, except when we'll be touching upon them to show how they affected the rounds. I can see by the number of heads being scratched that these terms are muddy to most of you. I shall wash away your bemuddlement at once.

"To begin with, the term 'social dance' is a catchall into which have been put recreational dances, from all countries, performed by both sexes. Now that that has been cleared up, I'll define the social dances I mentioned a minute ago; they are three distinctly different types. If you like, you may take down the definitions. Whoever needs paper and pencil will find some in those cardboard boxes at the corner of my desk. Help yourselves, but quickly."

In order to quell his impatience Normand strummed his fingers on his binder while he waited until everybody was ready to write, then he said, "So you won't have trouble keeping up with me, I shall dictate slowly:

> A roundelay is any European folk dance which males and females perform encircled by others. Hands clasped the circlers spread out and face the performers in the center. Or all turn outward to dance in the formation of a circle with couples, each pair facing the Line of Dance.

"Instead of writing out that term let's be professional and use its abbreviation L.O.D. Incidentally, if by now anyone here doesn't know we dance in a circular line opposite to the direction in which the hands of a clock rotate, you are in the wrong place. To continue,

> A square is any American folk dance which an even number of males and females perform under the guidance of a caller. The dance takes the form of two lines, a circle, or the usual square or squares, that is, one or more sets of four couples.

"Am I going too fast?" asked Normand. "Raise your hands if you want me to slow down. Would you like me to explain something?"

"Yes, I would," came a shout from the last row of seats. To attract the supervisor's attention, Bert Craig was waving his hand like a flag blowing in the wind. "What does a caller say?"

"You needn't be concerned about it, Mr. Craig. What a caller says is of course important; it sets the mood for the dancers. What is most important is a caller's timing. The words, the figures, the music—all should be synchronized. Calls and movements vary in different regions of our country. Time doesn't permit me to go into the variations." Normand laid his binder on his desk.

"Nevertheless, to answer your question"—he pulled out the top drawer and removed a book on square dance—"I shall read a few lines from a typical call, Bachelor Mill, arranged by a Texan, Jimmy Clossin of El Paso:

> Gents swing out, ladies swing in;
> Now, you're heading against the wind.
> Ladies swing out, gents swing in;
> Now, you're heading home again.
> Stir up the dust and sweep out the sand,
> Plant your 'taters in a sandy land,
> Promenade your Partners 'round,
> Square your sets and settle down.

"So much for the squares and roundelays. Now we come to the rounds, the social dances with which we are specifically concerned. I am sure all of you are familiar with rounds. Don't shake your heads in doubt. They are the commonly known ballroom dances. Probably what throws you is that they do not have all characteristics in common. Simply defined,

> A <u>round</u> is any social dance which males and females perform independently in separate pairs. For the most part a couple are closely embraced, dancing in unison under the male's guidance as they travel counterclockwise in and around a ballroom—or wherever.

> Certain rounds are distinguished by other things. Some rounds are performed in open position. Some are performed in place. Some are exhibited in the corners of a dance floor.

"I should caution you that the definitions of the social dances I have given you are general, and obviously brief. However, they will do as a starter for the purpose of our study. Be aware, too, that while roundelays and squares are prearranged formation dances requiring teamwork among the couples, rounds are performed by individual couples dancing on their own spontaneously. In the old-fashioned round such as the varsoviana and schottische, the man must conform to a fixed pattern. In the modern round, or ballroom dance if you prefer, he is free to lead his partner into whatever figure strikes his fancy.

"The excellent patterns of the modern rounds contribute to first-class styling. Each round is special and serves individually as an outstanding representative of its kind. The originals are classics. So greatly are they appreciated in America and abroad as well, they are setting standards for other dances in their class. Rounds have advanced beyond social dance to stage and screen. A case in point is the exhibition ballroom dancing witnessed in the flawless art form of Fred Astaire—a master beyond compare—and one of his terpsichorean partners, Ginger Rogers. Anybody with a degree of expertise should be able to recognize the classics among the ballroom dances.

"At separate hours I intend to expound totally on the classics—no punches pulled, one round at a time." Normand grinned at his play on words; a few trainees chuckled. "My talks of necessity will cover in toto all North and South American dances currently performed by everyone (who can dance or attempts to) in the halls and clubs, private and public, across the land. Today I shall familiarize you with the beginnings of dance in general. The next day I shall discuss the waltz. At later sessions I'll go into the fox trot, and so forth."

The preliminaries disposed of, the supervisor seated himself, opened his binder, and adjusted it to reading distance. Before commencing to lecture from the reference at hand, he referred the class to the topic outline on the blackboard. Printed in capital letters was the all-inclusive title of his lectures. Directly below was a subtitle indicating a specific subject, the one about to be discussed.

Chapter 3

A HISTORY OF THE CLASSIC BALLROOM DANCES

Prelude to the Dance

Despite prohibitive decrees and anathemas, the ageless art of dancing has been passed down to us by the spoken and written word through myths and chronicles across the world. The Dance belongs to every country as well as to every period. All peoples, whether ancient or modern or barbarous or civilized, have shed tears of joy and sorrow over this prized possession. Countless lives have been regulated by it. No matter how often reconstructed, with old parts or new, like the wheelwork of a finely adjusted clock, the delicate movements of the Dance run continually in time with its era.

Prophesying about the restoration of Israel, the Hebrew prophet Jeremiah, who rebuked the nation for idolatry, said (Jer. 31:4, 5, 13):

> Again I will build thee, and thou shalt be built, O virgin of Israel: thou shalt again be adorned with thy tabrets, and shalt go forth in the dances of them that make merry.

> Thou shalt yet plant vines upon the mountains of Samaria: the planters shall plant, and shall eat them as common things.

> Then shall the virgin rejoice in the dance, both young men and old together: for I will turn their mourning into joy, and will comfort them, and make them rejoice from their sorrow.

Thus in biblical times choreography was not merely a form of worship but also a way of life. An agricultural people, the tribes of Israel arranged dances for the hour of planting and the hour of harvesting. Via the dance ritual the Israelites rejoiced at births, grieved at burials. They danced during circumcision, puberty, and marriage rites. After wars women did victory dances; in peace maidens did wooing dances. A dance was performed for all hours of the day.

Pertinent words of *Koheleth* (the "Preacher"), the son of David, King in Jerusalem, expressed a mood of the times which affected the Hebraic way of life (Eccles. 3:1, 4):

> To every thing there is a season, and
> a time to every purpose under the heaven:
> A time to weep, and a time to laugh;
> a time to mourn, and a time to dance.

While the Egyptians had dances round the clock, too, choreographic art usually functioned as a mainspring in the religious rites of the hierarchy. Pharoah—high priest, mighty king—was the revered emblem of the son-god Ra. On an ancient monument unearthed in Egypt has been found this inscription: "O Ra! in thine egg, radiant in thy disk, shining forth from the horizon . . ."

The Egyptians attributed sunrise or sunset to Ra who was believed to boat each day over the celestial Nile from horizon to horizon, a hazardous voyage. To safeguard the worshipped god of light against hazards such as solar eclipse, Pharoah would ballet ritualistically around his temple walls to stave off the forces of darkness. Sun worship since time immemorial had inspired circular movement in dance.

Related to Ra ritualism was the mystical Dance of Stars: a ballet in which priestly dancers (the stars), led by the king-priest, circled an altar (the sun) to demonstrate the motions of the celestial bodies, sacred secrets entrusted to king and priest. This ritualistic portraiture of the stars dancing round the sun was aesthetic but unscientific.

Mystifying the ignorant population through deceit, the priesthood pretended that supernatural ability was required to perform the astral dance. In turn the Egyptian priests were deceived by their own ignorance; they thought the stars were fireballs flung furiously from the demonic bowels of the earth up into the sky.

Across the Mediterranean Sea, with the passage of time, mysticism was put into question by Greek philosophers. Meanwhile mythological thought had become dominant in Greece. The myth-minded Greeks placed dancing in a godly domain on a cultural pedestal amidst the rest of the fine arts. Grecian mythology immortalized Terpsichore—goddess of the Dance. Her attribute the cithara, she was also an adored muse of lyric poetry. So, in ancient Greece where belief was prevalent that gods imparted the arts of life to men, it was only natural dancing was idolized as poetry in motion.

In Homer's <u>Iliad</u> (an epic poem, twenty-four books long, about the siege of Troy) at the end of the eighteenth book the lame artisan-god Hephaestus, who taught men metalworking, forges a suit of armor for the youthful hero Achilles, to Greeks a model not only of strength and valor but also of beauty and chivalry. The artisan-god decorates Achilles' shield with various scenes from life. Dancing is naturally the motif of one scene:

> There, too, the skilful artist's hand had wrought,
> With curious workmanship, a mazy dance,
> Like that which Daedalus in Cnossus erst
> At fair-haired Ariadne's bidding framed.
> There, laying each on other's wrists their hand,
> Bright youths and many-suitored maidens danced:
> In fair white linen these; in tunics those,
> Well woven, shining soft with fragrant oils;
> These with fair coronets were crowned, while those
> With golden swords from silver belts were girt.
> Now whirled they round with nimble practised feet,
> Easy, as when a potter, seated, turns
> A wheel, new fashioned by his skilful hand,
> And spins it round, to prove if true it run:
> Now featly moved in well-beseeming ranks.
> A numerous crowd, around, the lovely dance
> Surveyed, delighted; while an honoured Bard
> Sang, as he struck the lyre, and to the strain
> Two tumblers, in the midst, were whirling round.

Without a background in the literature of ancient Greece equal to Edward Earl of Derby, who in 1864 rendered the <u>Iliad</u> into English blank verse, none of us can be expected to understand Homeric passages completely. What we should look for in the "Shield of Achilles" are reflections of attitudes Grecians held toward the Dance. We see that their dance and song were almost as inseparable as one's body and voice. And sound accompanying movement resulted in romantic rhythms inspirational to the poet in his verse.

Still any reflection in the "Shield of Achilles" may easily be distorted if proper light is not shed on the <u>Iliad</u>. It was not a popular poem but a court poem, composed to be sung in the palaces of the Grecian aristocracy. For the commonality to join in song at court was ungodly. When Homer spoke of an ordinary Greek in relation to an aristocrat, the poet's language by contrast expressed sheer scorn for the commoner. In the second book of the Iliad a character Thersites, portrayed as a personality with an unpleasant temper and a penchant for argument, was degraded as the ugliest, most scurrilous type of human being imaginable. A member of the Greek army in the Trojan War, he is the only common soldier mentioned in the Iliad.

The brilliant satirist Lucian of Samosata (born circa 120 A.D.) voiced Grecian sentiment about dancers in his dialogue "Of Pantomime": Like Calchas (supreme augur in the first book of the Iliad), the dancer must be able to tell the past, the present, the future. The dancer must be able to cite the mythology of the classical Greek world from the time when it first emerged from formless Chaos down to the days of Cleopatra, shapely queen of Egypt. Also, and unquestionably, the dancer must be able to reproduce figures—all the noble spirits of Attica no less.

As for Roman mythology it appears to be nothing more than a poor imitation of Grecian mythology. The so-called Roman pantheon (state deities) while lacking the originality and quality of the Greek pantheon nevertheless is identified with it. The most original of the Latin deities is the war-god Mars who fathered Romulus, legendary founder and first king of Rome.

During Romulus' time, 753 B.C., the warmongering Romans considered devotion to dancing as an art form beneath the dignity of men. They should train their limbs to kill, not to dance: how else could men prove their reverence for god and state?

The second king of Rome, Numa Pompilius, was supplied a divine answer by his advisor Egeria, a goddess with whom he would have intercourse in the Muses' grove at night. She reminded him that Romulus had joined his soldiers in the *Bellicrepa saltatio* (a dance of conquest) after they raped the Sabine women. Since men did dance to celebrate, Egeria advised Numa to dignify the fact—exploit it.

For greater glorification of war, the dance art was thrust upon the cult of Mars. Twelve priests, their number probably derived from the ancient lunar year, were pressed into the god's service. It was their solemn duty to perform a sacrificial dance military in form. The soldier-priests were designated Salii, and the war dance Salian.

Headed by trumpeters, the Salii—Roman citizens of the first

rank—clad in red and purple tunics with gold embroidery, strutted proudly through the city to Mars' Temple atop the Palatine Hill. (Here rich, red-blooded Romans had feast and fun fit for the gods.)

The Salii paraded in full battle array: they also wore brazen apexed helmets and breastplates, and swords hung from their hips; they carried violin-shaped shields on their left arms and javelins in their right hands. Halting before an altar of the Temple, they clashed their shields and sang with raptures as they danced the sacred Salian in three measures.

At the same time one of the Salii drew his sword and proceeded to cut out the vital organs of some mortal, mere flesh and bones, who had the honor of dying as a Salic sacrifice; only if he were anti-Mars would he fail to endure the agony in silence. Next the soldier-priest, having sprinkled the honored mortal's blood on the altar, dutifully set fire to his lifeless body; the sweet stench of death was a simple gift, perfume for Mars' marble nostrils.

So well did the Salian serve the martial cause that thereafter the Salii embraced any form of dance useful in bringing offerings to all the different deities in the *Indigitamenta* (a Latin catalogue listing the godly statuary). The Romans as usual took such dance forms from the Greeks. But the former debauched dancing with bloodcurdling orgiastic stylization which the latter lacked the barbarism to conceive.

After the Roman Empire fell apart like badly cracked statuary and Christianity replaced paganism as the official religion in the fourth century, many pagan ritual dances seemed too valuable to eliminate from rites or ceremonies. For all that, the dance rituals of the Jews were legacies more highly valued by the early Christians. Georgory Nazianzen, a Cappadocian father of the Church, suggested in effect: Why dance like the pagan—to destructible idols—instead of—to an invincible god—the way King David did when he brought the ark to Jerusalem (Samuel 6:14, 15):

> And David danced before the
> Lord with all his might; and David
> was girded with a linen ephod.

> So David and all the house of
> Israel brought up the ark of the
> Lord with shouting, and with the
> sound of the trumpet.

Thus within the confines of ecclesiastic function performers of the dance were sanctified. In all Christian churches a portion of the ground divided from the altar was elevated somewhat like a stage. Here, in imitation of the Levites of old, the priesthood of the new faith joined with the laity in various dance ceremonies; seldom if ever were the people not participants.

By the fifth century, however, religious dances had been reduced to slow and stately processional performances through town streets or around church altars. These processions were performed by colleges of priests, and only on occasion by laymen. Dancers outside the sacred walls of the church were excoriated: the clergy in implied words preaching, Do as I say—not as I do. Unable to comply with such hypocrisy, people danced where and how they pleased. As a consequence clergymen received substantial revenue selling dancing indulgences to conscience-stricken persons.

Could the procurement of church funds, to be shared with the Crown, have been the reason why in 554 Childebert I, King of the Franks, interdicted dancing throughout Frankish territories? Whatever the reason, dancing became discredited. Interdict followed interdict. A notable one issued in 744 by Pope Zachary, who succeeded Gregory III, banned dancing in the vicinity of all churches. Again, as late as the twelfth century Odon, Bishop of Paris, prohibited the Dance in his diocese.

Pontifical bans having stigmatized dancing for so many gloomy centuries, advancement of the art was impeded. During this period, well described as the Dark Ages, literature concerned with the fine arts fell into obscurity.

[On the last gloomy note Ralph Normand ended his Prelude to the Dance. The supervisor's tone now seemed somewhat somber as he spoke to the group of trainees: "Unhappily conceivable writings about the Dance perished as the result of some seven hundred years of cultural deprivation. It is really a shame because such writings might be very helpful in determining the source and origin of the waltz, our next subject.

"Not until the revival of arts and letters in Western Europe—two hundred years subsequent to the Italian *Risorgimento* (literally, "new arising," in the 1300s)—were rays of light shed upon the waltz. Still, records, too often obscure in the Middle Ages, are not always intelligible. That explains, also, why the waltz's lineage is a subject of much controversy.

"Moreover, a careful study of all the material on dancing which I could obtain convinced me long ago that frequently those who know do not write, and those who write do not know. In summary, with questionable data confusing the issue, I had no easy problem evaluating the different views historians hold in regard to the *fons et origo* of the waltz.

"That's it for today. Tomorrow we'll examine what is said to be the waltz's possible or probable sources and origins." Expressing his regret that he had no time to answer questions, the supervisor dismissed the trainees. The following day, not to miss a word, everyone arrived early for Normand's lecture.]

Chapter 4

A HISTORY OF THE CLASSIC BALLROOM DANCES

<u>European Dance</u>

I. The Waltz (to improve balance and turning ability)

Some historians maintain that in the sixteenth century Catherine de Medici, wife of Henry II of France, brought the waltz in its initial form from her native Italy to Provence. What she introduced was an Italian dance *la volta*, 'the turn.' Obviously the main figures consisted of turns, but leaps and lifts were included, too.

Immediately we have disagreement from a French nobleman Vincent Carloix. For thirty-six years he served as a secretary under a marshal in France, François de Scépeaux, Sire de Vieilleville. The secretary, who prepared the memoirs of the marshal's life (1509-1571), informs us that the real introducer of the waltz or volta to the Parisian court was the Comte de Sault, and he made the introduction in 1556. That year young Sault, a native of Provence, was attached to Sire de Vieilleville's suite.

But the validity of the information put forth by Vincent Carlois is doubtful. Experience has shown that the memoirs of sixteenth-century noblemen generally abound with errors and omissions.

Before discussing the volta any further, I must clear up an ambiguity. In many transcripts it is written mistakenly as "the lavolta" or "lavolta" because the foreign definite article <u>la</u> erroneously became telescoped into the substantive <u>volta</u> in England. Shakespeare made the faux pas in King Henry the Fifth, Act III, scene v, line 33:

They bid us to the English dancing-schools,
And teach "lavoltas" high and swift corantos;
Saying our grace is only in our heels,
And that we are most lofty runaways.

As would be expected, in France "volta" took on the spelling "volte." The dance became so Frenchified it lost some of its Italian flavor despite Catherine de Medici's measured instructions. An indelicacy preserved in the volte for a time was the way in which a man helped a woman do leaps into the air: to lift her he placed his hand well beneath the busk of her dress and pushed upward.

When the queen's son Henry III wore the crown, his favorite diversion was to dance the volte—with an imposing touch—at the court of Valois, French royal house. The Valois dynasty occupied the throne of France from 1328 till the assassination of Henry III in 1589.

It seems the wayward, immodest volte had superseded the decorous, modest basse danse once most popular with European noblemen. The basse danse was solemn and slow in nature; the partners, at times pantomiming graciously, danced to moderate triple time. They held hands as they stepped across the room, their feet kept low to the floor. On the other hand, the volte, light and gay, was comprised of involved turns, springy steps, and fancy lifts executed within an imaginary circle. Using such movements while turning to the left—if giddy then turning to the right—the partners, in close proximity, danced to lively triple time.

A detailed description of the volte can be found in an antique French book Orchésographie, a treatise in the form of a dialogue. On the title page is the caption, "Whereby all manner of persons may easily acquire and practice the honourable exercise of dancing." Interestingly a comparative claim, or words to that effect, by a chain of American dance studios often appears in today's advertisements: "Arthur Murray can teach you dancing in a hurry."

Discussed in the antique book are the recreational dances practiced in Europe throughout the fifteenth and sixteenth centuries. Modish along with the volte and basse danse were the nizzarda (a version of the volte danced in Nice), almain, bouffon, branle, canary, courante, gavotte, morisco, pavan, and the galliard—a merry dance of Roman descent. The volte was a galliard of a kind.

Orchésographie, the best of the rare works on dances of that period, was published in 1588 by Jehan Tabourot, Canon of Langres, under the pseudonym Thoinot Arbeau. (Since he was a priest, he had to hide his identity when he wrote on such a ribald subject as the

Dance.) Arbeau's instructions on how to dance the volte are pragmatic and of incalculable value to chroniclers as well as choreographers, but nothing is mentioned in <u>Orchésographie</u> to justify the assumption that the volte is the *avant-coureur* of the waltz.

Some experts claim the waltz's ancestry originated among the Eskualdunak, as the inhabitants of the basque country call themselves. Offered as evidence is a resemblance, puzzling however, between the basic waltz step and the *pas de basque*: a movement important to theatrical dancing, classic ballet, and folk dances such as the Boston Two Step of the British Isles, the Nebesko Kolo of Serbia, the Neapolitan Tarentella of Italy, the Tsiganochka of Russia—and, of course, the Fandango Arin-Arin of the Basque country.

Historically embracing seven provinces, this romantic area of the Pyrenees is contiguous to the Bay of Biscay and lies in northwestern Spain and southern France. It is thus not surprising that there are several *pas de basques*. Outstanding are the French, Russian, and Spanish. But the experts are vague as to which one they have in mind. Let us see if we can make heads or tails out of this cosmopolitan jigsaw puzzle.

Since the waltz is in triple time (three beats to the measure), the French and Russian *pas de basques*, which are customarily performed in duple time (two beats to the measure), can be set aside at once. The Spanish *pas de basque* is the one with the same time pattern as the waltz. By virtue of geographic location and choreographic traits peculiar to the Basques, it may be rightfully claimed that the Spanish is the original from which all other *pas de basques* developed. As a matter of fact, the Spanish *pas de basque* is a standard ballet step today. Therefore, of the various *pas de basques* the one from Spain is the most likely predecessor of the waltz.

Having moved that piece of the timeworn puzzle into place, we questioningly pick up the next piece: Which basic waltz step, a new one or an old one, is to be used in putting the pieces together: After 1860, Americans, copying the elaborate dance styles of the French, embellished the waltz with postures and motions borrowed from ballet. Also, in backtracking to the 1830s, we discover that the basic waltz step danced at assemblies in the States was, except for its simpler styling, similar to the one which has become standardized in modern ballrooms. All this being so, today's basic waltz step should bear as close a resemblance as any to the *pas de basque* utilized in ballet.

[The supervisor deviated from the history temporarily. "I do not wish to get technical. It is impractical, however, to make an objective comparison between the two steps any other way. Besides, since you are training to be teachers, the sooner you acquire a working knowledge of technical dance terms and fundamentals the better.

"As we know, the time pattern (three beats to the measure) of the *pas de basque* matches that of the waltz. What we have to puzzle out is whether their dance patterns match up, basically at least. Let us compare the two." The supervisor went to the front of his desk to demonstrate the steps while he spoke.

> To do a basic waltz step, one starts in first position:
> (1) on the first beat of the music he steps forward with the left foot;
> (2) on the second beat he steps side-oblique into second position with the right foot;
> (3) on the third beat he closes with the left foot so that his feet end up in first position.

For a man of his height (over six feet) Ralph Normand was surprisingly light-footed. The trainees, watching with wonder, were about to be surprised still further by his agility, which rivaled that of an acrobatic artiste if not a ballet dancer.

> To do a *pas de basque*, one starts in fifth position, left foot front:
> (1) on the first beat of the music he does a *demi-rond de jambe* and a *jeté*, that is, with the left foot close to the floor he describes a half-circle outward to the side and leaps upon that foot into second position;
> (2) on the second beat he does a *glissé*, that is, he slides the right foot diagonally into fourth position;
> (3) on the third beat he does an *assemblé*, that is, he brings his feet together, left toes up to right heel, so as to end up on fifth position.

"Although the directions I have given for the basic waltz step and *pas de basque* do not indicate progression, needless to say, in available space both can be danced progressively backward or forward, with or without turning. But obviously the same cannot apply to a jigsaw puzzle; just because the pieces can be moved around from one irregular space to another is no indication they fit, unless twisted into place perhaps.

"Suppose you do lack special training in technicalities of professional dancing, particularly in ballet. Still no one needs to be a ballet master—or mistress . . . pardon me, girls—to understand from the comparison of the two dance patterns that any resemblance between the *pas de basque* and the waltz is distorted indeed.

"By your pained expressions I gather some of you must be dying to hear more about foot positions used in dancing. Let's put it to a vote. Those in favor of my taking a moment to brief you on the fundamental positions of the feet before I continue the history of the waltz signify by saying, 'aye.'

"Sh-sh, not so loud. Is anybody opposed? No 'nays.' It's unanimous. The 'ayes' have it. A wise decision, why not have your cake and eat it, too. Learning dance fundamentals is essential to improving technique. The more you learn and improve, the better will be your teaching ability as well as your dancing skill."

The supervisor picked up a sizable pasteboard leaning against the wall behind him. Reversing the pasteboard so that the right side faced the trainees, he placed the object on the ledge of the easel which stood nearby. On its white surface the pasteboard had instructions charted in bold, black letters.

FOOT POSITIONS: Ballroom & Ballet

First Position ....Heels adjoined, toes out; feet form a V.

Second Position........Feet about twelve inches apart, heels parallel.

Third Position ....Left heel against right instep, or right heel against left instep.

Fourth Position ....Ballroom—Advance left or right foot a natural pace, or step back with either foot. Heels are aligned.

Fourth Position ....Ballet—Left heel about twelve inches ahead of and in line with right toes, or vice versa.

Fifth Position ....Left heel in front of and against right toes, or right heel in front of and against left toes.

In order to make sure everyone had a good view of the chart, Normand dragged the easel a short distance forward, closer toward the first row of seats. "As you can see, ballroom dancing and ballet have five primary positions of the feet in common. In the former the toes are turned out conservatively, 45 degrees at the most; whereas in the latter they are turned out extremely, as much as 180 degrees. Let me give you a teaching hint. Instruct beginners when they practice the ballroom foot positions to assume first position each and every time before attempting to go into any one of the other stances. In the long run it speeds things up, especially for slow learners.

"I shall fully explain all of this, and more, at our next technique session, where you will have an opportunity to study the chart at length. Until then, if you don't want to look pigeon-toed on the dance floor, remember no matter which position you are standing in, your toes should be turned outward. Now to return to the history."]

A few theoreticians would have us accept the evolution of the waltz from the minuet—or as the French say, "main-way," spelled m-e-n-u-e-t. The name *menuet*, actually a diminutive, was concocted from the word *menu*, "small"; for *pas menus*, "small steps," were ingredients of the dance. They were a variety of common Gallic *branles* ("shakes" or "dances") found in Poitou, a province of west central France from 1416 till about 1789, the year the Revolution began. *Branle de Poitou* was a provincial form of minuet danced by Poitevins, whose plain *pas menus* lacked sophistication.

In 1653 Louis XIV, a balletomane, minueted publicly in Paris to confer distinction on his court musician Jean Baptiste Lulli. Lulli, who excelled as a composer and arranger of ballet-opera, was the first to set the minuet to music. At court the dance despite its artlessness gained refinement plus complexity. Introduced into ballets, the minuet became classical in form.

Unlike the provincials' *pas menus* which were rash and robust, the courtiers' were deliberate and delicate. In the courtly minuet a man and a woman, using well-planned *pas menus*, punctiliously traced an abstract figure eight on the floor. This configuration was modified before long, however. By degrees dancing masters curved and angled the Line of Dance so that it underwent geometrical-like changes.

["I'll show you how on the blackboard. Let me pull the easel back. I need a little more room. First I better remove the chart. . . . That takes care of that. I was a bit crowded. Hold on one second longer. I'll just get a piece of chalk. All set, here we go. Observe the gradual transformation in the series of numbers and letters I write on the blackboard: the L.O.D. for minuet figures simply was changed from 8 to S—S to 2—2 to Z."]

The figure zee, a modification by the dancer Louis Pécourt, proved the most realistic change, and the most welcome. He succeeded Pierre Beauchamp, original maître de ballet at the Académie Royal in Paris, when the latter retired in 1687. Arranging the minuet along angular lines tied into less intricate figures, Pécourt simplified the choreography to an appreciable extent. His modified form of the complex minuets performed at ballets was ideal for court balls. Appropriately one of his arrangements was referred to as *Menuet de la Cour* ("Minuet of the Court").

Looking up the *menuet* in The Encyclopaedia of Dancing edited by Chas. d'Albert in 1914, we find, despite Pécourt's insertion of the simpler figure zee as a principal movement, the dance steps retained their complexities. Mark well that in the minuet, to use the anglicized name again, although steps are utilized through the performance they must be distinguished from movements. Besides the figure zee the dance consists of two other principal movements, paraphrased here for clarity and brevity:

The introduction—it is preceded by two reverences, one to spectators, one to partners; both times the gentleman bows while the lady curtsies. (Steps are danced after the reverences are completed.)

The finale—it is followed by two more reverences, one to spectators, one to partners; both times the gentleman bows while the lady curtsies. (Steps are danced before the reverences are initiated.)

At the commencement of the minuet a prelude of music is played; in eight bars each gentleman escorts his lady by the left hand to a predetermined starting place in the ballroom; he releases her hand as they stand side by side in readiness to perform the introductory movement. After the introduction the figure zee is performed. Next the finale is performed; the steps danced, the minuet ends with two reverences—no more, no less.

Stage and screen performances showing powdered-wig versions of minuets in which scene after scene cavaliers with swords dangling at the sides endlessly perform gallant bows as ladies with spreading fans in their dainty hands overdo demure curtsies are counterfeit productions, tinseled to pass off on unsuspecting audiences.

The minuet story of reverences may be entertaining, but it tells us nothing about the waltz; the part we really are interested in. Let us take another look at The Encyclopedia and see what develops. Now we are getting somewhere perhaps. We learn at least that the dance, composed of a great variety of subtleties and nuances blended into its components, cannot be performed without an understanding of four composite steps peculiar to the minuet:

(a) *Pas de Menuet a droite* ("Minuet step to the right"),
(b) *Pas de Menuet a gauche* ("Minuet step to the left"),
(c) *Pas de Menuet en avant* ("Minuet step forward"),
(d) *Balancé de Menuet* ("Minuet balance").

That techniques from ballet appear is to be expected. After all, the choreographers of the minuet were ballet masters. Four paragraphs of instructions involving technical terms and postures are devoted separately to a, b, c, and d—that is, one full explanatory paragraph for each step. Yet not a single sentence gives information which makes it possible to infer any connection between the minuet and the waltz.

Moreover, the positions and the music of the two dances are unconnected. In the minuet the partners dance apart to triple time; the music is majestic with the accent well marked on the first and third beats; on occasion the man and the woman take or give hands, their fingers held in an elegant manner. In the waltz the partners dance together to triple time; however, the music is gay with the accent well marked on the first beat only; for the most part the man holds the woman's right hand with his left, and his right arm encircles her waist.

A text of historical compilation published in 1895, Dancing by Lilly Grove and other writers, states on page 256, chapter viii, that the minuet was derived from the courante, one of the sixteenth-century court dances discussed in Orchésographie. Here we get into an imbroglio because it is also stated in the text, same page 256, that some scholars suppose the waltz to be a derivation of the courante—not the minuet.

What about the courante? Well, it was imported from Italy where the Italians fished the name out of corrente, a "stream." Why the courante was named indirectly from "stream" instead of directly from "fish" is hard to catch. Execution of the dance called for short advances and retreats with supple knee movements. All of which was prompted by the way wriggling fish dive-and-dart about in water. To claim that the waltz derived from the courante outweighs most fish stories no matter how the scales read.

On January 17, 1882, articles began to appear in a Paris journal, La Patrie, stating—with patriotic tones—conclusive proof exists the waltz was born in southeast France. The proof was a dance description found in a twelfth-century French manuscript, from which it was concluded not only that dance had to be la volte of Provence but also that la volte had to be the original waltz.

In Provence the dance said to be la volte was accompanied by a tune entitled Pallada. An excerpt from the description in the manuscript sounds impressive, especially in French:

. . . en danse, un movement lent sur les deux premiers temps de la mesure, et en bref sur la troisième; en musique, deux notes, une blanche et une noire, font une mesure en trois temps.

(". . . for the dance, a slow movement of the first two beats of the measure, and a brief one for the third; for the music, two notes, one white and one black, making one measure in three time.")

According to the journal *la volte* was introduced to Parisians November 9, 1178, long before Europeans other than Frenchmen knew the Provençal dance. Charmed by its figures, the people of Paris fell in love with *la volte,* and royalty honored it as the princess of ballroom dances at the court of Valois.

Readers skimming La Patrie are bound to miss holes in the journal's articles on the origin of the waltz. A careful look at the proof presented raises the question of credibility. Written in the twelfth century before the literary and artistic renaissance of France in the 1500s, the manuscript is medieval. We have already learned documents of that period are not always trustworthy. Beyond that the manuscript was not quoted by the journal as describing the waltz per se; conclusions merely were drawn about the dance from a skimpy description in one of the passages.

As for the notable year when dancing *la volte* was reportedly dignified by the French Royal family Valois, 1100 is a historical faux pas. Their reign did not begin till 1328—two centuries after the so-called original waltz was said to have been received at the court of Valois.

In 1895 in Paris—over a decade after La Patrie stirred up that city's citizenry with sensational news that the waltz was French—a professor G. Desrat came out with Dictionnaire de la Dance. Russia was recognized in the dictionary as being the country which had invented a popular waltz, *valse à deux pas.* Such recognition could not be denied because the professor had it on the authority of his own father, who was a reputable dancing master, that he had been present the very evening Baron de Neiuken, an attaché at the Russian legation, first demonstrated and sold the *valse à deux pas* to the French aristocracy at a grand ball back in the year 1839.

Curiously this Russian-style waltz, and the music accompanying it, fits in principle the description found in the twelfth-century manuscript referred to by La Patrie in 1882, thirteen years previous to the publication of Desrat's dictionary. But to bring up embarrassing, dead questions is undiplomatic. May the professor's intellect rest in peace.

["As up-and-coming dance teachers, or dancers, it is important that you understand there are differences in waltzes:

"Although the French were waltzing before 1839, they did a dance known as the *valse à trois temps* ('three-BEAT waltz') in which a step was taken for each beat in a measure.

"The *valse à deux pas* ('two-STEP waltz') danced by the Russian attaché was an innovation whereby two steps instead of three were taken to a measure. The first step, receiving two counts—slow, was long; the second step, receiving one count—quick, was short."

Normand could not resist an impulse to inject a little humor into his talk. *"En passant*—if you play chess, that phrase shouldn't confound you in the least. Due to lack of understanding either of French or of music sometimes the *valse à deux pas* was and still is referred to incorrectly as the 'two-beat waltz' (*valse à deux TEMPS*). Be informed that regardless of the number of steps a waltzer takes, the musical time for waltzes, three beats or counts to a measure, remains unchanged."]

Tactful words have been written concerning the relationship between the waltz and an attractive dance somewhat similar, the long-ago-popular redowa. Composed of exact, rapid movements, it was difficult to control for unaccomplished waltzers. Nevertheless, whether or not they could get along with even a plain waltz, the dancing crowd among the American public often attempted to overcome the redowa in the latter part of the 1800s. Allen Dodworth, the Arthur Murray of the nineteenth century, thus observed, "Our (America's) beautiful waltz of to-day (1885) is a subdued redowa."

The redowa had strong Czechish as well as Bohemian features. It had been breast fed around 1800 by Slavic mother dances in the western region of Czechoslovakia, then the kingdom of Bohemia. However, there is reason to believe the redowa also was suckled in prepartitioned Poland. For one thing, like the Bohemians and the Czechs, the Poles are Slavs. Furthermore, we learn from a once prominent French dancing master Cellerius who in 1847 wrote (in his Paris publication La Danse des Salons) that the redowa evolved from the Polish *pas de basque*. In fact, before it changed, almost beyond recognition, the *pas de basque* was the main step of the redowa originally rearranged for the drawing room in the 1840s.

The redowa had a twin. Although the twins were offspring of the same Bohemian folk dances, they were not identical and quite different in character, but both were refined types. By the year 1845 they had become favorites at salons in capital cities on the Continent.

One type was the *rejdovačka* danced to duple time like a polka. The other type was the *rejdovák* danced to triple time like a waltz.

It is natural that the prefixes are alike: the prefix *rej* is Czech for "round dance." A common name for the *rejdovák* was redova, usually spelled with a "w" instead of a "v"; hence the name redowa became the most familiar. Both Bohemian dance types immigrated to New York and traveled to other cities in the states. Wherever they appeared the *rej* twins infatuated Americans.

Unfortunately the two were often confused. The heart of the redowa had tripartite action: leap-slide-change, leap-slide-change, on and on. Such movements functioned well to regular waltz rhythm with a lively tempo. Abused by clumsy laymen who could not distinguish a waltzlike *rejdovák* from a polkalike *rejdovačka*, the redowa degenerated into an ugly two-step. To complicate things its beats were irregularly accented. Impaired, the redowa soon passed away.

[Bowing his head in a seriocomic manner, the supervisor addressed the trainees: "Let us pause momentarily to say a few words in memory of the *rej* twin. Led astray by wrong company, the redowa's susceptible heart was damaged by sinful ways such as indulgence in heavy lunges and inadvertence to sudden changes in weight, lessons to be learned but not to be practiced. Look at the broken-down redowa; listen to the evils that befell it:

"LEAP; it was leaped, too often lunged, with a s-t-r-e-t-c-h! (Properly the leap—on either foot, forward or backward— was supposed to be unabrupt and not abnormally lengthened.)

"SLIDE; it was slid in a r-u-s-h! (Properly the slide was supposed to be in time with the music: speed of the forward slide had to be adjusted in bringing toes of sliding foot up to heel of leaping foot; speed of the backward slide, as well, had to be adjusted in bringing heel of sliding foot up to toes of leaping foot.)

"CHANGE; it was made with a j-e-r-k! (Properly weight was supposed to be transferred smoothly from sliding foot to leaping foot.)

"For those uncertain about it, you should realize that the male in starting a leap-slide-change stepped left-right-left, next right-left-right—and so on. And the female in starting a leap-slide-change stepped right-left-right, next left-right-left—and so on.

"Peculiar to the redowa was a hereditary form of pursuit: the pursuing male cunningly chased the fleeing female; on occasion directions were reversed, and the female pursued the male. Couples, who misunderstood the pursuit, conspicuously leaned from side to side as they alternated from foot to foot doing leap-slide-changes. In redowaing the dancers used waltz position, waltz turns, waltz patterns. Just the same, despite the way the movements were led or followed, the waltz remained gently graceful as a gazelle, while the redowa turned out gawkily graceless as a gorilla."]

Lloyd Shaw, an American writer with expertise on the subject of folk dance who is considered to be a genius in the art, theorizes in The Round Dance Book (first printing December 1948), "Our standard waltz seems to have stemmed from the Redowa, a member of the Mazurka family." One paragraph on page 242 in his book refers to the folk mazurka or mazur danced as far back as the sixteenth century by the Mazures, a Polish tribe occupying at that time the duchy of Mazovia. Several other paragraphs in chapter seven, however, indicate Shaw had in mind the ballroom mazurka.

In any case, it is hard to reconcile Shaw's theory with the fact that the choreographer of the dance, Polish master Markowski, did not introduce the mazurka into the ballroom until 1851—at least six years after the redowa became popular with Parisians. What is more, plans for the waltz were drawn at least six hundred years before Markowski resided in Paris.

Despite the tons of arguments the weight of authority and evidence reinforces the stand that the waltz's lineage traces back as far as the Middle Ages (circa 1000 A.D.) to the *Drehtänze*, or "turning dances," and the *Springtänze*, or "leaping dances," which were cradled in the Alpine areas of Bavaria and Austria. "Indeed," the German historian Curt Sachs informs us, "the first dance description of modern Europe comes from Bavaria, just at the turn to the second millennium . . ." Dancing of that place and period was described figuratively in the Lay of Rudlieb, a masterpiece written in southern Germany:

> The youth springs boldly up, against him is his maiden.
> He is the falcon like; she glides like the swallow;
> No sooner are they near then they shoot past each other;
> He seizes her with ardor, but she flees his grasp.
> And no one who beholds them both could ever hope
> To equal them in dance, in leap or gesture.

This passage from the twelfth-century Rudlieb is a classic example of the couple dance footed in medieval times by the pastoral peoples of the Bavarian Alps (range of the Alps between the south of Bavaria in Germany and the Tirol in Austria). Each summer on the mountains and in the valleys hot-blooded youths—shepherds, tillers, boors—would pair off with flirtatious village maidens to foot springy gyrations wildly as minnesingers warbled lascivious love lays under the widespread branches of the *Linde*. A "lime tree" providing songsters and dancers shelter from the sun was a familiar sight in the midst of villages.

Since southern Germany and Upper Austria have a common boundary, either one could be the fatherland of the waltz. Crossing and recrossing the German-Austrian border for centuries, its restless ancestors had been sprung and gyrated in so many unknown places that not till 1521 are we able to pick up the trail of gyrators. That year Kunz Has, a mastersinger of Nuremberg, in a lyrical complaint clues us in on the movements of gyratory males and females:

> Ytzund tanzt man den wüesten Weller,
> Den Spinner, oder wie sies nennen.

> ("And now they dance the wild Weller,
> the Spinner, or whatever it is called.")

Mastersinger Has' information may not seem much to go on, but we have learned two important things: In that Spinner is in apposition to Weller, it follows that the dance's characteristic movements were made up of spins or, naturally, rapid turns.

["If any of you feel the second alternative is groundless, try to spin without turning. Please! don't get up from your seats. This is neither the time nor the place. Take a whirl around the main ballroom when you are free. Also in the process try to turn slowly and still keep on spinning."]

As to the name, Weller is an obsolete dance term for *Walzer*, the German substantive for "waltz." Forms of *Walzer*, with such meanings as "trundle" or "rolling motion," were used in Old High German. But the word *Walzer* was not applied to dancing till about 1750.

["I shall explain how in proper chronological order. Note that the infinitive form *walzen* is related to ancient words, Norse *velta* and Latin *vertere*, both of which mean "to turn."]

Besides Spinner, the Weller was also called Dreher; in fact, any German dance characterized by turns was known as a Drehtanz. Unfortunately technical descriptions are not available. However, Montaigne, the French philosopher and essayist, in his *Journal de Voyage de Michel de Montaigne* mentions having seen Bavarians performing turning dances in couples when he visited Augsburg in the year 1580.

Montaigne was intrigued by the way partners held each other. They danced strangely embraced with, of all things, their cheeks often touching as they turned: the man's hands were well placed on the woman's back; her hands were placed on his back as well. Through Montaigne's eyes we see that the Drehtanz was not only a couple dance but also a close round, that is, a social dance performed by a pair in closed position.

In sixteenth-century Germany two distinct classes of dancing existed—lower class and upper class.

The lower class included the circular and jumping, hopping, or skipping kinds: social dances commonly performed by the peasantry during summer in fields or streets. Obviously the Springtanz as well as the Drehtanz belonged to the lower class.

The upper class included the measure, or glide, and similar gliding kinds: social dances customarily performed by the nobility during winter in halls or palaces. The measure must have had an influence upon the Drehtanz, for a less rapid variety of it later developed in which steps were glided. In fact, the slower dance was called the Schleifer, or "glider" in English.

Both classes of dancing were accompanied by singing. Song and dance were led by an honored Vortänzer, "opener" of a dance who traditionally did so with a mug of beer or a glass of wine in his upraised hand. To be the Vortänzer was a distinction sought by peasant and nobleman alike.

A generation or so later, well into the 1600s, it was customary on an occasion of dancing to perform at the outstart die Allemande, "the almain," followed in due course by der Hüpfauf, "the upspring."

Slow and dignified, in duple time, the almain was referred to as an "opening dance" (ein Auftanz): all the couples, facing each other yet well apart at arm's length, performed in two orderly rows with men in one row and women in the opposite row.

In contrast the upspring brisk and informal, in triple time, was referred to as "a follow-up dance" (ein Nachtanz): now the couples closely embraced hopped round and round at random.

Do not be misled by der Hüpfauf, especially by the English translation "the upspring." While in name and step it sounds like a Springtanz, in character it is a typical Drehtanz. Because of its timing, three beats to a measure, the upspring was most often spoken of as the "Tripla."

After 1700 the almain, rather restrictive, lost favor with the outcome that the hitherto dependent *Tripla* was no longer bound to following a leading dance. Conventional ties between *Auftanz* and *Nachtanz* loosened, the *Tripla* along with other *Drehtänze* in general gained greater and greater freedom as independent dance movements.

Such independence is jubilantly expressed, by one of the earliest recorded references to waltz words, in a mid-eighteenth-century musical comedy <u>The</u> <u>Newly</u> <u>Revived</u> <u>and</u> <u>Inspired</u> <u>Bernardon</u>. It was written by Joseph Felix von Kurz, a famous Viennese clown who performed under the stage name Bernardon. In the second act he sang and danced to a piece entitled *"Walzer."* Here are his jubilant lyrics which illustrate the point:

> Bald walzen umatum
> Mit Herirassa drum!

Translated freely the lyrics read, "Soon we shall waltz round and round hazzaing!"

["A brief note in review about *Walzer*, its Germanic ancestor *Weller* together with other ancestral *Drehtänze* had appeared not only in Germany but also in Austria; some appeared as early as the eleventh century. Almost always the dances were identifiable by their strongest characteristics, namely: turning—<u>der</u> <u>Dreher</u>, spinning—<u>der</u> <u>Spinner</u>, gliding——<u>der</u> <u>Schleifer</u>, jumping—<u>der</u> <u>Hopser</u>, leading—<u>die</u> <u>Führung</u>, hopping—<u>der</u> <u>Hüpfauf</u>, or, for the timing, <u>Tripla</u>.

"Rotating rounds of these kinds were classified *Deutsche Tänze*, 'German Dances.' Collectively they represent the family that gave birth to the waltz, but not entirely."]

Now to turn to the most prominent of the *Drehtänze's* relations, a member of a large family of Austro-Alpine dances plurally called *Laendlerische Tänze*. It seems because of variations in spelling, not in styling, this relation had besides the singular surname <u>Laendlerische Tanz</u> such other names as <u>Ländla</u>, <u>Länderli</u>, <u>Länderer</u>—and <u>Ländler</u>, which attained the greatest prominence in the waltz world.

[Struck by a thought, the supervisor quickly left his desk in order to chalk on the blackboard the last four names he had just mentioned. "If you ever have the occasion to do any reading about folk dances in Austria or Germany, you probably will run across the sign of an umlaut, two little dots above a vowel as you see in each of the examples here; the dots are used to indicate a change in sound; however, an umlauted 'ä' can be written 'ae' or vice versa: this can be confusing to someone who doesn't know German.

"In spite of the language barrier sight and sound should leave no doubt in your minds that the different names I referred to were all formed with the same element <u>Land</u>. And it came from an early designation for Upper Austria, *Land ob der Enns*. Literally *Land* means 'country.'"]

Musically as well as choreographically <u>Laendlerische</u> <u>Tänze</u> had a strong influence on the waltzing movement. Discordant as it may sound, before 1800 a <u>Ländler</u> was performed with unwaltzlike leaps often covering two octaves. This is not jarring when we recall the ancestors of the waltz—both <u>Drehtänze</u> and <u>Springtänze</u>—roamed into Austria circa 1000 A.D. Through the centuries they had been turned and leaped to *landla Melodien* ("country tunes") in *das Landl*: an endearment Austrians use when speaking about a countryside—in particular the small, mountainous part of Austria above the Enns river.

Although *laendlerisch tanzen* originated in *das Landl*, its performance was not limited to that area. An alpine country dance, moreover a peasant's way of dancing, the *Ländler* was performed in just about all the rural districts. At each locality it generally underwent alterations in accordance with indigenous dance patterns. Local changes notwithstanding, clear-cut lines of the *Ländler* still can be seen across Austria in such places as the following:

> Salzburg, where <u>laendlerische</u> <u>tanzen</u> took on the form of the <u>Schuhplattler</u> due to the introduction of <u>Platteln</u>, rhythmic slaps by the male dancers on various parts of their bodies coordinated with snapping the fingers, clapping the hands, and stamping the feet—
>
> Tirol, where <u>laendlerische</u> <u>tanzen</u> took on the form of the <u>Haiss-plattler</u> (an intricate <u>Schuhplattler</u>) due to the addition of <u>Trestern</u>, males' leaping up into the air or their lifting the female dancers over head and shoulder—
>
> Styria, where <u>laendlerische</u> <u>tanzen</u> took on the form of the <u>Steyrischer</u> due to the practice of <u>Gstanzln</u>, singing of improvised stanzas by the male dancers after they interrupt the dancing to assemble at the middle of the <u>Tanzboden</u>, a "dance hall."

The style of the <u>Steyrischer</u>—that is to say, the <u>Ländler</u> as it was danced by Styrians—inspired the lyric, epic poet Nikolaus Lenau to write a poem which he named *"Der Steyertanz"*:

High o'er the maiden's head
Then raises he his arm;
His finger as a pivot,
She circles round about
Like strength to beauty joined.
How straight ahead he dances
In noble attitude,
And causes then the maid
Light whirling from the right
To glide beneath the left.
His nimble partner now
Must circle at his back,
Dance round and round about him
As if he wished to be
Encircled by his love,
As if he wished to say,
"Describe for me the circle
Of all my hopes and joys."
And now the blissful couple
Take hold each other's hands
And with a supple movement
Slip through each other's arms.
His eyes are fixed on her
And hers see only him.
Perhaps they mean to say,
Why can't we two, united
In one another's arms
Spend all our life together
In such a dance as this?

Nikolaus Lenau was a Hungarian who apparently had mixed emotions about Germany and Austria; he resided in Stuttgart and Vienna at different times from 1833 to 1843. A dreamer, he visualized perfect love when he observed Styrian dancers performing a *Laendlerische Tanz*. In his poetry he captured the ideal spirit of the Ländler. But as a rule a spirit no matter how idealistic cannot exist in a maddening world without imagination. A sensitive genius, Lenau became insane in 1844, and died six years later.

In reality peasants not poets performed *Laendlerische Tänze*. There was nothing poetic about the way the peasant clung to his dancing partner, his cheek glued to hers with sticky sweat. On hill and dale during the performance of a Ländler unimaginative peasants whistled loud and shrill and smacked their lips in imitation of the blackcock's mating call to the gray hen. The herdsman and the milkmaid carried on like a pair of love-performing mountain birds.

Music was provided by young peasants whose fathers had taught them how to play wind and string instruments, an alpine art passed down from father to son generation after generation. *Landla Melodien*—some measures in duple time, some in triple time—were played not just by ear but by eye as well. Ever watchful, the music-makers alternated the rhythm, since spontaneous saltatorial steps the dancers took as they turned and twisted did not always follow a consistent pattern, odd or even. Whenever breaking holds and moving apart, couples clapped and stamped to the improvised rhythm, their hands hitting hard and their feet falling heavily upon each beat of the music.

In spite of the peasant's lack of inhibitions, the <u>Ländler</u> was a sluggish dance. For one thing dancers leaped so high that in order not to lose their footing they had to slow down their movements. And as if dancing outdoors on soil and stone was not awkward enough, the men word hobnailed boots. All such things proved obstacles to rapid mobility.

Near the end of the eighteenth century barges going on excursions up and down the Danube river, from Passau in Bavaria and from Linz in Upper Austria, transported small bands of wandering alpine musicians to Vienna. To earn food and lodging they played and performed *Drehtänze* of the Bavarian Alps and *das Landl* wherever the opportunity presented itself: at suburban inns, at county fairs, at peasant weddings. These itinerant bands let loose *landla Melodien* by the scores among the Viennese.

Soon *laendlerische tanzen* ran wild in the *Wienerwald*, the captivating "Vienna Woods," which encircle a great part of the Austrian capital. Alpine turning dances, most notably the <u>Ländler</u>, spread to wine taverns and beer gardens, to coffeehouses and open-air restaurants, to carnivals—to the Redoutensall, where masked balls were held. Inevitably, in moving to the grand sections of Vienna, the rustic <u>Ländler</u> was refined by society. Unlike peasants who leaped and spun in heavy footwear on rough stony ground, Viennese donned light shoes to turn and glide on smooth parquet floors.

So it was the laws of culture compelled the abrogation of elevated, abrupt leaps in favor of depressed, suave glides. The lowering of *Ländler* steps quickened the pace of rotation to such a degree that ballroom dancers' feet did not always have a chance to emphasize each musical beat as had been the practice by peasants. In

consequence emphasis was placed only on initial steps of basic figures in a *Drehtanz*, which now was danced consistently to triple time.
Also, dancers in Vienna found rotating from FOOT to foot to foot
with swift succession much more expedient than plowing around
flat-footedly STEP by STEP by STEP as peasants used to do in *das
Landl*.

To dance Viennese was to eddy like whirlpools in a ballroom.
Rippling from one whirl to the next, couples moved about
immersed in a blue Danube of music, their bobbing bodies bell
buoys agitated by rhythmic waves. Afloat on the balls of their feet,
without ever appearing to lower their heels, couples whirled rightward round and on, round and on—again and again—to a fascinating yet frightening tempo not in the least unlike the rapid eddy-
ing of a whirlpool.

By the buoyant way dancers treaded a measure, they accentuated the downbeat, the first beat in triple time, and under stress of
rapidity were forced to steal time from the second beat: so instead of
a ONE, two, three count, the ordinary timing of <u>Deutsch</u> <u>Tänze</u>, they
used ONE-two-three—the unique tempo from which emerged the
world-famous Viennese Waltz.

Emphasizing the first step of a basic waltz figure to correspond
with an accented downbeat of a waltz measure is a technique in
waltzing now as it was then. Nevertheless, an anticipated second
beat combined with a rapid tempo, twice as fast as a regular waltz,
remain the Viennese Waltz's rather special qualities.

["Mr. Normand . . . Mr. Normand, excuse me," one of the
trainees interrupted the supervisor's discourse. "I'm sorry to break
in, but I can't follow you very well. I am unclear about the meaning
of 'figure' and 'step.' What is the difference between the two?"

"That's a good question, and a troublesome one. Literally, of
course, 'step' in the simplest terms means a single movement of a
person's foot. The trouble is in ballroom-dancing jargon the term
'step' is often interchanged with the term 'figure.' Although the latter is preferred, both terms due to usage are synonymous. By definition a figure or a step is a complete set of dance movements.

"If you wish to refer merely to that part of a set which forms the
basis of a particular dance, in the present case, the waltz, use the
modifier 'basic.' Needless to say, a basic waltz step or a basic waltz
figure is composed of three steps—ONE, two, three. However, a
complete set of dance movements, a waltz turn for example, is composed of at least six steps—ONE, two, three, FOUR, five, six. In other

words, a pair of basic waltz figures or steps make up a full turn, 360 degrees.

"While we are on the subject of turns, the Viennese Waltz was characterized by pivoting progressively in one direction, to the right, and a rigid unbroken tempo, sixty to seventy-six measures per minute. Because of the great rate of evolutions waltzers actually took only one entire step to the measure in a half-turn, 180 degrees. To explain,

> First half-turn, basic waltz step: (ONE) with the right foot toeing out, the man stepped forward clockwise describing an elongated arc as he carried the weight of his body over that foot; (two) he next placed the left foot beside the right foot, (three) and pivoted in place clockwise on the balls of both feet.

I might add it was considered poor form to allow one's heels to touch the dance floor. Thus a waltzer balanced on the balls of his feet as he turned: incidentally, in some instruction books on social dancing the term 'toes' instead of 'balls' is used, which is incorrect. Only ballet dancers dance on their toes.

"So much for that, after completing a semicircle, on the next measure in undelayed continuity a waltzer executed another 180 degree turn.

> Second half-turn, basic waltz step: (FOUR) with the left foot toeing in, the man stepped backward clockwise describing a reverse arc as he carried the weight of his body over that foot; (five) he next placed his right foot behind the left foot, (six) and pivoted in place clockwise on the balls of both feet.

"The woman, as a matter of course, performed waltz turns with her feet in opposition to her partner's as they traveled alternately around each other. They did so in this manner: the man in moving forward traveled around the woman while she in moving backward acted as a pivoting point. Conversely the woman in moving forward traveled around the man while he in moving backward acted as a pivoting point.

"The couple circled clockwise continuously round an imaginary circumference on a dance floor. To obtain a picture of the pattern performed, visualize stretched along the Line of Dance a colossal spiral spring with its symmetric coils laid out flat at regular intervals, one wind of each coil representing a 360 degree waltz turn.

"In turning waltzers of old Vienna rotated on the balls of their feet without hardly, if ever, resting their heels on the dance floor. Remember it was considered poor form to do so. Perhaps that is why they lagged behind in the development or mastery of a dancing technique Rise and Fall: the elevation of the body by pressure upward from the balls of the feet, and the subsequent lowering of the body by dropping the heels flush with the floor; the rise and fall are gradual actions, almost in slow motion for smoothness.

"Eventually Rise and Fall was perfected in other lands and the splendid style of the waltz was enhanced still more by an attractive sway which counteracted loss of balance upon a waltzer's falling away from a turn. Also the tempo of waltzes was slowed down considerably. Current American waltzes in point of fact are danced as slow as thirty measures per minute, forty-eight at the most. Quite a difference from the nineteenth-century Viennese Waltz which was danced sixty to seventy-six measures per minute.

"Paradoxically in an atomic age where airplanes which surpass the speed of sound have been designed, people themselves are moving at a snail's pace, so to speak. Yet in Vienna of the 1800s through velocity of travel was limited to that of horsepower the whirlabout Viennese Waltz thrilled fast-stepping individuals. Nevertheless, whirling to a measure per second apparently was still too slow to suit such speedsters who became infatuated awhile with the Langaus, a stepsister of the waltz. Conceived somewhere along the Danube near Linz, the Langaus consisted of two instead of three basic steps. It was executed with long strides at a breakneck gallop round a ballroom no less than six to eight times in succession. Just the thought of dancing that way to a speedy tempo on a slick floor makes my head spin."]

For practical purposes the history of the waltz in Vienna has been covered. It would be inappropriate, however, to bid that nineteenth-century capital of music *auf Wiedersehen* without paying tribute to the royal family of the waltz, the Strausses—Johann (the father, who wrote 152 waltzes), Johann junior (acclaimed the waltz king, who wrote some four hundred waltzes), as well as Josef and Eduard (the slighted brothers, each of whom also wrote scores of waltzes). Of all bandmasters ever to wave a baton or composers ever to write a note, the Strausses played the paramount part in popularizing the waltz for posterity.

The royal family's contributions to dance, concert, and operetta music notwithstanding, a widespread misbelief must be rectified.

Waltzes were written and waltzing was popular long before the Strausses embarked upon their musical careers. By 1791, thirteen years before the birth of the family head Johann senior, Mozart had already written six Ländler and fifty Deutsche (primitive waltzes). Beethoven created twelve Deutsche in 1795 and subsequently wrote thirteen Laendlerische Tänze later redacted as waltzes by Czerny.

After the foundations of the waltz as orchestral music had been prepared, Schubert laid the cornerstone. From 1816 to 1827 he composed altogether twenty-eight Deutsche, forty-eight Ländler, and 113 waltzes, the earliest of which originally were in the Deutsche category but, undoubtedly because of the nature of their composition, at a subsequent date were reclassified as "First Waltzes."

An 1819 monument in classical waltz music, Weber's rondo, Invitation to the Dance, was influential in molding the form of waltz composition. Although this masterpiece served as an inspiration to the waltz king, and others deserving of a crown , its formal structure is unlike that of true Viennese waltzes. The rondo differs from such light, easily digestible waltzes as Strauss's "Southern Roses," "Vienna Blood," "Artist's life," "Voices of Spring," "The 1001 Nights," "Wine, Women, and Song."

As records indicate the music and figures of the waltz were loved greatly by Austrians and Germans who performed the dance everywhere waltzes were played. In that waltzing called for performance in public places, it was unavoidable for people in all stations of life to rub elbows with one another on the dance floor; dancers found little discomfort in this unheard of closeness. Vienna's rulers, however uncomfortable, tolerated the situation and voiced no outward objections to the waltz. Such was not the case in Berlin; familiarity between individuals of high and low rank really rubbed that city's rulers the wrong way. Ignoring the people's love for the waltz, they banned it. In fact, under the reign of Kaiser Wilhelm II, the waltz was verboten at the court balls of the German imperial house. Not until his abdication in 1918 did the ban on the waltz waver.

Circumstances in France were different. Before the Great War waltzing won solid popular approval but gradually—step by step. For all their faults French rulers were sophisticated enough to enjoy the waltz, and they felt their subjects' participation in it was as natural as intercourse. The rise to popularity of the waltz had begun with the French Revolution and had heightened during the Napoleonic Wars. Berlin's ban overlooked, the grim-faced Germans grumbled gutturally that by signing the treaty of Lunéville back in

1801 they ceded to the French their national *Drehtanz* along with territories of the German Empire on the left bank of the Rhine.

In France, as in Germany and Austria, turning was typical of waltzing. However, the Frenchman's way with the waltz had taken an intricate twist into a triad of diverse dances, consecutively executed. Throughout the course of an evening a program went in series like this:

> First dance, <u>La Valse Lente</u> ("the Slow Waltz") was waltzed in a stately style to three-eight or three-four time; the music was grand. After several rounds of dancing, the orchestra speeded up the tempo, a cue for the waltzers to go to the next of the series—
>
> Second dance, <u>La Valse Sauteuse</u> ("the Spring Waltz") was waltzed to six-eight time in a debonair style; the music was gay; leaping and springing steps were now used. After several rounds of dancing, the orchestra speeded up the tempo, a cue for the waltzers to go on to the last of the series—
>
> Third dance, <u>La Valse Sauteuse Jeté</u> ("the Quick Spring Waltz") was waltzed in a lively style to six-eight time; the music was spirited. Leaping and springing steps were continued, but the orchestra accelerated the tempo to a greater speed, a cue to the waltzers to speed up their movements in turn.

From the foregoing dance program we get a general idea of the kind of waltzing done in France at the beginning of the nineteenth century. There is no dispute that the waltz—which the French took possession of and the Germans laid claim to despite the kaiser's disapproval—was looked upon with approving eyes by both European nations.

Came 1812, the British were once more warring against us, the quondam rebels, and in stanch tradition were also waging a battle against the revolutionary "mazy" waltz which had crossed the English Channel to encroach upon the shores of the ceremonious monarchy. The antagonism this foreign innovation provoked in traditional Englishmen is illustrated in a letter sent at that time to a local press: With words of indignation to the editor an irate father stated that he rushed his daughter, the apple of his eye, away from the ballroom when he beheld her as she waltzed brazenly embraced by her swain in a position best described "the very reverse of back to back"—a euphemistic way of saying "dancing belly to belly."

Displeasure with the waltz was widespread among traditionalists who looked upon women as caryatids too priceless to be mishandled. Typical of such a view was that of the antiquary Sir Henry Englefield; he gave vent to his feelings in a poem:

"The Waltz"

What! the girl I adore by another embraced?
What! the balm of her lips shall another man taste?
What! pressed in the dance by another man's knee?
What! panting and recline on another than me?
Sir! she's yours; you have pressed from the grape its fine blue,
From the rosebud you've shaken the tremulous dew;
What you've touched you may take.
Pretty waltzer—adieu!

Writings in various forms accusing the waltz of being responsible for loose morals appeared in publications during this period. Several influential scribes wrote about unchaste performances by waltzers, commoners and noblemen alike. It should be understood, though, that usually these quill-and-scroll commentators were serving the vested interests of throne and pulpit.

Waltzing nevertheless was open to everyone and anyone. Independent of ancestry, status, wealth or denomination, the dance, in which all classes increasingly mingled, had an indirect effect of weakening barriers between religious beliefs and disbeliefs, materialistic advantages and disadvantages, birth rights and wrongs. Entrenched controlling factions must have had a premonition of doom for they reacted to the waltz as if it were a menace to their unlimited authority, reinforced by rigid church dogmas and strong class ties.

Thus it is not surprising to hear that the defenseless dance was often maligned not just in Great Britain but also elsewhere. In Prague of all places as early as 1785, where waltzing was extremely popular with common Czechs, an imperial edict forbidding dancers' disgraceful turning of women by men declared it to be,

Sowohl der Gesundheit schädlich, als
auch der Sünden halber sehr gefährlich

("Injurious to health as well as very
hazardous because of the sins.")

By "the sins" no doubt was meant promiscuity between the sexes who attended a dance. In line with such reasoning one is led to believe that meeting any other way would render males and females immune to natural desires.

Traveling through Bavaria in 1804, Ernst Moritz Arndt, a German poet, visited a village near Erlangen. At a social gathering of the villagers he witnessed, and later recorded, the way whirling waltzers were conducting themselves. The following translation of Arndt's account although not literal, since idioms posed a problem, is substantially accurate:

"The room in which the young couples were dancing was dimly lit. Like others a youth raised the full, long skirt of his partner supposedly to prevent it from dragging across the floor. His fingers entwined in the hem, he draped the skirt over both her shoulder and his as they snuggled up against each other. They proceeded to whirl wildly; their whirling increased and decreased while the pair, by now inflamed, worked into shockingly immodest positions. Grasping one of her breasts, the youth squeezed it erotically from whirl to whirl. With each turn in the waltz she became hotter and hotter. In heat, the girl appeared ready to succumb. Other couples dancing to one side of the dark room indulged in more daring dalliances, far beyond the hugging and kissing stage."

A question, if you please: Could it be testified that these young villagers were really waltzing? For argument's sake, let us grant that nineteenth-century reports about the most extreme cases of licentiousness by males and females in performing the forbidden dance are not exaggerated. Would we not be sinfully unobjective in defiling waltzing in a dance hall as immoral, any more than we could objectively defile swimming in a public pool as sinful because exhibitionists yielded to their impulses and performed sexual acts under the water.

What it boils down to is not what is done but rather by whom it is done that purifies matters. Therefore, roars of disapproval were quieted when the "mazy" waltz from Vienna was danced in 1816 by the Russian Emperor Alexander and his partner, the Countess de Lieven, at a Mr. Almack's supper-dancing suites in King Street, Saint James. Unhesitantly other social lions in attendance leaped to their feet to emulate the royal pair's performance. Inasmuch as Almack's was the assembly place for the *haut monde* of London and the balls held there had determined the fashion of the parlor dance for half a century, the waltz finally received its due acceptance in England.

We now leave the British Isles to discover how Americans received the waltz. Despite false reports by some of our literary works, from December 21, 1620—when the Pilgrims first settled in Plymouth, Massachusetts—mixed dancing between the sexes was not prohibited under Puritan rule. After all, knowing that dancing was sanctioned in the Holy Scriptures (Exod. 15:20, 21; Luke 15:24, 25), how could the Puritans with clear conscience condemn it. However, mixed dancing was regulated with the utmost strictness by their <u>blue</u> <u>laws</u>, which were enforced so severely the importation of "evil-fashioned" dances such as the waltz was bitterly opposed by puritanical groups for a prolonged period of time.

Sixty-one years after the pilgrims came to the New World to escape injustice, a French dancing master who dared attempt to teach in Boston was summoned by the ministerial authorities and denounced as "a person of very insolent and ill fame that raues and scoffes at religion." Mercifully the Lord saved the Frenchman; he merely was run out of town, not also tarred and feathered. Social dance was a safe subject to scorn—something to preach against. With an accusing finger pointed at satanic sinners, a skyaspiring minister, Increase Mather, publicized his condemnation in a tract: An Arrow Against Profane and Promiscuous Dancing, Drawn out of the Quiver of the Scriptures!

On into the 1800s hidebound American writers were still assailing a form of the social dance. New York, 1807—one of the bitterest assaults was made in *Salmagundi*, writings co-authored by the Irving brothers, Washington and William, and an associate James Kirke Paulding. A satirical miscellany, *Salmagundi* contained explosive poetry blasting the waltz:

> Scarce from the nursery freed, our gentle fair
> Are yielded to the dancing-master's care;
> And, ere the head one mite of sense can gain,
> Are introduced 'mid folly's frippery train.
> A stranger's grasp no longer gives alarms,
> Our fair surrender to their very arms,
> And in the insidious waltz will swim and twine,
> And whirl and languish tenderly divine!
> O, how I hate this loving, hugging dance;
> This imp of Germany brought up in France:
> Nor can I see a niece its windings trace,
> But all the honest blood glows in my face.
> "Sad, sad refinement this," I often say;
> 'Tis modesty indeed refined away!

Let France its whim, its sparkling wit supply,
The easy grace that captivates the eye;
But curse their waltz—their loose, lascivious arts,
"That smooth our manners, to corrupt our hearts!"

Salmagundi, conforming to the accepted essay style of the eighteenth century, was an extremely effective series; hundreds of imitations were soon to follow. Apparently *Salmagundi's* poetical outcry against the waltz was heard afar. United States Senator John Tyler, who had had occasion to observe the waltz firsthand in 1827, one day told his daughter in no uncertain terms: ". . . it is a dance which you have never seen, and which I do not desire to see you dance. It is vulgar I think."

One wonders if the Senator was speaking as a father or a politician, for after he became president April 14, 1841, he held dances every two weeks at the White House. Alienated by his Whig Party because he vetoed a controversial Bank bill, he was bitterly denounced. Without the Whigs behind him the President was subject to attack. Tyler's reputed "folly and dissipation," his critics said, "turned the executive mansion into a great ballroom."

In the South the attitude toward the waltz was opposite to that of the North. Early in the 1800s newcomers from Europe migrating below the Mason-Dixon Line introduced the waltz at social functions. The Europeans and their dance were received with gracious hospitality—in spite of occasional rejections by some prudish southern gentlemen. As our nation expanded welcome mats were laid out for waltzers at more and more ballrooms across the country. The waltz had arrived at last!

In a New York publication, issued 1885, Allen Dodworth wrote about the waltz: "We have arrived at the culmination of modern society dancing, the dance which has for fifty years resisted every kind of attack, and is to-day the most popular known. From palace to hovel its fascination is supreme . . ." Dodworth in writing figuratively was using a neat round number, "fifty years." Actually eighty-five years would have been a closer approximation. Very likely he used 1834 as his basis because it was the year another dancing master Lorenzo Papanti created a scandal by exhibiting the "disgraceful" waltz in Boston on Beacon Hill at the mansion of Mrs. Otis, a wealthy socialite. The exact date when the waltz was first performed in America is open to speculation. Most writers generalize the dance appeared here at the turn of the century.

Anyway, by the end of the nineteenth century several American versions were widely practiced; in favor were the Knickerbocker, Balance, Hop, and Caprice Waltzes. Still the favorite of all was the conventional, rightward turning Viennese Waltz, in recent times also called the Pivot Waltz. The slowing of its timing in the United States was conducive to variation of movement. As a natural outcome waltzing was diversified by turning leftward, a difficult feat for the average person to accomplish.

As a matter of fact, dancing schools in pre-World-War-I days exploited the layman's inability to turn in the unconventional direction—counterclockwise, that is. On conspicuous signs placed in front of the buildings where these establishments did business, managers advertised WALTZ AND REVERSE GUARANTEED.

Eclipsed for a time by the precursors of the fox trot, waltzing at the advent of the twentieth century was further perpetuated in a number of somewhat imitative forms. The most common ones were the New Society, the Diagonal, the Merry Widow, the Variation, the Lame Duck, the Dip, and the Boston (of which there were several varieties). Such dances, lacking the quality of the classic waltz, did not last too long. Timeworn, the waltz itself was all but discarded by a general public unappreciative of its value.

The popularity of the waltz receded to its lowest ebb after October 28, 1919, with the enforcement of the Eighteenth Amendment by the passage of the National Prohibition Act, authored by a puritanical congressman Andrew J. Volstead. Undisciplined Americans, liquor-mad, turned to drink in preference to dance as a pastime, and under the pretext of dancing toddled tipsily on postage-stamp floors in speakeasies. Whatever the reason—lack of space, lack of skill, lack of steps, lack of sobriety—people performed a one-step indiscriminately to just about every kind of music that musicians played. When the Eighteenth Amendment was repealed December 5, 1933, the public in general seemed less inclined to drink as a diversion and began to show an interest in the classic ballroom dances. The waltz, being one of the classics with the most interesting patina, was studied appreciatively in a clearer light, and with a clearer head.

Many factors explain this renascence. Following repeal of Prohibition, scores of roomy dine-and-dance places sprouted all over the country. First-class hotels opened roof gardens and dining rooms featuring dance music. Even disused theaters, such as the old Hammerstein in New York, were converted into continental restaurants on the order of the Wunderbar in Berlin. That exemplary eating house had long featured dinner dancing.

Employment of outstanding professional dance teams who exhibited the latest tangos, rumbas, fox trots, and waltzes, became a prevalent policy at hotels and night clubs. Whereas in the past orchestras were expected to provide dinner music, now bands were engaged to play dance music. Celebrated band leaders: Enric Madriguera, Bill Coleman, Paul Whiteman, Rudy (Hubert Prior) Vallée, and others arranged musical compositions to accommodate the dance teams. Inspired by top-notch exhibitions, enthusiasts took lessons to learn the new routines or tried somehow to pick up steps appropriate to specific dances. Untrained social dancers realized that to ride out rounds required preparation, for to attempt at half cock to fake a fox trot or a waltz on a spacious, wide-open floor could be disastrous.

Although waltzing had an attraction as a ballroom and drawing-room dance, it was far-removed from the center of public attention. Then practically overnight in 1938 the waltz was cast into the limelight. As a publicity campaign Metro-Goldwyn-Mayer sponsored waltz contests nationally to advertise a motion picture, The Great Waltz, in which a huge orchestra (ninety musicians in all) played selections from the masterpieces of Johann Strauss. Starred, to be sure, was his waltz of waltzes "The Beautiful Blue Danube"; costarred were "Tales From the Vienna Woods" and airs from "Die Fledermaus." Hollywood, Broadway also, palpitated excitedly with a langsyne through revived beat in three-quarter time, a waltz rhythm to which people responded heartily, experiencing the romantic fervor the revolving round roused in their grandparents long ago.

[Glancing at his wristwatch, the supervisor saw he had enough time to cover one or perhaps two more points of historical significance. Just as he was about to do so, he was stopped by a question from a member of the Training Class. "Is it true, Mr. Normand, in Europe men used to wear white gloves when they danced a waltz?"

"Well, yes; they wore gloves for a waltz, for other dances, too— not only Europe but also in America. As for the color I don't believe the gloves necessarily had to be white, unless required on special occasions. I'm really not sure. Maybe at different periods different colors were fashionable. Your guess is as good as mine. I do know in centuries past etiquette went hand in hand with dancing. Recently while browsing in a bookstore, I came across an old copy of an 1859 publication Art of Dancing in which the author Edward

Ferrero gave hints on etiquette under a chapter heading 'The Ethics of Politeness.'

"In the past other writers as well devoted chapters to the subject in dance books. Hints on etiquette were simply lessons in proper conduct. For instance, a man was instructed that it was ungentlemanly to place his arm around a lady's waist before the orchestra played a few preliminary chords to start a dance. To put a gloveless hand on a beautifully gowned lady at a ball also was considered an impropriety, unworthy of a gentleman. If he happened not to be wearing gloves, it was permissible instead to use a handkerchief, which he secured against her back with the palm of his hand as they danced.

"If there are no more questions, I shall continue." The supervisor instantaneously regretted he had not been emphatic about disallowing further interruptions, for a second trainee was quick to ask, "With which foot did the old-timers in our country begin a waltz, and which way did they turn?" "I hoped no more questions would come up at this time," Normand replied. "However, since your question ties in with what I was about to discuss, I'll answer—but briefly.

"As I explained earlier, in the decades of the horse and buggy the major waltz turn was to the right, and the turn to the left was subordinate; the left or reverse turn was a newfangled idea. Like modern man, great-grandfather started waltzing with the left foot. He slid it sideways, occupying two beats of a measure in the process; posthaste on the third beat, with a smooth shift of weight, the right foot displaced the left foot, which simultaneously was raised in an aerial position preparatory to his commencing to waltz with his flame. Since backing a lady at the start of a dance was also frowned upon as a breach of etiquette, on the count of one he leaped rearward with the left foot, on two slid the right foot back toward the left foot, and on three with an upward kick of the left toe cut under the heel of the right foot—sharply elevating it. Then he stepped ahead on the right foot to initiate turns clockwise, to the right.

"Nowadays a male's dancing backwards is outmoded. Great-grandson customarily starts in a forward direction (with the left foot) and, should he wish to turn, must do so to the left. Otherwise, unless he steps to the side and round the girl in a semicircle of sorts—as was done, by the way, during the old days in the performance of a Viennese Waltz—he will be compelled to cross in front of his right foot, thus tripping himself as well as his partner.

"No more questions now. I need to acquaint you with a couple of waltzing techniques not yet discussed. As future instructors you will find it of value to be informed of the fact that the European waltz was greatly enriched by an American movement, the hesitation: It is a modified waltz figure with variations. Basically on the first beat of a measure a waltzer steps with the left foot in the direction of his choice, say ahead; next bringing the right foot up to the left foot, he hesitates for the remaining two beats. His partner performs her part in the same way except, of course, with her direction opposite to his.

"In another variation a waltzer, having advanced his left foot on the first beat, leaves his right foot in place and sways (backward and forward) on the remaining two beats. Because of this swaying to the rhythm of the music, some sources suggest the hesitation is a steal from the tango, which has similar backward-and-forward motions. More likely the movement was born of necessity. In reversing directions in fast waltz turns, dancers ran into a stumbling block; seeking a solution, they contrived the hesitation. In other words, while turning they learned by trial and error that hesitating to reverse directions rather than stepping on the second and third beats prevented dance partners from losing their footing.

"Also a valuable asset to the waltz is the canter, wherein steps are taken on the first and third beats only. The canter resembles a like-named pace of schooled thoroughbreds, an excellent example of which is the Tennessee Walking Horse, whose third gait is a canter. Obviously the movement as well as the name was derived from the cantering of horses. In mimicking the tricky stride of these light-footed quadrupeds, dancers of yesteryear took uneven steps (long, then short) interchanged with dips. That practice was unsightly as it gave the appearance of limping.

"Now the steps are even in length, and the dip has been eliminated. A dancer invariably uses the same foot—the foot with which the cantering commenced—for the one count in canter after canter. To canter the dancer steps forward on the count of one; on two, without touching the floor, the other foot gradually advances; on three weight is placed upon it: This principle is applied in canter pivots, as you will learn when you receive advanced dance instructions in the Training Class.

"Animal movements as well as names had an even greater influence on the choreography and nomenclature of the fox trot. That, however, is a study in itself, which will be examined in subsequent lectures. Diversifications and modifications notwithstanding, the waltz lags far behind the fox trot in popularity. Still, waltzing rounds are performed quite often at folk-dance festivals today.

"You may have been wondering why I presented the waltz before any of the more popular dances. First of all, the waltz is older than the others. Also, the waltz's roots have grown steadily over the years into the rest of the modern ballroom dances. The basic waltz step—styled and rhythmed to the requisites of each—is an integral part of the fox trot, swing, and Latin dances: tango, samba, rumba, mambo. I'll go a step further and venture to say that parallelisms exist between the Austrian ländler and the American jitterbug. Or do you believe any similarities are merely coincidental?

"Of course not. I could go into specifics, but nothing is to be gained in belaboring the point. Anyway, the waltz has been covered thoroughly enough. This afternoon's session lasted well past the hour. Since you have no teaching appointments as yet, no harm was done. In the future, though, whenever my lectures run long, should any of you be booked, just walk out of the room. Needless to say, studio business has priority over extracurricular studies. For the benefit of those who are speed writing a mile a minute to make a copy, save your energy. There is no hurry. The outline of the histories shall not be erased from the blackboard.

"When you return next week, I will answer any questions you may wish to ask. However, I'd appreciate it if you would refrain from bringing up questions concerning dance definitions. They are not ideal subjects for discussion. In that the denotation as well as the connotations of a dance become clear and meaningful only after it has been viewed in its entirety, a particular dance cannot satisfactorily be defined in a dictionary."]

Chapter 5

The following Monday Bert Craig as usual the most eager of the trainees was the first to engage Mr. Normand in conversation. "I've been thinking all weekend about what you said at our last session. Why a dance can't be defined satisfactorily is beyond me. Also at the end of the lecture you used a couple of words that were over my head."

"Let me see, I'll check my notes. . . . You must be referring to 'denotation' and 'connotation.'"

"Right-O. I am. What do they have to do with the price of rice in China?"

The tasteless query irritated the supervisor, but considering the source, he let it pass with a grain of salt. "Mr. Craig, you should buy a dictionary. "Denotation' is a term's actual primary meaning; for example, the denotation of a home is 'a place where a person lives,' and it has many connotations. 'Connotation'—or secondary meaning—is what is suggested in addition to the primary meaning; for example, the connotation of a home is 'privacy,' or 'warmth,' or 'security,' or 'comfort'—all four senses or more may apply. To denote and connote in words a home, which is stationary, is one thing. To do so with a dance, which involves movement, is something else. In the final analysis, the only satisfactory way to define a dance is to demonstrate it."

With their hands raised high other trainees vied for the supervisor's attention. One by one, as they caught his eye, they shot questions at him. Alice Scott added a fast comment to her inquiry. "If my memory serves me correctly, some time ago in a music-appreciation course I learned that many Viennese considered the waltzes of a composer Franz Joseph to be superior to those of his rival Johann Strauss junior. Previously, though, in your lecture you said he was the waltz king. How did you determine that?"

Normand chuckled: "You have your facts confused. I never heard of a Franz Joseph. You must mean Josef Franz Lanner."

"I'm sorry. You are right. That was his name. I forgot."

"Another thing, Miss Scott, Lanner's rival was the elder Strauss, not Strauss's son who was named after his father. The story behind the rivalry between Johann Strauss senior and Josef Lanner is rather interesting.

"Lanner, the son of a middle-class glover, was born in Oberdöbling, a charming community near Vienna. He began his career as a violinist with a string quartet in the taverns and inns of the capitol city. Innkeepers customarily provided their guests with dinner music to listen to and to dance to. Lanner was the leader of the quartet; Strauss was the viola player. Strauss also was a violinist, capable of playing first violin. Nevertheless, the arrangements of the string-quartet's melodious moods and movements required a viola.

"Former boyhood friends, Johann and Josef were as a consequence close colleagues. Coincidentally in their early teens they had played and studied stringed-instruments under the same conductor, a Michael Pamer who had a penchant for Ländlers. From the old school, Pamer was a harsh taskmaster; he would virtually drill his band in the techniques of Austria's threadbare mountain music, which still proved useful—rewardingly so.

"Both Josef Lanner and Johann Strauss were gifted musicians and prolific composers, but in temperament, and appearance, the two were as different as day and night. Josef, who had a light complexion and hair the shade of a beige dove, was a soulful, pious person; his waltzes were poetic—sentimentally expressed by orthodox symmetry, a musical form kept inviolate; on the margins of his waltz compositions he always wrote, 'With God: Josef Lanner.' Johann, dark-complexioned with curly black hair the sheen of a raven, was a hot head—a strong-willed individual; yet he had a broad mind and the courage to deviate from the accepted principle of symmetry in the waltz, which besides being boring restricted variation in the music and the dance.

"An alehouse keeper's son, Johann, as a small boy lived in Leopoldstadt, an island ghetto in the Danube. He frequently strolled down to the banks of the river to look for barges which carried fiddlers from Linz. Johann loved to listen to them play *landla Melodion*.

The 'country tunes' of Upper Austria played by these nimble-fingered fiddlers made a strong impression on a boy from the Jewish quarter.

"To escape the stench of beer and stale smoke that permeated the noisy alehouse where he lived, Johann often sought refuge in the serenity of the Vienna Woods. Playfully he rummaged through the woods in search of dead branches from which he removed the foliage: Pretending he was leading an orchestra, he waved a branch—as if it were a baton—to the beat of three-four time. Next he would use two branches—one as a bow, the other as a violin—in order to imitate the wrist action and finger movements of a violin player.

"Unaware of Johann's talent but aware of his fondness for the instrument, his parents bought him an inexpensive violin, which was dull-toned. Interestingly, the boy had the ingenuity to pour left-over beer from mugs into the sound holes to brighten the violin's dull tone. The more he practiced the more beer he poured till it streamed out of the sound holes. Apparently he would have waded in gallons of the foamy liquid if it helped to produce a tone that was music to his ear."

Alice Scott found it difficult to believe what she had just heard. She told Mr. Normand that undoubtedly young Strauss had an ear for music. However, the thought of his pouring beer into a violin to improve the tone seemed so incredible she had to express her disbelief. Mr. Normand assured her the story was not fiction. The violin, he explained, was a mediocre Bavarian product with a tone as rough and hollow as a dry, marrowless bone. The beer moistened the inside of the instrument thereby giving it a comparatively smooth, solid sound.

A question nagging at him, Bert Craig broke in at this point to ask: "Didn't the beer damage the violin? It couldn't have lasted long. Surely the soaked wood warped."

"One would think so," replied the supervisor. "When I read about the incident in a biography on Strauss, I was puzzled myself. I wondered if anybody else had ever tried something like it. Mr. Craig, why don't you do a little research. Look up a violin maker and ask him about it. Let us know what he says."

"Great idea. I'll do that. Oh, may I ask one more question, Mr. Normand?"

"Certainly. Go ahead."

"What was wrong with symmetry in Lanner's waltzes?"

"Nothing." The supervisor qualified his answer: "That is, nothing from the viewpoint of thousands of Viennese. His waltzes reflected the spirit of life in Vienna beautifully. In the early 1800s, before he started composing, waltz music was deathly boring. The worn-out waltzes to which dancers drudged through in three-quarter time consisted of one accentuated and two unaccentuated notes, which if repeated over and over again sounds like this: UMtata, UMtata, UMtata, UMtata, . . . Waltzers circled to UMtata's until the music stopped. Imagine dancing hours to such uninspired, lifeless rhythm.

"Lanner enlivened his waltz compositions but within perimeters of the symmetrical form that the Viennese were accustomed to and could relate to. Moreover, his melodies were most sentimental. And many people loved him for it. When he died in 1843, twenty thousand mourners joined the funeral procession. As they followed the composer's coffin, they cried, <u>Lanner oder Kaner</u>! They wanted 'Lanner or no one.'

"But we are getting ahead of the story. Let's turn back to the days Josef Lanner lived. Almost overnight his string quartet grew into a full-fledged orchestra. It was so popular, he received numerous engagements to play waltzes at dancing parties. One day he became ill and was unable to attend an urgent engagement, requiring unique dance music. Incapacitated, he was in no mood to prepare waltzing arrangements. Josef requested Johann to conduct the orchestra and to compose music for the affair. A young man of high aspirations, he jumped at the chance despite the short notice.

"Under Strauss's direction the musicians performed magnificently. The dancers were enthralled with his music, which included the classic *Taeuberln Walzer* ('Waltz of the Doves'). As ill luck would have it, the laurels went to Lanner who got all the credit for Johann's work (Opus I). His ego bruised, Johann soon walked out on Josef.

"If beer babble is to be believed, their parting company ended in an episode as corny and crude as the scenes of free-for-alls often depicted in the movies. While playing at the Ram, a suburban inn, they exchanged harsh words—antagonistic differences about their music. In the heat of passion violist and violinist somehow crossed bows and a duel ensued. The rest of the orchestra members chose sides with the result that bedlam broke loose.

"Waltzers scurried helter-skelter off the dance floor. Some stopped dead in their tracks. Flutes and Clarinets flashed like shiny steel blades. Thrusting and parrying with instruments, mild-mannered musicians dueled one another with uncharacteristic violence. Luckily they lacked the skills of swordsmen: no mortal wounds were inflicted, but feelings were scarred for life. In retaliation Johann organized his own orchestra, which also became a phenomenal success.

"Josef and Johann's locking horns at the Ram, supposedly is how a rivalry began between the two. If so, it would have ended as fast as it started. For, despite their differences, they respected each other's musical talents. Moreover, in their hearts they wished to remain friends.

"Unfortunately they were torn apart by the people of Vienna, who had split up into two rival factions: 'Lannerianer' and 'Straussianer.' Not surprisingly both factions had their share of followers with selfish motives. Hangers-on following the successful musicians, like self-seeking politicians climbing onto a bandwagon, prodded Johann and Josef into bitter competition.

"Although they were reluctant rivals and begrudged each other nothing, they were driven mad by musicofanatics. Under great pressure to be the best, each felt compelled to outdo the other. For instance, when Strauss heard that Lanner was appointed Musical Director at the Emperor's Redoutensall (where fancy court balls were held), Strauss put other plans aside posthaste and entered into a contract to appear at the Sperl—the biggest bourgeois dancing hall in Vienna.

"On a local level the two were more or less equally successful. But, while Lanner preferred to stay in Vienna, Strauss, more ambitious, toured Europe with his orchestra to attain greater heights of success. . . ."

Vincent Armstrong, who throughout the discourse seemed engrossed in somber thought as though he were present in body but absent in spirit, instinctively perked up to volunteer a short statement: "My aunt recently visited Vienna where she saw statues erected on a large pedestal in honor of Strauss and Lanner. She told me that during the composers' heyday they were idolized by the Viennese people for their waltz music."

"They still are greatly admired," the supervisor acknowledged. "The monument is located in Rathauspark ('park of the city hall'). I have been to Vienna also. For all the bitterness, it is ironic that the statues of the rival composers stand side by side with sweet harmonious expressions on their faces.

"Musicologists are in accord that Viennese waltz music was

developed by Lanner and improved by Strauss—and perfected by his namesake: the oldest of Strauss' three sons, Johann II, successor to the 'Straussianer' throne. He was hailed not only as the waltz king but also as the uncrowned king of Austria for his musical conquests on a national and international scale.

"In Russia at the Vauxhall Palace (circa 1855) Czar Nicholas along with his subjects applauded so long and so loud at Johann's concerts that he was compelled to perform well past midnight week after week. In order not to miss the maestro's encores the audiences—thousands of Russians from distant St. Petersburg—deliberately missed the last train home. Intoxicated by Strauss' potent performances, aristocrats and bourgeoisie happily slept hours on tables and chairs in a park near Vauxhall Palace in wait for the return train to St. Petersburg scheduled to pull into the railway station later in the morning.

"In France at the 1867 World Exhibition held in Paris, Johann Strauss gave concerts in Cercle International, a hall within the exhibition. A publisher, Jean Hippolyte de Villemessant, who happened to attend one of the maestro's performances, was so impressed with the Austrian genius that the Frenchman published, in his politic-literary journal Figaro, a series of complimentary notices about the maestro.

"In a special edition of the journal Strauss was most eloquently editorialized:

> Music that harbors the devil and leaps from the rocks in a cascade. Strauss! What magic there is in the name! To the sounds of his music courtiers and soldiers dance, town and country rotate, dainty boots and wooden shoes alike, fairies and nurserymaids. His music penetrates into the spirit and animates the feet—it is original and universal. The waltzes of Johann Strauss resound across the frontiers of our culture over to America and Australia, and in China they awaken the echoes beyond the Great Wall.

"In America—the year was 1872—Strauss was persuaded to conduct concerts in Boston to commemorate a centenary of our country's struggle for independence from England: the hundredth anniversary of rebellious incidents such as the Boston Massacre and Tea Party that led to Massachusetts' throwing off the taxing yoke imposed by George III. Johann Strauss received a royal welcome in Boston beyond his expectations. Strategically placed in his path on street corners were huge placards depicting him majestically in a conductor's stance atop a globe of the world; in his hand he held a baton pointed toward the heavens as if he were a god-king wielding a scepter to direct orchestral angels.

"Boston's auditorium in which Strauss appeared was filled to capacity—100,000 seats. On the stage were numerous musicians and a colossal chorus—20,000 singers. The auditorium was so vast and noisy that a cannon had to be fired to alert everybody the concert was about to start. As the BOOM of the cannon died away Johann raised his baton and conducted the grand orchestra in the playing of the Blue Danube waltz. The moving strains of the music drove the women in the audience into a frenzy.

"After the concert while he was attempting to leave the auditorium women grabbed hold of his coat tails and kissed them madly. Not satisfied with his autograph, women pleaded for mementos: locks of his beautiful, black, curly hair. Pursued, Johann fled to his hotel suite where he instructed his valet to distribute locks of hair to the women clamoring outside on the sidewalk.

"Oh—I should mention the locks were snipped off Johann's black-haired Newfoundland dog. If any Bostonian descendants happen to have strands of the canine's hair, they could at least claim they have genuine mementos of a royal dog that belonged to the memorable waltz king Johann Strauss."

Chapter 6

As the session progressed Mr. Normand was peppered with a variety of incidental queries by the trainees. Their bringing up subject matter irrelevant to the history of the waltz tried his patience. Since the Latin-American dances were to be discussed in future sessions, Vincent Armstrong was ruled out of order when he asked, "Why is 'rumba' sometimes spelled with an h and sometimes without an h?" Despite his impatience generosity prevailed on the supervisor to answer the question, but rather pedantically: "The h in r-h-u-m-b-a is incorrect orthography."

Alice Scott (a Bible in her hand) questioned whether the Holy Scriptures clearly sanctioned dancing as Mr. Normand had stated earlier in speaking about the Puritans' not being able to condemn it with clear conscience. Last weekend at home she had looked up the scriptural passages he referred to and found dancing mentioned just briefly. At her request the supervisor gave her permission to read the passages contained in the Old and New Testaments:

> Exodus, chapter 15
> 20 And Miriam the prophetess, the sister of Aaron, took a timbrel in her hand; and all the women went out after her with timbrels and with dances.
> 21 And Miriam answered them, Sing ye to the Lord, for he hath triumphed gloriously; the horse and his rider hath he thrown into the sea.
>
> St. Luke, chapter 15
> 24 For this my son was dead, and is alive again; he was lost, and is found. And they began to be merry.
> 25 Now his elder son was in the field: And as he came

and drew nigh to the house, he heard musick and dancing.

"You are missing the point, Miss Scott. Brevity has nothing to do
with it. If you check your notes on the Prelude to the Dance, you will
find that in my initial biblical reference Jeremiah—under chapter 31,
Israel's restoration—it is clear dancing was a sanctified ritual.
However, I believe somewhere I made a notation pertaining to that
particular point which should eliminate any doubt in your mind.

"Let me see. Just a minute." The supervisor thumbed through a
stack of papers on his desk. "Here it is. Turn to The Book of Psalms,
chapter 149: Praise for Restoration of Israel. . . . Have you found it?"
"Yes," Miss Scott answered. "Very well," replied the supervisor.
"Read the first three verses—out loud, please":

> Praise ye the Lord. Sing unto the Lord a new song, and
> his praise in the congregation of saints.
> 2   Let Israel rejoice in him that made him: Let the chil-
> dren of Zion be joyful in their King.
> 3   Let them praise his name in the dance: let them sing
> praises unto him with the timbrel and harp.

Just as Alice Scott finished reading the last line of the verse
almost in the same breath she remarked, "It would be nice to know
how the ancient Israelites danced. Mr. Normand, do you have any
idea what kind of dance movements they performed?"

Perplexed, Ralph screwed up his face in annoyance. He disliked
being caught off guard. The supervisor replied her guess was as
good as his. He recommended, however, that she go to the main
library at the Civic Center and obtain a copy of *World History of the
Dance* by Curt Sachs.

"There is a chapter in his history on movements in which old
whirl dances performed by Jewish women are mentioned. But while
others also are touched upon in several chapters, I am not sure that
dance movements of the ancient Israelites are sufficiently discussed
or described—certainly not movement by movement."

With slightly stifled shouts and hands raised high, other trainees
were vying for Mr. Normand's attention so they could ask him more
questions. In that he had a great deal of ground to cover, he pretended not to see the upraised hands. Moreover, he was not in the
best of humor; consequently he told the class in no uncertain terms
to settle down and be quiet.

When he was satisfied that the class had come to order, the

supervisor proceeded with his talk: "Remember last week as I began the lecture on the history of the waltz, I mentioned parenthetically that it improves <u>balance</u> and <u>turning ability</u>. Every dance has something beneficial to offer. This fact, shrewdly utilized, can be pressed to a tremendous advantage in your efforts to sell the ballroom dances to students.

"Look up here at the blackboard. Observe the phrases printed in colored chalk which are enclosed by parentheses after the headings in the eight histories outlined. Note there are two special benefits to be derived from each dance. Take the samba. In practicing it, one can achieve <u>flexibility</u> and <u>abandon</u>.

"For instance Miss Adams, a beginner who has completed a five-hour introductory course, refuses to sign up for samba lessons with the argument that that dance does not appeal to her. Such an attitude is absolutely undesirable, because the fewer dances a student is interested in, the less hours she is likely to buy. Thus the smaller will be your pay checks, mine, and the studio managers' as well.

"No need to be concerned, you have the upper hand. Simply say, 'Miss Adams, the samba is a wonderful dance to assist you in achieving <u>flexibility</u>. It will loosen you up, help you to relax. You know how tense you get the moment you start dancing.'

"Miss Adams cannot help but agree with you, for as a rule beginners are tense to a certain extent anyway. Now that you've caught your fish, do not let her wiggle off the hook. Ask her if she is self-conscious in a ballroom. Nine times out of ten the answer will be in the affirmative; nearly all persons who can't dance imagine everyone is staring at them when they are on a ballroom floor.

"The rest is smooth sailing. Tell her that the samba is unconditionally guaranteed to bring about the achievement of <u>abandon,</u> that it is excellent therapy for self-conscious students. To wrap up your sale, assure Miss Adams she'll fling her cares to the wind and have loads of fun. A wallflower cannot resist such juicy bait."

By now the supervisor was in a better mood, engrossed in his sales talk and forgetting Alice Scott's exasperating inquiry which had taken him unawares. With a fatherly tone he advised: "Make the most of any valuable selling angles you may latch onto if you want to earn real money around here, not just petty cash. Remember the hourly pay for teaching is small remuneration in comparison with the large commissions available to you from renewals you write, or courses you sell to guests invited to the studio."

Normand rose to his feet, folded his chair, and leaned it against the wall; he next pushed the cumbersome blackboard to one side of the room. This act caused the members of the Training Class to perk up their heads and shift about in their seats to be more comfortable. Seeing how attentive the young men and women were, the supervisor smirked smugly, pleased he still held the interest of the group.

Ralph Normand—a tall, lanky individual—stood out in a crowd. Often judged to be in his mid-twenties, he actually was in his thirties. He was exceedingly handsome, almost on the verge of being beautifully boyish in physiognomy and physique, yet not to the point whereby he could be mistaken for a homosexual. When Ralph spoke his voice exuded masculinity. And his unyielding, matter-of-fact manner proved a direct contradiction to his puttied, pedantic personality.

Although a liberal on a few facets of life, Normand was a typical company man—a hardheaded one at that. His very existence revolved around the studio and its activities. Undeniably he was brilliant; but, like too many minor executives, he overrated his own importance. The supervisor never lost an opportunity to cram the merits of National Dance Studios down the throats of others.

The next twenty minutes Normand spoke in general about tested, studio teaching methods. Then surprisingly he introduced an entirely different matter to his audience, which had experienced six arduous weeks of intensive training: of learning under an abridged program all the modern ballroom dances, not to mention specialties like the balboa, or an occasional old-time round such as the varsoviana thrown in for good measure, of perfecting styling, footwork, continuity, and rhythm—of mastering countless dance techniques ordinarily requiring months if not years to perfect.

Without exception the trainees in the class were most eager to put their recently gained knowledge and skill into application, keen to become sharp ballroom dancers. But now a heaviness in Normand's statements was about to take the edge off their enthusiasm, or so it would seem from the dullness of their expressions.

"Teaching dancing is only part of your job in this organization. There are other things involved. I am sure you've never dreamed that many women—and men—have been driven to the studio by emotional problems they were not equipped to solve. If you are honest with yourself, I venture to say your being here also resulted from one form of personal perplexity or another. What was your reason for joining the studio? Was dancing your only motive? Give these questions some serious thought.

"Naturally dancing is the main commodity we have to sell, and you should constantly make it your duty to know your product. We put the most select materials at your disposal. If you use your initiative, the high quality of your professionalism will be demonstrated not only on the dance floor but also on your sales record.

"To come back to our patrons. Perhaps I can best convey what I am trying to get across to you by citing the case of a former student of mine, Mrs. Kathleen Robinson. She had signed up for one hundred hours of instruction right off the bat. A course of that length costs in round numbers approximately nine hundred and forty dollars at the present rates.

"When Mrs. Robinson was on the books, I had just broken in as a new teacher and wasn't too sure of myself. For the first few lessons the woman appeared sullen, not in the least responsive to my well-meant efforts. It was discouraging and tiresome to spend the long hours with her. Regardless of what I said or did, I couldn't inveigle her into cracking a smile, let alone could I teach her much dancing. I came to the end of my rope during a lesson one day and, no longer able to hide my irritation, asked my student point blank what in the world was wrong with her? Before she was able to reply, I told her quite sternly that nobody had twisted her arm to sign up for dancing lessons!

"To my astonishment, instead of being angered at my insolence, she was elated to find someone who wanted to know what was troubling her. Mrs. Robinson whispered what she had to say was confidential, and she did not wish to be overheard. Taking me by the hand, she pressed it innocently, I felt, against her breast as she led me toward an uncrowded area of the ballroom where she had left her purse on the wall bench.

"Out of the depths of her purse she fished a small but thick, maroon, tooled-leather book. Quickly flipping to a specific page in the book, which turned out to be Mrs. Robinson's diary, she handed it to me. With a tremor in her voice she said: 'Sit down and read from this entry on, and all shall be clear. I am too upset over worrying about the situation to discuss it.'

"Realizing the diary of the troubled woman might reveal information of great value in my working with her—a task which held in store the possibility of a fat commission for me—I eagerly scanned the pages covered with Palmer script that disclosed methodically, in full particulars, how and why Mrs. Robinson made her way to our studio.

"It seems Kathleen's marriage of thirty-three years, on the surface ideal, had fallen miles short of perfection. Her husband, a prosperous auditor—and, mind you, the direct descendant of an English baron—was from outward appearances a model husband. The Robinsons were the envy of their social set. Whenever Kathleen's friends nagged their lords and masters, they would whine: 'Why can't you be like Mr. Robinson! He is such a good provider, such a marvelous father, such a devoted man to his wife'—and other usual prittle-prattle of dissatisfied helpmates, who imagine the water is purer in the next hole. They would have been struck with apoplexy had they discovered as shocked Kathleen did, by accident without her husband's knowledge, that for years he'd been having an affair with his associate—a man.

"Too weak in disposition to confront the scoundrel with his unfaithfulness yet, beyond that, unable to face the dire consequences, Kathleen remained silent. Since her husband burned the candle at both ends, it was difficult to divide his time between his wife and associate; evidently he preferred his male lover, for Robinson stayed away from home at every opportunity. In the past she hadn't objected to being left alone because she took it for granted her husband was either tied up late at the office or out of town on business. Now that she knew the true story behind his frequent absences, she felt lonelier than ever and neglected.

"Not wishing to degrade her name which was, and still is I believe, highly respected in the community, the woman was ashamed to tell anybody about her marital woes. She dared not confide in her two grown daughters and risk the chance of a family scandal. Both are married to prominent men in the city. There was no one to whom she could unburden herself—nary a person did she trust to bare her soul to. How could she tell anyone that her husband was having sexual relations with a man. High-strung by nature, Kathleen found the tension unbearable.

"One Monday she attended a regular weekly luncheon in the Mural Room of the St. Francis Hotel. Neither the occasion or even the choice bits of gossip that her companions held forth could detract Kathleen from the agony gnawing within her.

"As she descended the wide staircase between the marble pillars at the Powell Street entrance to the hotel, a Yellow Cab starter blew his whistle; its shrill sound penetrated her aching head like the pierce of a needle. To contribute further to her discomfort came the clanging of a cable car, a noise she now cursed, but which in prior days had never failed to elicit from her a pleasant sub vocal response, 'clang, clang—clang, clang!'

"By force of habit Kathleen looked up at the clock on the Philippine Air Lines billboard perched atop the Soriano Building. Noticing the advertiser's suggestion,

THIS YEAR SEE THE ORIENT: MANILA
                                    HONG KONG
                                    TOKYO

ROUTE OF THE ORIENT STAR,

Kathleen Robinson decided, right then and there, to take a trip. If she didn't get away from her maddening situation, she would lose her senses. However, it had been ages since she had been anywhere; the woman remembered she was badly in need of new luggage.

"As she turned her head when she started to walk down the block, Kathleen caught sight of the miniature Eiffel Tower set upon the roof of the City of Paris. She had an impulse to go there to hunt for traveling bags, but was in no mood to mill around with shoppers in a crowded, stifling department store. Therefore, she exercised a womanly prerogative and changed her mind, promising herself to make the purchase in the near future.

"Mrs. Robinson's despair was augmented by a candy wrapper which somehow had adhered to the heel of her shoe. After several futile attempts to dislodge the sticky piece of cellophane by grating it with her heel back and forth over the edge of the curbstone, she crossed the street to Union Square, plopped on a park bench, and removed the messy wrapper with her fingers. Aggravated enough to burst into tears, still, not wanting to become a public spectacle, the woman fought to restrain herself when a couple paused nearby to feed the remains of a sandwich to some pigeons.

"She regained her composure by directing her attention to the Dewey Monument situated at the center of the square. As she scrutinized the almost one-hundred-foot granite erection, she focused her eyes on the apex, where she saw a bronze figure of the Goddess of Victory holding in the right hand a wreath (symbol of esteem) and in the left hand a trident (symbol of naval supremacy).

"Kathleen recalled her grandmother once told her that Ida Clark, a teacher in the early 1900s at the now defunct Lincoln Grammar School, was selected to be the model for the Goddess of Victory. The sculptor Robert Aiken was hopelessly in love with Ida Clark—an unforgettable lady. He had been her pupil in the eighth grade.

"It dawned on Kathleen that, although she had been born in San Francisco, she really had no clear conception what the monument signified. She had noticed it countless times from a building, a streetcar, an automobile, and even from a path in the square. Yet, in all the years she'd lived here, it never had entered her mind to read the inscriptions on the four plaques surrounding the Corinthian column near the base.

"Impelled by curiosity, Kathleen went over to the monument, walked about its huge quadrate pedestal, and acquainted herself with the different inscriptions chiseled into the plaques. A few days later, out of curiosity, I visited Union Square myself. Impressed, I returned the next day to photograph the monument for my collection of memorabilia. I also photographed all the inscriptions. It was a bit tricky to do for, I would say, the plaques alone are at least eight feet high and—oh, approximately three feet wide.

"If any of you are as interested as I was, you can of course go to Union Square and look at the inscriptions yourselves. Or you can borrow my negatives and have your own photographs developed. They are not too expensive." A curious trainee pleaded, "Couldn't you show us your photographs now?"

"Well, all right, but hurry," the supervisor qualified his consent. He opened his desk drawer and pulled out a manila envelope from which he withdrew several glossy photographs. Normand motioned the trainee to step up to the front of the room. When she approached Normand's desk, the supervisor handed the glossies to the trainee and instructed her to pass them around for everyone to see.

Eagerly the members of the class studied the various photographs. And this is what was learned about the Dewey Monument:

(east side—
parallel to
Stockton Street),

SECRETARY OF THE NAVY
JOHN D LONG
TO
COMMODORE
GEORGE DEWEY
APRIL 24 1898
★ ★ ★
WAR HAS COMMENCED
BETWEEN THE UNITED

STATES AND SPAIN•
PROCEED AT ONCE
TO THE PHILIPPINE
ISLANDS AND CAP-
TURE OR DESTROY
THE SPANISH FLEET

(west side—
parallel to
Powell Street),

ON THE NIGHT OF
APRIL THIRTIETH 1898
COMMODORE DEWEYS
SQUADRON ENTERED
MANILA BAY AND UN-
DAUNTED BY THE DAN-
GER OF SUBMERGED
EXPLOSIVES REACHED
MANILA AT DAWN OF
MAY FIRST 1898•
ATTACKED AND DE-
STROYED THE SPANISH
FLEET OF TEN WAR
SHIPS • REDUCED THE
FORTS AND HELD THE
CITY IN SUBJECTION
UNTIL THE ARRIVAL OF
TROOPS FROM AMERICA

(south side—
parallel to
Geary Street),

ERECTED BY
THE CITIZENS OF
SAN FRANCISCO
TO COMMEMORATE
THE VICTORY OF
THE AMERICAN NAVY
UNDER COMMODORE
GEORGE DEWEY AT
MANILA BAY MAY
FIRST MDCCCXCVIII
★ ★ ★

ON MAY TWENTY
THIRD MCMI THE
GROUND FOR THIS
MONUMENT WAS BRO-
KEN BY PRESIDENT
WILLIAM MCKINLEY

(north side—
parallel to
Post Street),

AMERICAN SQUADRON
MANILA BAY
★ ★ ★
OLYMPIA
flagship
BALTIMORE
RALEIGH
CONCORD
PETREL
McCULLOCH
★ ★ ★
ON MAY FOURTEENTH
MCMIII THIS MONU-
MENT WAS DEDICAT-
ED BY PRESIDENT
THEODORE ROOSEVELT

(north side—the base of the monument),

ERECTED 1901 • NEWTON THARP ARCHITECT • ROBERT I AITKEN
SCULPTOR   REPLACED 1942 FOLLOWING CONSTRUCTION OF
UNDERGROUND GARAGE • TIMOTHY L PFLEUGER ARCHITECT

Deciding the trainees had had ample time to look at the photographs, the supervisor continued his former student's story. "In concentrating upon the historic events of the Dewey Monument, Kathleen Robinson had forgotten about her troubles momentarily. She left Union Square a little less disturbed, to be delayed at the intersection by a changing signal. While she waited for the green light to appear, the woman faced the United Air Lines office at the diagonally opposite corner. Again awakened to the thought that she needed a trip to get away from it all, she vowed to fly off somewhere soon.

"Now dragging herself up Powell Street, Mrs. Robinson began to redwell on her hopeless predicament. Wretched, she was lured by the cocktail sign above the entrance to the Yankee Doodle into drowning her sorrow in drink. Uncertain whether or not she ought to, she passed the bar but faltered next door at the Press Club Building, before the window of the Exercycle Company. As she watched the mannequin displayed inside pedaling a bicycle going nowhere, its wheels revolving as though in progress, the mechanical movement made the woman's head whirl, and her headache returned.

"Mrs. Robinson was overcome by a dizzy spell: She remembered how ill she'd felt after she had a second goblet of sauterne at a Thanksgiving Day dinner party. No! a cocktail wasn't the answer, so she walked on.

"Upset and not knowing what to do with herself, Kathleen decided it might be a good idea if she had her hair shampooed. Anything to keep busy, to avoid thinking, to lift her morale! Because of her erratic state of mind, when the woman neared the wrought iron gate which distinguishes Elizabeth Arden's beauty salon from the other business establishments on Sutter Street, she experienced a locked-out feeling and forged ahead.

"At the Fine Arts Studio, in the adjoining building, Kathleen stopped to admire a display of Wedgewood. The exquisite collection of light blue ware, with its delicately made white cameo reliefs, had her marveling at the artistry of the potter. If things were only different, she engaged in wishful thinking, it would be nice to acquire a pottery set as lovely as that Wedgewood blue.

"The distressed woman might have commenced brooding anew over her unfaithful husband; but as Kathleen turned away from the show window of the antique store, she was attracted by our eye-catching neon sign, NATIONAL DANCE STUDIOS.

"There would be a good place to while away the tedium of the afternoon, she told herself. She had to do something to get her mind off her domestic crisis. Jaywalking across the street, Mrs. Robinson headed straight for our studio. In her mental state it hardly took any salesmanship by the interviewer to persuade the dear lady to put her X on the dotted line of a one-hundred-hour dance contract."

A mercenary glint was detectable in Ralph's steel-grey eyes as he spoke about the sale, a statement which he proceeded to justify. "My student later confessed to me that the course was purchased of her own free will and volition. For her wanting to learn to dance was really no whim; it was something she had always longed to do. In fact she now believed the instruction, the new contacts, and the responsibility of showing up for hourly lessons every Monday, Wednesday, and Friday afternoons (Kathleen's scheduled program): all might tally up to some form of deliverance from the tedious run-of-the-mill social functions she was fed up with and couldn't stomach any more.

"After I had unearthed Kathleen Robinson's story, I switched my method of teaching entirely. Upon approaching her every other weekday, I paid her compliments on the clothes she was wearing; instead of devoting much effort as before to technicalities and advanced steps, I simplified the dancing instruction to the point where Kathleen began to follow a bit better my forceful leading." Ralph grinned boyishly to make light of his bragging.

"Gradually I noticed a turnabout in her deportment. She would wear such accessories as unusual earrings and colorful scarves to entice my flattering exclamations of how becoming they were! She began to smile—not just with her lips but with her eyes, too. Often Kathleen remarked, I was the best teacher in the studio; she never would give me up for another, and she looked forward to her lessons each day with eagerness.

"I should not go so far as to prescribe such treatment for all people in Mrs. Robinson's situation. But tell me, at her age what else could she do? She was no spring chicken, you know. Dancing was her salvation, an outlet for her distress. In reality, I surmise, the woman was dragging her feet, forever clinging to the hope, however faint, her husband sooner or later would free himself from his homosexual entanglement and truly be hers, not merely in name."

Pressed for time, the supervisor abruptly ended the storytelling in terms of general percentages. "So you see, to be a success in the dance game you must be twenty-five per cent instructor, twenty-five per cent father confessor—and fifty per cent practical psychologist."

BOOK TWO

Chapter 7

Spontaneously fingering a smallish bump (a war souvenir) on his forehead, Vincent Armstrong pondered over Mr. Normand's discourse centered around emotional problems. It was coincidental that a similar theme had prevailed in the story of Vincent's life the past six years—squandered—vanished—never to be regained. He had wandered as listlessly as driftwood floating on a vast ocean . . . driftwood, tossed by waves to and fro, hither and yonder. Uneasy! Restless! Without purpose!

"Why did you come to National Dance Studios? Being a ballroom dancing teacher wasn't your object in life. That was one target you never aimed for. Be honest with yourself, Vincent. What in the U.S.A. compelled you to enroll in the Training Class? Was it simply the prospect of meeting exciting women?"

As he attempted to analyze his motives, his prominent features—resembling those of a youthful Abraham Lincoln—were marred by a forlorn frown lending age to Armstrong's characteristic countenance. Still fingering the bump on his forehead, he drifted back in thought five years to the day he was discharged from the army and released from Dibble General Hospital in Menlo Park; he had been shipped here after spending months recovering from war wounds in a French hospital overseas.

Quickly departing from the military hospital grounds, Vincent, a Purple Heart medal pinned on his uniform, found his way to El Camino Real, a main highway, where he was patriotically offered a ride into San Francisco by a talkative novelty-jewelry manufacturer. Or was the man a silverware distributor? Vincent was not paying attention, neither was the driver. With one hand on the steering wheel of his car and the other hand occasionally tapping Vincent on the shoulder, the man kept yakking about the war as if he were kibitzing about the World Series. Annoyed, the ex-soldier wished he had taken a bus.

Without taking a breath the gabby guy had the stamina to slide in, "What do you intend to do now that you are out of the army?" Armstrong cut him short with an edged, "I don't know!"

And he truthfully did not know. For a solid week he had been vacillating between two options. He seemed incapable of deciding whether or not to reap the benefits of the G.I. Bill of Rights (Public Law 346—78th Congress) and resume his education, or to seek employment in order to receive immediate earnings.

Several months ago Vincent had sent his mother a message on V-Mail from overseas; in the letter he wrote: "Give my clothes to Goodwill Industries. It will be a while before I can return home; there is no use letting my clothes get moth-eaten."

The upshot was he now needed an overcoat, suits, shirts, ties, underwear, socks, shoes; he could use a watch, a billfold, a candid camera, an electric shaver—a dozen and one things. He had a yearning for a car. There was so much he had missed. So many places to be seen. Girls galore to meet. Lost time—briefer than brief, scarcer than scarce—he must make up! Often when facing death on the battlefield, he had vowed that, if he were spared, in the future he would live each and every day as though it were his last.

On the other hand, he could not push the G.I. Bill of Rights aside. Nudging at him repeatedly was the fact that he was eligible for free tuition: laboratory, library, health, infirmary, and other such fees customarily charged; as well as books, supplies, equipment, and essential incidentals; plus sixty-five dollars per month allowance for subsistence. With the federal government footing the bills, it was a grand opportunity to complete his education.

Yet what if he should die tomorrow or even in the very next second—the sudden way he had seen soldiers drop dead in combat. Working for a college degree meant straining and self-denial. Was it worth that? Numerous graduates from college, to earn their bread and butter, were pursuing occupations as gasoline station attendants, door-to-door salesmen, waiters, drivers, and other kinds of employment not requiring degrees. In situations in which an academic parchment was mandatory the pay was too frequently on the same par with blue collar workers, or not infrequently less.

Where could Vincent Armstrong draw the line? How were the

scales to be balanced? Could it be that a garbage collector earned more money than a college man. In his frame of mind the young war veteran appeared lacking in proficiency to come to a determination.

While serving in the army, he had become accustomed to having his existence regulated by commissioned officers and dominated by noncom's. As a private he was ordered when to eat and sleep, when to wake and dress, when to move and stay, when to walk and run, when to stand and sit, when to talk and listen, when to do this and that, that and this, this and that.

Halt! Not that—this! This, this, this, and this. Double-time that, and that, and that—and that! Hurry up and wait. Police the area. Stop hosing the dog. Get your tail down! Isn't on the ball? Aching back. TS, gigged. Report to the mess sergeant. Yeah, KP. Dingles on a shingle. Chow hog. Forced march; blistered feet. Ninety-day wonder, second lieutenant: You'll live. Piece, not a gun. Piece! Weekend pass. Keep your pecker in your pants! . . . Short arm inspection: pull back your foreskin. Hey, wash off the cheese. How do you like those apples. And this and that. Dig a narrow trench—deeper! Pooh. Smelly latrine . . . , ticks on his behind; burn out the bloodsuckers. With what? With a cigarette. That burns. Sick call. Yes. What! No, sir. Louder. NO, SIR! Shavetail: field-strip that butt.

Bemuddled—psychologically teeter-tottering—his independence bruised, his sense of values blurred, Vincent found it hard to make choices. Unable to arrive at definite decisions he resolved, pending his readjustment to civilian life, the only alternative was temporarily to file away plans for the future.

Despite unpleasant, disciplinary pettiness servicemen are subjected to in their training and their fighting, historically, for whatever reason one cares to give, they more than often end up feeling or at least expressing great pride in their war service. Vincent Armstrong was no exception. Not only was he proud to have served in the armed forces but also he was proud to have served his country in its hour of need.

Although Germany had surrendered on May 8, 1945, not until the day after Vincent was discharged from the army did the war end with Japan. The United States had stunned the Japanese nine days before on August sixth when an American Air Force bombardier in a B-29 (the *Enola Gay*), piloted by Colonel Paul Tibbetts, unloosed the first atomic bomb in history over a city—Hiroshima, a major port and military stronghold on the island of Hunshu.

Within seconds the blast and heat rays from the atomic bomb

(containing 1,000 grams of Uranium 235) destroyed sixty per cent of the city: four and one-tenths square miles were reduced to piles of grey-white ashes and smoldering cinders. Scores of people were killed or injured by the blast. Scores of people were crushed or crippled by collapsing buildings. Scores of people were cremated or scarred by the heat rays, rivaling the sun's surface temperature. Scores of survivors exposed to ionizing radiation, a by-product of the A-bomb, were destined to die from such dreadful diseases as leukemia and cancer.

[On that disastrous day the population of Hiroshima was about 400,000, including an estimated 250,000 civilians residing within the boundaries of the city, plus military personnel, and some influx of suburbanites.

The first casualties report was made public November 30, 1945, by the Police Department of the Prefectural Government of Hiroshima. The report gave the following statistics:

killed 78,150
injured 37,425
missing 13,983

The foregoing figures did not include casualties suffered by the military personnel stationed in Hiroshima. It also should be taken into account that a large number of the survivors died of latent effects from radiation subsequent to the publication of this report.

A national census was conducted October 1, 1950, to survey the population of Japan, as well as to secure information on the exact number of Hiroshima survivors who were still alive. The census disclosed there were 158,607 survivors dispersed throughout the country; most were living in Hiroshima and the surrounding suburbs. Accordingly it was calculated that at least 200,000 deaths resulted from the atomic bombing of Hiroshima.]

After Hiroshima was bombed, an act of heroism was performed, dwarfing all the great deeds of survivors who fought against insurmountable odds to save the severely injured. Had the heroic performer been a soldier, his intrepidity would have earned him Japan's highest service medal, the Golden Eagle. Here are the impressions of one observer:

With buildings burning, smoking, and falling everywhere in the city, the greatest concern that the employees in the General Affairs section of the Hiroshima Communications Bureau had was for the safety of the Emperor's picture, which hung in a room on the fourth floor. Above all else the likeness of Tenno, the Heavenly Sovereign, must be saved. In spite of danger from rapidly spreading fires, due to a whirlwind caused by the intense heat coming up from the ground, a long-drawn-out conference was held in the office of the Chief of General Affairs to determine where the Emperor's picture could be safeguarded. Nearby Hiroshima Castle was the place finally selected as the best haven.

His imperial image was removed from the Communications Bureau with the fanfare and fuss found in a guard of honor. Extra care was taken in placing the bulky picture upon the back of a Mr. Yasudo. As he loyally carried his burden through an inner garden of the Bureau, another General Affairs employee, cupping hand to mouth, bugled:

"The Emperor's picture will be transferred to the West Drill Field at Hiroshima Castle by order of the Chief of General Affairs." At the sound of the bugled words everybody in the garden bowed with humility.

When he marched off the Bureau grounds into the streets, Mr. Yasudo was escorted by four employees who had enclosed him in a diamond-shaped formation; they were bent on guarding the Emperor's picture against all hazards. One employee, the advance guard, led the way at a point up front. (Meanwhile, were there any men trapped in burning buildings who could be saved?) A second employee, the rear guard, trailed behind to maintain a point at the back. (Meanwhile, were there any women trapped in smoky buildings who could be saved?) A third employee guarded the left point. (Meanwhile, were there any children trapped in fallen buildings who could be saved?) A fourth employee guarded the right point. (Meanwhile, were there more and more trapped people perishing?)

In the great concern over the safety of the Emperor's picture, an inexcusable oversight had occurred. No one remembered to bring the Communications Bureau flag: it is unritualistic not to accompany the imperial image with a flag whenever His location is changed. The right guard was sent back to the Bureau for the flag; however, Mr. Yasudo and the other guards were forced to move on without him when flaming wreckage started crashing down into the street.

The faithful group of subjects trembled. With the flag omitted from the picture-carrying ritual, what would the Emperor think! By the time Mr. Yasudo and the others reached the gates of Hiroshima Castle, the fires had spread to the West Drill Field. Since the castle was unsafe, a message explaining the necessity to alter their course was relayed to the Chief of General Affairs. The alternative arrived at was that the Emperor's picture would be out of danger on the east or other side of the Ōta River.

(Flowing through Hiroshima from north to south, the Ōta is a deltaic river with seven estuaries which separate the city like sticks divide an open fan.)

Traveling northeast, the three escorts and Mr. Yasudo who bore his burden with stoutheartedness, marched across Hiroshima in the direction of Asano Sentei Park, which fringes the banks of the Ōta River.

Mr. Yasudo had to watch his step every foot of the way, for wherever he walked there were bloody puddles, tricklings from the wounded lying in the streets. He carefully stepped over the live bodies to make sure not to land in a puddle. What would the Emperor think if Yasudo splashed blood on the picture!

Near Asano Sentei Park the escorts and Mr. Yasudo were stopped by a roadblock built from hundreds of hurt humans hardly able to stir. The human obstruction was impassable. Only a miracle could save the picture now. The four weary men hung their heads in despondency. They felt so sorry for the Emperor.

Seeking solace in the sky, they saw a vision of Tenno holding a miraculous lantern. A ray of sunshine shone on the Emperor's picture. And the Heavenly Sovereign spoke. And the faithful subjects heeded his words. And they repeated his words again and again and again, "The Emperor's picture be saved, the Emperor's picture be saved, The Emperor's picture be saved, . . ." And they held the picture up for all to see.

Shamefacedly the hurt humans prayed to the adorable likeness of the Emperor. They were naked. The forceful flash of heat from the atomic blast had seared the clothes from their bodies.

In accordance with the way they happened to be positioned, the hurt humans prayed; as they sat, as they stood, on their knees, on their backs—or prostrated before His imperial image. Regardless of their positions everybody worshipped in pain. Flash-burned, their flesh was red and raw and moist and mushy.

Sacrificing their last bit of energy, the hurt humans moved aside to help save the Heavenly Sovereign's likeness. Except for torsoless heads and limbs blasted onto the road by the atomic bomb, which were avoided, Mr. Yasudo and party made their way to the Ōta without encountering any further obstacles. At the riverbank the Emperor's picture was handed over to the Chief of General Affairs, who had rushed ahead of the employees to prepare a reception befitting royalty.

While a host of subjects above the bank bowed with reverence, a body of soldiers escorted the Emperor's picture to the edge of the river, where an officer in command helped the Chief of General Affairs put the honored object aboard a boat he had in readiness. The military honor guard snapped to attention and saluted when the officer flourished his sword deftly, a signal for the boat to set sail.

As the boat sailed farther and farther from the riverbank, the gentle subjects bowed lower and lower. By contrast the rough river flowed swifter and swifter. The currents were so swift it was feared the small vessel would be overturned. A shudder ran through the stooped subjects at the thought of the Emperor's picture falling overboard into the waters of the Ōta.

Not too far upstream, before the boat got under way, scores of less fortunate subjects had jumped into the river to escape the ever-spreading fires on dry land. Caught in the swift currents many men, women, and children were swept downstream. In crossing the Ōta, the boat sailed past people splashing about in the water who were struggling to stay afloat...a sad sight to behold.

Back on the riverbank subjects not yet threatened by fire watched with wonder. Some stronger swimmers swam after the boat. Would they be able to reach the small vessel in time to board it? If they did, it might capsize. Had the end come; was the Emperor's picture doomed? Miraculously no: the people drowned before they could catch up with the boat. The subjects safe on shore signed with relief. His imperial image was saved!

Three days later, after Hiroshima was bombed, the sons of Nippon, having been slow to accept previous ultimatums, with due respect quickly asked Uncle Sam for honorable surrender terms when on August ninth an American Air Force bombardier in a B-29 (the *Great Artiste*), piloted by Major Robert Sweeney, unleashed an "improved" atomic bomb over another city—Nagasaki, a seaport on the island of Kyushu.

In spite of the fact that the second atomic bomb (containing 1,000 grams of Plutonium 239) was designed to be more powerful than the first one, damage caused by blast and heat rays in Hiroshima and Nagasaki were approximately the same magnitude. Yet only thirty per cent of Nagasaki, including one square mile of its harbor, was destroyed—why?

At Hiroshima destruction of buildings by the blast was complete within the radius of one and a quarter miles from the epicenter, partially within two and a half miles, and slightly three and three-thirds miles from the epicenter. Heat rays burned almost all wooden houses within the radius of one and a quarter miles from the epicenter and produced burns on human bodies within two miles. Unfortunately there were no mountains or other shelters to provide some protection against the A-bomb.

At Nagasaki the epicenter was in a valley near the Urakami Catholic Cathedral. Whether it provided anything but spiritual shelter against the blast and heat rays is doubtful. Substantial physical protection against the A-bomb undoubtedly was provided by the mountains in the area, for the central part of the city remained intact. Nevertheless, thousands of people were killed, injured, and exposed to ionizing radiation.

[Records at City Hall in Nagasaki (obtained through the Tokyo office) show the population was about 210,000 on August 9, 1945. Also recorded was the approximate number of casualties on the date of the atomic bombing. In 1956 the statistical information was updated in the Nagasaki City Administration Directory as follows:

> killed 73,884
> injured 74,909
> missing 17,358

The foregoing figures did not include future fatalities that in all probability resulted from residual radioactivity, which was effective a long time after the explosion of the Atom Bomb.]

Unwilling to admit defeat, die-hard samurai in Japan's Supreme War Council refused to surrender. But Hirohito their emperor argued Japan was in danger of annihilation. To continue the war was suicidal.

Seppuku is for subjects not for sovereigns. Is not honorable surrender better than 'honorable suicide'? All he asked of the victor was that the capitulation should not contain "... any demand which prejudices the prerogatives of His Majesty as a sovereign ruler." Hirohito's prerogatives included four main powers*:

> * the Emperor is the central authority of civil government;
> * he is supreme commander of the army and navy;
> * he is head of the state religion (Shinto);
> * he has supreme authority in foreign affairs, declarations
>   of war, and the making of treaties.

The President of the United States, Harry S. Truman, was displeased. He felt the Emperor should bow to the victor without reservations. In any case, President Truman realized it was significant that only Hirohito had the powers to order the surrender of the heavily armed Japanese forces, which were strongly entrenched and strategically dispersed across warworn Asia and the Pacific.

Truman conferred with his cabinet to study the overtures of peace put forward by the enemy. As soon as the wrinkles in the surrender terms were ironed out, the president communicated by telephone with America's allies in London, Moscow, and Chungking. His message was well received; he unanimously was authorized to be spokesman for the Big Four—England, Russia, China, and the United States.

On the morning of August eleventh the president had Secretary of State James Byrnes send a note to Tokyo accepting the Japanese overtures of peace, with the proviso, however, that the Supreme Allied Commander, General of the Army Douglas MacArthur, govern Japan through the ascendancy of the emperor.

Secretly Hirohito must have been pleased with this peace pact. He would not have to renounce his title. He would not have to stand trial as a war criminal. He now had no need of a war chest. He could devote all his resources to filling his treasure chest.

America's statesmen were pleased, too. They now possessed a valuable antique, a genuine puppet-mikado with priceless silk strings attached. Never mind that the strings were frayed. The American people could afford the expensive repair bills. Is not America the richest nation in the world. The political puppeteers were in a generous mood. Their government possessed the two-billion-dollar atom bomb.

Two billion dollars was indeed the price paid for the recondite experimentation that went into the development of the A-bomb. Yes, under the guise of secrecy, without the taxpayers' knowledge or consent, hundreds of millions of dollars were lavished on a deadly weapon—which can kill mankind any day now. In fact, the congressmen who generously signed blank checks to finance the atomic project (called the Manhattan Project) were as much in the dark about it as were the people whom they were supposed to represent.

Yet, with all the gold in Fort Knox and genius in the United States, the atom bomb could never have been built if the labor (secrets) of scientists of every nationality had not been exploited.

Well, perhaps not all nationalities. What is about to be revealed is fiction based on fact...or something else?

Not until a Second World War year, 1941, after international revelations in the field of nuclear physics shed light on the way titanic atom bombs as well as atomic power plants could be manufactured at a profit, was the Manhattan Project started. Said undertaking, by an ambiguous agreement between two top company executives, Mr. Ulysses S. Wirepuller of Republic Incorporated and Sir George B. Majordomo of Monarchy Limited, was a joint enterprise in which the returns (information about nuclear energy) were to be shared equally. Since the North American Continent was out of flying range of the German luftwaffe and the aerial buzz bombs, the board of directors, to protect the investments of the Manhattan Bomb Company, located its main offices, laboratories, and production plants in the States.

As the wheels of the war gained momentum, Sir Majordomo, living up to his end of the business arrangement, sent Mr. Wirepuller progress reports on nuclear experiments conducted at the company's laboratories in England. When weeks went by and G. M. did not hear from U. W., the former cabled the Yank executive officer for updated information on development in the fission of the atom and the manufacture of atomic bombs. A believer in the dictum "possession is nine-tenths of the law," Mr. Wirepuller felt under no obligation to comply with Sir Majordomo's request. So U. W. put off G. M. with twiddle-twaddle that wartime regulations did not permit information of such a strategic nature to be divulged at random. He stopped short of saying the information was classified, Top Secret.

Unbelievable as it seems, the anecdotic Anglo-American relations paragraphed above illustrates that distrust can be sillier than trust. A jocose example, demonstrating preposterous measures taken in attempts to conceal the power of the structure of an atom, was found in occupied Japan. The staff in General MacArthur's headquarters suspicious of Asiatic intrigue, censored with a steel stamp any scientific journal printing references to the A-bomb or nuclear fission (the principles of which were contained in textbooks on physics studied by Japanese schoolboys).

If Democritus, the "laughing philosopher," were alive today, he would split an atom laughing at the formula, A-bomb stories told about spies stealing secrets. For Democritus had disclosed atomistic theory in ancient Greece. The philosopher even named the atom.

Since Democritus' time (circa 460-370 B.C.) learned men from all parts of the world have had a finger in the development of the principles behind the atom bomb. In scholarly private diaries it is written that exciting nuclear-fission secrets are concealed in Madame Nature's womb, not in Man's brain box. Naturally, curious gentlemen, desirous of carnal knowledge, had to come up to her standards of sophistication before she permitted herself to be probed. She is coy, a damnable tease. They could never have gained entrance to her boudoir had they not had a gentlemen's agreement to compare notes, of partially successful seducers, from which the proper techniques to use on the lady was learned.

Morally, bellicose Man progressed as far as he could throw a flame the day after he stumbled upon the incendiary energy in fire. The day after he discovered the explosive energy in the atom he progressed morally as far as he could throw a bomb. Man—the genius, the moralist—has used long-wished-for gifts of power well in progressively depressing and destroying his kind. Ovid, an outspoken Roman poet (43 B.C.–A.D. 17?), who was exiled for his unpopular views, dared criticize gifted Man's morals in pointed poetry, "Ovid's Metamorphoses" (The Story of Phäeton):

> Choose out a gift from the seas, or earth, or skies,
> For open to your wish all nature lies;
> Only decline this one unequal task,
> For 'tis a mischief, not a gift, you ask;
> You ask a real mischief, Phäeton: . . .

Shortly after hostilities between Germany and the Allies ceased in Europe, on Tuesday, August 14, 1945, at 4:00 p.m., a joyful announcement came from the White House: "Japan surrenders—unconditionally. World War II is officially over!"

At the approach of evening on that momentous Tuesday, Vincent Armstrong, our young war veteran, walked with cadenced steps along Market Street; his whole being swelled with pride. Like a peacock flaunting his pretty, preened feathers, he paused at street corners on occasion—carefree...erecting his lean, sinewy body...puffing out his chest. From time to time, as his sky-blue eyes stole glances at himself in the glass of store windows, he inspected his neatly pressed olive-drab army uniform.

His coat on the left side had an abundant serving of "fruit salad"—colorful decorations, ribbons with battle stars—truly aligned above the seam of the flap over his breast pocket. The garrison cap jauntily tilted on his head covered most of his thick wavy hair, dark brown in color. He marched smartly in his combat boots, shined to a fault with ox-blood polish.

Vincent halted to strike a match on a hydrant; he cupped his hands to protect the flame from the wind as he lit a cigarette, and was careful not to lip it. If there was anything he detested, it was the taste of tobacco dampened by spit-soaked paper. Forming his lips into the shape of an oval, he blew smoke rings while he strutted along, his head held high. The former soldier boy magnified his five feet ten inches enormously, fancying himself a giant blowing clouds over the forty hills of San Francisco.

By now Market Street, the main downtown thoroughfare, was crowded with crowds of people celebrating the end of the war. Disgracefully, flagitious incidents followed that were to turn the celebration into a mockery of the sons and fathers and the daughters and mothers sacrificed by the millions in the Allied nations' struggle for universal peace and freedom, for law and order—for human dignity.

Seated in a late-model convertible Cadillac, observing the passers-by rejoice, a distinguished-looking man, with an attractive woman sitting beside him, was accosted by a sailor reeking from alcohol, and behaving in a boisterous manner. Good-natured individuals, the man and his companion tried to humor the drunk but to no avail. He had a nasty disposition.

"Better put th', th', th' Cad and da', and the dame away, bub," sputtered the drunken sailor, his chin beaded with drops of saliva. The top folded down, he was able to lean over into the convertible; in doing so, he brushed against the woman's head and messed up her hairdo. "Ta', take off, bub," the drunken sailor spat out an order. "Or," he warned the man, "they'll take 'em away from you."

The sailor, staggering as he suddenly stepped back from the Cadillac, collided with Vincent Armstrong who happened to be passing by. The impact knocked the cigarette out of Vincent's hand. "Watch where you're going, you bastard!" the drunk uttered an insult instead of an apology.

Ignoring the base bluster because the sailor was intoxicated, Vincent kept moving till he reached the Paramount Theater. He stopped to see a marine corporal, assisted by other marines, climb up onto the marquee where a brood of usherettes were perched near the edge watching the celebrators. On the marquee ad board hung in large metal letters were the words JAPS QUIT. The corporal plucked off some of the letters, let out a bloodcurdling yell, and waved the letter J menacingly in the direction of the usherettes. Startled, they scattered like frightened hens looking for shelter in a chicken coop. Next the moronic marine started chucking letters at passers-by below. One of the letters grazed Armstrong's ear lobe; luckily the metal letter left only a slight gash, but it did sting. He used a clean khaki handkerchief to stop the bleeding. Angered when he saw the blood, he threw the stained handkerchief on the sidewalk already littered with debris, including miscellany reminiscent of New Year's Eve celebrations: serpentine throws, adding machine tapes, typewriter ribbons, calendar leaves, and shredded telephone books tossed out of windows by spectators in buildings, and confetti flung from bags by participants in the streets.

Some servicemen running in a pack, the way wolves on a hunt stalk a helpless prey, seized a middle-aged woman who was walking alone waving a little American flag. She was too stunned to scream. In their pursuit of the unprotected woman, they had pushed Vincent Armstrong aside nearly knocking him off his feet.

One of the servicemen squeezed the woman's breast; to justify his outrageous familiarity, in the man's unjust mind, he lied idiotically to her: "Lady you remind me of my mommy back home. She always fed me milk." He put his finger in his mouth, pretending the finger was the nipple of a baby bottle. The serviceman made a sucking sound and said, "I'm hungry, you got any milk for me, mommy?" Before he could say, or do, anything else, she was snatched away by others and passed around from one pair of outstretched hands to another as if she were the carcass of a doe. At the moment she was ambushed, the woman involuntarily had dropped the American flag, which now was being trampled on.

That night downtown was transformed into an insane asylum in which orderly sane people were indiscriminately locked up with disorderly insane people. Females; adults...and minors, single...and married, unescorted...and escorted, inebriated...and sober, acquaintances...and strangers, were expected to submit in good graces to lecherous hugs and lickerish kisses.

Civilians and noncivilians—soldiers, sailors, marines—exchanged hats in a crazy comedy of wrong sizes. Removing his garrison cap before anybody could snatch it, Vincent Armstrong folded and stuffed the soft headpiece into his pocket. A loud, crashing, splintering sound sent him scurrying for cover in a doorway.

Brazenly, rioting maniacs were shoving automobiles through plate-glass store fronts. Although the rioters were enjoying it, to vandalize valuable property at random or to loot expensive merchandise in general was not their primary objective. They were particularly interested in the displays of Scotch and bourbon whiskey.

As he zigzagged in a turbulent sea of swaying humanity: arms swinging, elbows swerving, hips swiveling, legs swaggering, Armstrong skillfully steered his way clear to Market and Taylor Streets...though he very nearly tripped over a slender, silver-haired lady sitting on the corner curb. She was weeping and sobbing pathetically. On her bosom, next to her heart, was a gold star. (Her only son had been killed in the Battle of the Bulge.) The bereaved mother's tearful lamentations were drowned out by the wailing of a fire-engine siren.

In the middle of Market Street pyromaniacs, fueled with alcohol, had started a bonfire. They were stoking the fire with all the things they could lay their hands on—ripped off awnings, rifled goods, stolen purses; lost garments, most of which had been taken by force; cardboard and wooden signs, wrongfully removed from their rightful places; unpaid for magazines and newspapers—anything and everything burnable.

Firemen arrived on the scene in ample time only to be prevented from extinguishing the dangerous bonfire. As the firemen assembled their equipment, the engine was stripped of its reel line, or hose, by the pyromaniacs, cheered on by a wild crowd of their peers. In order to perform their duty the firemen grabbed hold of the reel line in an attempt to retrieve it. But that was no easy task because the reel line had been stretched out almost two hundred feet.

Inevitably a tug of war ensued. Tugging the reel line at the far end with a good grip on the nozzle, were the "lit firebugs"; and tugging at an opposite section of the reel line attached to the water tank on the engine, were the fire fighters. The leaping flames, the red fire engine, the two groups in conflict, dramatically with blood-flushed faces struggling over a length of rubber hose, might well have been cast and prop for a scene in Dante's *Inferno*.

Appearing from nowhere, a bearded sailor on roller skates leering stupidly all but churned Vincent Armstrong's stomach when the sailor dangled a dead rat on a string under Vincent's nose. Trained to react to the unexpected, Armstrong the soldier side-stepped the stupid, salty sea nut, and gave him a non too gentle shove. He went rolling out of control at high speed toward some girls who, repelled by the sight of a dangling dead rat, dispersed pell-mell.

Pudgy hands of a big-boned fat female pulled Armstrong by the waist into a crooked file of parading people following, in conga-line fashion, a man half blinded by gin. His attraction was a large American flag on a pole that he supported at an angle on his shoulder. To him the entire episode was just a game, the players leader and followers: The patriotic goatherd led the stray goats as far as Powell Street; then since he had no sense of devotion he abandoned them for different sport farther along Market Street. Reeling, he stumbled and the flag slipped off his shoulder and dropped to the sidewalk. Gradually The Star-Spangled Banner was kicked into the gutter by feet whose owners did not look where they were going.

What had won the pie-eyed defector's allegiance was a woman about forty years old, clad in tight slacks and a sheer blouse. She was entertaining a gathering audience with simple sexy songs sometimes heard at smokers during social intercourse. At the moment the woman was warbling words she made up to the tune of "Pistol Packin' Mama":

> Frazzin' in the bedroom, and were they getting kicks;
> But then she got all steamed up
> And wore out poor old Dick.
>> Pull that peter out, Babe,
>> Pull that peter out.
>> Peter lovin' Mama,
>> Pull that peter out.
>
> Next night he saw the blondie, and she would frazz no more.
> She jacked him off—
> Changed her mind. Gad! His balls were sore!
>> Pull that peter out, Babe,
>> Pull that peter out.
>> Peter lovin' Mama,
>> Pull that peter out.

Sis-s-s-s-s-s-s-s-s-s-s, BOOM!!! Pop! Pop! Pop! Pop! Pop! . . . ! Illegal firecrackers—cannons and tiny poppers—were being exploded at the heels of celebrators by childish characters among the crowds. Armstrong, his ears ringing, paled a ghostly white. Shocked by the suddenness of the exploding firecrackers, the war veteran momentarily thought he heard machine guns and artillery shells being fired, which are hellishly terrifying, for the shells make a loud, sharp, piercing sound seconds before they explode. Combat soldiers call the shells "screaming minnies." Vincent Armstrong was still haunted by their sounds, unearthly silent sounds only he could hear.

To escape the deafening cannons and tiny poppers he ran across the street to the corner of Eddy and Powell Streets. He found cover at the entrance to the Bank of America Day and Night Office, where he squeezed himself into a plate-glass section of the four-sectional revolving door. With his hands placed over his ears Vincent remained standing between the glass panels till the firecracker barrage died down. All unfortunately was far from tranquil.

Piratical sailors, just released from boot camp, had taken over a cable car on the Powell Street turntable. A grandmother who was not well and a bit unsteady was afraid to step off the cable car's narrow footboard by herself; nevertheless she was forced to disembark unassisted. Two giggling bobby-soxers, too foolish to see the seriousness of the situation, were fluttering their eyelids, flirting for fun. Led on, the sailors prevented the two from disembarking. Despite their protests, seemingly mild, they were pushed back into the enclosed section of the cable car, where they were held against their will. Realizing they had been courting disaster, the silly bobby-soxers, now serious, demanded to be set free at once. Their demands were not met, not immediately anyway.

Subsequently, with much, much more energy than the municipal starter, conductor, and gripman exert each trip in order to reverse the cable car's direction, the sailors joined by a crew of other pirates began spinning it violently on the turntable. Why the iron-rimmed, wooden, circular platform did not collapse is a wonder.

Riot squads, overworked by constant trouble-chasing from Van Ness Avenue to the Embarcadero, were summoned to quell the disturbance that was turning violent around the Powell Street turntable. At the advent of The Law some sailors commandeered an empty police car and began rocking it from side to side as if it were a cradle; as they rocked they sang "Rock-A-By Baby." Instead of being angry at the sailors to everybody's amazement the police were amused by the riotous acts. Laughing, the bluecoats stood by permitting the bluejackets to stick out their tongues at The Law.

Before Vincent Armstrong knew what was happening, two sailors a short distance ahead were crouching over a female lying on the ground in an immodest position—willingly! Not only did she allow them to hoist her feet up into the air but also she voiced no objection to their looking between her legs. A third sailor, his sexual appetite whetted, snuck up and all of a sudden tore off her panties. The snatcher sniffed the female's panties and exclaimed, "Fish! phooey fish." With a perverted gleam in his eyes he twirled the panties on a finger as he started to run away. Furious because the sailor snatched her panties, the slut chased after him yelling, "You like fish, I'll make you eat it!"

Thoroughly disgusted, Vincent decided to move on. However, he was not sure where he should go next. It was fortunate that he hesitated, for he missed stepping under a waterfall by inches. A paratrooper walking a few feet in front of him was drenched with a shopping bag full of water tossed from the six-story Hotel Powell. On the paratrooper's sleeve was a row of "hashmarks," gold stripes signifying years of faithful service to our country, overseas. The gold stripes were soaking wet.

Keeping an eagle eye on the sixth floor, Vincent gave the Hotel Powell a wide berth as he walked up the block. He turned right on Ellis Street, headed in the direction of Roos Brothers Clothiers. At the intersection of Ellis and Stockton Streets an informal ball was in progress. Dancing on the blacktop were males and females costumed in uniforms from all branches of the armed forces and costumed in civilian attire were males and females from all occupations of survival.

Vincent looked for a band but found there was none. He was unaware that earlier the city's V-J Day Committee, appointed by the mayor, Roger D. Lapham, had instructed a band assembled at the Ferry Building to parade up Market Street in an effort to calm the crazy crowds with harmonious music. The committee's tactic proved futile. Evidently the victory in Japan drove people out of their minds; they manhandled the musicians forcing them to disband and flee to safety.

Band or no band, the couples were dancing to their own music, improvised versions of popular melodies hummed over and over again...off-key if not off-beat. Just the same the couples were having a ball. Some jitterbugged. Some fox-trotted. Some did goofy dances. Some danced apart. Some danced close, very close. A lanky army lieutenant who had been glued to his partner abruptly backed away from her. The left trouser leg of his pinks had a wettish, sticky stain below the crotch. On the lieutenant's pallid face was a most peculiar expression, almost lifeless. Maybe he was suffering from anemia.

Alongside the makeshift ballroom an F streetcar had been wedged in near the intersection crowded from curb to curb with celebrators, "I double-dare you!" Vincent Armstrong heard a sailor challenge a group of his mates. Accepting the challenge, six sailors scaled the streetcar's bulkhead. In short order all were undressed down to their skivvies. To show off, with hands on their hips the sailors attempted to impersonate bathing beauties as they awkwardly posed and waddled back and forth on the top of the streetcar.

His throat parched from chain-smoking, a reaction brought on by the disconcerting sights he was witnessing, Vincent had a thirst in need of quenching. In that Lotta's Fountain was only two blocks away at Market and Kearny Streets, he went there for a drink of water.

[Lotta's Fountain, a rococo memorial, was presented to the citizens of San Francisco in 1875 by Charlotte Crabtree, an idolized American actress born in New York. She died at the age of seventy-seven, leaving a fortune of nearly four million dollars to charity. Half the money was willed to a foundation for the relief of needy World War I veterans; bequests were given to hospitals and to funds for the care of stray dogs and old horses.

With the fountain as a backdrop Luisa Tetrazzini, noted Italian soprano, sang "The Last Rose of Summer" for San Franciscans on Christmas Eve, 1910. A medallion was placed on the south side of the fountain in remembrance of the occasion.

In 1916, On October 4th and 5th, the Path of Gold Festival Committee reconstructed the fountain. Periodically public indignation meetings have been held: outcries against the ugliness of the outdated rococo memorial. Throughout the years artists had given it a face lifting in vain. Also artfully bronzed, it is still looked on as an eyesore in a modern municipality mesmerized by flat façades and barren walks. To venerable native San Franciscans, Lotta's Fountain will always remain beautiful, a magnificent obsession.]

Upon approaching Lotta's Fountain, Vincent Armstrong saw another performance displaying the body beautiful. Several servicemen, roaring and ready to pounce like a pride of hungry lions, were watching a wild woman strip off every stitch of her clothes, but she partly covered herself with a cheap fur wrap. When the wind changed directions and animalistic servicemen got a whiff of her scent, they pounced on her, ripped away her fur, and pawed at her naked body. Instinctively, to avoid their scratchy fingernails, she leaped onto the cast-iron fountain so that she could gain a toe hold on the low ridge around the base. Then she tried to shin up the fountain's shaft, an eight-foot curlicue. Unable to hang on she jumped back down to the sidewalk.

In her desire to be the center of attention the woman, stark naked, did a dirty dance with postures assumed by a wildebeest in heat, which brought roars of approval from her ring of admirers. She had picked a most appropriate stage for her lewd performance. Any traveler on safari in San Francisco's concrete jungle, in search of the fountain, will find each of its four flanks is studded with a lion's head. The beastly bellows from the servicemen eyeing the nude rivaled the roars of Leo himself, king of the beasts. The curtain rang down on the vulgar vaudeville when a husky petty officer, who had been standing off stage in a wing, broke up the act and cloaked his pea jacket over the burlesque queen's bare shoulders. Arm in arm the pair left the fountain site and waded into the depths of the engulfing confluence on Market Street.

Vincent wondered how well they knew each other, if at all, as he observed the pair disappear. But he put the thought out of his mind for, with his mouth dry and his tongue fuzzy, it was more urgent to quench his thirst than to satisfy his curiosity. While drinking from a water faucet in the fountain, he almost had his teeth bashed against the spout. Quavering like a wind bell, a baby-faced pinup, her lipstick smeared, had accidentally run into him.

"I'm...I'm sor'...I'm sorry," she apologized having caught her breath. "I didn't mean to bump you. Would you help me?" Afraid he might refuse, she burst into tears and pleaded: "Please! please help me! Those sailors back there are after me. They've taken my purse. And they threatened to take my dress off."

His balance regained, Vincent turned around to see some sailors cutting across Kearny Street. They were coming too close for comfort. Quick to grasp the danger she faced, Vincent made a quick decision: "Sure, I'll help you," he assured the terrified girl. He slipped his arm protectively under hers and said, "Let's get going."

Hastily Vincent guided the girl up Market Street. The object of his maneuver was to conceal her among the dense crowds of celebrators. Unable to converse in their haste, breathless and perspiring, they plowed ahead silently, struggling hard to elude the pursuing sailors. Fate foiled their escape however. The density of the crowd had, for the moment, thickened to an impenetrable mass in the area outside the Billiard Club. A marine private was stretched out on the sidewalk near the foot of the terrazzo staircase leading to the club.

Whether he was drunk or sober, or an idiot, was not determined; the marine making the sign V for victory with taut fingers while skipping down the flight of stairs, with about as much restraint as a loose boulder rolling down a steep cliff, had lost his hold on the handrail attached along a wall on one side of the staircase. The leatherneck had tumbled and landed squarely on his head. His skull fractured, he lay at the bottom dying on the cold cement.

People, shoving and pushing, impatient to view the death scene, allowed Vincent and the girl some space to squirm through the massive crowd. Despite their desperate efforts to flee from danger, the delay proved disastrous. On Mason Street, approximately half a block north of Market Street, they were overtaken by their pursuers. Vincent did his utmost in the friendliest terms to persuade them not to molest the young girl.

As a token of good will, he pulled out a pack of cigarettes and offered each of the sailors a smoke, which was accepted. He also offered to shake hands with one of the sailors, which was a mistake. Without warning the sailor grabbed Vincent's left arm by the wrist wrenching it unmercifully, a second sailor twisted Vincent's right arm behind his back, a third sailor clutched Vincent by his hair; the bravest of the lot, a fourth sailor, pelted Vincent with blows to his body.

Spotting a policeman, the girl screamed to attract his attention. He must have been too far away; he did not respond to her screams. She yelled for help louder and louder to men passing by. Her yells fell on deaf ears. Before she could utter another sound, a cockswain clamped his callous hand over the girl's mouth and dragged her into the dark vestibule of the Garfield Building. Breaking free from his attackers, Vincent, in a spontaneous action, ran toward the vestibule with determination to rescue the girl.

"I guess the doughboy hasn't had enough," a sailor shouted to his shipmates, who immediately gave chase. The sailors caught Vincent—ganged up on him—kicked him viciously—knocked him to the ground—and left him helplessly battered. He was lying face down barely conscious when his forehead pressed against the ice-cold pavement, it had the effect of a cold compress. Vincent was revived somewhat, but benumbed and blear-eyed. Propping himself up on an elbow with great effort, he saw shadowy images of the gobs, gang-raping the baby-faced pinup.

Her unspeakable torments expressed by her cries were muffled by the ungodly murmur of the multitudes, not to mention the damnable honking of automobile horns. The backfiring of an automobile ejected puffs of black smoke from the exhaust pipe. Vincent got a whiff of carbon monoxide and lost consciousness. . . .

Stiff Pacific breezes, reviving Vincent Armstrong, cleared his head of the gaseous fumes and soothed his contusions. Coming to with a start, he rose to his feet and hobbled over to the vestibule of the Garfield Building where the criminal copulation had been committed. Gone were the felonious sailors and the violated girl. As he stepped away, Vincent heard something spongy squish under his scuffed boot. Could he have crushed a snail? He never had come across one in this neck of the woods. Lifting his foot, he saw a shriveled condom. To vent his frustration he booted it out onto the sidewalk.

Once more our war hero battled his way through the crazed crowds of celebrators. Before the defilement of the victory celebration, he had the lofty pride of a robust conqueror. Now, sore in spirit as well as in body, he was sadly—oh, but sadly crestfallen, his self-esteem shattered. As he trudged up Market Street, Vincent was jostled block after block. No respect whatever was shown for the awards of valor so conspicuous on his army uniform. Enraged...with hair disheveled, with head bowed, with teeth gritted, with shoulders hunched, with fists clenched...he glared defiantly around him, wanting to tongue-lash the celebrators for their unforgivable behavior.

"Stop! Stop this madness! You are behaving like uncaged wild animals, not like civilized human beings—not like patriotic Americans": Vincent Armstrong wanted to shout much more at the rabid rejoicers. It was useless; his words would have been wasted. Choked up with emotion, his watery eyes reddened and blurred, he could taste salt as tears dripping down his cheeks fell upon his lips. He hurried home in a haze. Removing his badly soiled, olive-drab uniform, he hung it in the farthest part of a basement closet; never would he wear the uniform again. His medals he put in a tool box, locked it and threw away the key.

Piqued, upset to the pit of his stomach, Armstrong brooded immaturely. He formed a low opinion of himself; he blamed himself for allowing his experience in the army to turn him into a worthless misfit. Armstrong did not realize that the war years had been aberrant, that he had lost irretraceable steps needed to advance in a normal way from boyhood to maturity. Who cared to inform him, an ordinary citizen, that the cause of his sick feeling of worthlessness was a bit of scum spooned from a polluted world seething with unrest.

War affects nations as a whole and persons individually, seldom for good, often for bad. (Riddle: When is a worthy war not a worthy war? Clue: Dead men do tell tales.) A compote of dissatisfaction, stewing a long peacetime in a depression pot full to the brim, is sure to boil over and make a mess on the country stove, which instead of being cleaned with a fresh cloth is always wiped up with a smudged rag and covered with the wrong paint—red liquid manufactured by Ares and Associates.

The smug administrative masters of subservient men, since the Bronze Age, have been neither intellectually equipped nor equitably minded in seeking an agent other than warmonger Ares to counteract economic chaos. If this statement sounds apocryphal, history was written with weasel words. Hence it is small wonder that Intellect and Equity are hopelessly blinded in societies dazzled by the superficial beauty of Nicene and the false appeal of Bolshevik.

Ares' enormous spear had inflicted wide wounds: Acquaintances were slain, lying buried in ocean beds and in foreign plots. Girls, married in the heat of war, were out of circulation to their regret, the available ones widowed, burdened with children or painful memories. At last a childhood sweetheart, next a high-school classmate, soon former friends were encountered. They exchanged warm greetings but cool farewells. Attitudes were different. People had changed. They seem less friendly—distant. Vincent Armstrong had nothing in common any more with his old cronies.

ANONYMITY:

"Did you hear about Harry Britt? You remember that dumb little jerk that used to pull hairs out of his nose. He's fat as a goose. Didn't have a nickel to his name before Hitler and Mussolini started all the fuss and ruckus. The lunkhead didn't even go through the eighth grade. He's now worth a hundred thousand smackers in cold cash. All he did was walk around with a ten-cent cigar between his teeth, trying to look like a big shot (spelled with a capital 'I'). We was batting the breeze the other day, and he told me he still didn't know how it happened. On the q.t., I'll bet you dollars to doughnuts Harry chiseled on his income tax. Imagine making all that loot selling hand-painted live turtles at those two-by-four concession stands on Fisherman's Wharf.

"Eddy Nims struck it rich, too. He was starving on the road, without a pot to piss in, peddling a line of baby clothes. The war came. His commissions added up. Sleepy Eddy's eyes are usually half shut. So one of those wiseacre real estate brokers buffaloes him into putting a deposit on a pair of commercial buildings in the

Marina. Speculators said they were white elephants—real, sour lemons. Nims tried to back out of the deal, but the broker held him to the contract. Property values skyrocketed in the Marina District after San Franciscans wised up to the fact it was just an idle rumor that the Japanese would fly over the Golden Gate and bomb Yacht Harbor. You know, like they attacked Pearl Harbor."

Yes, the philanthropic war had bought all kinds of people porterhouse steaks. Even the poor Negroes, who had migrated from the South to find work in defense plants and shipyards, received a juicy bite or two...well, in a way, if we count leftover scraps of fat and gristle.

Many orthodox and nonorthodox Jews, descendants of penniless immigrants driven by cultural bonds into the Fillmore District, had left the area, which before the war was a well-maintained neighborhood and now was run-down, blighted blocks filled with deteriorated Victorian houses and dilapidated obsolete flats. Educated, some self-employed—thanks to their industrious parents—the children of Israel in search of a better life spread thinly throughout San Francisco's desirable residential areas.

A colony of Japanese, trustworthy individuals, a credit to the community, also had lived in the Fillmore District for generations. Nevertheless, at the outbreak of the war the government interned Issei, Kibei, Nisei, Sansei alike: whether born here or not, whether educated here or not—whether American citizens or not. Despite the physical hardships, financial losses, and human indignities the Japanese suffered in relocation camps, their men volunteered to fight...to die...for the United States of America.

Scarce, sorely sought shelter was at long last available to the Negroes. And their migration into the Fillmore District was becoming obvious. FOR SALE signs suddenly appeared on Victorians and flats everywhere in the neighborhood.

Property owners in other parts of the city, apprehensive that real estate would decrease in value now that the war was over, panicked along with the rest of the landed gentry into putting their property up for sale. To facilitate sales, Chinese renters, another minority desperate for housing, were evicted from tenements in Chinatown, where large families often occupied only one room. Overcoming their fear of hostile Italians, the Chinese invaded adjacent North Beach, "little Italy." As expected they met prejudicial opposition in the Italian stronghold. While landlords refused to rent to Chinese, the former had no qualms about selling to the latter highly priced buildings, none too few of which were steps away from the wrecker's ball.

Backed to the wall, Chinese families had little choice except to buy at outrageous prices shabby structures forty or more years old, not always free of wood rot and termites. Still more outrageous was the fact that the new owners had to keep their fingers crossed, praying that the restriction clauses which forbade Asians from living on their own property would not be enforced. Said restrictions clauses were formerly written into deeds by Caucasians who failed to understand their country's Constitution.

San Francisco was swarming with strangers. From Vincent Armstrong's perception they appeared to be taking over the city. They were to be sure unaware of his existence; yet by their very presence the newcomers gave the native son a complex, made him seem a stranger in his home town.

At Alta Plaza Park, an old haunt, better players snubbed Vincent off the tennis courts. His feelings hurt, he sulked as he departed down the path of the hilly park. In prewar days, when he was in top form, they would have kissed his ass for a game of tennis. He tried to console himself by reaching into the past and stretching a foul point not exactly in line with reality.

Myriad petty annoyances piled up to a mound of disturbances within Vincent's mind. No longer did he have a clear course in life. With the completeness that rain washes away footprints, his ambition to become a lawyer (a boyhood dream) was obliterated. His enthusiasm for a bright future was mired in a mindless gloom. Still he had to survive. He needed to work, to accomplish something, but he was unstable.

For over five years Vincent found and lost one position after another. Each time he filled out a new employment application, he concocted plausible reasons why he had quit his previous jobs. Outright lies could not get him by indefinitely. He started encountering firms that checked applicants' references.

Upon inquiring, the prospective employers were informed, "Mr. Armstrong was discharged because of the complete lack of enthusiasm he showed toward his work." They refused to hire him. After a few more unsuccessful attempts, almost glad for an excuse to be idle, he simply stopped seeking employment.

Eventually a day of reckoning came; while downtown on a spending spree, Vincent withdrew his last twenty-five dollars from the bank. His savings spent, he had to find a job. At the corner of

Geary and Powell Streets he stopped at a newsstand. After glancing at the headlines, he bought a San Francisco Examiner. Seeing that he was about to miss a speedy B streetcar, he dashed into the safety zone, where he caught the conveyance as he skillfully hopped onto the running board and simultaneously grasped the center post for security—a dangerous practice of some males in a hurry to be on their way home.

That evening Vincent looked through the classified section of the Examiner. Under the job-opportunities columns he saw an advertisement that attracted his attention.

NATIONAL DANCE STUDIOS
needs
energetic individuals
to train
in career positions as
ballroom instructors
*Experience not necessary
*Must be over 20 yrs of age
*Single persons preferred
If you want to work in a
congenial atmosphere in
pleasant surroundings
apply in person
5-10 p.m.
Monday thru Friday
625 Sutter Street
Ask for Mr. Galloway

"Why not?" Vincent asked himself. "Until the right setup develops, teaching dancing may tide me over. 'Experience not necessary,' they say. They're willing to train. That is just the ticket. For once I'm ahead of the game. Not only do I dance well, but I enjoy it."

Vincent Armstrong was rationalizing. The idea of being in a situation which could bring him in close propinquity with women charmed the young man subconsciously. It had been willed his would be the judgment of Paris. He found irresistible Aphrodite's magic cestus, the power of prurient pleasure—delightful dalliances a seductress invites.

Excitedly Vincent's mind began to churn: creamy desires long suppressed stirred within the man. The psychic content of him separating from adulthood, he became immersed in luscious memories of his puberty.

As early as the eighth grade, Vincent recalled, he had had strong sexual urges. They grew still stronger when he heard other young-sters in the schoolyard tell dirty stores plagiarized from adults, or when he and his playmates sneaked into the boys' toilet to ogle at pictures of nudes torn out of discarded art magazines.

Recess ended, one again in the classroom, Vincent would day-dream about all the naughtiness which had transpired during the play-period.

Chapter 8

The new term had begun at John Muir Junior High School. Windows out of which one could not have seen clearly at the end of the previous semester now, like polished diamonds, sparkled and glistened in the sunlight of Indian summer, which beautifies the city by the Golden Gate every September. Scrubbed and washed away from woodwork and walls were the messy smudges; the telltale fingerprints; the spatterings of ink; the childish, misplaced efforts at artistry and wit. The dullness of gummed corridor floors, daily tracked over by hundreds of youngsters' feet (with grimy galoshes when it rained, with dusty shoes when it was dry), had given way to the sheen of hard wax. Indeed the custodians had been alert at their posts.

Entering through front and side doors, the schoolteachers were returning from their three months' holiday. First the early birds, then the regular flock, then the slow-winged stragglers fluttered around the main office to sign in before the 8:30 a.m. deadline. Individual mailboxes (cubicles built into a wall of the office for the teaching staff) were emptied of publishers' listings, outdated announcements, mimeographed communications from administrators, dittoed schedules, book lists, and other miscellany that had accumulated during the summer.

Out in the corridor vacation experiences as well as the merits, or demerits, of in-service and graduate courses were discussed. Above the steady drone of voices came squeals of real and occasionally feigned delight as different arrivals entered the scene.

A few frugal fogies wore the same old things, sweat-stained dresses and suits: uniforms so long associated with the wearers that their true personalities were indiscernible. A number of individuals, up-to-date schoolteacherly types, were dressed in stylish garments from which the store tags had been removed that morning. Wearing new clothes, refreshed bodies were all primped for a crisp, clean start.

Despite the apparent gratification in once again rejoining colleagues, most of the teachers were not overjoyous at the disappearance of the carefree months—June, July, and August. However, there was one unwed educatress, Roxanne Davis, who was glad that the long summer vacation had ended.

Now she would not have to share vicariously the benefits of married life by paying calls to relatives—visits denied as such, still intrusions; attend stage plays at the Curran or Geary Theater without an escort; eat veal scaloppine al marsala or sweet-and-sour spareribs by herself, a lone connoisseur to praise the culinary talent of the Italian or Chinese chef; shop for trinkets neither needed nor wanted; and putter about her home to fill the empty days when school did not keep.

Long ago donated to an educational library, Roxanne's *White Years of Womanhood*—an unused set of reference books, lettered alphabetically—had been placed on the wrong shelf in the stacks, because of poor light no doubt. Desiring one day to refer to the S volume (her "Suppressed Passion"), she searched through the dimly lighted stacks. After a fruitless search Roxanne began to wonder if the missing set of books possibly might have been shelved beyond reach. In frustration, with the hope of finding the S volume, she used as a stepladder a wobbly pile of works on abnormal psychology which were lying by her feet. Although *White Years of Womanhood* had never been fingered, she was shaken when she opened the S volume and saw that it was no longer immaculate; its withering pages had turned brown and musty.

As they dilly-dallied in front of their respective home rooms, the pupils of John Muir Junior High School seemed to have the same question in mind: The new teacher, with whom the next four months had to be spent, what was she like?

Vincent Armstrong was worried about Miss Davis' being assigned to him as his English teacher. He had not had her before; and, according to the way everybody was talking, she was very very strict. Even the troublemaking smart alecks had to admit Miss Davis was no pushover, a tough opponent. It was obvious that the boys and girls were scared to death of the teacher.

Vincent dreaded going to her class, especially since English was a difficult subject for him; needless to say, the boy had no choice in the matter. Bolstering his courage, like the proverbial soldier who became a hero in the face of fire simply because it appeared better to be shot advancing than retreating, he went to brave the battle with Grammar, Punctuation, Composition, and Miss Davis!

Miss Davis' classes were always the most orderly in John Muir Junior High School. All she had to do was raise an eyebrow or lift a finger, and a puerile rebellion was quelled immediately. Since wagging little tongues, loosened with slime, had spread disgusting rumours that the teacher was a terrible tyrant, her pupils feared reprisals (God only knows what) if she was angered.

Surprisingly Vincent soon held views quite different from his classmates. He saw no reason to fear Miss Davis. The awful stories he had heard about her absolutely were not true. She was really nice. In fact, she was beautiful!

Although he was merely a stripling of fourteen years, Roxanne Davis' physical properties had drawn Vincent to her with the force of a magnetic body attracting a small strip of tin.

To him she was neither a typical schoolteacher nor an ordinary woman. Miss Davis was what this teen-age boy pictured to be his ideal...a sweet, soft-spoken sultana out of *The Arabian Nights*:

Like the royal maidens in Oriental tales Roxanne was well-formed, sensually alluring; her bright ivory countenance had the fascination of a shining full moon (she used no powder on her round, cream-white face); her exotic dark eyes were fringed by long, silken, black lashes (she had to use mascara because her eyelashes were so light and frizzy); her cheeks, red delicious apples, were a lovely vivid color (she wore rouge well); her lips, enticing as ripe cherries, were exquisite (she applied her lipstick artistically); her teeth were precious, perfect pearls (she had a permanent bridge and some gold inlays). Roxanne's brunette hair was done up smoothly in a pumpernickel-like roll. Just as he had seen in prints in storybooks, Vincent visualized her glossy locks, the darkness of night, falling over her shoulders and trailing down to her slim waist.

Unlike a fanciful princess of the Orient, shapely as a trim porcelain figurine, Roxanne was *saftig* like a plump German peasant girl. By watching her diet, which consisted of low-calorie foods; doing exercises, which tightened the stomach muscles; wearing foundation garments, which were made to order; and maintaining proper carriage, which took constant vigilance, Roxanne slimmed her figure amazingly. That is, she did not appear to be so big in certain places as she actually was.

Dutifully Roxanne Davis looked after her class. Each day, red marking pencil in hand, she made it a practice to walk up and down the aisles between the rows of desks to see if the boys and girls needed individual help with their lessons. But the unappreciative juveniles, fearful of being caught misbehaving, would react to the teacher as though she were a policeman patrolling a beat. Guilty of stealing into dreamland for the hour or, perhaps, pilfering answers to homework from neighbors, the pupils settled down to honest efforts the instant Miss Davis approached. Heads cowered when the teacher swung her pencil and left red marks to make corrections on pupils' papers.

While his classmates were disciplined by the policeman's billy club (Roxanne's red pencil), Vincent Armstrong was merely amused by it. Feeling that he would not be called to account, still at the schoolboyish state of mentality, he behaved accordingly. The little devil diagrammed his English exercises in red ink instead of the preferred blue-black color. He wore a red beanie, which he twirled on his forefinger devilishly whenever he removed the skullcap. On his desk he always had a good supply of heart-shaped candies with red wrappers. And, last but not least, he inked fancy red Rs on the backs of his hands.

Had Roxanne been affected with protanopia, she could not have seemed less able to recognize the color of the deviltry Vincent flaunted in red. Only in making her usual rounds did the teacher show any awareness of the boy. The times she stopped at Vincent's desk at the rear of the classroom, she stayed long enough to check his (red-ink) diagrams: visual aids for determining the relation of sentence parts. Before she moved on to assist the next pupil, she would however explain briefly the relation of sentence parts such as prepositional phrases that were unclear to Vincent. Yet, no matter how correct or incorrect they happened to be, Miss Davis never expressed an overall judgment, critical or complimentary, about his diagrams, their redness notwithstanding.

Oh, yes, there was something unusual the teacher did do on occasion. In coming to Vincent's assistance, Roxanne planted herself beside him; then, while she checked his schoolwork, she leaned far forward over his desk so that the neckline of her dress dropped low. As a result the swell of Roxanne's full breasts were visible. Vincent, straining his eyes, sometimes could faintly see raspberry nipples in the cups of the woman's brassière.

"Holy peepers! Is Miss Davis giving me free sights on purpose? Naw. I must be having hallucinations":

To assure himself he was imagining things, the youngster in his thoughts misused the sesquipedalian word he recently had heard an actor use in a motion-picture thriller. One afternoon, though, when Roxanne tickled the nape of his neck with her fingers, he became convinced he had not been hallucinating. She really must have intended him to see her bare breasts. They were tempting to taste but her raspberry nipples surely were forbidden fruit. Could she just be playing with him?

If he were a man—in any case, an experienced virile man—very likely Vincent would not have hesitated to accept Roxanne's offer to play a game of sex. Since he was after all a boy, an active one at that, sports (which burn up energy) were his predominant interests. Thus he indiscriminately dismissed the teacher from his mind along with his distasteful lessons, as most youngsters are prone to do after school lets out for the day. [So it will be until educators begin taking pains to season learning in order to make flat brain-food palatable to knowledge-starved children.]

It was reality, not a play of his mind; Roxanne was impassioned with Vincent, quite heatedly so. She had her heart set on seducing him and would not be denied. To break down the substance of his devil-may-care yet angelically aloof attitude, she applied heat and pressure. The woman despite her virginity had the years to know her chemistry. Bending over Vincent at an opportune moment, she would press hard up against him and blow hot breath into his ear.

She often whispered delightful endearments. Her voice was soothing as the sound of water flowing from a fountain. On the verge of manhood Vincent's libido came into play.

Many a night Vincent dreamed that he was a Persian prince, and Roxanne was one of his dancing girls—unveiled. Her eyelids darkened with kohl, the whites of her mystical eyes highlighted her dark irises, the way stars illuminate the night sky. Her waist-long tresses, the shade of the feathers on a raven's wings, flew about wildly as she danced before a fountain in the palace garden to maddening chants by eight eunuchs in red turbans. The eunuchs chanted over and over again in a strange tongue the parts of speech fundamental to English grammar.

Driven into a frenzy by the repetitious chants, Roxanne, clinking bracelets and anklets, swayed snakelike from side to side. Suddenly she struck a tantalizing pose as she eyed Vincent, who reclined on cushions made of pure silk and drank refreshing sherbet out of a silver goblet. Vincent reached for her leg. Roxanne twisted and turned away and disappeared behind the fountain. She reappeared quickly and now her dancing was even livelier, her movements turbulent. Her beauteous breasts heaved like waves on a stormy sea. The chanting ceased, as indifferently as it had commenced. Calmed, Roxanne fell to the floor, crawled over to the cushions, and spoke with adoration:

"Oh, Vincent, master of all you survey, taste my raspberry nipples. Allah himself has flavored them to please your palate. Let me serve you. Here, dear prince—take a handful. Umm! are they not delicious. . . ."

The classroom drama, starring pupil and teacher, at John Muir Junior High School, was climaxed by a surprising incident, the first of a series of incidents that began on All Fools' Day.

Vincent's Uncle Walter, a bachelor, was both sole and star boarder at the Armstrong residence. A practical joker, he had hunted in the novelty shops up and down Market Street until he found a suitable article, a hard-cover handbook with which to play jokes or tricks on April fools.

From the outside the handbook looked like a real one, perfectly harmless. Do not be misled, judging the contents of this edition by its title would have been unwise. Instead, what appeared to be full pages between the covers—was actually a rectangular border of partial pages with the inner hollow space containing a built-in spring and hammer, which could be cocked to strike a giant cap when the handbook was opened.

A healthy curiosity impelled the first goat to nibble at the leaves around the edges of the trick handbook. Uncle Walter planted it on the kitchen table just as the members of the family sat down to have their breakfast. While they were eating, Mr. Armstrong casually flipped open the handbook. Did the gunlike gadget inside work? It worked only too well. After it fired, there were three irritated individuals: father scalding the roof of his mouth with piping hot coffee, mother spilling maple syrup all over her freshly laundered linen, and son spattering melted butter on his polo shirt.

Uncle Walter burst into such painfully deep laughter that tears came to his eyes. "April fool! April fool!" he cried with sheer bliss. In the next breath he had the audacity to look to Mrs. Armstrong for sympathy because the bottom of his potbelly hurt from his laughing so hard.

Furious, Mr. Armstrong snapped at his wife's brother: "God damn it, Walt! How two peas from the same pod can be as unalike as you and your sweet sister, is beyond my comprehension."

For all the good it did, the head of the household might as well have been talking to a brick wall. Doubled up, clutching his potbelly, Walter laughed louder than ever at the slapstick scene he had created. If he heard his brother-in-law, the family comedian chose to ignore Armstrong's quip.

Determined to milk All Fools' Day dry, Walter squeezed out an overflowing pail of belly laughs on his job at the Borden Dairy Company. Using an unscrupulous barker's patter, he tricked his co-workers into opening the handbook. They were aware they would receive a shock all right, but it was not the kind they expected. The April fools had been led to believe that the handbook contained cartoons of nude men and women depicted in a number of obscene positions—among others position 69.

When he came home after work that night Vincent's uncle, having had his fill of fun, put the trick handbook away into a drawer of a chest in the sunroom. Vincent—who was stretched out on a couch nearby, his ears glued to the radio—glanced up and caught sight of what Uncle Walter did. Overcome by an irresistible desire to possess the handbook, the boy rose bright and early the next day so he could steal the gunlike gadget from the house. He ran all the way to school with it, his pulse beating a mile a minute.

Printed in big, black letters on the flesh-colored cover of the handbook were the words SPICY VARIETIES, making it as embarrassingly conspicuous as a nose covered with blackheads. Therefore, Vincent kept the handbook hidden in the repository of a desk wherever he attended his respective morning classes.

At noontime young Armstrong, overanxious to try out the stolen article, outdid Uncle Walter numerically and otherwise. It was palmed off on Vincent's schoolmates; none were spared, the frightened youngsters throwing it back at him with the funniest reactions: one girl shrieked and wet her pants. If Vincent failed to trick any boy into accepting the handbook, he held it up in front of his victim's face and released the gunlike gadget without warning. One is not surprised that the wide-eyed youngster whoever he happened to be jumped away like a terrified frog. Fortunately the bell rang indicating the end of the lunch hour, or Vincent might have terrorized all the youngsters at John Muir Junior High School.

Later that afternoon, during the English period, he again hid in his desk the conspicuous handbook. Also he placed a composition manual on top of it. This precaution was necessary because the catch, which prevented the cover of the handbook from opening accidentally, had become loosened.

As had been her procedure for some weeks, Miss Davis began the class by reading two chapters from Herman Melville's *Moby Dick*, or *The Whale*. Powerful in suspense and adventure on the high seas, the novel always held the undivided attention of the girls as well as the boys. Vincent was no exception. He listened with such intensity and grew so engrossed that the trick handbook was completely forgotten while Miss Davis read Chapter XLI: Here Ishmael, the narrator, describes how a ferocious, white, sperm whale...with a sickle-shaped lower jaw...had...as a mower reaps away a blade of grass in the field...chewed off the leg of a Captain Ahab, who was trying to kill the whale with a line-knife from the prow of his broken boat, the gunnels floating in pieces on the ocean.

After she finished reading Chapter XLII, "The Whiteness of the Whale," Miss Davis discussed briefly, and simply, Melville's parodies and puns, his metaphors—and the mastery of his composition. These few points touched upon, she laid the novel aside, a sure sign she was about to tell the class to get ready for the composition exercises.

Reflex actions went to work. Still awestruck by the ferocity of the great whale (a white monstrosity the size of a ship), Vincent without thinking removed from the repository of his desk the composition manual he had placed on the trick handbook as a precautionary measure.

"Quick. Plug your ears." The cover flew up, tripping the hammer. BANG! The unexpected noise the giant cap made in that quiet classroom could not have been much less shocking than the burst of a bombshell.

Dumbfounded girls and boys, including Vincent, stiffened in their seats. All the pupils turned the whiteness of Moby Dick, not to overlook a white-faced teacher. Upon recovering somewhat from her shock, she asked with a tone as hard as her question, "Who fired that cap pistol?"

No response—dead silence. . . . Was the room a morgue! What an odd phenomenon: muscles twitched, blood circulated, lungs breathed, hearts beat; yet not a body stirred.

Probably the person guilty of causing the firing never would have been discovered, for his face was the picture of innocence, a perfect copy of a Giotto saint. In this case, however, the services of Sherlock Holmes were not needed. Smoke—the dirty informer— escaping from the repository of the pistol-owner's desk, pointed an accusing finger at him. It was pathetically amusing to watch the frantic efforts of Vincent as he attempted with puffed-up cheeks to blow away the telltale smoke, and at the same time tried to look saintlike.

"Vincent Armstrong!" Miss Davis' voice cracked with the severity of a whiplash.

Her tension released, the astounded teacher got hold of her faculties. Now that she could think clearly, she was elated. The boy had played into her hands. A game-plan formulated in Roxanne's mind. To disguise her elation she put on a rigid, expressionless mask.

The teacher demanded of her pupil, "Vincent, you will kindly come in after school and explain the meaning of this!"

Chapter 9

Vincent masked his feelings, too. Outwardly he looked somber. Inwardly he smiled. He was not at all intimidated by Miss Davis' stern demand. The youngster realized he would have to explain why the smoky discharge occurred...that it was accidental...that he had not fired a cap pistol. But he was fairly sure he would not be punished other than being subjected to a lecture on the dangers of bringing gunlike gadgets to school or being scolded for disrupting the class.

What else could Miss Davis have in mind? Perhaps she wanted to be caressed. Beyond this horizon he could not see. An inexperienced traveler, he was a shade solicitous as to just how pleasurable would be a journey into love land with his adult school teacher. So far her endearing whispers and loving touches indicated to Vincent that she was affectionate, apparently an able guide. As yet pupil (and teacher) had an unknown distance to travel.

Up until the present Vincent had had insignificant physical experience with members of the opposite sex. On occasion he had mustered up courage to hold hands with shy girls at Saturday matinees in the neighborhood motion-picture theaters. And on occasion he had kissed bashful girls at birthday parties where courageous youngsters played Postman and Spin the Bottle.

Vincent's earliest awareness of his sexuality was when he first experienced a nocturnal wet dream: The whitish, viscid fluid he secreted on the bed sheet frightened him. Ashamed to discuss the matter with his parents, he sought the counsel of easy-to-talk-to, crude boys who sold newspapers on a street corner near his house. Between bragging and chaffing they gave him a liberal education in the obscenities of sex, to a certain degree enlightening despite their vulgar explanations. Before long he graduated with a good grasp of the art of "jacking-off," or to state it on a higher level—self-gratification (?) by one's masturbating.

That afternoon subsequent to the three o'clock bell, the hour school let out, Vincent, having re-entered his English classroom, stood vis-à-vis with Roxanne Davis. Suddenly he got cold feet, a chill ran up his spine, and his tongue froze. Suppose he had misconstrued the teacher's intentions. If she had motives other than he had predicted, what a calamity it could be! For the time being his fears were suspended by the timely, untimely arrival of two girls in want of extra help with their English.

"Have a seat, Vincent, while I see if I can give Josephine and Lucy some assistance," Miss Davis said. By a nod of her head she indicated that he should sit down in a chair placed next to hers.

Both girls had endless questions about grammar. Ill at ease, Vincent became fidgety and picked at a hangnail. Tired of trifling with it, he tugged at the bit of irritating skin with his teeth, biting it off too close to the cuticle.

"God, my finger throbs! Will those darn girls ever run out of wind," he complained inwardly as he sucked the cuticle to alleviate its smarting.

"Isn't the word railroad always a 'noun'?" asked Josephine. "I mean, is it not the only one of the eight parts of speech that is the name of anything?"

Miss Davis replied: "True, a 'noun' is a name. And every word that occurs in speech is classified as one of the eight parts of speech. But few words are at all times the same part of speech. That is, a word which is a 'noun' in one sentence may be a 'verb' in another sentence and still some other part of speech in another sentence.

"Simply stated, the class to which a word belongs is determined by its use. Therefore, unless we know how it is used in a sentence we cannot classify a word as a 'noun,' 'pronoun,' 'verb,' 'adjective,' 'adverb,' 'conjunction,' or 'preposition.' . . . Let me see, have I mentioned them all." She repeated the parts to herself, giving her memory a jog. "Oh, I omitted the word 'interjection.'

"Isolated by itself railroad could be any one of three parts of speech. Granted, in most sentences the word railroad usually does the work of a 'noun'—as a subject, for example:

This railroad is the longest one built in the west. Or as an object:

Transporting goods by <u>railroad</u> as less expensive. Yet it may be a 'verb':

Why not <u>railroad</u> the informer to the penitentiary. Also it can be an 'adjective':

Late last night the <u>railroad</u> station burned down.

"In *Rape Upon Rape* (Act II, scene xi) the playwright Henry Fielding used the word *but* both as a 'verb' and as a 'noun.' Although *but* is commonly classified as a 'conjunction,' he wrote in his dialogue this unusually constructed sentence, <u>But</u> me no <u>buts</u>."

The quotation from Fielding's play brought to a finale the explanations by Roxanne Davis. She suggested the girls go home and select a word from a magazine and write several sentences using the same word but in different classifications of the parts of speech, if not eight at least three. Thanking Miss Davis for her help, Lucy and Josephine departed.

At last they were alone, the woman and the boy. Roxanne seated in a chair beside Vincent's, benignly requested him to explain the cause of the big bang which had disturbed the English class earlier that day. His confidence somewhat restored by her speaking in a gentle manner, Vincent with a tremor in his voice started to tell the teacher a straightforward story about the trick handbook.

It did not matter; she did not hear a word he said. As he spoke his words became less and less discernible: Roxanne was staring at Vincent with captivating desire. Spellbound by the concupiscent glare of her wide-open orbs, the boy babbled on incoherently. The woman pressed her knee against the boy's leg, and he placed a hand on her lap. Seconds elapsed yet he dared not stir. He was too timid to move his hand lest he touch her in a most forbidden place.

Vincent's body remained as motionless as the case of a clock, while his heart beat excitedly with the quickness of the escapement ticking in a timepiece. Upon shifting her legs, which were cramped, Roxanne's skirt had crept up well above her knees. Vincent finding the bareness of her flesh a fascinating sight, was unable to wrest his eyes from her exposed thighs.

Roxanne, in desperate need of passion, to encourage Vincent took his hand and slid it along her thigh onto her abdomen; the smooth sensation set his fingers in motion which was fingertip by fingertip, very cautious.

"Darling," she said sweetly, "how far would you like to go!"

Trembling with excitement, Vincent put caution aside: "I want to touch you all over. Your skin is so silky, so nice and warm. It feels good. I like it. Only...why did you chose me for this?"

(In spite of the fact that it seemed to be implied, it never entered the youngster's mind to bring up the difference in their ages.)

"Most of my life," answered Roxanne. "I have had a deathly fear of men. When I was eleven years old I saw my father, in a drunken stupor, give my mother a brutal beating with a fishing rod. I won't ever be able to blot from my memory the terrible, bluish-black welts he inflicted on her frail body.

"Since then I have avoided men, and spent my years in nothing more than a hollow shell. It has been frightfully lonesome without companionship, never having loving arms embrace me." She was quick to add, "not that I haven't had the opportunity." Although Vincent was an adolescent, he nonetheless was a male. Her womanly pride compelled her to let him know other males had desired her.

"Every once in a while men would make advances. I shunned them. My stomach loops with revulsion when a man so much as intimates that he is going to lay a hand on me. I am reminded of mother's terrifying screams as my drunken father beat her. Once, aboard the Lurline on a vacation sea voyage to the Hawaiian Islands, I attempted to overcome this childhood nightmare by encouraging the friendly approaches of a fine gentleman I met in the ship's dining room. But it was no use. Each time he came near me on deck my insides tied into knots. I put an end to the affair by confining myself to my cabin for the remainder of the crossing.

"To make a long story short, you attracted me the moment you walked into the classroom." Vincent blinked his eyes in bewilderment, which Roxanne sensed. "Don't ask me why, dear one. It is not easy to explain. The only thing I can say is day after day the attraction grew stronger and stronger.

"My heart would flutter with joy should I think of you. Pretty soon I began looking forward to seeing you with great expectancy. A feeling of safeness—of secureness—stirred within me at your presence. How I longed to cuddle in your arms! It was such delightful, wishful thinking. Now that it is really taking place it's heavenly yet frightening."

The realization that her deepest desires were abut to be fulfilled made Roxanne shudder. Overcome emotionally the woman began to weep for joy. In commiseration the boy wiped away with his fingertips tears running down her flushed cheeks, and said: "Don't be afraid. I won't hurt you."

Intensely aroused by heat radiating from Roxanne's body, Vincent persisted, "I want to touch you all over."

"Wherever you like," Roxanne consented in words and then in actions; she leaned back, relaxed, and spread her legs apart. Free to do as he wished, Vincent lowered his hand to finger the inner sides of her thighs, his thumb gradually inching upward.

Anticipating where his roving fingers intended to roam, Roxanne murmured: "Precious, I have too much clothing on. My girdle is too tight,"

Vincent barely heard her. He was a fervid explorer burning with the desire to enter virgin territory—a hidden vale wherein the petals of an exquisite, pink flower glistened with silvery dew. Obstructive barriers would not stop him. He was determined to penetrate a dense forest concealing the vale of ecstasy he felt was within reach.

Pangs of conscience abruptly brought the English teacher to her senses. After all, they were in a public schoolroom. Anyone could walk in without notice and catch them in their imprudent behavior. The blame would be entirely hers, for he was a pupil, and underage. There would be a scandal. Her position—her reputation was at stake. Dismissal! Contributing to the delinquency of a minor!

"Please stop. Oh, my god! Forgive me. This isn't the place or the time." Reluctantly the woman tore herself away from the boy.

Having come as far as he had, Vincent was too worked up to be sensible. He was interested in right *here* and *now*, not what was wrong with *where* and *when*. He insisted on being given a reason for her change of heart. Tearfully Roxanne explained that it was not fair of her to take advantage of someone as young as he. Moreover, she informed him how dangerous the situation was, and how fearful she was of the consequences.

Vincent was beyond listening; he tried to put her fears to rest. Was he not tall for his age. Could he not pass for sixteen...maybe seventeen, if he wore his double-breasted suit. He was grown up enough to understand what was going on. Nobody had to know about their intimate affair. It would be their secret. Unable to convince her, Vincent appealed to her compassion, telling her about the nights he had tossed and turned in bed, losing sleep, aching for the comfort—the pleasure of her company.

"Sooner or later a fella had to stay with a woman." This statement Vincent Armstrong quoted with confidence (the neighborhood newsboys had said so). Continuing to plead, he told Roxanne that he cared for her—that he must have her! The youth shook with frustration.

His heavy pleas, on top of Roxanne's hunger to be loved and her uncontrollable affection for Vincent, outweighed her concerns. The teacher was moved by tender feelings. Comforting her pupil with a caress, she agreed to satisfy his desires and hers but elsewhere. It would be prudent, also, in the long run, more satisfying to bide their time and go to her home so that they would have complete privacy. Consoled by the prospect of engaging in sex with the woman under favorable conditions, the boy regained his composure—and impatiently asked, "When?"

Some relatives were visiting her from Los Angeles. As soon as they left, Roxanne promised to make arrangements for a rendezvous, which unexpectedly was not soon. Her relatives were not cooperative. Despite subtle hints that they had worn out their welcome, they found excuses to prolong their visit. Ultimately, after what seemed three endless weeks, they took their departure. Both Roxanne and Vincent lived through those slow-dragging days, hours, minutes, and seconds in a continual state of anxiety.

Always in her English classes Roxanne Davis used a procedure analogous to climbing a stepladder when teaching her pupils. She was well aware she had to contend with haphazard educational systems starting as low as the first grade in grammar school. Consequently, whenever she found that a step or steps had been missed at the lower part of the "learning ladder," she exerted every effort to review, unhurriedly, for her pupils the fundamentals they needed to advance to higher levels of education in English. If only more teachers were that conscientious, how fortunate learners would be.

Of late, though, the pace of Roxanne's helping pupils to climb up the "learning ladder" had quickened step by step. Her co-teachers passed remarks at luncheon about the way she now gobbled her food, which was uncharacteristic, for she was the type of personality that masticated her food thoroughly. More talk was caused when Roxanne, who routinely had been the last to lodge at faculty conferences, recently had come to be the first to vacate. It was wondered why the woman's nerves were strung up to such a high pitch. A certain boy knew the reason. And he would never tell.

Of late Vincent's other teachers, particularly in Math and History, had to chide him for his lack of attention in class. During the Physical Education period in the locker room the word was passed around that something had gone haywire with Vincent. Normally a live wire in the gymnasium, he now appeared dead on his feet. Also, there was a noticeable decrease of enthusiasm toward his extracurricular sports activities.

At home Mrs. Armstrong soon sensed a difference in her son's demeanor. She mentioned it to Uncle Walter who offered his opinion, "Our youngster is suffering from growing pains." The cliché alleviated the mother's concern, more or less. Still she could not help wondering why her son, a carefree youngster, was suddenly so serious, as if he had the weight of the world on his shoulders. A certain woman knew the reason. And she would never tell.

One school day in the morning Miss Davis announced joyfully to her pupil: "My relatives have gone back to Los Angeles!" The time at last had arrived for Roxanne and Vincent to rendezvous.

In the afternoon young Armstrong attended to a slight formality on the telephone: "Mom, this is me," the boy identified himself. "A classmate of mine and I are going to compare notes on our homework. He invited me for dinner. I'll be home about eight o'clock tonight. Is it okay?" Vincent gave his mother a few more pat explanations, and wheedled permission from her to stay out late.

Precisely at 4:12 p.m. Vincent and Roxanne met in the Bay Bridge Transit Terminal; she resided across the bay in Berkeley. To avoid possible detection or suspicion each of them had taken separate streetcars to the prearranged meeting place. Since Vincent did not know his way around the university city, he could get lost. The pair decided time would be saved and confusion prevented if, instead of making the trip separately, they traveled together from the terminal to Roxanne's dwelling.

Chapter 10

Roxanne and Vincent, sitting side by side, rode in silence on the electric train which by now was almost midway across the Bay Bridge...the longest bridge in the world. It was a bright, sunny day. She was dozing, lulled into a dreamy semi-sleep by the warmth of the sun. He was wide awake, agitated and anxious, awed by what awaited him.

Rays of sunshine flooding the coach through the windows illuminated a stream of dust particles. Gazing at the minute parts of matter, Vincent amused himself by endeavoring to keep track of their chaotic movements while he observed the particles darting about in the air. Eventually he grew tired of this monotonous diversion and looked down at the bluish-gray water below the bridge.

A clumsy ferryboat was chugging along, leaving a disquieting trail of ripples in the placid bay. Only yesterday the vessel had been the Bay Area's lifeline to San Francisco. Its usefulness starting to fray, the ferryboat was living on borrowed time, before long to be broken up for scrap in a boneyard—the salvageable parts disposed of, the worn-out hulk left to rot among other wooden antiquities.

The train sped along the bridge toward the bore tunnel cut through the rock islet called Yerba Buena on which the west suspension span and the east cantilever span are anchored. Like a Pacific Humpback's dorsal fin projects from amid the ocean, the little island juts up from the middle of the bay (325 feet above sea level). Yerba Buena, a United States naval reservation, is neatly landscaped, paved with narrow, tortuous roads that wind around its craggy slopes, uniformly terraced and thickly wooded with eucalyptus foliage, live oak, and a variety of evergreens. Besides a lighthouse or signal tower displaying a luster-blue glass lookout, Marine detention barracks and trim quarters of Navy and Coast Guard personnel were presently situated about the islet.

Vincent now was focusing his vision upon the sea a short distance beyond Yerba Buena's northwesterly lateral. Here just beneath the surface of the water were shoals—sand banks roughly 735 acres in expanse. For over a century they appeared on marines' maps a hazard to navigation. The shoals were isolated, separated from the Yerba Buena bank by a nine-hundred foot channel. Today it is bridged by a wide viaduct which might never have been constructed if the Bay Area had not needed a centralized airport.

After reviewing architectural plans and feasibility studies, an appointed committee of San Francisco citizens concurred that the Yerba Buena Shoals would be an ideal location for the airport. The Corps of United States Army Engineers was enlisted to assist in the reclamation of the shoals. In February 1936 huge army dredges began pumping black sand from the bay's shallow body of water in preparation for filling the shoals. Eighteen and a half months later they were systematically filled within the enclosure of a sea wall formed from 287,000 tons of quarried rocks. Thus the shoals were raised from their dateless depth of two to twenty-six feet below sea level to an elevation thirteen feet above the mean low-water line.

A total of four hundred acres was elevated to the eminence of an islet honored with the title "Treasure Island" (inspired one imagines by Robert Louis Stevenson's renowned novel). To commemorate the erection of the Golden Gate and San Francisco-Oakland Bay Bridges, this humanly created terra firma was duly designated as a temporary fairground convertible to a permanent aviation field. Overnight on Treasure Island a lively magic city appeared, bustling with crowds of sightseers from around the world.

In his reminiscing Vincent's thoughts turned to 1939, the year the Golden Gate International Exposition opened on Treasure Island. His parents had taken him to the exposition so that they as well as he could see industrial developments and artistic productions. But there was much more to see than was anticipated. As his father drove the family sedan down the causeway leading to the islet, Vincent's eyes flew about faster than flying saucers. Architecturally arranged upon the landscape were spacious, spectacular sights.

"Christopher Columbus! Mom...Dad, look! Just look!" their son exclaimed. Seated in the back of the sedan, he rolled down a smudged glass and stuck his head out the car window to get a clearer view. Gaping, he said, "Honestly, I didn't expect the place to be so wonderful. Why, the Palace of Fine Arts at the Marina doesn't hold a candle to it."

The youngster was comparing the singular building art of but a few burned-out civilizations, which is comparing the wick to the wax. The Palace of Fine Arts, preserved to this day, was one of the eight main structures of the 1915 Panama-Pacific International Exposition held in San Francisco to celebrate the completion of the Panama Canal. The architecture of the Palace of Fine Arts is ancient Roman with traces of Greek influences. By contrast the structures of the Golden Gate International Exposition were modern merged with Mayan, Incan, Malayan, and Cambodian architectural remnants.

A cartograph of Treasure Island showed sixteen areas in the exposition containing, among other splendors, magnificent structures, gardens, sculptures, and courts. Of all the courts, eight in number, the central court—the Court of Honor—Vincent Armstrong recollected the clearest. Compass-like in contour, the Court of Honor at NW, NE, SW, SE points led through arcaded pavilions to vast exhibit places: Electricity and Communications Building, Hall of Science; Vacationland; Mines, Metals, and Machinery Building; Homes and Gardens Building; International Hall; . . .

Reeling about rapidly in young Vincent's recollection were scenes of exhibitions which had been on display within the long halls of the great buildings. Favorite shots of exhibits began to project upon his mind's screen.

The electric robot Willie Vocalite created in man's image—who stood up, sat down, spoke, and smoked like a smokestack— appeared along with Sparko, the mechanical dog that looked real enough to bark and bite. A giant Big Ben with a star-pocked face symbolically portrayed regeneration of the solar system throughout eternity. And Big Ben's dial, six feet in diameter, was designed to create a prismatic effect, constantly changing colors which intrigued Vincent the boy despite the complexity of the exhibit. Television: watching it in a lounge, his mother and he, separated from his father in the crowded hall, were surprised, to say the least, when they saw him appear on the picture tube.

But there were other things to see, interesting exhibits everywhere. Looking at a duplication of Thomas Edison's laboratory, Vincent saw an obsolete blower used by the inventor to fabricate the first electric lamp. At another exhibit the boy observed the Time Capsule, a replica of the original message and contents which had been buried in the East and would supply historians, five thousand years into the future, keys and tools to unlock the mysteries of twentieth-century life on earth.

Earth the way it appeared aeons ago also was on display. Standing before double glass doors to the remote past—geology and zoology—the boy had a marvelous view of a paleontological, pristine panorama: He saw Texas in the Permian period approaching a glacial climatic condition about 250 million years ago; the remains of the giant salamander, the ship lizard, and many other crawling reptilians in fossil shale, rock, or conglomerate; the chalk beds of the Cretaceous period, marking the end of the gigantic reptiles about fifty million years ago; the Painted Arizona Desert, a wide polychrome range of plateaus and low mesas as it was about 150 million years ago; the flood levels and forest heights in Southern California...and the viscid death trap at the bottom of the necropolis for prehistoric fossils of the La Brea Tar Pits, which still exist in Los Angeles' Hancock Park.

Next Vincent came to Treasure Mountain—one of the major exhibits—contrived to demonstrate methods of mining, methods of extracting ore from underground, methods of manufacturing machinery with pure and alloy forms of metal processed from ore. In just fifteen minutes Vincent passed through twenty-five hundred miles of mining country (including five hundred feet of tunnel) which, of course, was a simulation on a small scale of the West's mining district. As for the mountain it was rather big: fifty feet high, and four hundred feet long.

Along his way through Treasure Mountain the boy stopped briefly to watch miners manning an underground hoisting station: he saw, on the cage platform, skips that were loaded with ore being hoisted up a timbered shaft toward the surface. Elsewhere in the mine, men were operating pumps to remove leakage seeping out from between logs and boulders. Other miners on dry ground were wheeling ore carts on rails to hoisting stations. This exhibit represented the Mother Lode country and California gold mining as well as Montana, Utah, and Arizona's Copper country.

Vacationland! wherever it might be the youngster pictured it a fantastic fun place. His notion of such a place came from motion pictures. And he found it in this exhibition building, which covered four acres. There was so much to see that he roamed all over the place, but hurriedly as if he were afraid he might miss something. The upshot was he saw quite a lot yet very little. Like in the movies, man-made scenery in the exhibits looked real. Like in westerns, a trading post stocked saddles and other riding gear. Like in rodeos, rough-riding cowboys rode bucking broncos. Like in modern movies, pleasure craft from outboard motorboats to cabin cruisers were shown, as well as modernized buses with air conditioning...with all the latest comforts passengers on vacation could have while traveling across the country.

At an informational counter the National Automobile Club offered a complete touring service in conjunction with an electrified relief map. By the push of a button a sightseer could illuminate on the map the shortest or more scenic route to any part of the country, from coast to coast. Vincent and his father had a terrific time pushing the button and lighting up a desired transcontinental route. Each attempted to guess the other's selection. To Vincent's chagrin his father outguessed him three times in a row.

Vincent did not want to be outguessed again so he subtly edged his father toward some other exhibitions, which had models and dioramas of Railroading that seemed to interest Mrs. Armstrong much more than they interested her husband and son. With the scrutiny of a railway engineer, she inspected bolt by bolt a model railroad system: It comprised ten locomotives and one hundred cars, including station houses and equipment such as turnouts...crossovers...switches, yards...sidetracks, water tanks, bridges, semaphores...block signals, terminals—everything needed for a carrier to operate.

Of particular interest to Vincent's mother was the California-Nevada Railroad diorama. It included a miniature whistle stop common to the Sierra region in 1870. The floor plan of the railroad station despite its smallness was an authentic layout: One could see the station agent's dingy den, the baggage room, and the waiting room. Strict attention had been paid to detail: One could see the glow of oil lamps, a scale for weighing gold dust or nuggets, a push broom (well-worn) and, of all things, in the den on a shelf a corncob pipe filled with tobacco.

After viewing the tiny corncob pipe, the Armstrongs had to believe they had just seen the ultimate miniature. What could be tinier. Shortly after entering International Hall, a building due east off the central court, they exclaimed almost in unison, "Unbelievable!" The hall contained a quarter of a million miniatures. Among the hand-carved exhibits were thirty thousand silver spoons in an acorn, thirty elephants in a seed, a table and two chairs on a pinhead, a four-inch rifle and one-inch dueling pistols which actually could be fired, . . .

Now returning to the central Court of Honor, Vincent's mind moved from the minute to the mammoth. Within the central court was the Tower of the Sun, a colossal campanile. It stood four hundred feet into the air, and thus soared far above the rest of the structures on the islet. Dominating the exposition in stature, the tower, supporting a forty-four bell carillon, commanded admiration from whomever looked upon its magnificence.

The Tower of the Sun made the deepest impression on Vincent. Without exaggeration, native-born or not, San Franciscans in particular had to be impressed the most by the bell tower, and for a significant reason. We are, however, overshooting the mark. Let us set our sights and take accurate aim.

Its name obviously derived from the mythical Greek god Helios, the 'sun.' Is not the sun the foe of darkness and cold, of infertility and famine. Destroy Helios and these treacherous demons would march under the cover of night to sack our beloved earth. Indeed the magnificent tower was nobly named...a respectful tribute to the sun god's championing the cause of humankind's survival.

Arranged about the foot of the tower, like handmaidens in attendance, were urns; each held an olive branch (the familiar gesture of peace). And highly visible over each urn was a ram's head...which in mythology represents the Egyptian deity Amen-Ra who had the force of reproduction, and who fused with the sun god to propagate animal and plant life. Aqua, a godling that is part of the sun god's work force, was not overlooked. Fountains positioned close to the base of the tower—to the north, to the south, to the west, to the east—heralded the powerful influence water also bears on fertility.

Well-watered gardens in the central court were laid out below the sun tower like vivid tapestry carpets spread around a majestic throne. As though they had been summoned to give a command performance, groups of Pacific madrones planted near the tower's base presented a symphony in orange- and cinnamon-colored trunks, and cucumber-colored leaves. *Magnolia grandiflora*, an evergreen tree bearing glossy leaves undercoated with rusty orange or golden brown colors was the Court of Honor's symphonic poem, expressed by gold and bronze tones.

Boxwood hedge borders, spacing off the central court, and Valencia orange trees, composing two concentric rings, performed in perfect harmony to accent annuals around the area. Seasonal flowers such as blooming violas (White and Radio), hyacinths (Queen of the Blues and Innocence), tulips (Moonlight), pansies (Lord Beaconsfield), and daffodils (Pseudo-Narcissus), along with thousands of other harmonious varieties, blended beautifully with the chromatic concerto.

While the central court was circular—the sun tower was octagonal, all eight sides of which were ivory-coated and textured with metallic materials that reflected rays of sunlight whenever Hēlios, rising in his empyreal domain, beamed radiantly down on the tower. The wide octagon tapered skyward into a pyramidal pinnacle surmounted by a gigantic bird, twenty-two feet high. It was fabricated from wrought iron and gilded so lavishly a predacious goldsmith might have considered the possibility of stealing the bird off its towering perch.

Perched almost four hundred feet in the air, equivalent to thirty stories, the bird appeared indistinguishable to observers on the ground, the Armstrongs included. Vincent placed a hand over his forehead in the formation of a sunshade and strained his eyes to get a clearer view. The boy's orbs nearly bulged out of their sockets as he tried to telescope his sight by stretching his neck to the limit. Despite valiant efforts he could distinguish only a glittering object atop the Tower of the Sun.

Vincent asked his mother and father if they had any idea what the object was, but they had none. Mrs. Armstrong suggested asking a guide in the exposition. Perhaps one of them knew something about it. She wondered whether there were guides posted at strategic spots on Treasure Island. Her husband volunteered to find out while his wife and son waited by the tower. Mr. Armstrong departed and before long returned accompanied by a smiling, uniformed chap.

Seeing the guide was pleasant, Vincent, sometimes shy, did not hesitate to satisfy his curiosity. He pointed to the glittering object and asked, "What is that supposed to be stuck way up there on top of the tower?"

"It's a wrought-iron phoenix covered with gold leaf," answered the guide.

"Did you say, a phoenix?"

The guide assured the boy he had heard correctly.

"What's a phoenix? And what does it have to do with the Tower of the Sun?"

The guide still smiling said: "Let me explain. In Egypt there's a fable that the sun, which is a god, is a beautiful bird called a phoenix. It is ten times as big as a bald eagle, and has brilliant plumage. Every five or six hundred years, when approaching death, the phoenix builds a nest of sprigs and myrrh and sets it on fire. The hoary bird fans the flames with its withered wings. As the flames get bigger and bigger the bird is consumed by fire. Magically, just as the genie in Aladdin's lamp rises in a glimmer, the phoenix flies glimmering out of the ashes—renewed, young and beautiful again."

Vincent, not too satisfied with the story, gave a boyish response: "But I live in San Francisco. There are seagulls at our ocean beach, real ones. What does a make-believe Egyptian bird have to do with anything?"

"Since you are from San Francisco somebody at one time or another must have told you about the 1906 earthquake."

"Yes, my grandfather did say something about it. Was it very bad?"

"It was horrible. That cataclysm struck with such tremendous force it caused dreadful death and destruction in the city—as well as in smaller cities within a radius of fifty miles. To add to the horror, great fires, flaring up in a number of isolated sections of San Francisco, could not be controlled. The tragic fact was the earthquake shock completely incapacitated the city's water system so that the fire department was powerless to fight the rapidly spreading fires.

"On the morning of April eighteenth at 5:13 o'clock the main shock, the first one, occurred. The second shock . . ."

Vincent interrupted, "How do you know the exact time?"

"I may be off a few seconds," admitted the guide. "The clock I'm referring to hung in an insane asylum, the Agnew's. Records show the hands on the clock were immobilized by the furious shaking of the earth's surface. 5:13½ a.m., the time the asylum clock came to a stop, was estimated to be thirty seconds fast. Other clocks in the city had stopped a few seconds after 5:12 a.m.

"Five minutes after the first shock, a second stronger shock occurred. Tall buildings started to sway like wind-blown willowweeds. Next, three aftershocks also followed in close succession. Buildings collapsed—cornices and chimneys toppled into the streets. Among the ruins fires broke out resulting in powerful bursts of flames swept by the wind inward from the bay toward land beyond the Embarcadero.

"Although old wood or brick buildings constructed on man-made land east of Montgomery Street and several buildings south of Market Street, including the Mission District, were ruined by the earthquake, it was fire (unchecked due to broken salt-water mains) that was responsible for much of the death and for most of the destruction. Three-quarters of the city was reduced to a charred pile of ashes.

"In spite of the fire...the earthquake...an act of God: loss of life and property, loss of livelihood and possessions, sickness and suffering, a confused citizenry, low in spirits, somehow rebuilt their lives along with their city. Like the golden phoenix San Francisco ascended from the ashes anew, but richer and more beautiful than ever.

"That is why Arthur Brown, Jr., the architect, had a phoenix-casting placed on the spire of the tower. It is symbolic; yet it serves as a sad and sentimental remembrance for all San Franciscans."

The guide's statement proved to be true in more ways than one. Vincent Armstrong has neither forgotten the story of the phoenix nor the Tower of the Sun to this day.

As the train sped on toward Berkeley, Roxanne, still in a dreamy semi-sleep, stirred in her seat. Sitting side by side with Vincent, her full hip pressed firmly against his. Miss Davis' hip felt hot, like an electric heating pad. The heat from her hip felt so good he buried Treasure Island in his mind and looked forward instead to the hidden sights his teacher had promised she would show him in her bedroom at her home in Berkeley.

The boy could hardly wait to play with the woman's naked body the way he had often played with a smooth pillow between his legs in bed at night, while he pretended the pillow was she. Anxious, he asked her twice, "Do you live very far from the University of California?"

When he received no reply, Vincent nudged her to see if she was awake. Roxanne, bothered by the brightness of the sun shining on her face, blinked several times, her eyelids moving with the rapidity of a butterfly's flickering wings. Opening her eyes, her visage sweet and promising, she inquired, "Are you all right, dear?"

"I'm fine," he assured her. "I just wondered if we were almost there."

She smiled and said, "Yes, we get off at the next stop."

Roxanne Davis' house rested on a hill in north Berkeley, a serene residential neighborhood within walking distance of the university campus. The house had the air of a country retreat so many pine for yet so few ever acquire. Two stories, detached on all sides and surrounded by ample grounds, the dwelling offered the benefit of seclusion—seclusion at times needed to retreat from self-righteous society.

The exterior of the house was rustic, covered with hand-split shakes, dark bark; the gabled roof was shingled and stained grass green; a bulky chimney of faded red brick indicated, and correctly so, that in the parlor sat a spacious open-hearth fireplace. Since the house was constructed long ago, as wine ages in an oaken vat, its bucolic flavor had become more potent over the years, which one could easily be addicted to.

Lush growths of shrubbery, rose bushes, jasmine, poppies, a large spruce, and pepper trees were rooted all about the grounds. Roughly lined along both sides by cobblestones was a wide path that led to solid brick steps ascending to an ivy-entwined porch with a clapboard covering slanted protectively above the front door, before which Miss Davis and young Armstrong were now standing.

Under one arm the pupil clung to his schoolbooks; under the other he had the teacher's briefcase, to free her hands. Her door key was missing. She rummaged her coat pockets, pulling the linings inside out, and ransacked her purse, disrupting the contents, in a frantic search for the missing door key.

"I can't imagine where I could have lost it!" she sounded quite annoyed with herself. (At what seemed a possibility that his fantasies might be lost, too, Vincent showed signs of distress.) "Don't worry," the woman consoled the boy. "I have an extra one hidden. Probably I left the key on my dresser this morning. I've been so absent-minded lately."

Miss Davis stuck her fingers into a clay flower pot sitting on the porch floor and dug out a key covered with bits of damp dirt. After blowing the dirt off the key, she unlocked the door...much to Vincent's relief.

No sooner had the door closed behind the pair when Roxanne flung her arms around Vincent with such suddenness that he lost muscular control: the result was he involuntarily dropped his schoolbooks and her briefcase onto the hallway rug. In the impetuous embrace the boy's forehead bumped the woman's bosom. She tightened her hold, spurred on by excitement, pressing his nose flat up against her. Smothered, he had difficulty breathing. Too shy to say anything he used his mouth a few seconds for respiration. Needing to ease the pressure on his crushed nostrils, he backed away by bracing his palms against her full-blown breasts.

Their resilience stunned the stripling. He gave way to a compulsion, parted her unbuttoned coat, and proceeded to knead the swellings beneath her dress. The more they yielded and heaved the more he manipulated them with his agile fingers. Dreadfully stimulated, both souls were completely beside themselves. They pawed and hugged with unrestrained fury. But their cumbersome clothes were torturous obstacles preventing the pair from deriving the carnal gratification each sought, each yearned to give.

"Vincent! Oh, Vincent. Wait! Wait, dear-heart," reluctantly Roxanne implored him to desist. "Come upstairs to the bedroom. We'll be more comfortable there."

The teacher took her pupil's hand to lead him toward the staircase. Just as she began to walk, she accidentally trod upon one of the schoolbooks lying open next to her foot. Blinded by passion, she was unaware that she had stamped a heel mark on a spotless flyleaf. . . .

"Vincent, the house is kind of chilly," Roxanne remarked with a shudder. "I'll turn on the heat. It will be quick. The thermostat is nearby, down the hall. Go ahead into the bedroom. I'll be right back."

Quickly joining Vincent, Roxanne went over to a dormer window, closed the curtains, and exclaimed: "Now we are alone, shut off from the whole world! You may be young—untouched, my darling. In a way I am young, too; for I have never been touched either. Isn't it wonderful! You shall be the first to pet my private parts, as I shall be the first to pet yours."

All the while she was speaking, Vincent was fiddling with the tab of the zipper on his windbreaker. It appeared the slide fastener was jammed. Seeing he was having trouble unzipping his windbreaker, Roxanne offered to help, "Here, let me do that."

After she succeeded in releasing the zipper, Vincent removed his windbreaker and the rest of his clothes, except his socks; his feet were cold. The woman, bothered by a sense of incompleteness, kneeled and slipped the socks off the boy's feet. Her minuscule mental manacle gotten rid of, she felt freer.

With nothing else to restrain her, she freed herself from the confinement of her clothes, which she tossed in a disorderly pile on an upholstered armchair. To complete her abandonment Roxanne removed her combs and hairpins and put them on a linen doily pushed askew across an end table. In leaning down to straighten the doily, her long tresses fell primitively over her breasts.

Vincent, who stood shivering, had goose flesh. Roxanne wrapped her hair around his neck, and they warmed each other with their bare bodies. Too excited to remain in one spot, they moved about the bedroom while pawing each other.

The woman and the boy soon stopped in front of a cheval glass mounted in a walnut frame held by swivels. As they stood side by side, she tipped the full-length mirror forward, then swung it back and forth ever so slowly. "See us," she purred. "See us in the mirror!"

Chapter 11

Too soon, much too soon to suit young Armstrong, had another summer come round. Roxanne's relatives from Los Angeles were visiting her once more...for a prolonged period of time. His ardent affair with the woman very likely could not be resumed before summer vacation was over. Having to wait till the fall semester to see more raw reflections of Roxanne and himself in her mirror was, from his view, hard on his sexual make-up.

Rest assured there were other things to occupy the boy's mind. Vincent's best friend, Jack Haig, in exploring the ocean shoreline, had stumbled upon a small, secluded beach below the cliffs of Lincoln Park (near China Beach). Since the beach was free of pebbles and flat as a mattress, sunbathing on it promised to be superexcellent. Jack told Vincent that the beach was too small to accommodate but a few sunbathers and too obscure to be detected from the park above. Therefore, the sandy strand was a safe place to bask in the sun without swim trunks. Completely exposed, they could tan to their hearts' content from pate to toenails without fear of being observed. By the end of the summer vacation they would be bronzed Tarzans in the flesh.

Although the country was not at war, Haig was by no means a perfected product of peacetime: his predilections were the antitheses of what pacifism purports to produce in a plastic population. In the impending global battle the country's political leaders were to scour the States, combing their fair-haired man power for youths of Haig's high military caliber.

Name any war involving the country. Go back to the American Revolution and advance forward: the War of 1812, the Mexican War, the Civil War, the Spanish-American War, World War I—not to mention undeclared wars, which may be challenged. Is it correct to call <u>wars</u> "undeclared"? One would think that war is war, declared or undeclared...just as death is death, announced or unannounced. Whatever! you can wager a silver dollar that members of Jack's family fought in one war or another at one time or another.

There is a private, scary joke among the Haigs that the stork was bribed to deliver males only, the wives fearing if they had daughters, the girls also might be soldiers. No member of the Haig family, to its discontent, had had the ability to rise above the highest rating of an enlisted man, master or first sergeant. Unspoken yet strong was the hope of the Haigs that some day one of their stock would become a commissioned officer in the United States Army.

An obedient son, Jack did not question his father's way of life. It was right because his father was his father. What could be more logical! Following in his father's footsteps, he pursued the art of warfare with the determination of a hungry predator. If warfare were edible, he greedily would have consumed every bit of it even if the stuff gave him indigestion. So sold was Jack on becoming a soldier, he failed to understand why his chum Vincent did not want to join the army as well, for duty's sake if for no other reason.

Later on when they were in high school, Haig harped on the subject to aggressively that Armstrong in self-defence signed up for R.O.T.C. (Reserve Officers' Training Corps) instead of Gymnastics. Of all the courses offered to the students. R.O.T.C. turned out to be the most boring as far as Vincent was concerned. He could not swallow the whole corps: military organization and courtesy, reading maps and aerial photography, use of weapons and marksmanship, drill and more drill, plus the concomitants—button polishing, rifle cleaning, petty discipline, and parading stiffly in scratchy wool uniforms.

"Baskets not bullets!" was the civilian cry of Vincent Armstrong who was relieved that he was only studying about soldiering. Never, never would he serve in the regular army, so he thought. (His resolve was not set in concrete as he could not foresee the future.) The next term he transferred back to his former gym class. After that Vincent spent more time than any other player shooting basketballs through hoops in the gymnasium, which he preferred a hundredfold over shooting bullets at a target on a rifle range.

In San Francisco's Richmond District at the intersection of El Camino Del Mar and Twenty-Seventh Avenue on three corners stand, over nine feet high, masonry columns resembling metronomes in form. An oblong metal plate with a little, bossed, sea lion's head is embedded in the stonework of two columns, one on the northwest corner and one on the northeast corner. Driving or walking past these landmarks down Twenty-Seventh Avenue, a winding street, we come to Sea Cliff Avenue where we turn west and continue on a very long block rightward to an incline; descending it we ultimately arrive at a dead end—a big cliff overlooking the ocean and China Beach.

[In April 1935 the name China Beach was officially designated James D. Phelan Recreation Beach, for the deceased Senator Phelan had left a bequest of fifty thousand dollars toward the purchase of the property. In that transaction the State of California acquired title to it. Nevertheless, China Beach, the storied name, is still preferred by native-born San Franciscans, most seniors if not most juniors.

The appellation "China" was used to identify the beach because in the early days Chinese fishermen camped on the stretch of sand, which offered some shelter from ice-cold trade winds. Semicircled by the big cliff, China Beach's surface is not too different from the shape of a crescent. At night the fishermen lit bonfires to keep warm or to fry fish they had caught offshore. The flames and sparks from the bonfires appeared so eerie in the darkness that rumors spread the beach sheltered a pirate's den. Dark deeds inexplicably attributed to the piscators from the Orient rivaled the bloody acts of Blackbeard and his crew of cutthroats. Why the Oriental was falsely accused of being sinister is more mysterious than the slander itself.]

Beyond China Beach to the west we find more cliffs. The cliff which leads down to the small, secluded beach Jack Haig had told Vincent Armstrong about—is dangerously steep. On the slope of the cliff was a faint footpath. Mountain goats would have hesitated to use, for it was unsafe. All but disappeared, the footpath had been made long ago by daredevil youngsters who defied death. Ignoring the danger, Jack and Vincent, convinced life is forever as were their young predecessors, descended the footpath recklessly: it crumbled beneath their sneakers, and an avalanche of dirt and rocks slid down the slope. Fortunately there was nobody below.

Jack was the guardian of a bottle of olive oil, quart-size, which he held protectively in his right hand, balancing himself as best he could with his other hand while slipping and sliding every few feet. Vincent, carrying a blanket, accompanied him on the hazardous trip downward. Through it all, Jack at the risk of his own safety was careful not to drop the bottle. Its contents were too valuable to spill. Somewhere he had picked up a notion that skin if drenched in pure olive oil could be immunized against sunburn. Who will deny Jack's intentions were unadulterated, indisputedly as pure as the olive oil, when he transmitted his supposition to Vincent.

By sheer luck the boys dropped to the bottom of the cliff onto the beach with bones and bottle intact. They soon undressed and draped their clothes over a flat boulder close at hand. Several yards away, nearer the shore line, they chose a favorable spot on which to recline. They smeared their bodies with olive oil; each applied some to the other's back. Confident they were going to tan with immunity, they spread-eagled atop Vincent's blanket, which he had placed on the sand. Gradually the soothing warmth of the sun's rays and the comforting sound of the ocean's waves lulled the boys to sleep.

After an indefinite lapse of time Vincent, in a sleepy state, thought he heard voices near the cliff. His body, with the blanket, had sunk so snugly into the soft, hot sand he was too lazy to stir. But before long he was compelled to move. An arm that he had been lying heavily on was asleep, and it felt painful...as though it were a live pincushion, chock-full. While moving his arm about to get rid of the pins-and-needles sensation, he looked up and caught sight of three boys scaling the cliff. Vincent glanced at the area where he and Jack had put their clothes on a boulder. Articles of clothing were scattered all over the ground.

"Hey, Jack, wake up!" Vincent shouted to his chum stretched out beside him on the blanket. "Hurry, gosh darn it! Wake up before they get away!"

Jack raised his head, his eyes drowsy and his voice cranky. "What do you want? I was sound asleep."

"Never mind your beauty rest, Snow White. Something has happened to our clothes. Those guys over there must have been monkeying around with them!" Vincent stormed, shaking his fist at the three boys now almost half way up the slope of the cliff.

Aroused by this disturbing news, Jack jumped to his feet. "We'd better check it out."

The two sunbathers ran over by the boulder and gathered up their clothing. Upon inspecting the coin pockets of their trousers, they discovered what little cash each had had was gone. "Can you beat that!" Jack exclaimed. "Those rotten punks stole our money!"

Donning trousers and sneakers posthaste, Jack and Vincent pursued the fleeing boys as quickly as it was possible for any creature to climb up the steep cliff. Having vanished from Lincoln Park, the three thieves were nowhere to be found. Resigned to the fact that to continue the pursuit was futile, both chums who had been chasing neck and neck stopped to consider their predicament.

Jack tried to paint a positive picture: "Well, suppose we look at it from this angle. At least we still have our clothes. We'd be in a fine fix stranded out here naked as baboons."

Vincent painted a negative picture: "Don't you see. We won't be able to board a streetcar without paying a fare. We'll have to walk home."

Jack had a bright idea. "What do you say we hitchhike?" Vincent consented halfheartedly. "I guess so—if we can thumb a ride. Might as well get started. Let's go back down to the beach and get the rest of our things. My mom doesn't know I borrowed her blanket."

Homeward bound—afoot—Vincent and Jack were not in the best of spirits. What should have been a sweet day had turned sour. However, their spirits improved after a goodhearted chap, touched by their attractive thumbs, gave the boys a lift in his light delivery truck. Vincent, who did not second the motion enthusiastically, was nominated to bear Jack on his lap in that the seat contained a stack of packages, and thus was not wide enough to accommodate the driver plus two other persons sitting side by side.

As they were riding along, a few times Vincent asked Jack to ease himself up a bit, because his weight was causing Vincent considerable discomfort. He would have liked to exchange their places so that he could sit on Jack's lap a while. But since they were not very far from home, he decided for the rest of the way to grin and bear it..."like a brave trooper," a phrase he had often heard Jack utter.

That evening Mrs. Armstrong made an urgent telephone call summoning a doctor to her house. Her son Vincent was in agony. The boy's skin was fiery red and his thighs were swollen. After examining his patient, the doctor diagnosed his symptoms as "dermatitis due to the actinic rays of the sun"...or, as he put it prosaically to Mrs. Armstrong, "second-degree sunburn." For over a week the corner drugstore did a booming business. Vincent's mother patted and dabbed her pride-and-joy most tenderly with wads of cotton soaked in gallons of calamine lotion.

Sunburned so badly he could not tolerate the bedclothes against his skin, Vincent spent ten miserable nights and days assuming a prone or push-up position in which he tried, with limited success, to stay on the tips of his toes and fingers. By the eleventh day, his sunburn sufficiently healed, he was able to leave his bed. Exercising the utmost care in putting on an unstarched shirt (the sleeves shorn off) and a pair of laundry-softened corduroys, Vincent set forth from his house.

On the outside he greedily gulped fresh air, while he sauntered ahead in a taut manner to prevent his shirt and corduroys from rubbing against his peeling skin, still sore and sensitive. As he carried himself tautly, he was hunched over, ambulating like a tortoise. Of all people, there was Jack Haig a short distance up the block. He spotted Vincent and proceeded to stroll toward him. Jack was moving tortoise-like, too, as though he were mimicking Vincent, who took offence:

"Swell pal," Vincent muttered angrily, "poking fun at my misery. It was his fault. Why the heck did I listen to him. Oil is for frying not tanning."

When Jack came within speaking distance of his chum, Jack registered a complaint, loud and clear: "Keyrist! have I been sick. I just got out of bed. I was burned to a crisp. Whoever told me olive oil guards against sunburn was way off base. That sad-sack will never rise above the rank of yardbird."

Now that he realized Jack was not mimicking him, Vincent simmered down. How could he remain angry at his best friend. After all, he also had been badly sunburned. Rationalizing made Vincent feel somewhat better. Perhaps there is some truth in the old saying "Misery loves company," yet not for long—and certainly not without consequences.

Thereafter Vincent Armstrong waved over Jack Haig's head a sword which was wielded when he straddled his high horse with overbearing pride in a soldier's profession. All Haig had to do was to sound off about glory on the battlefield, and Armstrong stabbed him to the hilt with the cutting edge sharpened at China Beach. His pride wounded, Jack would be stilled after attempting, ineffectively, to retaliate with weak, weary words: "That has nothing to do with the price of rice in China."

Notwithstanding Jack's defeat at China Beach, he retained his confidence and went on to uphold the family military tradition. Day by day he conditioned himself in the art of soldiery. Eventually, when he attended high school, R.O.T.C. training further fueled the fire for his martial passion. The love and affection he bestowed upon his issued army-type uniform would have brought tears to an orphan's eyes. Speculation ran high among his classmates as to the actual number of hours he devoted to polishing the brass buttons on his uniform...all shone brightly like polished gold. Schoolboys being schoolboys, they have a peculiar sense of humor which they sometimes express by concocting coded nomenclature in referring to one another's peculiarities. Ergo, it was no military secret that Jack Haig was nicknamed Golden Nuggets.

From outward appearances a pompous posture and a stilted strut accompany an arrogant air. Jack, who walked with a soldierly gait with head held high, fitted this description to a T. Golden Nuggets was noticed by some students, unnoticed by some; liked by some students, disliked by some. Whatever was thought of him, Jack had to be respected. In his R.O.T.C. class he fought his way up from the nadir rank of recruit to the zenith rank of lieutenant colonel. He maneuvered his battalion to first place in the city's inter-high-school military competitions by leading the reservists in the capture of every group trophy, and by singlehandedly winning every individual merit award.

Valedictorian at the high school's graduation exercises, highest honor student, Golden Nuggets was valuable officer material. Someone in command at West Point must have mistaken Golden Nuggets for fool's gold, Jack Haig's application to enter the United States Military Academy was rejected. To his disadvantage, he had been born with a wooden spoon in his mouth, and had neither direct nor indirect political pull.

To say Jack Haig was born years too soon is, in the light of changing times, an understatement. He, however, had to contend with the reality of his times. Despite a broken heart, Jack picked up the pieces and reinforced by his father's and grandfather's strong adherence to service in the army, joined the colors as a buck private. If he could have foreseen the future, Jack would have spared himself much anguish.

World War II was just around the bend of the road. Frothing at the mouth, diseased dogs—German, Italian, Japanese breeds affected with 'race' rabies—were digging up putrid bones of aggression that threatened to ruin soil and living things on the entire earth. Unprepared lands had to be saved. But how, there was a shortage of expertise in the field of warfare.

America, among other lands, needed all the officers it could muster. Commissions were handed out by the numbers, on or off the battlefield. Men who had military skills acquired in such units as the National Guard and the Reserve Officers' Training Corp (or Camp) were at a premium. At last Jack Haig had an advantage!

After Vincent and Jack graduated from high school, life's circumstances parted the two boyhood chums. They were destined never to meet again. To be separated forever from people and places pleasantly associated with our youth, is a heartache almost as tragic as the creeping up of old age and senility. It is a hard fact that life extracts a heavy toll for adulthood.

Now and then, here and there, we encounter or hear about former friends and experience deep within ourselves an emotional twinge of gladness for their successes and achievements...or grief for their failures and misfortunes. The last Vincent ever heard of Jack was that, shortly after becoming a full-fledged colonel in the infantry, he was killed October 20, 1944, on Leyte: the focal point of the United States invasion of the Philippine Islands.

The memory of Jack Haig blurred as Vincent refocused his vision back onto Roxanne Davis. With the advent of autumn Armstrong was again in attendance at John Muir Junior High School. He could hardly wait for Miss Davis' English class to start. Not since waiting to open gifts at Christmas had he been so impatient. Often in unwrapping a gift of dry fruitcake, Vincent was disappointed; glazed fruit in crumbly cake did not satisfy his taste buds. Having learned what to expect underneath Roxanne's wrappings, he knew he would find an enjoyable gift, a moist love treat.

But it was not the gift-giving season, Yuletide was too far off. Unfortunately—or fortunately for the boy—depending on one's empathy, if any—the woman was nowhere to be found. She was not in her classroom. In fact, she was no longer at John Muir Junior High School. Upon inquiring at the principal's office, Vincent was informed Miss Davis would be replaced by another English teacher. Miss Davis had been transferred to a school in an outlying district.

Transferred! Roxanne had been transferred. Great, real great! What a letdown. He must do something. If only he could talk to her. That's it! He would phone her tonight and make a date.

Vincent was in for a bigger disappointment yet. His parents having left the house to visit neighbors next door, he took the opportunity to call Roxanne and tell her that he wanted to see her. She replied she would like to see him, too, but was unable to at this particular time. Her brother Phillip, a civil engineer, had arrived from Alaska where he had been designing and directing construction of harbors and highways. The job completed, he came home to rest a few weeks. Phillip planned to stay till he was assigned a new project.

In three weeks Vincent called Roxanne again, merely to donate a dime to the Pacific Telephone Company. Lucklessly his telephone call was answered by a man, "Hello—hello, speak up." Click! the boy without saying a word dropped the receiver back into its cradle. The schoolteacher had prepared her pupil for such an occurrence: "Should my brother ever answer the telephone when you call, hang up."

Eight days later Vincent had some luck. Roxanne answered the telephone this time. Coming to the point bluntly, he asked, "Has your brother returned to Alaska?"

"No," was Roxanne's terse reply. She added, "He is still in Berkeley."

"Will he be home much longer?" In his next breath Vincent, a bit nervous, asked a redundant question, "Will he go up North soon to work on a project?"

Roxanne replied with uncertainty: "I'm not sure where or when he is going. Phillip hasn't said anything specific about his plans."

"You are speaking so softly. We must have a bad connection. I can barely hear you." It suddenly dawned on him that her brother might be within hearing range. Suspicious, Vincent tried to determine if he was actually there: "You are not alone. Somebody else is in your house."

"Yes," Roxanne confirmed Vincent's suspicion. She spoke a little louder, sounding panicky, "Why don't you give me a jingle in about a month. Good-bye for now," she cut short their conversation, and instantly stifled a sigh of relief. At that instant her brother had entered the room.

To comply with Roxanne's request, Vincent delayed a month before telephoning her. No longer did her brother present a problem; he was far from California; he had accepted an engineering assignment in the Midwest. She now presented a problem, which perplexed Vincent. After some soul-searching the woman had decided it was better that they forget the whole thing. Truly she was sorry and begged the boy not to think too harshly of her. Never would she forgive herself. Vincent swore no matter what happened he could have nothing but loving thoughts about her. He failed to understand why she was filled with remorse.

Roxanne explained: "You were innocent. I did a terrible thing. I robbed you of your virginity."

"You did not. I wanted you to have it. Besides, you were a virgin also. You gave me a precious part of yourself...a gift nobody else can ever have." Although Vincent was a mere minor, he properly used words with wisdom, which many mature men misuse in similar situations.

Since the schoolteacher had no answer for her former pupil, she resorted to argument as a solution: The differences between them were insurmountable; they were miles apart in age; it was beyond her comprehension what he wanted with a woman of her age when young girls were available, plentiful as the shells on the seashore.

In rebuttal Vincent said he did not want others. He desired her. The boy was sexually frustrated and not at all interested in arguments based on right or wrong facts. He pushed hard but she refused to budge. Convinced she would not change her mind, Vincent stopped calling her on the telephone; and his contact with Roxanne Davis ceased, at least for quite a while.

Chapter 12

Uncomfortably warm due to the closeness of the limited space filled with newly trained instructors, Ralph Normand went over to a window and opened it to let some fresh air into the studio in which the supervisor had just finished answering a barrage of questions pertaining to his lecture on the importance of using practical psychology in teaching ballroom dancing...and selling lessons. A sudden gust of wind, blowing several sheets of a loose-leaf notebook off Vincent Armstrong's lap, cleared the man's head of reflections on his past boyhood, abruptly bringing him to a clear realization of the present.

As Vincent slid down from his seat to retrieve the notebook's sheets strewed about the floor, Bert Craig, who sat next to him, volunteered to help: "Hold on, I will give you a hand. You pick up the ones by your chair. Let me get the ones by the door. We'd better hurry. The session is almost over."

While the pair were busily gathering up the strewn sheets before departing instructors could step on them inadvertently, Bert's fiancée Alice Scott dipped into her suède bag. She scooped out a lipstick and a mother-of-pearl compact, applied powder to her face and rouge to her parted lips, stood to her feet, and put on a beige flannel coat that she had previously spread across the back of her chair.

"See you later," she addressed both Bert and Vincent. "Have your dinner without me, won't you. I'm trotting along to the White House. The department store closes at six o'clock tonight." Looking at her wrist watch, she exclaimed: "Gosh! it's four-thirty already. That allows me an hour more or less to shop. Oh, well, if I shake a leg, I should also have enough time to grab a bite to eat on my way back to the studio. Bert, sweetie, you know our wedding day isn't too far off. No point waiting until the last minute to buy my trousseau."

Placing her fingertips lightly to her mouth, puckered into the shape of an O, Alice blew a kiss to Bert and tossed a wave to Vincent, "Bye now, I've got to run." Turning on her spike heels, she scurried away, leaving the two friends to themselves.

Handing Vincent some slightly soiled sheets Bert picked up from the floor, he remarked: "They are not too bad. You can use the clean sides to write on. Boy, my stomach is growling. And it is still half an hour till the dinner hour. Am I hungry. I hope we don't have to stand in line. Let's leave earlier today so we can avoid the crowd. What do you say we eat at Fosters Cafeteria."

"Nothing doing," Vincent refused. "We ate there last week. Is it necessary to go to Fosters all the time. I would like to feed my face somewhere else for a change. Suppose we eat at Mannings. The food at that coffee café is very good."

"Sure it is. But I hate paying inflated prices. Mannings is too damn expensive," protested Craig.

"Aren't most downtown eating places. Wake up, buddy boy. We are living in a period of creeping inflation. Food is dear." Armstrong stated an irrefragable fact, inflation or deflation notwithstanding.

"Since I am compelled to pay high prices anyway, I'd rather go where there is a better variety of dishes to select from. More important, my palate is addicted to wholesome, grade-A food. My mother has always prepared nothing but the best for me." Vincent's mouth watered; he could almost taste her delicious dishes. The man expressed an opinion, however childish, commonly shared by sons of all ages: "Her cooking is beyond compare in the whole wide world."

"Gee, Vince, that covers a lot of territory. I sure would like to have dinner at your house sometime. Don't get me wrong. I'm well fed at home. But my stepmother isn't the greatest cook in the world. You are lucky to have a mother who is a great cook. No wonder you are so finicky about food."

"I guess I am," Vincent agreed. "Too often people sacrifice taste for cost. When I see some of them eating in grease-joints around town, I wonder how they can digest the greasy food dished out over the counter.

"What floors me is the tightwad who can afford to eat well yet tries to save money by frequenting popularly priced restaurants just because they serve big portions. True, he gets plenty to eat; but chances are the food is low quality and poorly prepared. Either he was born with a cast iron stomach, or the glutton must enjoy spending a fortune on doctor bills. If you ask me, saving at the expense of one's health is being penny wise and dollar foolish."

Taking personally what Vincent Armstrong was saying, Bert Craig raised his voice in objection. "Fosters doesn't serve such big portions!"

"Who's talking about Fosters," retorted Vincent. I am only speaking in generalities to bring out the point that when it comes to my stomach, money is no object."

"Vince, be reasonable," Bert pleaded. "People have to live within their means."

"I know, I know! But how about splurging this once. Christ! life's too short. There will be opportunity enough to save money on your meals after the preacher locks the ball and chain around your waist. You may as well take advantage of your numbered days as a single man. Come on! Be generous to your stomach. Treat yourself to a delicious dinner. The devil with filthy lucre. Splurge! Live dangerously."

Armstrong burst out into laughter at his playful mockery of Craig. By needling his friend, however, Armstrong had unwittingly pricked him in a most sensitive spot. A pained expression appeared on Craig's face. He looked downcast.

"Don't take it to heart, Bert. I was just pulling your leg. I'm hungry, too. When I'm hungry, I get grouchy and unreasonable. To tell the truth, if my folks weren't helping me out, I would be in a hell-of-uh pickle. Pickle," Vincent interjected. To cheer up his friend, he engaged in wordplay. "The sour...the dill...the dilly of a joke is I'd be fortunate to be eating dill pickles. Can you beat it! I'm not worth a plugged nickel. I haven't five cents of my own to buy a cucumber pickle."

In response Craig exchanged puns with Armstrong: "Tug away, Matey! I can stand lots of leg pulling. My legs are sturdy as an anchored tub." He slapped his solid thighs to give credence in jest to his words. Despite the jolly punning, he sounded far from cheerful as he said, "Vince, you kidding me is the least of my woes."

"Really, Bert, what is wrong? Even though we have only met recently, be assured you can talk to me about anything. Perhaps you will feel better if you get it off your chest. We, all kidding aside, are friends. You can confide in me."

Before replying, Craig looked around. He wanted to make sure nobody was within hearing distance of his voice. Seeing everyone had left the studio, he spoke freely:

"Vince, I'm standing at confusing crossroads, uncertain which way to turn. You might be able to set me in the right direction. I hope so, anyhow. In the short time that we have known each other, you've impressed me as a guy with good sense. I would like your advice about something very serious."

"Thanks for the vote of confidence, Bert. If I can, I'll be glad to give you my advice, for whatever it may be worth."

With a look of embarrassment, Bert asked a surprising question. "Do you think I ought to marry Alice?"

"You are not serious...you are?" Vincent could hardly believe he had heard correctly. "Holy smoke! I would have sworn on a stack of Bibles you were very much in love with her."

"I am, I am! That isn't the thorn on the rose. Uh, let me explain. Where will I start. You see . . ." Bert combed his fingers uneasily through his bushy brown hair in groping for the proper words.

"To begin with, I've never told you that Alice, her mother, and I were in an automobile accident by Golden Gate Park on Fulton Street, not too long ago. Alice's leg was fractured. The doctor put a plaster cast on it. The cast was removed shortly before we came to National Dance Studios. That's why in the early stages of our training she used to rest so often. Her leg was still weak. You probably noticed her sitting out dances every once in a while."

Nodding his head in affirmation, Armstrong replied: "Now that you mention it, I have. So that's the reason she would always be rubbing her leg. I asked her a couple of times if she was okay. All she said was that she was a little tired. Poor kid, she didn't once complain of discomfort when we practiced together. What did the doctor say? Is it all right for her to plan on teaching ballroom dancing?"

"Sure, just as long as she rests between dances, so that her leg has a chance to strengthen. He thought dance exercises might even help."

"The doctor is right, Bert. Exercise can be very helpful. In army hospitals I have seen G.I.s exercising to gain back the strength in their arms and legs which had been broken during combat. Here is one of the exercises they did that you can show Alice." Armstrong pushed a chair aside and demonstrated a leg exercise. "This is not too hard. But tell her not to overdo it. Was anyone besides Alice seriously hurt in the automobile accident?"

"Nope, she was the only one who got banged up bad. Her mother was more scared than harmed. She suffered some superficial scratches. As for myself, I pulled a muscle in my shoulder when I turned the wheel sharply in order to avoid a head-on collision.

"Vince, I'm curious. I know American soldiers were called G.I.s. How did they get that name?"

"Well, G.I. stands for 'government issue.' So I suppose that's where the name came from. I can't give any other explanation. Now getting back to the automobile accident. Who caused it?"

A righteous beam lit up Craig's blue-green eyes. "The other driver caused the accident. He was absolutely in the wrong. He failed to stop for a red light. And he speeded across the intersection so fast, his car swerved and smashed into mine. We were lucky to escape with our lives. A woman who witnessed the whole thing signed an affidavit in our behalf. It was an open-and-shut case. His insurance company arrived at a settlement with our lawyer in a hurry. Mrs. Scott and I received two hundred fifty dollars apiece. And Alice was given thirty-five hundred dollars."

Expecting to hear larger sums, Armstrong grimaced, his disapproval apparent. "In addition to the thirty-five hundred dollars did the insurance company at least pay the medical expenses and the attorney's fee?"

"Medical expenses—yes! Attorney's fee—no!" Caught off guard by his friend's unfavorable reaction, Craig raised his voice defensively yet his tone was apologetic:

"Oh, I'm sorry we didn't get more. Maybe if we had taken the case to court, we would have done better. I...we were afraid to fight the insurance company. Our lawyer said that in spite of us having a strong civil suit, there was a possibility we could net still less money if we went to court. Perhaps we would have ended up with nothing but a jumbo-sized goose egg. You see the guy who caused the accident claimed to be on some kind of medication that affected his driving ability.

"Also, lawsuits, it seems, can drag on a long time—weeks—months. And attorney's fees and court costs can run into a pile of dough. So, deciding to play it safe, we accepted the settlement. I think we made a wise decision. Don't you agree?"

"Of course, since that was the situation," Vincent Armstrong felt compelled to agree. "The injustice of it, though, is enough to boil a body's blood. It's a stupid shame that plaintiffs in the right cannot be assured of winning in a court of law. Either we need wiser judges or wiser lawyers—or both."

Baffled, Bert Craig shrugged his shoulders as an indication that an explanation of the injustices of the justice system was beyond him. "I'll never be able to figure it out."

"Nevertheless," Vincent went on with wise words, "I suppose one should make the best of a bad situation." To lighten the conversation, he injected a little offbeat humor: "As Confucius might have philosophized, 'A grain of rice on the tongue is worth a mouthful in the mud.' Yet how does the business with the insurance company affect you and Alice? I still don't know what's bothering you."

"Nothing," replied Bert, "well...nothing except the same old family troubles. You're probably sick of hearing me complain about Alice's and my problems. But I have to unburden myself to somebody. I'm being pressured from left to right, from right to left...from side to side!

"On one side, my future mother-in-law is giving me the usual hard time. Like I often told you, she's sore because Alice quit her job to train at the studio almost two months without pay. Her latest gripe is that I'm marrying her daughter for the insurance money.

"Alice, you see, has worked since she was knee-high to a grasshopper. In the bargain, she's always handed over her pay check to her mother. This wasn't fair by a long shot. Alice's mother and her brother Bob, too, were healthy, perfectly capable of earning a living. Bob...who is a year younger than his sister...had to finish high school, but not Alice—oh, no!

"Now that Alice intends to get hitched, Mrs. Scott will obviously lose a soft touch. Boy, is she acting up something awful! The woman plays on her daughter's sympathies all the time, making a pretense at grieving for Mr. Scott. Whenever I visit Alice, her mother creates scenes and carries on miserably. She's forever bitching that their circumstances would be different had her husband not died of sep'-ti-, uh, ce'-mi-a, some sort of 'blood poisoning.' From the way Mrs. Scott acts toward me, you'd swear I had poisoned him.

"On the other side, my parents haven't let up riding me, either. My dad and...my mother continue to take the stand that I'm unprepared financially, that I should learn a dependable vocation. Needless to say, they aren't pleased with my wish to be a dancing instructor. In that I have had a couple of years at San Francisco State, they insist it's a crime to waste my schooling in a dance studio. Actually, they are determined that I complete my college education.

"The two of them treat me like a four-year-old instead of a grown man of twenty-four. They talk to me as if I were an infant, as if I have no mind of my own. 'You are inexperienced...too impractical to grasp the values of life'; my parents keep belittling me.

"What's more, they say I'm a fool for wanting to marry someone who isn't on a par with me educationally and below our standing socially. They're always eating out my heart about Alice coming from a penniless, low-class family living in an old flat south of Market Street. And the hard fact that she used to work as a laundress at Cerciat Laundry doesn't soften matters.

"Without exaggeration the whole thing has me wound up like a tight ball of yarn. I am unable to figure out whether I'm being tangled or untangled. Sometimes I rue the day I was born. One minute I console myself, 'Marry Alice. Everything will come out in the wash.' The next minute I ponder, 'If there are so many complications and such commotions prior to the wedding, what will happen later?'

"Probably the simplest solution for me is to join the Merchant Marine and ship out of the country. I don't know. What would you do if you were in my shoes?"

Armstrong hesitated before replying to Craig. Armstrong had not expected Craig's problems to be so serious, so deeply involved with his parents and Alice's family.

"Criminy, Bert, you're putting me on the spot. There are limits to my mixing into someone else's affairs. It isn't that I have any qualms about giving a friend advice of a personal nature. But I just can't let you shift the onus to my back. If I tell you to marry Alice and afterward things go wrong, I'll feel responsible. On the other hand, if I advise against the marriage, you may some day regret you listened to me. One way or the other I will be at fault.

"Perhaps a tip or two from my Uncle Walter would be helpful. Get an earful, and a belly-laugh, about what that character spouts on the subject of marital bliss:

"'Going to the church altar to tie the nuptial knot, isn't very different from going to the racetrack to play the horses. At the races you put all your chips on a lively and high-spirited filly because she looks good to you...or because a tipster leads you to believe she's a champion, a cinch to pay off. Quite often men also choose mates by their good looks...or by the prospects of their winning charms. Getting married, like betting on the races, is at best a gamble. In both ventures while some win, many lose.'

"And he ends up by saying: 'You needn't take my word for it. Statistics show that the divorce rate in the U.S.A. is the highest in the world. Yet people continue to cling to the belief (or hope) that the odds are in favor of a marriage being successful.'

"You must bear in mind, now, Uncle Walter's views are not typical of the average American. He is a confirmed bachelor. Consider his tips for what they may be worth.

"In all fairness to Alice, I must tell you if you are not absolutely certain you ought to marry her—that is, should you have any reservations about being married—don't prolong your engagement. Sure, when you break it off she will be hurt. Still imagine how much more she would be hurt if the two of you married, and later fell out of love and divorced. What if a child was in the picture. That would be an unforgivable tragedy. Bert, you owe it to your fiancée to be aboveboard with her."

"Haven't I been trying to be. That's the reason I'm asking for your advice, Vince. I have no desire to be unfair. You've got to understand I can't help being upset over Mrs. Scott's fiery attitude toward me. The old spitfire should have a damper put on her. Alice is too easygoing with her mom."

"I am not implying by a long shot that you are being unfair." At this point, too irritated to speak subtly, Vincent could not avoid wounding his friend's feelings. "It strikes me you are thinking of yourself alone. Here you sit on your behind mooning, undecided whether or not you should marry Alice while she is out shopping for a trousseau in preparation for the wedding.

"If you really and truly love her, you shouldn't blame Alice for Mrs. Scott's selfishness. So the woman is selfish; you are marrying the daughter, not the mother. How would you feel if Alice blamed you for your folks' attitude—for their snobbery—for their throwing cold water on her engagement. Let's face it, you are neither a university professor nor a member of the Four Hundred. Suppose you were, that wouldn't cut any ice."

(Bert Craig froze, chilled at Vincent Armstrong's cutting statements. Subconsciously he had an inferiority complex about his lack of a profession and social status. Although during the conversation he was the one who in unmistakable words stated his father and step-mother were snobbish, he did not appreciate hearing Armstrong say it. Moreover, despite Bert's immaturity, deep inside he perceived that his parents had his best interest at heart in insisting he obtain a college degree instead of a marriage license. His own worst enemy, he was too rebellious to admit they were right.)

Vincent continued lecturing Bert: "Incidentally, speaking of class and of character, Alice has more compassion and more sense than some of those insensate coeds I met when I attended the University of California. As for society gals, would you want to be married to someone like Barbara Hutton? Or would you rather have Alice Scott as a wife?

"Without overestimating, Alice is an exceptionally rare jewel. If I loved her, nothing could blind me to her true value. Now you have my opinion. Of course, whether you should complete your college education is another matter. I suggest you take guidance from a person smarter and older than I."

Vincent smiled for he was attempting to be humorous. "A very clever person who comes to mind was an ancient Roman by the name of Marcus Cicero. He said, 'Nobody can give you wiser advice than yourself.'"

With a forthright look into the eyes of his advisee, Vincent Armstrong stubbornly sealed his lips. The taut, rigid line they formed indicated beyond a doubt he did not have the slightest intention of uttering one more syllable about the dilemma Bert Craig faced.

Like on depressing headlines in boldface, gloom could be read on Bert's lineaments. Out of strained politeness the little fellow murmured an unintelligible acknowledgment, a halfhearted acceptance, of all his adviser had elaborated upon. Quite manifest was his dissatisfaction with the well-meant yet, in his mind, brutally frank counsel he had received. In self-pity he thought, "Vince could have been just a bit sympathetic."

One wonders why some of us oftentimes beseech others for advice about a problem requiring a decision, but regardless of how prudent an opinion is offered, we cannot accept it. Consequently, the same as Bert Craig, we remain dissatisfied, locked in the identical state of indecision which we sought to escape. Nothing being gained (?)...nothing being lost (?), the two young men went silently on to dinner.

The following day, the trainees at National Dance Studios assembled in supervisor Ralph Normand's studio for another one of his discourses on the history of social dances and subtle selling of dances. Alice Scott sat as usual between her fiancé, Bert Craig, and their mutual friend, Vincent Armstrong. Bert, reflecting upon the discussion he and Vincent had the day before, and feeling guilty, exchanged uneasy glances with the latter who, embarrassed for Bert, was ill at ease, too.

In the meantime Alice, oblivious to the unspoken conflicts stirring within the breasts of the disquieted duo, raved with excitement over the lovely wedding gown she had bought at the White House. To alleviate Craig's as well as his own mounting tension, Armstrong interrupted her with a hastily concocted question far afield from hymeneal rites.

"Alice! before I forget. I left my notes on the dance histories at home. Do you know which dance Mr. Normand is going to discuss this afternoon?"

Distracted with such suddenness, the bride-to-be was momentarily at a loss for words. "Hmmm . . . How—which dance—how could you forget, silly. We have been talking about it all week. And at the last session Mr. Normand said he would take up the fox trot next."

His purpose accomplished, Vincent was greatly comforted. "That's right. I wasn't thinking. I'm a blockhead." Now he was being funny: "I better sweep the sawdust out of my head. Do you have a brush in your suede bag?" To humor him, Alice fished out a hair brush. He pleaded in fun, "Lend it to me, please." "Here, Vincent, you may use it," she obliged, bursting into laughter when he began to brush his thick head of hair with sweeping strokes.

Although Bert was relieved that the subject had been changed, he was self-conscious. Slumping down in his chair, he drew his chin against his breastbone, suggestive of the way a turtle withdraws into its bony shell to hide. Then by force of habit, he looped his arms over his head, interlocked his fingers, and planted the palms of his joined hands on the nape of his neck. He might have succeeded in appearing inconspicuous if it were not for his elbows protruding winglike. Nevertheless, nobody in the group noticed Craig, nor had anybody an occasion to do so, particularly after Ralph Normand hustled into the room and attracted everybody's attention.

"Our assistant manager," announced Ralph, "will join us later to demonstrate the methods of conducting a dance analysis often given in conjunction with an introductory course or a trial lesson. Analyses, though hardly spoken of as such publicly, are presented as prizes in the management's advertising schemes to draw people into the studio. On second thought, perhaps a better choice of words would be 'programs'—not 'schemes.'

"For example, on musical radio programs sponsored by this organization, disc jockeys periodically broadcast that should the listener identify a mystery tune being played and phone in the name within ten minutes, the lucky person would receive, or win, <u>eight</u> dancing lessons free of charge. This isn't so generous an offer as it sounds. While a regular lesson consists of a full hour, the free course is comprised of half hour lessons; therefore, in actuality only <u>four</u> are offered. Still and all, complaints are nil, since our commercials do not state the length of each lesson, just the number a winner is entitled to. Need I mention, the recordings played on the radio are so common and simple to recognize only a numbskull could miss naming one.

"Coming in flocks to claim their free lessons, the pigeons are thus decoyed into the studio. Now a clever analyst neither teaches too technically nor tests to tyrannically. His main purpose is to convince our patrons that dancing is very easy, quickly learned, and that lessons are a must—that they are needed. Unfortunately, too many untrained and unskilled individuals seem reluctant to admit that they could benefit from instruction; yet ninety-nine per cent of them either cannot dance or dance improperly. All of which causes three basic problems in the selling of ballroom dancing."

Ralph energetically raised his right arm in mid-air with his hand forming a fist. Uncurling his index finger, he pointed it, like a baton, straight at his audience and enumerated successively:

> "The first problem is to prove there is a need for people
> to improve their dancing, and to convince them to do so.
> If they aren't able to dance, matters are less complicated.
> Simply sell them on the idea of learning how."

Next he extended his middle finger:

> "The second problem is to create the illusion that danc-
> ing is easy. This is harder than it appears, because danc-
> ing isn't easy; it is difficult. And, to complicate the situa-
> tion, few are willing to work hard at mastering the art."

He then straightened another finger:

> "The third problem is to persuade people to sign up for
> as long a course as possible, and to discourage the break-
> ing of their contracts afterwards by inveigling them into
> making a substantial down-payment."

"Here supersalesmanship is essential. Since for practical purposes socially, if not professionally, learning to do all the ballroom or drawing-room dances takes at least two years of concentrated effort, I would estimate. This unpublicized fact is quite comprehensible when we realize, disseminated propaganda notwithstanding, people in general require a number of hours to master a single step-combination.

"Of course, merely learning the directions of dance steps doesn't demand too much time. Anybody with two left feet can learn to step forward, backward, or to the right side as directed. Obviously, mastery of a dance involves technical methods of performance such as follow-through; weight placement and balance; dexterous movements of knee, hip, and shoulder...as well as the hands; interpretation of music, accenting the proper beat, and phrasing steps in coordination with musical phrases:

"And, it is only natural that the time to teach these techniques will be shortened greatly if an instructor has talent to work with. Moreover, talented students after practicing a year or so may become proficient in some dances. Untalented students, however, might practice hard twice as long and never really attain proficiency in any dance."

From one of the recently trained teachers in attendance, a hand was raised indicating she had a question. Recognized by Ralph Normand, she asked, "Is the technique of follow-through, which you just mentioned, comparable to that used in sports?"

The supervisor answered: "That's right. In sports 'follow-through' is the carrying of a motion to natural completion after a ball has been hit—as in baseball with the stroke of a bat, as in golf with the stroke of a club, as in tennis with the with the stroke of a racket. Following through not only enhances a player's accuracy but is good form as well. In ballroom dancing we call it style, and skill.

"Unlike a golfer, a baseball or tennis player, a dancer uses his feet (and legs)—not his hands (and arms)—in following through. Briefly defined, in dance 'follow-through' is the continual brushing by of the in-steps as a dancer moves either foot in any direction. Novice ballroom or drawing-room dancers unfamiliar with the technique rarely if ever follow through except by hit and miss. Most of the time they even fail to dance with their feet close together.

"Watch me," instructed Ralph. Leaving his chair, he went around to the front of his desk, turned his back to the group of new teachers, spread his feet wide apart, and walked (awkwardly) backward a few steps and sideward a few steps...his feet all the while remaining well-parted. "See! as the novices plod about a dance floor, this is how their posteriors look, bigger than hippopotamuses." At the sight of the supervisor's ridiculous appearance, amused young men and women began to laugh loudly. Ralph Normand was on the brink of laughter; however, he restrained himself. Keeping a straight face, so that he could resume his talk, he quieted the noisy group with motions of his hands.

"The follow-through technique not only lends a streamline shape to a dancer's form but also is an asset in assuring one's sure-footedness on a dance floor. Sometime as an experiment, standing with your feet far apart, try to take a step in any direction. It is a very awkward thing to do. You'll discover the closer your feet are brought together the better will be your balance, and the more definite will be your steps, whichever way—"

Just as he was about to complete his sentence, the supervisor lost the rest of his words when Vincent Armstrong, thinking Normand was finished with what he had to say, abruptly voiced a query in reference to an earlier statement by the supervisor. Vincent found it hard to understand how spun-out courses were able to be sold to individuals who had been led to believe ballroom dancing could be learned in a hurry.

"That is a good question," Ralph Normand complimented Vincent. "Once they enter our studio—which has the décor of a dream world—most everything under the sun is discussed with prospective patrons, except how long it takes to learn to dance. We avoid giving a direct answer and remain noncommittal by telling the dreamers, who expect to become accomplished dancers overnight, that they can learn to dance as fast as their heart desires. It usually works because they have the desire.

"In addition, after laying out an extensive dance course for a student, we divide it into small blocks of hourly lessons. When a block is completed, the student is induced to sign up for more lessons. Our objective is to sell the entire course, or as much of it as possible. Our incentive is do-re-me. The notes ring as true as the arithmetic: the more blocks we sell the more money we make."

Ralph wondered if his wit with words made sense to the members of the group. Losing his trend of thought, he paused momentarily to find words relevant to the subject under discussion. "Now what was I going to say? It must have been a lie. . . . Oh, yes...never overlook the fact that whether or not patrons can afford lessons is no concern of yours. The receptionist at the desk downstairs will arrange a budget plan on credit for your student.

"Remember, when the assistant manager arrives be alert. Sharpen your pencils; it'll pay you to take notes. He's a crackerjack of a salesman, tops in the business. He will present profitable pointers for you to use in selling dance courses.

"While we are waiting, I'm sure there will be sufficient time to cover another phase of my chronology on recreational dancing." The supervisor pulled open his top desk drawer and withdrew a notebook. Flipping to the desired page, he commenced to read.

Chapter 13

A HISTORY OF THE CLASSIC BALLROOM DANCES

American Dances

II-A. The Fox Trot (to perfect timing and smoothness)

I take issue with dancing masters, historians, other writers in the field, and the like who hypothesize that the fox trot and its forerunners are of African or Negroid origin. It is impractical to go on a safari to hunt for elusive proof of these theories from country to country on the Dark Continent when the fox trot's forerunners can be tracked roaming in large numbers from coast to coast across America, an enlightened continent.

In the early 1800s during the years of the rancheros, and dominance by Catholic missionaries on the Pacific Coast in California, public fiestas were sponsored by the Spaniards to celebrate important affairs of state. As a major event in such festivities padres conducted religious processionals and invited participation of the Indians, who performed indigenous tribal dances, numerous in form.

A variety of dance forms grown naturally in different areas around the country were abundant among all American Indians, not just among the Californians. Tribes characterized dances by areal characteristics. To name some: 'snake dance' of the Hopis of Arizona and New Mexico, 'buffalo dance' of the Jemez of Santa Fe, 'rabbit dance' of the Otos of southeastern Nebraska, 'crow dance' of the Sias of New Mexico, 'beaver dance of the Blackfeet of upper Missouri and the Saskatchewan Rivers, 'pigeon dance' of the Cherokees of central New York, 'deer dance' of the Ojibways of the Great Lakes, and 'bat dance' of the Papagos of southern Arizona.

[Apologizing for the interruption, one of the newly trained teachers admitted he was ignorant as to where the Great Lakes were located. Impressed by the teacher's candor, the supervisor responded: "No need to apologize. I have met college graduates who were not well-versed in the geography of their country. The Great Lakes are a chain of five fresh-water lakes in central North America, through which four run a stretch of the United States-Canada boundary." Ralph Normand could not resist making a satirical comment. "Notice that while I indicate the original habitats of the various Indian tribes, they are not necessarily located there today."]

Besides dances in which creatures of the lakes and forests were imitated, the tribes, often as a means of communicating with their spirits used other dances of a different nature: the Ghost Dance of the Paiutes of southwestern Utah; the Rain Dance of the Kickapoos of southern Wisconsin; the Harvest Dance of the Zuñis of western New Mexico; the now-forbidden Sun Dance of the Sioux, south and west of Lake Superior; and the Devil Dance of the Arizonian, New Mexican, and Texan Apaches.

Each of the countless Indian dances had its characteristic choreography and chronicle, plus special song and symbolism. In many dances the members of both sexes performed individually. Dances requiring strenuous activity were performed solely by the males. Other dances required that the females perform together as a group. Finally there were the dances in which males and females danced with one another.

Among the most vigorous to be found anywhere, the dances of the Indians, wildly natural, were too often misinterpreted by outsiders as being frenzied as well as artless. Rhythmic precision merged with dramatic action presented itself constantly in an Indian's dance. Using his muscles freely, he vibrated virtually his entire body. Never did he indulge in uncontrolled or meaningless tittups.

["In the light of this information, one wonders if ash-blonde Gilda Gray, songstress-dancer of the twenties, deserves to be credited as the originator of the once popular shimmy. In doing the dance she shook every part of her anatomy as though it were lemon jello *shimmering* in a bowl. The trick she used when *shimmying* was muscular control, the technique developed by feathered autochthons, aeons before Gilda's time."]

Whichever befitted the occasion, Indians danced with spiritual fervor or joyous abandonment. Indications exist that from the tendency of whites and redskins to assimilate in a fluid society, however small, soft substances of the Indians' ceremonial dances by osmosis diffused into pioneer folk dances: most familiar are The Circle, Chase the Squirrel, Pop Goes the Weasel, Green Mountain Volunteers, Arkansas Traveler, Jennie Crack Corn, Shoo Fly, Red River Valley, Chorus Jig, Rustic Reel, Fishers' Hornpipe, Old Dan Tucker, and Oh! Dem Golden Slippers. . . .

GOLD! California, the Golden State—gold: 1849...James Marshall's epochal discovery...gold at Sutter's mill, wrought a dramatic change in the dance of life. Throughout the gold rush, migrants, blinded by the shiny, bright-yellow, precious metal, went wild with worship over the golden idol pedestaled in the mines of the auriferous Sacramento Valley. Itchy, they could not wait to go to San Francisco, where they blew their gold dust to the winds. In their jubilation a generation of Argonauts drank and did dirty dances with strumpets (gold diggers) in the concert saloons and dance halls of Sidney-Town, a violent waterfront district where murder was a common occurrence.

["San Francisco's Barbary Coast, a bloody cesspool, was built around Sidney-Town, notorious for its crooked, gambling houses and contaminated, slave brothels. Fumigated year by year in the 1900s, one block of the Barbary Coast received a clean bill of health and survived as the International Settlement on Pacific Avenue, between Columbus Avenue and Montgomery Street."]

Despite the danger...the death...the disease in the Barbary Coast, at the turn of the century (before the Great War) San Franciscans— young and old, men and women—packed the dance halls on Pacific Avenue, and elsewhere in the district. The largest dance hall, the Thalia, attracted wall-to-wall crowds. On display at the Thalia were zoological dances, artless copies of the Indians' original dance classics inspired by wild animals in their areas.

From the Barbary Coast the zoological dances sprang far into sections of the land. Popular were such dances as the bunny hug, the chicken glide, the turkey trot, the pony prance, and the grizzly bear. Performed by dancers (?) in a smutty manner, the dances got a bad reputation which they did not deserve, for they were domesticated. Feared by hygienic social groups, the domestic animal dances were fenced out of some so-called sanitary places: certain-clubs, –churches, –cabarets, et cetera.

[Scratching his head in a witty way as he was about to show off a bit of his knowledge, Bert Craig brushed back the mussed-up strands of his hair, raised his hand, and asked Mr. Normand for permission to speak, which he granted. Bert put a cupped hand to his mouth, coughed, and cleared his throat before he spoke. "It looks like the grizzly bear dance was named after the symbol on the California flag adopted during the Bear Flag Revolt in 1846."

The supervisor smiled briefly, then replied with a sober expression. "True—and that incident is a sad commentary on a chapter of American history!"

Surprised by the supervisor's statement, the dance teachers in the recently trained group found it hard, without a challenge, to accept Mr. Normand's accusation. They reacted noisily, clamoring in a chorus for an explanation.

"It is far, far afield from the history of the dance. Nevertheless, since you insist, I shall explain:

"Backtracking to June 14, 1846, we find thirty-three uncouth soldiers of fortune (grudging, meddlesome, adventurers...drifters, hunters, trappers, and sailors who had deserted their ships). That day, bent on plunder, the thirty-three men, Americans, invaded by stealth a peaceful, defenseless hamlet in Sonoma. Under the guise of liberating California from Mexico, they imprisoned a Mexican colonel, Marino Guadalupe Vallejo, and plundered his property, a prosperous rancho.

"To cover up their outrageous acts against Colonel Vallejo, the leader of the soldiers of fortune simply said the Mexican was a captive of the Bear Flag War (or Revolt). But, for their cause they needed a cover, a flag; so they devised one. The flag was crudely made from materials that happened to be at hand.

"A five pointed star—familiar to the sailors as being symbolic of a state—was outlined in ink on a piece of coarse, unbleached, cotton cloth; the outline was filled in with red paint. The hunters and trappers were great admirers of the grizzly (large and powerful with an ugly temper); thus a grizzly bear facing the star also was outlined in ink on the cloth, and that outline was filled in with red paint, too. Next, sewn on the bottom of the cloth was a strip of red flannel which contained the words CALIFORNIA REPUBLIC.

"The outrage is that Colonel Vallejo, despite the criticism of his countrymen, always had been hospitable to Americans. The irony is that he was a strong advocate for the acquisition of California by the United States. The fact is that the Bear Flag Revolt had little, if anything, to do with the acquisition of California from Mexico. The reality is that the Revolt was a hindrance (lives were lost); with the Mexican War in progress, it became much more difficult for the United States to annex California. The tragedy is that not one drop of blood would have been shed in the acquisition of the state if the thirty-three soldiers of fortune had never set foot on the soil of California."

Saddened, the teachers suddenly sat stone-faced and silent. The supervisor resumed his discussion on the history of the fox trot.]

Black men as well as redskins played starring roles in the movement of American social dance. In antebellum days three-piece Negro bands were an integral part of life on many southern plantations. The musicians accompanied their singing with a fiddle, banjo, and bones (or clappers) held in pairs between the fingers to produce musical rhythms. After the Civil War, in 1867, an informative book was published entitled <u>Slave Songs of the United States</u>. The book not only was timely but also was ahead of the times. It is an authentic collection of Negro spirituals, reels, and dance tunes. Most important, the collection contains vivid descriptions of a variety of black men's music.

Before I discuss the Negro's contribution to dance music, a dance called cake walk should be looked at. The combination of cake-walk rhythm and banjo technique was the forelooper of ragtime, which Negroes from the South nurtured. The choreography of the cake walk, however, was inspired by Indians, the beleaguered Seminole. The name Seminole was derived from a Creek word, *simanoli*, meaning 'separatist,' or 'runaway.'

The Seminole, an offshoot of the Creeks, belonged to a large confederacy of Muskogean Indians. As could be expected by their designation, the Seminoles separated from the confederacy, and overran Florida in the 1700s after the British destroyed the native Floridian tribes. Meanwhile the Seminoles amalgamated with congenial Yamasses, whom the British had driven out of Carolina. The population of the Seminole tribe increased further as African bondsmen fleeing the lash in Georgia were welcomed into the redskin's fold. Unmolested by the Spaniards, generations of these unchained blacks raised herds and cultivated the soil in relative peace. The blacks were disturbed only on odd occasions when white slave makers, Georgians or Carolinians, raided the Florida peninsula to seize escapees and to enslave others.

On October 28, 1835, the United States government, having earlier acquired Florida by cession from the Spanish Crown, undertook a full-scale campaign to deprive the Seminole of their land and to remove their people from the peninsula to designated "Indian Territory" in Oklahoma. This callous campaign was met with violent resistance. The upshot was, the wronged redskins waged war with whites!

During the Seminole War, which lasted seven years, Negroes were able to watch firsthand the war dances of the red-skinned braves, dressed in battle array and trappings. Their tempestuous dances, created to stir the spirit of massacre in warriors on the warpath, were so rousing that every dancer's very being raged with homicidal intent. Tomahawks poised menacingly overhead, they rushed one by one toward a blood-red post, an emblem of hostility, and struck it a vicious blow.

While they gyrated and gestured waiting for their turn to strike again, the braves let out at the top of their lungs a weird battle cry: "Yo—ho—ee—hee—eeee!" Over and over they shrieked the cry of battle as they sprang spiritedly into the air. Landing lightly on the ground, the braves stepped high with a dancer's agility, executing quicksteps around the blood-red post.

Dancing themselves into a fighting frenzy had the psychological effect of reinforcing the braves' determination to survive, in Florida, as an independent Seminole nation. Unified in purpose, they were emboldened to face any enemy. Now, keyed up to fight to the death, with self-induced courage acting as a tranquilizer, the dancers grew calm, paired off, and walked in solemn serenity to cadenced drum beats.

Fascinated Negro bystanders from southern plantations, unable to remain still while the Seminoles danced, instinctively made up movements of their own: in cadence with the drum beats, they did high-stepping struts, a form of fanciful walking. But instead of assuming the Indians' natural posturing in their war dance, the black slaves in their fanciful walking assumed the affected posture of white slaveholders, who stood like peacocks and strutted like pigeons.

Some spectators said the slaves were putting on airs, acquired from the southern aristocracy. Some spectators said the slaves were making fun of their masters; if so, the masters never realized they were being mimicked, fortunately for the slaves.

Soon fanciful high-steps were strutted at shindigs in the big plantations throughout the South. Recreational activities centered around the plantation where slaves attending shindigs (sometimes festive frolics, sometimes crop celebrations) sang songs and danced dances. Contests were held to see which black couple 'cut the best figures.' Usually the judges were the plantation owners: the master would announce the winning couple; the mistress would give the winners a decorated cake. Hence the high-stepping dance had received the name "cake walk." Often the name is combined "cake-walk."

[On the assumption that some members of the group he was addressing might be unclear about a colloquialism he had used, Ralph Normand decided to clarify it. "In case you are not sure about the phrase 'cut the best figures,' or as the darkies in the Old South would say, 'de best cuttn' of figgers,' it means obviously 'the best intricate steps performed.' And from that, I would imagine, today's colloquial expression 'cut a rug' (to dance) was adopted by drawing-room dancers."]

In post-bellum years (circa 1903-1914) hotel operators, capitalizing on Florida's balmy weather, turned the Gulf State into a fashionable winter resort. Socialites attending balls at high-class hotels, displayed the newest styles in evening clothes. Negro servants, who at times were expected to put on cake walks as entertainment for such occasions, emulated the wealthy vacationers by parading pompously in formal attire.

Thereafter, when competing in cake-walk contests up and down the state, colored entrants primped and posed in borrowed finery. The men would wear black swallow-tailed coats and high, stiff collars. The women wore white diaphanous gowns adorned with colorful bouquets. From Florida the top high-steppers went to Georgia, to North and South Carolina, and to Virginia. Ultimately the latest versions of the cake walk appeared in New York, the showcase of America. On display were two styles: Grand Straight and Fancy Cake Walks, which were performed to syncopated rags...heartbeats of Negro dance music.

Leaving New York Harbor and sailing down the Atlantic Coast to Louisiana in search of more information about the part that Negroes played in the story of ballroom dancing, we sight at the shore line of the twentieth century the first popular wave which washed up a lively form of the black man's dance music, ragtime. The music was so named because it was frequently referred to as "ragged," by whites in the 1900s for want of a better word. Yet it should be noted that since the days of slavery in the Georgia Sea Islands secular songs have been synonymous with the expression *rags*, which means 'sinful.' Ragtime—nickname, rag—was conceived with the intermarriage of the music of New Orleans Creoles and the airs of Dixieland Negroes. Their conception, ragtime, is rhythm characterized by steady <u>syncopation</u> in the melody, with improvised embellishments.

["For those of you who are unfamiliar with the term, *syncopation* denotes a temporary dislodgment of the usual accent or beat of musical composition. Regular accent is a basic element of most music. As we listen to it, we experience recurring beats which systematically fall into units of two's or three's. The first beat of each unit is slightly emphasized. Whenever this sensation of regularity is fixed upon our brain and irregularity is for an instant interjected, *syncopation* occurs.

"Ragtime is somewhat similar to a Scotch catch, or snap, which is characteristic of some Negro as well as Scottish music. Therefore, it would be worthwhile to familiarize ourselves with the catch. The Scotch catch is a pair of notes played with liveliness, one being extremely short and the other being longer than the first: the second is still short nonetheless."

Normand stepped up to a blackboard and drew two musical notes, a sixteenth note (♪) and a dotted eighth note (♪.). He again addressed his attentive audience, "If you can read music, that's fine; if you cannot, do your best to follow my explanation, which I shall try to simplify:

"The note with the two hooks is a sixteenth, the note with the one hook is an eighth. An eighth note indicates a tone twice as long as a sixteenth note. And adding a dot to an eighth note increases its duration value half a length more.

"Keeping all that in mind, a Scotch catch is the cutting short of the first two notes in a melody by placing a sixteenth note in front of a dotted eighth. By doing so, a musician playing an instrument, whether a bagpipe or a piano or a horn, produces an electrifying, snapping sound...a sound heard wherever dance bands played snappy rags."]

In reality through what medium ragtime was initially transmitted to the American public is a tug of words: Some writers pull in the direction that the spiritual sung by the plantation and levee slave was the medium. Some writers pull in the direction that it was the Negro brass band on the steamboat chugging up and down the Mississippi. Some writers pull in the direction that the southern darky strumming on a banjo inside the tavern was the medium.

Some writers pull in the direction that it was the soul brother shuffling around the cat house. Some writers pull in the direction that the black itinerant musician ragging in the honky-tonk was the medium. Some writers pull in the direction that it was the blackface of the minstrel show. None seem to have the strength to win this tug of words.

However, the arm of authority pulls strongly in the direction of Benjamin (Ben) R. Harney, a white song writer and dance-hall piano player born 1871 in Middleboro, Kentucky. It appears he was the person who started the process of getting the public to pay attention to ragtime as an American art form. Well-publicized appearances can be misleading. If the makeup is removed, we can see that he was an imitator on the ragtime stage. Harney may be applauded for composing a tune, "You've Been a Good Old Wagon but You've Done Broke Down," published 1895 in Louisville, Kentucky.

The tune was the first rag music ever copyrighted. It was composed of elementary elements of ragtime. But it was not basic black rag. Harney's tune lacked the deep feelings of the Negro's soul buried in his music. Nevertheless, at the age of twenty-five the song writer won the hearts of New Yorkers when he appeared at Tony Pastor's Variety Theater in 1896. To unversed, northern white audiences Ben Harney's imitation of the southern black and his piano ragging seemed remarkable authentic.

One of the most respected musicians, in America and in Europe, believed to be responsible for the rise of ragtime was Scott Joplin, a Negro born 1869 in Texarkana, Texas. While Ben Harney was a writer of ragtime songs (which were impractical for dancing), Joplin was a writer of piano rags (which were practical for dancing). He had training in classical music, but his heart and soul was devoted to ragtime music. In 1899 he published a sensational, successful piano piece, "Maple Leaf Rag." Thereafter, Joplin gained the reputation as deserving a place in the musicians' hall of fame as a pianist and composer of syncopated rags.

Another notable Negro associated with the rise of ragtime was Thomas (Tom) Million Turpin, also an outstanding pianist and composer of syncopated rags. It is said Turpin possessed arcane rag techniques inherited from musicians who preceded him, his soul brothers. He was the first black man to publish a piano rag, "Harlem Rag"; it was danceable, the year was 1897.

The genius of ragtime was a Negro piano player, Louis Chauvin of St. Louis. He had a natural ear for music, which he could not read or write. In their *History and Analysis of Ragtime*, co-authors Ernest Borneman and Bartlett D. Simms maintain that many of Chauvin's original tunes and syncopations were transcribed by Tom Turpin and later by Scott Joplin without giving Louis Chauvin due credit. That, unfortunately, is a smear on the record of the Negro's struggle to achieve recognition as a contributor to dance music on the American social scene.

[Alice Scott whispered to Vincent Armstrong, who was sitting beside her, that she wanted to ask Mr. Normand a question, but she hated to interrupt him. Curious about her question, Vincent nudged her, egging her on to ask: "How come you omitted George M. Cohan and Irving Berlin? Didn't they write ragtime?"

"Not really," replied the supervisor. "What they wrote was synthetic...not real rags. Sure, Cohan attempted to write syncopated songs: he was a Jack-of-all-works—a singer, a dancer, an actor, a manager, a producer—but he was not a master of ragtime.

"On the opposite side of the footlights, Irving Berlin was a specialist in popular song writing. Southern syncopation was not his specialty, despite the fact that he wrote a song with the title, *Alexander's Ragtime Band*. Originally Irving Berlin's name was Israel (Izzy) Baline. Whether he changed his name because of apprehension about anti-semitism, or whether it was because he wished to anglicize his name, is not clear. Being Jewish, his musical culture was worlds apart from that of the Negro's. The differences in their cultural backgrounds were clearly reflected in their music."]

In spite of the fact that ragtime could be played artfully on brass as well as on string instruments, most rag artists preferred to show their skill in pianistic art. Thomas Edison patented the phonograph in 1877: Yet within the next three decades, the actual heyday of rag music revolved around the player-piano period when rags on cylindrical rolls were the kitten's purr and the puppy's yip. Piano pieces written to ragtime for nickelodeons rarely if ever had lyrics. Although wordless rags were not singable, they were danceable. But not in the conventional way, that is, unlike the way formal, turning figures were performed in the waltz to three-quarter time.

Rag was not just black music, rag was black dance, which white writers stereotyped as 'shuffling movements.' Rag movements were not fixed in form: They were fiery! Hot rags, in the vernacular of musicians, prompted overheated couples to caper as though they were stamping out floor fires. What happened to the movements was that professional hacks constantly pounded on out-of-tune pianos producing inferior ragtime music. By 1910 rags started to smolder and smoke, and burned out with the eruption of World War I.

In movements—musical and dance—rags are played and danced to quick two-four and four-four time. The jig, a very fast dance of English origin, and the reel, a lively dance of Scottish origin, are danced either to two-four or to four-four time. Excluding syncopation, there are certain similarities between rags and reels, and between rags and jigs.

A quotation from Shakespeare sharpens the point in *Much Ado About Nothing*, Act II, scene i, lines 72-79:

> The fault will be in the music, cousin, if you be not wooed in good time: if the prince be too important, tell him there is measure in every thing and so dance out the answer. For, hear me, Hero: wooing, wedding, and repenting, is a Scotch jig, a measure, and a cinque pace: the first suit is hot and hasty, like a Scotch jig, and full as fantastical; ...

In the southern slave states just as pigments of English and Scottish psalms blended into Negro spirituals, just as pigments of English and Scottish airs blended into Negro tunes; so did pigments of English and Scottish dances blend into Negro dance steps, decorating patterns of ballroom and drawing-room dances. Thus it is not surprising that Anglo-Celtic features are discernible in American music. Many of the tunes to which folk dances are gamboled in America were old English-Scottish-and-Irish jigs, reels, and hornpipes: be they roundelays, quadrilles, squares, longways, running sets, or clear-cut variations.

Over the years, through long association, Americans have come to regard these dances as their own. For example, the Virginia Reel, believed to be most representative of American folk dances, is nothing more than the familiar English contra dance, Sir Roger de Coverly. Brought in colonial days to Virginia by Englishmen as a society dance, its name later was changed to the Virginia Reel and, under the American appellation, grew popular as a country-dance presumably homespun in rural areas of the States, in valleys and on mountains.

Stopping at this high place to take a sweeping look at the historical panorama unrolled thus far, ranging from sights of zoological dances of the American Indians to sounds of ragtime rhythms of the

Afro-Americans, we hear neither woodnotes nor do we see footprints of the fox trot. At the turn of the century we catch sight of animal-like dances that appeared again: camel and fish walks, elephant and humpback rags, kangaroo and snake dips, crab step, horse trot, chicken scratch...and some native dances: Gaby Glide, Gotham Gabble, Toddle, Texas Tommy, Chicago, Frisco. What was the Americans' fascination with movements of animals! Could it be that a developing democratic nation—raw and inelegant in its illiterate grouping toward freedom of individuality and motility—was straining to hurl off the restrictions and formalisms of shackling European dancing masters?

We must temporarily delay our hunting expedition for the fox trot to meet a multitalented man, Vernon Blyth Castle. No history on twentieth-century ballroom dances would be complete without the inclusion of at least a thumbnail sketch of his life. Blyth was an electrical engineer, a pilot, a comic-conjurer, a drummer, an actor, and an exhibitional dancer.

Subsequent to graduating from Birmingham University, but before ever entering the field of engineering, Blyth decided to take a vacation in the United States. He sailed from England to New York City with his sister (Coralie Blyth) and her husband (Lawrence Grossmith), who were to rehearse there for a play, *The Orchards*. Since Blyth was filling in his leisure time by watching the rehearsals, his brother-in-law convinced producer Lew Fields that he might as well give the young Englishman a bit part in the production.

Vernon did not want to trade on his sister's laurels by going under the family name Blyth which Coralie used in the theater. Consulting with Grossmith, he assumed instead the stage name Castle, borrowed from Windsor Castle in Berkshire. The Englishman's choice was quite suitable even though he was born in Norwich (1887-1918).

One role after another led to *The Hen-Pecks*. It was a comedy in which Castle impersonated Zowie, Monarch of Mystery, the first of a series of highly successful theatrical appearances.

One day in New York, while attending a swimming party, at the Rowing Club in New Rochelle, Irene Foote (a doctor's daughter) was introduced to Vernon Castle. She, too, was interested in acting. After almost a year's courtship they married on May 28, 1911.

Pursuing their career, the newlyweds went to Paris in the springtime to join *Enfin . . . une Revue* ('At Last a Farcial Piece'). Unprotected by a workable cash umbrella, they got caught in a shower of bad luck as delay upon delay in rehearsals washed away their limited, liquid funds. When the revue finally opened, the situation did not look too bright; for the French had not acquired a taste for the Castles' kind of comedy, a slapstick skit in a barbershop, they had imported from America. (Not all Americans find slapstick palatable, either.)

Besides the distasteful barbershop skit, Vernon and Irene had performed in the revue, unsuccessfully, a pantomime with stiff, simple steps to a fairy tale, "The Lead Soldier and the Paper Doll." In seeking to improve their act, they hit on the idea of presenting to their French audiences two recent American crazes—the Grizzly Bear and the Texas Tommy. Irene's mother had mailed her newspaper clippings describing the dances.

However, the descriptions were very skimpy, which is typical of the way newspapers describe things: here is one example, "a dancer lurches like a bear in doing the Grizzly Bear." Anyway, when they were in New York during a performance of *The Hen-Pecks*, the Castles had seen musical comedy star Blossom Seeley, an entertainer from the Barbary Coast, perform the Texas Tommy as a solo dance in so-called 'Frisco style.' Between the clippings and Vernon's recollection of Blossom Seeley's steps and style, he arranged a rough-and-tumble acrobatic version of the two American dances to the tune of "Alexander's Ragtime Band," which they sang for a finale. French audiences were delighted with the dances but more so with the music (few understood the lyrics). The Frenchmen clapped and clamored, "Encore!"

The rainfall was over: There was sunshine: The sky had cleared for the hitherto hapless honeymooners. An agent, who saw the Castles' unique dance exhibition, booked them into the Café de Paris, a small, still select supper spot, patronized by a clique of international royalty and socialites. Performance after performance the Castles stylized their dancing with more and more refinement, from which resulted an elegant Castle Walk.

The pair's performances were so pleasing to the patrons at the café that the dancers' services were in great demand at opulent soirées. The new style of dancing they had stumbled upon was soon to lead Vernon and Irene to a pot of gold at the end of the rainbow.

The Castles sailed back triumphantly to America arriving at New York Harbor in 1912. News of their achievements in France having spread, the pair received top billing at Louis Martin's exclusive Café de l'Opéra. While performing at the café, Mr. and Mrs.

Vernon Castle soon reached such status that they were engaged to direct an elite dance academy, which was named Castle House, where they taught the latest dances.

Vernon and Irene came to be admired in the United States not only as the best ballroom and drawing-room dancers of the day but also as the best dancing teachers. They rinsed out the abuse of animal actions set free in the country and ironed out the misuse of colored rags that made care-less Americans appear ugly on a dance floor, public or private.

By popular demand, they toured the cities...Rochester...Buffalo... thirty-five in all. Wherever they entertained, the Castles' program was presented in two parts: the first half (traditional or folk dances), Pavanne, Furlana, Lulu Fada, Polka; the second half (modern or modified dances), Tango, Maxixe, Hesitation Waltz, One-Step.

A former official pianist to the president of Haiti, a Negro, Ford Dabny, was an arranger of syncopated music for Vernon and Irene Castle. In the States or abroad they would be joined on their tours by an indispensable black band.

["As yet the fox trot had not appeared. With the field of its forerunners almost cleared, it will be much easier to pursue the fox trot, but the wind is blowing in the wrong direction to pick up its scent. Luckily we are on the right trail."]

The development of American society was not always an orderly process; the same holds true for social dance. There are no doubt Americans, noteworthy ones, who were orderly in their conduct and their occupation. One in particular was a New Yorker, dancing master Allen Dodworth. In 1885 he had a book published entitled . . . Take a big, deep breath:

DANCING
and
Its Relations To Education
And Social Life
With a New Method of Instruction
Including a Complete Guide to
The Cotillion (German)
With 250 Figures

Dodworth was an intellectual giant in the art of social dance; although in that respect he has been neglected by many historians. Fraudulent claims non obstante, Dodworth wrote the first practical textbook on dancing, including philosophical observations on the subject. The 302 pages of text are filled with diverse dances delineated by the diagram method of instruction. In his book he devotes a chapter to the galop, a fast forerunner of the fox trot. To be sure, others had written about the galop before. Yet none described it as methodically as Dodworth did.

The galop (a dance and music) was bred under the name "die gallopade" in North Germany, according to Victor Junk's *Manual of the Dance*. Henry Ford, the automobile designer, in a handbook on old-fashioned dancing (*Good Morning*) places Hungary as the breeding ground of the galop, in 1815. Ford does not give his source. In a book published in Cologne in 1829, writer Joseph Franken refers to "die gallopade" but not to its grazing ground. The historian Curt Sachs intimates the galop was seen watering circa 1835 at the Vltava River in Bohemia.

Chas. d'Albert in *The Encyclopaedia of Dancing* maintains the galop is ancient, much older than it appears. At the tail end of the eighteenth century in Europe, it functioned as a finale to voltas and contredances in a set order that became a formality for ceremonial dances into the future. During Mardi Gras, in the year 1829, Caroline Fernande Louise, Duchesse de Berry, had reintroduced the galop to Paris.

At the outset the galop was a rapid round in two-four time leaped light-footedly in serpentine sequences. Parisians changed the footwork of the dance by shoeing it with the chassé, composed of a dual step-pattern: *glissé-coupé-glissé* ('slide-cut-slide'); the 'cut' acts as a displacing technique not as a step. Thus a chassé is the chasing of one foot from its place by the other foot—in two steps.

[On impulse the supervisor deviated temporarily to treat the teachers to a spicy slice of history. "In the 1830s a Parisian interpretation of the galop, *La Saint-Simonienne*, was as popular as free love. The dance was named after Count de Saint-Simon, a socialist philosopher and soldier who had served with the French army in America. Upon his return to France, he surrendered his title because of his revolutionary ideas and Bohemian life style. The unrestricted figures of *La Saint-Simonienne* allowed dance partners to be interchanged freely. This extreme, free-and-easy style created the perception that doing the dance was tantamount to the trading of mates(?)."]

In its final stages the galop was performed by a series of sliding steps (chassés) in the Line of Dance broken at equidistances by turns (semicircles): the directions of the steps and turns could vary...forward, backward, to the sides, but in a fixed pattern. Taking the name literally, couples, like runaway horses, to the horror of precise dancing teachers, galloped the galop out of time with the music (quick two-four time). Still worse, couples raced around a slippery dance floor sliding precariously as they jockeyed for the best positions in the ballroom. Having slipped out of the reins that had restrained them, social dancers balked at patronizing strict teachers, whose pocketbooks quickly were emptied.

Now, the laws of economic survival overpowering the rules of proper social dance, teachers of the performing art were forced to cast aside their traditional views. That is, they closed their eyes to the revolting way people were galoping. Desperate for patrons, dancing teachers put their ability to work for the dwindling dollar instead of for the diminishing dance. Ultimately the wild galop was lassoed and corralled. Nevertheless, the spirited nature of the dance was by no means subdued. Quite the contrary! Its tempo was enlivened by a momentous innovation that revolutionized a rigid form of social dance and music on two continents, American overnight, European a few nights later.

June 15, 1889, as part of the exercises to award school children prizes won in a literary contest, *The Washington Post* sponsored on the grounds of the Smithsonian Institute a musical program, which went into full swing. John Philip Sousa conducted the United States Marine Corps band in the playing of a surprisingly novel march. He had been requested to compose something original for the occasion, in honor of which he entitled his composition "The Washington Post March."

The music, to the amazement of a crowd of thousands, commenced in lively six-eight time, the usual signature for some dance numbers. Traditionally marches were played in two-four time. Applying within an arrangement the six-eight time signature to a march instead of to a dance was sensational in effect. The spirit of every man, woman, and child on the grounds was stirred with excitement as they listened to "The Washington Post March." Bandmaster Sousa's composition stole the show, so to speak, and he received a standing ovation!

Audiences everywhere were soon to hear—and cheer—Sousa's spirit-stirring marches. They were not his complete repertoire. On his European and world tours (between 1900 and 1911), in London, Paris, Moscow, and other major cities, Sousa featured a drummer who was a specialist in syncopation. As an encore the band played ragtime and performed the cake walk. So well-received was this

American music in Russia and in France that it inspired Igor Stravinsky to compose "Ragtime for Eleven Instruments" and Claude Debussy to compose "Golliwog's Cakewalk."

Quick to seize a golden opportunity, American National Association of Masters of Dancing at a convention in the early 1900s selected "The Washington Post March" as ideal music to commercialize a 'new' dance, the two-step, a simplified form of the 'old' galop. Re-formed still more by snappy two-stepping to a military cadence, the galop lost its identify. In dancing the two-step couples, maneuvering quickly in most directions, did a double-quick march the way soldiers in ranks skip to get into step, counting "one, two, one, two..." or "left, right, left right..." and vice versa (in dance terms: step, skip, step, skip—forward, backward, and turn—as often as desired). The two-step remained popular for an indefinite period of time, attributable to the fact that John Philip Sousa wrote almost one hundred popular marches.

After 1911 progressive reforms in social dance occurred: Foot placements (such as pointing one's toes) which in the past had approximated those of ballet, at last were less theatrical. Also, the conventional waltz or polka position, previously compelling a gentleman and a lady to maintain a respectable distance, now permitted body-to-body contact on the floor of the ballroom. Following on the heels of the two-step, came the one-step, whereby a pace was taken to each beat of the music. This was perfectly simple for dancing to a march, or to ragtime.

It should be revealed that Vernon and Irene Castle gave the one-step a face lifting and an alias. The dance on which choreographic surgery was performed went under the assumed name Castle Walk, a dance already mentioned. Cutting away personalized styling, the Castle Walk differs in description from the one-step: (Modern Dancing, 1914) "First of all, walk as...in the One-Step. Now raise yourself up slightly on your toes at each step, with the legs a trifle stiff, and breeze along happily and easily, ...To turn a corner you do not turn your partner round, but keep walking her backward in the same direction, leaning over slightly—just enough to make a graceful turn and keep the balance well—a little like a bicycle rounding a corner."

["For the sake of following a chronological order, we shall drop the one-step as well as the two-step. However, these dance movements will arise again when referred to briefly in relationship to the fox trot. Despite one's inclination to imagine so, this dance did not

receive its name from <u>Reynard</u> <u>the</u> <u>Fox</u> of the satirical, medieval
beast epic wherein the fox is used as a foil to jab at the upper classes
and the Church. Nonetheless, it is fact not fable that historically they
treated with cruel criticism dances of the common folk.

"By the way, the spelling R-e-y-n-a-r-d is a medieval form of
French. To clear up another misconception about the derivation of
the fox trot. Neither the name nor the dance was derived from the
French, *faux pas* ('to stumble'), though it is true that some people
stumble not only when they speak but also when they dance."]

To find the fox trot's lair we have to backtrack a distance to
1904...to the den of vice, the Barbary Coast. That year Harry Fox, a
song-and-dance man who had entertained in concert saloons along
the Barbary Coast, stepped up to the Belvedere Theatre where he
had a role in a comedy, "Mr. Frisky of Frisco." Entertaining was in
Fox's blood. Born 1882 in Pomona, California, he was the son of an
actor and the grandson of a clown, the circus star George L. Fox.
Harry's real last name was Carringford; but he appropriated the surname of his maternal grandfather as a stage name, with the purpose
of following in his footsteps.

In 1906 the San Francisco earthquake and fire disrupted every-
body's life, including Fox's. He soon set out on the road for the East
Coast to pursue his career in show business. Success came to Fox in
New York. After four favorable seasons he produced his own show,
"Harry Fox's Merry's." Next he played a part in "The Pet of the
Petticoats," followed by a successful vaudeville tour. Subsequent to
returning to New York City, Fox performed in two musicals, "The
Passing Show of 1912," and a year later in "The Honeymoon
Express," which was a big hit.

Starred in Florenz Ziegfeld Follies at the New Amsterdam
Theatre in the winter of 1913, Harry Fox, dancing to ragtime in an
extraordinary manner, performed trotting steps which were as exciting to watch as the trots of a thoroughbred on a race track. So
impressive was his fast footwork...so striking was his style that
Harry received standing ovations from the audiences. In anticipation of benefiting financially from this innovational performance, the
management engaged a prominent master of stage and social dancing, Oscar Duryea, to present Fox's trot atop a roof garden of the theatre. The garden surrounded a swanky night club.

In presenting the new dance to patrons of the roof garden,
Duryea was assisted by a rag band and sixteen chorus girls with
whom he danced individually, that is, one at a time. Each girl had

been instructed to do the same sort of short, speedy steps that Fox had trotted. As the band played, Duryea leading his respective partners in closed dance position swiftly bypassed the tables of seated patrons.

After running rapidly round and round the roof to quick four-four ragtime, conscientious Oscar ran out of breath. When changing to his next partner, he told her he was going to reduce their fast pace by dancing a couple of measures slowly and a couple of measures quickly, whereupon they proceeded to walk awhile and run awhile.

Naturally the time signature of the music governed the order of their steps. Duryea instinctively guided his individual partners into a uniform pattern whereby they fox trotted two measures taking four long (or slow) steps and two measures taking eight short (or quick) steps. His phrasing was used basically by fox trotters for a number of years to come.

Thus, through a twist of fate, we had a Californian (Harry Fox) as the virile procreator and a New Yorker (Oscar Duryea) as the obstetrician, who successfully performed a caesarean section resulting in the birth of a dance christened Fox Trot. Loved from infancy, it was adopted warmheartedly by the American family. Too often the young dance was mishandled, yet for the most part it remained unspoiled.

Time's fleeting foot worked changes in the fox trot. The American dance married movements of foreign extractions, divorced most. Nevertheless, the polyandrous dance is easygoing, one with which persons who have difficulty getting along in ballrooms can be compatible if they are willing to try. The true character of the fox trot cannot be properly appreciated unless certain qualities of the matured dance are understood.

A characteristic or basic fox-trot step—technically, a step-combination—is composed of four separate paces varying in direction (forward, backward, or sideward), in length (short, medium, or long), and in shape (straight, curved, or angled). As is standard, the man starts with his left foot, the woman with her right. And she, of course, moves in the opposite direction to him. The woman's movements described below illustrates a basic fox-trot step:

(1) Take a long step backward on the right foot,

(2) Take a long step backward on the left foot, brushing by the right foot,

(3) Take a comparatively short step sideward with the right foot (be sure it brushes the left foot before moving to the side),

(4) Close, that is, move the left foot next to the right foot.

["As dancing teachers you should be aware that the components of a fox-trot step vary in length of TIME as well as in length of PACE, a fact which brings us to the basic rhythmic count of the dance. Teachers in general, if at all, instead of saying 'basic rhythmic count' say 'primary rhythm pattern.' This term, though traditional, is confusing, especially since rhythm, meter, cadence, and beat are loosely interchanged as synonyms. To avoid confusion, basic rhythmic count will be used from now on.

"Rhythm, you are reminded, is the regular recurrence of accents in musical measures. A measure is music contained between two vertical lines called bars. For the fox trot, relatively speaking, the first beat of a measure is accented strongly and the third beat slightly in common or four-four time, which has four quarter beats or their equivalent units to a measure. Ordinarily the fox trot is in common time. Bearing that in mind, let us study the dance's basic rhythmic count in detail."

The supervisor walked over to the blackboard and chalked on it a comprehensive formula for the teachers to follow:

SLOW	SLOW	QUICK	QUICK
(1st step)	(2nd step)	(3rd step)	(4th step)

Since slow = two counts and quick = one count,

slow, slow, quick, quick = six counts or a measure and a half.

"I must explain: in terms of dancing neither 'slow' nor 'quick' is to be interpreted literally. 'Slow' and 'quick' refer to count, not to rate of motion (or speed). So, when using the basic rhythmic count, if dancers step on SLOW, they consume TWO COUNTS; by the same token, if they step on QUICK, they consume ONE COUNT. In both instances the rate of motion, regulated by the tempo of the music, remains constant.

"From the illustration on the blackboard you can see that the basic rhythmic count of the fox trot equals a measure and a half of music. Assuming an orchestra is playing and dancing is going on, whenever two basic rhythmic counts are completed by the dancer, three measures of music will have been played simultaneously by the orchestra.

"Such an arrangement is desirable because dancers are not compelled to start on the first accented beat, as in waltz time, for example. They have the freedom of beginning to fox trot on either the first or third beat of a measure. Simply stated, a dancer is not hamstrung by having to wait for a particular note of fox-trot music. He, and she, may start dancing—stop, and start again—on just about any note, a liberty which gives comfort not only to the poorest dancers but also to the best."]

Inasmuch as key properties of the fox trot have been unlocked, archives of other historical records of the dance are accessible to us. We learn that steps danced to ragtime in the 1800s often are alluded to as 'jazz steps.' Such usage of 'jazz' is an anachronism, since before 1913 there were no bands, songs—or dances—described as 'jazz' in the specific meaning of the word. That year a columnist used 'jazz' in a San Francisco newspaper to describe his enthusiastic reaction to a baseball game; but the word had nothing to do with musicians, singers—or dancers. Typically he never revealed where he dug it up.

North Africa is where the word 'jazz' originated, according to W. F. Raffé. In his Dictionary of the Dance he states it is of Arabic derivation, "From *Jazba* ('Delight'), *Dzhajasbah* in Islamic ritual prayer; used of ecstasy produced by circle dance and chant in mosque." If Raffé's hypothesis is correct, in 1619 when a Dutch ship first transported several Africans to Virginia to be sold as slaves in Jamestown, the Arabic word *Jazba* very likely would have been the dialect of their region...or religion, granted they were Muslims.

The Virginia legislature exercised its powers to the fullest extent to persuade Islamic black slaves—indeed, all slaves—to convert to Christianity. Other southern states soon followed suit. In 1670 a Slave Act of Virginia mandated that slaves who had been baptized into the Christian faith prior to their being transported to the States, were not subject to lifelong servitude. Slaves thus were converted by intimidation to Christianity, thereby suppressing their native religious beliefs. Consequently, Africans went underground in the Deep South with their ritual prayer but *Jazba* surfaced in rural songs and dances, and was concealed among urban musicians and bands.

In the state of Louisiana, predominantly in New Orleans, the soul of *Jazba* lived in the black man's music expressed through his instruments, however in a secular not in a religious tone. Negro bands which played unnamed (jazz) music, really ragtime, inevitably appeared in New Orleans: in 1890, Buddy Boldon's Band...in 1911, Eagle Band...in 1912, Original Creole Band...and other great bands in other years. Yet, despite the fact that black music was loud and clear, the name 'jazz' was not heard so far.

[One of the more inquisitive teachers in the group wanted to know when jazz separated from ragtime: what was the difference between the two; was it the rhythm? The supervisor patiently explained that though jazz was an offspring of ragtime, the day or decade of the demarcation line between these two types of music was difficult to determine. Clearly there were differences, but in the rhythm they were minor. The major differences were in harmony, melodious mode, and instrumentation. Jazz evolved into a vocalized form, smooth and melodic, whereas ragtime had been a pianistic technique, staccato and turbulent.]

June 28, 1914, Austrian Archduke Francis Ferdinand met a violent death, by assassination at Sarajevo, Bosnia: an international community was enflamed! The world was on the eve of a hot war. And America was on the eve of the Jazz Age. The Negro's music was hot—predictively a winner by a landslide! White musicians jumped onto the black musicians' band wagon, traveling all over the country with a musical message, phrases of promise.

June 1915, Tom Brown, improviser on the trombone, arrived in Chicago, Illinois, from New Orleans with his white band: Raymond Lopez, cornet player...Gus Mueller, clarinetist...William Lambert, drummer...Arnold Loyocano, bass and piano player. The five-piece combo played Dixieland music (white man's jazz) in imitation of Creole music (black man's jazz).

Brown's band was engaged at Lamb's Café. The first night the combo's unheard of improvisations, fervish propulsive rhythms, stunned the men and women in the café. They could not make up their minds whether to sit and eat or whether to stand and dance. However, the fresh beat of the hot music whetted the diners' rhythmic appetites and stimulated them into decisive action on the dance floor. Thenceforth was launched a tuned-up American craft—hot, improvisational music—that in record time steamed across the Atlantic Ocean to Europe.

The five-piece combo was publicized on the café's billboard as Brown's Jass Band. Jass (jazz) earlier was hypothesized to be a derivation of the Arabic word *Jazbo* ('Delight'). If you will recall, associated with it is the feeling of ecstasy.

To experience the feeling, ribald but real, we return to the 1800s in Storyville, the infamous red-light district of New Orleans, housing twelve square blocks of prostitution behind the French Quarter. The houses of joy provided their clientele two delightful services: a handsome Negro who played ragtime on a piano in a reception room with plush furnishings, and a voluptuous girl who 'jassed' on a bed in a private room furnished with mirrors.

Degraded to a vulgar vocable, 'jass' was commonly pronounced with Z sounds in lieu of S sounds, by 1917 through usage a refined meaning had been applied, and the spelling j-a-z-z became the accepted way. A quotation from a <u>Literary</u> <u>Digest</u> issued that year substantiates the last statement: "A strange word has gained widespread use in the ranks of our producers of popular music. It is 'jazz,' used mainly as an adjective descriptive of a band." Jazz (jass), it should be understood, also was used thereafter to describe music and dancing.

At the tail end of World War I (1914-1919), modish orchestras, equipped with instruments of jazz, played abnormally fast fox-trot numbers to conform with the requests of dancers who had tantivy mania. Crazed by the conflict, couples rushed excitedly through wartime dance routines. Jazz music playing at the fastest rate, the two-step, now combined with the fox trot, of necessity developed into a multidirectional quickstep so that the couples could keep pace with tempo (presto!). Dancers in quickstepping sped along the Line of Dance nonstop; some occasionally swerved to the left or to the right performing a series of four, side step-combinations: step-close (quick, quick), step-close (quick, quick)...again and again. The four-part rhythmic count was repeated for as many measures as couples cared to quickstep in doing the Fast Fox Trot.

After the war, due to the input of brass bands, the one-step as it previously had been used to tread a measure, was publicly scrapped. Just the same, a bit of the one-step was saved a number of years by private groups of dancers from the old school. But bit by bit the one-step almost in entirety was salvaged by a modern clique of ballroom dancers in San Francisco. "Smoothies," as they were called, melted down the bits of the one-step into the fox trot, forming a style of smooth-slicker dancing. As they fox trotted, like ice skaters, they glided smoothly around a dance floor slick as ice.

Smooth-slicker dancing was cast with the same time signature as the Fast Fox Trot. Both are danced to the fastest music in common time or measure, where the tempo (to reiterate, rate of speed) ranges from forty-five to sixty measures per minute. To be in rhythm with this faster tempo, dancers instead of taking four short steps (quick-steps) to a measure, take two long steps on the first and third accented beats of a measure.

Another form of Fast Fox Trot is the Peabody. Strange as a Ripley oddity, it was named after William Frank Peabody, a man with a bad reputation who was a captain on the New York City police force. That the name of the dance was in his honor, is hard to believe. Perhaps it was because he played fast and loose with the law. Linked to the underworld, he was dismissed from the police force on two occasions but was reinstated. He claimed he was framed by mobsters, whom he might have double-crossed(?).

The Peabody, smooth running step-combinations, is performed with fancy footwork to fast four-four time. The main movement is the crossover (moving forward or backward, the right foot crosses in front of the left foot or vice versa). A variation of the crossover is the grapevine (moving sideward, the right and left foot cross front and back alternately).

[The supervisor walked over to a cabinet at the back of the room and removed a stack of mimeographed sheets which he handed to one of the female teachers seated closest to his desk. He asked her to distribute the sheets among the others in the group. After she complied with his request and returned to her seat, he resumed speaking:

"In performing the Peabody, couples used the outside and open positions to a great extent. However, neither the fox trot nor the rest of the ballroom dances are restricted to just two positions. While you have been exposed to the different dance positions, you were not sufficiently schooled in their application and classification.

"Look at the mimeographed sheets. You will see classified in detail five primary positions of the body that are essential to ballroom dancing. I shall explain in greater detail the first three positions indicated on the sheets:

"The man circles the woman's waist with his right arm as she places her left palm high on his back. He raises his left hand (to her shoulder level), and she places her right hand in it lightly. For a beginner it is best, when learning the positions, to assume closed position each time before attempting to go into any of the other positions."

As he was speaking, the supervisor noticed that some members of the group had blank looks on their faces. It occurred to him they could be having a problem following what he was saying and studying the dance positions at the same time. He decided, before proceeding with his explanation, to wait a few minutes to give the teachers an opportunity to absorb the details on the sheets:

(1)	Closed	Position:	Partners stand in close proximity, toes to
	or		toes, chest to chest.
	Waltz	Position:	They embrace.
(2)	Parallel	Position:	Right; man steps directly to his left side
	or		so that his right shoulder is parallel to
	Banjo	Position:	that of the woman.
	or		(Their right hips are aligned.)
	Outside	Position:	They remain embraced.
			Left; man steps directly to his right side
			so that his left shoulder is parallel to
			that of the woman.
			(Their left hips are aligned.)
			They remain embraced.
(3)	Conversation	Position:	Man and woman stand so that their
	or		bodies form a forty-five degree angle.
	Conversational	Position:	His right side and her left side are
			tangent.
			They remain embraced.
(4)	Open	Position:	Partners stand apart, almost at arm's
	or		length. The man holds the woman's
	Left-Hand		right hand with his left hand.
	Contact	Position:	(Sometimes he holds her left hand
	or		with his right hand.) Also, he may
	Two-Hand		hold both her hands.
	Contact	Position:	
(5)	Shine	Position:	Partners stand well apart without any
	or		contact at all.
	Break	Position:	

Feeling that he had allowed the teachers enough time to examine the mimeographed sheets, the supervisor spoke out: "To better visualize the fine points of the five dance positions, requires the use of photographs. Still they would be imperfect, or at the least incomplete. Live, actual demonstrations, and your being participants in the positions under the directions of an experienced dancing teacher, would be the best way. That, needless to say, is reserved for your technique classes, which you will be attending soon."]

Besides the Fast Fox Trot a slow strain of the dance meanwhile was bred. In order to understand why this was done, it would be helpful to turn back the pages of history to the Civil War period. During the 1860s, and for decades onward, black folks' laughter and lament (singing the blues) was heard from back roads to riverbanks.

More and more self-taught Negro minstrels with lyrics on their lips and guitars in their arms, began wandering around the countryside in the Deep South where they strummed folk music and sang folk songs. Some were improvised, some were memorized. Neither the words nor the notes were recorded; but they were registered in the memories of other Negroes, especially their children's with a strong attraction for minstrelsy.

Such a child was William Christopher Handy who was born November 16, 1873. As a youth he learned to play an oldfangled rotary-valve cornet...over the objections of his father, a preacher. After practicing the cornet a few years, he left his birthplace (Florence, Alabama) and joined a minstrel road show. Before long Handy outgrew minstrelsy. Eventually he made his way to Tennessee establishing himself as a leader of a black band in Memphis.

A political campaign in 1909 for the election of a mayor of Memphis was organized by sponsors of their candidate, Mr. E. H. Crump. They employed Handy's band and instructed him to compose a theme song for the campaign. He went to work and wrote the song, which was entitled "Mister Crump." The campaign strategy worked. Candidate Crump won the election! In 1912, wishing to benefit from his successful song, Handy published it under a more appropriate name, "Memphis Blues."

Handy was a propagator of the blues, not an originator. With great success he also published: "Beale Street Blues," "Yellow Dog Blues," and in 1914 "Saint Louis Blues," the basis of which he had dug up from the depths of his childhood memories. The 'blues' were slow, sustained solo songs of his peoples' past and present, of their pain and pleasure.

In subsequent years white music writers climbed on the blues band wagon pulled by Handy. 1916...Jerome Kern, composer of musical comedies, wrote "Left-All-Alone-Again Blues"; 1920...Irving Berlin, composer of popular music, wrote "School-House Blues"; 1924...George Gershwin, composer of music with jazz idiom, wrote "The Half of It, Dearie, Blues."

Between 1929 and 1936, in the midst of the depression, extravagant dance bands were flourishing. (Good musicians were not too costly.) Influenced by blues composers, bands featured singers that could sing the blues, reflecting sentimental moods while couples danced romantically under moonlight chandeliers.

In the nature of a music-hall song, the blues is marked by slow tempo and frequent occurrence of blue notes. A blue note (or flatted note) is 'a minor interval interjected into a melody where a major ordinarily occurs.' Thus it is that the scale structure of the blues is founded on the blue note, and the fundamental tonality of the blues is in the major. Understandably musical compositions in the blues scale and intonation had the effect of slowing down the tempo of fox trots, thirty-three to twenty-eight measures per minute.

Moreover, slow ballad music played by nationally renowned orchestras created a natural desire for slower fox-trot figures. To name some of the outstanding orchestras: Casa Loma, voted the best sweet, 'arranged and rehearsed,' band in the country...Rudy Vallée, his sentimental voice was accompanied by an orchestra of languid strings and reeds...Guy Lombardo, whose saxophone tone rivaled the trembling sound of a human voice...Paul Whiteman, pretender to the jazz throne, was a specialist in symphonic orchestrations.

A slower fox trot was created—however, at random. It was referred to as the Westchester. Its figures, including peculiar postures and deep dips, were unattractive. The random figures were called the Westchester because they originally were performed by a dance set of the upper crust in New York's Westchester County. In short order, a transformation took place, and the figures became attractive. Consequently the figures, with certain modifications, were standardized. Also their name was changed to the Slow Fox Trot. The most appealing form of the fox trots, it is danced in common time to an auxiliary rhythmic count, spoken of by professional dancers as secondary fox-trot rhythm pattern.

["So that you will be able to make a comparison between the two, below the Basic rhythmic count (slow, slow, quick, quick) already on the blackboard, I shall now chalk the Auxiliary rhythmic count. . . . See the difference":

SLOW   QUICK   QUICK
(1st step)   (2nd step)   (3rd step)

Since slow = two counts and quick = one count,

$$\text{slow, slow, quick, quick} = \begin{array}{c} \text{four counts} \\ \text{or} \\ \text{a measure} \end{array}$$

"In the auxiliary rhythmic count is hidden a magic formula where waltz steps may be converted into fox-trot steps. As you have learned, each basic waltz step, or step-combination, is composed of three separate paces. In discussing the history of the waltz, it was emphasized that waltz music is in three-four time; and a waltz step occupies a full measure, which means that each of the component parts gets one count.

"Therefore, when applying the auxiliary rhythmic count to convert a basic waltz step into a fox-trot step, lengthen the timing—not the distance— of the first pace so that it takes two counts (slow); and, of course, the second and third paces retain a value of one count apiece (quick, quick). Presto! you have magically turned a waltz step into a fox-trot step.

"More magic! reverse the auxiliary rhythmic count of the Slow Fox Trot from slow-quick-quick to quick-quick-slow, and you have the auxiliary rhythmic count of the Medium Fox Trot. It is danced to common time at a rate of speed ranging from thirty-four to forty-four measures per minute. The figures are graceful, performed extensively in outside position."]

In New York City the Medium Fox Trot is known as the Roseland, where the name if not the dance originated. Roseland, the world's largest ballroom, opened to the public in 1919. Unforgettable black and white musicians played there: among the jazzmen the best were bandleader Fletcher Henderson and his cornetist Louis Armstrong, and later bandleader Jean Goldkett and his cornetist Bix Beiderbecke.

Since the intrinsic beats and accents of the slow, medium, and fast fox trot are in four-four rhythm, fox-trot steps fundamentally are interchangeable, no matter under which category they fall. In other words, they may be adjusted to any of the three tempos, slow, medium, or fast. Still two conjoint qualities, smoothness and continuity of movement, should be perpetually present in performing the dance. All through its growth x-steps extracted from folk, waltz, and tango dances, were accidentally or deliberately injected into the body of the fox trot.

A number of persons have applied temporary treatments to the dance: the best known are Maurice Talmadge, choreographer of the Talmadge Fox Trot, and the team of Charles Collins and Dorothy Stone, who choreographed the Collinstone Fox Trot. Others, too many to mention, applied band-aids to the fox trot's occasional scratches. Of importance, though, are the choreographic life-givers who were acknowledged in this history including Vernon and Irene Castle with their Castle Fox Trot.

The greatest exhibition ballroom dancer of the silver screen, Fred Astaire, admittedly was inspired by the Castles' stage performances (1913-1914): 'The Sunshine Girl,'...'The Girl From Utah,'...'Watch Your Step.'—all inspirational successes. Fred and his sister Adele adapted into their fox-trot routine some of the steps and style of dancing performed by the Castles. In turn, Astaire's dignified yet daring, different yet divine stylization of terpsichorean art was, and still is, an inspiration to generations of ballroom dancers on two continents, and beyond.

[Ralph Normand, realizing that the discourse had taken longer than he anticipated, pushed back the sleeve of his coat to expose his wrist watch. He saw by the time on the face of the watch that the assistant manager was long overdue. Just as he was about to send someone downstairs to the receptionist's desk to find out the reason for the delay, the interstudio telephone rang. He lifted the receiver to his ear and heard the voice of the receptionist at the other end of the line. She gave him a message which he conveyed to the teachers in the group:

"The assistant manager was unavoidably detained, and he won't be able to be here today. He sends his apologies for canceling his talk on salesmanship. He will try to arrange another appointment soon." Let down by the cancellation, the teachers expressed their disappointment a bit noisily. As a sort of consolation prize Normand dismissed the group early for a coffee break.

Later, after National Dance Studios closed, on his way home Vincent Armstrong kept thinking about the supervisor's dismissing him and the others early from the oral session. Vincent was reminded of his high-school days when classes were dismissed early as a reward for completing assignments, or was it for turning in assignments on time...which was it? His uncertainty of the triviality triggered Vincent's thoughts to shoot straight back in time! . . .]

BOOK THREE

Chapter 14

Senior high-school days, Juvenility's jeweled era, herein lies buried the map to sought-for treasures, chests upon chests of rare enlightenment. Oh, Youth! with thy strength thou hast but to spade a short while 'neath the rocky surface, and the invaluable learning of the sages shalt be thine to dispense as thou see fit. Whiten none thy hairs brooding over the toil. Callosity cometh into one's cranium no way from laborious meditation, rather from the lack of applying one's self to it.

Thine art sucklings' efforts, incomparable to the drudgery scholarians of old endured in order to unearth priceless wisdom, without which Truth is nought attainable. Deprived of knowledge vital to the comprehension of Truth, mankind throughout time hath been impoverished, unfree, forever shackled by modal equality bolted with damning insecurity.

Were ye to desist the cowardly turning away of the head or the fearful peering out of the weak eye, reality wouldst show you that headstrong champions of learning conquered but few witless dragons guarding the way into the cavern wherein Truth is imprisoned. By lord's reason, the dragons must be vanquished altogether should humanity once and for eternity be unshackled intellectually. These words spoken through infirm lips mayest go unheeded, for Father Time, weakened by resistance, long ago hath forgotten puissant linguistics. Pray on bended knee, some season, nae sooner, there cometh a wise wayward warrior who will have the facility—yea, as needed, the dauntlessness—to transmit this despatch to Youth:

Youngling, light up a candle. Thy vision is dim. Steady! the flame flickers. Watch thine eyes! Were thou nought blinded by youthhood itself, thou wouldst store thy mind now with the wealth of lore most easily discoverable in thy prime. The morrow or the day after is chance lost. At no other time will thou find so much time as today, this very instant, 'cause in the next thou hast that much less. Heed, the wick is burning low! Quickly, observe all about you unlettered elders, envisage thoughtfully their mistakes, their misconceptions. Believe nought as foolhardy failures long ago did, that thou will side-step life's dark pitfalls by avoiding the bright path to knowledge.

* * * * * * * *

* * * * * *

* * * *

* *

Of Vincent Armstrong's memories, at Commerce High School, his sophomore semesters were the most unforgettable. In his second year he formed a friendship with a girl, that proved pleasingly beneficial to him yet distressingly heart-rending, the sour seeping into the sweet. It was in Geometry I where he met her, Mildred Stensley. Wrestling with Euclid's methods and assumptions had been a dreadful struggle for Vincent. The measurements and relationships of points, lines, angles, and figures in space threw him for a loop, and he began falling dangerously below the rest of the class.

Fortunately Mildred came to Vincent's rescue. She was a "brain," declared to be so by her admiring classmates, none of whom were having an easy time with the Euclidean propositions. Like clockwork, an hour each morning before school started, Mildred corrected Vincent's attempted solutions to their assigned geometrical problems. Drawing points and lines, she patiently would reiterate for his benefit: "Geometry is based on the postulate that only one line may be drawn through a given point parallel to a given line." With her assistance he managed a day at a time to hang onto that branch of Mathematics.

Since the final examination in Geometry I was just a week away, Mildred invited Vincent to her home so they could review together the subject matter covered during the semester. Fond of the boy, the girl sincerely wanted to help him get over his fear of geometry, which includes theorems, corollaries, and axioms. The strange sounds of such Euclidean propositiions were in Vincent's words, "scary as the devil!"

Mildred's fondness for him stood out like a salient angle, presenting a complicated proposition. It is a given that Vincent needed her help. He was too crippled by a mental block to pass Mathematics without a crutch. In Mildred Stensley he had a staunch staff. Tangent to the plot, was a problem almost as hard as geometry; he could not return the affection she needed.

"If only Mildred didn't have a crush on me," he wished. But she did, and it weighed heavily on Vincent's conscience. Feeling unworthy of her friendship, he assassinated his character, comparing it to a dirty dog's. Armstrong did not act alone. Accomplices to the conspiracy of one's self-abasement harbor a belief, influenced by devout dogma, that humility cleanses human failings.

Although Mildred possessed a beautiful mind, and an appealing personality, she had no idea she lacked the type of physical beauty Vincent found attractive in a girl. It is a pity that despite her gray matter and personal appeal, all he could see, with a critical eye, was Mildred's light-brown hair, which was rather streaky; her nose, which was turned-up a bit much; her eyes, which were very gray; her breasts, which were too small for his taste. That Mildred remained unaware of how Vincent observed her physically, was a good thing.

On a Monday afternoon, classes having let out, Vincent and Mildred met in front of the school building and proceeded south on Van Ness Avenue in the direction of her home. While they were walking along, it suddenly dawned upon Vincent that he did not have a clue as to where Mildred lived. They always spent their time together on the grounds of Commerce High School. In their discussions about geometry he had no reason to ask Mildred for her address.

Two blocks beyond the school they crossed Market Street continuing now on South Van Ness Avenue a short distance to Natoma, a narrow back street. Natoma Street as well as other thoroughfares between the middle of blocks south of Market Street contained one and two story light industrial and obsolete residential buildings among the poorest to be found anywhere in San Francisco. Most of the buildings, wood frame, ages ago had been painted a brownish-gray color; the old paint was drab and cracked. To Vincent the buildings' surfaces looked like the hoary hides of mud-spattered elephants.

"Here is where I live," announced Mildred as they approached a two-story building consisting of two flats. She opened the door to the upper flat (the door was unlocked) and beckoned him to follow her up a flight of stairs covered with threadbare carpeting. As he started to walk up the stairs, Vincent detected an odd odor. Step by step the odor grew stronger and stronger. By the time he reached the landing at the top of the stairs, the odor was overpowering to his sensitive sense of smell.

"Cripes!" Vincent said to himself, "there must be a dead rat wedged between the walls." What the boy was smelling was must and mold. Cheaply constructed, not well rainproofed, besides old-ness the building was reeking not only from plaster walls dampened by wet slats but also from rotted studs, to which the clapboard siding of the structure was nailed without tar-paper lining.

Concerned about offending Mildred, Vincent did not show his intolerance of the flat's musty-moldy odor, despite an urge to hold his nose. Instead the boy held his breath now and then as best he could while he stood in a dimly lit hall off the landing. Mildred told him to wait, that she would be right back after she let her mother know they were there. Before his eyes could become accustomed to the poor light in the hall, the girl returned from the front part of the flat where her mother was.

Wanting to introduce Vincent to her, Mildred led him by the hand down the hall to a front room. It was quite small; all the rooms in the flat were small. Upon entering the room, he was unpleasantly surprised. Cracked plaster on a wall was partly concealed with a section of newspaper featuring comic strips, which for the first time in the boy's middle-class life seemed far from funny.

By the wall below the comics the girl's mother was seated in an old-fashioned rocking chair. Slowly yet steadily she rocked back and forth. This made Vincent uneasy. He wished she would sit still while they were getting acquainted with each other. Although the rocker was old, it was not an antique but a collectible of sorts, the same as the rest of the furniture in the room. Since the woman sat slumped in a relaxed position, the boy could not estimate her height. Had she stood, he would have seen that she was inches taller and pounds thinner than her daughter. Mrs. Stensley's profile, her pug nose in particular, left no doubt she was Mildred's biological mother.

The woman wore no make-up, thus the blemishes on her face were easy to spot. She had unsightly traces of hair on her upper lip. Her pale-pink gums clashed with her teeth, stained tobacco brown (she was a heavy smoker). The discoloration of the woman's teeth and her mustache, however faint, repelled Vincent. She was a sorrowful sight, obviously unhappy. Her sad eyes were arid, thirsting for tears that refused to flow.

Perturbed by the sadness of her expression, the boy was on the verge of shedding a compassionate tear for the woman. He was spared the embarrassment of doing so when Mildred's baby sister, who had been crawling around on the floor, yanked his pants cuff. At first Vincent thought it was a cat tugging at his pants; instead he saw a red-headed tiny tot grinning like a Cheshire cat. He was moved to bend down and rub her affectionately with his fingers.

In her hand the child clutched a blue and purple crayon as if she was holding on to stilettos. Fortunate it was indeed that the crayons were not weapons with sharp, pointed blades; or the carrot-top would have been sliced to shreds: across her cheeks, on her arms, about her knees, she had mercilessly wielded the crayons, leaving gashes with ugly colors of purple and blue.

She was scribbling in a back issue of "Murder Mysteries" in which she had created pages upon pages of her own mysterious writings. Drawing Vincent's attention to her colorful handiwork in the magazine, she pointed to it with pride indicating she wished to be praised. "My, my! aren't your pictures pretty," the boy pretended to admire her scribblings. The compliment switched on the child's green orbs; they lit up brightly, the brightness of circular neon tubes. Encouraged, she resumed her scribbling with zeal!

While Vincent was occupied with Mildred's baby sister, Mildred had gone to her room at the rear of the flat. Mrs. Stensley hardly said anything from the moment he met her. All she seemed to do was stare at him. The silence in the room was a bit eerie. Never before had Vincent been in such a strange situation; it troubled the boy. He was too young to understand she simply was not a talkative person. At a loss for words to carry on a conversation with the woman, Vincent had welcomed the intrusion of her child.

She provided him with a polite excuse not to face the mother. His back turned to her, he imagined that he actually could feel Mrs. Stensley staring through his clothes, through his flesh—into his bones. Bent down uncomfortably low to be nearer the tiny tot's size, the boy could stall no longer: his legs were tired, and the stone silence was burdensome, dead weight on his nerves.

Vincent straightened up and, difficult as it was, faced the woman as he strained to say something sensible to her. He was spared the ordeal. Opportunely Mildred called to him: "Come back here with me, at the end of the hall, Vincent. We can begin studying now. Bring my geometry book, will you. I left it on the sofa, by the arm closest to the hall door, I believe."

No sooner had Mildred spoken when Vincent sprang over to the sofa, snatched the geometry book as eagerly as a dog seizes a bone, and hurried in the direction of Mildred's voice. Upon locating her room, he breathed a sigh of relief. She was sitting on the floor with a pencil and ruler in her hand and a pile of scratch papers by her feet. The girl asked the boy to sit down beside her. He promptly complied with her request.

Settled down, they waded into the sea of confusing, on the surface, but, in depth, orderly system of Euclid's "Elements." Upset by the poverty he was witnessing, Vincent, his mood pensive, had difficulty concentrating on geometry. He wondered if he every could conquer the subject. Still, do not fret. Point by point, line by line, triangle by triangle, parallelogram by parallelogram, under the girl's tutelage he received proof that Euclidean geometry is not invincible. One by one he attacked the fierce "Elements" with fresh fortitude, and in the raging battle grew inured toward the poverty-stricken environment in which he found himself.

In the interim an unset alarm clock ticked away on a shelf. Seconds turned into minutes and minutes turned into hours on the numbered dial till the big hand and the little hand formed a 180 degree alignment, agreeing it was six post meridian, at which time Mildred's father returned home to interrupt the schoolmates' study session. Since the Stensleys usually had dinner during this hour, the head of the household insisted his daughter's friend join them for their evening meal.

Vincent was not at all happy about the idea of having dinner with the Stensleys. As a result he tried too hard and too fast to think of plausible reasons to refuse the man's hospitality. Entangling his thoughts, he got a knot in his vocal cords. He became tongue-tied. His silence implied consent. Thus he was obligated to stay and eat...potluck, no less! We are not a bit surprised.

From the moment he set eyes on Mr. Stensley, Vincent disliked his looks. While Mildred helped her father serve dinner, the boy itemized mentally the features that bothered him most about the man. First, there was his misshapen nose, which must have been battered in a dozen fistfights. Second, there was his unkempt hair; very likely he was too slovenly to comb the coarse, matted strands. Third, there was the man's haggard jowls, sprouting sandpaper-like whiskers darkened by a five o'clock shadow. The least he could do was shave! No doubt Stensley was a shiftless roughneck, the boisterous type who hung out in taverns and guzzled beer morning, noon, and night.

Going over Vincent's itemized list of critical observations, we see Mr. Stensley in a different light. First, the man absolutely abhorred brawls. His misshapen nose was broken in an automobile accident; an intern at the Emergency Hospital failed to set the man's nose properly. Second, a few minutes before meeting Vincent he had been walking in the street, where a wild wind played havoc with his hair; in the flat, baby sister did the same with his brush and comb. Unaware Mildred was studying with a friend, he had entered her room to ask her if he could borrow a hairbrush, not mentioning it when he saw Vincent. Third, an allergy had caused his face to break out in a rash; that accounted for his not having shaved.

In checking out the last part of item number three, we find the man was a confirmed teetotaler; alcohol undoubtedly would have killed him. Stensley, pour soul, had heart disease. So critical was his condition, doctors forbade him to do heavy manual labor. As the pick and shovel were the tools with which he worked most of his life, he had difficulty in finding other means of earning a livelihood. Jobs he was physically capable of doing were unattainable.

Once in a while he came across an employer who offered a job requiring light manual work, only to lose out to younger, more experienced, or healthier men. Stensley became demoralized, resigning himself to his bitter fate. Up against it, he sought public assistance through county agencies. They put him including his family on relief. In this degrading manner the Stensleys existed. Fortune favors some people; for they are blessed, often not deservedly. Mr. Stensley was not one of the favored ones. Undeservedly the man was cursed.

Portions of food having been dished around the kitchen table, Mildred's father said grace. Dinner consisted of canned cuisine she had overheated on a gas stove in pitted aluminum pots. That particular day Vincent had not eaten lunch. Needless to hear his stomach growl, he was very hungry. Although the dishes served to him were unappetizing, he hunted and picked unburnt particles of food from his plate to satisfy his hunger. As he ate he could not help but think of his mother's wonderful cooking, which he sometimes was not hungry enough to eat because he had been snacking before a meal. Whimsically he resolved never again to spoil his appetite nibbling chocolate-coated, frozen bananas on a stick, or pink-colored candy floss while wandering about in Playland at the beach.

In silence Vincent praised God for the manna he was fed in his father's house. With emotion he thanked God that he was not Mr. Stensley's son. Perhaps if he were a girl, he would have thanked God that he was Mr. Stensley's daughter. Upon finishing high school, Mildred Stensley enrolled in a university on a scholarship and graduated with the highest honors. She became a world-famous scientist. After several years she received a Nobel Prize for her outstanding achievements in Physics.

Chapter 15

About the time that Vincent Armstrong was attending high school, Hollywood studios in Los Angeles released a number of stereotyped motion pictures across the country. Included among the batch, said to have box-office appeal, were sensational gangster films, overnight productions with stale plots freshened up by rewritten scripts and turned out as quickly as retreaded tires.

As a rule the main characters were comely clever counselors, crime-cleansing specialists quite often overly glamorized and glorified above realistic men's wildest expectations. Vincent, a child of celluloid culture, had the national habit of attending movies regularly. So infused was he by the noble exploits of the Thespian barristers, he vowed to pattern himself after these neoteric knights in jurisprudential armor.

Whenever anybody asked Vincent what vocation he planned to pursue, he declared with vainglorious braggadocio, "I am going to be a criminal lawyer," never simply saying "lawyer" without the modifier. Invariable the boy had to have the word "criminal" attached. The combined descriptive adjective and substantive sounded majestic to his ears, if not to anybody else's.

Recklessly using sciolism, Vincent was guilty of gross ignorance. He thought all he had to do was put in four years of earnest effort in an accredited law school—just a fast flick of the wrist; pass the state bar exams—just a simple snap of the fingers. And, with a lawyer's license he could acquire a legal weapon: a magic sword at his disposal to cut out lawlessness in the land, the way actors extirpate foul play in scenarios on the silver screen.

Eager, Vincent could hardly wait to begin his journey on the road to becoming a criminal lawyer. Upon the recommendation of his high-school advisor, our up-and-coming Clarence Darrow furrowed his prelegal groundwork early by enrolling in Public Speaking I. There is no debate the boy had every intention of applying himself body and soul to learn the power of speech (that trial lawyers use to wipe crime from the face of the earth while defending innocent-looking criminals).

Oftentimes being too zealous can be painful. One tries very hard to do right; yet things always seem to go wrong, despite one's best intentions. Those of us who have been hurt by Fate, will not be astonished to see that Vincent, his sincerity notwithstanding, got started on the wrong foot in the public-speaking class. Unexpectedly the cause of his misstep was not due to something serious but rather to something ludicrous.

At the beginning of the course on Public Speaking I, Vincent Armstrong and a few others, who strolled into the classroom early, found plenty of unassigned, empty seats to choose from. All the would-be Ciceros selected seats in their favorite places. Vincent occupied a seat centrally situated. Putting his elbow on the paddle-shaped surface of his tablet armchair and resting his chin in his hand, he eyed the handful of students sitting around him.

A quick count showed a total of seven students: five girls and two boys including Vincent. He surmised the number would increase by the end of the period, or surely by the end of the week. His conjecture never did materialize. Besides the fact that public speaking was not compulsory, the vast number of students at Commerce High School had an aversion toward participating in oratory, be it public speaking or debating.

The public-speaking teacher, Mr. Du Puy, marched into the classroom punctual to the minute. His physical appearance commanded everybody's attention. Broad is the most appropriate word to describe the man. Everything about the man's body and face was broad: He was broad-nosed and broad-jawed, broad-shouldered and broad-chested. His buttock was broad. He had a broad smile but the temperament of a bulldog.

Even Du Puy's voice contained an element of broadness. To put it broadly, the range of his voice, like his stalwart physique, was extensive yet well-leashed. Seldom did he have an occasion to raise his voice. Du Puy was someone people were hesitant to antagonize. Crossing him—that is, arguing a viewpoint contrary to his— appeared to be fraught with peril. In spite of his aggressive personality he was surprisingly broad-minded. Protective of fruitful discourse, the pedagogue's manner of expression was that of a scarecrow's which keeps off flighty cawing crows.

Mr. Du Puy had hoped for a larger class. Exceptional speakers and debaters being few and far between, he reasoned the more students there were, the more effective would be The Law of Great Numbers, increasing the probability of his having at least four or five outstanding runners-up and hopefully a winner in the season's city-wide oratorical contests.

Predicting by percentages and plausibilities, unless he could develop into public speakers no fewer than six of these boys and girls, Commerce High School was bound to put up a poor showing in the forthcoming public-speaking contests, not to speak of the debating competitions. To test their aptitudes, Mr. Du Puy usually had his new students come to the front of the classroom and give a talk on their respective backgrounds.

The teacher addressed the class: "Suppose we break the ice and acquaint ourselves with one another. To the best of your ability I want each of you to tell the rest of us something about yourself. Begin by stating your name and the reason or reasons you are taking this course. Are there any questions?" (No one of the seven students had a question.) "None. Very well, which of you will volunteer to be the first to speak."

Before Vincent or any of the girls could consider volunteering or had a chance to volunteer, the other boy in the class without thinking raised an arm covered with freckles. He could not make up his mind whether to pull back his arm as soon as he realized his was the only one extended. Anyway it was too late! Having seen the raised freckled arm, Mr. Du Puy had already asked the boy to step forward. When he hesitated, the teacher told him to move along quickly so that there would be time for everybody to speak before the hour was over.

Half-heartedly he trotted to the front of the classroom. Skittish as a colt sensing the presence of a rattler, the youth was having difficulty controlling his limbs. He put his arms behind his back. He placed his arms across his chest. He dropped his arms to his sides. He shifted his weight from leg and foot to leg and foot until he managed to compose himself sufficiently to start speaking.

"My name is Herbert Ruport, Junior. I would like to go into law and politics. I decided to learn public speaking because the vote getters are slick lawyers with gift of the gab, real smooth speakers. The lawyers and politicians can talk their way out of anything. In the dog-eat-dog field of politics a guy can step into slippery messes that...that, messes that...messes that . . ."

Herbert's thought mechanisms broke down. He could not stop repeating himself. He hemmed and he hawed. Game to the core, he put forth a heroic effort to proceed. It was catastrophic. His repetitious utterances were raucous, analogous to the rasping sound of a cracked phonograph record.

Meanwhile Vincent Armstrong was squirming in his seat with indignation, nettled that Herbert had the audacity to trespass on Vincent's private ground of obsession, which was to him hallowed. How dare this Simple Simon, Junior, utter such drivel! How dare this simpleton, this—this ham, imagine he could play a lawyer's role! How dare he presume he could wear the suit of an honorable attorney at law as portrayed in courtroom scenes by handsome, motion-picture actors!

"I—I—I, . . ." Herbert stuttered and stalled as he struggled to say something. In his effort to speak he opened his mouth wide; a gap appeared revealing that he had an eyetooth missing. Like his arms his face was covered with freckles. His wiry red hair was cut flat as a red-berry pie. A skinny youngster still in an awkward stage of development, he looked comical.

Although Vincent's indignation had been aroused, he could not help being hilariously amused by the predicament of his classmate. Vincent tried not to laugh, but he was pushed over the edge when Herbert, instead of returning to his seat, stood speechless and grimaced a silly grimace. Losing control, Vincent let slip an avalanche of sidesplitting laughter.

Mr. Du Puy ejected from his desk chair with the speed of a rocket. An angry glare blazing from his orbs illuminated Du Puy's disapproval of Vincent Armstrong's rude behavior. The teacher fumed, "What is so funny, young man!"

Vincent turned crimson. His embarrassment was unbearable. If he just could have dropped through the floor and disappeared that very instant, he never would wish for anything again. Sadly it was not a day for miracles. No opening appeared in the floor. Still worse, there was no way to explain his outburst of laughter. Not knowing what else to do, he sealed his lips, praying his silence might pacify the angry teacher.

However, Mr. Du Puy had no intention of being easily pacified or pacified at all. "I believe you were laughing with us and not at us.

I am glad you find public speaking so enjoyable. You must be itching to stand behind the lectern. I beg your pardon for not calling on you to speak first. Far be it from me to deprive a body of his earthly pleasures.

"Therefore, I trust you will be more than pleased to prepare a speech on 'Human Equality, Fact or Fiction, in Relation to Individuals at Large, With Emphasis on America and Asia.' Your presentation is to cover two entire class periods. Be sure to divide the subject matter into two parts so that you can present your views in reference to the American Continent at one session and your views in reference to the Asian Continent at the other session. To help you remember, I shall write down the assignment for you."

Mr. Du Puy scribbled the title of the two-parts topic and his instructions on a sheet of paper. He then had Herbert hand it to Vincent, adding to his discomfort. "The first part of the speech will be due three weeks from today. Do you understand Mr.—uh, what is your name?"

While Vincent did not agreeably understand, he nodded his head signifying "yes." The student was afraid to tell the teacher that he understood but disagreed. After stating his name in a low, unmodulated voice, he had to speak louder, enunciate, and repeat it twice more before Mr. Du Puy admitted the syllables comprising "Vin'cent Arm'strong" were distinctly audible.

The remainder of the day was ruined for Vincent. Describing his frame of mind in a few words, he was utterly discombobulated. What a sorry situation at school! Nothing could be more upsetting to a conscientious student than to be in Dutch with his teacher. Oh well, the bottle already had been broken; crying over spilt soda water was a waste of tears. But that scary speech could not be ignored. It was intimidating, frightening as a strange, barking dog.

"Du Puy, you hound, you damn hound!" Vincent hurled insults upon the man—a display of emotionalism which proved futile, since the boy did not feel better after his verbal onslaught. Now, to add to his misery, he felt foolish for having cursed at thin air. In his distress he had crumpled up the sheet of paper containing the punitive assignment, which he would have liked to throw away. On a rational thought he smoothed out the crinkled paper and reread the topic: 'Human Equality, Fact or Fiction, in Relation to Individuals at Large, With Emphasis on America and Asia.'

"Brother! what have I done to deserve this?" Young Armstrong lamented his lousy luck: "I know less about happenings on Earth than I know about what is happening on the planet Saturn. Where would I even rub elbows with people who discuss social subjects such as equality in the world? At home all Uncle Walter does is glue his ear to the radio. Sometimes he turns on the news. Mostly he only listens to programs like Jack Benny's. And Dad, he never reads anything in the newspapers except the headlines or the sports page."

In retrospect Vincent recalled there was often a bunch of soapbox agitators hanging around Jefferson Square. They would rant and rave, yelling their heads off regarding something or other. When passing by, he had observed them trampling the green blades of grass as they gathered in the hilly square. Occasionally he overheard bits and pieces of their heated conversations, but he never stopped to get the gist of what they were talking about, until the time that purely by chance he encountered the lanky old man.

Chapter 16

On a Sunday afternoon, after an active morning of Vincent's playing touch football, while departing from Margaret S. Hayward Playground, he saw a commotion across the street in Jefferson Square. A large crowd had gathered, and several police patrol cars were parked along the north line of Turk Street. Crossing the street to satisfy his curiosity, he mingled with the crowd. Soon he discovered the mainspring operative in producing the hubbub was some character perched on a branch among the dense foliage of a big eucalyptus tree located in the westward part of the square.

Closer observation revealed to Vincent that the man had only one leg. How he managed to climb up the tree and work his way out on a limb was inconceivable. People in the crowd speculated that a few seedy individuals, who stood nearby cheering, must have helped him ascend the eucalyptus tree. Probably the man wanted to use it as a platform to agitate a riot. He had been arrested for starting riots in the past.

A burly policeman, boosted up the thick trunk by two fellow officers, attempted to crawl along the branches to grab hold of the one-legged man. Determined to avoid arrest, he proceeded to swing menacingly a crutch he had braced under his arm. As he swung the crutch, the branch supporting him shook. The branch was not too sturdy. Overweighted, it began to crackle. Fearful the branch would break, the policeman was forced to retreat. Shouting at the top of his lungs, the cripple vehemently upbraided the Police.

"Is this your idea of freedom of speech? You Gestapos, strong-arm men in blue uniforms. You muscle sconces. Brass knuckles for the chicken-livered capitalists! Sure, any old citizen is entitled to bitch all he wants to about being exploited by the high and mighty wealthy class. Yeah, just as long as he don't go and stub their smelly, pedicured toes. Pretty god damn smart! The Constitution to every party guarantees the right to criticize the capitalistic system. Hogwash! Kiddies in kindergarten are learned, 'Sticks and stones will break my bones, but names won't hurt nobody at all.'

"Leave the workers bang their lunkhead against a brick wall, hollering they ain't getting a fair shake. That's no skin off the pluto-crat's nose. His pockets bulges yet with silver dollars which he has filched from we wage slaves. Yeah, I said wage slave. And don't you kid yourself for a second that you're less of a slave even if you do happen to belong to a union. Economic shackles is economic shack-les. It matters hardly nothing whether you're forced to wear them ten hours a day or eight hours a day, six days a week or five days a week, for sixty cents an hour or seventy cents an hour. Nine out of ten union members dies poor men just the same.

"What's more, their widows and orphans are lucky if they don't have to go in hock to pay for their funeral expenses. C.I.O. or A.F. of L., one is no saintlier than the other. They're both run by a gang of highbinders—labor fakers, that's what they are. Labor leaders are nothing but middlemen that for a cut make deals with bosses to put down and hold in check the restricted union membership. And those members doesn't by a long shot cover the whole of the miserable working class.

"If and when any workers—not dues hungry unions and fat-salaried executive officials, no! not these marrow-sucking despots—if workers show a smidget of a sign of uniting, of taking action to get their deserved slice of the loaves of bread they've labored to bake, the panful of money grubbers with itchy palms, whom really rule the roost, grow panicky and cry copper. Then flat-footed assholes like yourselves, that are paid off in swill, come charging to smash the sweaty brows of your brothers with billy clubs.

"Wasn't it enough that in the World War my leg was sacrificed on the filthy altar of lucre to your god of greed Tycoon, that the prof-its of the Sixty Families could be increased a thousand per cent. They made barrels and barrels of lucre out of the blood bath. Those blood-suckers, less useful than a roll of used toilet paper, have sent you to drain me of the only thing I got left in life, my liberty.

"Hell! all the cops in San Francisco can't scare me or shut me up. I'm going to blow and blow and blow and blow my bugle till the working stiff savvies the tune of my music and get T-bone steaks.

The Sixty Families can afford to eat their fill of not only expensive T-bone steaks but rich mushroom gravy, too. These vultures are yet picking out of their gold-filled teeth the remaining bits of choice meat they devoured greedily all the time the doughboys were tasting mustard gas in a capitalistic war to protect the fine silver and fancy linens of these privileged few. Workers, you're not workhorses, you're men. Throw away your blinders. Don't you see the scraps the Sixty Families dumps into the garbage can . . ."

In his rage the fantasized soul waved his arms wildly. His grip loosened on the crutch, it fell noiselessly upon the carpet of grass below. Before the cripple could finish his last sentence, the burly policeman, who again inched his way along the branch of the tree, caught hold of the man's one leg. Losing his balance as the policeman pulled his leg, he fell off the tree. It was miraculous, he hit the ground hard yet was not injured. Three policemen pounced on the cripple to subdue him. He struggled viciously, as viciously as an infuriated leopard struggles when a hunter captures it by clinging to the tail of the wild animal. In a matter of minutes the wordy captive was handcuffed and hauled away in a patrol wagon.

Meanwhile Vincent Armstrong, bewildered by the entire episode, sought to find out more about what happened from a friendly-looking man in his seventies—impressively long in stature, lean in flesh, large in bones, and loose in joints—who had been a spectator at the scene for quite a while. He admitted he had not been there from the outset. Therefore, he only could surmise that the crippled war veteran was apprehended for disturbing the peace.

Inoculated with an infectious spirit of friendliness, none too prevalent nowadays, the elder's warm manner put Vincent in a frame of mind to converse with him, though Vincent did all the talking at first. He expressed disbelief regarding the frightening, vituperative statements uttered as factual in the cripple's abusive language, blasted loudly like rock dynamited in a quarry. Wisely exercising forbearance of a sage, the old man listened to the young man ask and answer his own questions, each reply a negative one to the assertions hitherto made by the embittered, one-legged man.

"Who ever heard of such a cock-and-bull story. That guy must be cuckoo, getting onto a tree and spreading terrible lies. How the devil did the screwball worm his way up its wide trunk? The branches must be twenty feet above the ground." (The boy overestimated the height.) "You wouldn't dream a person with a leg missing could be capable of climbing so high unassisted. I bet some communists helped the nut. He's probably a Red himself. If he doesn't like it in the United States, why the heck doesn't he go live in Russia?

"Can you imagine a sane person expecting anybody to believe sixty wealthy families in America could be so cold-blooded that for profits they'd send American soldiers to die on the battlefield. Neither six, sixteen, or sixty families have that kind of influence here in the first place. Sure, we do have wealthy families," Vincent stated positively...without his considering 'wealth' is a relative term. "All around the country big corporations are in the hands of millions of stockholders. I know. My dad has some United Airlines stock."

Not understanding anything about the stock market let alone corporative functions, the boy wavered, saying what sounded plausible to him: "My dad, he—well, he's often mentioned that he voted by proxy on the airline's business affairs of terrific importance to many, many of the owners of the airline. That nutty, crippled guy sure can slice the baloney thin. Does he really expect people to believe sixty families control our nation's money and buy special privileges with it? I'll eat my football helmet if the Sixty Families even exist.

"That guy is full of baloney. My history teacher told me we tried to stay out of the World War. But the straw that broke the camel's back was Germany's violation of our rights as a neutral on the high seas. Anyhow, we felt it was our moral duty to make the world safe for democracy. To create such a falsehood that any Americans heartlessly planned to profit from the war, is as bad as the act Benedict Arnold was guilty of—treason! If some made more money, it must have been a coincidence of the times. They certainly did not intend to use the misery of war to fill all their pockets with coins. That crazy Bolshevik should be locked in the booby hatch, and the key thrown in the Pacific Ocean. He wants to cause a bloody revolution! Nobody has a right to revolt against the government."

After listening patiently to the young man, the old man replied: "Granted, climbing a tree and making inflammatory accusations about one's country isn't a sensible way to behave. Nevertheless, if a man fights for his flag and is incapacitated for life in the conflict, and in all probability is shell-shocked, which American could be so ungrateful as to want to ship him off to a foreign land because of his differing opinions, senseless or not. The Russians gloat over that type of incident. Stalin and his comrades in the Kremlin are liable to broadcast to the world that the truth hurts, and we haven't the nerve to face it.

"Any man, in particular a man who has fought for his country, should have a right to object to what he believes is wrong. If he is mistaken, he ought to be enlightened, not punished. Really, sonny, people don't complain when they have every reason to be perfectly satisfied.

"No government on earth, past or present, has proven itself elevated to that stage of perfection it did not need immense improvement. America, irrespective of our patriotic bias, isn't an exception to the rule by a long stretch of the imagination. If you are unshakenly convinced I am full of baloney, like that disabled war veteran appeared to be, a few random questions carefully considered may well offer better food for thought.

"Why in every state of the Union do scores upon scores of underpaid Americans cling desperately to jobs they loath?

"Are national minimum wages established by the Fair Labor Standards Act adequate to allow most, if not all, Americans to live according to the high standard of living said to exist in the United States?

"The fact is sad indeed that the minimum hourly wage (forty cents an hour) regulated by the Act is monstrously low, and the hours too long. Still worse, it neither pertains to nor protects all our citizens. True, on October 24th of this year 1940, a forty-hour week went into effect. But it applies to interstate—not to intrastate—commerce; and, moreover, it applies only to specific industries. So, if a business operation doesn't cross a state line, the majority of workers employed within a state fail to fall under federal jurisdiction.

"Additionally the numbers of that group affected by interstate commerce is greatly reduced by provisions of the Act which excludes of all people seamen and persons such as those serving in an executive, administrative, professional, local retailing or outside salesman capacity. Also excluded are those persons in horticulture, agriculture, and the making of dairy products; those in certain newspaper publications; and those in local air-carrier transportation systems.

"Here is another part of the whole thing that reeks to high heaven. The Act authorizes an administrator to issue a certificate permitting minors and the physically handicapped to be hired for still less than the scant salary scale set up in section six of the statute.

"What a joke! Minors and handicapped persons are either capable or incapable of handling jobs performed by able-bodied adults. If they are inefficient, why are they hired in the first place. If they are competent, why legally permit an employer to utilize their services for a mere pittance. The present Fair Labor Standards Act needs to be radically reformed and revised.

"Sure, one can argue that this Act is better than nothing, a very poor argument indeed. No fair-minded American can deny all working people in the United States should be assured by legislation, without chicanery, as a benefit of their labor a minimum wage with which they are able to afford simple pleasurable pursuits. A legislature expecting people to labor simply to exist is in a sorrowful state of affairs."

Pausing momentarily, the old man formulated the next question for the young man. "Do the numbers of jobless persons run into the millions? I am not including in the millions housewives and children, of course."

The catechizer's method of questioning, used by the old man to draw forth his self-serving answers, was alien to Vincent Armstrong. He did not know just how to respond. A thought struck him, and he was on the verge of expressing it. The elder, however, started to catechize anew before Vincent could utter a word.

"Obviously the number of unemployed in our country is very high. There is no question about it. Let me rephrase the question. Is our political-economic system structured to completely eliminate unemployment now and forever?"

With his body the tautness of a cub fox crouching in readiness to pounce on a hoary bear, the youth snapped: "Heck no! It's unheard of. What are you driving at? Our Representatives in Washington haven't shut their eyes to the unemployment situation. They are honorable, honest men. I listen to their speeches. Always they promise the future will be brighter. I hope you are not saying they are liars."

"Please, sonny," the old man replied, gently touching the youth's shoulder as a conciliatory gesture. "I didn't accuse the members of the House of Representatives of anything. All I am attempting to get across to you is the fact that our form of government is far from perfect. It will be difficult for me to explain what I mean if you insist on putting words in my mouth.

"Here, incidentally, lies the trouble with a lot of people who are opinionated. Without realizing it, their stubborn stand is an obstruction to mankind's progress because they refuse to hear somebody else's opinion, be it about imperfection or unfairness in government or whatever. When an idea expressed is not in accordance with theirs, right away opinionated people become argumentative instead of examining the other fellow's point of view for what it may be worth.

"Too many of us are scared to death our heavily populated planet will topple forward; and we shall have to lock arms in a joint brotherhood to live in an equitable world as a harmonious family. Coerced over the centuries, from one stage of society to another, by the terrifying reins of those who somehow sat in the saddle, from father to son, we've obediently built up such a resistance to the concept of sharing equitably that we frown upon the principle as unrealistic, blaming human nature—a convenient generality—for our cowardice in failing to come down to earth."

Unable to grasp the old man's meaning, Vincent commented but not to the point: "Have not men served as soldiers and fought for their rulers through the centuries. They certainly were not cowards. Besides, you can't change human nature."

"Perhaps not," the elder's words had a condescending ring. "You can, however, change rules to harness human nature for cooperative behavior. Before I say more, sonny, it might interest you to know I was a reporter in Saint Louis several years ago. As a freethinking humanitarian I came to the realization that a newspaper was not a front where someone with my ideals could depict truthfully the plight of the underdog. Since then I have been doing freelance writing, which leaves me disengaged to express the truth as I see it, uncensored by opportunist editors and their superiors, venal publishers.

"You would be amazed how many news items become distorted or never reach the press. Reporters don't in all cases uncover the complete facts. Some blow up incidents beyond sizable proportions. Others deflate them. If there is a chance that an article is apt to irritate the advertisers, it is altered or even squashed. Doubting Thomases pooh-pooh this practice to be unlikely. They discount the fact that most of a newspaper's revenue is derived from advertisements, probably as much as seventy-five per cent, if not more.

"Editors tailor facts to suit the paper's policy. Policy is designated by the publisher. He may be a big-buck elephant in finance, or a two-bit baby elephant fancying himself a financier. Naturally both are organs of the moneyed man. Thus editorials are aimed at readers (the People) so that they are persuaded to act in conjunction with those dictates perpetuating the position of the species Capitalist, who are relatively few in number.

"And the tragedy of history is that from the dim dawn of civilization to the present day, the human race, in a twilight state, has been ruled at times with cruelty, at times with corruption, by an exceedingly small percentage of men, and women. In each era a ruler—or a figurehead—and a comparative thimbleful of cohorts: militarists, false prophets, courtiers, land barons, politicos, traffickers in vendibles of war, and other mercenaries have formed alliances based on their mad quest for more and more power for the attainment of affluence.

"Maddened by an insatiable appetite to gobble up riches, they banded together directly or indirectly to rob, by a devious device, with impunity, the gullible majority (subjects or citizens). Just like an heirloom of personal value, it was handed down from chieftain to chieftain, from god-king to god-king, from queen to queen, from president to president, from dictator to dictator, from and by every type of hierarchy history records.

"You may wonder, what this devious device is. It is as misleading as a doctrine of Ethics called meliorism. (George Eliot used the term in her book 'Cross Fire.') Paraphrased in essence, meliorism is the belief that within nature everything, including Man, steadily and necessarily tends to improve the world. In reality the belief lacks basis in fact. Earthquakes, volcanic eruptions, and floods certainly do not bring about improvements.

"However, hierarchy after hierarchy state as certainty that under their brand of meliorism the world will improve, but hopefully conflicts and famines, like natural disasters, will not occur. With the tenacity of the giant squid Architeuthis extending propagandizing tentacles over every land, each hierarchy or political body tantalizes overtaxed multitudes into perpetuating its existence on the assumption that it intends to improve the world for unborn generations—never mind about the generations already born.

"To sail the same sea, still at the same time strike an alternate route...misquoting the Bible of Judaism and Christianity, the Koran of Islam, the Kojiki of Shinto, the Tao Tê Ching of Taoism, the Scruti of Hinduism, the Avesta of Zoroastrianism, and other allegoric writings capable of as many interpretations as stars in the skies, shells in the seas, and sands in the shores...holy men throughout the murky mist of the ages have inculcated their flocks with the absolutism that when a Divine Mind wills it, his creations are to live in a virtual paradise in the hereafter, never on earth. Heavens no! Earthly happenings can be confirmed. From an imaginary place in the far beyond nobody ever could appear to disprove such baseless preachings.

"A parallel line of preaching, which insults one's intelligence, is drawn-out, tiresome talk about the decayed stuff that people place too much importance on material possessions and little importance, if any, on spiritual matters. To me it sounds suspiciously like a revival of antiquated asceticism or, as I see it, black-and-white magic which shrieks scaringly: 'The carnal world is critically evil. Only by mortification of the flesh—by abstinence, by self-denial—is salvation to be gained.'

"The gain is never monetary. Hell no! Rather the assumption is that someone's sick soul should be saved. Such is the applesauce that witch doctors feed the Many Sinners while the Few Saints, who are blessed, employ brokers to invest their capital, bookkeepers to compute their returns, and bankers to safeguard their enormous profits, which a billionaire couldn't spend within several lifetimes, unless he stupidly squandered his money on bad investments."

The old man's forehead wrinkled, and he stared with a blank look. He appeared to be depressed, as though the burdensome cares of the seven continents were weighing heavily on his bent shoulders. Moved by the man's low spirits, Vincent smiled a kindhearted smile at him. Pleased to see this indication of compassion from the young-ster, the elder's spirits were raised.

Before Vincent could comment on what he had just heard, the old man remarked: "I must have been carried away momentarily. Be a good boy and listen a little longer. I must say, sonny, you are sadly mistaken in your comments about the Sixty Families. They do indeed exist. In fact, a book titled 'America's Sixty Families,' that has become a best seller, was published a few years ago, in 1937. The author, a former Wall Street reporter for the New York Herald Tribune, is Lundberg. His first name is Ferdinand.

"The book contains statistical data which show the mint of money the families have. Page upon page is filled with information showing who controls the largest American fortunes, and how the Family fortunes are used. That is—the way they affect economics and politics in America. The lives of all Americans are touched by their monetary influence. The times it is good we survive. The times it is bad we suffer. Now, sonny, do you have any questions?"

Vincent was quick to ask: "By the Few Saints do you mean the Sixty Families? If so, where did you get the idea they were blessed? And aren't the many shareholders in big corporations wealthy?"

In reply the old man explained: "Few Saints is simply a figure of speech. I'm sure multimillionaires believe they are blessed. The late John D. Rockefeller, one of the wealthiest members of the Sixty Families, was quoted as saying, 'God gave me my money.'

"No person can dispute the fact that there are numerous individuals who are shareholders in America's multimillion-dollar corporations. However, how many shares individuals own, and the unit value of their shares is something else. At best playing the stock market is a risky game. As a rule, investors' votes are limited to the kind of stock and the number of shares they buy. For example, to reduce risk, if they buy instead of common- preferred stock, a safer stock, they generally do not have the privilege of voting.

"The upshot is the stockholders are voiceless in the administrative affairs of the corporation. Besides their lack of authority, they receive very little cash dividends and none at all if no profits are realized. On the other hand, subordinate officers of the corporation unfailingly vote themselves undue compensation: a low estimate in a poor year would be $30,000 (minimum)—plus bonuses, liberal expense accounts, and lavish pensions.

"In a financial statement issued by General Motors Corporation, I recently read that an executive William Knudsen received for one annual period a salary of $150,000. As if it wasn't enough, Knudsen—he's the president—was awarded a bonus of some four thousand shares of common stock. The president of another large corporation, I read about, is due to receive at his retirement $75,000 a year, and $25,000 for his advice alone.

"To spoon ice cream onto the pie, not only will he receive $100,000 annually as long as he lives, but when he dies, this executive's widow is to be paid from corporate funds $50,000 a year the rest of her life. Subordinate officers of the corporation also voted one another pie à la mode: mounds of benefits and salaries heaped on a scale according to rank. The small stockholders, the silly asses, many of whom have invested their last penny, passively grin and bear it. There isn't a hell-of-a-lot they can do about it, anyway."

Having laid a concrete foundation, the man was ready to build on his argument. "Tell me, sonny, how many shares of United Airlines stock does your father own?"

"Eighty shares, if my memory serves me correctly," the ingenuous youth answered. "Maybe less, I'm not sure."

The old man was prepared with another question. "Do you remember how much your father paid for the shares?"

"Not exactly, but . . . Vincent paused to search his memory. "I believe Dad once mentioned to my mother he paid seven or eight dollars a share."

"Hum, let's assume eighty shares is correct, and they cost him eight dollars per share. Multiplying eight times eighty, we arrive at a total cost of six hundred and forty dollars. What dividends, or profits, did he receive," the elder demanded to be told.

"I think Dad said that he received twenty cents profit a share." The triviality of the figure had the blunt impact of a fast flung boomerang on the boy's head. Biting his lip, he tried to ease the hardness of his chagrin with a rapid retort. "It may have been more!"

The old man refrained from chuckling as he replied: "That's good enough. Again I'll give you the benefit of the doubt. We will assume the dividends were twice the amount you overheard. The short and long of it is, at forty cents a share your father would have realized a profit of thirty-two dollars." Having hit the spike hard and true, the man had driven his point well into the ground.

Ill at ease, tired of listening to the long-winded talker, Vincent was bored and restless. Still worse, he had to urinate. He fidgeted from foot to foot for boyishly he was too shy to say he had to answer the urgent call of nature. Painfully uncomfortable, he glanced at an avenue of escape: the roughly paved path leading out of the square.

On the path he caught sight of a gray squirrel. A bicyclist riding nearby rang the bell on his bicycle. Frightened by the shrill ring of the bell, the squirrel darted away into a thicket of dark green bushes. At that second he envied the squirrel's size and speed. Vincent wished he could flee and disappear in an instant, too. Cornered, he racked his brain trying to find a way to part company graciously with the elder. Vincent's anguish was all for naught. The talk was about to come to an end. "Sonny, I have with me an informative weekly publication you might enjoy reading." The old man removed a folded newspaper from inside his overcoat, which was well-worn and fit him like a gunny sack. "You will find the paper publishes world and national news with a liberal slant, but nothing nonsensical. Unlike the Examiner, Chronicle, and the Call-Bulletin, the paper's editorials can call a spade a spade without fear of retaliation, simply because the publisher is not dependent on advertisers. Business firms, as a matter of policy, aren't solicited for advertising in this paper."

Pulling a short, stubby pencil out of a vest pocket, the old man said: "I shall write my name and phone number above the headline. Should you care to discuss any of the articles, feel free to phone me.

Here": the man handed the boy the newspaper after writing <u>Russell Evans</u> – <u>WEst</u> <u>4846</u> across the top margin of the front-page.

Despite a reluctance to do so, Vincent accepted the paper. He half-heartedly muttered, "Thanks." Jumping at the chance to leave without seeming impolite, he promised insincerely, "I will go right home and read it." Worried he would wet his pants, he turned away, immediately departing without saying, "good-bye." Although surprised by the abruptness of the boy's departure, the aged gentleman did not hesitate to bid him a fond farewell. Vincent must have taken the farewell (Godspeed) literally, for he ran off as fast as a fleeing squirrel.

Chapter 17

Weeks later when young Vincent Armstrong thought about his chance encounter with the old man, he had to smile. He vividly recalled running down the path of Jefferson Square in a desperate dash for home, where he could hardly wait to lift the toilet seat in the bathroom and pull aside his fly to unbutton his pants, so that he could relieve the painful pressure on his urinary bladder.

"Betcha," Vincent wagered with himself, "the ancient chatterbox would have plenty to chatter about Human Equality (uh—uh) . . . Balls! agates for baseball cards, bottle caps, milk tops, or whatever to remember the whole shitty thing." Having ejaculated in a juvenile manner unbecoming a lad of high-school age, Vincent studied hard the slip of paper preserving the lengthy topic of the homework punitively administered by his public-speaking teacher, Mr. Du Puy.

Upon reiterating, "Human Equality, Fact or Fiction, in Relation to Individuals at Large, With Emphasis on America and Asia," Vincent blasphemed, "Jesus Christ, damn it! It's too complicated. I won't be able to write a long speech about such a deep subject. Everyone knows God created all men equal, all over the world. What more is there to say?

"I wonder what the old man would say. Perhaps I should get in touch with him." Vincent was indecisive, his thoughts negative. "Maybe I shouldn't—just maybe I'd better stay clear of that chatterbox. He is so talkative if encouraged he'd beat his gums till my eardrums busted."

Haunted by a vision of Mr. Du Puy's broad brow, his froggy dark eyes bulging with wrath when he had meted out as punishment the arduous multiple-assignment, Vincent moaned: "All I did was laugh at Ruport. You'd think I maimed freckle face or something worse. A thug would have received a lighter sentence." Self-pity prompted the schoolboy to draw a dramatic parallelism different from the reality of his situation.

His feelings farfetched, he imagined himself falsely imprisoned on Alcatraz. Attempting to escape, he was on the verge of drowning in the treacherous waters of the San Francisco Bay. Desperation stirred him as if he had been splashed with cold water. Vincent made up his mind at once to call for help before it was too late.

"Man-oh-man, I wouldn't ever have thought that I would be dying to see the old man again. Who cares if he chatters a bit much. He is an angel compared to that devil Du Puy."

Now that Vincent was decisive, his thoughts were positive; although he was uneasy. "I have to get in touch with the old man. I'm sure he can help me. Whew, is he deep. And the man's vocabulary is great, really great. I know he will come to my rescue. I just know it. He must...he will."

Vincent breathed more easily, relieved that help was in sight, or so it appeared. He also was relieved that he had not disposed of the newspaper on which was written the elder's telephone number. By a fluke Vincent, instead of carrying out his intention to toss the newspaper—unread—into a trash can, used the paper to line his clothes-closet shelf simply because nothing else was close at hand.

But Vincent's relief did not last. He panicked: his mother had been housecleaning the other day. She might have relined the two shelves in his clothes closet. Usually she burned all the old shelf paper. What if she had burned the newspaper, too? Vincent gasped, "Jesus...extinguish the possibility!"

Vincent rushed into his bedroom and grabbed a rather rickety chair, the first thing handy to use as a stepladder. He lifted the chair over to the clothes closet where he stepped up onto the chair, for the shelf with the newspaper lining was the highest one, too high to reach from the floor. The shelf, Vincent could see, had been newly lined with clean butcher paper.

"Well, that's that, I am sunk." Be it manly or unmanly, the youth would have wept if he was not instantaneously distracted. Warned by creaking of the rickety chair on which he was standing that it could topple under his weight, Vincent was quick to place his palms at the top of the solid shelf to brace himself; by doing so he accidentally slid the butcher paper off to one side.

Lo and behold! sheets of the newspaper were exposed on the

shelf. The sheets were still there, and in place as he previously had secured them with steel thumbtacks. Probably that was why his mother had left the newspaper intact. He tried to remove one of the thumbtacks with his fingernails; he did not succeed. The flat head of the thumbtack was pressed too snugly against the wooden shelf. After tugging futilely around the edge of the thumbtack, his fingertips felt numb, they hurt. He abandoned this painful method and resorted to brain in lieu of brawn.

Withdrawing from his jacket pocket a thin mailbox key, he worked it like a crowbar to pry loose the stubborn steel head of the thumbtack. It was dislodged in short order. The rest of the thumbtacks offered no resistance. Vincent removed the newspaper from the shelf without tearing a single sheet. Across the top margin of the front-page he found the old man's name and telephone number clearly written above the boldface caption, WEEKLY PEOPLE (a Socialist Labor Party publication).

In a matter of seconds Vincent was at the telephone dialing West 4846. After several rings a woman answered. He told her that he needed to speak to Mr. Evans. She replied she was not sure if the old man was in, but she would knock on his door and find out. Vincent continued holding the telephone receiver to his ear as he waited patiently. Before long his patience was rewarded when he heard someone speak. The voice sounded much like the old man's except it was unexpectedly harsh.

"Hello, who is this? What do you want?" The man had been asleep, still drowsy he seemed cranky. His voice was harsh-sounding for his throat was congested with phlegm.

"Are you Mr. Evens—Mrs. Russell Evans?" Vincent asked, ignoring the man's questions. Vincent did not respond directly to him because Vincent wanted first to determine the true identity of the voice coming over the telephone.

"Why, yes, my name is Russell Evans," confirmed the puzzled elder, scratching his head. "Who is this? How did you get my telephone number?"

"I am the young fellow to whom you gave a Weekly People newspaper. It was on a Sunday, in the afternoon...at the part, on Turk Street."

Half awake, the old man upstretched his free arm and then lowering it rubbed his eyes. After digging away dry grains of bothersome hardened fluids that had collected in the corners of eye sockets, he expressed mild regret: "Sorry, I don't recall. I honestly don't...

On which occasion did you say we met?"

Vincent persisted: "Surely you remember. You know, the day the guy with one leg climbed up a tree and blew his top. And the police arrested him, and you and I talked about the incident."

"Hold on a minute. Let me think..." The man stifled a yawn. "That was in Jefferson Square, some time ago. Yes, of course, it comes back to me now. I'm glad you called. What can I do for you, sonny?"

Vincent was instantly moved by Evan's friendliness. The floodgates of his heart opened, the youth poured out his troubles to the elder. Vincent related everything that had taken place in his public-speaking class: How he had lost control and laughed at his schoolmate's funny gestures while giving a speech. Mr. Du Puy's angry reaction to Vincent's outburst of laughter. The teacher's meanness in assigning as punishment for Vincent a very hard, long talk; the first part of which he had to prepare and give in front of the entire class in just three weeks—without fail!

Hell's bells, he was only a high-school sophomore. Du Puy, the tyrant, knew darn well the subject matter of the assignment was way over the head of any second-year student, especially one without experience in public speaking. To prove his point Vincent read the title of the two-parts topic over the telephone. ('Human Equality, Fact or Fiction, in Relation to Individuals at Large, With Emphasis on America and Asia.')

All the time he was on the telephone Vincent spoke rapidly with a high-pitched voice, an indication of how worried he was. Realizing that the boy was in an agitated state about the difficult assignment, the man diked the boy's rapid flow of words with the assurance his task was not insurmountable. As a matter of fact, the man chuckled cheerfully, he had on file reams of material which, refined and edited, should fit the bill.

To further console the boy, Evans advised, "Always bear in mind, worry is interest paid on trouble not due: That is a self-evident truth." Their conversation culminated when Vincent was invited by the old man to come to the rooming house where he lived so that they could work on the speech.

Chapter 18

Before the unfortunate episode in Public Speaking I, a girl at school had invited Vincent Armstrong to a house party the coming Saturday night. He gladly accepted her invitation. Disheartened by the harsh method Mr. Du Puy used to punish him, Vincent's zeal for attending the party had deadened. He decided to skip the party. However, now that the old man, a prince of a person, generously offered to help him, the youth felt his lease on life was renewed. Youthful, vigorous in mind and body, he had a change of heart and went to the party.

Upon arriving at her home, the girl, who was the hostess, escorted Vincent downstairs to a large social room. In sharp contrast to the hardwood floors—dark oak—the ceiling and walls were finished in knotty pine. A bar trimmed with black and red molding occupied a far corner of the room. Four matching stools, upholstered red Leatherette, were set close to the brass footrest at the front of the bar. On glass shelves attached to a wall behind the bar were displayed toby and beer mugs, a few knickknacks, and miniature liquor bottles (their fluid contents a little evaporated). Otherwise, except for a phonograph sitting on top of a record-laden bridge table, the social room was unfurnished.

Orderly arranged on the bar were big oval platters with savory snacks: assorted crackers and cheese, pitted olives, dill pickles, coleslaw, potato salad, and some bags of potato chips. At one end of the bar was a tray stacked with homemade cookies. At the other end of the bar, paper plates, cups, forks, and napkins had been placed beside a huge cut-glass bowl filled to the brim with unspiced punch containing slices of lemons and ice cubes. Hooked over the rim of the punch bowl was an indispensable silver ladle by means of which the young people attending the party served themselves cups of refreshing punch.

When the boys and girls were not quenching their thirst, they were dancing away to their hearts' content. Each time a record was changed on the phonograph all but inseparable pairs exchanged partners. As the even progressed everybody had a fling around the social room—everybody but Vincent. Seated at the bar, he had a ball munching snacks and sipping punch. He remained rooted to his bar stool like a stump in the ground; nobody was able to budge him the least. Eventually the other youngsters started to poke fun at Vincent.

"Say, Mr. Wallflower, why aren't you dancing? Don't be a party-pooper."

"What's the matter. Do you have a pebble in your shoe?"

"It's even worse. He probably has bunions...right, killjoy?"

"You're not tied to that bar. Trot out here and shake a hoof!"

At that moment reaching for a dish of olives, Vincent growled, "Aw dry up! I don't want to dance." Not so much hungry as he was irritated, he grabbed a doomed olive and attacked it with his teeth, devouring the olive's leathery meat. Other olives quickly met the same fate.

Belching mutely (his hand over his mouth), Vincent right away ladled himself a cup of punch to aid his digestion. In spite of being badgered, he controlled his irritation and moved nearer to the bar. Someone theorized for all ears to hear that Vincent Armstrong had never learned to dance. Proof, presumably in jest: The glutton never dances. He spends all his time at parties gorging himself with free food.

Jest or no jest, the last jibe hurt Vincent's pride. He lost his tolerance for the teasing. Eyeing a girl within reach floating by herself to the music, he slid off the stool with the smoothness of a shark, seized her, and nosed his victim toward an uncrowded corner of the social room.

She was pulled along so swiftly the girl caught the heel of her shoe in Vincent's trouser cuff. As she struggled to release the heel, she tripped, almost falling to the floor. Her mishap, funny yet not funny, filled the room with adolescent laughter. Onlookers were treated to a good time at the victimized girl's expense. Regaining her balance, the girl thrust her arms into the air, a display of dismay. With a scornful look she turned on her heels to walk away from Vincent. He darted ahead to face the girl, grabbed her shoulder with his left hand, and pulled her toward him none too gently.

It was fortunate for the girl that she had the suppleness of a Raggedy Ann doll. Her footing unsteady she flopped up against Vincent's body. Wrapping his right arm around her narrow waist, the boy held the girl tightly. By superior strength he forced her to dance straight back, but the girl resisted after a few steps.

She swerved. She stopped. She stood her ground. She spat out syllables: "Ooo, please! Darn you! Don't break my back! You...you...you roughneck! Not so tight. Be a gentleman. Let me breathe."

Vincent loosened his hold around the girl's waist. Urged on by hilarious onlookers to be a good sport and dance, she ceased her resistance. Now that the girl was cooperative Vincent led her into a fox trot doing simple steps, nothing spectacular.

Next he did something that stilled the laughter of the teasing teen-agers. Taking her right hand in his left, he lifted it above the girl's head. Just as a rodeo cowboy rotates a lasso, Vincent spun her round and round in different ways. She followed his twists and turns surprisingly well—not counting her two or three missteps.

One of the youths among the onlookers exclaimed with a tone of admiration: "Why, he's doing The Box Twirl! I go to public dances pretty often in San Francisco at Walohan's and Trianon, and at Sweet's across the bay in Oakland. Seldom have I met anybody at ballrooms who knows that routine. Very few of the best dancers can do it."

From his peripheral vision Vincent could see other teen-agers at the party gathering around to watch him dance. The peacock in the young man manifesting itself, he began to show off more than ever. Vincent strutted every dance figure he had previously picked up. Led on by his colorful exhibition, the girl gave her all to keep pace with him in her own showy fashion.

Bar none, the on-looking youngsters, though uninstructed in the art, judged Vincent's social dancing to be first-rate. Qualified or not, many in admiration declared, "Boy oh boy, is he a terrific dancer!" or complimentary words to that effect. Record after record was played before Vincent and the girl finally stopped dancing and refused to continue despite much coaxing from their admirers.

That he needed a rest was the reason Vincent gave for his refusal to go on dancing. (The real reason was he had exhausted his supply of dance steps.) The girl said she loved doing The Box Twirl, but she also needed a rest. (False pride prevented her from admitting she had been overcome with dizziness in twirling like a top.)

Seated again at the bar, Vincent now was joined by the giddy girl. She sat silently several seconds struggling to stave off a disagreeable sensation that the floor was moving beneath her as if she were on a raft afloat in an ocean. Gradually recuperating, she spoke: "I guess we should introduce ourselves. My name is Martha Tisland. What's yours?"

As soon as he told her his name, Martha praised Vincent Armstrong in a melodious voice: "I adore your style. It's so wonderful. You are so light on your feet. Where did you learn to dance so heavenly?"

Vincent just smiled, saying nothing. The girl's question opened the door to memories of Curly, a cherished childhood chum who had been the springboard for Vincent's learning to dance. He always smiled a pleasurable smile when thoughts of Curly entered his mind. He wished Curly could have heard the girls and boys at the party complimenting his performance of The Box Twirl.

Vincent wondered what had become of Curly. Would they ever see each other again. Probably not. Several seasons had passed since Uncle Walter brought Curly Dillingsworth to the Armstrong residence as a guest for Christmas dinner. It was not of the greatest significance, but Uncle Walter, the practical joker, while puffing on a pipe mumbled something droll with a straight face about how he happened to meet Dillingsworth. Vincent made a mental note to ask Uncle Walter to clear up that smoky detail.

Also out of curiosity he would ask Uncle Walter what Curly's proper first name is. Vincent had never heard it mentioned. Uncle Walter often jokingly called him "Curly." In amusement the young man replied that it was as good a nickname as any. Anyway, he should have been christened "Curly," so appropriately did the appelative delineate his hair. Curly's brownish locks, curled like the scroll on a violin's head, were in texture stiff and glossy as the hair of the bow.

Dillingsworth's features were in tune with his personality: Similar to the small bridge that raises the strings on a violin, the raised bony structure of his thin, short nose curved subtly. And the curves of his nostrils paralleled the curves in the fine S-shaped sound holes on the front of a violin. His eyes, solid resin-brown tones, were softened by a warm, winsome grin which was as captivating as a catchy tune. By measure a degree under six feet, two inches tall, he was a little taller than the largest member of the violin family (the double bass). Neither a Stradivarius nor a Guarnerius could be compared however to the design of a Dillingsworth, whose priceless twenty-year-old body was masterfully crafted.

Vincent delighted in listening to Curly talk. Born in Boston, accustomed to using the broad "a" and eliding the final "r" in words, his manner of speaking sounded noticeably different from San Franciscans' speech sounds. He explained to the Armstrongs that the way he pronounced words had historical origin in the speech of southern England where his ancestors came from.

Dillingsworth's delightful accent to an impressionable youngster seemed expressive of sophistication, something boys strive for too soon. On opportune occasions when conversing, Vincent affectedly broadened his "a's" and elided his "r's" in vain efforts to sound like a true Bostonian. This amused Dillingsworth no end. Feigning offense, he would shout in sport: "Put up your dukes you black-guard! I'll teach you to massacre the king's English."

Thus forewarned, the boy set himself, assuming the stance of a pugilist. After a playful round of fisticuffs, wherein the friendly fighters exchanged harmless blows, the challenger, to bolster his small friend's ego, conceded defeat. For Vincent's win Curly gave him a prize, a silver quarter which the young man tossed to the boy with a snap of finger and thumb. Vincent would catch the coin in mid-air as one snatches a fly buzzing by.

Scurrying off to the ice-cream parlor to buy his favorite treat, an Eskimo pie, Vincent thoughtfully returned with two. The second pie symbolized Curly's consolation prize. So strong was their attach-ment, the young man and the boy never appeared to be apart. It was sort of ridiculous: in looking for Vincent the tall one had to be found, and in looking for Curly the small one had to be found. Uncle Walter—leave it to that wit not to miss a butt—in jest dubbed the pair "Mutt and Jeff," after the comic-strip characters.

Social dancing was Curly Dillingsworth's preferred pastime. Whenever a club or a church or any organization held a dance, he was certain to attend; unless, of course, he happened to be ill. Married people sometimes brought their children with them to these dances. Using this fact as an argument, Mutt and Jeff persuaded Mrs. Armstrong to let her son Vincent go dancing with Curly.

Personable, well-mannered, looked upon as a beautiful dancer, Curly was an adored young man. At dances all the Aphrodites, their passions aroused, fell in love with Adonis, unlike the myth to no avail. Scoff if you wish, he was one masculine human who went to a dance to dance, not to seek companions for coition. His aloof yet polite indifference toward women as women illogically increased their desire for Dillingsworth. (Still more illogical was the tragedy that though normal virtually in every respect, he was undersexed.)

Unaware of his abnormality women at dances, goddesses of love and beauty, whose charms were irresistible, believed their powers would be effective on the young man if they could approach him without being obvious. Aware of the closeness between Curly and Vincent, they went out of their way to make a fuss over the boy.

In him the Aphrodites imagined they had an Eros to pierce Adonis' heart. To gain Curly's favor they would corner Vincent, place their alabaster arms on his shoulders, and dance the small boy around a hall with spicy steps, conspicuous to put it mildly. He—flattered and half-flustered or half-flattered and flustered—flounced along to the lively tempo of the orchestra as best a beginner could.

Thus it was that Vincent Armstrong was introduced to Terpsichore arrayed in one of her art forms—social dancing. By 'do or die' he learned to hold his own on a dance floor. In time by 'trial and error' he developed a style of sorts that to mediocre social dancers looked great.

"My, you look engrossed," remarked the girl sitting next to Vincent at the bar. "Your mind must be miles away. The party is getting a little noisy. Do you hear me?" To gain his attention she snapped her fingers under his nose. "Hey! a penny for your thoughts." With that cliché she woke him from his reverie of days long past.

Not in the mood to get into a drawn-out discussion, Vincent engaged in a bit of banter. "Sister, are you extravagant. My thoughts aren't worth that much. Aren't you rather loose with your money? What did you do, Martha, rob a bank."

She giggled and retorted: "No silly, I inherited a fortune. Let me see now. I wanted to ask you something. Fudge! I forgot. It's right on the tip of my tongue. But for the life of me, I can't remember what it was. I suppose you are going to tell me it must have been a lie. Oh, never mind..."

She chatted on and on trying to carry on a conversation. Vincent simply sat silent studying Martha. To his taste she was uninteresting and unappealing. He was biased, for he was comparing two different kinds of fruit—a green schoolgirl to a ripe schoolmistress. In Vincent's mind not only did Martha's constant talk seem dull but also her nates and breasts were as unappetizing as a hard Seckel pear. On the other hand, Roxanne's tempting talk together with her nates and breasts, the rotundity of succulent honeydew melons, stimulated his sexual appetite for forbidden fruit.

That night after Vincent left the party, and was at home snuggled in between the sheets on his bed, he saw reflections of Roxanne Davis' nakedness in a cheval glass. The mirror of his mind swung back and forth at different angles displaying all her forbidden fruit, which he hungered to taste. Sex-starved, he folded a puffy pillow in half; imagining both folds to be Roxanne's rotund breasts, he masturbated ravishingly.

Chapter 19

Unhappily the dreaded day had arrived in Public Speaking I. Vincent Armstrong's heart skipped a beat when Mr. Du Puy made a sudden entrance and accosted him: "Young man, the first part of your oral presentation is due today. Five hundred and four hours—that is twenty-one days, that is three weeks—have gone by since I asked you to speak on the subject of 'Human Equality, Fact or Fiction, in Relation to Individuals at Large, With Emphasis on America and Asia.'

"You can't complain you were not given ample time to prepare. If you have any notes, refer to them all you wish. However, I expect you to speak the entire period. And remember, the second part of the assignment is due tomorrow. That gives you an extra evening for review. Okay, let's get started," he ordered, sounding more like a casehardened army officer than a cultured schoolmaster.

As he had promised Vincent, the old man wrote a speech on the assigned topic. (The speech, extendible over two class periods, was a compilation of excerpts from his own diverse compositions.) Although Vincent had stayed up late nights memorizing the old man's material, he hoped Du Puy would forget about the punitive homework. Vincent's hopes were now shattered. He had no choice but to confront the dreadful situation head-on. Standing up, he squared his shoulders and strode to the lectern at the front of the classroom.

With such long strides did the boy approach the lectern (a dictionary stand), he was stunned suddenly to find himself at the front of the room facing his six classmates. Vincent's imagination went wild. Their heads were a short range of mountain tops. The room was mountainous, looming larger and larger the longer he looked. Vincent had a strange sensation of being a stray tot lost in the Grand Canyon, too choked up with fright to cry out for help.

Despair not. Stillness prevailing over the classroom came to his rescue. Terrified by the dead silence, he had a compulsion to yell at the top of his lungs. To quell his fears he felt the need to hear a reassuring voice (his own). He rallied his internal forces and spoke, daringly.

"In the preamble of the *Declaration of Independence* Thomas Jefferson, drafter of the American document, and his congressional colleagues unanimously declared—quote: 'We hold these Truths to be self-evident, that all Men are created equal, that they are endowed by their Creator with certain unalienable Rights, that among these are Life, Liberty, and the Pursuit of Happiness'—unquote. That all men are created equal is far from the truth. It is a misstatement, for it certainly is not in conformity with fact or reality."

The public-speaking teacher, who had slid into a tablet armchair at the rear of the room, and the six students, shocked at their classmate's sacrilegious statement, drew back in their seats: The man frowned sternly but said nothing. The girls snickered, the freckled boy sneered. By haughty looks and unintelligible utterances they expressed their displeasure with Vincent. (This scene brings to mind, depending on one's view, seraphs backing away in disdain from a fallen angel.)

Vincent's nerves were strained by the adverse reaction of his classmates. And the stern frown on Mr. Du Puy's face further increased the boy's tension. His body, which was bent over the dictionary stand, became taut, tightly drawn as an archer's bow.

In that he was very tense, Vincent closed his hands forming fists so firmly his knuckles turned white. Since backtracking was out of the question, he decided it would be easier to go on his course if he relaxed. Opening his hands to relieve the tautness in his fingers, he proceeded by way of an explanation (which the old man had prepared for him in anticipation it might be needed).

"Before you pass judgment upon what I have just said, grant me a fair hearing. Wait at least till I have finished my speech. Afterward should you find me wrong, I will stand corrected. Let us unemotionally and with open minds put to test this sacred self-evident truth. If it is in reality a truth, by definition a fact, there is not a thing to fear, because I won't be able to prove otherwise.

"Mind you, I am not taking issue with the principle that all men should be equal. In an ideal world they should be. Neither am I questioning the sincerity of the signers of the <u>Declaration of Independence</u>. They deserve their place in history among America's greatest statesmen. What I am saying is that no human being at any site on soil and sea has ever been created equal, was or is equal, or in the future will likely be equal to all others in every sense of the word.

"To begin with, we are not all born equal physically. Heredity, the genetic transmission of characteristics from parents to offspring, has no conception of equality. The science of genetics, a factor of heredity, informs us that physical variations in siblings passed on by both parents is the fortuitous, biologic and result of a definitely advantageous or disadvantageous combination of chromosomes. They are transmissible inborn qualities such as exceptional motor coordination or a tendency toward baldness.

"Undeniably certain viewpoints about heredity appear to be controversial. Nevertheless, realities are realities, and facts are facts. Some of us are born healthy. Others come into the world sickly. Some of us will grow up to be tall, some of us will be medium in height, some of us will be short. Some of us will be fat, some thin, others the right weight for their build. Right or wrong, not all will weigh the same no matter how well-balanced the scale, or their diet.

"Males and females are normally beyond comparison in physical strength. The muscle and bone structures of either sex have distinctive differences. None too few have congenital deformities. The hunchback of Notre Dame is not fiction for unfortunate individuals who happen to be born with his deformity. Only limited numbers of our population are physically capable of developing bodies as strong as the athletes of ancient Greece. Today as then, people possess bodily structures which vary in strength but, modern medicine notwithstanding, many are comparatively weak. The weakest of the weak...the weaklings, so to speak, do not fare well in society.

"Here are fashionable questions with obvious answers. Are all men equally handsome? Are all women matched in beauty? Matinee idols and Miss Americas are rare rubies. It is not uncommon for infants to be disfigured at birth. By what standards in adulthood will their looks be judged.

"All human beings—good-looking, so-so, or ugly—have different colored skin, hair, and eyes. Which color is in your opinion the most beautiful: just think about it. Also, humans have different odors, pleasant or unpleasant determined despite deodorants by noses big and small. Have not untold numbers of our species been treated as inferiors for centuries. In this century are they not living within the shameful shadow of inequality merely because of a difference in pigmentation.

"Approaching the physical question of equality in another light, we can educate a blind child to read Braille, and train a dog to guide him about. Lenses can be ground to accommodate the near- and far-sighted. Likewise we can teach a profoundly deaf child to speak and to read lips, and if he is only partially deaf fit him with a hearing aid. In addition, we can fashion for a disabled child an artificial arm or leg. But a seeing-eye dog, glasses, and an auditory device all put together can not compare to an organ of sight or of hearing. Neither is a...a pros—thet—ik device equal to a real limb."

Vincent breathed a sigh of relief that he had avoided a disastrous defeat in warding off the word 'prosthetic,' a terrible tongue twister as far as he was concerned. Many a dreary night when he was struggling to commit the speech to memory, he feared it would be his Waterloo at this particular place. Although a great number of uphill word battles were yet to be overcome, the lad now believed he stood a fighting chance of surviving further verbal encounters free of mishaps, at least noticeable ones.

"If from infancy to adulthood a physically normal being received a perfect diet, plenty of sleep, proper amounts of fresh air and sunshine, prescribed medical and dental care, and planned brawn-building exercises, his body should be strong and healthy, provided he isn't in the meantime incapacitated by a chronic disease or an accidental, crippling injury. Unfortunately disasters do befall millions upon millions of people in numerous ways.

"Supposing, though, they had no accidents and were reared under conditions as perfect as humanly possible for achievement of an ideal physique. We still couldn't make all people equal physically, even if one hundred per cent cooperation was had. The most we could hope to achieve—and by all means out to—is the development of a body to its highest potential. While it is an admirable goal, it does not end up in physical equality: for, like fingerprints, no two individuals' potentials are exactly the same."

At this point Vincent paused to run an index finger down a page of the typed copy of his prepared speech, actually an address, which he had earlier placed on the slanted surface of the dictionary stand. Upon locating the first line of the next paragraph he was ready to talk about, he thought what good luck it was that Mr. Du Puy had been the one who brought up the idea of Vincent's using notes.

The possibility the teacher would not permit him to refer to any written material, previously had worried Vincent. Slyly he cast his eyes downward viewing word by word the contents in the address. Straightway looking up, he rattled off the words to create the impression he was speaking extemporaneously (from few notes). Whenever he could, he continued the show as he read and spoke, and read and spoke.

"Secondly I propose to affirm that not all men are created equal mentally. From the beginning of recorded time, morons, imbeciles, and idiots have been born with each tick of the clock. A look at last year's statistics collected by prominent psychologists, reveals some pertinent numerical datum. In 1939 they found from two to three per cent of the American population were retarded:

"Although many in this classification were subnormal as the result of destruction of brain tissue by syphilis contracted from the mother, injury in the *uterus* at birth, childhood accidents, illnesses, extreme malnutrition, or an unbalanced supply of hormones produced by endocrine glands—many others were predisposed from the time of fertilization to feeble-mindedness."

With a tongue as thin as a reed Vincent's voice quavered when he uttered the word 'syphilis' and 'uterus,' words youngsters refrained from mentioning in polite circles of adults. His classmates' reactions to the unmentionable words were typical: The girls blushed, their cheeks aglow. The freckled boy grinned asininely from ear lobe to ear lobe. And his Public-speaking teacher raised a heavy eyebrow up into an amazingly high arch.

"So forth...excuse me...so far according to the findings of psychology, heredity determines the upper limits of one's intelligence. But one does not have to be a psychologist to discover a feeble-minded child could never become a genius, nor can a person rated superior in I.Q. be expected to become a genius. An Albert Einstein appears on the terrestrial globe almost as infrequently as a total solar eclipse appears over the North American continent.

"Psychological studies approximate our population falls into three general groups in mental ability: a small percentage below average, a large percentage average, the smallest percentage above average. There we have it in a pea pod. I see no point in straining the matter again, for it should be clear now. No man is born equal mentally to all other men, regardless which school of thought grades the levels of intelligence.

"However, an indispensable factor must not be ignored. Mental ability in and of itself without motivation is virtually valueless. Often individuals who are quite bright seem to accomplish nothing worthwhile. All environmental conditions being equal, their lack of accomplishment may be due to a deficiency of cortical activity, which psychologists say stimulates the use of one's intellect. Stating it another way, internal forces (commonly spoken of as 'drive') are vital elements in activating the brain to function at its maximum output.

"Seasons when Mother Nature is in a generous mood, she bestows an ample amount of drive upon individuals who are not too bright as well as upon others of her children. In fact, we often hear about a dull person accomplishing something worthwhile. Be that as it may, his intellectual feats never exceed the limitations nature has set for him.

"Psychologists observe in the growth of infants as their potentialities for perceiving, acting, and thinking develop, that they exhibit a natural impulse to use these capacities. In terms of psychology the foregoing is the primary law of inherent motivation, an inclination among children to apply aptitudes, according to their age and ability.

"Since the majority of individuals' machinery of maturation is equipped with a self-starter, psychologically designated as motivation or drive, we are with few exceptions in possession of a valuable indigenous property. Native drives, by the way, are as varied as auto parts. To turn on a motor, a driver must step on the starter. Can a machine run otherwise, of course not. In order to set intellect into motion, one must exercise some push.

"In addition, a mind cannot work properly if that all important inward efficacy of I.Q. is low grade. The higher the octane number of gasoline pumped into its cylinders the better an engine operates. Furthermore, if the weight of several cars is constant, the one having the most horse power will travel at the fastest rate of speed and is apt to cross the finish line ahead of all others. So it is with people. A vigorous body is a great advantage in racing toward a goal requiring the exertion of gray matter.

"Speaking of a vigorous body, a thought just occurred to me. I am sure you realize only in fiction does one hear of a strong or strengthless race. Within all races many a Hercules and Zephyrus are born. More about that later. Right now we are concerned with discussing mentality.

"Sheer ignorance has fostered the prejudiced thinking that particular races, especially American Negroes, are a dull lot. Nothing could be further from the truth. Their poor showing academically as a race was due largely to the fact that in the past they were not given the same opportunities to learn as Caucasians were. An educated black man equal in innate ability to an uneducated white man would outpoint him in intelligence tests which, for the most part, were based upon acquired knowledge. Dr. Otto Klineberg, instructor at Columbia University found in actual mental testing Northern blacks surpassed Southern whites.

"They needn't take this to heart, for in the present year 1940, as in past years, educational expenditures per capita is extremely low in the South. To shortsighted persons who from afar are unable to recognize blacks' high intelligence, I show the following snapshots of but a few brilliant Americans of Negro ancestry: George Washington Carver, educator and scientist; Ernest Everett Just, a pioneer and writer in biology; Carter G. Woodson, author of Negro history and education; and Charles Clinton Spaulding, financial genius and insurance magnate.

"Black or white, special talents may be manifested in persons falling into subclassifications of intelligence. In such a subclass is the idiot savant, a mentally retarded individual—not an idiot, as the term implies, but an imbecile or a moron—who, regardless of his abnormality, has a specialized ability that caps his determinable status of mentality. There are records of no less than four subjects in this category authenticated by psychiatrists: one was a top speller, one was an adept drummer, one could do delicate embroidery, one could recite the dates all American presidents held office.

"Mark well that these god-given gifts (or from whomever) are mechanically performed and steered one way unmindful of a specific destination. Because of the idiot savant's defective mentality, what motivates him in the scheme of things to do one thing better than anybody else, is unclear. The assumption is he gets some sort of satisfaction from succeeding in at least one thing. Monetary gain and social status have been proven meaningless to him. Since the development of his talent is usually accidental, the idiot savant doesn't drive himself very hard to become proficient in his specialty.

"At the other end of life's highway, we find a mental giant, Albert Schweitzer: doctor of medicine, doctor of philosophy, doctor of music. Scientists acknowledge him to be a distinguished experimental physician in the realm of tropical medicine. As a philosopher he takes exception to occidental suppositions as has no other sage since Spengler. Schweitzer compiled the deepest and most inclusive biography ever written about Johann Sebastian Bach, master composer.

"Albert Schweitzer is praised by musicians as one of the world's foremost organists. He is an authority on the structure as well as the construction of the organ. His accomplishments could be discussed forever. I'd better stop before I go too far afield. In the field of performing arts while high intelligence is always advantageous, individuals of low intelligence sometimes are well-endowed with talent.

"However, among the talented inequality also reigns. Examples are classic: The genius of a Charlie Chaplin, an intellectual entertainer, cannot be compared to a common circus clown, nor can the talent of an Anna Pavlowa, ballerina supreme, be compared to that of a chorine. Some might argue the comedian and the ballet dancer couldn't have achieved greatness if they had not slaved and sweated to perfect themselves in their respective professions.

"Granted. Still, how can any argumentation be reconciled with the grim reality that hundreds of aspiring comics and dancers—many highly intelligent—have worked like pack mules for years to reach the heights of stardom. Yet, because of mediocrity, they fell by the wayside never to be seen or heard of.

"Next to mull over a matter that muddles the minds of men: Personality—the personal or individual quality which causes one person to be different or act differently from another. A baby two weeks old has at the outset little, if any, visible personality; for it is a pattern of collective character...behavioral, temperamental, emotional, and mental traits of an individual.

"Inborn traits of people's personality patterns are as numerous as postage stamps, whose designs and colors appeal to some and not to others in a variety of ways. Dr. Gordon W. Allport of Harvard University and his collaborator, Dr. Henry S. Odbert of Dartmouth College, plowed through 400,000 words in Webster's *New International Dictionary*. They counted those words distinguishing the behavior of one human being from that of another. At the completion of their research they had a list of 17,953 terms describing characteristics of personality, or four point five per cent of the sum total of words in the entire dictionary analyzed.

"Of the thousands of words describing mankind's characteristics, 'magnetism' is rarely applicable. Few individuals are by fate ordained to be magnetic personalities. I can see by the expressions on your faces, you scoff at that statement as an exaggeration. It is understandable. After all, isn't the world inhabited by billions of people. Yes, there are people by the billions and, consequently, there are many different temperaments and dispositions. Yet only a hamlet full of men and women have been foreordained with attractive attributes bestowed on mythological deities.

"In spite of the array of talented actresses both here and abroad, Greta Garbo, rumored to be a recluse, magnetized the public into acclaiming her the most alluring female personality of the silver screen. In spite of the fact that contradictory politicians are more plentiful than sea lions on Seal Rocks, one man, a victim of polio, President Franklin Delano Roosevelt possesses a personality so magnetically powerful he has quieted the grumblings of a huge, hungry nation discontented because of the worst economic depression Americans have experienced in recent times.

"In positively identifying human disparity in a societal line-up, one must recognize that from cradle to coffin not all men are socio-economically equal. Before digging into the entrails of this unpleasant matter, I need to call your attention to a false bent which should be straightened out if we carefully separate fact from fiction. Simply because in a father's eyes his child is on a par socially with all others (rich or poor), doesn't mean the man's view realistically reflects the standards of society. A qualifying comment is no doubt in order.

"Every father cannot necessarily be said to have fallen prey to such wishful thinking, especially if he has ever looked into an uncracked mirror and asked himself what his socio-economic standing in the community is. Now that that heavy question has been lifted from my back, I feel unburdened and am able to proceed more easily. Since my statement is too big a chunk to consume in the time allotted, I shall endeavor to cut away the fat from the lean meat, masticate the social portion, and save a choice economic piece to chew on afterward.

"Page after page in history books reveal sickening, gory evidence from the earliest stages of civilization innocents looked down upon as society's dregs have been born of parentage cruelly branded worthless rabble. At the present stage of World's play, with civilized compassion, they are characterized 'the lower class,' which is a synonym for 'poor people.' Most people feel more secure, status-wise at least, if they believe they belong in 'the middle class,' a term nevertheless difficult to define. There is little difficulty in defining 'the upper class.' It is synonymous with 'well-to-do persons.' Of course, to be technical we should include two other terms: 'upper-upper class' and 'lower-lower class.'

"It is significant that social injustice perpetrated against humanity isn't uniquely a crime committed by any specific race. The Caucasoids, whites and light browns; the Negroids, dark browns and blacks; the Mongoloids, yellows and reds—all colors of the spectrum, all share the guilt of mistreating and regarding contemptuously not only people of skin coloring dissimilar to theirs, but also, glaringly, brother beings of their own complexion.

"Don't get the wrong impression, the classifications of race I've referred to are generalized and by no means the only ones. Joseph Deniker, a French anthropologist, from his distinguishing peoples' hair, shape of their heads and noses, together with their statures as well as hues of skin, came to the conclusion there are six grand divisions subdivided into twenty-nine separate races. Using color as a criterion, Carl Vin Linné (latinized *Linnaeus*), Swedish botanist, distinguished, by skin pigmentation, merely four separate races.

"The term 'race' itself defies interpretation, and invites disputes. 'Race' is ambiguous in meaning to anthropologists who are waging a cold war over the right definition of the term. Efforts to divide men into clear-cut races by anatomic structures have failed miserably and resulted in nothing but confusion. For instance, the Irish popularly are believed to be taller than the Japanese. However, on a trip to Japan and Ireland we would find a sizable number of Irishmen comparatively shorter than Japanese men. We don't need to travel very far to see much variance in height is found among all nationalities.

"Also we ought to see that color categories used to identify groups of people connected by descent or origin, serve simply as an expedient means of communication, not as an exact criterion. Otherwise our pale faces would turn red if we were asked how it is that some Caucasoids are darker than some Negroids. We would be spared this embarrassment were we familiar with the function of our integumentary system.

"From biochemistry we learn that the coloring of a person's integument, the external covering of the body, depends on the quantity of two chemicals in the skin: melanin, which darkens it, and carotene, which causes it to appear yellowish. Basically the skin consists of an outer layer, the epidermis, and an inner layer, the corium. Each of us has a certain amount of melanin and carotene in the inner layer. When these two pigments are combined with pinkish tones reflected from blood vessels in the corium below the epidermis, all the sundry shades under the sun are created on the countenances of earthly beings.

"Advancing a step further toward a still more analytic approach, we learn the blood structure of all humans is alike. Scientific findings show that our blood falls within four groups: A, B, AB, and O. In a family of four, according to Mendelian Law (formulated by Gregor Mendel theorist of genetics) all the members might belong to the same group. Or father and son might both be in group A, and mother and daughter in group B.

"As additional examples, a Chinese amah's blood could be in the same group as that of the queen of England. And the blood of an alabaster governor from one of Uncle Sam's southern states could very well be in a group identical to an ebony African native's.

"Wrapped in wrinkled white material, kluxers—members of a secret southern society, the Ku Klux Klan—spin out of whole cloth a strange story. Kluxers fabricate that Negroids' descendants were unlike those of *Homo sapiens*: 'human beings,' which include all existing races. Woven into kluxers' fabrication is an image of blacks with primitive traits of anthropoids ('manlike apes'). Scientific studies show the kluxers' imagery is distorted. Anthropologists concur that Mankind is not a descendant of any contemporary species of Anthropoid, but that both have descendants in common.

"Anthropology is in accord, too, that though none of the races is closer to apes than the others, Caucasoids rank first, Mongoloids second, and Negroids third in having traits similar to the simian animals. To wit, apes have brow ridges; so do Caucasoids; the brows of Mongoloids and Negroids are smooth. They have hairless bodies, yet those of apes and Caucasoids are hairy. In final contrast, Negroids have heads of woolly, black hair and Mongoloids have straight, black hair; Caucasoids' and apes' hair is curly and brown."

You can well imagine the boys and girls in Mr. Du Puy's public-speaking class were aghast when Vincent informed them that they—white Caucasians—of all people! possessed characteristics resembling primordial apes: gorillas, orang-utans, gibbons, chimpanzees, and other large tailless monkeys. Mouths open wide enough to admit a banana (whole), the students, doing their best not to be obvious, eyed one another to see if their classmate's statements were indeed factual.

"While all 'human beings' are *Homo sapiens*, none is an Adam or an Eve: that is, they are not thoroughbred—bred of pure stock, purebred, unmixed. There was interbreeding between races before the birth of Christ. As late as the fourth century A.D., barbaric, low cultured Huns, Magyars, and Avars from East Asia invaded eastern and central Europe. Squat, muscular figures with flat faces, the Huns (members of a nomadic Asian people) ravaged the land and raped the women. The Magyars (members of the principal ethnic group of Hungary) clashed in fierce fighting with European inhabitants; women were taken as the spoils of war. The Avars (members of a people originating in Asia) occupied Pannonia as well as other parts of eastern and central Europe, where they had their way with women. The Avars dominated the populations before their decline in the ninth century.

"And before the decline and fall of the Roman Empire, black slaves interbred with divers populations under the domination of Rome. From the history of Man's carnal knowledge we learn that only in the Garden of Eden could a pure race be conceived...if a golden apple was not forbidden fruit.

"Still some men crawl with the serpent. Screaming with madness, Adolf Hitler Schicklgruber, master of muck, made guttural utterances about race purity—all the while soiling it. In his Nürnberg racial laws he dictatorially distinguished the Germans as Aryans (pure and superior) as opposed to non-Aryans (impure and inferior). One of Adolf's nazi superminds must have been too terrified to tell <u>der fuhrer</u> that the term 'Aryan' was assumed by etymologists to be the prehistoric language from which Indo-European languages were derived.

"To assume the term 'Aryan' applies to descendants of an unadulterated race of prehistoric persons is more madman's muck. But this is not a discourse on etymology, so coming back to inequality . . ."

Almost too good to be true, the bell rang ending the session in the public-speaking class. O bliss, the first part of Vincent's ordeal was over. That night, exhausted from his trying experience, the conscripted orator slept soundly. A faint smile parted his lips. He was having a timely dream in which stars were revolving around his body. Vincent projected reality into his dreaming, as before retiring he thanked his lucky stars he escaped being bombarded with embarrassing questions by Mr. Du Puy, who had to leave the classroom right at the close of the period.

"Vince...Vincent Armstrong, where are you?" asked Bert Craig. "You've been staring out into space long enough to go to the moon and back. Come down to earth. You can't dance on the moon."

"In response Vincent gave him a friendly shove. "Okay, my mind was in orbit. I'm returning to National Dance Studios."

"Hurry. You are in for some rough weather. Take it slow and easy. I have you in sight. You're exactly on course. Look! Vince is landing, he's landing. He is here!" Bert exclaimed as he nudged his fiancée Alice Scott.

She laughed. "Don't pay attention to him, Vincent. My little sweetie is being funny as usual."

"I know," Vincent replied. "Bert is always auditioning for a comedy show."

Supervisor Ralph Normand arriving on the scene just then, dialogue among the three was cut short. Chit-chat among others in the studio stopped, too. As soon as they were settled in their seats, Normand addressed the fresh crop of dancing teachers.

"No matter how many steps you learn. No matter how much technique we teach you. If you don't practice, you will never perfect your dancing. The head-high mirrors on the walls of the ballroom downstairs are decorative. That, however, is not the main reason for the mirrors. Mainly they were installed for teachers to practice in front of. Watching yourself perform from the tips of your toes to the top of your head, is an excellent way to master dance figures and shape your style. An attractive appearance on a dance floor is worth working for.

"Those of you who promise to come to the studio early in the mornings to practice, raise your hands." (Not a hand was left unraised.) "Great! I shall now reward you with another historical presentation on the dance."

Chapter 20

A HISTORY OF THE CLASSIC BALLROOM DANCES

American Dances

II-B. The Jitterbug (to foster agility and self-expression)

Legmen's claims, seemingly substantiated, as to a definite date when the term 'jitterbug' was applied to dancing or dancers, have turned out to be nothing more than conjectures. For that matter, a hodgepodge of guesswork also seems to surround the source of the term. To separate fictional from factual ingredients—as much as obtainable information permits—let us temporarily skip the first and less jumbled part, 'jitter,' and analyze the last syllable, 'bug,' which etymologists tell us is of unknown origin, unless we accept a relationship between the Welsh *bwg*, meaning 'ghost,' and the use of the word 'bug' as in 'bugbear' or 'bugaboo.' But we are not ghost hunting.

[The supervisor chuckled. At that moment a more humorous thought hatched in his mind. He could not resist expressing it. In his eagerness he used the wrong words.]

If we were to catch some scary bugaboos . . . Don't laugh! I am referring to insects, not to shades of persons. I meant to say if we were to hatch some bugs, we would see they were notched or cut in the middle. In point of fact, 'insect,' the technical term for 'bug,' is derived from the Latin *insecare*, 'to cut into.' Just because bugs infest rugs, do not get a nutty notion that is how the expression 'cut a rug' originated. I suggest you review your notes on the history of the fox trot where the origin of that expression was discussed.

In popular cant (that is, nonstandard language), a bug is an enthusiast, a person who is carried away by his feelings: one kind is a devotee of swing music; the devotee is impelled by the rhythm to abandoned, athletic dancing expressive of vigorous youth. Moreover, usage has established another meaning of bug—a 'fanatic' or 'maniac.' We use such expressions as "he has a bug in his head" or "he is bugs." Well, we are getting warmer. Whenever an enthusiastic jitterbug on the dance floor is so lost in the mood of the music that he is beyond himself, the hepcats exclaim:

"Bounce me, brother, with a solid four! Beat me, daddy, eight to the bar! You're real gone, man! Break it down! Go, go, go!" Now do you hear how the newly hatched larva of the second half of jitter-'bug' underwent metamorphosis.

In order to ferret out the root of 'jitter' (U.S.A. slang: to talk and act in an extremely nervous manner), we shift to spoonerisms, which were the rage in Grandfather's generation. Spoonerisms are an unintentional transposition of sounds, usually the initial sounds of two or more words, typical examples, a "blushing crow" for a "crushing blow" and "our queer old dean" for "our dear old queen." They were named after an Englishman noted for such slips, William A. Spooner, warden of New College, Oxford. He was born in 1844 and died in 1930.

On encountering a person who had consumed an excessive amount of gin and bitters and was weaving from foot to foot, grandfather referred to the drunk by transposing initial letters of words, into a lingo somewhat similar to pig Latin. Grandfather spoke thus, "He's been and got the"...I'll spell it..."g-t-t-e-r-s"...pronounced jitters. Here we have the possible source of the first half of 'jitter'-bug.

Hence, if 'jitter' is indicative of a person having a fit of nervousness while spasmodically turning and twisting, and if a bug, as we have determined, is a fanaticized or frenzied dance enthusiast, it is conceivable that, at the gate of the 1930s, oldsters watching youngsters get heated up dancing to hot music, coldly showered the latter with the syllables 'jitterbug.' Whether the term was applied in the beginning to the dancer and next to the dance, or vice versa, is as much of an enigma as is the hackneyed "Which came first, the chicken or the egg?"

Although controversy centers around the circumstances leading to the creation of the dance, indisputable is the Afro-American's role as a contributor of jitterbugging to red-white-and-blue culture. Before the Civil War (1861-1865) and subsequent to his emancipation

(?), wherever he was at liberty to do so, the Negro strutted, stamped, skipped, and shuffled to some sort of syncopation played on string instruments, of the type indicated in the history of the fox trot.

Unfortunately his activities too often were restricted to vicinities of unsavory repute. The strut, the stamp, the skip, the shuffle—which are at present the basis for figures in the jitterbug—were performed by the Negro within the confines of the jook, a house of vice.

["Jook is a derivation from a regional form of language spoken by the Bambara tribe in Africa. Here is the way jook is spelled by Africans." The supervisor stepped up to his blackboard and wrote the word dzugu. One of the dancing teachers in the group remarked she failed to see how the word 'jook' could have been derived from the African word. Ralph Normand explained jook was an Americanized pronunciation of dzugu—the Bambara's word for 'wicked.']

Jook houses abounded in the segregated South. As a consequence, the Negro's dance movements were performed dissolutely. Nonetheless, they are artful in character and achieved a legitimate place on the stage and in society.

Jitterbugging is said to be a variety of an Australian native dance Corroboree. This contention throws branches across the trail walked by foreloopers of the Jitterbug. To clear the way, they were tribal dances with African ancestral features. One of the most prominent is the Charleston that bears a strong resemblance to an Obolo dance of the Ibo tribe in West Africa.

Contrary to popular belief the Charleston was named after a seaport in South Carolina, not after the city of Charleston in West Virginia. To entertain passengers on steamers docked along the Carolina Coast, black dockworkers performed their native dances intermingled with the Charleston. Eventually the dance set sail from Beaufort Island docks, off the coast of North Carolina. Voyaging to the mainland, the Charleston migrated northward in the nineteen hundreds.

It was in the twenties, the Jazz Age, that the black Charleston was to cross the color line into the white world. At the outset of the century jazz had infiltrated America's two major cities, Chicago and New York. Voices from the civic council were raised in censorship, from the clergy in condemnation, from the composer in contempt. Nonconformist jazz was blamed for the evils of the country, just as misnamed juvenile delinquents are blamed today.

Nevertheless, Americans—at least on a minor issue—were not

deceived. Jazz was the people's music, created by fellow Americans who had hurdled a barrier of race prejudice and, despite their lack of formal education, by sheer ingenuity delivered a musical message of creative freedom. Seeking escape from the stifling routine of life within the confinement of Civilization's bastille, humanity eagerly bent an ear to listen to jazz music, and freely bent a knee to dance in jazz motion.

By the time the Charleston arrived in New York its African features were almost unrecognizable, since previously defaced the dance had undergone plastic surgery. Introduced in Irving C. Miller's production *Liza*, the Charleston held little attraction for the public. However, in Harlem (the main Manhattan Negro quarter) children seeing familiar family features in the Charleston from the first had found the dance attractive.

It so happened Lida Webb, a dance director and arranger, one day on her way home caught sight of her ten-year-old niece charlestoning in the street with other children. Visualizing professional possibilities from the way they performed the Charleston, Lida made mental notes of their movements.

Lida Webb was the dancing mistress of *Runnin' Wild*, a colored musical comedy under production by George White. He asked her to arrange a dance number for it. Recalling the eye-catching way the children of Harlem did the Charleston movements, she arranged them into a number suitable for sixteen chorus girls and three boys. Lida's new routine was introduced in the Negro revue when it opened on 62nd Street at the Colonial Theater October 29, 1923.

While attending a theater party, Bee Jackson, an ambitious stage dancer, saw Miss Webb's interpretation of the Charleston and instantly fell in love with the dance. With coyness Bee induced Lida to teach it to her. In February 1924 at the Silver Slipper (a New York night club) she performed her own version of the dance to "The Original Charleston," the black pianist James P. Johnson's same successful score that had been used in *Runnin' Wild*. Miss Jackson thus was the first white girl professionally to present the Charleston to the city.

New Yorkers went wild over Bee's stinging performance. Copy cats charlestoned with abandonment at nightspots in alleys, in pubs, in public places, in private—wherever the Charleston was played. Like the Siamese twins the music and the dance were inseparable. Dancers of all ages, professional and nonprofessional, were driven to distraction by the racy rhythm, which along with the timing was the same as in the fox trot except the accent, emphasized out of the ordinary, created a strange syncopated sound.

["In case you have forgotten, syncopation denotes a temporary dislodgment of the usual accent or beat of musical composition. Simply stated syncopation is a shift of accent that occurs in a measure when a usually weak beat receives a strong stress. For a fuller explanation look again at your notes on syncopation in the history of the fox trot."]

People's ears were attuned to four-four, fox-trot time in which the accent occurred on the first and third beats of a measure. In the Charleston the accent occurred on the first beat, too, but an eighth before the third beat. That little jazzy eighth offbeat sparked the souls of dancers. Before long countless burning feet in the nation were stepping hotly to the Charleston.

Inevitably hot passion for the Charleston cooled, and lost favor with social dancers. Still as recently as 1949, when danced in Broadway's highly successful musical comedy *Gentlemen Prefer Blondes*, the Charleston staged a temporary comeback. The play, based on a novel by Anita Loos, portrays a gold digger who facetiously epitomizes a section of society in the Roaring Twenties.

Revival of interest in the Charleston was further demonstrated that year at Princeton University. Students held a Charleston contest instead of their annual Prince Tiger dance. Participants were attired in styles antedating the repeal of Prohibition. Each female wore an appropriate flapper's sack dress (sans waistline). And her male escort donned an enveloping raccoon coat.

Of course, the Charleston is danced quite differently at a social affair than in a theatre where fast forward and backward kicking steps are tapped on toes and heels. Foot steps such as 'wing' and 'lift' and such hand motions as 'cross over' from the stage version of the Charleston were modified and merged often with figures in the fox trot. These three terms, truly traditional or theatrical, perhaps will be comprehensible if I give a rudimentary description of the Charleston.

Dancers commence by assuming first position: heels together, toes out forty-five degrees. The steps are executed snappily but smoothly on the balls of the feet. The man as usual starts with his left foot. (The woman's footwork parallels the man's, except in the 'lifts' she uses the opposite foot from his. They perform side by side with the woman on the right side of the man.)

The movements in four counts to the measure are continuous—

nonstop. For variety, between repetitious movements, the hands are placed on the knees and 'crossed over' alternating from knee to knee as the knees swing inward and outward a number of times. In starting,

> <u>Count one</u>: Twist ('wing') the heels outward so that the feet are spread apart (pigeon-toed), simultaneously raise ('lift') the left foot off the floor; the lifting action brings the bent left knee close to the right knee.

> <u>Count two</u>: Instantaneously resume first position...heels together, toes pointing outward.

> <u>Count three</u>: Twist ('wing') the heels outward so that the feet are spread apart (pigeon-toed), simultaneously raise ('lift') the right foot off the floor; the lifting action brings the bent right knee close to the left knee.

> <u>Count four</u>: Instantaneously resume first position... heels together, toes pointing outward.

The movements from which 'wing' and 'lift' have sprung also are found in preparatory tap-dancing exercises intended to give strength along with flexibility to ankles and knees. However, to assume the 'wing' and 'lift' I described, closely resembles the original steps would be a gross error indeed. I applied the term 'crossover' to hand motions only as a matter of convenience to describe a style of charlestoning.

Actually the Crossover was a traditional step by which a dancer crossed one foot in front of or in back of the other in a variety of ways. In principle the Charleston of the twenties was more or less a series of variations of four-count basic movements. In practice the dance was combined with other movements. The Charleston Walk, for example, was a combination of the walking step in the fox trot and the theatrical 'wing' and 'lift.'

As I stated before, the dance and the music were inseparable, bonded by note and by step. Toning down one tones down the other. Tones can be harsh, tones can be soft. Let us listen:

On February 12, 1924, jazz magnate Paul Whiteman premiered George Gershwin's "Rhapsody in Blue" in New York at the Aeolian Hall, where was conducted <u>An Experiment in Modern Music</u>. To elevate jazz to concert level—and at the same time to sell symphonic syncopation, so to speak—proved to be Whiteman's primary purpose. The occasion symbolized the summit of a schism in Jazzland that had started to split a decade ago.

Back in 1914 the trend was for musicians to play jazz loud. A popular product of the period was clarinetist, Ted Lewis. His dance band consisted of a clarinet, cornet, trombone, piano, and drums. While the brass instruments blared and blasted away, Lewis, the leader, strutted across a bandstand showman-like and blew sharp, shrill sounds from the mouthpiece of his clarinet. Down on the dance floor couples stepped lively to Lewis's jazz music.

On another bandstand, Art Hickman, who gained distinction as a versatile orchestra leader at the St. Francis Hotel in San Francisco, approached jazz in a different direction from Lewis. Well-equipped with reed, brass, rhythmic arrangements for jazz ensembles, Hickman had organized a combo consisting of two saxophones, a cornet, trombone, violin, banjo, piano, and drums. Utilization of the mellow-toned saxophone in jazz bands was a rarity in those days.

Feeling that he could retain the effects of jazz yet enhance it musically, at rehearsals Hickman devised quiet, harshless arrangements whenever tender treatment was appropriate for dance numbers. Thus was formed a schismatic body of musicians who, during an evening's engagement, entertained couples by playing jazz softly and soothingly. In consequence, an unusual caliber of music arose to command the attention of not only dancers but listeners as well.

Contemporary jazzist speak of the music Hickman played as "sweet," and the music Lewis played as "hot." The latter is an improvisatory art, sometimes spontaneous, whereas the former is predeterminative, that is, arranged and rehearsed. It is beyond coincidence near resemblances of both kinds of jazz are found within the rituals of Negro religious music (or holy dance): Hot jazz is not too far distant from body-swaying, hand-clapping impulsive shouts vocalized by a colored Southern congregation. Sweet jazz comes close to prepared arrangements of Negro spirituals sung by a trained choir or concert artist.

Like Art Hickman, Paul Whiteman advocated sweet jazz. Besides being a magnate of the music, he was an ambassador extraordinary in Jazzland. He presented jazz in a comprehensible form on paper, hitherto unscored by others. A large man with a rotund body, he made an impressive figure when he wielded a baton on a podium. The sweet jazz his orchestra played was suitable for sentimental fox-trot dancers and was acceptable to conservative listeners. As a result, intricacies in the techniques of arranging jazz music and increases in the dimensions of the dance orchestra expanded significantly.

In 1926, however, there was resistance to expansion of orchestras or bands. Gifted instrumentalists inspired by Bix Beiderbecke (cornet master with a superb tone and smooth style of extemporization) developed an individualized form of jazz which called for smaller instrumental combos and greater liberty of impromptu inventiveness. Their freedom to play unrestrained, as never before, was enjoyable for appreciative listeners, but was frustrating for dancers accustomed to adhering to fixed fox-trot figures in step with musical arrangements.

In the interim big black bands—led by Duke Ellington, Louis Armstrong, Fletcher Henderson, and other exceptional musicians—were sending a masterful message about the enjoyment to be derived from authentic Negro music. At the same time, commercialization of the phonograph was selling hot jazz door to door. Heretofore it had been carried to the parlor of the piano-playing public in the lifeless form of sheet music. With recordings bringing live jazz to Mr. and Mrs. Richard Roe in their home, appreciation of popular music, sweet as well as hot, greatly increased.

Soon a strange, suggestive dance, the black bottom, stepped into the shoes of the Charleston. People love sex, without which populations would perish. Thus despite the immodest nature of the dance, it immediately won approval in many circles when its wicked wiggling and bottom-banging antics were performed by Ann Pennington, a Broadway hoofer, in George White's *Scandals* of 1926 at the Apollo Theatre.

In its rude beginnings the black bottom was a vigorous dance with sexual overtones. The name was dug up below the muddy banks of the Mississippi River. At the outset of the nineteen hundreds in the black-bottom lands of the lower Mississippi Valley, native-born Negroes performed the black bottom as a solo dance. The dancers, shaking their shoulders and twisting their torsos vigorously, beat time slapping knees, thighs—and bottoms.

Picked up by troupers performing with minstrel shows that traveled through towns of the Magnolia State, the black bottom eventually was brought to northern cities where it appeared in vaudeville. On the stage the black bottom became a clog dance with shuffling and stamping steps spiced with saucy knee and hip actions.

Similar to the Charleston, like other dances that were too rugged or risqué in their preliminary phases, the black bottom underwent a purging process. Cleared of primitive impurities, the dance was palatable to the prim-and-proper public. In his *Scandals* of 1926, George White had presented a version of the black bottom which led to versions appropriate for social dancers to do in a ballroom or at a party. Fundamentally the purged black bottom consisted of three movements: stamping, swaying, and shuffling.

[Not wishing to leave any loose ends, Ralph Normand decided to delve deeper into the black bottom. He explained to the group: "There isn't time to go into great detail; however, as teachers of dancing you should know something more about the movements. They were danced to musical measures in four-four time—two slows (four beats) and four quicks (four beats).

"Specifically stated in dance terms, two slow steps and two quick half-steps (equal to a beat) plus two quick steps and a pause on the fourth beat. As you have learned, a quick step is equal to one beat; a slow step is equal to two beats.

"Here I'll put a skeletal description of the three movements on the blackboard. To touch upon the bare essentials, the fleshly form of the black bottom is stripped away." The supervisor spoke as he wrote:

"1. Stamping Steps...alternating from foot to foot, the heels were raised, knees bent, and stamped slowly, then quickly.

2. Swaying Steps...the knees were kept together and swayed extremely from side to side as the shoulders tilted in the direction of the knees, left to left, right to right, or vice versa.

3. Shuffling Steps...as the feet were dragged forward, the body leaned backward, and as the feet were dragged backward, the body leaned forward."]

In 1927 the year after the black bottom appeared on the horizon—following Charles Lindbergh's sensational, solo transoceanic flight (May 20-21) from New York to Paris—some nimble-footed colored couples, heated by an evening of hot jazz, energetically improvised knee-bending steps as they moved from corner to corner across the dance floor of the Savoy Ballroom in Harlem. In the stag line, with lifted eyebrows, George (Shorty) Snowden, a champion Negro dancer famous for his fast footwork, stood observing the couples drenched in perspiration.

The FEAT of the daring American aviator who had hopped in his airplane The Spirit of St. Louis nonstop over the Atlantic Ocean, fresh in Shorty's mind, he exclaimed in awe: "Look at them kids hoppin' over there! I guess they're doin' the Lindy Hop." With reverence Shorty administered the sacrament of baptism to the dance.

However, it was not new. It was the rebirth of an old southern dance the Texas Tommy, similar to the one that Irene and Vernon Castle had borrowed from the entertainer Blossom Seeley, whom I referred to in the history of the fox trot. She had acquired the Texas Tommy while she was in San Francisco where in 1910 the Texas Tommy was a dance craze at Lew Purcell's a black cabaret catering to white customers on the Barbary Coast.

[Concerned he would tire the teachers, the supervisor lightened his lecture. "Factually Hop was a misnomer used in conjunction with the Lindy by Shorty Snowden. The colloquial definition of the verb hop is 'to dance': and its slang meaning is, loosely, 'to go,' as 'to hop to it.' He undoubtedly meant either one or both of these definitions.

"The fact remains that the literal meaning of hop is 'to move by a quick, springy leap or by successive leaps,' as do birds, toads, grasshoppers, and kangaroos...not to slight fleas. The word also means 'to spring' or 'jump on one foot.' But the couples at the Savoy Ballroom were not springing, leaping, or jumping on one foot. What they were doing were basic movements of the Lindy Hop and the Texas Tommy.

"The Lindy Hop's basic movement was a two- or box step in which a couple achieved emphasis by bending their knees after a step, thus accenting the offbeat of the music; that is syncopation, pure and simple. The Texas Tommy's basic movement was a kick plus a triple hop from foot to foot. Common to both dances was the breakaway, which allowed a couple to separate and, in shine position, improvise steps freely to dance music, syncopated or not."]

A colored choreographer, a concert dancer, a credit to our country, internationally acclaimed Katherine Dunham maintains that the Lindy Hop performed at the Savoy Ballroom was a secularized form of ancient dance sacred in Africa. Nevertheless, she is not of the opinion the Lindy Hop was conceived in the United States. Specializing in the origins of Negro dance and music of the West Indies, she observed on field trips to the islands the natives performing in their ritual dances movements and rhythms characteristic of the Lindy Hop, which were transported to Jamaica by African slaves in the sixteenth century.

As did its black forerunners, during the maelstrom of the Jazz Age, the Lindy Hop floundered in darkness, for approximately five years...after which the dance emerged from obscurity. In the thirties the shag, a dance that helped the Lindy Hop regain footing, was in a state of ascension. Jazz men, particularly the New Orleans Feetwarmers, had a hand in the ascent of the shag while they played at the Savoy Ballroom, stamping ground of the Lindy Hop.

The New Orleans Feetwarmers' band was under the leadership of Sidney Bechet, a great soprano saxophonist. A gifted trumpeter Tommy Ladnier was also a member of the band. On September 15, 1932, the New Orleans Feetwarmers cut "Shag," a record rated by critics as a classic. In the record Bechet and Ladnier coordinated style and tremolo so effectively the resultant strongly pronounced rhythm of their priceless disk was instrumental in accelerating the popularity of shagging.

Characteristic of the shag were springy, hopping steps...repetitious step-hops, short and close to the floor. A peculiarity of shagging was striking a pose similar to the Statue of Liberty: in closed position as a couple shagged, with his left hand the man held the woman's right hand high above their heads. Their bodies remained erect and motionless.

Tilting their upright bodies, like leaning coupled statues, in unison to four-four rhythm they also did dips, in different directions. The woman's shag steps were the same as the man's except she started with the opposite foot, the right one. Whether shagging in place, traveling forward or backward, or turning left or right, the basic step-combination was shagged to a measure and a half consisting of six quick counts:

> Count one-and (quick-quick): On count one-, spring lightly onto the left foot. In an instant, on the and count, hop with the same foot. (The trick is to combine the hop with a short sliding movement on the sole of the shoe.) Simultaneously kick the right foot back and up behind the left leg. (The toe of the right shoe should be up only a fraction from the floor.)
>
> Count two-and (quick-quick): On count two-, spring lightly onto the right foot. In an instant, on the and count, hop with the same foot. (The trick is to combine the hop with a short sliding movement on the sole of the shoe.) Simultaneously kick the left foot

back and up behind the right leg. (The toe of the left shoe should be up only a fraction from the floor.)

Count <u>three</u> (quick): Spring lightly onto the left foot.

Count <u>four</u> (quick): Spring lightly onto the right foot.

When college students started to shag on campuses across the country, couples danced in conversation position unconservatively by not holding hands. Freed of the hand holds, their bodies were positioned at a wider angle than the usual forty-five degrees. They still remained embraced, of course. Although they did so less often, couples continued to dance conservatively in conversation as well as in closed position.

[Vincent Armstrong, Alice Scott, Bert Craig: all three (who sat side by side) were puzzled by the supervisor's words. Going into a quick huddle, they agreed Bert should ask him to clarify what he said. "Mr. Normand, I'm sorry to interrupt, but we can't understand how couples can be embraced in conversation position if they are not holding hands."

The supervisor replied: "Perhaps I should have explained that the couples remained partially embraced. In other words, while they were not holding hands, they were still in conversation position because the man's right arm was around the woman's waist, and her left hand was on his shoulder. For your clarification, I suggest you re-examine the detailed descriptions of the five dance positions on the mimeographed sheets that were passed out to you and the others the day the history of the fox trot was discussed."]

On college campuses shagging was appropriately called the Collegiate Shag or Hop. In different areas of the country different appellations were applied to the shag; also, as with all dances, various interpretations of shagging were put into practice. The hops of assorted localities expressed distinct flavors of the heady dance analogous to the way hops, conelike flowers, communicate distinct flavors to beer.

The state of New Jersey labeled the shag, the Jersey Jump. The city of Saint Louis labeled the shag, the Saint Louis Hop. To San Franciscans' chagrin the shag was referred to in their city as the <u>Frisco</u> Hop. Across the country many Americans poked fun at the dance by calling it the Flea Hop. But the shag was not squashed.

Meanwhile, a modernistic movement advocating hot jazz (originally a black improvisatory art) was ascending in the nonclassical, white musicians' world. Benny Goodman, a young man of indigent Jewish parentage, became this movement's most admired advocate, and not without good reason. A marvelous clarinetist, his phenomenal technical proficiency was unequaled by other musicians. And his improvisation—personalized, pragmatic, and precise—served as an exemplary model for aspiring clarinet players.

In his role as a bandleader he led the way to freedom of expression and individuality in musicians' playing hot jazz or modish music not only to dance to but also to listen to, enjoyably. Goodman's free style embraced popular along with standard musical compositions: he assimilated the two into a typically American mode of music—swing! As a human being who believed in brotherhood he earned a place in the humanitarians' hall of fame by integrating, in advance of fellow bandleaders, black brother musicians with white members of his group.

To a great degree Benny Goodman's musical pursuits were steeped in the southern tradition established by the Original Dixieland Jazz Band, perpetuated by the New Orleans Rhythm Kings, and elaborated on by the Memphis Five as well as various other combos, white and black. Negro bandmaster Fletcher Henderson—an unexcelled arranger in the New Orleans tradition—reset with variations a number of tunes for Goodman's band:

To name some, "Down South Camp Meeting," "King Porter" and "Sugarfoot Stomp," When Buddha Smiles," Sleepy Time Down South," "Blue Skies," "Sometimes I'm Happy." Henderson's arrangements played an important part in shaping the swinging, syncopated style of Goodman's clarinet playing. He was a fascinating figure to watch wielding a woodwind instrument on a bandstand despite the fact that he wore spectacles.

Summer 1934 the bespectacled clarinet player had received his first engagement as a bandleader in New York at Billy Rose's Music Hall. The coming fall he contracted to lead his band over the NBC network in the Saturday night radio series "Let's Dance." Several months later Music Corporation of America booked his ensemble, a hot band, into the Rooosevelt Hotel, which previously had a policy of engaging only sweet orchestras during the dinner hour.

Unfortunately the hotel's guests lacked an appetite for unsweetened music. It appeared diners, while dancing, were not accustomed to hearing a hot band that featured soloists who played free-style swing on wind instruments. Benny Goodman's engagement was terminated after two unsuccessful weeks at the Roosevelt Hotel.

Determined to succeed, Goodman decided to accept an offer for his band to play at the Palomar Ballroom in southern California next year about mid-August. En route to the West Coast he filled the intervening periods with a series of cross-country bookings. On the road the response to his swinging hot band was lukewarm, if not cool. Again couples were not used to listening to a soloist's improvisations while they were doing set steps on a dance floor.

Nevertheless, the members of the band traveled on to the Golden State. In San Francisco their swing music was welcomed warmly. On radio programs previous performances by Benny Goodman and his topnotch musicians had sold the hot band to listeners of all ages across America. Additionally, Columbia and Victor records that he had cut were selling western states solidly on swing. When Goodman with his retinue of musicians arrived in Los Angeles, they were rendered a royal reception at the Palomar Ballroom.

There were still some musical moats to be swung over; however, the rightful instrumentalist was well on his way to being proclaimed "King of Swing" by loyal, imaginative admirers. Although his throne may have been a fantasy, the inauguration of Benny Goodman on August 21, 1935, at the Palomar Ballroom in the city of the Angeles symbolized de facto a new period in America's music—the Swing Era.

[Anything to do with what occurred in San Francisco was of interest to Bert Craig. He interrupted Ralph Normand to ask, "Where did the Benny Goodman band play in our city?" His talk momentarily stopped, the supervisor searched for the answer in his notes. Upon finding it, he answered: "Goodman's band played at MacFadden's Ballroom. The place is no longer in existence."

Before other teachers in the group could ask any questions, Normand resumed talking: "To facilitate your understanding how the Swing Era affected social dancing, I should make you aware of certain facts. Swing music, or simply stated 'swing' wasn't completely a novelty. Swing was new and yet it was old. As far back as 1911 jazz musicians used the term in heated jam sessions. For twenty-four years swing had drawn breath from hot jazz.

"The complete novelty was that white Americans in most social strata were acquiring a taste for a black man's menu of musical variety. Formerly, while sweet jazz was regarded as a delicacy, hot jazz was looked down upon with distaste because it was the specialty of Negro musicians in dark dives and dance halls, vilified as 'cheap jig joints.'

"It is not surprising swing music appealed mostly to the youth of America. Swing, a purer improvisatory art, was wilder, freer, and more emotional than hot jazz. Swing is difficult to define but may be expressed easily as strong inward feelings musicians convey on impulse through their playing. (Is that not the way youthful feelings are often expressed?)

"Benny Goodman himself could not define swing music in brief words. The best he was able to do was to explain <u>swing</u> in terms of action: 'A band swings,' he said, 'when its collective improvisation is rhythmically integrated.'"]

The Swing Era in full swing, musicians were less restrained and more inclined to improvise freely on original melodies. Large dance bands were formed that in free style played popular music with simple harmonic and rhythmic patterns. Accordingly stiff ballroom dancers were imbued with the spontaneous spirit of swing, allowing couples to move about on a dance floor unhampered by rigidity and restraint. Suitable dances for swing music were thus sought or invented.

After the mid-thirties the Shag lost its identity when it was merged with the Lindy Hop by inventive dancers. Also they shortened the name to just plain Lindy. Dance by dance the Lindy had incorporated into it a number of step-combinations, including movements, which fell under three classifications, generically called 'Jitterbug.' The step-combinations are constantly changing as they are always being shuffled and reshuffled, and the faded ones discarded and replaced. All the step-combinations in the three classifications, like a fresh deck of playing cards, are far from faded at this hour of the game.

The first classification, FLOOR STEPS—performed, as a rule, fairly close to the ground and with the dance partners maintaining some bodily contact—include for the most part

a. <u>Jockeying</u> (preliminary step: basic rhythmic action of the knees, a carry over from the Charleston)

> Body Position: open and conversation

> Jitterbugged to the steady beat of the bass—four counts to a measure. The man starts by stepping back with his left foot; the woman steps back with her right foot.

> Count one: The man steps back onto the ball of his left foot with a straight leg. (His right foot is held slightly off the floor.)

Count <u>two</u>: He bends the knee of his left leg with quick action.

Count <u>three</u>: He straightens his left leg with his weight still on the ball of his foot.

Count <u>four</u>: He again bends the knee of his left leg with quick action.

The partners repeat all four counts. This time the man starts with his right foot; the woman starts with her left foot.

b. <u>Twist</u> (a figure containing tantalizing traces of the black bottom)

Body Position: open, left-hand contact

Leading the woman by sharp, left-to-right, left-to-right, half turns of the wrist, the man leads her straight ahead as he moves progressively backward; she follows doing twist-abouts. Or he leads her rightward so that they move in a circular direction; she follows doing twist-abouts:

She bends her knees, keeping her body low as she executes twist-abouts on the balls of her feet. When she twists with her weight on her right foot, she straightens her leg to raise her right hip (and heel). When she twists with her weight on the left foot, she straightens her leg to raise her left hip (and heel).

Except for minor modifications the twist appears to be one and the same dance figure as the sugar foot. It used to be performed by both the man and the woman. Today she, not he, ordinarily performs it in their routines.

While the modern version of the twist and sugar foot is American, they were derived from traditional Haitian dances: the sugar foot from Haiti's *Yenvolou* and the twist from Haiti's *Coye*. Actually they originated in Africa, not in the West Indies.

The Haitians are proud descendants of African tribes, the royal Dohomey, who did different dances for specific occasions. They danced skillfully, using all their bodily parts. They danced with their fingers and toes...with their abdomens, derrières, and limbs...and with their knees and hips, of course. The twist and sugar foot covered, it is fitting to slip into

c. <u>Swing-out</u> (partial separation of the dance partners)

Body Position: open

Usually at once, but occasionally after they have been
dancing in closed position, the man swings his partner
out almost at arm's length so that they are in left-hand
contact, or in open position, as they jitterbug.

[Alice Scott raised her hand indicating she had something on her
mind. "Yes, what is it?" the supervisor recognized her desire to speak.
"A little while ago you mentioned the breakaway. I can't see that there
is much difference between the swing-out and the breakaway."

"There is a vast difference between the two movements, Miss
Scott. In the swing-out the couples are always in contact by hand-
holds, limiting their freedom to break loose on the dance floor. In the
breakaway the man and the woman have no contact whatsoever,
leaving each to improvise steps at will.

"As a historical note in the early 1900s complete separation during a couple-dance was at times performed on stage by black enter-
tainers. Eventually complete separation of couples doing the
Jitterbug off stage became a characteristic of the dance. The breakaway movement gave a woman independence on the dance floor
she never had experienced before." With his observation on the
breakaway completed, Ralph Normand felt free to proceed.]

In the second classification, SHINE STEPS, the partners—facing
in the same direction—stand independently side by side. The
woman's left side is in proximity to the man's right side, but they
remain separated. Both start to dance with the same foot. The steps
include mainly

a. <u>Shorty George</u> (or the Sabu, named after a Hindu character in a movie
because of its oriental flavor cooked up by Snowden)

Body Position: break, shine

Pointing index fingers to the floor, keeping the knees
tightly together, and facing directly ahead, the dancers
begin traveling with deep, alternating dips by turning
left oblique to right oblique, right oblique to left oblique,
and so on.

While advancing, the dancers teeter-totter their shoulders. When they dip to the left, the dancers lower their
left shoulders. When they dip to the right, the dancers
lower their right shoulders.

["The next shine step I am about to describe is imitation cake walk. It lacks practically all the natural ingredients of the cake walk concocted by Negro slaves on southern plantations before the Civil War. In 1877 the cake walk containing unlabeled artificial coloring was a favorite treat in New York where it was served on stage by a musical comedy team, Harrigan and Hart, in a saccharine number called 'Walking for Dat Cake.'

"If you care to partake of the real thing, directions for the genuine cake walk are given in the history of the fox trot, as you must be aware. Now to give you a quick recipe of a white extract from the black cake walk."]

b. Tip (the term may have derived from Tip Tap and Toe, an acrobatic tap act engaged in the thirties by the comedy star Eddy Cantor)

Body Position: break, shine

Couples, assuming cocky postures and snapping the fingers of their right hands rhythmically to the music, strut ahead with their bodies turned at an angle—right shoulders well forward. The couples' right arms are held out in front, forming wide Vs. Their left arms are extended obliquely sideward above their waistlines. Here is how one struts:

Count one-and (quick-quick): On count one-, step forward briskly on the toes of the left foot. In an instant, on the and count, come down firmly on the heel.

Count two-and (quick-quick): On count two-, step forward briskly on the toes of the right foot. In an instant, on the and count, come down firmly on the heel.

Count three-and (quick-quick): On count three-, step forward briskly on the toes of the left foot. In an instant, on the and count, come down firmly on the heel.

Count four-and (quick-quick): On count four-, step forward briskly on the toes of the right foot. In an instant, on the and count, come down firmly on the heel.

After a tour of America in 1842 the English author Charles Dickens, advocate of international copyright and abolition of slavery, wrote *American Notes*. In his book he describes in literary terms a dance he observed a young Negro performing in a minstrel show at Five Points, a depressed district in old New York. The youth was William Henry Lane, billed as Master Juba the finest minstrel dancer on the face of the earth. One of the movements he performed in his dancing was a flat-footed Shuffle, an African fore-runner of the Afro-American shine step with which we have just caught up to:

c. Trucking (footwork inherent in native Congo dances of Africa, Brazil, and the West Indies)

> Body Position: break, shine

> Note: trucking is danced in an identical way by both partners but individually.

> Facing forward, the dancer turns his body obliquely to the right. His shoulders are uplifted and tilted: the left shoulder is forward and higher than the right shoulder. Holding his hand head-height, he wigwags his index finger which is pointed toward the ceiling. With swaying hips he "trucks on down" a dance floor in a straight line.

> There are loads of trucking steps. The simplest is the shuffle in which a dancer advances from foot to foot by swiveling short slides on his soles.

["The next shine step, Suzie-Q, that we want to get acquainted with is usually seen in a dance hall during a trucking number. Miss Suzie Q's origin eludes us until we look more closely at her petite form. Suzie we see is a diminutive for Susanne, a girl's given name. And Susanne is a French form, which shows us where to look for her roots, theoretically.

"At the beginning of the French Empire in the eighteenth century, styles from France influenced life styles in America, including dress designs and dance designs. In New Orleans throughout the French Quarter white masters commonly had intercourse with their black female slaves: Mulatto babies were born. Susannes were baptized. Mulatto dances were conceived. Suzie Q was christened, dressed in the latest fashions."

His audience hummed tones of astonishment at the supervisor's theory. Was it possible, they wondered. "Oh my—oh, my suz!" exclaimed Normand. He was surprised the teachers were so surprised at his tongue-in-cheek statements. Seeing nothing to be gained in expanding the point, he forged ahead.]

The Suzie-Q is executed as smoothly as trucking, and is timed to offbeat syncopated music. The Suzie-Q can be danced at will any place in a routine if it is not disruptive. The woman's part is the same as the man's except they perform in opposition. They face each other, and may suzie-q in two different ways...holding hands or without holding hands:

Holding hands, they remain erect. Without holding hands, they bow (Japanese style) remaining unerect. Their bodies are motionless, but if not holding they coordinate their hands and feet with syncopated motions. To be more descriptive of

d. Suzie-Q (performed in vaudeville as part of a tap-dance routine, it was worked into the Lindy subsequent to 1936)

Body Position: break, shine

Each clasping their own hands with fingers interlocked, the partners swing their hands pendulum-like in time to the music. Their bodies are bowed and their knees are bent. The partners suzie-q accordingly:

They zigzag four times clockwise: toe-heel-toe-heel (1-2-3-4). This is accomplished by swiveling alternately on the toes and heels. The dancers may repeat the four-count pattern as often as desired in the same direction. Or they may reverse directions, and suzie-q counterclockwise.

Boogie-Woogie, the last shine step to be discussed, is also a style of music which was significant in the last phases of Jazz. Musically boogie, short for boogie-woogie, is nearly as important as swing is to jitterbugging. Boogie dates back to the birth of the blues: hot jazz fathered in the days of slavery by Negro southern secular songs.

Boogie's acceptance to society in the South was inevitable. However, that hot-jazz music did not make its debut nationally till December 23, 1938. Boogie-woogie's formal appearance before northern society occurred in New York at Carnegie Hall.

There a trio of ebony-ivory keyboard artists—Meade Lux Lewis, Pete Johnson, and Albert Ammons—was holding a cutting session. "Cutting," or to use the infinitive "to cut," means to outplay a soloist or combo in competition.

Mr. Lewis and Mr. Johnson were seated at the traditional grand piano. Mr. Ammons sat at a timeworn upright piano converted into a one-man band by the addition of a banjo and drum. So stimulating was the musicians' boogie beat that enraptured listeners, bouncing up and down in their seats with excitement, figuratively hit the ceiling.

Boogie-woogie is expressed as jazz in the form of instrumental blues, especially for piano. The essential element of blues figuration (melodic or harmonic unit) is conveyed to the keyboard in boogie-woogie, which is distinguished by a perpetual percussive pattern persistently performed by the piano player's left hand. At the same time his right hand, improvising rhythmically, riffs:

That is, his right hand repeats two- or four-bar phrases in counteraction to the strong, steady rhythm generated by his left hand. The consequential rhythmic crossings are as intricate as the numerous intersecting tracks in a railroad yard. And the dynamic melody is as rousing as the sound of an oncoming locomotive.

We turn the music sheet to James Yancey an American Negro who was a blues pianist, a jazz singer, and a tap dancer of such stature he entertained the royal family of England. The event was palatial, for it was a command performance by King George V. Yancey ran the boogie-woogie express on the way to heights of popularity in Chicago at the hub of the twenties. The boogie-woogie bass, a musical tool of Yancey's, was patently designed along the lines of train-engine rhythms with highly powered force that increased melodic momentum.

Among his piano blues (or boogie) recordings is the "Five O'Clock Blues," commonly called "The Fives," which created an impression so powerful many musically minded Americans instead of referring to boogie-woogie as such, speak of it as "The Fives." Yancey has been a guiding genius followed by practically all boogie-woogie pianists since the 1920s.

For all of James Yancey's brilliant contributions to piano blues, he cannot be credited with naming the music "boogie-woogie." Rather it was an apprentice of his, another Negro pianist-singer-dancer, Clarence (Pine Top) Smith who attached the brush-handle to this style of jazz.

A resident of the Windy City, Smith was familiar with the South-Side neighborhood expression "Let's pitch a boogie," an old stand-by for "Let's throw a party," in which music and money were donated to help a soul brother who was unable to pay his room rent. The origin of the word "boogie" is obscure. However, it is clear that Smith made the brush "woogie" in December 1928 to fit onto the handle "boogie" when he needed a label for a new recording. His record, "Pine Top's Boogie Woogie," preserved on wax Smith's solid solo piano playing and some silly soliloquizing.

We must not be fooled by the nonsensical, rhyming brush-handle Clarence Smith applied to his music. The man's accomplishments in boogie-woogie should be taken seriously, and they are by hot-jazz music lovers. Smith perfected the pianistic style of playing rich, rhythmical, rolling bass figures that are fingered eight eighth notes to the bar. So it is we hear. musicians play and see jitterbugs dance eight-to-the-bar.

Because of the intensity of the drumlike rhythm beaten by the pianist's left hand, boogie-woogie casts a musical spell over jitterbugs. With greater force than swing, boogie goads them into fancy...frenzied...foot-loose frisking on a dance floor. Yet fascinating four-four beats booming and reverberating from a piano keyboard typify both kinds of hot jazz. Also, except for impromptu variations, swing and boogie beats are of equal value and are stressed equally by both the musician and the jitterbug. Here is how dance partners boogie-woogied to the beating bass of a band:

e. <u>Boogie-Woogie</u> (at the turn of the century piano boogie was built by talented black workers in the lumber camps of Texas; later in the 1900s the musical parts were used by professional dancers as material to form boogie figures.

Body Position: break, shine

A distinctive boogie feature is the springy ball-change, a quick transfer of a dancer's weight from the ball of one foot to the ball of the other foot.

Standing side by side, the partners individually spring forward a short step onto the ball of the left foot. Without losing a beat, they also spring forward onto the ball of the right foot, which lands well apart to the side of the left foot. They do the same thing again but in a backward direction.

Next they repeat both forward and backward combinations. While boogieing the partners hold their arms out—with hands palms down—as if set to row a boat.

[In that the dancing teachers in the group had no musical background, they were unclear how dancers doing the boogie counted eight eighth notes to the bar. Ralph Normand explained while he chalked an illustration on the handy blackboard. "Repeating as many step-combinations as they wish, the dancers count a boogie measure of music like this:

one,	TWO,	three,	FOUR,	five,	SIX,	seven,	EIGHT
(left,	RIGHT,	left,	RIGHT,	left,	RIGHT,	left,	RIGHT).

"The action is continuous. In stepping ahead, the knees are bent, deeply; in stepping back, they are straightened. Bending and unbending of the knees coordinated with the ball-change creates a sinuous swinging of the hips, by which the upbeat is sexually accentuated with a downward thrust of the pelvis. There you have it, style and step in brief of the basic Boogie-Woogie.

"The knee-action Jockey (or Jockeying), discussed under floor steps, before long was supplemented with a breaklike movement (two simple, short snappy steps) similar to breaks used in tap dancing, a technique that involves a change of rhythmic pace at the end of a series of taps. Eventually the breaklike movement was molded into a variety of jitterbug figures, as you are about to see.

"In order to make it easy for you to follow me, I have had mimeographed descriptions of three Lindy rhythms upon which jitterbugging is structured." Pointing to a small stack of papers on top of his desk, the supervisor asked a teacher to pass the papers out to the group.

"Look at the descriptions. See the timing symbols Slow, Quick-Quick and Quick-Quick, Slow; they are used in a number of dance arrangements to set steps to the time of music. This particular arrangement, for fast tempos, is common to the three Lindy rhythms utilized as a framework into which directional patterns have been fitted for the Jitterbug.

"Notice that each slow (two counts) is bridged by a pair of Quick-Quicks (one count + one count). They are symbols for the breaklike movements that were added to jockeying. The woman's footwork, of course, is opposite to the man's. I'll demonstrate the rhythms as they are shown in the mimeographed descriptions for the man. Watch":

Single Lindy Rhythm

Slow: Step short to the side on the left foot,
(Quick: Tap on the ball of the right foot (close behind
(the left foot),
(Quick: Tap in place on the left foot;

Slow: Step short to the side on the right foot,
(Quick: Tap on the ball of the left foot (close behind
(the right foot),
(Quick: Tap in place on the right foot.

"For the sake of thoroughness you should be informed that there are two categories of the Lindy, Eastern and Western. In the East a dancer in doing the jitterbug steps forward on the quicks. In the West a jitterbug steps backward on the quicks as is indicated in the mimeographed descriptions. To continue the demonstration":

Double Lindy Rhythm

(Quick: Tap on the ball of the left foot (close behind
(the right foot),
(Quick: Tap in place on the right foot,
Slow: Step short to the side on the left foot;
(Quick: Tap on the ball of the right foot (close behind
(the left foot),
(Quick: Tap in place on the left foot,
Slow: Step short to the side on the right foot.

"By the way, the term *tap* is regional not standard. Dancers in southern parts of the country and in the Midwest use *dig* instead of the Easterner's *tap*, and on the West Coast *touch* is used. Still each of the terms means the same in relation to social dancing. That is, when tapping, digging or touching a dancer puts no weight on the foot...or minimum weight if necessary. I use *tap* to tie it in with the stage term, consistent with professional hoofers' jargon but inconsistent with their tap-tap sounds which are not heard in ballrooms or dance halls. So look at my footwork, do not listen for light taps as I demonstrate":

Triple Lindy Rhythm

Slow: With alternating small shuffles step sideward:
              step left—close with the right foot—step left
              again (one-and-two count),
(Quick: Tap on the ball of the right foot (close behind
(the left foot),
(Quick: Tap in place on the left foot;
Slow: With alternating small shuffles step sideward:
              step right—close with the left foot—step right
              again (one-and-two count),
(Quick: Tap on the ball of the left foot (close behind the
(right foot),
(Quick: Tap in place on the right foot.

"It is important to round off a few fine points pertinent to the performance of the three Lindy rhythms. In addition to being danced side to side, they also are performed clockwise and counter-clockwise. Regardless of the direction, the body, like a piston, moves up and down under pressure from fluid flexing of the knees. Since the Jitterbug is not a traveling movement, on the dance floor couples select a steadfast vantage point where they can best show off their figures."]

Although the Jitterbug had strong appeal in America, not everybody received it with open arms. Dancing masters and ballroom operators did not put out the welcome mat for showy jitterbugging upstarts. They posted signs prohibiting jitterbugging. Couples caught doing it were ejected from the ballrooms.

In an attempt to make the Jitterbug acceptable a circle of students at the University of South Carolina while watching couples jitterbugging in a Columbia night club run by Negroes, got the bright idea of transforming the city Jitterbug into a country square dance. The night club, originally a synagogue (the House of Peace), had been remodeled and named The Big Apple after a dance popular with young southern blacks in the early 1900s. Therefore, the transformed Jitterbug was also named The Big Apple. Stuffed into it together with other jazzy figures were the shag, trucking, suzie-q, and pecking.

Pecking is an odd floor step, I omitted mentioning earlier. It is a movement peculiar both to tame and wild birds that appears comical in the eyes of a modern society. But in Dahomey, an ancient West African kingdom, the inhabitants, who were fetish worshippers, did not see anything comical about the peculiarity of birds' ways, in or out of the wilderness. By movements of their necks and shoulders the Dahomeyans performed a serious dance in which they imitated with reverence the way birds peck.

By some strange coincidence pecking happened to be more suited to square dancing than to jitterbugging. A domesticated bird's eye view of how pecking was performed in the thirties will put this movement into focus. The couples faced beak to beak. The man, a strutting rooster, and the woman, a posturing hen, pecked at each other in imitation of the behavior of barnyard fowl.

Since calls were used in square dancing, the same method was used in The Big Apple. The caller called: "cut that apple, peck 'n pose, truck around, do double stomps, kick the mule," and so on. The dancers responded by shagging, trucking, suzy-quing, pecking, and whatever else they were instructed to do.

Ultimately, having formed a large circle, couples were called by turns to enter the center and shine (strut their stuff). The shining couple, encircled by the rest of the dancers, improvised to swing music the strangest dances, everything from sand steps—chicken scratches—to a countrified jitterbug.

A choreographic bumper crop grown in some southern states, The Big Apple was crated and shipped autumn of 1937 on a whole-sale scale to New York. From there the dance was sent to several other northern states that had received orders for its fresh figures. In spite of the demand for The Big Apple, the Jitterbug per se contin-ued to be met with opposition and was accepted by comparatively small factions throughout the land.

To cite a specific case, that year the members of the North Carolina State Baptist Convention unanimously decreed the unorthodox dance was to be banned from all educational institu-tions belonging to the membership. As late as 1939 stiff-necked stu-dents' feelings against the Jitterbug were still so strong dance stu-dios reaped little benefit commercially from displaying the dance. The wrath of the teaching trade was aroused.

At the fifty-sixth annual convention of Dancing Masters of America, Incorporated, war was foolishly declared on the nation's jitterbugs. The battleground was the Hotel Astor in New York City. Field battery dating back to World War I was rolled out under the command of Irene Castle who a generation before had been part of a unit successful in wiping out the last of wild, animal-like dances rampant on home territory in 1914.

Assisted by her second-in-command, the male half of an adagio team (Alex Fisher and Ruth Harrison), Mrs. Castle opened fire on defiant jitterbugs. The main weapon with which she planned to dis-place the advancing enemy was the Castle Rock and Roll, a so-called new dance. Actually it was the old Boston Waltz executed to medi-um fox-trot rhythm and tempo. To boost the morale of weary dance troops bogged down by timeworn movements, she modernized the nomenclature of her obsolete choreography.

Mrs. Castle's stockpile of ammunition, reconditioned steps, was camouflaged by three divisions: one...Kicking the Bucket, two...Banking the Turn, three...The Sideslip. Their concealment notwithstanding, one could see they were old-fashioned waltz fig-ures with a modern twist. However, historical documents show that the Castle-directed dance shells misfired. The jitterbugs were neither destroyed nor stopped. They gradually marched onward to victory.

[Alice Scott could not resist asking, "Whatever became of Mrs. Castle? After her husband Vernon was killed in an airplane crash, did she remarry?"

"Yes, she did," Mr. Normand confirmed the nuptial fact. "The dear lady is married to a Frederic McLaughlin. I don't know anything about him!" Not pleased to engage in idle talk, the supervisor cut off his student's inquisitiveness with a sharp comment:

"Perhaps Irene Castle should have stayed out of the limelight. All she succeeded in accomplishing by her rock-and-roll tactics was to step up the advance of the dance-music that is really Rock 'n Roll. With the defeat of her mistimed cause she cast a shadow on a luminous legend—The Brilliant Castles."]

It is now time to train our sights on AIR STEPS, the third classification of the Jitterbug. To untrained eyes they may appear the same as LIFTS performed onstage by professional exhibition dancers. But there is no comparison between the two movements, just as there is no comparison between the movements of kites and gliders.

Air steps had been performed by Juke-box Janes and Johnies as early as Christmas 1930 (and earlier by other jitterbug jumpers). Whether in an ice-cream parlor or in a barroom, they did air steps to the music of juke boxes. By July 1943 all around the United States professional performers and contest competitors were exhibiting air steps in their jitterbugging routines.

They were exhibited around the globe, too. Leon James and Willa Mae Ricker, creative colored choreographers, voyaged overseas to exhibit the American art of jitterbugging. Here are but a few of the air steps the internationally famous dance team performed:

a. <u>Round-the-Back</u>: (specialty of a galaxy of black stars, outstanding jazz dancers, at Harlem's Savoy ballroom established March 12, 1926, in New York City)

Body Position: left-hand contact

From open position the man pulls his partner toward him and flips her, feet first, under his right arm. (As she is flipped her body is curved.) Still in motion, the woman flies over the man's back and lands on her feet agilely to face him once again in open position.

Note: In preparing to flip the woman, the man starts bending his knees till he is in a crouched position. Just as she comes full circle, he straightens up so that they face each other.

Occasionally before the forties nonprofessional dancers performed a limited number of air steps: Over the Back, The Snatch, Hip to Hip, Side Flip—all of which indicates the way a man elevates a woman in executing air steps. Preferring the standard floor steps, seasoned ballroom dancers shunned air steps, yet not for long.

Fred Astaire appeared on the scene. That suave American theatrical dancer, who conquered gravity (on film), frequently leaped from the floor up into air as he danced. Unseasoned dancers, high-school and college students, were thrilled by Astaire's great performances. He set a sensational style. At proms and public dances, wherever there was space, they did or tried to do air steps.

In the Old Testament (Eccles. 1:9) it was said, "there is no new thing under the sun," which if true applies to the last air step, the Pirouette: The ancients borrowed it from the revolving astral bodies; European ballet masters borrowed it from ancient Grecian dancers. American choreographers borrowed it for chorus girls; contemporary dancing teachers borrowed it for jitterbugs.

b. Pirouette: (a pirouette often is performed on the toes by ballerinas; technically a pirouette, tour en l'air, is performed 'in the air')

Body Position: break, shine

In pirouetting, to gain momentum the man, who breaks away from the woman, swings his arms leftward as he kicks out with his right foot to start spins by pivoting on his left foot counterclockwise. Meanwhile the woman stands in place marking time. (Their roles could be reversed.)

This completes a well-rounded summary of the three jitterbug classifications: floor steps, shine steps, and air steps. There are several other combinations of such steps that were not discussed. Although they are of much value to a jitterbug, they are of negligible value to a historian.

[For all intents and purposes the supervisor had covered the history of the Jitterbug. However, he had yet to discuss a dance which was closely connected to it but was definitely diverse from it. He decided to allow the group of student teachers a brief interval to stretch their limbs and clear the cobwebs from their heads.

A stiff, stale audience could not be very attentive. Normand wanted the teachers to be relaxed, in a fresh listening mood when he spoke on the history of the next American dance—The Swing. The supervisor asked the group if they would like to take a coffee break. All the teachers raised their hands and voiced their approval, all except Vincent Armstrong who was too engrossed in thought to respond. In his mind's eye he was looking back...back to a period in high school where he was a speaker not a listener.]

BOOK FOUR

Chapter 21

Less jittery than he was the day before in Public Speaking I, Vincent did not wait for his teacher, Mr. Du Puy, to comment or to ask him to begin talking on the second part of the oral presentation. He deliberately avoided eye-to-eye contact with Mr. Du Puy. Just as soon as Vincent's classmates were settled in their seats, he hurried to the front of the room and placed his notes on the slanted surface of the dictionary stand.

Relieved that the teacher said nothing so far about the first half of the talk Vincent had presented yesterday, he took a deep breath, braced himself for the ordeal of his punitive assignment, and stated the subject to be discussed: 'Human Equality, Fact or Fiction, in Relation to Individuals at Large, With Emphasis on America and Asia.'

"We cannot express our view of equality in America, or anywhere else, with our eyes closed to the past. Let us take an eagle's eye view of the mountainous historical records of slavery in our country to see what we can spot. The first slaves, black slaves, were transported by a Dutch ship to Jamestown, Virginia, in August 1619. The blacks, twenty in all, were auctioned off to the highest bidders as if they were choice cattle.

"The selling and buying of black men and women (Negroes), was a business engaged in by self-styled southern gentlemen for generations, and slavery was not discontinued with the outbreak of Civil War. It occurred April 12, 1861, at Charleston, South Carolina, over an incident in which a Confederate, General Beauregard, ordered his troops to fire on Fort Sumter under the command of a Northern officer, Major Anderson. Not long afterward, on January 1,

1863, to be exact, President Lincoln issued an Emancipation Proclamation declaring that all slaves held in states in rebellion against the Union to be then, thenceforward, and forever free!

"Clearly the Emancipation Proclamation was a war measure and did not apply to the states that had not seceded from the Union. Unfortunately the proclamation failed to stop states in the South from reinstituting slavery after their readmission into the Union.

"On April 2, 1866, President Lincoln publicly announced insurrection was ended in several southern states. And on August 2, 1866, President Lincoln announced insurrection was at an end in the state of Texas as well. Civil authority according to his proclamation existed again in the United States. But did civil rights exist—and for whom?

"Embittered Texans refused to permit an expired beastly issue of the Civil War lie buried in peace. In the Lone-Star State regressive statutes, masked as 'separate but equal,' were enacted with a vengeance against the Negroes. Texas was not the only state beating a dead horse.

"States in the Confederate heartland—Alabama, Georgia, Mississippi, South Carolina—were getting their licks in, too. I will read verbatim a typical enactment, a misdemeanor in the Deep South punishable if violated by a fine as high as five-hundred dollars.

"Code of Laws of South Carolina, Title 5, Section 19: 'Any circus or other such traveling show exhibiting under canvas or out of doors for gain shall maintain two main entrances to such exhibition, one for white people and the other for colored people. Such main entrances shall be plainly marked For White People and For Colored People. All white persons attending such show or traveling exhibition other than those connected with the show shall pass in and out of the entrance provided for white persons, and all colored persons attending such show or traveling exhibition shall pass in and out of the entrance provided for colored persons.'

"Living in the year 1940, ruled by a civilized (?) government, it is hard for us to believe laws have ever been enacted in our country which are a throwback to the Stone Age. Yet we find man's beastliness to man still worse in another body politic, the Union of South Africa. So beastly is prejudice in Cape Town, the legislative capital, Europeans (whites) have forced non-white medical students interning in a hospital to stand facing a wall during an operation on a European. One is forced to ask, why would it be unlawful—or shameful—for interns of color to observe naked bodily organs of white patients undergoing surgery?"

(Younglings react to glimpses of nudity in a number of pert ways. To state two for the sake of brevity: They mimic the saucy red-eyed vireo that seems to sing, "I see you. You see me. I see you...so what!" Thus younglings tweet away their bashfulness. Or, they mimic the impudent blue jay that seems to sing, "Lee-oh-la. La-oh-lee. Lee-oh-la...who cares!" Thus younglings tweet away their embarrassment.

In the situation of the South-African interns there is nothing to chirp about. The image of a naked body lying on an operating table was obliterated from the minds of Vincent's classmates by the heart-rending mental picture of the colored interns lined up with their faces pressed flat against a hospital wall. The expressions on the faces of the boys and girls changed from disbelief to pity. In their innocence they could not understand God's indifference to men mistreating men.

An exceptional jurist in His Majesty's commonwealth once said: If a white man oppresses a black man, that is criminal; if a black man oppresses a white man, that too is criminal. And if a white man abuses a white man, or if a black man abuses a black man, that is incestuous.)

"While we are nearby, let us look in on Basutoland, a British high commission territory partially surrounded by the Union of South Africa. Basutoland is occupied by various African tribes many of which collectively are called Basuto. The dominant tribal peoples claim to be original Basuto, the genuine article to use a figure of speech. By virtue of such genealogical factors as the best breeding, birthplace, and background, they fancy themselves the crème de la crème among the tribes in the territory, certainly of purer stock than the Matebele.

"Matebele in general refers to tribes of non-original Basuto. Humiliated because their ancestors came from lands outside Basutoland, and degraded socially, the Matebele are lowered to the level of servile occupations. Also crushed under the Basuto's elite, social heel is the Bathepu, another non-original generic group. This uncivil treatment by bona-fide Basuto is their resentment over the fact that each tribe within the Bathepu obstinately clings to its respective tongue and folklore.

"Let us leave the dark continent and go to South America, as far as Ecuador where Indians heavily populate the Andean highlands above the valley of Otavola. For generations Spaniards and Indians have intermarried with the result that differences in their coloration are of little consequence. Whether anybody's color is brown or red, light or dark, is not a basis for prejudice. In that respect the people are color blind. However, societal distinctions are a fact of life in Ecuador.

"As ridiculous as it appears the natives' station in the highlands is determined by their mode of dress. Light-skinned Ecuadorans have the highest status not because the color of their skin is white but because the color of their currency is green. They can afford to be well-dressed in the latest fashions.

"In the lowlands poorly dressed Ecuadorans, mestizos, persons of mixed European and Amerindian ancestry, are looked down upon as guttersnipes. They often are positionless, propertyless, and penniless. They wear shabby, outmoded Spanish garb. Yet the mestizos lord it over the backward Cholos, unadulterated descendants of the Incas, who dress in their outworn Indian costumes.

"The poor Indians are terrorized and illegally subjected to involuntary servitude. Mestizos attack and rob the Indians with impunity. About all the action the authorities take against the crimes is to turn their heads and stick their fingers in their ears. Thus they are not disturbed by distressed cries echoing across the Otavola Valley.

"Shifting the scene to Asia, we now focus the spotlight on Japan in an era designated Meiji, literally 'enlightened reign?' (under Emperor Mutsuhito from 1867 to 1912. The Meiji era is held to represent the modernization of the Japanese islands' social scaffolding which was reinforced by law on three levels: the tiptop, nobility...the top, gentry...the undermost, commoners. It was mandatory under the law of the land that every householder attach to his front door a card showing his name and class. The law, a socially rigged framework, may have been modern Meiji, but it was oppressively enforced by the nobles with the blessing of the emperor.

"Merchants often acquiring ill-gotten yens at the expense of other commoners, gained enough economic strength to rise above the lowest level of society. For a number of years the highest levels, nobility and gentry, represented five per cent of the entire population. Circumstances and conditions in Japan reduced this percentage somewhat. Still the oppression was not reduced.

"Instead of concerning ourselves with the oppressors—the gradual diminishing nobility and gentry, and thriving dishonest merchants—we fastidiously wash our hands of the parasites and, more important, concern ourselves with a few million classless human beings, the most socially oppressed. Scattered throughout the slums of Tokyo we see *burakus*, 'blocks' of broken-down dwellings occupied by the poorest of the poor. Spat at as if they were vermin and hatefully called *eta*, a derogatory epithet, the occupants are driven into the *burakus* where they find refuge—in poverty. Horrified, we are compelled to inquire: Who in the Land of the Rising Sun are the *eta*? Other Japanese, is the shocking answer!

"In the minds of Japan's snobbish sons marriage with the *eta* is unthinkable. Paradoxically many of the *eta's* womenfolk are exceptionally beautiful. *Eta* are despised and disowned simply because of the occupations, once considered unsanitary, that they, as did their fathers, engage in for a livelihood. So the 'unclean' *eta* plying their trade as butchers, tanners, leatherworkers, shoemakers, et cetera, are rejected by other yellow people claiming to be of immaculate stock.

"That prejudice wades in contradictions is borne out by the fact that *eta* are also engaged in farming, a clean occupation. In Karako (part of the prefecture just north of Tokyo), in Obie (in south Honshu), and in Honami (in north Kyushu) are villages typical of many to be seen in Japan thinly spread over the countryside. In these villages most *eta* barely eke out a living. They till tiny tracts and, like their urban kin, are excluded from community life, and are forbidden to worship with the pharisaic villagers.

"But Nipponese behavior of brother against brother, bad as it is, is beyond comparison in not too distant Indic Asia, where we shall now cast our western eyes. More so than elsewhere, we would be at a loss ventilating our view of India's complex social organization, unless at the same time we aired its principal religious persuasion. The two flow together analogous to a large body of water, feared and revered, which runs downstream descending into an awesome cataract...Hinduism.

"Brutally frank observers impudently have described that form of devotion: 'a mystical maze of myths,' 'a superstitious culture of savagery,' 'a masochistic theology of madmen.' No matter how much one is offended by or disagrees with such metaphors, the stark reality is that Hinduism, orthodox Hinduism, was structured upon a system of uneven caste-stratification. Hinduism without castes is as inconceivable as fire without flames.

"Question with the utmost tact an orthodox Hindu about his creed in reference to caste inequality, and you will consistently receive a dogmatic reply: 'Nobody! absolutely nobody save a Hindu is capable of understanding his ancient of ancient faiths, which has sanctified the most superb societal system of all ages.'

"Arya Samajista, the fanatical extremists of the polytheistic Hindus, advocate strict adherence to the gospel of the Vedas, antiquated Sanskrit literature professed by their holy men or Brahmans to be supernaturally inspired scriptures. Broadly the Vedas consist of four collections: Rig-, Yajur-, Sama-, and Atharva-Veda. The first one, Rig-Veda, is to Hinduism what the first book of Moses, Genesis, is to Judaism and Christianity. Turning to the famous title, though infamous text, Purusha Skuta—ninetieth hymn of the tenth mandals ('book') of the Rig-Veda—we peruse the numbered verses explaining Brahmanic conception of Man's creation":

> 'Number two: Purusha himself is this whole universe, whatever shall be. He is the Lord of immortality.
>
> Number eleven: When the gods divided Purusha, into how many portions was he cut? What did they call his mouth, his arms, his thighs, his feet?
>
> Number twelve: The Brahman was his mouth; the Rajanya (or Kshatriya) was made of both his arms; his thighs became the Vaisya; and the Sudra was produced from his feet.'

(So badly did the beardless orator mispronounce the Hindi words, a pundit wandering into the schoolroom might well have winced upon hearing his mother tongue abused. Inasmuch as such a foreign visitor was unlikely to appear, Vincent was not particularly perturbed at this stage of the speech. After all, his ghostwriter, the old man, while coaching the youth on his delivery, had assured him when he expressed concern about his wrong pronunciation of Hindustani that neither Mr. Du Puy nor Vincent's classmates would know if he happened to blunder.)

"Embodied within the twelfth verse is the hard matter out of which the Hindu caste-stratification was formed. Let us dig up its strata layer by layer and see what is to be discovered. But, before doing so, we should be equipped with a factual tool, a scoop that Brahmans either wrote or edited the Vedas.

"The top stratum—the layer that emanated from the mouth of Purusha—is the Brahmanic priests and pundits who head Hinduism in the sense that they are the revered hierarchy and the reputed intelligentsia. Traditionally they are the real leaders. Theoretically all mankind is subservient to their will.

"Various hereditary Brahmanic chieftains prevail. Sanadhya,

Audichya, Sarasvat, and Gaur comprise some of the influential groups. At present the leading Hindu communal society is the Mahasabha, which is reactionary and militantly rightist. The Mahasabha, controlled by bank barons and landlords, is led by a model Brahman, Pandit Madan Mohan Malaviya. He praises with frothing mouth the divine goodness of the priestly instituted caste system, and with snapping jaws upbraids nonsectarian reforms.

"Centuries of enforced ignorance and wholesale torture have persuaded primitive peoples that Brahmans are one step removed from heavenly deities and, moreover, only through their eternal wisdom and benevolence may loving things subsist in this world and the next. Unbathed or not, blood-smeared hands or not, the bodies of Brahmans are spotless and stainless.

"The priests and pundits are believed to be saintly and sacred, privileged to enjoy every exemption, every immunity. It is sacrilegious even for mighty maharajahs to refuse to treat them with the most profound respect. Offenders against Brahmans are said to suffer agonizing deaths and, among other horrors, to be reborn as vultures craving the flesh of men!

"The second stratum—the layer that emanated from the arms of Purusha—is the Rajanya (or Kshatriya), the warrior caste corresponding since ancient times to the Rajputs of Rajputana, and in current times to the Gurkhas of Nepal. They are the Brahmans' protective armor and iron gauntlet that has so effectively smashed the permissive population to a pulp in the hallowed name of Hinduism. To seek the favors of the gods, which naturally only Brahmans are empowered to grant, the hardhearted warriors stand ready to draw their swords against those who would dare repulse the priests raving for alms or the pundits ranting for tuitions.

"The third stratum—the layer that emanated from the thighs of Purusha—is the Vaisya (more recently called Bais): originally they were the pastoral, later the agricultural, in time the mercantile caste. Nowadays some are powerful industrialists such as the Banias, Khatri, and Aroras who lifted packs of heavy fortunes from the backs of their people. Tossing ill-gained rubies and rupees to the gods, buying spiritual blessings, the modern counterparts of the Vaisya support Brahmans to the hilt, and profitably supply warriors with weapons.

"The fourth stratum—the layer that emanated from the feet of Purusha, is the Sudra, the lowly servile caste, created to do the menial tasks of the three upper strata, especially the Brahmans.

Unlike their superiors, Sudras are not permitted to witness national sacrificial rites, nor are they permitted to hear the revelations of the Vedas that the Brahmans say would be a defilement of the godly scriptures. A Sudra may never be invested with the sacred thread which is supposed to bring regeneration to the members of the higher castes in an initiation ceremony wherein rigorous acts of devotion are performed.

"As a finale to this religious service symbolizing spiritual birth, a member of the warrior or mercantile caste is blessed as twice-born. As for a Sudra, he is doomed to remain once-born (*dvija*), incapable of purification. The Sudra cowers in utter debasement; although in reality he may be the epitome of virtue.

"So stupefied is a devout Sudra by the preachings of his priests, he believes walking across the shadow of a guru (divine preceptor) is a transgression. Often at the end of a fast the *dvija* will still decline to eat food until he can wash it down with water in which a Brahman is gracious enough to dip a purifying toe.

"Despite its sweet-sounding metrical Sanskrit, the Rig-Veda sourly sings of the Sudra as, 'the servant of another to be expelled at will, to be slain at will.' Such violent phrasing is almost gentle compared to that of other Indic writings, specifically the blood-curdling Code of Manu, reputedly written by a mythological progenitor of the Hindus but more probably concocted by hoary practitioners of priestcraft to put the people at the mercy of the Brahmans and, in turn, the Kahatriyas and Vaisya. How many human beings were and continue to be suppressed under the authority bestowed by this drummed-up canonic code, grows frighteningly apparent when we learn in 1940 out of about 204 million followers of Hinduism upwards of 191 million are Sudras.

"Planned with mathematical precision, the Code of Manu was coldly calculated to keep the castes solidified on the assumption human upheaval thus will not occur to break up the four-layer stratum of society in India. Many of the laws in the Code are inhuman, too vile to cite. However, I have selected a few which are discussible and give some indication as to the exacting measures resorted to by the Brahmans to deter social intercourse and marriage between the lower and upper castes":

> 'Manu, Ch. IV, v. 245: A Brahman who always connects himself with the most excellent ones, and shuns all inferior ones, himself becomes most distinguished; by an opposite conduct he becomes a Sudra.

> Manu, Ch. III, v. 110-12: A Kshatriya is not in actuality called a guest in a Brahman's house, nor is a Vaishya, nor a Sudra. If a Kshatriya comes in the manner of a guest to that house, he may be fed, however only after all Brahmans have eaten. Even a Vaishy or Sudra who comes in the manner of a guest should be allowed to eat, but with the servants, thereby displaying the kind disposition of the householder.

> Manu, Ch. III, v. 15: A twice-born man marrying a Sudra out of infatuation will quickly bring his family and descendants to the condition of Sudras.'

"Brutally beaten into the benumbed brains of the Hindus is a self-serving doctrine involving successive rebirths (transmigration of the internal soul?). Brahmanic advocates of the doctrine hold it is governed by <u>karma</u>, ethical consequence of past and present actions, good or bad. They advocate that in the grandeur of the infinite cosmological scheme a speck of life, soiled by sin, is reincarnated again and again and again.

"The soiled speck is transferred from vegetable to insect, from insect to animal, from animal to human, from least human, to unfit human, from unfit human to fit human, ofttimes up a metamorphic scale, ofttimes down the scale. When the soiled speck is sufficiently purged, it ascends to the highest degree on the metamorphic scale and enters the holy form of a Brahman. Thereby a cycle is completed which culminates in the speck's return to its source of spiritual sublimity.

"Listen to the dialogue of a common scene in India: Prostrating himself at the feet of his guru, the *dvija* wails out of frustration, 'Oh merciful sire, since I cannot escape the effects of my bygone black deeds, I beg you to impart to me the knowledge of the sages. Pray tell me how to save myself from being bound in a future existence to the same dog's fate to which I am now deservedly roped.'

"Looking pious, the divine preceptor instructs: 'Follow faithfully step by step every direction of your <u>dharma</u> (the caste's rigid rules of conduct). Behave until your dying day as a perfect servant to your betters. Pity not yourself. Do not ever forget, you through your own doings are a despicable, lowly creature. Unquestioned obedience toward your master's slightest wish, without complaint, is a Sudra's only road to salvation.'

"In the excavation of each of the four beds of religious rock comprising India's stratified social structure, it must be realized winds of despair have gradually eroded the top layers of the Vedic formation. Eventually heavy rains of dissension washed away tons of loosened rock fragments with the result that an estimated three-thousand castes and tens of thousands of subcastes are scattered about the famine-ridden land.

"Centuries of diabolic inculcation by the Brahmanic priesthood has developed in the leadership of these lithoid caste-subcaste divisions hard characters resistive to any and all change unless they personally benefit. Progress would inevitably lead to their expulsion; hence little reform, if any, is permitted. Therein is an underlying reason why the uneven caste-stratification of Hindu society carved out by the Purusha Skuta circa twelve-hundred years before the advent of Christ is still as solid as ever in the year 1940 A.D.

"At this time a parenthetical statement seems opportune. In order to hoard power, the Brahmans have deliberately kept their flocks lost in darkness. By nature pedantic and pompous, they have shrouded Hindu metaphysics in mysticism. Therefore, the most learned scholar could slip up on some element of the shadowed subject.

"To illustrate, a word for 'caste' is varna. Confusingly, Max Müller, author of A History of Ancient Sanskrit Literature, refers to varna as 'the coloring or modulation of the voice.' Yet a number of distinguished writers define varna as 'color or complexion.' A theory based on their definition is the assumption that since near-white as well as brownish invaders overran the subcontinent around 3,000 B.C., conquering the black aborigines, men were separated into castes by skin shades and were forced to live within designated geographic boundaries. It would be less complicated if one referred to varna in practical application as order—that is, societal order—ranging from the lowest to the highest in equality.

"Although varna may be an arcanum arcanorum or mysterious 'secret of secrets' unrevealed to outsiders, it is no profound mystery in India. And, to reiterate, caste distinction is a petrified principle of Hinduism. However karma (rebirth) or dharma (rules) is construed, each perversely preserves the wickedness of varna, together with its inherent pleasures for a privileged minority and pains for a plagued majority.

"Dissatisfied just to trap and half-starve in the fourth varna some 191 million bedeviled persons, the Brahmanic brotherhood had to satiate still more its demoniac spirits by outcasting close to fifty-one million additional underfed human beings. Imagine nearly fifty-one million people shooed away from society as if they were a swarm of anopheline mosquitoes screened off at the entrances to populated communities. In the bloodshot eyes of Hinduism, as low as a Sudra is—and that is rock bottom—an outcast, muddy clay, could never reach up high enough to scratch a *divija's* thickened sole.

"While he is considered impure because of sins committed during a former life, a Sudra's contact does not contaminate other Hindus. But a pariah, no matter how clean or chaste, pollutes by his very touch. A fanatic Hindu believes he can be polluted by the mere sight of a pariah. Obdurate orthodoxy requires an outcast to wear a bell around his neck so that the bell's ringing as he walks will give warning an untouchable is in the vicinity. Thus caste men have time to avoid the polluting scum or else, one by one, they be put through the inconvenience of performing purificatory rituals.

"An abject Sudra may console himself that in his next transmigration there is a possibility of ascending to a loftier order, whereas an accursed pariah labors under no such delusion. According to Brahmanic teachings, an outcast and his mate and issue, alive or dead, cannot ever be saved. Their destiny sealed, eternally they must remain filthy, impious, beef-eating panchamas, unworthy of breathing the same air as Hindus who pay homage to the sacred cow and out of reverence to this dumb beast's holiness are confirmed vegetarians.

"Fed up with Hinduism's doctrines sanctifying the subjugation of millions of innocents, we are compelled to wonder what Great Britain has done about this deplorable situation. To be sure, His Majesty's propaganda ministers have highly publicized altruistic England's indignation the times his viceroys reprimandingly slapped on the wrist rebellious rajas or badgeringly shook a finger at belligerent Brahmans.

"In reality these showy gestures are a farce as far as humanitarianism is concerned. The British government usually indicates disapproval when her forceful reign or raj is threatened. Tolerating no misbehaviour, Father England always has been a stickler for maintaining discipline among the headstrong children in his colonies. A lax display of sovereignty, he fears, would endanger his control.

"For 150 years up to and including the present year, 1940, the British government has had the potency, the authority, the facility, and the opportunity to express its objections to the evils of <u>varna</u>. The Crown's propagandists declare the government has done so; but the facts refute their claims. Archaic, unfavorable Hindu domestic and inheritance laws as well as customary, inequitable laws affecting the nether castes, are still administered in the courts of British India.

"Moreover, Parliament has not condemned the caste system as a criminal conspiracy against the lower strata or stratumless Indians, nor were acts passed to abolish the discriminatory practice of varna. That the parliamentary body would is quite improbable inasmuch as Great Britain in principle finds no fault with castes. Snubbing social scientists findings, England accepts without compunction caste or class differentiation by blood types, type B (blue blood) being the rarest and richest in the opinion of the sovereign state.

"The English aristocracy can be compared to the crown of a masonry arch over an opening with a locked, steel gate: The keystone is the monarch who holds the stonework together, and upon which the extrados, princes and princesses, depend; and the abutments that receive the thrust of the arch are dukes and duchesses; and supporting the crown arch are the peers, supportive lords in parliament.

"Beyond the arched gateway is exclusive power and wealth protected at all times by the royal guard. Shouting from the gilded balcony of the palace down below to their subjects, the aristocracy mouths poetic words in a nasal tone annoying to one's sensitive ears:

> Commoners assembled in clusters out there,
> England's our heritage. Cheers to the crown!
> Don't storm the palace; bold vassals take care.
>
> Now that all's quiet, to you we'll explain,
> Trespassing never was part of the bill.
> Outside the gates you will kindly remain;
> Keep to your places as noblemen will.
>
> You have your duties, and we the estate;
> These are the birthrights no subject must wrong.
> Loyal men, heed what your masters relate:
> Fight on for glory; serve for a song!
>
> Duteous commoners, you need not sigh.
> Only the slackers in prison we fling.
> If you are ready to toil and die,
> England endures for us. God save the king!

"Where are the minds of Englishmen, who Sudra-like stand by with blind devotion while the king and queen, riding in a golden coach, are extravagantly glorified at a costly coronation, a wasteful expenditure that could be spent prudently to give a humanitarian hand to miserable unfortunates unable to find shelter from the damp London fog? Where is the pride of Englishmen, who Sudra-like bow with bended knee before starchy humans, lavishly attired in jeweled crowns and ermine cloaks, who, more often than not, are unable to come up to the bootstraps of their subjects' productivity, creativity, and ability, despite the advantages bestowed on the crown? God save the commoners!

"At once a chilling reality awakens us as though cold water were splashed on our faces. Negroids do not disapprove of individuals because they are black-complexioned, yet many a Negroid debases other Negroids socially. Mongoloids do not disapprove of individuals because they are yellow- or brown- or red-complexioned, yet many a Mongoloid debases other Mongoloids socially. And Caucasoids do not disapprove of individuals because they are white-complexioned, yet many a Caucasoid debases other Caucasoids socially.

"Something is strange in society's social column. Let us stretch our imagination and look up at its monumental capital of gold. We observe persons holding on to it for dear life. The sun shining in our eyes blurs our vision so that we cannot see their complexions. But by shading our eyes we can see that they are few in number, and that they are grasping priceless antique scrolls only affordable to wealthy individuals.

"Notice time and time again some lose their hold and drop off the capital to fall hurtfully below on the copper base. Frantically clinging to the edges of it by their fingertips are masses of indigent people, most of the human race, sunk chin-deep in mire surrounding the base. Also we observe around the fluted stone shaft several stouthearted individuals desperately seeking toeholds in scant-and-sparse cracks by which to climb up to the capital. For every one who succeeds in reaching it, countless numbers swiftly slip back down into the mire, spattering slime.

"Although erected in our imagination, this monument depicts only too realistically mankind's plight. In a weird world of wrongs being lofty or low in social status is not determined by the worth of a person's character but by the worth of a person's currency. Consequently color is not a criterion for placing a person in society's high station.

"If you disagree, be prepared to answer a long delayed question. Are all whites socially equal in the United States? Resist replying hastily and consider a matter or two. One thing is certain, presently in the year 1940 relatively few members of the white population are listed in the Social Registers circulated in such major cities as Baltimore, Boston, Chicago, Cleveland, New York, Philadelphia, Pittsburgh, St. Louis, San Francisco, and Washington.

"The hard cash fact is, a family's eligibility for entry in a blue-book listing socially prominent people depends mainly on the patriarch's Dun and Bradstreet rating. So it is that Social Registers include golf-playing Mr. Tycoon, his socialite wife and their heirs, and limited numbers of carbon copies of families in country clubs. On the other side of the tracks, pool-playing Mr. Toiler, his housewife and children, and unlimited numbers of carbon copies of families in city communities are excluded from the bluebook.

"In the light of all that has been related in class during yesterday's and today's periods, it should be illuminating to glance again at the topic we have contemplated: 'Human Equality, Fact or Fiction, in Relation to Individuals at Large, With Emphasis on America and Asia.' Now that you have some insight on the subject, you can decide for yourself if human equality is fact or fiction in America...in Asia...or anywhere else in the world."

Chapter 22

At last Vincent Armstrong's lengthy discourse had ended. His arduous task in Public Speaking I behind him, he was joyful. It was nevertheless too soon to rejoice. A new difficulty awaited the youth. While walking home after school, he worried about a demand Mr. Du Puy shouted at him as he scooted past his classmates to exit the room in a hurry when the bell rang indicating class was dismissed.

In a stern voice Mr. Du Puy had demanded: "Just a second, young man, before you gallop off in a cloud of dust. Come to my registry room during your study period tomorrow morning. I want to have a few words with you privately. The room number is 313. Remember now, I'll be expecting you—without fail!"

Troublesome thoughts plagued Vincent each step of the way. Could anything be wrong. How did Du Puy find out he had a study period. Did the public-speaking teacher go to the trouble of checking Vincent's program card in the attendance office. Maybe Du Puy suspected Vincent had not written the speech. Or maybe the talk was too outspoken. The old man had warned Vincent its hard facts were not easy to swallow and digest. Just the same, why the devil did that so-and-so Du Puy insist upon seeing him in private.

Chance would have it the high-school student never learned the answers to his perplexities. The next day, as he approached Room 313, a teacher passing by in the hall informed him that Mr. Du Puy had been in an automobile smashup on Sixteenth Street near Mission Dolores Basilica. Incapacitated by his injuries, he would not be back at school until the following semester. Vincent was very sorry to hear the man had been injured in an accident. Still, under the circumstances, the youth was not entirely lacking in elation at the fortuitous turn of events.

After that harrowing trial in Public Speaking I, he resolved to avoid putting himself again in a position which could lead to a similar experience. Thenceforth Vincent was extra cautious in all his classes, minding his P's and Q's to the letter and behaving exceptionally well. He made every effort not to attract the teachers' attention. Being attentive and of good demeanor was painless for Vincent to endure. However, holding on to his resolution to be inconspicuous sometimes could be as unbearable as holding on to a red-hot poker.

Occasionally while he sat in his classrooms, sunlight shining in through the windows penetrated Vincent's clothing. The rays warming his skin reminded him of the delightful glow that had radiated from the body of Roxanne Davis the afternoons they lay naked in bed fondling each other. Vincent was dazzled by the bright sun; the classroom appeared in his mind's eye to be her well-lit bedroom.

Envisioning the woman's nakedness, the youth grew sexually excited. Blood flowed rapidly into his male organ, which became saturated with the hot, red fluid. Distending till it was elongated and erect, Vincent's organ throbbed tormentingly within the confined space of his underpants and pressed hard against a thigh, almost burning the flesh beyond endurance.

So tremendously did his organ distend, Vincent was ashamed to move away from his seat lest the bulging contour on his pants be observed. By cruel coincidence, at such times he would be summoned to the front of the room to recite. Dangling a large binder in a casual manner near the fly of his pants, the schoolboy attempted to conceal the object of his embarrassment. He dared not remove the binder before the protuberance between his thighs dwindled down to unnoticeable dimensions.

Naturally Vincent's erections were not confined to the schoolroom. They were bound to occur on a streetcar, in a swimming pool, just about any place should something stimulate Vincent to think of Roxanne, and cause him to reflect upon the carnal thrills she was equipped to provide. Thus far he had respected her wishes, admirably restraining himself from pursuing her. But the virile youth was straining at the bit.

Early one Sunday morning when he awakened from a torrid wet dream, Vincent decided come rain or come shine he had to see the woman. Perhaps instead of telephoning Roxanne, if he went to her home, he could convince her that she and she alone was capable of gratifying him sexually. She would not be able to deny he gratified her, too. Very likely Roxanne remained at home on a Sunday. Also it was possible her brother might be there. Vincent was willing to take the risk, that frantic was he.

Upon arriving at Roxanne's house, Vincent ascended the steps to the front door, oh so quietly, and pushed the doorbell, every so gently. After several seconds, when nobody responded to his fainthearted approach, he realized it was foolish, for the sound of the bell was too soft to be heard. If Roxanne's brother happened to be at home, a timid signal to gain admission into the house would not prevent him from coming to the door. Pouring caution down the drain, Vincent carelessly gave the doorbell a hard push. That worked, he could detect someone stirring about in the house. As the youth desperately had hoped, Roxanne was the one to open the door.

She greeted Vincent with an expression of surprise yet, to his delight, voiced no objection to his unexpected visit. Roxanne invited him into the house. The place was dark. Evidently she had been asleep. Her hair was disheveled, spread untidily over her shoulders. All Roxanne was wearing was a housecoat. She told him that her brother was away, which was good news to Vincent. He relaxed, sinking down into a squat, leather armchair near an ash-littered fireplace in the living room.

The room was awfully stuffy. It seemed there was a bad odor from the ashes or whatever else was still smoldering in the fireplace. He would have liked to open a window to get a whiff of fresh air. Roxanne drew the drapes to let some light into the room. Seeing her more clearly, he became perturbed. Geez! she looked tired. Her lids were droopy, and she had dark circles under her eyes.

Vincent sat back in the armchair, immobile. Forcing himself to speak, he begged her forgiveness for dropping by unexpectedly. The youth explained he just could not put her out of his mind. He was haunted by the unforgettable exciting moments they had shared in front of the long swivel mirror in her bedroom. While talking, he struggled to hide his alarm over Roxanne's haggard appearance.

His blood boiling, Vincent was too hot to see straight. He was tempted to slip his hand through an opening in her housecoat, where he eyed the enticing curve of a puffed-up, pale breast. Suddenly the bad odor—a strange, sickening stench—hit him again, stifling his puissant passion. To dissipate the smell he brushed the palm of his hand back and forth over his nose as if it itched.

Apparently Roxanne had not heard a word Vincent said. Despite his explanation why he had dropped in on her unannounced, she asked what prompted him to come to see her. As in the past she repeated her favorite lines that the world was filled with lovely young girls, fresh blossoming flowers. He had so many to pick from. She simply could not understand how he could be interested in a shriveled-up old lady like herself. With a dramatically sad gesture she directed his attention to her hair, streaked with telltale gray.

Vincent tried to console Roxanne by saying that she was far from old, that she had always appealed to him strongly, that he had not been able to find the same strong appeal in girls his own age. All right, so she surpassed him by a number of years. He had never given their difference in age a second thought.

He reminded her that she was the one who said their sex was exceptionally wonderful because of his youth and her maturity. "People are only as old or young as they feel," Vincent argued, quoting a warmed-over platitude. "You must not imagine yourself as being old. Why, you have a long life ahead of you."

At those words Roxanne started to cry, weeping hysterically. Tears poured heavily from her moist eyes, two cloudbursts precipitating torrents of rain. Upset by her tearful downpour, Vincent attempted to calm Roxanne. He asked her why she was crying and reached out to wipe the teardrops from her cheeks. She pulled away and did not reply. Vincent attributed the cause of Roxanne's tears to his unexpected presence. He apologized for not telephoning before he came to see her. The last thing he wanted to do was to intrude. In a slighted tone he said he would depart at once.

Between deep sobs she told Vincent that he was really welcome, begged him not to leave, and assured him he was not the cause of her grief. Crying had not flattered the woman; her face and figure were drawn. (An image of an eviscerated hen flashed across Vincent's mind.)

The schoolteacher had mixed emotions about having initiated Vincent into the sex act when he was a pupil in her class at John Muir Junior High School. But she confessed she stopped feeling guilty about their affair some time ago. Her despondency had nothing to do with him. It was due to something else.

"I am terribly, terribly ill!" Roxanne blurted out the reason for her unhappiness. "Truly, my dear, I am not well."

With a pang of sympathy in his heart Vincent tried to be helpful. "Oh, I'm sorry. Shouldn't you see a doctor."

"God is my witness, I have. I have seen many doctors. Two were specialists, the best in California."

Puzzled, the youth pressed the woman for details. "Can't they help you. What did they say?"

Staring at him with gaunt, hollow orbs, her expression conveyed the feeling of a dreadful dissolution in the offing. Roxanne reluctantly answered, "They...they said I have incurable cancer."

Life is fragile material stitched together by fine threads easily frayed and severed. Perhaps it was because their intercourse was cut off; perhaps it was because his libido was ripped to pieces; perhaps it was because her existence was worn beyond repair: regardless of the possibilities the final chapter was written on their tragic affair. Nonetheless—whatever the reader's sentiment about that leitmotif might be—after the heart-rending episode with Roxanne Davis, the youth had neither the desire nor the occasion to go to Berkeley again until nearly three years later when he graduated from high school and aspired to matriculate at the University of California as a prelegal major in preparation for law school.

He was eager to enroll as a student in this famed educational institution but was apprehensive about returning to the little city across the bay from San Francisco. Since Roxanne's house was within walking distance of the university, he feared, due to her nearness, he constantly would be subjected to disquieting memories of her the days he had to be on the campus to attend classes.

However, you can rest assured the young man was needlessly concerned. A heavy chain of events, interlinked with occasional light ones, was to submerge Roxanne so deep below the surface of Vincent's mind that, like a rhapsodical dream, she soon faded from his consciousness.

Vincent Armstrong was awakened instantly to reality by the aroma of freshly brewed coffee. "Here is the java, no cream or sugar. Careful! it's hot," Bert Craig cautioned Vincent in handing a cup of coffee to him. "There were no chocolate doughnuts left. Too bad, that's your favorite kind. You should have joined Alice and me on the coffee break. See, Mr. Normand only just now returned to the studio. You wouldn't have missed anything."

Vincent thanked Bert and blew into the cup to cool the steaming coffee. He slowly sipped it while waiting for Normand to begin discussing the next dance, which the supervisor had said was closely connected to the history of the jitterbug.

Chapter 23

A HISTORY OF THE CLASSIC BALLROOM DANCES

American Dances

II-C. The Swing (to cultivate sure-footedness and personality)

By the time we started exchanging blows with the Axis, jitter-bugging had won the sanction of Army Morale Divisions, Defense Recreation Authorities, and high-class hotels. But, although the handwriting was on the wall in 1941, the jitterbug's conversion into a dance of respectability did not occur until the final stages of the war. Such, too, had been the case when Johnny came marching home in 1918, and dances once objectionable were accepted.

Another interesting historic parallel can be drawn between conditions preceding World Wars I and II, conditions which had a like effect on the dancer, and, in turn, on the dance. The GI, identically to the doughboy, lived in daily dread of the much-revealed, much concealed horrors awaiting him upon the battlefield.

With each war bulletin bringing news of shocking fatalities, far behind the lines packs of jittery dogfaces—clinging to soothing females' hands—attempted in the peaceful atmosphere of the dance floor to escape the turmoil of combat. Trained in the ways of war, not in the art of dance, the tense and edgy soldiers broke out in a rash of rapid movements to scorching hot jazz. The resultant steps were rough if not ridiculous in character.

Under both the Wilson and Roosevelt administrations, dancing away one's cares was a panacea many Americans used in seeking release from neuroses or hysteria induced by the frightening international scene. However, just as dancing had calmed down to some semblance of normalcy at the time of Kaiser Wilhelm's dethronement in 1918, jitterbugging simmered down and became somewhat sane in its execution when the Land of the Rising Sun was eclipsed in 1945.

Shortly after the cessation of hostilities on all global fronts, the elixir of the jitterbug concentrated into a newly manufactured dance, labeled swing. Its name obviously was derived from that of swing music. Unlike jitterbugging, swinging, if properly performed, gives an appearance of dignity to the dancer. Because swing is highly refined and subtlized, it sometimes is described as 'sophisticated swing.'

["Although in the swing most step-combinations are formulated from three rhythmical arrangements also, they are by no means identical to those in the jitterbug (arranged on Lindy rhythms)." Normand removed from his desk drawer a bunch of mimeographed sheets which he distributed among the teachers.

"Illustrated on the sheets are the three swing rhythms that I am referring to. You can see their COUNTING FORMULA—Slow, Slow, Quick, Quick—consists of six beats whereas the Lindy's consists of eight beats as was detailed in the history of the jitterbug. Since one and one-half measures of music are a requisite for swing steps, it is evident they are different from jitterbug steps for which two measures are required.

"Rhythmical differences notwithstanding, the DIRECTIONAL PATTERNS of the swing were cut from the same choreographic cloth as was the jitterbug. Such material we already have examined thoroughly. Therefore, delineating swing steps—something I shall not attempt to do—would be a waste of time at present."

While the supervisor was talking, some of his curious listeners looked at the mimeographed sheets he had distributed. They read as follows:

Single Swing Rhythm

Slow:	Step to the side on the left foot, and then with the toes of the right foot touch the floor near the heel of the left foot,
Slow:	Step to the side on the right foot, and then with the toes of the left foot touch the floor near the heel of the right foot,
(*Quick*:	Step back into fifth position on the ball of the
(	left foot,
(*Quick*:	Step in place on the ball of the right foot.

REMINDERS: A Slow equals two counts, a Quick equals one count. The woman's footwork is the same as the man's except she steps with the opposite foot to his. Of necessity the knee is bent before the toes, slightly raised, touch the floor. Be sure to start in first position, heels together and toes pointed outward comfortably. Review the foot positions in your outline of the history on the waltz.

Double Swing Rhythm

Slow: With the toes of the left foot touch the floor near the heel of the right foot, and then step to the side on the left foot,

Slow: With the toes of the right foot touch the floor near the heel of the left foot, and then step to the side on the right foot,

(*Quick*: Step back into fifth position on the ball of the
(left foot,

(*Quick*: Step in place on the ball of the right foot.

REMINDERS: The two Slows are simply the reverse of the two Slows in Single Swing Rhythm. The Quicks are the same in the single, double, and triple rhythms.

Triple Swing Rhythm

Slow: With alternating small shuffles step sideward: step left—close with the right foot—step left again (one-and-two count),

Slow: With alternating small shuffles step sideward: step right—close with the left foot—step right again (one-and-two count),

(*Quick*: Step back into fifth position on the ball of the
(left foot,

(*Quick*: Step in place on the ball of the right foot.

"In spite of the difference in phrasing between jitterbugging (two measures) and swinging (a measure and a half), the history of the jitterbug is the history of the swing. Correctly or incorrectly, that is why the phrasing as well as the names of both are often interchanged.

"When you were in the Training Class, at technic sessions the dance director taught you how musical phrasing is rendered in a sequence of movements making up a swing step-combination. It was not his job to delve into the historical aspects of the swing. Furthermore, since National Dance Studios considers the jitterbug to be passé, he refrained from teaching you techniques used in the performance of that dance.

"It is my job, nevertheless, to point out to you the dissimilarities between jitterbugging and swinging in their practical execution so that you will be properly equipped to teach your prospective students. A necessary though frequently overlooked piece of equipment in social dancing is etiquette, for just as a discourteous driver cannot drive well on the highway, a discourteous dancer cannot dance well on the dance floor.

"Therefore, I touched on social behavior, good and bad, in a chart of comparisons based on my personal observations in ballrooms and dance halls. I ordered copies of the chart at the same time the ones on jitterbug and swing rhythms were mimeographed. Unfortunately, the girl in the office was too busy with her regular work to run off the last stencil. So I shall read my copy to you. No. Better yet, I'll have one of you do it."

The supervisor snapped open the metal rings of a binder lying on his desk and took out the chart. Next he selected Alice Scott to read it to the other teachers in the group:

COMPARATIVE CHART

Jitterbug	Swing
1. Jitterbug is not restricted to any one spot or direction in its performance on the dance floor. In other words, its movements are erratic. They may take little or a great deal of space. But generally they demand much elbowroom. As a result, jitterbugs (particularly the unskilled ones) monopolize space on a floor, jostle non-jitterbugs, and crowd them out. Here is a reason why the dance and the dancer often are disliked and barred.	1. Swing, on the other hand, is restricted to a comparatively small area on the dance floor—an imaginary narrow slot extending approximately two yards in length, depending upon individual stride and arm reach. The couples, in consequence, never move about erratically but dance back and forth on a straight line between two hypothetical points. If any jostling occurs, it is usually caused by careless non-swingers failing to avoid colliding with those who are swinging.
2. The bending of the knees in jitterbugging ranges from slight to extreme—the latter being the rule, not the exception. Also, since hopping, jumping, and leaping are prevalent in the	2. The bending of the knees in swinging is quite subtle. In that the knee is naturally flexed when a dancer steps, constant effort is made to minimize the flexion. For the most part, there is no hop-

dance, the stepping lacks solidity and is not close to the floor. As a consequence, jerkiness becomes evident in the movements, and dignity of execution is nonexistent.

ping, jumping, or leaping; the stepping is solid and close to the floor. Emphasis is put on smoothness of execution and dignity in movement.

3. Jitterbugs frequently stamp or tap their feet and can be rather noisy.

3. Swingers never stamp or tap their feet and are as quiet as possible.

4. In jitterbugging the rhythms are interchangeable. That is, any given step can be done in either single, double, or triple Lindy rhythm. The choice is a matter of individual preference; ordinarily, however, the rhythm—once selected—is maintained throughout the entire dance.

4. All that holds true for interchanging the rhythms in jitterbugging also applies in swinging; but, in addition, the rhythms may be mixed. This means that a swing step—besides being performed solely in single, double, or triple swing rhythm—may be done in combinations thereof. For example, a step might contain parts taken from both single and triple rhythms.

Miss Scott's reading concluded, she handed the chart back to Mr. Normand. He thanked the young woman, who promptly returned to her seat.

The supervisor replaced the chart into his binder and said: "Should anybody want a copy of the Comparative Chart, let me know. I'll save you a copy, if ever I get some mimeographed.

"I might add a couple of points worthy of being noted: First, due to the swing's inter-measure phrasing it lends itself to interesting innovations in dance patterns. Second, swing is a smooth dance appropriate for all ages, youngsters and oldsters alike.

"Now you have heard the whole story of the swing. Paradoxically, despite the fact that it is sterling American, the latest product of our folk dances, only a limited number of us are able to distinguish swinging in a ballroom from swinging in a hammock."

Still seated in the studio, Bert Craig, Alice Scott, and Vincent Armstrong were engaged in conversation. "I can't imagine," Bert laughed, "anyone not knowing the difference between swinging in a ballroom and swinging in a hammock. Surely Mr. Normand was kidding. Or was he serious?"

Alice responded to her fiancé: "Honey, don't be silly. Of course, he wasn't serious. He was merely making a point. It is true, most people are not familiar with the latest American dances."

Vincent agreed with her, "They not only are unfamiliar with the new American dances but also they are unfamiliar with the old ones...present company included."

His ego a bit bruised, Bert was miffed: "Speak for yourself. I listened very carefully to Mr. Normand's lectures on the histories. I remember all the dances, new and old. He covered all the old ones."

The supervisor, Ralph Normand, on his way out of the studio, happened to overhear Bert. "Pardon me, Mr. Craig. I only discussed the dances that were relevant. There are many outdated dances I did not mention. A couple of examples comes to mind, the Collegiate Hop and the Varsity Drag."

"They sound interesting," Alice commented. "They must have originated on college campuses. Were they difficult dances?"

"Not really," Normand replied. "The Collegiate Hop was simply a step and hop from foot to foot. Gleaned from the Charleston, The Varsity Drag's basic movement was raising the feet up on the toes and lowering the feet down onto the heels in the performance of steps. It did not originate on college campuses. The Varsity Drag was introduced by a stage dancer, Zelma O'Neal, in a 1927 production 'Good Times.'

"I have to run. I am late for an appointment. See you tomorrow morning."

That night after going to bed, Vincent Armstrong had a dream. He dreamt he was on the varsity in tennis and debating at the University of California. In his dreaming he relived the days bygone he had spent on the campus.]

Chapter 24

whistled Vincent spontaneously as he lay stretched out on a lawn of the University of California campus. The shrill, birdlike sounds his pursed lips blew were an accompaniment to the bells in the tower of the campanile which were chiming Yradier's musical composition *La Paloma*. In between notes he inhaled fresh, invigorating air and mused how gratifying it was finally to be at the university on the way toward realizing his boyhood dream to become a criminal lawyer.

Unexpectedly, though, the scholastic road upon which he had set forth appeared bumpy, rather rough in reality. Vincent was somewhat shaken up by the ruggedness of his new educational experience. Highly elevated, it turned out to be more arduous to ascend that he hitherto had visualized.

Looking around the campus at other students reclining on the blanket of grass, he wondered if they also were having difficulty starting off on a smooth journey toward their academic objectives, whether in the liberal arts or in the professional fields. His fellow students seemed cheerful and unconcerned about their studies.

Judging by appearances, Vincent was inclined to believe he alone was finding courses at the university not easy to grasp. Upperclass boys and girls certainly sounded cocksure of themselves in their attempts to attain academic achievement. They had the superior look of wise owls hooting about classical literary works and complicated scientific principles that were, among other subjects, very deep. It was hard for an academically tool-less freshman to dig into the base of doctrinal matter.

None of the owlish upperclassmen showed outward manifestations of being the least bit disturbed about their studies. Evidently they found university easy, since, as far as he could see, they scarcely opened a book. Instead they whiled away their time discussing everything from who or what created God to mindless experiments with an Ouija board.

Oh, very likely it was the newness of university life that was troublesome to adjust to. There was no use worrying prematurely. Getting jittery and jumping the gun could disqualify a fellow from a competitive race. In the long run he was bound to make much more mileage—progress further in his courses—if he slowed down and paced himself. Undoubtedly, while endeavoring to secure a lead, he had been burning the midnight oil too long, hitting the books too hard. The monotony and strain of overstudy had dulled his perspective.

Yes, that must be why he had been having trouble staying on track. He was bored, on edge. Under stress, he had become keyed up till he was ready to snap—a taut wire drawn too tight. Well, he must relax somehow, rest his mind a little, let himself go, unloosen his emotional self. What he urgently needed was diversion, a solid dose of it. To a male possessing Vincent Armstrong's virility, of necessity this signified staying with a woman...an ardent woman...an uninhibited woman, a strongly sexed woman who was capable of relieving the terrible tension pulling him apart inwardly.

However, with commuting back and forth between his home in San Francisco and the university in Berkeley, studying evenings on weekdays, and working Saturdays and Sundays (partly to pay tuition but mostly to maintain a car), he had neither five minutes nor five cents to spare. Seeking out female companions was a time-taking, expensive proposition that he could ill afford. Still, what would be the good of it if, for the sake of speculation, he put a bite on his father and filled his wallet with a few greenbacks. His address book was empty, blank as the back of a business card.

Come to mull over the situation, it did not add up. Of the hundreds of females flitting around the campus, he did not have one telephone number—not a solitary one. Periodically he had attempted to strike up an acquaintanceship with certain ones. But, he struck out. The coeds who attracted Vincent were not attracted to him. They refused to give him the tiniest tumble, let alone a date, though his advances toward the girls were no more brazen or no less polite than any of the other freshmen.

How come, he pondered, the limited number of girls he liked, the ones whose forms furnished fuel to his inside furnace, just were not interested in him. To aggravate the situation their attitude was standoffish when he spoke to them, as if they were annoyed at his attempts to become acquainted. Nothing he did to establish friendly relations worked.

Brother! he tried every line in man's get-acquainted manual. Unsuccessful, he discarded it and tried time-tested animal's approaches. Regardless of the method Vincent used: the worldly wolf's approach, the slow snail's approach, the lovable lamb's approach, the cautious cat's approach, the rapid rabbit's approach, the teasing turtle's approach, the dear deer's approach...all failed to attract an appealing mate.

Yet, to Vincent's irritation, the females he was not fond of persistently got into his hair. And brushing those twists out was an unpleasant thing to do. It mattered not how little he encouraged some or how much he discouraged others, they would take the initiative in acquainting themselves with him. Some smiled so sticky sweet that he felt demoted in self-esteem to the lower class of a heel when he pulled away with a distasteful sour look.

Why, oh why, Vincent wondered, was life so tormentive. Did other people undergo the same trials and tribulations? Feeling sorry for himself, he hoped such was the case, as though that might ease the pain of his anguish if it were endured by others also.

Still, to fool around with college girls was nonsensical. The career-minded bookworms were sickening to the stomach. They were domineering females wrapped up in themselves. And the good-time "rah, rah, rah" chicks were a headache to put up with. All they wanted to do was dote upon football players while being wined and dined. On top of that, irrespective of type—serious, flighty, or otherwise—the girls had mainly one passion in common: they itched to hook a husband. Hell! this fish was not swallowing any female's juicy bait. A fellow had to be ripe for marriage.

Vincent Armstrong was unripe as a stone-hard avocado.

Carrying on a school romance with some coed could become involved, could interfere with his studies as well as hers. What if they were not right for each other. Suppose she was negligent in taking care of herself, and her belly bloated. He would be a sacrificial lamb led to the altar. Might as well cut off his head; that could not be more painful. Without a doubt it would be a safer, a lot smarter to meet someone experienced sexually who was not a student at the university, someone on the outside.

Now then, where shall I look? Vincent asked himself. Searching his mind, he had a recollection...of course, at Bunny's in San Francisco! He should have thought of the downtown coffee shop earlier. It was the place where a pleasingly plump, blonde waitress worked.

True, her hair appeared to be bleached, and she was no beauty queen. Still the way luscious parts of the waitress' body oozed out of her snug-fitting uniform, like whipped cream oozing from the tube of a canvas pastry bag, made his mouth water. He could not be positive, but he suspected she had cast a sexy eye in his direction the times he dropped in at Bunny's for a strawberry waffle. Or else why had she rushed over to serve Vincent first when other customers were seated ahead of him: That was something he ought to find the answer to, and soon.

Chapter 25

Although it was out of his way to go downtown, Vincent did not care. On pins and needles to become intimate with the amiable waitress, at his earliest opportunity he started to frequent the Bunny Waffle Shop. The first few times he patronized the place Vincent and the waitress exchanged friendly eye-to-eye glances. Before long they were engaged in words with warm overtones of intimacy.

Speaking to a waitress with familiarity across the counter of a busily buzzing coffee shop fronting Market Street was awkward for the college boy. Everybody—customers sitting on stools flanking Vincent's left side, the cashier to his far right, couples in booths behind him—seemed to have their attention directed at Vincent.

Self-conscious, he felt his every action was noticed, his every word heard. Nevertheless, during their snatches of conversation he managed to tell the waitress some things about himself that he believed interesting, which they were if one happened to be interested in Vincent Armstrong.

From their brief chats he learned the waitress' name was Elsie Martin. She mentioned her home town once, but it did not register on his brain; the crowded coffee shop was too noisy at the moment for him to concentrate. Also, Elsie told Vincent that she had resided in San Francisco only four months; that she had expected the bay city might be foggy though not so windy as the area was; that San Franciscans were chilly, chilly cold—damned unfriendly.

Elsie confided she was either awfully homesick or awfully lonesome. She could not make up her mind which bothered her the most. What did Vincent think it was? Her question was left unanswered. He had to leave in a hurry for his classes at Cal. Urged on by a sweet tooth, or whatever, Vincent returned to Bunny's the very next day. He craved a strawberry waffle covered with fluffy whipped cream (or something scrumptiously soft and sapid).

When the waitress served Vincent his order, he spoke to her. "Elsie, yesterday you said you were undecided as to whether you were lonely or homesick. After thinking it over, my diagnosis is that Miss Martin ails not because she is away from home. Her sickness is loneliness.

"People could come down with it even in their own backyard. My case is a good example. I was born in San Francisco. Except for occasional short trips out of the city, I've lived here all my life. Most of my relatives, including my mother and father, live in San Francisco. Just the same, I found a fellow's family is a poor substitute for a woman's company. So you see, I am lonesome, too. In fact, I have the stag blues now. Jeez! I dread the idea of spending tonight alone."

Sympathetically patting the college boy's hand, Elsie picked up the hint as quickly as a waitress picks up a tip. "There is no reason you should. You are really right, Professor Armstrong." Her playfully jocular address was intended to brighten his blues.

"I'm sick and tired of being my own babysitter, shut in by four walls. Not that I dislike staying home. I prefer a quiet evening lounging around in comfort, but not by myself. That's no fun. Look, we can't talk here. The manager is stretching her rubber neck all over the place. I'll be through work at six-thirty. Meet me in front of the stairs of the Hibernia Bank. It's not far, just up the block at the corner of . . ."

Vincent, who took a native's pride in his knowledge of San Francisco, interrupted, informing Elsie he knew the location. "The bank is at the northwest corner of Jones and McAllister Streets."

"Swell," she said and went from behind the counter toward a customer motioning for service in one of the booths. As she passed by Vincent, she had an afterthought, which she whispered in his ear. "We better meet a little later, about seven o'clock. I'll need time to check out and change clothes. See you, hon."

That evening upon Elsie's arrival at their designated meeting spot (by the staircase of the Hibernia Bank), Vincent, who was waiting, greeted her with a customary Yankee "hi" on one hand and on the other with an unexpected query. "Tell me, young lady, do you like chicken?"

The waitress, who had rushed to keep their date, after catching her breath, exclaimed, "Chicken! why, yes, I like it." Before she had a chance to say she was not hungry, the U.C. freshman retorted, "Then grab a wing on the house." In jest he cackled and flapped his arms.

"You're a cutie-pie," she responded, laughing heartily. As Vincent extended an elbow winglike, Elsie slipped her arm under his.

"Where do you live?" he asked. Vincent's voice had a tremor. His utterance sounded cracked. His throat was desert dry, hot.

Elsie replied: "I live at 1539 Franklin Street, between Bush and Pine. I rent a furnished apartment. We can catch a streetcar at the next intersection. Or would you rather walk. It isn't too far."

"Oh, I have a car. I'm parked nearby." While they were walking with their arms interlocked, firmly, Vincent could feel the woman's full-rounded breast bouncing up and down almost in rhythm to their spry steps. She wore no brassière, and no slip.

The waitress sighed...and said: "I'm glad you have a car. I get fed up riding streetcars. At times when I board one after my shift at the coffee shop, it's a battle royal with the rest of the riders for a little space to breathe. Half the time, offer love or money, a seat isn't available on those rolling sardine cans. And I have to stand all the way home, bony elbows poking me left and right. Streetcars stink, if you want my frank opinion."

"I agree with you on that score, Elsie. I am not an ardent streetcar fan, either. The smell of sweaty bodies boxed in like cattle on a freight car turns my stomach. Anyhow, I guess driving his own vehicle spoiled this plutocrat. The poor peasants are welcome to my share of public transportation," he joked. "There's my carriage, the blue Chevy on the same side of the street as the main public library."

Vincent guided Elsie toward his automobile and opened the door to let her in. Considerate, she insisted he enter first instead of walking all the way around to the driver's side. Some cars were coming and she was afraid he might be hit. Pleased by the woman's thoughtfulness, he smiled, stepped in, slid across the front seat, and settled behind the steering wheel. Elsie followed, sliding next to Vincent. He started the motor and drove off. They rode in silence. Sweet-sounding words were not needed, their thoughts were harmonious, they were in tune with each other.

At Van Ness Avenue the waitress moved still closer to the youth. This distracted him to such an extent he inadvertently failed to stop his automobile, crossing the broad thoroughfare against a red light.

Luckily he was not tagged for the traffic violation; no motorcycle policeman lurked in the shadows. As Vincent shifted gears, he grazed Elsie's knee. Her immediate reaction was to raise her leg higher. Thus the U.S. freshman felt free to cup his hand over the woman's knee.

The contact was electrifying to both. They began breathing heavily. On impulse he slipped his hand a fingertip at a time up her skirt. Since she showed no signs of disapproval, he fingered her ivory thigh with the nimbleness of a pianist fingering a keyboard in playing an exciting movement for an appassionato. Stirred emotionally, Elsie—to embolden Vincent still further—spread her legs wide apart.

Loud blasts caused by an infuriated driver's banging a fist on an automobile horn startled Vincent. His Chevrolet was straddling a white line and blocking the lanes. Instinctively he turned his steering wheel sharply to the right, permitting the automobile at Vincent's rear to zoom by. Shaking his head in anger, the driver in the passing vehicle glowered at Vincent.

Although he was unperturbed by the angry look, which city drivers are accustomed to receiving from others on the road, it had a sobering effect. Coming to his senses, Vincent realized sex play with the woman in an automobile while driving was unsafe. He had to exercise control and keep his hands off her until they were in the privacy of the woman's apartment.

Elsie Martin's quarters were very clean and smelled good despite the mustiness of the old building in which she lived. It had been cheaply converted into studio-type apartments. The age as well as the condition of the used furniture were on a par with the building, a relic of the 1906 San Francisco earthquake. Paper drapes hanging from angle irons and bordering a large bay window, mismatched the chenille spread on the mattress of the brass bedstead protruding into the middle of the one-and-a-half room apartment.

A large bureau with high legs stood on claw feet against a wall; on top of it was a beveled-glass mirror in a round frame. A reupholstered armchair occupied a corner of the room. Beside the armchair was a black wrought iron floor lamp with a yellow shade, which had a floral design that clashed with the faded pattern of the worn rug on the floor.

In the kitchenette was a nearly new gas stove, an old model refrigerator, a wooden folding table, two mismatched chairs, and a painted stepstool for reaching high shelves in a built-in cabinet.

Beneath the sink, alongside the chrome-plated trap, sat a small galvanized garbage can. A leaky faucet above the sink was in need of a washer.

Elsie told Vincent to have a seat and make himself at home. She wanted to go into the bathroom to freshen up. Upon going, she said she would not be too long. While he waited, annoyed by the drip-drip of the leaky faucet, Vincent killed time trying to stop the dripping by turning the porcelain handle as tight as he could at the shut-off position. It was useless. The dripping did not stop.

Ultimately, having found one on the drainboard, he placed a dishcloth over the spot where the drops of water were falling from the faucet into the sink. The sharp plipping of the dripping flattened out to a plopping. That was a little better. The flat sound was not so annoying to his ears as was the sharp sound.

Impatient and hot, hoping to hurry her, Vincent called out to Elsie: "Would you mind if I remove my jacket. It's kind of warm in here."

"Be comfortable, hon," she replied from behind the bathroom door. "Hang your jacket in the closet. There are some hangers on the clothes rod."

After hanging up his sports jacket, Vincent sat down, loosened the Windsor knot in his necktie, and undid the button of his shirt collar. He jumped up, his heart skipping a beat, when Elsie came out of the bathroom clad in nothing except a towel. Approaching the woman, the young man slipped his arms around her waist and pressed his lips against hers. The towel became loose and fell to the floor. He placed his hands on the woman's well-padded hips. Smacking of a rollmaker's handling dough, he kneaded her flesh heartily.

"Wait—wait!" she cried, breaking away. "Are you clean?"

"Absolutely, I'm squeaky clean. I'm in excellent health. I swear, I'm clean," he answered tersely and truthfully.

"Let me look at you," she demanded. "A girl can never be too careful."

Vincent quickly stripped, tossing his clothes on the armchair. Elsie took hold of Vincent's penis squeezing the tip hard, causing him to wince. Although the experience was new to Vincent, he realized she wanted to see if he had gonorrhea. He had heard from fellows familiar with prostitutes they did something similar to be sure their clients were not infected with 'the clap.'

The college boy was thinking of asking the waitress how she learned the trull's trade trick but decided he better not. Satisfied

Vincent had no venereal disease, Elsie proceeded to play with his protuberance. All of a sudden Vincent needed to urinate.

He excused himself and hurried to the bathroom. After urinating, Vincent pulled the long chain of the hopper (near the ceiling) in order to flush down the toilet bowl the amber fluid that he poured into it. The din from the flush sounded like the roar of a waterfall. A bit embarrassed, he delayed opening the bathroom door till the noise died away.

Elsie seemed to have remained standing in the same place where she had been before he left the room. But obviously she had moved: the blankets were tossed back over the foot of the bedstead. His primitive passion triggered by the implication of this fast preparation, Vincent grabbed the naked woman and flung her onto the bed. He fell on top of her bracing himself with the palms of his hands not to squash her. Consequently the thin bottom sheet was torn. Elsie's legs got entangled with it as he twisted her about wildly. She voiced no object to Vincent's savage behavior, since in her aroused sexual state she found it thrilling.

Now Vincent struggled, unsuccessfully, to remove the torn sheet tangled around Elsie's legs. His efforts were hindered because she was lying flat on her back weighted down by his body. Besides, he was too excited, in too great a hurry. Frustrated, he uttered a profanity.

She giggled, amused at Vincent's outburst. "Take it easy, hon, if you will just let me up a second, I'll pull the sheet off my legs."

With the torn sheet out of the way Vincent felt freer to enjoy the nakedness of the woman. He was spellbound by her breasts, silky as petals. Her nipples were two rosebuds waiting for a bee to extract their nectar. On the breast nearest her heart she had a honey-colored nevus the size of a small gold coin. Vincent was fascinated by the birthmark, which did not distract an iota from the loveliness of her succulent breasts.

Elsie's body set afire, her orbs glowed with excitement. In a heated tone she commanded the young man, "Open your mouth, lover!"

He obeyed in an instant. To his amazement she pushed her breasts together and put both nipples between his lips. Vincent growled greedily, imitating a gluttonous bear licking honey.

"Ouch! Be careful! Don't bite! Your teeth are sharp. Just use your tongue. That's good. Ooh, you hairy bear!" the woman cried out in sheer ecstasy, digging her nails into Vincent's bare shoulders while he continued to lick her more and more . . . !

Chapter 26

Despite the fact that Vincent had every intention of seeing Elsie Martin again soon, his studies at the university—merciless taskmasters—thwarted any plans he had for an early rendezvous with her. Monopolizing the freshman's time or thoughts twenty-four hours a day seven days a week, the hard studies tormented him whether he tried to sleep or whether he tried to stay awake.

Vincent had no peace of mind unless he devoted his spare moments on and off the campus to the acquisition of academic knowledge, which could not be obtained overnight. Therefore, pressed for time and pressured to study, he procrastinated about dating the waitress till, before he realized it, several weeks had elapsed.

Late one afternoon Vincent drove to the San Francisco Public Library to return some books that were due. On Larkin Street, by the Civic Center across the street from the library, he found an empty space to park his blue sedan and wheeled it in between two other automobiles. As he got out of the sedan, Vincent caught sight of a familiar female figure coming his way. Of all people it was Elsie Martin. He walked onto the sidewalk red-faced and spoke to her apologetically.

"Elsie! fancy bumping into you here. I bet you think I'm a real stinker for not getting in touch with you these past weeks. Well, it wasn't because I have forgotten you. Cross my heart and hope to die if I am fibbing."

Vincent's countenance was that of a cherubic choir boy the while he gave the solemn oath and made the sign of the cross with a swift sweep of his left hand. (The other hand supported a load of books under his arm.)

"My studies at Cal forced me to hibernate. I've been holed up for the winter like a bear." Vincent smiled believing Elsie would appreciate the humor in the simile. "School work has had me snowed under. I needed to take these books back to the library. So I crawled out of my den—on my paws, ha-ha.

"Seriously, I'll admit I should have given you a jingle on the phone to ask, 'What's cooking,' or at least to say, 'Hello.' But I hated to disturb you during your working hours at Bunny's. Besides...'hells bells.' You know how it is."

The woman eyed Vincent coolly, as though she was unsure whether or not she should accept his excuses. Warmed by his radiant smile, she melted and said she understood. "I know school work can keep you busy. A cousin of mine who went to dental college always had his nose to the grindstone. He complained his lessons interfered with his pleasure. Anyway, it is nice to see you again."

"You're a good sport, Elsie Martin. The best!" Vincent was relieved now that his explanation was accepted. The natural color quickly returned to his flushed face.

"Say, how come you are not at Bunny's. I thought you worked until six-thirty. Is today your day off?"

"My day off. Yes. I am off today. I just came from Market Street. I was downtown window-shopping."

"You had quite a walk. The blocks on Market Street are long. Each block in my estimation is equal to three regular city blocks. Are you headed anywhere special?"

"No. Nowhere in particular. I am on my way home. I have had it with looking at shop windows for today."

"Would you like to go for a spin and see our San Francisco scenery? Some of the views from the hilltops are splendid."

She said nothing for several seconds, trying to make up her mind. Her desire to see the views overcame her lack of certainty. "Okay. Why not."

Vincent was delighted. "Hop into my car. I shall scoot across the street to the library and turn in these books." He unlocked the sedan's front passenger door, opened it wide, and waited for the woman to get into the sedan, then he closed the door. Vincent's parting words were "Be back in a jiffy."

True to his words he returned very soon. Settling down behind the wheel of his automobile, he drove in a northerly direction. Vincent's destination was Russian Hill. As his automobile ascended its sharp incline via Green Street, the woman, as if imagining she was stepping on the brakes, pushed her feet down hard on the floor-board. She was fearful the sedan would roll backward.

"Goodness me! she exclaimed, "I simply can't get over the hills in Frisco. They sure are high—and steep! One has to be a mountain goat to climb them."

Joking, Vincent replied: "Young lady, you can call a San Franciscan a mountain goat all you want. But never call San Francisco...Frisco. The members of the Chamber of Commerce would have a conniption fit if they heard you."

"I beg your pardon," the woman humored Vincent politely, though she could not comprehend why anybody should be upset over her calling the city, Frisco. After a bit of pondering, she asked out of curiosity, "Tell me, what's wrong with the short name Frisco?"

"For one thing," Vincent answered, "it is considered disrespect-ful in that the term is a carry-over from the disorderly days of the Barbary Coast, which before the 1906 earthquake was a district of San Francisco notorious for its gambling houses and brothels. Frisco—like the term 'dump,' for example—is hardly appropriate in referring to a well-ordered, modern municipality.

"And another thing, using the slang synonym is in a sense sac-rilegious, since San Francisco was named after St. Francis of Assisi." (Vincent detected a puzzled expression on the woman's face, so he proceeded to elaborate.) "St. Francis was the founder of the Franciscan Order in the thirteenth century. One of their ideals—unworldliness—seems strange. Yet his life story is quite interesting."

"Oh, I see." In the tone of her remark the woman did her best to conceal disinterest. Not wanting to listen to a saint's life story, she switched to another subject. "I still have to marvel at the dizzy heights of the streets in San Francisco."

"Not all the streets are hilly. There are flat areas in the city, too. Really, do the hills here amaze you that much, Elsie?"

"Hills! they are mountains. My ears are beginning to pop." Grimacing cutely, she swallowed in pretense of needing to open her Eustachian tubes. "I read in a magazine that San Francisco is a city of seven hills. Just imagine!"

"Without a doubt the magazine writer was not a native San Franciscan. Otherwise he would not have used that small number. He probably had in mind the seven hills upon which ancient Rome was erected. The fact is, Elsie, a great part of San Francisco consists of forty hills."*

"Honestly, that many!" The woman was wide-eyed with aston-ishment. "That is a lot of hills to climb."

Vincent grinned and conceded: "Of course, some are not excep-tionally high in altitude. By the way, I must show you something spectacular on Russian Hill. I'll wager dollars to doughnuts it will knock you for a loop." He stepped on the accelerator and drove his sedan to the intersection of Hyde and Lombard Streets.

He made a sharp right turn, eastward, on Lombard Street, shift-ed to second gear, and depressed the foot brake but gradually released the pedal to permit the vehicle to roll slowly down the street. The sight his passenger beheld caused her to gasp in disbelief. She blinked her eyes to be sure they were not deceiving her.

The hilly block she and Vincent were on (between Hyde and Leavenworth Streets) looked like a gigantic boa lying dormant on the side of a cliff. The bricks set in the pavement were the reddish scales of the block-long snake, the eight sharp turns of the winding way was its flexuous form. Landscaping surrounding the street on a small scale rivaled Mexico's picturesque flower gardens in Xochimilco.

Most abundant were the beds of hydrangeas...shades of pink, lavender, and red...hedged with privet and similar shrubs. Also

---

*Below, alphabetically arranged, including a hill (Strawberry Hill) within Golden Gate Park, is a list of the hills in the city especially compiled for those persons skeptical about the correctness of the number stated by Vincent Armstrong.

Alamo Heights	Hunters Point Heights	Presidio Heights
Anza Hill	Lafayette Heights	Presidio Hills
Bayview Heights	Laurel Hill	Red Rock Hill
Bernal Heights	Lincoln Heights	Rincon Hill
Buena Vista	Lone Mountain	Russian Hill
Castro Hill	McLaren Ridge	St. Joseph Hill
City College Hill	Merced Heights	Strawberry Hill
Corona Heights	Mt. Davidson	Sunset Heights
Dolores Heights	Mt. Olympus	Sutro Heights
Edgehill Heights	Mt. Sutro	Telegraph Hill
Excelsior Heights	Nob Hill	Twin Peaks
Fairmount Heights	Noe Hill	Washington Heights
Gold Mine Hill	Pacific Heights	
Holly Hill	Potrero Hill	

observable was an olla-podrida of ice plants, Boston ivy, geraniums, veronicas, candytufts, and fuschias. California poppies raised their golden heads flirtatiously in various places. And blushing roses agilely climbed a north wall near the base of the hill.

Concrete walks comprised hundreds of steps (numerous as those archeologists have discovered leading to the Palenque temples in the ruins of the Mayans) fringed that block of Lombard Street on both sides where palm trees and others stood. Palm fronds joined tree branches in a graceful dance whenever stirred by rhythmic breezes. Upon this hillside modernistic homes with balconies and sundecks had been constructed, typical of structural-site designs of the extinct Yucatan Indians who built their dwellings on supernal terraced mounds secured by retaining walls plastered with stucco colorfully painted.

"Whew! now I have seen everything," Vincent's passenger expressed awe as she glanced around the wondrous winding way. Not until the automobile had rounded the last of the eight curves did she take her eyes off the landscaping and homes nestled in the hillside.

Hearing his stomach suddenly growl, Vincent estimated: "It must be about 5:30. I am hungry as a bear." Stopped at a traffic light, he got a look at the dial of a clock through a window of a store. Beaming at the closeness of his estimate, he said, "I wasn't very far off; the time is exactly 5:20 p.m."

"Is it that time already. You better drive me home, cupcake. My next-door neighbor has to prepare dinner for her husband. She's watching my baby. I should go and pick her up."

"Baby!" Vincent exclaimed. He was so rattled he nearly stripped the gears of his automobile. "You didn't tell me you have a child."

The woman put her hand to her mouth to shut it—too late! She realized that she had closed the door of the bird cage after the canary had flown out. Unable to spin a fabrication on the spur of the moment, she spoke straightforwardly. "I did not see any point in bringing it up. Besides, I'm divorced. What difference does it make that I have a child."

"None, none whatsoever," the college boy replied with a complete lack of concern. (He spoke thusly for he was not contemplating marriage.) "It just did not occur to me that you had ever been married. So you are a mom. That's great." Restraining a smile, Vincent increased the speed of his automobile and joshed, "We are well on our way to your Franklin Street mansion, Madame Martin."

"Goodness, Vincent, how silly of me. I forgot to mention I don't live on Franklin Street anymore. A couple of weeks ago I moved to a flat on Oak Street...corner of Laguna Street."

"This is really a day of surprises." He smiled freely now. "We haven't gone out of our way, though. We'll cut across Pacific Heights and be there in fifteen minutes."

When they arrived at her flat, the woman invited Vincent in and asked him to wait while she went next door to fetch Betty Ann, her baby. Presently she returned, reading a note that her neighbor had put in the mailbox:

> "My mother-in-law phoned us to come over for din-
> ner. Couldn't wait. You know how she is. Took Betty Ann
> along. No need to worry. Will be back earlyish, by nine
> o'clock.
>
> Esther

"I'm disappointed. I wanted you to see my beautiful baby girl. She is the sweetest, cuddlesome roly-poly." The mother folded her arms into a cradle and moved them from side to side pretending she was rocking her little baby. In her rocking the woman unintentionally poked Vincent's ribs with an elbow. For a second he felt the poke, which was a bit painful.

To make light of it, he gave her a hug as he flattered her: "My grandmother used to say 'an apple doesn't fall far from the tree.' She is your little girl so she must be beautiful. Lovable, too."

Vincent planted a kiss on the woman's lips and placed his hands on her breasts. She pushed him away abruptly. "I thought you said you was hungry, mister. Let's have something to eat before we get all hot and bothered. That is if you wouldn't mind potluck."

"Why, thank you. I would love it." At the moment the college boy's mind was far afield from food. But he reasoned the woman was keeping him at arm's length to teach him a lesson for his not having showed up the past few months.

Wisely he played the woman's game and refrained from touching her. After they had eaten their fill of potluck, she led him into the bedroom. In record time the pair were undressed standing front to front stark naked.

Savoring the deliciousness of her nudity, he was stunned to see the honey-colored nevus no longer garnished the woman's left breast. "My god!" Vincent uttered in utter amazement. "What the devil happened to your birthmark?"

In an instinctive reaction she placed a palm upon her breast where the nevus was supposed to be. The woman stared silently into space before she answered: "Uh, uh, I had it taken off. Wasn't the plastic surgeon a whiz. Look, he didn't even leave a scar."

"You should not have had your birthmark removed. What a hell of a shame! It was a honey." Vincent took hold of the woman's breasts to taste their sweetness.

Her nipples had a strong honeyed aftertaste of buckwheat, not the light honeyed taste of clover which he preferred. Perhaps she needed a shower. Soon weary of sex play, the college boy bid his female playmate adieu.

Although he had had an orgasm, he did not feel gratified. Something was amiss. How could the woman be a lively wiggly pussy during intercourse on one occasion and on the next be a lifeless lay figure. The last time her love-making had been delightful, wickedly exciting.

Elsie simply was not herself. He must have caught her at a bad time. Possibly she was having a mood swing, the scholar in him theorized. Or was it, as he had heard older fellows say, that the second sexual experience with the same woman seldom came up to their expectations and oftentimes turned out to be a letdown for both bedroom players.

Chapter 27

Not anxious to see Elsie Martin again, Vincent, walking along Market Street several days later and hungering for a strawberry waffle, to avoid the waitress went to a different Bunny's location (on Powell near Ellis Street). Lucifer, howbeit, machinated a devilish scheme to thwart the U.C. freshman. Who should be working at the Powell Street coffee shop, none other than Elsie!

Cornered, Vincent masked his true feelings. Undesirous of hurting her, he acted as though he was pleased about the chance encounter. "Hi, gorgeous. What are you doing in this neck of the woods?"

Elsie greeted him with a wink and explained: "There is a shortage of waitresses here. The gossip is one of the gals quit because she was sexually harassed. Another caught the flu bug, or something. I don't know exactly. Anyhow, I was transferred here from the Market Street shop the first of the month."

"I am glad I dropped by this Bunny Waffle Shop." The collegian continued conversing: "Or I would have missed you. Tell me. How is the baby?"

"The ba—by!" Elsie seemed surprised by Vincent's inquiry. "Oh, my little baby daughter. Betty Ann is in the pink. She is fine...I believe so."

"You believe so. Aren't you sure?" Vincent waited for an answer. When she said nothing, he was insistent that she reply. "It's kind of noisy around here. I guess you didn't hear me." He repeated the question. "Aren't you sure your baby is okay?"

"Huh...SURE? Sure I'm sure. You see, I have been on irregular shifts lately. And I haven't had any luck in finding a reliable baby sit-

ter to look after Betty Ann. Since my neighbors—we are real friendly—were going to the country on vacation, they offered to help me
out. So they carted Betty Ann along with them. She's in good hands.
They are swell people. By the way, hon, what brings you downtown,
out of your dark den?"

"My dentist's office is in the Flood Building. I had an appointment to have my teeth cleaned. See how white they are." He parted
his lips wide like a snickering stallion. Then to Vincent's regret, he
lowered his guard, remarking offhandedly: "I guess I'll go to a
movie and relax today. I'm not in any mood at all to do homework."

"That's perfect," the waitress expressed her approval of how he
intended to spend some time. "My shift is almost over. Let's take in
a movie together. Enjoy your waffle. Don't rush. When you have finished eating, wait for me outside the coffee shop. I won't be long."

Vincent's tender soul did not have the heart to reject her over-
ture. Making the best of an awkward situation, he prevaricated to
save them both embarrassment. "Great, I'll get a triple treat, Miss
Martin plus a double bill at the movies."

Whereas Vincent was not overjoyed at the idea of resuming intimate relations with the woman, by the time the motion pictures had
ended, he had a different feeling about her. The main feature, a four-
star musical in Technicolor, depicted scenes aboard a navy destroy-
er which was manned by a crew of sensual, smiling show girls wearing scant sailor outfits. Endowed with alluring busts, the chorines'
cleavages were suggestively exposed. Their slender arms, shapely
legs, solid thighs, smooth backs, and skin-bare midriffs enhanced the
sexuality of their high-kicking dance routines. Directed to tantalize,
the filmed sexy shots stimulated Vincent's libido.

Too agitated to be upright, Vincent pilfered for the nonce a rationalization of nautical origin: 'Any port will serve a seaman in a
storm.' Who cares if Elsie is colder than a mermaid swimming in icy
ocean waters. With that attitude he dropped anchor at Martin's flat
on the windy corner of Oak and Laguna Streets.

Once again Vincent Armstrong, the collegian, and Elsie Martin,
the waitress, were disrobing beside a bed. The room was brightly lit
but it was chilly. She had put a match to a gas heater which was slow
in warming up the room. First to undress he stood shivering with
goose flesh. He watched her as she removed the last of her under-
garments, a brassiere. The hooks unfastened, she slipped it off and
turned to face her companion.

His wide-open orbs feasted ravenously on her white, meaty

body. All at once Vincent gagged as if he had gulped down a fish-bone that lodged in his throat. Clearly perceivable on Elsie's left breast was what appeared to be a honey-colored nevus.

Partial perplexity plus partial peevishness prompted Vincent to grab the woman by the shoulders and shake her like a perturbed parent punishing a puzzling problem child. Vincent shook Elsie so hard her breasts persisted in quivering naughtily even after he had released his hold on her to speak his mind.

"All right! what in hades is going on! One time you have a birth-mark, the next time you don't. Now you do. I'll bet you paint it on with some sort of light-brown color. Maybe it is make-up? I shall find out now...no more diddling around." Moistening his fingertips with saliva, he rubbed her breast vigorously in an attempt to clean off the brownish spot.

Elsie laughed. "You can't rub that off. The birthmark isn't fake. Believe me. It is real. Come, lie down. I'll explain."

Vincent was too miffed to listen to her. He stepped aside and mulelike refused to budge.

Paying no attention to the stubborn way he was acting, she tossed back the bedclothes. Still laughing she said: "This is only the second time we have been together. When you were here before, you just imagined you were with me. But you were not."

To tease the U.C. freshman instead of explaining further she sang:

> Imagination is funny
> It makes a cloudy day sunny,
> Makes a bee think of honey,
> Just as I think of you.

Vincent hardly appreciated the song. He yelled at the woman, "You are not making a bit of sense!" Exasperated, he called her singing 'Imagination' idiotic. "What utter nutty nonsense."

Becoming serious, Elsie stopped teasing him. "Shush! Be quiet. Just listen. The gal you bumped into at the Civic Center is my sister. She is the one without a birthmark. We are identical twins."

"You're kidding! What kind of a game are you playing?" Disbelief was plainly written on the lines of the collegian's counte-nance. "If what you say is true, how did she know who I am? We never met before that day I went to the public library."

"Hon, remember you spoke to her first. We have had sister-to-sister talks about you. I told her what a wonderful lover you are, and how handsome you are. She recognized you from my description of you...you black-haired, blue-eyed Casanova.

"Also I told her that you owned a blue Chevrolet. As a clincher, you mentioned some things about me. She quickly put two and two together, which added up to Vincent Armstrong. She—dear college boy—is a smart cookie."

More or less convinced, though very suspicious, Vincent interrogated Elsie. "How come you have a key to your sister's place?"

"I live here, too." Elsie replied in an unintimidated manner. "If you had taken the trouble to telephone me, you would have found out that I moved in with her quite a while ago."

Continuing the interrogation, he asked: "If everything is as you say, where is your sister now? And where is her baby daughter?"

"They are both in Los Gatos," Elsie answered, her tone had a ring of deep sincerity. "You see, one of the things I didn't tell you earlier at Bunny's is that our next-door neighbors invited my sister, as well as Betty Ann, to join them on their jaunt to the country town."

Coming to the conclusion he had copulated with two consanguineous women who compared notes about his behavior in bed, the young man was disquieted indeed. For his peace of mind he faced the music and muted his feelings to soften the sound of his dual sexual performances. "Still aren't you sore that I fiddled around with your sister?"

Empathy twinkling in her bright dark eyes, reflecting the sparkle of luminous stars in the night sky, the worldly waitress replied: "Certainly not! Boys and girls desire one another. Life has been so ever since Adam and Eve covered their naked bodies with aprons of fig leaves.

"Besides, you thought it was me that you were with. As for my sister, she is an adult and unattached. Okay, she had hot panties. Does that mean the poor kid was supposed to use a candle in place of a cock."

"Elsie Martin, you are a peach, a peach of a person." The broad-minded woman's words spelled instant relief for Vincent. He plunged into the bed directly between the cold sheets and rolled over toward the woman who radiated the heat of a hot-water bottle. Snuggling up against her body, he embraced her lustfully.

"Brrr! your hands are a couple of icicles." She shuddered, wriggling away. "Wait until they warm up."

Vincent withdrew his hands, which he cupped. After blowing hot breath into his cupped hands, he patted Elsie's plump posterior.

With each pat he playfully gave her a tongue-lashing. "That, that, that...and that is what you get for the prank you and your sister pulled on me."

Elsie laughed and laughed and laughed..."Oooh, don't tickle. My stomach hurts from laughing too hard. Betcha," she predicted, "my sister and I are a red-hot twosome you will never forget."

Despite destiny's determination they should lose contact with one another in the future, her prediction proved to be true. From time to time throughout Vincent Armstrong's lifetime he relived in reminiscing his incredible affair with the identical twins.

Chapter 28

The University of California turned out to be the worst disillusionment of Vincent's younger years. Yet he failed to understand the hard reasons for it. Some of which he was able to partially digest had been served piecemeal to him by bitter U.C. undergraduates long before Vincent had registered at the university. Initially he came to the defense of the educational institution whenever it was criticized. He accused the faultfinders of offering him rotten sour grapes.

Now that he was in a position to judge from actual experience, he discovered, he had erred greatly in alluding to Aesop's fable as a motive of spurious scorn for the critics' unattained scholastic achievements. Consequently, Vincent reversed his opinion about the teaching methods at the university. Chilling to the bone was the university's apathetic attitude toward students experiencing difficulty in the lecture halls who, nevertheless, had intellectual abilities far beyond average. Chilling to the brain was the professors' placement of academic ice blocks indifferently freezing creative students from moving beyond the field of established higher learning.

How quickly, Vincent wondered, had such an icy attitude cooled the fervor of other enthusiastic undergraduates, as it had in a single semester cooled his fervid enthusiasm to study and to learn—and to create. He shuddered in massive, glacial Wheeler Hall, where, lecturing through microphones, distant professors (not all intelligible speakers) minute by minute flung shovelsful of subject matter at students desperately trying to grasp everything, despairingly trying to write down everything, and hoping against hope that all the while the subject matter was snowballing not a flake of a fact, possibly to be the basis for a question in a midterm or final examination, had been omitted in the scribbling of one's notes.

Examination time! it was extremely gelid. Vincent experienced a tingling sensation; he paled and became numb, almost as if he suffered from frostbite. In reality it was not his being exposed to examinations that brought about this condition. The freshman feared the consequences of receiving failing grades in courses. They had to be completed for credits toward a degree.

He was caught in a cold circle: in order to complete his courses he had to have passing grades on his written examinations. Should he fail, he would be flunked out of the university, be branded a brainless baboon, be humiliated before his family, and his friends. Never would he realize his ambition to become an attorney. He was as good as decapitated! Thus without a head he studied.

If Vincent Armstrong had entered the university with a hunger for higher learning—to acquire knowledge extensively, to attain it explicitly, to absorb it clearly, to utilize it sagaciously—that desire now seemed lost. If he had entered the university with a thirst for learning how to use his intellect—to reason logically, to analyze thoroughly, to create constructively, to think idealistically—that desire now seemed gone. Instead the drive for self-preservation seemingly developed in the youth a single-minded appetency: Above all else to survive his examinations with high grades.

Usually, despite professors' habitually overloading students with assignments, the desire for survival presented relatively little difficulty of fulfillment provided a student could steal sufficient time to memorize the enormous bank of lecture material adequately enough to give it back under pressure in bluebooks or in test papers. The Sisyphean task lay in being able to put one's hands on copies of a course in comprehensive and concise form.

Doing so necessitated the mastery of a certain craftiness which Vincent never learned. He did not know where to look off campus. And obtaining such concentrated fat facts from the academic icebox bearing the U.S. trademark was as painfully difficult as pulling barehanded a fast-frozen tray of ice cubes from a refrigerator that needs defrosting.

Growing a bit more campus-wise after exchanging views with fellow students, Vincent concluded the only way to accomplish the foregoing feat, from start to finish was to write down word for word as speedily as possible the lecturers' profound utterances...ad interm forcibly stopping his gray matter from interfering with the wording of the lectures by not attempting to understand (or remember at the moment) what was being said. In this respect, according to educational standards, he earned an "A" for effort but a "D" for achievement.

When reviewing his notes at home, he invariably found that vital details were unclear or that important parts of his handwriting were illegible, or that words were missing. Fit to be tied and ready to bite nails, Vincent would be mad with anger at himself for not having learned shorthand. How he envied students who had and, ergo, with the complete lectures at their disposal, were able to memorize virtually verbatim the professors' stiff words, a sure-fire way of getting high grades on examinations.

Moved to mad moods, Vincent engaged in fanciful thinking, imagining how wonderful it would be to have a wire recorder like the ones he had read about that were being used lately in some lecture halls at schools in Italy and Germany. Armed with a wire recorder, facing fierce exams in the bleak University of California atmosphere would no longer make him feel as though he were encountering polar bears around the North Pole.

Chapter 29

A cleverly lodged parable, representing one thing real in life or nature from which one moral is drawn for instruction, has been maintained since of old to be worth ten clever debates, discussions, disputations, and dialectics. Should there be two shreds of plausibility in this ancient assertion, what is the value of a timely parable representative of a hundred things in life or nature, from which a hundred morals may be drawn?

In the thirteenth century descendants of predatory nomads, Western Tartars, members of the Mongolian tribes, had conquered China; and for the first period in history the Celestial Empire passed under the sway of an alien potentate. No specific episode was in itself instrumental in the transference of the imperial omnipotence. But a momentous turning point was seen around 1210 when the mighty Mongol chieftain Genghis Khan, after subjugating all the little countries north and south of the Gobi Desert, repeatedly assailed the northern Chinese Golden Tribe, the Chin.

Towns and villages were sacked, women raped, men tortured, infants mutilated in the ensuing forays led by Genghis Khan. The slaughter of human flesh continued on a sweeping scale as the ferocious Tartar drove his fighting forces head-on unrestrained, analogous to herds of wild horses stampeding over thickly inhabited terrain. Multitudes of Chinese people were trampled beneath the hooves of the nomadic Mongol beasts.

Beastly Genghis Khan, feared by friend and foe, won battle after battle but died in his tracks before the Chin were totally defeated. Circumstances surrounding the Mongol chieftain's departure from the scene of the onslaught, remain to this day an enigma to historiographers. However, their studies show that his successors eventually overpowered the remnants of Chin, the resisting Golden Tribe. Treacherous, the Tartars also slew their allies, tribesmen of the dwindling Southern Sung who unwisely had allied themselves with the Mongols to wage wars of aggression against the Chin.

On a fixed course of plunder and pillage, the Tatar-Mongolian conquerors marched across two continents, leaving death and destruction in the wake of their every victorious inroad. They overran much of central and western Asia from the coast of the blue Pacific Ocean to the core of dark eastern Europe.

By 1279 Kublai Khan, a grandson of Genghis, had completed the subjugation of China. As the spoils of war Kublai took the seat of the Dragon Throne, thereby setting the stage for a Mongol Yüan Dynasty. During Kublai's administration the empire, a gigantic xanthous balloon soaring majestically in the sky, had been blown up to its ultimate limits. His sovereignty was supreme, sumptuous, superb, supereminent...splendiferous. So the storytelling scribes stately swear, *ad hominem*.

Dignitaries, far and near, paid tribute to his luxurious court at Khanbalic, the capital city. Khanbalic (named Peking, 1421; styled Peiping, 1928; renamed Peking, 1949) was acclaimed the most magnificent and dazzling place on the terraqueous globe. His plethoric palace and pleasure parks—built by countless slaves, of no earthly use in the eyes of their masters—were exquisite, spectacular sights to behold. Without a doubt the Grand Khan was the wealthiest ruler alive.

Apparently to curry favor high-ranking Orientals, occidentals too, yesterday and today have venerated him along with his tinseled kind as paragons of glittering greatness. Shunted have been the tragic realities that Kublai's predecessors, not to mention his demoniac majesty, used the sinews of war and the tendons of peace to fill their coffers, seized or stolen (by stealth) from scores of kingdoms whose rulers had—as rulers tend to do—purloined their excessive treasures from senselessly staunch subjects.

Despite the overwhelming power and wealth fortifying the Yüan Dynasty, it started to rot and crumple like a rain-soaked, termite-infested log structure. Intoxicated with the potency of the staggering empire bottled up, sealed tight, delivered gratis, and served lavishly to them in golden goblets, nine emperors succeeded one another in cursory, Sybaritic reigns which endured less than a century, a paltry eighty-nine years to be precise.

Under the emperorship of the last Mongolian authority, Tohan Timur the Docile, who had assumed the title Shun Ti, ill-treatment of the subjugated Chinese populous was revolting. Public officials were authorized to confiscate private property at will, without justification. Merchants were paid for their goods with worthless paper currency issued by the authorities. Villages of famine-stricken peasants, dying in swarms like flies, were swatted again and again with squashing demands for land and grain taxes.

Time-honored Confucianists, custodians of Chinese virtues and values, were kicked about viciously: mongrels received better treatment. Chinese were condemned creatures, receiving neither jurisprudential justice nor scholastic standing. The teachings of Confucius were laughed at and spat upon.

China's custom of conferring rank in government service on the basis of literary qualifications was ignored. Discrimination by the decadent Mongols was widespread. Important offices of the realm were handed over on demand to uneducated Tartars, military men who replaced learned Chinese officials (kuans or mandarins). Naturally, these poisonous mushrooms of irresponsible and oppressive government vegetating in China grew out of a fungus of intrigue and debauchery that had been planted on Khanbalic behind the palace walls.

Peering over the palace walls, we see a train of attendants bowing and scraping before a slouched figure, the lord and master sitting on the Dragon Throne. Shun Ti was the absolute sovereign of the greatest empire on earth. At his feet crawled Cathay and such protectorates as Korea, Tibet, Burma. India, Persia, and Russia were under his domination, too.

So far did the Mongol's domination extend, his regal rod reached beyond the boundaries of Lower Silesia. True, Shun Ti was master of much and many. But he was not master of himself; for he was infirm of mind and soft of body—easily moldable kaolin. He appropriately was named Tohan Timur the Docile, something he himself could not glaze over despite his having assumed the title Shun Ti.

Although he sat on the Dragon Throne and held the reins of the empire, he did not control it fully. Shun Ti's ministers had a good grip on its tail. Lamas—mendacious Mongolian monks—contended with his ministers for complete control of the empire. The ministers' and monks' behavior was not in the least dissimilar to that of a pack of dogs fighting over bones. The Lamaites, cunning and corrupt, had seized the legs of the throne by perverting the thinking of Shun Ti.

By degrees the lamas craftily worked on his clay composition until it became hard as porcelain, and with a shaman's skill put a glasslike glaze on his make-up...glost-fired at a very hot temperature. Thus they were able to see through Shun Ti and dominate his will, making a figurehead of their emperor who had as much value as a badly cracked, ceramic figurine.

Since childhood he had been tutored in Lamaism with an admixture of fetishism, having elaborate rituals. Mad monks muddied his mind by initiating him into fetishist rites. They taught Shun Ti irrational devotion to inanimate objects and blind regard for bodily parts—fetishes. The monks solemnly said that they, the objects and parts, were the embodiment of potent spirits with magical potency residing within the fetishes.

At the age of fourteen puberty having come to the boy emperor, in his honor there was constructed a concealed chamber called The Room of Harmlessness; it sounded like a paradox if one happened to be nearby. Inside the chamber a harem of naked virgins performed a Heavenly Devil's Dance in varied vile positions. Contracting muscles and manipulating fingers, the dancers would begin vivaciously vibrating voluptuous parts of their bodies (sometimes their own, sometimes each other's) whenever an obese eunuch announced Shun Ti was about to enter.

In the chamber he displayed his feelings of awe for the fetishes. The potent spirits, he was told, had requested his highness not to trouble himself with petty matters of state, which the monks obligingly volunteered to assist his ministers in looking after. Here amidst the concubines his desires to acquire the spirits' magical potencies would be heard when he uttered a prayer to a fetish of his choice, one by one. Should Shun Ti's desires not be fulfilled, the explanation was pure and simple: a spiritual antagonist was hidden in the fetish with the residing spirit's help.

Then he, The Emperor, in the exercise of his imperial duty, was to punish the trembling, traitorous thing that had betrayed him by harboring an enemy spirit. Shun Ti must dismember the traitor and banish it forever from the sanctuary of The Room of Harmlessness. When a fetish was punished, horrible screams penetrated the walls of the chamber and echoed throughout the palatial halls. The screams were so loud, at the gate to the palace they pierced the eardrums of hardened guards who cringed in horror. Invariably the mutilated fetishes were the virgin maiden's bodily parts.

With a clod of clay as Shun Ti enthroned, it was inevitable that the Mongol governmental structure fell into disrepair, giving the flea-infested, diseased rats of officialdom still bigger holes to crawl through. Spreading their droppings, they inflicted misrule and misconduct and misery upon the Chinese people. Boundless bubonic brigandage plagued China.

One day word reached the palace that Chu Yüan-chang, a poor farmer's son turned guerrilla, had unified under his command independent bands of Chin revolutionaries into an alarmingly large army. He fearlessly had attacked the emperor's outposts in southern sections of the country. Chu Yüan-chang now planned to mount a full-scale offensive against the Dragon Throne. It was undetermined where he intended to wage warfare next in China.

An alarmed Mongolic royal court convened at once for an emergency session to determine what strategy should be used in counteracting an attack by the Chin revolutionary forces. Only a highly select group, the inner circle of Tatar-Mongolians, were permitted to attend the meeting. In attendance were ministers including their superior the prime minister, generals, monks, and emperor Shun Ti (a voiceless participant). After the customary courtly formalities and faultfinding, tactics were discussed.

All functionaries at the court agreed with the prime minister, who had the loudest if not the greatest voice, that the unexpected...the element of surprise...was the strategy to use in staving off the anticipated offensive. To defeat the guerrillas should be easy if they were ambushed. Were not the Tartar troops the best trained in the Orient. Did they not have the swiftest steeds and the sharpest swords to outrun and outfight the fastest, fiercest foes either side of the Great Wall of China.

There was a problem, however, more information was needed for the strategic operation to be effective. Unknown was not only where but also when Chu Yüan-chang planned to mount the full-scale offensive. Also it was not known how many men he had at his disposal. The prime minister decided a spy should be sent to find and infiltrate the rebel leader's garrison to obtain the needed information. Most functionaries were in accord, though they had their reservations.

Questions arose: Who will the patriotic spy be? Must he not be young, strong and bold? Would he not need to have a fluent knowledge of Mandarin, the standard Chinese language. Certainly no Mongolians except a few tired elders understood the language, let alone had mastery of all the other dialects spoken in China. Some functionaries suggested using a Chinaman loyal to the emperor as a spy.

The prime minister objected on the ground that it would be sheer folly to trust a Chinese subject to spy on his own people. Instead the prime minister had in mind to carry out the mission a young Mongol who descended from sturdy Tartar stock. He was someone that could be trusted. Moreover, he spoke Chinese fairly well. In any event he had enough command of the tongue to slide by with the gods' willingness. Still, if peradventure he should have the misfortune to run into unfamiliar Cantonese or other dialects, it would not matter a swish of a yak's tail.

Bewildered functionaries looked at the prime minister with disbelief. They had a troublous thought in common: "What manner of madman's talk be this!"

Monks started to argue pretentiously, ministers to approve prejudicially, generals to object pompously, and Shun Ti to chatter pointlessly. Outshouting the noisy official body, the prime minister called for order, demanding in no womanish words that comments be reserved until his position had been stated fully. In short order calm was restored, and a sullen yet curious court listened.

The individual whom the prime minister recommended to act as spy was named Lieou Koukai, a student at the Imperial Academy. Because of the high marks he received at his last Advanced Scholar Examination, he had been listed atop the roll of honor. It was widely recognized, to be foremost on the list was in itself a commendable accomplishment.

Howbeit, the youth had done something many times more praiseworthy. He was the first Tartar since the immortal Kublai Khan founded the academy to receive a tally of one hundred percent on the examination, which consisted of questions acknowledged by the most erudite persons to be extremely difficult and exceedingly lengthy.

In fact, when Lieou Koukai's answers to the written test were being checked, the examiner discovered not only that they were devoid of error but also the characters that had been brushed on the rice paper were identical in the minutest stroke to the answers in the key. So unbelievable, so utterly impossible did this duplication appear, the examiner was positive the student had cheated.

Somehow he must have procured a copy of the key, hidden it on his person, and slyly as a jackal copied down its contents right under the very noses of unsuspecting monitors stationed in the testing area.

Confronting Lieou with his base dishonesty, the examiner berated him, demanding to be enlightened as to what trickery the cheater had used in order to perpetrate the clever act. Lieou's pained visage indicated how deeply the sharp thrust of the humiliating accusation wounded his pride. Nevertheless, he put the lid on a heated urge to make a retaliatory outburst, and he extinguished the flame of his temper, thus preventing it from boiling over. With a cool head the youth denied he was guilty of any wrongdoing. As for his extraordinary test results, he offered a perfectly natural explanation which all the same was fantastic in nature.

Years ago during an early stage in his boyhood, Lieou learned he possessed a wondrous endowment, verily a heavenly-awarded gift: the prolix power to remember over extended periods, character by character or image by image, whatsoever his ears or eyes perceived just once. He surmised the sages in drawing up the key to the questions on the examination had meticulously brush stroked characters (stroke for stroke) duplicating the lessons (word for word) imparted orally to the students.

He never missed a day at the academy and not a word in an oral lesson. Need more to be explained. Clearly there could no longer be any doubt about Lieou Koukai's veracity.

As far as the examiner was concerned, he had heard enough. Where was the proof. He wanted the youth's explanation verified now! Unconvinced, and scowling suspiciously, the man stepped over to a book-filled recess in a nearby wall. Thumbing through various volumes, he selected forthwith a novel titled *Hai Yu Chi* (Record of Travels in the West).

Facing Lieou, the examiner mockingly forewarned the youth that his remarkable gift, the product of supernal regions, was to be evaluated straightaway—put to a crucial test. He was advised to listen closely with both ears; for he would be expected to brush stroke in entirety by memory an episode from the novel about to be read aloud.

Ere commencing, the examiner indulged in fat falsity. He pretended a softness of heart urged him to give Lieou Koukai a verbal précis of the episode so that he could become familiar with it in advance. Thus he would have a head start in affixing the events of

Hai Yu Chi on his celestially-blessed brain. The preceding deception served a twofold purpose:

Firstly, feeling certain Leiou would fail, the examiner sought to prevent the student from later having an excuse that he had been given absolutely no leeway. Secondly, the examiner saw a way of making a monkey out of Lieou via an inferential lesson. Seemingly, to the sardonic man, the episode in *Hai Yu Chi* he was going to read manifested a similar situation between himself and the youth with his unmitigated lie.

In his brief summary the examiner paraphrased the episode as he was reading to the student. The main character in it was Wu-k'ung, erstwhile king of the monkeys who had metamorphosed from a stone egg brought forth and deposited on a desolate mountaintop enveloped by dark clouds. The long-tailed creature in quest of the lore of witchcraft descended from his elevated birthplace and came across a mischievous magician's path. From him Wu-k'ung learned black art, which he practiced lightyear after lightyear.

A chronic evildoer, Wu-k'ung caused so much mischief throughout the cosmos that the godhead commanded minor deities to capture the creature. Outwitted time and time again, the godlings could not hold Wu-k'ung in a cage. He was too evasive and smooth for his own good.

Henceforth, the stone monkey's ego grew larger than his little body. Full of egocentric pebbles, he proclaimed himself the brightest being in the universe. He had grand illusions of becoming the great I AM. But fret not. At tail end Wu-k'ung was crushed to dust whilst waging a war of weighty words with the wisest of the wise, Buddha.

Portraying a look of Buddhistic sagaciousness, the examiner next started to read the rest of the passages in *Hai Yu Chi*, character by character. When at long last he completed his reading, he slammed the book shut and slipped it under an armpit. By a flick of his hand he signaled Lieou to begin brush stroking. With Argus-eyed watchfulness the examiner sometimes stood and sometimes sat observing the youth. All the while as the liquid in a clapsydra flowed at rhythmic intervals through a small aperture into a vessel of the water clock, he patiently kept time with tapping movements of his foot.

After several hours, the examiner's patience exhausted, he grabbed the youth's memorized brush work the instant he finished. The examiner lost not a second in comparing it with the passages in *Hai Yu Chi*. Running a forefinger down the vertical columns (right to left), the man saw to his astonishment that the characters of both works were a perfect match, the same to the slightest stroke as if the youth had had the novel in front of him to copy from. A geyser of words gushed apologetically out of the gaping mouth of the man, who now bowed with deep respect before Lieou Koukai.

Lieou's prolix powers of memorization aired, the select group of high-ranking officials applauded the prime minister for recommending the youth to do the spying. To expedite matters, a courier was sent to the Imperial Academy to summon Lieou Koukai. Upon his arrival in court, following a few formalities, he was sworn in as a spy for Emperor Shun Ti, a duty he was honored to perform.

The youth dropped to his knees in a posture of thankfulness for the privilege of serving his emperor on the dangerous mission. Did not the honors outweigh the dangers. Lieou's scholastic achievements were rewarded beyond his wildest dreams: Shun Ti promised him everlasting gratitude—and a choice concubine. The monks promised him immortality in nirvana. The ministers promised him an appointment in the academy. The generals promised him gold in his palm.

(With a retentive mind such as his, Lieou was not oblivious of the fact that to refuse the spy duty meant his testicles would be torn from his body. And he would be thrown into a snake-filled pit to die in agony.)

The prime minister, delegated spokesman, briefed Lieou on what intelligence was to be obtained. Because of the urgency of the situation, he was ordered to go at once to the region of Kwangchow disguised as a peasant. A speedy horse and appropriate rustic clothes would be provided for him. In Kwangchow he was to mingle with the inhabitants. Wherever he went he should hint he wanted to join the rebel Chu Yüan-chang in his effort to unseat the tyrannical Tartar occupying the Dragon Throne.

Lieou was to spread word that the Tatar-Mongolians were sucking the blood from the veins and the marrow from the bones of the Chinese. . . . On reconsideration, avoid spreading vicious lies about us; as he spoke the prime minister by a brush of his brow eluded eye-to-eye contact with the youth. Untruths could infuriate dull people who are cowlike in their submissiveness to turn their sharp horns against the authority of the Mongol regime. More peasants might join forces with Chu Yüan-chang.

Sooner or later some of the rebellious dogs are bound to get wind of your seditious smell and welcome you into their pack. Once recruited, learning the location of Chu Yüan-chang's center of operations and the details of his planned offensive should be but a matter of opportunity and observance. That in a litchi nut was the extent of the preparatory instructions. His briefing concluded, the youth departed for Kwangchow.

Time passed and Leiou Koukai returned safely to Khanbalic palace, reporting his mission had been accomplished. He informed the functionaries at the court that Chu Yüan-chang had no specific headquarters nor a hide-out. It was the strategy of the rebel leader to divide his army evenly into several separate units strewn far apart in diversified directions. Except for Chu Yüan-chang none of the rebels knew where the dispersed army encampments were situated. A slippery eel, Chu Yüan-chang under the cover of darkness constantly shifted his headquarters from unit to unit.

It so happened that Lieou was put into an army unit encamped near the bank of the Yangtze Kiang. By a stroke of luck, while fetching water from the river, he overheard two sentries talking on the far side of dense underbrush. One said, that week Chu Yüan-chang would be making nightly tours of inspection at all the campsites.

For seven nights, stealthily pursuing the rebel leader on horseback, Lieou strained his eyes in the dim moonlight memorizing the locations of all the dispersed units constituting the revolutionary army. (The functionaries of the court murmured with satisfaction.) Out of a clear sky on the eighth day the rebel leader changed the locations of the encampments. Tactics he habitually used which afterward became apparent.

Ergo, the intelligence Lieou Koukai had obtained was worthless. (The functionaries of the court murmured with dissatisfaction.) Nonetheless, his mission had not been unsuccessful. Just before Lieou deserted the enemy, an underling passed the word to the men in the encampment that Chu Yüan-chang had arrived. He was holding a high-level security meeting with their superiors. Sneaking behind the meeting place, Lieou listened; his ears perked outwardly as the plan of the rebels' offensive was discussed in detail.

Functionaries at the court exhorted the youth to bring forth his findings without further dawdling. Obligingly he proceeded to reveal from memory the rebel's plan of attack *tzŭ* by *tzŭ*. With amazing accuracy his voice reproduced rising and dipping tones characteristic of the Chinese language, eloquently spoken. However, it was not appreciated by the functionaries. They wanted to hear the plan expressed in Mongolian, not in Chinese which none understood.

Their angry voices shouted for Lieou to verbalize the plan in the

Mongolic tongue. That was impossible, the youth replied. He did not understand a thing he was saying. (Unluckily the rebel Chu Yüan-chang in discussing the plan divulged the details in a dialect which was meaningless to Lieou Koukai.)

Albeit steamed by the youth's inability to decipher the data recorded on his brain, the court, if the reader will recall, had anticipated that possibility, and cool heads conferred. The problem boiled down to a simple matter of selecting someone to translate the Chinese wording of the plan into Mongolian so that the Tartar troops could be informed how many were needed to wait in ambush; and when and where to spring the deadly trap on Chu Yüan-chang's revolutionaries.

Chinese interpreters came and went through the palace gates. Yet none were able to translate the words of Chu Yüan-chang. While time streaked by with the rapidity of a shooting star, the gods, without rule or reason, engaged in gamesmanship. They swung open the palace gates at the last hour court was in session. A farmer appeared who was formerly from Chung-li, the rebel leader's birthplace. Familiar with the dialect of Chung-li, the farmer easily translated Lieou's recitation of the planned offensive.

Of all places, the one where the rebel leader intended to begin his assault was a district bordering the banks of the Yangtze Kiang, tantalizing close to the Chin campsite where Lieou had been inducted. The intelligence that the young spy had acquired was letter-perfect, but ill-timed.

The onslaught had been scheduled to occur the day before the functionaries heard the Chinese translation by the grace of their gods. A precise, punctual person, Chu Yüan-chang had his fighting forces attack Mongolian strongholds at the exact predetermined hour, systematically overpowering them one by one with overwhelming numbers.

In relatively short order Chu Yüan-chang controlled the Yangtze Valley as well as the surrounding territories. After a time the rest of Southern China surrendered to him. Marching onward to the North, he progressed steadily year in and year out, securing province after province.

The subjugated Chinese people aided him everywhere he fought. In 1368 Khanbalic, the last Mongolian stronghold, fell into the rebel leader's hands. He transferred the capital to Nanking and declared himself emperor of China under the title Ming Tai Tsu. Thereby he established a new dynasty, the Ming or...the Bright.

As for the dethroned emperor Shun Ti, he with his herd fled like frightened llamas to the steppes of Mongolia, whence had migrated his ancestor Genghis Khan. Thus it was that this twig of the tyrannical Tartar tree snapped, and the Yüan Dynasty fell to the ground to be used as kindling to fuel historic tales for fireplaces in China.

The history of the Ming Dynasty never would have been written if the gods had not made a grave mistake. Since superhuman beings are purported to be paradigms of perfection—incapable of making errors—to save face they have kept their mistake a closely guarded secret the past centuries.

Lest they hear me reveal it and seal my lips forever, lower your ear nearer the page. I shall whisper the secret to you. Sh, sh! I implore you not to rustle the page so loudly. Do not repeat this to a soul if you wish me well. Now to be brief and to the point: When the gods, while puttering around in their firmamental workshop, created Lieou Koukai, in lieu of a mortal mind they mistakenly put inside the high-grade student's vacant skull the brain of a parrot.

BOOK FIVE

Chapter 30

Teachers' training at National Dance Studios was an ongoing policy. To keep up with the state of the art, they were required to attend technique classes taught by Chandler Corey, the dance director, whose job it was to refine the coarse mannerisms in the dancing of newly trained teachers. Also they were taught advanced steps and style. At times they were exposed to choreographic theories.

Corey was not only a superior director but also he excelled in ballroom-dancing artistry. Whether performing with a partner or doing school figures, he always looked perfectly natural. He practiced school figures (steps danced without a partner) for years to perfect his skills on a dance floor—or a stage.

When he was a child, rheumatic fever affected Corey's heart. As a consequence, he weakened it practicing too strenuously. That he had a heart condition in his case happened to be a twofold tragedy: He was forced to set aside his aspiration of studying ballet, of becoming a great dancer and choreographer. Corey's balletic idol was the fabulous Vaslav Nijinsky.

Chandler Corey certainly had the physique of a ballet dancer. His graceful physical likeness can be seen among the male figures Nicolas Lancret immortalized in a painting, La Camargo Dancing. In contradiction, Corey was unappreciative of his classic frame. Since his teens he coveted the powerful, athletic build of a football player.

Whenever he sat in the bleachers watching his high-school team play football, he indulged in reverie, conjuring up a vision of himself as a fullback charging through the opponent's line of defense to make heroic touchdowns. To bolster his ego, he wore double-breasted, navy-blue suits with extra padding in the shoulders. In contrast to the color of his suits Corey's blond locks stood out like a golden harvest. (It was not generally known, but he dyed his hair.)

Despite the dance director's desire to be a man's man physically, his temperament smacked of the delicate artist. Ordinary, of average mentality, Corey on the surface appeared to be a proud, profound personality. The matter-in-hand way he carried a portfolio—full of dance notes—as if it contained philosophical papers, gave people the impression that he was indeed deep.

Seldom did the dance director talk to anyone outside his classes. Always in a hurry, should he encounter a trainee or a teacher, Corey claimed he had to be somewhere, so he could not stop to chat. Being pressed for time was a defense mechanism Corey used to cover his intellectual shallowness. Except when discussing The Dance and related forms of the art, he had little to say. Cornered into a conversation about any other subject, he side-stepped it by getting around to his favorite field—dancing.

Looking owlishly wise, as he adjusted his horn-rimmed spectacles which slipped off the bridge of his nose, he hooted: "Ho, hum, such is life. Dancing, you know, isn't merely an instinct of mankind. In animal life The Dance is instinctive, too. Surprisingly the chimpanzees, similar to human beings, participate in communal dances. And let me tell you, I was flabbergasted to learn the South American cocks of the rocks, the antelopes, and even the spiders during courting season seduce and win mates by performances of fantastic love dances.

"And listen to this: The marmots engage in tag dances not too unlike people's. Should a marmot wish to dance, he taps another on the shoulder. That preliminary over, the two rise up on their hind legs, place front paws pad to pad, and with noses touching dance roundabout. Finally they separate, whirling away. Darting back to reassume original positions, both marmots crack their teeth together noisily as a finale to the revels, which include somersaulting downhill, of all things.

"Most intriguing to me are the courtship dances of the gooney birds. That, you know, is what blackfooted albatrosses are called. The birds pair off, bow with outspread wings, and cross their bills which they rattle like sabers. They then utter whistling cries as they rub their stretched necks against each other's, necking the way lovers do. Next they straighten up, puff out their breasts, and strut around leisurely in rhythm. The albatrosses' web-footed movements are no less artful than the foot movements of humans dancing a minuet.

"The same as humans, apes have costume balls for a particular purpose or season. With twists and turns of their bodies they interweave vines and twigs, material for costumes donned during dances in which challenges are thundered with rage at electric storms. The apes aggressively beat their chests as if keeping time to sound and step. Incredible, don't you think."

Having almost exhausted his information on the nature of animals' dancing, Corey, looking at his wristwatch, would exclaim, "Oops! I had no idea it was that late. Gotta run. Remind me sometime to tell you more about the dances of not-so-dumb animals." Pivoting on his toes, he quickstepped away to wherever he was headed.

While Chandler Corey was unsteady in the scholarly world, he was sure-footed in the world of social dance where he stood on solid ground in his command of dancing fundamentals that he exhibited to his class members, thereof thoroughly teaching them technique. When introducing an advanced step- or combination, Corey demonstrated it with style so that the members could see exactly how it should be executed in final form.

For their benefit he did a step over and over, simply and slowly with and without music. Corey's deliberate bodily movements were analogous to a motion-picture actor's movements filmed in slow motion, giving the class a clear mental image of the dance director's school figures, step...by step...by step . . .

The record player set at low speed, Corey's school figures were easily followed. During the demonstrations he stood at the head of the class with his back to the members, who were lined up behind him across the width of the studio. Everybody imitated his movements to the slow music. Some imitations were well-expressed, some were expressionless.

Mechanical in his movements, stocky Bert Craig, strongly desirous of becoming an impressive ballroom dancer, looked unnatural while he mechanically attempted to duplicate the original style of the gifted dance director. That Bert had a strong desire to excel in the ballroom was ironic, since his mother's bad case of dancing fever was the cause of Bert's parents getting a divorce.

Mrs. Craig was unhappy with Mr. Craig, and the feeling was mutual. She was displeased because her husband could not dance. In defiance of the woman's braying that he at least try to learn how to dance, the man, just as stubborn as she, at social affairs refused to budge from his chair, neither for a fox trot nor a waltz. Dancing, he argued, was the least important thing in her life. She argued she was born to dance; he was too mulish to admit it.

To snap his suspenders, Mrs. Craig squandered Mr. Craig's hard-earned savings on private lessons. On a dance floor (when the orchestra played 'Imagination'), she pictured herself a graceful white swan floating on a lake. She was in reality graceless as a jenny ass trotting on a road.

By contrast, Alice Scott in her dancing exhibited beauty of form and elegant motion. Besides being endowed with perfect grace, she had a flair for coordinating, in flawless harmony with the rhythm, movement to music. However, her perfection was a bit flawed. Seemingly she lacked her fiancé's retentive capacity. Alice on occasion forgot the pattern of a dance step whereas Bert never did.

It was small wonder that Bert remembered patterns of dance steps. His ability to memorize notwithstanding, he thought about nothing else but step-combinations day and night. If he was having difficulty falling asleep at night, he counted steps instead of sheep. In the morning he rose from bed before the cock crowed so that he would be the earliest arrival at National Dance Studios, whereupon he hurried to the ballroom to practice school figures in front of wall mirrors without being disturbed. When the other teachers arrived, he would have to follow standard procedure and practice dancing with a partner. Bert wanted to be a step ahead of the others.

Since they were engaged to be married, it was only natural that Bert and Alice paired off with each other the most. Should she bungle a step because she failed to remember the pattern, Bert stiffened, and his displeasure was apparent from the surly sullen expression on his face. Irritated by his fiancée's forgetfulness, the little fellow felt frustrated. He could not realize his full capability practicing with her. She stood in the way of his progress. He blamed her, not himself, for his shortcomings as a dancer.

Still tied together in practice, Bert roughly recaptured for Alice the directional pattern which had escaped her mind. With impatience he showed her how she had spoiled the step. If she did not do it right the second time, he snapped at her doglike. This mean attitude upset the girl. She became tense and lost her concentration. Disconcerted, she was unable to follow the patterns he led her into. Alice was making too many missteps. They had to quit practicing together right in the middle of a dance number.

While they waited for the music to stop so that they could change partners, Bert sulked with his eyes glued to the floor. Alice tried to console him. Squeezing his hand affectionately, she said: "I'm sorry, dear. I promise to do better next time." She was quite aware of Bert's swing moods from boyish humour to childish ill humour. Blinded by maternal instinct, she tolerated his immaturity. Oh, yes, the foolish female loved Bert. She loved him doggedly.

As for our protagonist Vincent Armstrong, his inflated opinion of himself as a finished dancer had burst like a pierced balloon the instant he ran up against the sharp criticism from the dance director, who showed him how ridiculous were the antics of unschooled performers on public dance floors. Having spent many evenings in San Francisco ballrooms (notably El Patio and Wolohans) where professional dancers almost never appeared, Vincent—an amateur among amateurs—had been influenced by all sorts of artless exhibitions by superficially skilled dance-hall masters, social dancers at best.

Confronted with the hard fact that he was not the 'terrific' dancer his friends in the past described him to be, gouged his vanity. Now that he had professional instruction and was better qualified to pass judgment on his dancing, he had to admit they paid him an undeserved compliment ('terrific' was complimentary assuming his friends were using the descriptive adjective in the colloquial sense of the word).

Vincent, unlike Bert Craig, had no illusions of grandeur about developing into a local Gene Kelly, national dancing star of stage and screen. Having slowly but surely progressed in the Training Class, Vincent was satisfied to move along at a tortoise's trudge in the Technique Class. Still, he made more progress than seriocomical Bert, whose hare's hops were so tiring he could not keep up with advanced steps.

By no means was Vincent Armstrong's progress unnoticed. The studio managers had an eye on him throughout his training. But Vincent was not being observed to a great extent for his skill as a dancer or for his ability as a teacher. To the contrary, what they were interested in was Vincent's personality.

He was the type of manly individual that inspired confidence in the opposite sex. Wealthy widows, wistful women, would buy expensive dance courses for the privilege of being in his embrace within the romantic atmosphere provided by National Dance Studios. In view of such lucrative prospects, he was the first among the newly trained teachers to be assigned a student.

Chapter 31

"Tonight at eight o'clock you are going to have a student," Ralph Normand informed Vincent. A beam of satisfaction illuminated the supervisor's countenance. "I requested that you be placed under my wing. There is no doubt in my mind you've got what it takes to succeed in the dance game. And the managers agree with me. The individuals on my team—all of whom were well-trained—surpassed the rest of the teachers in sales the last quarter. I feel confident you will help us maintain our lead: the bigger the sales, the bigger the commissions.

"One more thing before the matter escapes me." Mr. Normand now spoke in a stern voice symbolic of authority. "You are expected to conduct your lessons in the ballroom, not off the dance floor in the side studios or in the ones upstairs on the second floor."

Peeved over that policy, an unwritten law of the management, Vincent made suppositions: "Suppose I am teaching a student swing in the ballroom while swing music is on, and it changes to a waltz. Or suppose I want her to do school figures so I can stand back and evaluate her performance. With inappropriate records playing and people circling around us, I'm afraid student, not to mention teacher, might be thrown for a loop."

"No, she won't and neither will you," assured the supervisor. "Simply pretend you are alone with your student in the ballroom. Tell her to turn a deaf ear to the different music and a blind eye to the other dancers around her. Whichever steps she is doing, she is to continue regardless of what dance number comes over the sound system. You will be amazed how well it works out.

"Let me put it this way: Can you picture the plight of an amateur boxer stepping into the ring at jam-packed Madison Square Garden after being trained to fight in a cramped basement. The same applies to a dilettante dancer. If she learned to dance in a big ballroom filled with couples, she would be able to perform better than if she was taught in a small room."

Vincent could not swallow the comparison. From Vincent's side of the table, it seemed the supervisor was comparing orangeade to applesauce. With persistence Vincent asked, "What if the student is shy and insists she be taught in private?"

"In that case," responded Ralph reluctantly, "you have no choice, do you?" Not wanting a reply, he intimated by his tone the subject should be dropped. "Well, I'm sure the question won't come up with Matilda Gump, the doll you will be teaching tonight. She is a spinster pushing forty. Miss Gump recently returned from a vacation in Oregon.

"Albert Cole used to be her teacher. You have never met him. He departed from the studio while she was on vacation, before you were here. Anyway, he said she'd spout in spurts about religion. Perhaps it was astrology. I don't know. Cole never did get the story straight.

"He claimed she is withdrawn and unfriendly, which may or may not be true. Cole wasn't the easiest person in the world to get along with. See if you can find out what's eating her. It may be useful in persuading the gorgeous gal to extend her dance course. She does not have too many hours left.

"Here," the supervisor handed Vincent a large folder, "this is her dance-course plan. On the back are notes Cole wrote which show the ground they covered. Notice his comment in the lower left-hand corner: 'Spent part of the hour on timing and balance. Both need improvement.'

"It would be worthwhile to read everything in the folder. However, keep an open mind. I am not sure how objective Cole was about her dancing. You judge for yourself." Normand shook Vincent's hand and wished him luck.

At a quarter to seven that night in a busy reception room, Vincent Armstrong was hastily introduced to Matilda Gump. Without dawdling he escorted her into the ballroom where engaged in conversations a host of teachers and students stood about the dance floor or sat on the built-in benches along the walls.

Since he was a new teacher, Vincent surmised he was the subject of everybody's conversation. A few teachers glanced his way but they were not discussing Mr. Armstrong. While they waited for the music to start, the teachers for the most part were giving their students pointers on how to improve their dancing.

Not too familiar with the seasoned teachers, unsure of his instructional methods, Vincent was self-conscious. To add to his discomfort, Miss Gump was silent as a mummy. A blank look was written on the lines of her face, marked by a lifeless expression. Her deadpan manner was not very pleasant. To put some life into her, Vincent gave Matilda an electrifying smile. It was ineffective; her dead pan remained unchanged.

Intentionally or not, Ralph Normand in one respect had ushered Vincent down the wrong aisle. Matilda was far from gorgeous. Unattractive facial features was not her main drawback. Although she was tall and thin, her bodily parts were disproportionate. The pleated skirt she wore could not hide her hipless hips nor her protuberant posterior. Visible through her sheer, pink blouse was a slack bra which cupped the woman's breasts, two small plums.

A wart beneath her undershot jaw caught Vincent's eye. He quickly looked away so as not to embarrass her. After a brief pause he uttered the first thing that popped into his mind.

"How did you enjoy your vacation in Oregon, Miss Gump?"

"Sort of...somewhat...so, so," she solemnly spoke.

He did not hesitate to ask, "Did you visit any place in particular?"

"Portland," was her terse answer.

To keep the dialogue alive Vincent again questioned her. "Were you in the city during the Rose Festival?"

"Yes. The flowers on the floats were exquisite. They were every color imaginable." The woman's tone now contained an animated ring.

The lively sound of his student's voice, raised the teacher's spirits. He felt encouraged to talk: "I have seen only black and white shots of the Rose Festival in newsreels. But I can imagine how colorful the processions must be. The floats decorated with colorful arrangements and carrying all those beautiful, shapely girls posing in swim—a . . ."

Swallowing the syllables he was on the verge of blurting out, Vincent's face turned red as a rose. He realized, too late, that he had made a faux pas. Matilda glared at Vincent and sarcastically said:

"Just because a female exposes her figure in a bathing suit, doesn't mean she is beautiful. If there were any beauties on the floats, I was too uncomfortable to notice. The weather was sweltering. My clothes stuck to my skin like Scotch tape. Portland in the summer is miserable, a blazing furnace."

Burned up by the woman's sarcasm, Vincent fumed internally. She had a nerve! He was thinking of giving her a piece of his mind. Instead he counted to ten to cool off. Gaining control of himself, he was tactful.

"Believe me, Miss Gump, I share your dislike of hot climates. There is nothing comparable to the weather in San Francisco. The ocean breezes are a pleasant relief on a hot day."

At that moment music came over the sound system in the ballroom. It was an opportune time for Vincent to hop off abrasive subjects onto the smooth one of dancing.

"There goes the music. Uh, oh, the tempo is a little fast. Shoot! I wish a slower fox trot had come on. It will be all right, though. Let's take it easy for this number. If we cut down our pace a bit, we still can coordinate our steps with the timing. In the meantime I shall be analyzing your strong and weak points. Should any problems arise, we'll work on solutions in the next number."

Vincent, grinning saccharinely, faced Matilda and placed his arms about her in dance position. However, when they turned their heads to acute angles so that they were no longer positioned face to face, his lips puckered distastefully at the spinster's sour expression. Ignoring her unpleasant attitude as he faced leftward over her shoulder, he concentrated upon the business at hand.

Ten minutes after dancing with her, Vincent discovered Matilda's repertory of steps was limited, more so than had been indicated on her dance-course plan. That her timing and balance was in need of improvement was a gross understatement. She did not dance to the musical tempo, she ran a race to it. She stepped at such a rate of speed, she slipped twice, almost losing her balance as if she had skidded on a banana peel.

Still worse, Vincent's student, who continuously danced on her toes, bounced within his arms. Her bouncing was so vigorous it seemed wire springs were attached to the soles of her shoes, laceless flats. While they tripped the light fantastic, the man's right hand unavoidably kept sliding off the woman's waist to a lower region near her big bottom, which he could feel bumping against his hand each time she bounced. Peering out of the corner of his eye, he got a glimpse of her profile. It was discernible from her side view that she was now in a rapturous state. Quite a change! to Vincent's surprise.

When the music temporarily stopped, the teacher took his student aside to discuss the difficulties with her performance. He chose his words carefully. "Do you mind if I make some suggestions? You are handicapping yourself by wearing flat shoes. They are suitable for ballet—not for ballroom dancing. If you wore shoes with heels, your balance would be improved.

"Dancing on the toes all the time is tiring, especially in going backward where you must stretch your leg to touch the floor with your toe. In flats this can't be done without difficulty, because the hind part of the foot has to be dropped rather far before it lands on the floor. That mainly is what causes you to lose your balance.

"Also, staying on your toes prevents you from stepping solidly. The result is you tend not only to be unsteady on your feet but also to use your body to an extreme. Using one's body in performing a dance may or may not be appropriate.

"For example, in Hawaii a hula-hula wouldn't be a hula-hula without undulating movements of the hips. And in European folk dances a jig wouldn't be a jig unless the body bobs up and down. But in modern dances such as the American fox trot, body action distorts the style. In other words, a fox trot is not a fox trot if it is performed with unsteady movements."

Although Matilda was listening to Vincent talk, she was not hearing him, at least not clearly. Her mind was fleecy and remote as a cirrus cloud. Eager to put into practice all he had learned in the Training Class, the inexperienced teacher was unaware that students' thoughts often drift during their lessons.

"Miss Gump, do a few steps by yourself. I would like to watch you dance." She complied with Vincent's request but started off on the wrong foot.

"Oh, no, my dear lady! Get into the habit of starting with the proper foot, even when you are practicing. Remember, the man always starts with his left foot and woman with her right foot."

In an attempt to put Matilda at ease, Vincent said: "I find amusing the fact that in England the exact opposite is the case. The woman starts with her left foot and man with his right foot. Yet, unlike us, Englanders drive on the left side of the road. Speaking of twist-abouts, women button their clothes from right to left and men from left to right. Or is it the reverse? My tongue is getting twisted! A person could lose his hair trying to comb out the knots of life's inconsistencies."

Vincent must have pressed Matilda's funny bone. In spite of her vinegary disposition, she simpered sweetly.

By now couples on the move invaded the isolated area of the ballroom that Vincent and Matilda were occupying. The danger of collision becoming imminent, the teacher decided his student doing school figures where she stood on the dance floor was precarious.

"Our spot is getting too crowded, Miss Gump. We'll delay your giving me a demonstration until we have more room. By the way, do you have any questions?"

Turning her head from side to side, in universal sign language she gestured "No." Her teacher thus presumed his explanations had been lucid. He glowed within, elated over the success of his efforts. "All rightie, the music is starting again, let's dance," he said, extending his arms—the right one waist high, the left one up high.

Hardly had the man put his arms about the woman in dance position when she swung her right foot halfway rearward in anticipation of his stepping straight ahead with his left foot. She returned her foot to the proper place posthaste upon the teacher's cautioning her, "Wait! Wait for my lead!"

This time she waited, and they began in unison. "Good. Just try not to hurry. Slow-slow-quick-quick, slow-slow-quick-quick . . . ," he regulated her speed to the tempo of the fox trot, his voice functioning as a metronome while they advanced in the line of dance around the ballroom.

After a while Vincent's metronomic utterances attracted attention. He had the feeling other teachers nearby were laughing at him. Out of embarrassment he stopped voicing 'slows' and 'quicks' to assist his student, leaving her to regulate the tempo by herself, which proved disastrous. On her own she got carried away and speeded up her pace, fox trotting much too fast for music in a medium tempo. To boot, her erstwhile bounce recurred.

Irked, Vincent insulted Matilda in the privacy of his think chamber. "Miss Gump, you must have a rubber ball for a brain!"

Presently, concluding that allowing himself to become exasperated was insensate, unwise if nothing else, the man ceased fighting a futile cause and, discontinuing his attempts to lead her, permitted the woman to dance at will, which she did with abandon.

Applying practical psychology, the teacher cheered his student on: "Hooray, you are doing great. Just dance a wee bit slower. Take your time. That's better. I've been catching glimpses of you in the wall mirrors as we have been dancing around the ballroom. Your style is unusual...very unusual, indeed."

Then, conscience-stricken, worried Matilda might separate the chaff from a grain of truth, Vincent regretted having commented as he had. However, his worry was for naught.

She unexpectedly remarked, "Uh-huh, I know it. My style is out of the ordinary." With the smug look of a child revealing a secret, she whispered in his ear, "Mr. Armstrong, I was destined to dance."

Not anticipating such an incredible statement from her, Vincent was temporarily voiceless. (Suddenly it flashed across his mind that Bert Craig had mentioned something similar about his mother: Mrs. Craig swore she was born to dance. Bert was convinced she would say so just to irritate his father. But Vincent wondered why Matilda Gump believed as she did.)

The teacher fox trotted with his student for several minutes debating with himself whether he ought to ask her to explain what she meant. Bursting with curiosity, he decided to ask her. "Miss Gump, how did you arrive at the conclusion that you were destined to dance?" By the firmness of his tone it sounded as if he demanded an answer.

A slow thinker, she was easily flustered and disliked anybody pressuring her to converse unless she had things she could talk about readily available. Finally finding the words, she answered his question with a question. "Have you read 'Mansions of the Soul' by Dr. H. Spencer Lewis?"

Frowning, Vincent replied: "Why, no. To tell the truth, I never even heard of him. Is he a contemporary writer?"

"No, he isn't. Until his demise, Dr. Lewis was the imperator, or supreme executive, of the <u>Ancient</u> <u>Mystical</u> <u>Order</u> <u>Rosae</u> <u>Crucia</u>, popularly called the Rosicrucian Order." Matilda could not resist mentioning the complete title, the very sound of which gave her a vicarious thrill of participation in the esoteric.

"The Rosicrucian Order? I Never heard of it," Vincent had to admit. "What is it? and where is it?"

She knew her subject so well, Matilda had a ready reply: "The Rosicrucian Order is a fraternal organization in the sense that it operates on a lodge system.

"According to tradition, the Rosicrucian Order, worldwide in scope, originated amidst the arcane schools of learning in Egypt around 1350 B.C. during the reign of Pharoah Amenhotep IV. The first member-students met in the secret chambers of the Great

Pyramid of Khufu. Later in the majestic temples along the Nile, learned members initiated candidates into the great mysteries of the cosmos.

"Amidst the mysteries uncovered by this early secret fraternity of Rosicrucians was the doctrine of reincarnation. Dr. Lewis treats rebirth in a new body in his book. In one chapter he refers to a meeting with a business man who testifies that as far back as his boyhood he found pictures of places in the Holy Land and Egypt remarkably familiar. Yet in his present lifetime he never traveled to either place."

Bewildered by Matilda Gump's strange story, Vincent confessed his state of perplexity to her. "It is confusing, and beyond my comprehension. Anyhow, what does all that have to do with your ballroom dancing?"

"Shush!" she said: "Don't interrupt my trend of thought. I will explain everything. Just listen."

Only too happy to comply, Vincent gave his undivided attention to Miss Gump. He welcomed the opportunity to gain some insight into her emotional defenses. Thus he would be supplied ammunition to break down her resistance against buying more lessons.

Still Vincent was reluctant to use the hard dollars-and-cents psychology of National Dance Studios to sell students expensive dance-courses. He had an internal conflict over the propriety of the ethics in the psychological warfare he was preparing to wage against a weak woman.

"Sorry, Miss Gump," Vincent apologized. "I didn't mean to interrupt you. Please, go on. Tell me more."

Her voice overly tightened to a high pitch, Matilda continued to unwind. "Like the man that Dr. Lewis met with, I also found pictures of places in the Ancient World remarkably familiar. Ever since I was a little girl, travelogues of Egyptian cities have fascinated me.

"I am not referring to scenes of modern Cairo: the maze of narrow streets lined with yellow limestone houses...the bazaars...and Ismaîlîeh...or the European quarter. I am referring to such places as the ruins at Memphis and Thebes.

"Deep within my soul I've always had the feeling that if I were to visit Egypt, I'd find out something about myself both of interest and personal value to me. Could it be possible I was having recollections of a forgotten past experience? It was a question I asked myself many times.

"Probably I wouldn't ever have found an answer if I hadn't happened to notice glued onto the inside back cover of the book,

'Mansions of the Soul,' a little green slip which had printed on it: Rosicrucian Order, San Jose, California.

"Eager for more information on reincarnation, I sent a letter to that address. A few days later I received literature, including a membership application, which I filled out and returned to the San Jose address. That's where the Supreme Grand Lodge is located.

"To my delight, I was accepted as a member in the Rosicrucian Order. Next I exercised my privilege to affiliate with the Francis Bacon Lodge in San Francisco.

"While attending convocations at the local lodge, I learned that other members, too, had had vague recollections of residing in foreign lands that they never in their lifetime visited. Learning that others experienced psychic visions as well, strengthened my belief in the rebirth of souls. Along with weekly instructional monographs mailed to me from San Jose, I began reading history books on Egypt."

Vincent was skeptical of Matilda's strange story; it seemed pointless. Nevertheless, he was interested in hearing the conclusion. To encourage her to continue, he told a white lie colored with a green hint. "It sounds like an intriguing correspondence course—almost as intriguing as a ballroom dance-course."

Matilda smiled a strange smile, and said: "I believe they go hand in hand. Don't be misled, Mr. Armstrong. The monographs are not the same as an ordinary correspondence course. They are lessons which reveal, fascinating mysteries of life, awaken dormant talents, and develop personal powers.

"Wishing to perfect my personal powers, I read additional books—books about the customs of ancient Egyptians. Coming across passages describing temple dancers who lived during the great Rameses II's time, stirred up in my mind a strong sense of familiarity with the pictures as well as the book's descriptions. They were exactly as I had visualized in my girlhood."

Not hearing in Miss Gump's divulgences anything useful for a sales pitch, Vincent broke his silence, suggesting they leave the floor and sit down on the wall bench where they could talk without being jostled by other dancers. As soon as the teacher and student were seated, he told her that he was unable to see the connection between what she had related and her statement 'she was destined to dance.'

"It's quite simple," Matilda replied. "I always wanted to learn to dance. But, fearful of making a spectacle of myself, I lacked the courage to try. The thought of people staring at me while I stumbled around on a dance floor was too disturbing. I had migraine headaches. And I couldn't sleep.

"Seeking help, I telephoned for an appointment with the lodge master of the Rosicrucian Order in San Francisco. At his private office I consulted him about a peculiar phenomenon I had experienced on a sleepless night:

"I had a dreamy vision that I was a dancer in the Temple of Amon-Ra at Luxor. My body was scantily covered; ribbons crisscrossed my bosom. I wore a biblike necklace, wide bracelets, rings on my toes, and garlands in my braided hair.

"The end of my long braid was weighted with a large ball that pulled my hair and bounced against my back the while I danced to the clapping hands of maidens. The louder they clapped, the harder the ball bounced. Between the weight of the ball and the loud handclaps, I felt excruciating pain in my head as I danced faster and faster. So vivid was the vision that my head still ached hours after the dream faded away."

(Could Matilda Gump have misread chronicles on Egyptian dances? Or did she confuse her incarnations? It appears that hand clapping as a means of beating time, and the type of hairdo she describes—a pigtail ending in a weighty ball—was typical of the Third and Fourth Dynasties. In the Nineteenth Dynasty, under the rule of Rameses II, Matilda would have danced to the rattle of a sistrum, not to the clapping of hands.)

With an expression of adoration she digressed: "You have no idea of the sublimity of the lodge master. After a few moments in his presence I was exhilarated. In listening to him, I had imparted to me knowledge of the mystics, knowledge which has been cloaked in secrecy over the centuries, knowledge...uh—uh. Glory be! It is hard to explain to the uninitiated. Let me put it this way . . ."

The woman proceeded to verbalize virtually verbatim a phase of Rosicrucian ideology. "'Within us there are constructive creative forces always at work and always attuned with the most perfect wisdom of the immortal self. These forces must repair the damage done to the body, overcome the strains and stresses upon the mental system, and guide the indecision of our minds in the right direction.

"'A strange, potent force, unsuspected except by a few, is lying dormant in every one of us. It is man's fifth estate—a sovereign heritage—a dormant, potential, personal power. The fifth estate of man is creative evolution. It is the inherent power within the very being and essence of each of us to create for ourselves individual mastership in all things—our environment, our talents.'"

Unable to think of any more material she had learned by rote, Matilda stopped speaking. She looked at Vincent smugly, as though she had passed on the wisdom of the ages to him.

The teacher resisted the temptation to ask his student to define the third and fourth estates, which he vaguely recalled from his days at college. He doubted Miss Gump understood what she was quoting. Obviously she could not put any of it into her own words. With tongue-in-cheek, he remarked, "I have never heard anything so remarkable."

Not realizing his remark was facetious, she was pleased and said: "Oh, there are many things, many mysteries, many unexplained happenings people have not heard of. Thank heaven, life is no longer a mystery to me." She raised her hand abruptly, and dangled it in front of his nose.

"See this ring? Lucky me! I discovered it in a Rosicrucian student-supplies catalogue. The ring was imported from Cairo. In the silver mounting, as you can see, is a scarab. It is an exact copy of the antique rings on display in the Rosicrucian Egyptian Museum." She turned the scarab, which was fastened by a swivel, to show Vincent hieroglyphics inscribed on the ring.

"The scarab, an image of a beetle, was regarded as sacred by the Pharoahs. In ancient Egypt the scarab beetle was believed to have supernatural powers and was worn as a magic charm."

Vincent searched his mind. Where had he heard the word <u>scarab</u> before? Of course! he had heard it from his grandfather who used to call a 'worthless, contemptible person' a <u>scarab</u> or <u>dung</u> <u>beetle</u>. Vincent would have liked to tell Matilda that, but he bit his tongue to refrain from offending the woman. He did want her to renew her ballroom dance-course. Gad! what a rancid way of buttering one's bread.

Turning the scarab back in place, Matilda went on to say: "This ring is the best investment I ever made. It has worked miracles for me. I wear the ring day and night. In my nightly visions of a former life the heavy ball attached to my braid no longer pulls my hair or bounces painfully against my back while I dance in an Egyptian temple. In my present life I seldom experience sleepless nights. And I seldom awake with painful migraine headaches.

"The fear of being hurt as a dancer was perpetuated in my rebirths. I have conquered such fear with the help of the scarab, which was venerated by the mighty Pharaohs as a symbol of the sun-god Khepera. I now have knowledge that I was born and bred to perform for the deities, to dance eternally in the temples of my destiny."

At that moment a waltz came over the sound system in the ballroom. Vincent stood up indicating they were to resume dancing. As soon as Matilda arose from the wall bench, she pirouetted imagining she was an exotic temple dancer. She lost her balance and fell into Vincent's arms at an awkward angle. He straightened her body and placed his arms about her in waltz position.

While they were waltzing (to a slow tempo), Vincent had several thoughts he would have liked to express to Miss Gump. But he was doubtful that she would be interested in his opinions. Moreover, he was irritated by her infernal bouncing. Disgusted, he let the woman bounce...her buttocks bumping his hand time and time again as the music played on.

Chapter 32

"Good morning, Vince. Where have you been keeping yourself? I haven't seen you very often lately."

"Oh, I have been around. I guess we don't run into each other often because our teaching schedules are different."

"That's the way the cookie crumbles." Bert Craig dropped the small matter. "Tell me. Are you working Saturday night?"

"Yes. But I'm only booked for two hours. I will be free at nine o'clock."

"Alice and I will be free at nine also. The extra change we pocket teaching Saturdays certainly helps supplement our meager earnings during the week."

"How true," affirmed Armstrong. "The money we receive in this glamorized dance mill is barely enough to nest and feed a bird."

"You aren't just whistling to the wind." Craig rationalized, "It is a consolation, at least, that National Dance Studios makes up for the low pay by giving us all the high-cost instructions in advanced dancing we want."

Vincent challenged Bert's rationalization. "That's highly debatable."

"It is?" Puzzled, Bert asked, "What do you mean?"

"Merely this: Ever since the new Training Class was formed, the studio staff members have been paying less and less attention to us. When we started here, the entire staff used to go out of their way to help us improve our dancing and to teach us new steps.

"Now that we are no longer trainees, we're brushed off like dandruff on a collar. Every time I approach a member of the staff for assistance with a difficult dance step, instead I am given the usual reply: 'a dancer learns by trial and error—practice, practice, and more practice.'"

Craig's countenance registered displeasure. "Come to think of it, I have been told the same thing."

"Bert, do you remember when we were still in training. Everybody in National Dance Studios said we topped all the classes that had preceded us."

"You bet your sweet life I remember that compliment." Suddenly short, stocky Bert Craig's long facial expression widened to a gratified one. He seriously believed that he had been the most responsible of all in making their class the best ever.

Armstrong resumed talking: "Yesterday I had some business to discuss with the assistant manager. I went to his office, but he wasn't there. He was on the second floor in the Training Class. He had just left. So I chased up the stairs after him. When I entered the room, I happened to overhear him feeding the same old baloney to the new trainees that he fed us. I heard him say they were the greatest group National Dance Studios has ever employed.

"Obviously all newcomers are handed a routine song and dance. They are praised, pampered, and promised pie in the sky. It is the management's foxy method of keeping greenhorns contented while they sweat through the training period without pay. To put it mildly, we are given soft soap instead of hard cash."

Craig's wide facial expression of gratification lengthened to a glum look. "You mean they play upon our emotions to work not for money's sake but for art's sake. The same sort of icky stuff we were instructed to apply to our students to cajole them into renewing or extending their ballroom dance-courses."

"Exactly, my enlightened comrade," Armstrong smiled as he concurred, making light fun of a heavy fact. "Taking advantage of our desire to master dancing, they appeal to our emotions. We are actually paying for the lessons with our labor."

Unwilling to face the reality of the situation, Bert quickly picked up on the comical vein Vincent brought into play. "Comrade, I see the light. Still, I am a love slave to The Dance. Woe is me! I'm chained by a year's contract and must serve the Studio to the bitter end. But all is not lost. I can improve my dancing in Chandler Corey's technique class. He better devote some time to helping me. Or I'll plant a bomb in the seat of his pants."

Armstrong, seeing no point in arguing, indulged his determined yet unrealistic friend. "More power to you. No doubt if you are that insistent upon being helped, the dance director will be compelled to spare you a little instruction once in a blue moon. The question is how many moons. Corey just sold a lifetime dance-course to another wealthy widow. He is booked solid and is too busy to conduct teacher's technique classes—not many, anyway."

"That's better than none at all. Beggars can't be choosers. I will take what I can get. Vince, you sound as though you are thinking of quitting National Dance Studios."

"Later on, Bert, not right away. Teaching dancing is a stepping stone for me. I have no other prospects presently. Besides, the consequence of breaking my contract with the Studio stops me cold. Two hundred dollars is quite a sum for a pauper like me to toss down the drain." Laughingly Armstrong added, "Believe me, brother, I need the cash more than the management does."

Craig also had something to say about the forfeiture clause of the agreement with National Dance Studios. However, he was distracted from expressing his opinion by Alice Scott who entered the scene.

"Is Vincent going out with us Saturday night?" the girl inquired. As she spoke she placed a hand on her fiancé's shoulder affectionately.

"Gee, I didn't get around to asking him. How about it, Vince. Would you care to join us after work?" Receiving an affirmative answer, Bert exclaimed, "That's great! We'll have a ball."

Alice had a thought. "Let's go dancing someplace where we can nurse our drinks." She delighted in using that expression not only because Bert had taught it to her but also because she knew being economical pleased him.

"Swell! I'll date one of the other teachers. And we'll all take a postman's holiday," Vincent teased a bit.

"Which one will you date?" Alice's curiosity craved to be satisfied.

"Umm, I probably will ask Ruth Gowen. We can learn a lot from her. She has been teaching ballroom dancing almost three years."

Approving of the choice, Bert Craig then suggested with eagerness. "What do you say we start the ball rolling Saturday night by dropping by Bimbo's 365 Club for a drink."

Bert's fiancée started to giggle. "He wants to see the naked lady in the fishbowl."

A tinge of red appeared on his chubby cheeks. Wondering if she might have been overheard by others in the area, Bert glanced around uneasily. "Why must you always blurt things out like that?

Go ahead! Broadcast it all over the state of California." While sarcastically reprimanding Alice, he threw his hands up in dismay.

The girl, believing the distraught young man's anger was justified, remained quiet. This was not the first time she had embarrassed him. On occasion Alice Scott was too outspoken, particularly in regard to her betrothed who filled her thoughts constantly.

Vincent Armstrong came to her rescue. "Bert, for crying out loud! Alice was only kidding. Don't excite yourself so. You'll burst a blood vessel. I've gone to the 365 Club myself for the same reason. I even met one of the nude mermaids in the flesh." Vincent punned, "Perhaps I should say in the scales."

At the mention of the nude mermaid, Bert was all ears. Despite the unattractive pun, his frame of mind changed from irritation to expectation.

"The introduction did not do me a bit of good, though. She was off duty, fully dressed, and—worst luck—married!" Vincent went right on speaking, and resisted an urge to laugh at Bert, whose disappointment was clearly written on his face.

Vincent thought he might cheer up Bert with an attempt at humor. "Oh, well, there are plenty of unmarried mermaids in the ocean. Married or single, she is still a sexy sight."

"The lady told me how her act is pulled off. She lies undressed on a rug in a room in the basement beneath the bar. At the center behind the long counter of the bar is the fishbowl, which is actually a six-sided tank. The sides are about fifteen by twelve inches.

"In the tank, or fishbowl, a simulated rock formation conceals a tunnel containing mirrors in which her image is reflected from a mirror down below the basement room. The reflection of the lady's body appears in miniature at both ends of the tunnel. The fishbowl revolves so that everyone seated at the bar can get a full view of her.

"Whenever the lady wishes to create an illusion of her swimming, she wiggles her arms and legs. From time to time she winks to flirt with goggling male customers."

"Doesn't she get cold and embarrassed lying in the nude on a rug?" questioned Alice naïvely.

"Except for backstrokes she lies flat on her stomach. I imagine the room is well heated." Vincent stopped short of saying "What a silly question!"

Chapter 33

Saturday inevitably arrived—but not without complications occurring. It happened to be the wrong time of the month for Ruth Gowen, who had accepted Vincent Armstrong's invitation to go to the 365 Club. When she menstruated, Ruth experienced severe backaches and cramps. They became so unbearable by nightfall that she notified management she was too ill to carry on with the teaching of dances.

As soon as Miss Gowen's remaining appointments were turned over to accommodating exchange teachers, she was granted permission to leave the Studio. Before her departure, Ruth, having located Vincent, explained she was not feeling well and regretted she was unable to keep their engagement.

In replying, Vincent proved very understanding. "There is no need to apologize. What's most regrettable is that you are ill. Let us hope it isn't anything serious. We can always arrange to get together another time."

(The tender verbal intercourse between Vincent and Ruth notwithstanding, they did not date in the future. He never found a reason to ask her out socially. She could not care less because she was interested in someone else.)

Earlier in the week, after learning what Alice Scott intended to do Saturday night, Joanne Armond, also a teacher at the Studio, included herself along with her husband Bob in the plans to visit the nightclub. Joanne used any pretext she could invent to escape the Armonds' conjugal dream-castle.

Built on quicksand, the foundations of their marriage had been gradually sinking. And the additional weight of her vocation teaching dance, objectionable to him, was hastening the calamity. Strange bedmates were Joanne and Bob, cruelly trapped by fate, not knowing how to break away from each other.

"I'm so glad we're joining you in your get-together. It will be wonderful for Bob to meet some of my coworkers. According to my husband, anybody who teaches ballroom dancing is a brainless nincompoop.

"He will change his tune tonight. If not, he'll pay the piper. The poor boy is suffering from collegitis. Will he be floored when he tries to match wits with Vincent or Bert. I can just picture Bob's puss after he is outclassed in book learning by a pair of dancing teachers."

Left in the lurch at the last minute, Vincent did not have time to date another girl. Uncomfortable about the possibility of spoiling their evening, he decided against going out on the town with his friends. He excused himself saying, "A fifth wheel is only in the way." They dismissed Vincent's excuse as nonsense and insisted he join them.

Outside the Studio where Bob Armond was waiting in front of the entranceway, Joanne introduced him to her three friends (Alice, Bert, and Vincent). The customary handshakes disposed of, Joanne proposed they skip the 365 Club. She was not in the mood to sit through a floor show in North Beach. One voice in opposition was raised, but in the end Joanne had her way.

The group also accepted a second proposal of hers: to go to El Portal, a dine-and-dance nightspot in the Richmond District. Joanne's preferences for El Portal ranged from "parking presents no problem...more space to dance...less formal atmosphere...to an inexpensive bill of fare."

Ordinarily Bert Craig, the sole dissenter, would have been happy going anywhere as long as the place had a band and a dance floor. Now he unhappily went along in martyrdom. Considering himself, not Vincent, the real fifth wheel, Bert suffered silently: "Yeah! real wheel, real wheel—real, real wheel," dizzy notions reeled and rolled roundabout his brain. Pouting, the martyr felt abused because he was not going to see the lady in the fishbowl.

El Portal had been recently remodeled, with a resultant doubling of the bar and restaurant business. Despite the sizable outlay for modern improvements including the latest equipment, one essential item—an air conditioner—was omitted. Patrons having begun to complain about the stagnant air in the establishment, the owners ordered an air-conditioning system, soon to be installed. This improvement might have contributed to the comfort of future customers, but at the moment it offered none to the two couples and the stag seated in a U-shaped booth near the bandstand.

"Whew! It's hot as a steam bath in here. My shirt is soaking wet," Bert complained. Since their arrival an hour ago the perspiring fellow had danced every number with his fiancée. Wiping his sweaty brow with a handkerchief, he replaced it in the breast pocket of his coat, raised a highball glass to his parted lips, and sucked out a small piece of ice, which melted as he moved it about in his dry mouth.

Somewhat refreshed by the liquid from the melting ice, he was content to sit still for the next fifteen minutes, the length of the band's intermission. No longer was Bert brooding over his earlier disappointment. To the contrary, he was enjoying himself immensely, even though the lack of cool fresh air lessened the pleasure of his dancing.

As for Vincent Armstrong, he was not enjoying himself at all. His back to the booth, he found himself in a ticklish situation. Alice and Bert having stepped out onto the dance floor whenever the band started to play, Vincent had been left at bay—alone to face the Armonds, confronting him like a lynx and a dragon from across the table.

"That was a rumba." Minutes later, "That is a samba," Joanne, unable to restrain herself, would excitedly identify aloud the different kinds of music.

"Ah, now they are playing 'Orchids in the Moonlight,' my favorite tango number. I know you dislike to tango, Bob dear." (Slyly she exploited his inability to perform Latin-American dances.) That the question was a demand was quite apparent from the ferocity of her tone and feline defiance of her glare.

Joanne's irate spouse, not daring to object lest she spring and shriek, consented between clenched teeth. As our hero rose to dance with her, his gaze met Bob Armond's. If Vincent had suspected something was awry before, now he was certain.

The green-eyed monster seemed ready to snap his invidious jaws. Bob's physiognomy—a long, quivering chin; thick, locked lips; and pain-filled, deep-set eye sockets, their hollowness accentuated by his close-cropped haircut—was not pleasant to behold.

'Miserable' aptly describes Vincent's reaction to the jealousy Bob displayed. Still worse, Joanne refused to dance at a decent distance (for a married woman). She persisted in thrusting her body directly up against his. Ordinarily he would have welcomed such physical proximity of a woman. Under the circumstances he was unreceptive to it but behaved properly: he backed away, which was futile.

"Tango close to me—tango close!" The wildcat spat heatedly while again and again she molded herself like hot wax into his bodily form.

In desperation Vincent tangoed past other couples on the dance floor to the opposite side of the room behind a large pillar that hid Joanne and him from her husband's view. Upon returning to the booth after the music stopped, Vincent—in an attempt to allay Bob's antagonism—commented in a friendly fashion, "I understand you are studying at the University of San Francisco."

"A flirty little birdie must have told you!" Bob snapped with hostility. "What else did she chirp about!"

Coolheaded on the surface, Vincent pretended to be unaware of the insolence. Underneath the surface his blood boiled: "You jealous jerk! Don't get smart with me. I'll knock you flat on your fanny.

"I can't help it if your wife is loose because you do not have the right tool with which to screw her well in bed." To avoid voicing his heated thoughts, Vincent held his tongue and bit his lower lip, forcing himself to simmer down.

Meanwhile, Alice, Bert, and Joanne were busily engaged in a threesome conversation about ballroom dances, the central topic of the evening. One too many cocktails had dulled Joanne's claws, so that she forgot her desire to scratch Bob's mind by pushing him into a scrappy contest of quick wittedness with Armstrong and Craig, who she believed had more brain power.

Still, in constantly bringing up the subject of Dance, which he was not well versed in, she had wounded her husband's pride effortlessly. Armond was compelled to remain silent, as the college man had nothing to contribute to the subject under discussion. And he did not want to sound stupid.

In consequence, Bob Armond's moodiness was intensified. Eventually his bad humor on top of his resentful attitude became unbearable, difficult for the others sitting at close quarters to tolerate. Tension permeated the atmosphere in the crowded booth which was marked by stony silence.

Alice prompted the group to disperse when, hinting her bedtime was past due, she sleepily placed her head on Bert's shoulder. Although the individuals in the group went home in four different directions, there was a oneness in their ruminations: glad the get-together was over, sorry it had occurred.

Chapter 34

Much sooner than had been expected, Bert Craig was to lead Alice Scott to the altar. The circumstances precipitating their marriage were not in the true sense romantic. A friend of the Craig family, who worked in the advertising department of the Call-Bulletin, had received a pair of passes to the Embassy Theater.

Invited to an early Sunday dinner at the Craigs' home, the newspaperman, a grateful guest, hearing Bert mention he was on his way to see Alice, offered him the passes. Too great an economist to refuse, Bert accepted the free passes with expressed appreciation.

Later, in the evening, Alice and Bert went downtown to the Embassy Theater. Approaching the box office, he turned in the passes and paid a minimal service charge. In return, besides two admission tickets, he was handed four small colored cards upon each of which was printed Ten-O-Win: two cards were orange with the numbers 52 and 53, two were purple with the numbers 86 and 87. Without bothering to inspect the cards, Bert slipped them into a pocket of his jacket.

Alice and Bert entered the motion-picture theater and were seated in the darkened auditorium. After the featured cinema ended, the lights were turned on. A man could be seen sliding onto the stage a large, round, wooden contraption attached to a solid stand and divided into three concentric circles.

The center circle, a multicolored pattern of wedges, was stationary with a movable arrow on it. Lines separated the next or middle rotatable circle into sections numbered to one hundred in multiples of ten; an immovable arrow was affixed to the circle. On the outer rotatable circle were numbers signifying sums of money from two to eight dollars; also the outer circle contained four metallic, red triangles indicating percentages of a jackpot, if one was accumulated.

From out of a wing, microphone in hand, stepped the manager to announce that the game of Ten-O-Win (a special attraction at the theater seven nights a week) was about to begin. He asked the people in the audience to hold in readiness their Ten-O-Win cards issued at the box office.

The manager explained, in case anybody was unfamiliar with the game, that each winner was determined by spinning the middle and outer circles of the Ten-O-Win board as well as the arrow of the center circle: After the spins, the arrow pointing to the center circle would indicate the winning color, and the arrow pointing to the middle circle would indicate the winning number. When the outer circle stopped spinning, a third arrow affixed at the top of the stand would indicate the amount won.

While the manager was addressing the audience, Bert started to complain to Alice. "I wish they'd run the next picture and not kill the evening playing phoney-baloney Keeno games."

Alice corrected Bert. "The game is Ten-O-Win, not Keeno."

"Whatever they call it. I hope it's over soon. I've never won a darn thing in my entire life."

"You never can tell, dear." Alice squeezed her fiancé's hand lovingly. An optimist, she said, "You might win something."

(The manager continued his explanation of Ten-O-Win: "In all there may be ten winners, any one of whom could be lucky enough to carry home the jackpot, which has accumulated to seven-hundred dollars.")

Again Bert complained, "Fat chance I have of winning the jackpot!"

His fiancée remained optimistic. "You have as good a chance as anyone else here."

"I'll tell you what, Alice. If I win the seven-hundred dollars, I will buy you anything your heart desires. You just name it, sweetheart."

Alice smiles sweetly. "Anything?" she asked.

Certain he would not win, Bert felt he could afford to be generous. "Yes—anything."

"Even a honeymoon in Acapulco?" She still smiled, but she was serious.

"Yes, in Mexico or on the moon," was Bert's spontaneous answer. Inwardly he rationalized: "What do I have to lose. Hi diddle, hi diddle, the cat and the fiddle, the cow didn't jump over the moon. And I won't win the jackpot."

Meantime the manager spun the rotatable parts of the Ten-O-Win board. Occupied with his childish rationalization with a nursery rhyme, Bert did not hear the voice of the manager booming over the microphone:

"The color is...orange—the number is...53." Next the manager watched the outer circle slow down. As soon as it stopped, he exclaimed: "It is...a one-hundred percent jackpot! Wow! on the first spin of the evening the winning number is orange 53. I repeat, the winner is orange 53!"

Alice was so animated by the manager's enthusiasm that she tugged excitedly at the sleeve of her fiancé's jacket as she entreated: "Bert, Bert, what are our colors and numbers? Where are the Ten-O-Win cards?"

"Don't get in such an uproar. They are somewhere in my pocket. I'll find them." Bert fumbled around in his pockets.

"Hurry," urged Alice. "Hurry, before it is too late!"

"Okay, okay," Bert retorted to calm her. Removing the cards from a pocket, he hardly could believe it when he saw that one of the cards was orange 53. A second look convinced him his eyes had not deceived him.

He sprang to his feet shouting "Here! Here! Here, I have orange 53!" Like a peculiar mask the oddest expression of amazement covered Bert's face as he fought his way against laps and legs to the aisle. He rushed to the stage where his claim was verified.

Congratulating Bert Craig, the manager asked him what he intended to do with the seven-hundred dollars. On the spur of the moment, in his excitement, Bert committed himself:

"I am going to get married right away and take my bride to Acapulco for our honeymoon."

"How soon is right away?" inquired the manager.

The jackpot winner blurted out with bravado "Oh, in a few days—a week at the most."

"Is your bride here tonight?" the manager questioned further. Informed that she was in the theater, he requested her to stand up. Upon handing Bert a check in the amount of seven-hundred dollars, the manager prompted the audience to give a round of applause for the lucky couple. By Bert's public announcement, ready or not, he had made the immediateness of their marriage a *fait accompli*.

With Bert and Alice on their honeymoon the past week, life at

National Dance Studios had seemed empty from Vincent Armstrong's outlook. The daily routine of practicing and teaching ballroom dances was rather wearisome without his two friends around to break the monotony.

Students recently assigned to Vincent, in accordance with his taste, were unappealing—except for one student. She was Lucile Hardin, a strikingly beautiful woman that he found irresistible. Her dancing lesson was scheduled in the evening at seven o'clock, the next hour.

Vincent stepped into the men's restroom to groom himself before the lesson. While he was particular, he was not always overly fussy about his appearance. But whenever he was to teach Miss Hardin, he took extra pains to look his best. After washing his hands and face, he parted and reparted his hair and knotted and reknotted his tie till he was satisfied both were perfectly even. The way he saw it, an uneven part or an uneven knot was an eyesore.

From the studio supply Vincent had received a bottle of chlorophyll pills, which contain a deodorizing, green coloring matter found in leaves and plants. He downed a double dose of the pills despite the fact that he was unsure of their effectiveness as a deodorant. Goats graze on grass yet they have a bad odor. Nevertheless, Vincent had high hopes chlorophyll might be kinder to humans than to animals.

How he looked forward to giving Miss Hardin lessons! Especially in closed dance position. Never had Vincent met a woman so refreshingly clean. Her scent had the fragrance of a fresh gardenia moistened with dew. Her skin was velvety smooth as the petals. Her hair, fine fern, turned golden when exposed to bright light. Any part of her perfectly proportioned person would be kissable. A tremor surged through him at that salacious thought.

Moved by a wave of passion, he decided he had to ask the woman for a date. Of course, propriety—subtlety, too—should be used in his approach. If offended she might report him to his supervisor. He was not afraid of being fired, but it would be embarrassing to be discovered ignoring the rule that prohibited fraternization between teachers and students. Although she did not appear to be the type to say anything, it was a possibility. With his determination to take a calculated risk for a date, Mr. Armstrong went into the ballroom where Miss Hardin was waiting.

A half hour of dancing and lighthearted conversation having elapsed, the teacher felt the time was ripe to invite his student out on a date. Guiding her away from hearing range of other dancers, he quietly asked, "Miss Hardin, can you keep a secret?"

"What kind of a secret?" She appeared not so much surprised as mystified by the unexpected question.

He had a ready reply. "I can't explain what kind without revealing the secret. If you will answer me one way or the other, I'll know whether or not I ought to reveal it."

"Very well, I can keep a secret." Curiosity compelled her to concede.

He was still cautious. "Do you promise?"

"Yes, Mr. Armstrong. I promise."

Convinced the woman's word was her bond, Vincent spoke in a straightforward manner. "You are probably unaware we teachers are not allowed to date our students. In spite of that, I'd like you to go out with me. There you have the secret."

Miss Hardin's luscious lips—red as sunripened apples and, apparently, just as juicy—parted into a delicious smile, which did not last. Concern crept into her carefree countenance. "I would not want you to lose your job on my account."

"Heck! I'm not concerned about losing my job. Naturally, nobody relishes the idea of being fired. If we are discreet, we won't be found out. Besides, to get a date with you would be worth the risk."

An element of distrust was evident from the woman's response. "I bet you tell that to all your students. You do. Be truthful."

"I am telling you the truth. Cross my heart and hope to die if I am not." (Vincent made the sign of the cross over his heart, an act he learned as a little boy to show he was being truthful.)

"What about a date tomorrow night. Since I don't have an eight o'clock teaching appointment, I could pick you up between eight-thirty and nine."

Because of the relative lateness of the hour the woman was hesitant to accept the date. But a barrage of persuasive ammunition from the man weakened her defenses. "All right. I shall expect you by nine o'clock."

Lucile Hardin's residence was in St. Francis Woods, a hilly maze of irregularly laid out streets which, to one's utter distraction, twist and turn up and down in seeming chaos, notwithstanding the orderly, expensive, custom-built older homes that predominate over the area.

So confusing is the topography of this exclusive residential neighborhood, even native San Franciscans can lose their way while driving in it on a foggy night. Lavish growths of shrubbery, quite often concealing house numbers, make it difficult to locate a desired address.

Of all nights, the one Vincent Armstrong had selected was unusually foggy. Just the same, he was not distracted by the fog. Sexually worked up, the man was prepared if necessary to cut a path through a dense rain forest to capture the breathtaking creature that awaited him.

When he finally found his way to her doorstep, the fog was thick as clam chowder. Consequently, she—and he—came to the conclusion it would be messy to go out into the souplike mist. Anyway, staying at home was the safe thing to do.

Flames in the living room fireplace dying down, Lucile placed more logs on the andirons. She brushed fragments of bark off her palms and sat on a leaf-colored *metelassé* couch, upon the opposite end of which her guest had settled. In conversing with Lucile, he learned that the sole person, an aunt with whom Lucile lived, was away on a visit to a son in Texas.

"Wow! What a setup." Vincent had to use restraint to keep from exclaiming his internal glee aloud. He hardly could believe he was alone in the company of body beautiful herself.

As the woman talked, her hands rested on a cushion that was leaning against her thigh. Vincent wished she would push the cushion aside so he could better study her curvilinear lines underscored by a black blouse she was wearing. The man's mind, entranced by lustful visions, longed to savor her gardenia-white bodily parts beautifully arranged in a corsage unwrapped on the green *matelassé*.

Bent on seduction, Vincent suggested they go over some dance steps she recently learned at the Studio. That was a good excuse to put his arms around her. She was delighted for the opportunity to practice with her teacher. Getting up from the couch, she walked across the room to a radio on an occasional table and turned the dial to a station playing fox-trot music. The guest having trailed the hostess, he was by her side when she finished adjusting the volume on the radio.

They embraced...much too intimately for proper dance position. While they were sort-of fox trotting, Vincent drew his left hand along with Lucile's right hand onto her breast. Through her blouse and brassiere he could feel a hardened tit. It reminded him of a rosebud. "Are her titties the color of red or pink roses," he wondered.

Step by step she started singing to the music. On impulse as her lips parted Vincent kissed her. And his tongue darted into her mouth with the suddenness of a thunderbolt.

She muttered something about a French kiss, but her English was unintelligible. If she objected, it was halfheartedly. Lucile closed her mouth only a fraction. In ebullition Vincent pried her mouth open wider with his tongue.

A bit of saliva ran into the corner of Lucile's mouth. "Ooh!" she exclaimed, "We mustn't do this." Gently pulling away a step from their close embrace, she wiped her mouth with the back of her hand. She said she wanted his respect. "You are rushing me. I barely know you."

Vincent posed a rhetorical question to convince Lucile he was not being disrespectful. "How can we truly know each other unless we share our dreams, the desires we never dare fulfill except in the solitude of our love-starved hearts? Let me touch your heart," he pleaded as he attempted to unbutton the woman's blouse to expose her breasts.

Removing the man's hand, she argued: "You don't understand. True, I have desires. But I desire to be loved for myself, not just for my body. I want our friendship to be beautiful. You are making it ugly."

"How can you say that?" Impassioned, he avoided the issue. "Lucile, believe me, you are beautiful."

"Do you really think I am beautiful, Vincent?" "Of course, I do," he assured her. She seemed receptive so he French kissed her again; his moist tongue plunged deep into her mouth to challenge hers.

Lucile rebelled. "Stop! Don't kiss me that way. You are mean. Do you want to make me cry?"

For an instant, animalism in him being dominant, he was indifferent to her feelings. "Why should you cry? Are you frigid? Or is it that you dislike French kisses!" snarled Vincent.

"No—yes. No, not such wet ones. Can't you understand? I crave love." She began to tremble.

"Come close to me, if you crave to be loved," he demanded, trying not to sound overbearing. She complied by pressing her body up against his. Vincent held her securely and carefully lowered her onto a rug near the fireplace.

Lucile lay limp. The flaming heat from the fireplace elevated his passionate fever to a high degree, almost beyond endurance. He proceeded to unbutton her blouse.

"Please," she implored him. "I...please—let's talk. I should tell you something."

Her words were so softspoken, Vincent did not hear her. He continued to unbutton her blouse feverishly.

"Oh, dear God! Please," she cried. "Please wait."

It was too late. The blouse unbuttoned, he had quickly removed her brassiere. At last! She was stripped to the waist.

Vincent abruptly froze. A pained expression appeared on his face. It was the chilling look of a warmblooded man stabbed with an icicle in the abdomen. Lucile Hardin—beau ideal with skin as lovely as an unblemished rose petal—had embedded in between her breasts hideous scar tissue, reddish masses of fibrous growth crablike in form.

"See," she sobbed. "See why I need to be loved not just physically? Now you have seen my keloids. Do you still want to make love to me?"

"You know I do," he lied out of pity. "Really?" she expressed doubt. "Yes, really," again he lied. Since she stopped sobbing and showed a willingness to engage in sex, he now felt obligated to perform the act.

Vincent Armstrong, however sensual, nonetheless was a tender soul who could not deliberately hurt a woman's feelings. Although her keloids were disgusting, he gritted his teeth and never once looked away while they were undressing in preparation for the sex act.

But when they had intercourse, he clamped his eyelids so tightly shut, saline liquid secreting from the lacrimal glands burned Vincent's eyes. And when they opened, his vision blurred. As he ejaculated, the man had the sensation that a sticky string was being drawn right through the most delicate part of his anatomy.

During the discharge of his seminal fluid, Lucile had clung to Vincent with strength surprising to a member of the self-styled stronger sex. Not surprisingly, her strength sprang from fear. The woman was terrified she was fated to a life of loneliness and despair.

She was too panic-stricken to let go of a symbol of security, a superficial one notwithstanding. To prolong the fleeting moment, she pressed the man to her bosom as hard as she could. Lucile's keloids ground into Vincent's flesh, the ridges rubbing like coarse sandpaper against his hairy chest.

Weakened by his climax, the repulsive physical contact was

unbearable. Withdrawing from the woman, he cut it short. But he could not shorten or immediately withdraw from his mind the unpleasant bodily sensation of the sticky string, which seemed to be yards long.

The next morning, when Vincent arrived at the Studio, he was in a state of depression over his misadventure in St. Francis Woods. However, he was not to remain depressed the rest of the day, for the Craigs had returned from their honeymoon. Their return raised Vincent's low spirits almost as quickly as one can say "Acapulco."

Anxious to relate their experiences at a resort in Mexico, the newlyweds invited Vincent to join them for coffee and Danish pastry. Bert, though usually frugal, insisted they go to the Golden Pheasant, no less.

At the restaurant Alice, bursting with enthusiasm, monopolized the conversation. "We stayed at the El Mirador (she repeated the definite article, not realizing El means 'the'). It is the oldest and one of the best hotels in A-ca-pool-co."

Alice used exaggerated, round lip movements as she rolled out the Aztec word. Inability to pronounce the strange names of the Mexican places had been a source of frustration to her the first few days of the honeymoon. Finally a sympathetic guide came to the young bride's rescue by helping her with words she mispronounced.

"Gracious, is A-ca-pool-co colorful! It is a quaint seaport. The waters are brilliant blue. And the mountains are the greenest green that I have ever seen. The views are heavenly. We had a magnificent view of the Pacific from the hotel windows. The El Mirado, you see, is perched high up on the Que-bra-da Cliffs. They are not too close to the beaches, yet very near the center of town.

"It was thrilling to stroll through the shops and around the plaza. You should have heard the velvet voices of the handsome natives, many of whom, we were told, have Negro blood. The rhythm of their singing was enchanting."

Bert chimed in: "The full name of the seaport town is . . . Gee, I forgot. Just a second. The Mexican guide wrote it down for us." From his wallet Bert removed a scrap of paper, which he showed to Vincent. On it was written Acapulco de Juárez.

Putting the scrap of paper back into his wallet, he added: "At the southwest end of the town is an ancient Spanish fort. In recent times it served as a military prison. The place gave us the willies."

Alice had more to say: "I must tell you about our tours. We went by taxi-metro along the coast to Pie de la Cu...esta." She stumbled over the pronunciation of the name despite the help she had received from the guide in Mexico.

"Pie Cuesta? sounds like custard pie to me." Vincent teased her. "Maybe I should have ordered it instead of a Danish."

"You are being silly." Alice was unruffled by his teasing. "Pie de la Cuesta is a beach. But nothing like Ocean Beach in San Francisco.

"Sand ridges interspersed with coconut palms stretch as far as the eye can see. While we rested in hammocks shaded from the sun, we watched the foamy breakers and sipped refreshing coco milk.

"Pint-sized youngsters tried to sell us beads and shells. For a peso apiece the bigger kids offered to dive beyond the breakers. We would have enjoyed a dip in the ocean. Unfortunately, the powerful waves and undertow are dangerous to swim in.

"Next we were driven a short distance to the jungle village of . . ." Alice rattled on and on about the sightseeing she and Bert had done on their honeymoon. She was on the verge of talking herself hoarse.

Vincent saved her from that discomfort by interrupting to announce Ralph Normand was going to discuss another dance that day—in ten minutes, as a matter of fact. Vincent hated to miss the discussion, not even a minute of it, because the histories were one of the few features which still held his interest at National Dance Studios.

Therefore, the young bachelor, along with the newlyweds, hurriedly headed back from their coffee break to their place of employment. They arrived in the supervisor's studio in the nick of time, sliding into their seats a split second before the supervisor started his discourse.

Chapter 35

A HISTORY OF THE CLASSIC BALLROOM DANCES

Latin-American Dances

III-A. The Tango (to develop control and poise)

Latin-American dances have been performed on both hemispheres of the globe ever since the tango traveled to London via Paris, where it had migrated from Buenos Aires at the turn of the nineteenth century. Not too long after the dance arrived in the city on the Seine, tales as to the *fons et origo* of the dance shot up like tall weeds in a garden.

In 1913 Sem, an ingenious French caricaturist, presented—in Le Petit Journal, a popular Parisian morning newspaper—a startling satire dealing with the tango. According to the account accompanying the artist's cartoon, the place of origin of the dance was the Barrio de las Ranas, once a section of Argentina's capital disparagingly referred to as the Frog Quarter. The newspaper stated:

> In this section brothels, dance halls, and drinking resorts are constructed of flattened oil cans and preserved meat tins. The quarter is devoted to the lowest forms of vice; and the tango is only the development of the cautious, tiger-like, pliant, and treacherous steps of the disreputable frequenters of the Barrio.

The statement in Le Petit Journal seems to have been perpetuated. At any rate, the gist of it is consistently repeated as if factual by many writers. But the commonly accepted view that the tango originated in Buenos Aires, or anywhere else in the Americas, is as incorrect as is the belief that a bull becomes infuriated at the sight of a red cape. (The stimulus, of course, is its fluttering when waved, not its color.)

Documentary evidence proves, beyond a shadow of a doubt, that Spain was the birthplace of the rudimentary choreographic essentials of the tango; though the multiform dance has altered with period, locale, and incident. Yet Spaniards alone cannot be said to be the tango's procreators; a potpourri of peoples helped father the dance, directly or indirectly. To appreciate this fact, in addition to understanding the nature of the tango and its choreography, one must also know something about early Spanish history as it pertained to the dance.

It should be clarified, nevertheless, that the twentieth-century ballroom and exhibition tango is not related to another dance called the Spanish Tango. The coincidental sameness of name notwithstanding, the two dances are dissimilar in choreography. Specifically, the type of dance in Spain to which the present day tango happens to be akin is the folk dance, and the Spanish Tango is not included in this classification.

Indications are that, for the most part, medieval and modern Spanish dancing inherited the attributes of *las Andalucas delicias,* 'the Andalusian delights,' as dancing girls from Gadir were spoken of. (Gadir, an ancient province familiar in modern times as Cádiz, was in Andalusia, a region of southwestern Spain.) Because of their terpsichorean artistry the girls from Gadir, stylists in sensualism, had achieved wide recognition in the Western World even before Rome wrested control of Spain from Carthage (218-133 B.C.).

While the Roman Empire was disintegrating in the fifth century A.D., Spain was invaded by the Suevi, Vandals, and Alani; beginning in 415 they, in turn, were displaced by the Visigoths. Data on the barbaric ravishing of the country is comparatively plentiful; but, outside of the possibility that the Visigoths brought with them the well-known sword dance, for the next 235 years, information in reference to dancing is nil.

In 711 seven thousand Arabs, Syrians, and North-African Berbers—summoned from Africa by political enemies of Visigothic King Roderick—were led across the Straits of Gibraltar by Tarik, a Moslem general. In the decisive battle on the Rio Barbate the army of the Islamitic empire brought about the downfall of the Visigoths on the Iberian peninsula.

The capital of the Islamitic empire was Damascus. Hence, Spain became subject to Damascus' caliphate, and remained so till 756 when Prince Abd-er-Rahman I set up an independent emirate in Córdoba, the founding of which laid the groundwork for the establishment of the Caliphate of Córdoba in 929. Its sway extended over almost all of Spain.

Under the caliph's patronage, dancing and music were a nightly form of diversion. This entertainment was not confined strictly to the alcazars, however. For instance, the zarabanda—a song-dance licentious in character—appeared at festivals of that time. Authoritative sources claim remnants of the zarabanda still exist in the bolero. We shall soon see a link to the tango here, since it, in turn, contains traces of the bolero.

Although the Arabs, Syrians, and Berbers had embraced the same faith, Mohammedanism, they were not a harmonious body. Despite an outward appearance of order, there was only a weak central authority, and violent disputes were carried on. Finally, early in the eleventh century, the Caliphate of Córdoba, undermined by continual discord, broke up into a number of petty Moorish kingdoms.

Then, in the eleventh and twelfth centuries, Spain was overrun by new Mohammedan invaders, the Almoravides (1086-1110) and the Almohades (1110-1212).

Vanquished Spain, in the interim, had been establishing small, independent states which slowly and laboriously were reconquering lands seized by the Moors. This took eight hundred years—eight additional centuries wherein the Moorish influence was creating a bold imprint on Hispanic music and dancing.

Meanwhile, during the last two hundred years of this reconquest, what remained of the Moor's sovereignty on the peninsula had been consolidated into the kingdom of Granada. With the marriage of Ferdinand of Aragon and Isabella of Castile in 1469, most of Spain was at last under one command.

Then these monarchs instigated a campaign to gain control of the Moresque stronghold. In 1492, after being subjected to prolonged attacks, weakened Granada surrendered to superior force. The beleaguered city conquered, the last vestige of domination by the Moors was wiped out.

During the reign of Ferdinand and Isabella, The Dance was introduced into the newborn Spanish drama. The latter art came to life when its founder Juan del Encina produced his *églogas*, pastoral dialogues between shepherds and shepherdesses. Each playlet was terminated by means of a *villancico* ('Christmas carol' or rustic song) to at least one of which professional actors danced. They were from strolling lay companies traveling the countryside. Thus The Dance made its debut in the secularized theater and was viewed in a new light.

With the expanding power of sovereigns (*los Reyes Catolicos*) the Roman Catholic Church was concerned about control. In order to keep the people's behavior under strict surveillance, priests had no alternative save to permit dancing as part of the ritual within the church.

Before long dancing at masques as well as at fiestas become the modemodel, not only in Spain but everywhere else on the continent. Spanish dances were performed by courtiers to win the favor of royalty.

Now, lest we stray too far afield, we must turn to another group—the Gypsies or *Gitanos*—who played a role in the chronicles of Iberia's dancing. While the Moors' strong sway was significant, that of the Gypsies was important, too.

Historians inform us Gypsies lived in Spain before the fall of Granada. As late as the 1600s large bands of *Zingaros* (Gypsies from Italy) were wandering into Andalusia, where music and dance had been heavily enriched by Moorish-Arabic culture. Realizing the preciousness of the Andalusian art, the Gypsies adopted it but added rich qualities of their own.

Rhythmic traits of dancing, already amatory and aesthetic, were intensified, and swift, spontaneous steps evolved which were characterized by sudden stops. Moreover, the dancer's movements portrayed complete abandon, a yielding to natural impulses whereby an impassioned *Gitano* gave vent to thrilling outbursts of emotion. As a finale the deep tragedy of a homeless yet spirited people was artistically expressed in the gesticulations of their dance to *cantos handos*, a type of tragic Andalusian music that had great appeal to the *Gitanos*.

The part the *Gitano* played in the dancing of the Spanish folk thenceforth is legendary. His choreographic contributions in certain respects is said to have surpassed the Moor's. Be that as it may, both their influences had an effect on the dances of the populace to one extent or another.

Bearing the foregoing facts in mind, we view the Spaniard's folk dances with some insight. At the beginning of the eighteenth century the seguidilla, fandango, and bolero began their ascent to an apogee of popularity. Yet they were by no means young dances.

An esteemed composer and musicologist of Spain, Mariano

Soriano Fuertes, in his voluminous History of Spanish Music published in 1855, contended that the seguidillas could be considered as being among the oldest of Iberian dances, which are prehistoric in iconography as well.

Carmelite Father José Marti, Dean of the chapter of Alicante (a province in southeastern Spain), before he died, in 1705, said the fandango had its roots in the choreography of *las Andalucas delicias,* and the bolero has been traced to the zarabanda—as was mentioned earlier.

Relationships to the tango are found among Spanish folk dances, in particular the forenamed ones by Fuertes and Marti. Since the seguidilla is typical of virtually all national dances of Spain, let us look into it first.

Almost every region, province, and district lays claim to its own seguidilla. In La Mancha it is called the Seguidilla Manchega; in Aragon, Seguidilla Aragonésa; in Seville, Seguidilla Sevillana; in Valencia, Seguidilla Valenciana; in Galicia, Seguidilla Gallega. The name of the dance in Andalusia is Sequiriya. To Santander belongs the Pasiega; and to Guipúzcoa, one of the Basque provinces, the Quipuzcoana.

Inasmuch as these seguidillas originated in La Mancha, the Seguidilla Manchega would be an excellent dance with which to start tracing the genealogy of the tango. In a book *Espagne* ('Spain'), printed in 1874, the French historian Baron Charles Davillier gives the following description:

> One day at the fair of Albacete, one of the principal towns of La Mancha, we saw seguidillas Manchegas characteristically danced. . . . The guitarist . . . began in a minor key with some rapid arpeggios; and each dancer chose his partner, the various couples facing each other some three or four paces apart. Presently two or three emphatic chords indicated to the singers that their turn had come, and they sang the first verse of the copla; meanwhile, the dancers, toes pointed and arms rounded, waited for their signal. The singers paused, and the guitarist began the air of an ancient seguidilla. At the fourth bar the castanets struck in, the singers continued their copla; . . .

["Notice in the Seguidilla Manchega just described the guitarist played music in a minor key, and the singers sang verses of a copla, Spanish for a 'popular song' or 'melody.' Additionally, in the

Spanish language tango is defined as 'music' or 'dance.' And the tango is also danced to popular melodies in a minor key. Also there are major likenesses we shall see as the dancing progresses."]

> and, with agility, all the dancers began enthusiastically turning, returning, following, and fleeing from each other. At the ninth bar, which indicates the termination of the first part, there was a slight pause; the dancers stood motionless, and the guitar twanged on. Then, with renewed energy and a change of step, the second part was introduced, each dancer taking his original place again. . . .

["Early elementary elements of the tango can be seen in the Seguidilla Manchega at this stage in the dance. The pause and pose, the turn and return—all are tango basics."]

> It was then we were able to judge the most interesting and graceful part of the dance—the *bien parado*, literally "well stopped!" . . . The *bien parado* in the seguidilla is the abrupt breaking off of one figure to make way for a new one. It is a very important point that the dancers must stand motionless and, as it were, petrified in the position in which they are surprised by the certain final notes of the air. Those who managed to do this gracefully were applauded with repeated cries of "*Bien parado! Bien parado!!*"

Twenty-twenty vision is not needed to see that the *bien parado* is an inherited feature of the tango. Without well-executed stops or well-timed pauses, the tango's character would be weakened. In fact, such basic steps as the tango close, often used—and quite effectively—in phrasing, are punctuated with a pause.

[The supervisor was interrupted by one of the teachers in the group he was addressing. The teacher admitted that she was unclear about the distinction between dance phrasing and music phrasing.

Mr. Normand explained: "Phrasing is a manner of rendition or interpretation. In music a phrase is a segment of a composition as a rule containing four or eight measures. In dance a phrase is a series of movements interwoven to form a unit in a choreographic pattern. Historically, however, we are concerned with the pause."]

To appreciate the effectiveness of a pause we must understand how it relates to a basic step. Since the tango close is a characteristic one, suppose we examine it. But first an explanation is in order. The fast tempo to which the Seguidilla Manchega was danced was completely dissimilar to that of the tango. In olden times it was danced to an extremely slow tempo, and in modern times the tango is danced to a moderately slow tempo.

In the tango, unlike the fox trot, individual steps usually receive different counts from one another. Therefore, the Counting Formula (quick, quick, slow) of the tango close, simplified here for illustrative purposes, should not be construed as applying necessarily to other figures in the dance.

That fundamental factor figured out, let us proceed with our initial objective and study the component parts of the basic step being examined:

<u>Tango Close</u> (man's footing)

(Quick: Step either forward or backward (according to
(choice) on the left foot.
(*Quick*:   In one sweeping motion pass the right foot by
(the heel of the left foot and step sideward into
(second position.
Slow: Draw the left foot next to the right foot.

On the second <u>quick</u>, weight is placed and retained on the right foot. On the <u>slow</u>, no weight is placed on the left foot. (Needless to say, the woman's footing is in opposition to the man's.) The tango close completed, the dancers pause: they are poised in readiness to perform other steps.

The relationship between the tango and the seguidilla thus having been determined, let us see what a look at another of the previously mentioned Spanish folk dances shows. Contained in a History of Dancing, by the nineteenth-century French analyst Gaston Vuillier, is a vivid description of the fandango:

> The young men spring to their places, rattling castanets, or imitating their sound by snapping their fingers. The girls, beating the exactest time with tapping heels, are remarkable for the . . . lightness of their movements, the voluptuousness of their attitudes. Partners tease and entreat and pursue each other by turns. Suddenly the music stops, and each dancer shows his skill by remaining absolutely motionless, bounding again into the full life of the fandango as the orchestra strikes up. The sound of the guitar, the violin, the rapid tic-tac of heels (*taconeos*), the crack of fingers and castanets, the supple swaying of the dancers fill the spectators with ecstasy. . . .

At first blush, except for the appearance of the *bien parado*, the fandango seems to be unrelated to the tango. But on close inspection a striking resemblance between these two dances is detectable in Vuillier's colorful portrayal, intensified by his final touches:

> All is flutter and glitter, grace and animation—quivering, sonorous, passionate, seductive. *"Olè! Olè!"* Faces beam and eyes burn. *"Olè, olè!"*

Voluptuous attitudes, seductive postures, and passionate gestures typifying the fandango are also typical of the tango. In the modern dance, however, its erotic characteristics instead of being stressed are toned down, that is, subtly insinuated.

If the tango's eroticism were completely subdued, the dance would become expressionless and lose its identity. Waldo Frank, author of Hispanic America, aptly summed up the nature of the dance when he wrote: "Within the chaste contours of the tango figures rages the desire of sex."

So much for the tango's affinity to the fandango. Next let us scrutinize the bolero, chronologically the youngest of the oldest Spanish folk dances. In that descriptions of the bolero are vague and incomplete, to fill in details we shall start with a look at a ballet version created in 1780 by *bailarín* Sebastian Cerezo, a distinguished 'dancer' of Càdiz (formerly ancient Gadir).

He is said to have re-formed the bolero by combining extreme movements from ballet with the cachucha (a combination of the zarabanda and the chacona). The zarabanda, we have already learned, was danced in Spain during the Caliphate of Córdoba's reign (909-1031). Some latter-day writers contend the chacona is of Basque origin. Apparently they are unaware of the fact that Fernandez de Cordova, El Gran Capitán of Spain in the 1500s claimed the chacona originated in Gadir where it was danced circa 200 B.C. by *las Andalucas delicias*.

Here is a plausible explanation how the bolero received its name: While visiting La Mancha, *bailarín* Sebastian Cerezo performed the dance with the grace and vitality of a bird in flight. Since at times he appeared to be flying, the young men of the town named his dance <u>bolero</u>. It is a derivative from the Spanish <u>volar</u>, which is an infinitive meaning 'to fly.' (Note that <u>bolero</u> per se is a word for 'Spanish,' masculine gender.)

When describing the dance in his Code of Terpsichore written in 1823, Carlo Blasis—an outstanding ballet composer and *premier danseur* of the Imperial Academy of Dancing and Pantomime at Milan—said:

> The bolero . . . is executed by two persons. It is composed of five parts—namely, the *paseo*, or promenade, which is a kind of introduction; the *traversias*, or crossing, to alter the position of the places, which is done both before and after the *differencias*, a measure in which a change of steps takes place; then follows the *finales*, which is succeeded by the *bien parado*, a graceful attitude, or grouping of the couples who are dancing.

Before the colonization of the New World by the Spaniards, the music of the bolero was in triple meter. However, later on in the sixteenth century after Cuba was colonized the bolero was set to two-four time—a characteristic of popular Cuban music and, notably, the same rhythm as the tango. Eventually the bolero, influenced by Cubans, returned to Spain as a dance in duple meter. Thereafter in Europe the bolero was performed more often to two- than three-four time.

[Vincent Armstrong broke in on the supervisor's talk. "Excuse me, Mr. Normand. But I am not clear about the meaning of 'meter.'"

Exercising patience, the supervisor replied: "Perhaps it would have been clearer if I had used the term 'rhythm,' instead. It is, as you know, the musical arrangement of accented and unaccented short and long sounds. And in dancing 'rhythm' is measured movements.

"Briefly 'meter' is the arrangement of rhythmic units, in terms of number of beats. In tempo—loosely time, or rate of speed—the Spanish bolero is played (or performed) allegretto, that is, blithe, graceful and moderately fast. There we run into a divergence from the tango. Ideally the tango's tempo is adagio, that is, by comparison performed slower and in a leisurely manner."]

The kinship between the tango and the folk dances of Spain is most evident in the bolero. Besides *bien parado*, another family characteristic *el paseo* appears in the bolero. Ever since the tango's inception *el paseo*—'the walk'—has been an essential movement in tangoing. True, from time to time *el paseo*, capable of being danced in various combinations, underwent changes. Still, it was never discarded, as were less flexible tango figures.

["Incidentally, the customary practice today in referring to 'the walk,' is to use the French term la promenade, not the Spanish el paseo. I shall describe for you an elementary variation of la promenade, which is simply two walking steps plus the tango close. The

Counting Formula is slow, slow, quick (tan'), quick ('go), slow (close). Here is how to do that variation:

La Promenade

Slow:	Walk forward on the left foot,
Slow:	Walk forward on the right foot,
Quick)	
Quick):	Tango close.
Slow)	

Note: The walking steps may be done at will in closed, in parallel, or in conversational position. Nevertheless, the tango close must always be done or end up in closed position."]

Thus far we have discussed the lineage of the tango. What about the dance's etymology: Webster's International Dictionary states that *tango* is a Spanish word (meaning a 'gypsy festival' or 'gypsy dance' or 'gypsy music') derived from ancient Spanish, *tangir*: 'to touch' or 'to play an instrument.' However, not everyone agrees with Webster. In his treatise Cosas de Negros, Vincente Rossi, an Argentine writer, theorizes that the word *tango* is onomatopoetic. Rossi's theory cannot be dismissed as supposition.

To arrive at the derivation of *tango*, we must go to the Dark Continent. In all probability the dance term was conceived in the vicinity of Tanganyika, a great lake in Central Africa, where the next phase of our history starts.

In the remote past, while thumping a drum, a Bantu native—possibly of the Masai or Haya tribe living near or upon the lake—produced a series of two-beat units in which the second beat was somewhat accented. At the same time he had the impulse, as he so often had before, to imitate vocally the sounds registering on his brain.

The dissyllable inspired by the Bantu's primitive drum beats was 'tan-go,' an African name for percussion instruments. With the passage of time the two-syllable onomatopoetic utterances were expressed in the form of chanting. Accompanied by drums, chants were frequently heard in the jungle during mating dances. A drummer stressed the ultima as he chanted "tan-gó, tan-gó, tan-gó, tan-gó . . .!"

In the course of her commercial expansion in the 1440s, if Portugal had not begun the Negro slave trade on the European west coast, it is inconceivable what the ballroom tango of today would be like. An explanation is in order.

African tribal chiefs customarily sold captives of raped villages in Tanganyika Territory to Arabs who penetrated the jungles in Africa toward the end of the fifteenth century. These devout descendants of Mohammed drove barefoot black captives, shackled by the neck, miles from Tanganyika up to the Mediterranean Sea.

At the shore they were turned over to traders for goods and gold. The traders penned their human livestock less humanely than pigs in a sty within the filthy interiors of ships. The slave ships sailed under the flag of Portugal to predetermined ports in Europe, where their live cargo was auctioned off at flesh markets owned or patronized by spiritual sons of Christ.

After the Portuguese navigator Cabral discovered Brazil in 1500, blackamoors, chained in the holds of ships, were waterborne by Portuguese across the Atlantic to their new colony in South America. They were not satisfied just to enslave the Negroes, many of whom had been converted from fetishism or animism to Islam. The European slavers had to humiliate them even more.

Mohammedan Negroes (Malês), culturally superior to their Christian tormentors, were stripped of their tunics and made to wear instead the tanga or loincloth. The fact that the root tang became attached to tanga and Tanganyika as well as to tango supports the claim that the name of the ballroom dance is of African derivation.

Came 1516, Spain, entering into the slave trade, transported blackamoors by the thousands to her colonies. In the New World the enslaved African Negroes, unequal in freedom yet equal in talent to the Spaniards, mastered the folk dances and music of their masters.

In 1911 Albert Friendenthal, a specialist in the Negro's rhythmic techniques, commented in his book Voices of the People:

> Now the African Negroes possess great musical talent. Their passion for music can amount to frenzy. . . . It must be admitted, though, that in the invention of melodies, they do not come up to the European standard. . . . The greater is their capacity as inventors of rhythms. The talent exhibited by such African Negroes as the Bantus in contriving the most complex rhythms is nothing short of marvelous.

For two centuries African Negroes superimposed attributes of their own upon the performing arts until as practiced in the colonies music and dance were no longer unique either to Spain or Africa. Consequently, hybrid music and dances sprang into being in Latin America. The tango is a perfect specimen of such hybridization.

But to begin at the beginning. Negro slaves who labored on the plantations in Cuba and Haiti had transplanted a barbaric dance, the tángano, which they uprooted from soil deep within the pit of the Dark Continent. The tángano as enacted on the plantations was a vulgar dance with back-and-forth pelvic thrusts similar to in-and-out movements performed during coitus.

By the first quarter of the eighteenth century the tángano spread to Central American countries where it attained considerable popularity. Ad interim Negroes migrating from Cuba and Haiti conveyed the tángano to the ports of Buenos Aires and Montevideo, at the mouth of the Rio de la Plata. On the Argentinean and Uruguayan coasts the tángano also was known as the candombe.

On both coasts over the next century, segments of the tángano, commonly called the "Tango of the Negroes," were crossbred with the seguidilla, fandango, bolero, and other dances. The end product was a distinctive dance singular to Latin America. Still, in spite of the predominance of its Hispanic features, the inherent African rhythmical traits or characteristics of the Negro's tango remained exceptionally strong.

In Argentina an outgrowth of the dance was labeled Tango Argentino; in Brazil, Tango Brasileiro; in Cuba, Danza Habanera; in Peru, Tanguino; in Venezuela, Tanguito. Regardless of their common roots, these dances developed marked regional differences. As the Tango Brasileiro, the Tanguino, and the Tanguito, they in no way affected the tango, past or present.

In the Cuban capital, the Danza Habanera, the first refined copy of the tángano, did have an effect on the tango. The Dance from Havana had a dreamy, swaying rhythm which displaced that of the tángano. The habanera rhythm reflected the wild, syncopated, two-four rhythm of the Negro on the plantation and the musical tradition of the Creole. When the habanera rhythm arrived in the Silver Republic, it was wedded with the Tango Argentino, prefigurement of the classic ballroom tango. And therefore, the Tango Argentino is of immediate interest to us.

[The supervisor paused, had a thought, and decided to express it to the group that he was addressing. "Just as oxygen is vital to life, music is vital to dance. As dancing teachers the more knowledge you have about music, the more vitality you can put into teaching, especially Latin-American dances. So it would be beneficial to take a few minutes to inject the history of the tango with some musical vitamins.

"To opera buffs the habanera is a well-known musical form in Georges Bizet's opera, Carmen. She sways slowly to and fro singing *L'Amour est un Oiseau*—'Love is a Bird'—based on the rhythm of a habanera. Contrary to common conception, the French composer was not the creator of the habanera. He borrowed it from an aria *El Arreglito* written by the Spanish composer Sebastian Yradier.

"The habanera's musical form is a combination of Spanish melody and African rhythm, according to Friedenthal. As he put it in a book (published in 1913) Music, Dance, and Poetry of the Creoles of the Americas":

> Here (in Havana), then, two races confronted each other, both highly musical but reared in different musical worlds. No wonder that the Spaniards also benefited from and promptly took up these remarkable (African) rhythms into their own music. Of all these rhythms, however, the simplest which can be heard from all Negroes is this . . .

Walking over to a blackboard close at hand, the supervisor drew a rhythmic unit in duple time and explained it was a measure of music repetitively played in a pattern with a dotted eighth and sixteenth note followed by a pair of eighth notes. Next, as he pointed to the measure, the supervisor continued to quote Friedenthal:

> which . . . is the rhythm of the habanera. The melody of the habanera, which we would derive from Middle or Southern Spain, and the rhythm, which accompanies it and had its origin in Africa, therefore represent, in a way, the union of Spanish spirit with African technique.]

Because of the earthy element in the Tango Argentino's background, the dancing of it previous to 1910 was confined to the slums of Buenos Aires, two in particular: La Boca, the older part of the city's harbor, was a beehive of taverns and bordellos swarming with seamen, and the other part of the city steeped in squalor was the ill-reputed Barrio de las Ranas. Persons who frequented such slum sections often described the tango as baile con corté, 'dance with a stop.' A relation bien parado, 'well stopped'—prominent in Spanish folk dances—comes to mind here.

Among the frequenters of La Boca and Barrio de las Ranas were gauchos, who vied with seamen for the favors of *mestiza habituées*.

Stories, not too improbable, have circulated for years that coming to the city to escape the loneliness of the pampas or to dispose of a wagonload of hides, gauchos habitually went to the barrios to drink *mate*, if not something more potent, and to dance the <u>baile</u> <u>con</u> <u>corté</u> with the half-castes. While tangoing, the gaucho and mestiza both had a hand in shaping the choreography of the dance.

The lengthy, swashbuckling, swinging strides of the hard-riding gaucho from the vast grassy plains of Argentino and the sharp, silver spurs he wore on his boots contributed to the style of the dance. When dancing with the long-stepping pampean cowboy, in order to keep out of the way of his spurs a frisky female would twist and turn and kick up her legs trickingly, causing her full skirts to flare fanlike. Then tricks, today techniques, spectacular movements such as The Fan are exciting to watch in the performance of the ballroom and exhibition tango.

It appears that the rough cowboy from the pampa and the hot half-caste from the barrio in their lovemaking variegated tango body positions. As the two tangoed, she got into an enforced habit of straddling his right side where she would be arduously drawn and firmly held. Mounting on the man's thigh by the woman is a position colorfully applied by professionals in modern tango exhibitions.

Late in the 1800s inhabitants of a *barrio bajo* while drinking and dancing intermixed tango ingredients with the ingredients of another dance, the milonga, which was also popular in Buenos Aires' slums. As a result, the tango became mixed with milonga rhythm, presumably derived from melodies of folk songs sung by gauchos.

The swaying habanera rhythm of the tango was set aside by the rhythm of the milonga. It also was in duple time but the rhythmical signature had a more even beat and thus was much smoother than habanera rhythm. After the mixing of the two dances, they were named tango-milonga. Before long the second part of the hyphenated name was dropped. Thereafter the dance rightfully was called "tango."

Records of the early 1900s show that young sons of wealthy Argentineans often hung around Hansen's, a German beer garden of unsavory repute in the Palermo resort area of Buenos Aires. At Hansen's the youths would pass the time dancing with wanton women from whom they learned the art of tangoing, regarded as immoral by the city's eminent families.

When traveling abroad to Paris, Argentinean youths, despite parental objections, tried to introduce the tango to high society. The youths were snubbed. Parisian socialites turned up their noses at the licentious figures of the *Tango Argentino* ('Argentine Tango').

In 1907 an open-minded, up-and-coming French writer and composer, Camille de Rhynal, who had a passion for dancing, fell in love with the tango. He approached George Edwardes, the father of musical comedy, with the idea of featuring the tango on the London stage.

Gabrielle Ray, having swung onto the crest of stardom as a singer and dancer, was summoned to assist Camille de Rhynal demonstrate the tango to Edwardes. The theatrical producer liked the dance. But he did not believe it would be palatable to London audiences because the tango was too raw—in bad taste to say the least.

Seeing merit in Edwardes' objection, Camille de Rhynal set forth to dilute the highly spiced flavor of the Argentine Tango so that it would appeal to the taste of the public in general. Journeying to southeastern France, he found the right seasoning that was not too spicy to put in the tango.

In Nice he collected a small but choice group of influential epicures, including the Grand Duchess Anastasia of Russia. Bit by bit, at the Imperial Country Club, they strained out the unsavory sediments in the tango, and seasoned it mildly to please their cultivated palates. Now that the tango was tasteful, it was suitable for public consumption; although some figures were Frenchified.

Soon the tango appeared at a café La Feria on Rue Fontaine in Montmartre, a hilly section of Paris by the right bank of the Seine river. La Feria in short order was the chief haunt of tango dancers. Next the tango became quite an attraction at El Garron, a cabaret nearby where were discovered Almons and Odette. They were on their way to being acclaimed among the best of tango exhibition teams on the European continent.

In 1909 an illustrated newspaper Excelsior sponsored a dance contest which included the tango, giving it a big boost. The tango received high recognition in the 1911 World's Dancing Championships at the Théâtre Fémina on the famous boulevard Champs-Elysées when a well-known dance master Louis Bayo, tangoing with one of his students, Lemaire de Villars, won first prize.

It is also of significance that an American dancer, Maurice Mouvet, was a participant in the competition. He was privileged to have as a partner the renowned French actress and dancer Mademoiselle Mistinguett. They walked off with top honors in the waltz category.

Maurice (known professionally by his first name), while dining at the Café de Paris, observed a party of Argentineans dancing the tango. He was intrigued by the exotic dance. A few months later, after working up a routine with his partner, Maurice transported it to the United States where he first exhibited the tango in New York City at Louis Martin's restaurant.

More about the tango in the States will be discussed in due course. For now, one last comment concerning the Argentine dance in France. Gradually the round started rolling toward the Eiffel Tower in popularity. And it reached national heights by 1912, greatly attributable to the efforts of Bérnabe Simarra and Mademoiselle Gloria, an outstanding dance team who performed tango exhibitions at Magic City, the most popular of all the dance halls on the Parisian wharf, Quai d'Orsay.

Across the English Channel, back in 1911, a magazine The Dancing Times printed photographs of a French dancer, Monsieur Robert, showing his rendition of the tango. The article was delightfully descriptive, but it stirred little interest in the dance. At most, like a French novelty, it served as a conversation piece during the tea hour.

Englishmen who loved to gamble and dance often visited casinos in French towns such as Dinard and Deauville. At the casinos they heard tango music and saw tango dancers. Before long orchestras in London received repeated requests to play tangos, not just to listen to, but to dance to as well.

Consequently, tango teas became the vogue, though only within limited private circles. General public interest in the foreign dance was aroused among the people of England in 1912 when, at the Gaiety Theatre, George Grossmith (as Lord Bicester) and Phyllis Dare (as Delia Dale) performed the tango on stage in *The Sunshine Girl*.

By summer of 1913 the love-dance evidently had stolen too many Englishmen's hearts to suit the clergy; for on August 24 (at St. Paul's Cathedral in London) a sermon against the tango fulminated from Canon William Newbolt. "Such modern dances," the Anglican charged, "are evils which flourish unrebuked."

Not only in the British Isles but all over Europe both church and crown commenced condemning the tango that year. On November 17 the following decree was sent by Kaiser Wilhelm II to heads of the German military forces: "Officers of the army and navy are hereby ordered not to perform the tango in uniform, and to avoid families where it is danced." Also, he warned members of the ballet of the Royal Opera House not to participate in charity affairs if tango competitions were to be conducted there.

On November 20, in Rome, Pope Pius X issued a statement that the tango must be considered an immoral dance. Therefore, it was prohibited to Catholics throughout the world.

On December 15, it was announced that King Louis III of Bavaria had circulated among the commanding officers of the Bavarian army a secret Cabinet order informing them he would look with disfavor upon any officer who, during the coming Christmas festivities, attended parties at which the tango was danced.

On December 30, King Victor Emmanuel formally barred the tango from a forthcoming state ball in Italy. Following His Majesty's example, the British, Austrian, German, and Spanish ambassadors decided to exclude the Argentine dance from their entertainments.

Since the rudiments of the tango originated in the folk dances of Spain, a historic question arises. Was the Spanish ambassador being diplomatic or hypocritical?

Earlier it was mentioned that the American dancer Maurice Mouvet, upon returning to the States from overseas, conveyed an elaborated tango routine. In 1912, teamed with his wife, Florence Walton (her stage name), Maurice put on striking exhibitions which created sparks of excitement over the tango on the East Coast.

Politic authorities, true to type, tried to stamp out this rising fervor. Mayor John F. Fitzgerald, for instance, on October 11, 1913, promulgated an order requiring every public dance hall in Boston to have a matron and a policeman stand guard to prevent dancers from attempting to tango.

Bans against the tango notwithstanding, its popularity spread across our country like fire over a prairie, though it was not until 1914, when the Castles became leading figures in the tango movement, that the dance achieved nationwide acclaim.

The Castles, along with others, tilled the fertile soil beneath the red-white-and-blue flagstone, reaping a golden harvest of tango enthusiasts. Still, in spite of the prestige they enjoyed, Vernon and Irene had to toil under heated denunciation to gather tangos for the marketplace.

Here, as abroad, religious and regional regimentators continued to deal the tango debilitating blows. A typical view of the opposition was that of Clergyman William A. Brothers, from Montclair, New Jersey, who averred that indulgence in the tango is as much a violation of the Seventh Commandment as is adultery (Exodus 20:14).

The dance was blameless. The fact is tango tea time turned into a cocktail hour in which married women met garden-variety lounge lizards, lovers who tangoed as slithery on soft smooth sheets as they did on solid slick surfaces.

In spite of the critical wounds inflicted upon the dance, it refused to succumb. The great popularity of the tango gave it strength to survive. The extent of its high regard was demonstrated by the incredible manner the dance affected the American public. Time not permitting presentation of the whole picture, just select pertinent parts will be presented:

Silk dresses being a *sine qua non* at tango teas, many millions more yards of that fabric were imported into the United States than ever before. Tango red was the latest color of the day. Moreover, fashions in dress along with headdress underwent changes.

Costumes of professional tangoists such as Irene Castle—wearing chic toques, short coiffures, and pleated or slashed skirts—were copied painstakingly. Men's styles changed, too. The conventional, stiff shirt (treated with starch) which did not allow enough freedom of mobility, was replaced by the soft-bosom or tango shirt.

Flexible performance of intricate, beautiful figures of the tango made a trim shape desirable. To appear aesthetic and agile on the dance floor, the slimming down of one's figure became a fad. Thus the diet-conscious American stepped into the national scene.

Now for the dance itself. In 1914 not only were tango dancers on the increase but so were tango steps. Multiplying with the rapidity of rabbits, the steps were as long as rabbits' ears or as short as rabbits' tails. Of these countless steps ninety-nine and nine-tenths were inauthentic and unstandardized.

Since no authoritative manual on the subject of the Argentine Tango had ever been written, American and European teachers—competent or not—taught the dance whichever way suited their fancy. We can imagine the outcome: few students really learned to tango.

[Concerned, some member of the group in attendance would fall on one of the facts, the supervisor proceeded to prop it up. "You may have heard that an authoritative manual on the tango appeared in the nineteenth century. The title is The Fashionable Dancer's Casket; it was put to press by Charles Durang in 1856.

"The manual, a Philadelphia publication, contains a line referring to an arrangement by master dancer Monsieur Markowski which reads—sic—'originally (the tango) was a South American dance in two-fourth time, arranged for the ball-room.' Whether in a modified form or otherwise, the idea that this laconic statement is a description of the tango is far-fetched beyond words."]

Accustomed to American ragtime or Viennese waltz time and lacking an understanding of tiempo di habañera, many people raced through tango steps. In fairness, dancers were not always at fault. Musicians unfamiliar with Latin-American music tended to hurry the beat. To be in step with the rhythm the tango was performed slowly to a dreamy cadence twenty-eight measures (fifty-six beats) a minute.

At the outset tango music was written authentically in two-four time as was typical of such musical works as *Ché, Mi Amigo* ('Ché, My Friend') composed by Valverde-Herpin in 1911; *La Conchita* ('The Dream Tango') composed by Uriel Davis in 1912; *El Clavel* ('The Carnation') composed by Pedro de Zulueta in 1913; *Marigny* ('Inner Circle Tango') composed by M. Sarablo in 1914.

["At this juncture I shall jump ahead in the history a short distance," the supervisor told the teachers. "You should not be surprised that our lively fox-trot tempo overtook the leisurely tempo of the tango at a point where it was speeded up to thirty-four measures (sixty-eight beats) a minute, an ideal speed for tangoing in the ballroom, which is a reason more and more tangos would be written in four-four time for bands or orchestras to play at dances.

"A good example can be seen in a 1924 instrumental arrangement of the tango 'Isle of Capri' composed in tiempo di tango by Will Grosz. His composition, featured by the nationally known orchestra leader Xavier Cugat, is in four-four time, the common signature of fox-trot music."]

In the early 1900s the tango frequently was connected with amusement to a newfangled funny fad, twin beds. Playwrights Salisbury Field and Margaret Mayo successfully exploited the silly public mood about the tango in a farce 'Twin Beds.' The plot was spun around the bedroom and a dance-crazy young wife.

As of the days of that stage play—and far beyond—social dancers irrationally introduced dramatic exaggerations into the tango: inordinate posturing (often laughable), deep dizzy dipping, jerking of the neck-and-head, and tawdry torso twisting unfortunately became in the public's mind synonymous with tangoing. Just the same, it cannot be emphasized enough that true and tried tangoists executed the dance with dignity and grace—not with crude, exaggerated bodily movements.

A case in point: Lew Quinn and Joan Sawyer, among America's foremost terpsichorean artists of the period, danced a dignified tango which was lauded by the elite of New York society. The extent of the pair's prominence was such that the composer J. Tim Brymn in 1913 wrote the tango number *La Rumba* especially for Quinn and Sawyer. (The music is not to be confused with the Cuban dance, rumba.)

Nevertheless, excesses in the performance of the tango were denounced with ever-growing indignation. Battered by waves of protest, interest in the dance was now at a low ebb. Ticket sales at theaters featuring tango dancers, and students at dance studios fell off at an alarming rate. To stem the loss of currency, the Academy of Dancing Masters of Europe and America called for a special session of an international congress of teachers to be held in the fall of 1914 at Paris, France.

Despite the outbreak of World War I in Europe July 28, the congress met that fall and drafted strict rules for the proper execution of the tango, which were codified. In an attempt to standardize the tango, representatives of France and England compiled a list of the simplest authentic steps (or the most sanitized figures); some were originally from Argentina and Spain; a few had been devised in France.

["Also the representatives clarified the tango's nomenclature. This was a big step forward because in the past misuse or misunderstanding of the French and Spanish names had caused much confusion."]

The supervisor picked up a large poster-like cardboard leaning against one side of his desk. Finding a box of thumbtacks in a drawer, he affixed the cardboard high on a wall to ensure it was visible to the members of the group.

"Listed on this cardboard chart are nine steps selected by the congress to be officially standard in the tango. You should familiarize yourselves with the Spanish and French names as well as the English. Later on in the day, you may make a copy of the list at your convenience. For now, I shall read the Spanish and French names aloud so that you will have an idea how they are pronounced:

Spanish	French	English
El Paseo	La Promenade	The walk
El Corté	Le Coupé	The Dip
El Medio Corté	Le Demi-Coupé	The Half-Dip
La Media Luna	La Demi-Lune	The Half-Moon
La Rueda	La Roue	The Wheel
El Ocho	Le Huit	The Eight
Las Tijeras	Les Ciseaux	The Scissors
El Paseo Oriental	Les Pas Oriental	The Eastern Step
El Paseo con Golpé	La Promenade avec Piétinement	The Walk with a Stamp

"Most characteristic of the pre-World War I tango was el corté ('the dip'). Directions for the man's footwork were precisely as indicated below on the chart:

> Count one-and: On count one- step forward with the right foot. Hold that foot position on the and count;
>
> Count two-and: On count two- step side-oblique with the left foot. Hold that foot position on the and count;
>
> Count three-and: On count three- draw the right foot next to the left. Hold that foot position on the and count;
>
> Count four-and: On count four- step back with the left foot; dip by bending the left knee. Raise toes of the right foot on the and count, but leave the edge of the heel in contact with the floor.
>
> Mark well: count four-and is one simultaneous action. The right leg, on the and count, is kept straight.

"Perhaps you find it unusual that the man started el corté with his right foot instead of his left. In former days it was the proper thing to do. Nowadays, as you know, the man starts with his left foot, and properly the woman starts with her right foot.

"La promenade, les pas oriental, and la promenade avec piétinement were traveling steps. Progression while tangoing was a French innovation. Originally, since the figures of the Tango Argentino were performed more or less in place, dancers traveled very little around a dance area.

"It is worth digressing briefly to observe that traveling steps are a means of putting style into the tango. As dancers advance by slows and quicks, they prolong each slow step as long as possible before taking the next step. They take the quick steps, though, without delay.

"By stepping timely with the beat on the quicks, and—in contrast—by dragging the slows, dancers create the illusion of being a fraction behind the musical beat on every slow step. In so doing they impart an air of mystery and stealth to the tango.

"Although stealth (a prowling panther-like walk) was a movement in the tango attributed to Parisians, it is often mistakenly assumed to have originated in the *baile con corté* of the Barrio de las Ranas in Buenos Aires. Heavy tracks show the stealthy walk was acquired from Danse d'Apache requiring the agility of a panther. Early in the 1900s Danse d'Apache would be presented nightly at the cabaret Moulin Rouge by an acrobatic dancer Max Dearly who had teamed up with Mille Mistinguett.

"The origin of Danse d'Apache sounds like a Hollywood scenario. One night in Paris two pimps engaged in a heated brawl over a prostitute. Feelings about the affray became so violent that members of a gang to which the brawling pimps belonged split into warring factions in sympathy with one side or the other.

"A journalist, sensationalizing the incident in his column, branded the gangs 'apaches.' He saw a resemblance between their battling and those of the warlike American Apache Indians. The gang members retained the name apache with great pride, yet dishonored it by committing criminal acts.

"The apaches' rough, secretive way of life was reflected in their dancing. When doing the Danse d'Apache, they tossed their prostitutes around roughly like soiled rag dolls, glanced about slyly as if looking for easy prey, and moved cautiously to evade predatory *gendarmes*."]

All the steps listed in 1914 by the Academy of Dancing Masters of Europe and America are still practiced. Of course, various new figures have appeared. Today, however, one of the listed steps, *el paseo con golpé*, 'the walk with a stamp,' is used in the main by stage and folk dancers. Despite its seemingly limited use, to underestimate the historical value of the stamp step would be a mistake. *El paseo con golpé's* origin is believed to be in the barrios of Buenos Aires, where gauchos began their tango steps with an *arrancada* which literally means 'a starting with force.' In tangoing it is a sharp stamp of the heel.

Even though they utilized the technique, gauchos did not invent the *arrancada*. Long before the pampean cowboys existed, rhythmical clicks of the heels was a dance art among Arabs. The stamping of a dancer's heels being Arabic in character, the real source of the *arrancada*, then, is ancient Arabia, via Andalusia.

No matter how we twist and turn, at every bend of the road we run across signs that point to Spain as the homeland of the tango's fundamental choreography. We see another sign in the Innovation. Quite the rage in 1914, it was a type of tango danced without bodily contact.

The Castles, masters of the Innovation, frequently used it in their performances. Defining this form of tangoing, Vernon said, "The much-talked-of Innovation is nothing more or less than the tango danced without touching your partner."

Actually the name Innovation was a misnomer. There was not anything new about the dance. The Innovation's steps by definition were simply those of the tango. Moreover, the positional stance of a man and woman being separated yet performing together was not new.

As far back as two thousand years on Spanish soil, in the performance of the fandango, couples danced at arm's length, which is confirmed by an authoritative author Curt Sachs in his World History of the Dance. Without wasting words he states, "The fandango is danced by only two persons, who never touch each other even with the hand."

In spite of the fact that Vernon and Irene Castle exercised strong influence on the tango, the world looked to Paris to set the styles in tangoing, just as she did in women's clothing.

When France became embroiled in hostilities with Germany in 1914, the decorated French soldier in blue military coat, red trousers, and polished knee boots was suddenly the idol of the year—not the social dancer in abbreviated black jacket, expansive shirt bosom, and white-topped patent leathers.

Patriotism having taken precedence over pleasure, Parisians' desire to tango withered. And as parched men lay dying in trenches on the western front, world interest in the dance shriveled up, too.

After the war, the death toll for peace paid, attention in Paris was showered once more on the pleasurable dance. Inventiveness of tango technicians budded anew, reaching full bloom in the development of the French Tango. It was a less intense dance and more appropriate for ballroom dancing than the Argentine Tango. Regardless of nationality the tango failed to recapture its former universal appeal.

In 1921 fleshly passions boiled over with zeal for the dance in the United States when Rudolph Valentino, romantic Apollo of the silent silver screen, danced a torrid, thespian, tango sequence with Helena

Domingues in The Four Horsemen of the Apocalypse. But the heated zeal apparently was for the actor, not the dance, because the tango's popularity, like Valentino's life, was of brief duration.

However subdued and scorched the tango may have become in the twenties, it still had recognizable inherent features: rise and fall, sway, and contrary body motion (or torso torsion). They were predominantly Negroid in character.

On the Dark Continent the African natives displayed practically an exclusive preference for music with a double beat that they retained centuries after arriving in Cuba. The Negroes preferred duple meter since in their singing and dancing they customarily swayed their bodies laterally, a motion that could not very easily be fitted to a triple beat. The lateral swaying of the body has been carried over into the Argentine and French tangos as well as into the English Tango which I shall touch upon now.

The English Tango is a dance of the utmost precision, and small wonder, for in Great Britain, a figure (combined steps and movements) before receiving a stamp of approval by the Imperial Society of Teachers of Dancing must meet rigid requirements which include a detailed description of the configuration. A figure—or a step, in the vernacular of dancers—having thus been standardized, the Society members strive to attain nothing short of perfection in performing it. Tangoists in Britain will go to extremes to master beyond a fault not only the prescribed pattern of a figure but also pertinent body-motion techniques.

The belief that perfection is an exclusive quality of the gods brings to mind a quotation from Frank Veloz, one of the greats in the history of the tango, who compliments yet in the same breath criticizes the dancing of the British:

> The tango, danced by an expert couple of British dancers, is perfect—almost too perfect—for they are so concerned with the rises and falls, the sways, and the counter body motion that they don't seem to be enjoying the dance.

Still, Veloz's statement should not be misinterpreted. He believed in the utilization of body-motion techniques. Just the same he felt that if, when tangoing, a dancer experienced a lack of enjoyment, something was lost in the performance of the dance.

During the early thirties Veloz and his wife Yolanda tossed a life buoy to the tango, which—since the death of Valentino—had been drowning in an ocean of disinterest. Americans had failed to recognize that ballroom tangoing was a true art. The people's eyes were opened by Frank and Yolanda Veloz's artistic exhibitions. Their style of tango could be compared to the classic dances of Greece and Rome.

Rome was not built in a day, neither was the artistry of the Velozes. They took extraordinary pains to perfect their exhibitions. Booked into the Sevilla Biltmore of Havana, the two later traveled far inland to study the way native Cubans danced. Also the atmosphere surrounding the performances of Veloz and Yolanda had to appear authentic.

At the Embassy Club in Miami, following their Havana engagement, they initiated the concept of putting on exhibitions under simulated tropical moonlight reminiscent of that in the darkened jungles of South America. The lighting effect accentuated the tango's glamour while creating an air of mystification peculiar to primitive ritual dances. Complementing the exotic aura in step and stance, the tango team in formal attire was the epitome of sophistication. Their portrayal of each movement profoundly conveyed the deep, ardent feeling that typifies the tango.

Professionals, intrigued by the highly sophisticated style of the Velozes, looked in a brighter light at the possibilities the dance provided. Nonprofessionals, spellbound by Veloz and Yolanda's fascinating exhibitions, were reawakened to the charm that the tango possesses, for all ages.

Nevertheless, despite the resurrection of the dance, the return to practice of tangoing by Americans was minimal across the nation. The glamorous tango was, after all, just too emotionally demonstrative for an inhibited American public. Most people enjoyed watching exhibitors indulge in some feverish tango, but to partake of it themselves was considered as chilling as a cup of cold coffee.

Ironically, what more than anything else prevented an upsurge in the popularity of tangoing was the mutation by Argentineans of the normal or traditional tango. Altered in 1933 by artificial implants, the performance of the dance necessitated leg actions that were unnatural and jerky.

Hitherto the tango had been performed with smoothness. Musically the term for it is *legato*, that is, connected—in a smooth style. The opposite term is *staccato*, that is, disconnected—in a non-legato style.

Inasmuch as the dance was performed unnaturally in a smoothless manner, it was called the Staccato Tango. The manner of performing it had been copied from a Spanish stage dance, Paso Doble, depicting a quick-stepping matador engaged in a fight with *el toro* ('the bull').

The Staccato Tango, upon growing popular in Germany, became still more non-legato when the smart stepping of German dancing masters treaded a measure. The German's precise legwork in the execution of the Staccato Tango appealed to English tangoists, which is understandable, were they not accustomed to perfection in the dance.

By now staccato movements were no longer restricted to the legs. Staccato movements also could be observed in such theatrical actions as an abrupt toss of head and shoulders with each change of direction or position held by tangoists on a dance floor.

Consequently, global controversy was stirred up over the Staccato Tango, the theatrics of which were amusing to some people and embarrassing to others. One might say, there existed two camps: those who favored the smooth tango, and those who favored the Staccato Tango. The former camp prevailed. Their triumph, however, was a Pyrrhic victory. The tango's image was distorted so severely that it never regained the popularity it once had in America and Europe.

BOOK SIX

Chapter 36

With the conclusion of Ralph Normand's talk on the history of the tango his audience departed, except the Craigs and Armstrong. They had remained behind to thresh over something that was concerning Alice. The supervisor, who was standing nearby, could not avoid overhearing bits of their conversation. His curiosity aroused, he cut in and asked whether the three teachers had a problem he might help solve.

Appointing herself spokesperson, Alice addressed him: "Mr. Normand, they think I am worrying needlessly about Joanne Armond. No one at the Studio has seen her since Monday. Something is wrong."

"Why don't you check downstairs at the receptionist's desk in the lobby," Ralph suggested. "Joanne has probably phoned the Studio and explained her absence."

"I did inquire this morning. She hasn't called in. The receptionist tried to reach her at home by telephone, but nobody answered." Alice looked hopefully to Mr. Normand for an explanation.

"That is strange. I am at a loss what to tell you, Mrs. Craig. One thing I'm sure of is that Joanne had her heart set on hearing today's lecture. Last week she stopped me in the hall to find out the date and time I planned discussing the tango."

In that there was a matter Normand wanted to go into with Bert, the supervisor dropped the subject of Joanne Armond. "Say, Mr. Craig—before it slips my mind—what the dickens happened between you and Mrs. Keller during her dancing lesson yesterday afternoon? Your student complained to me that you were too inquisitive about her personal affairs."

Threatened by the accusation, Craig became defensive. "I was just trying to use applied psychology. My experiment backfired. That's all! Mrs. Keller's course is due to expire soon. I thought I would take another whirl at persuading her to renew it.

"My previous efforts to do so have been unsuccessful. She keeps dismissing my sales spiels with the old stall that she can't afford more lessons. Then she shuts up as if she had lockjaw.

"I heard somewhere about a psychological trick that supposedly works like magic in keeping a conversation going. The idea is to repeat the word spoken by a man or woman whenever she hesitates after completing a statement. Urged on by her own words, more often than not she will offer a response, which can be favorable.

"While I was giving Mrs. Keller her lesson, she let slip a statement that I latched onto as a crowbar to pry from her an admission she has the ready cash to lay out on dancing lessons. You are aware, no doubt, she sells real estate. She's with some outfit on Geary Boulevard. I can't recall which one."

"It is Green and Kaufmann Realtors. Mrs. Kaufmann and Green, a colonel, are partners." Ralph Normand was well-informed about particulars regarding students of the teachers under his supervision.

"Uh-huh, that's the company. Well, anyhow, Mrs. Keller was beaming all over the place. I remarked that she seemed in an unusually jovial mood.

"'Indeed I am!' the woman confirmed my observation. With a smug look of satisfaction she said, 'This morning I closed a neat package deal.'

"That she received a good chunk of dough dawned upon me at once. So, in order to make the most of the situation, I put psychology into play. Deal? I repeated her last word questioningly to draw out a reply.

"Mrs. Keller replied without hesitation: 'a real-estate transaction.'

"Transaction?" I was quick with my cue.

"'You bet your boots,' she affirmed, and added, 'It included a trade.'

"Trade? I was really lost in the woods.

"Now she decided to go into details, many of which were over my head. Real estate is a field completely foreign to me. Still, part of it was clear enough: two pieces of property were involved, and she received a double commission.

"Here was exactly the point I had been moving toward. With the expectation of hearing Mrs. Keller own up to the fact that she had some money to spend on dancing lessons, I eagerly echoed the woman's words, a double commission?

"Instead of replying, she glared at me. I had the feeling she was thinking the size of her commissions was none of my business. Since she volunteered no further replies, I had no choice but to cease playing psychologist. It never occurred to me that she had caught on to my little game, or that I'd ruffled her feathers—at least not to the extent that she would lodge a complaint against me."

Craig's motive won the wholehearted approval of the supervisor. "Luckily Mrs. Keller was in the dark as to the actual object of your game. I believe her complaint was intended to cover up her wounded pride at allowing herself to be squeezed into a tight corner.

"In the future, consult me when you want to try a new sales approach. Real-estate and car salespeople are so conscious of selling gimmicks that they are ticklish to deal with. At your next appointment with Mrs. Keller, act as though nothing out of the ordinary has occurred. Simply see to it that her lesson is enjoyable.

"You might show her an advanced step or two. Also, compliment her once in a while. The woman is rather vain about her appearance. She wears expensive, showy dresses. Tell her how lovely she looks. Perhaps she will convince herself that she should buy an additional dance course.

"Keep me posted on her reactions—and on her progress, fast or slow. Either way, it is sometimes a persuasive point in selling a student dancing lessons. If Mrs. Keller's reactions prove unsatisfactory, we'll use a different strategy."

At that moment Alice Craig, who had gone to the receptionist's desk to inquire again about Joanne Armond, returned with a sudden burst into the room. Breaking in on the conversation between her husband and the supervisor, she spoke in an emotional state:

"I just talked to Bob Armond on the telephone. He told me that he had been to the Golden Gate Park Police Station to report Joanne missing. He is worried sick. They had a tiff last Monday night, and she ran off. Joanne never came back to their apartment. Poor kid! I wonder if she's all right."

Vincent Armstrong, having been seated all the while, stood up and patted Alice on the shoulder to calm her down. "My dear," he said in a paternal tone, "nothing is to be gained by getting upset. It is no secret Bob and Joanne are always quarreling. She's stormed out of their apartment before over an exchange of hurtful words.

"Very likely, to throw a fright into her spineless husband, she spent the night with a girl friend. When Joanne is satisfied the jellyfish has lost his sting, she will put in an appearance. You mark my words."

Bert agreed with Vincent. Still Alice had her fears. But she conceded she could be needlessly concerned. That was the way matters remained as the three teachers left Normand's room and headed in the direction of the ballroom downstairs, where their respective students waited for their hourly dancing lessons to begin.

The student Vincent was to teach that hour was Mrs. Bonnie Braunbinn, a homely middle-aged widow. He wondered what any man could have seen in this female to marry her.

In physical structure Mrs. Braunbinn bore resemblance to the hoop ash: Her curveless body was as narrow as the trunk of the tree, her limbs as long and straight. Like the top of the hoop ash, Bonnie's head was large and ovid. Her lank hair, combed back tightly on her scaly scalp, was the color of blackberries.

Thin-lined eyebrows were curved in natural arches high above her orbs—two big, dark knotholes. She had a twig of a nose hanging over a tiny mouth with sliver-thin lips. Comparing Bonnie to a hoop ash was not in a grove of Vincent's vision. Within the scope of his sight he could compare her only to Olive Oyle—Popeye's lady love in Sims' and Zaboly's comic strip.

Teaching Bonnie Braunbinn ballroom dancing was a terrible, tedious task. She was exceptionally gawky. Her arms crooked at extreme angles, and—should Vincent discontinue his prompting—her legs branched out in diverse directions. Ungraceful, she encountered difficulty in performing the simplest steps. Bonnie's big problem was her inability consistently to remember plain dance patterns from lesson to lesson.

After weeks of effort, although Bonnie tried his patience all that time, Vincent finally had her doing limited school figures. This was well and good when she ran through the basic steps by herself. However, when they danced together, every so often she would balk in the middle of the dance floor and grumble "I'm mixed up." Next followed the usual demand, "Show me that step once more."

That Vincent was up in the air with her is an understatement. To add to his irritation, whenever Bonnie (who wore false teeth) opened her mouth to speak, he would almost be asphyxiated by disagreeable denture odors. Attack gas sprayed from an airplane could not have been much more asphyxiating.

In seeking an avenue of escape, he would turn his head aside. Since his speed was hampered by the necessity to move slyly, not always did his olfactory organ reach a safe distance in time. At the start of each lesson he prayed she would be quiet. Be he sinner or not, his prayers remained unanswered. She never failed to find something to talk about (with full parted lips).

Week by week Vincent's resentment toward Bonnie grew increasingly greater till he developed an utter dislike for the woman. Oh, yes, he complied with the socially imposed fiat that one hides his antipathies behind sweet smiles and sugary words. Nonetheless, a trace of true flavor of the teacher's feelings sometimes revealed itself to his student. On occasion, by the way he looked or sounded, she could tell he was not particularly pleased with her.

Fortunately for Vincent, if not for Bonnie, she did not comprehend the nature of his displeasure. She had no idea that when he avoided pushing her to extend her dance course, Vincent wanted it to expire so he could be rid of her. In Bonnie's eyes he was different from the rest of the teachers, who were continually after their students to buy more and more lessons.

"Dear, wonderful Mr. Armstrong" was only interested in her welfare, was beyond attempting to loosen a lonely widow's purse strings. One might say, in a loose sense, that she was right. Teaching her was objectionable to Vincent to such an extent he would rationalize, "I guess money isn't important enough in every case to contend with a toothless cunt like Bonnie Braunbinn."

This day, as in past days, Vincent tried to refrain from making a display of his repugnance toward being entangled in the long, bony limbs of the widow Braunbinn for a seemingly endless sixty minutes on a hardwood dance floor. Nevertheless, his student became cognizant of the fact that all was not as it should be, since he was even more tense than usual.

His tension was too great a strain on her nerves. "Mr. Armstrong," Bonnie interrupted their dancing to ask bluntly, "Are you mad at me?"

"No, not at all. Where in the world did you get that notion?" As Vincent was not entirely oblivious of what had prompted his student to pose the question, he struggled to strike a ring of sincerity in his reply.

"All along during my dancing lessons, I have had a feeling you were cross with me. Many a night I cried myself to sleep because I thought I said or did something to offend you. Mr. Armstrong, I would rather die than hurt you in any way whatsoever. I admire you from the very bottom of my heart. Not only are you the best teacher in the Studio, but you are also the grandest person."

Overpowered by emotion, Bonnie was a pathetic sight to behold. Moisture formed around the woman's big dark eyes, and her twiglike nose began to run. Bringing forth a brightly printed handkerchief that had been tucked away under a sleeve of her dress, she apologized in a high-pitched voice, "Excuse me. I'm so upset!"

Vincent, stricken by his conscience, offered an explanation he hoped would soothe as well as make amends to the overly sensitive woman. "Why, Mrs. Braunbinn, I'll admit at times I may have seemed stern when you've had trouble learning to dance. But I was peeved at myself—never at you—for not putting the lesson across in a clear manner. Really, if a student fails to master a step, it is the teacher's fault."

Having blown her runny nose, Bonnie dabbed at her nostrils with the soggy handkerchief. She cheered up with a sigh. "O my, I feel much better now. You are such a dear, Mr. Armstrong. It was foolish of me to think you were mad at me. I should have realized how much someone as conscientious as you takes your work to heart.

"You mustn't be so serious. Life is too short. Don't be hard on yourself if your students are slow in catching on to dance steps. I for one have had a miserable time with my coordination since I was in pigtails. I always have been slower and clumsier than a turtle."

Bonnie simpered faintly at her next thought. "Here am I preaching to you about being serious, yet I'm guilty of the same sin myself. I'm as solemn as a Sunday sermon. We are so alike in that respect. I am certainly lucky to have you for my teacher. Sincere and understanding people are rare birds these days."

Vincent Armstrong was greatly relieved when the lesson ended—however, not because of former reasons. Now he was too ashamed to look Bonnie Braunbinn in the eyes. He felt remorseful that he had held an unkind attitude toward the woman. Still worse, the man was crestfallen over stooping to the low level of acting the hypocrite.

Chapter 37

Friday evening, a little after six o'clock, Armstrong and the Craigs were seated in a downtown restaurant within the vicinity of National Dance Studios. No sooner had salads been served when Chandler Corey entered the restaurant. Catching sight of the three teachers, he approached their table with giant strides.

As the members of the trio glanced up to greet the dance director, he exclaimed, "Look at this!" In his hands was a newspaper, on the front page of which was a picture of Joanne Armond.

"Good god!" gasped Alice. Apprehensively she grabbed the newspaper from Chandler and read the headlines aloud:

WIFE FALSELY REPORTED MISSING
SLAIN BY U.S.F. STUDENT

———

Trussed Body
Unearthed On
Twin Peaks

———

Full Confession Obtained
After Police Investigate

"It's terrible! Just terrible." Alice shook her head in sorrow and shed tears.

Anxious to learn the grim facts that caused Alice's tears, Bert urged, "Well, honey, go on. What the heck happened?" Alice wiped away a teardrop and with a tremor in her voice resumed reading:

"'At the break of dawn today a young husband, Bob Armond—who'd taken the life of his beautiful 17-year-old wife Joanne in a fit of anger—led police to a secluded spot atop Twin Peaks, where he had buried her remains.

"'Elements in the circumstances leading to the murder bore a relation to the misty legend which—like fog—has enveloped the mount since before Gasper de Portola's expedition reached San Francisco Bay in 1769.

"'Costanoan Indians of the area held the belief that long ago the mountain peaks were a single entity—brave and squaw. However, the pair did not live in harmony, but wrangled moon after moon.

"'In time the Great Spirit, provoked by their conduct, decided to put an end to the incessant bickering once and for all. With a loud clap of thunder he sent down a bolt of lightning to split the mountain in two. And to this day the divided peaks remain as a warning of the punishment which may be meted out to quarrelsome couples..

(Crude Grave Located)

"'For hours subsequent to his confession of the murder Armond stuck stubbornly to the story that he could remember neither how he had killed Mrs. Armond nor where he had hidden her body. Finally he broke down and admitted he vaguely remembered driving around until, in a daze, he stopped somewhere on a hill.

"'With the purpose of refreshing the youth's memory, homicide inspectors then took Armond on a cruise of the city. When they were well into the Western Addition, he muttered, I remember now.

"'At his direction the police car was driven to Haight and Clayton Streets, turned up Clayton to Twin Peaks Boulevard, and ascended the winding road to a southwesterly shoulder of the 910 foot elevation. Approximately 50 yards from one turn in the road Armond directed the driver to a recently spaded patch of the rocky ground.

"'It isn't very deep,' he commented, his voice as expressionless as his face.

"'In short order the loose, damp dirt and broken pieces of rock were shoveled away from the shallow, make-shift grave.

(Corpse Identified)

"'A young woman, her auburn hair crusted with blood, lay on her side. Her arms and legs had been bound so tightly by a clothesline that it had cut deeply into the flesh.

"'She wore a knitted navy blue dress with pumps to match.

Beneath her body were found a beige flannel coat and a flowered silk scarf.

"'The articles of clothing in which the corpse was clad corresponded to those listed by Joanne Armond's husband in his Missing Persons Report at Golden Gate Park Police Station, Tuesday of this week.

"'Standing at a distance, the handcuffed youth was elbowed over to the grave by one of the inspectors, who ordered authoritatively, Look at her. Is she your wife?'"

All of a sudden Alice came to a stop. Impatient to hear the rest of the tragic incident, Bert demanded, "Go on. Why don't you go on?"

"Hold your horses!" Alice's reply sounded sharp as the crack of a whip. "The article is continued on page seven, column four." She turned to the sheet indicated and, upon locating the proper place, commenced reading again:

"'Armond stared into space, sullenly silent. I asked you a question! the policeman barked at him.

"'Meekly the youth answered, Yes, sir, she's my wife. Then he dropped to his knees, covered his eyes with the palms of his hands, and started to snivel disgustfully.

(Alibi Cracked Open)

"'Police suspicion of Armond was aroused after a routine door-to-door check within the apartment house at 2950 Turk Street, where the couple had resided. A tenant mentioned that she'd seen Armond backing his coupé out of the garage around 11:45 P.M. Monday. Quizzed by inspectors, he had denied leaving the building at any time during that night.

"'Next a search of the Armond apartment revealed a suspiciously spotted pillowcase at the bottom of a pile of clean ones neatly stacked in the linen closet. The ticking of a pillow on the bed had what appeared to be bloodstains. In the laundry hamper was a pair of Levi's, the cuffs of which contained an excessive amount of soil.

"'Confronted with overwhelming evidence during an interrogation at police headquarters, Armond had no alternative but to confess to the crime.

(Fatal Fight)

"'It seems Bob Armond had had a bourbon and Seven-Up at a neighborhood bar, to relax, following a mid-term examination. He is a student at the University of San Francisco.

"'Going home, he had several more drinks before he was visited briefly by his father, who joined his son in a highball. After Armond Senior left, the youth drank steadily until Mrs. Armond, a dancing teacher, returned from work.

"'She chided her husband for being intoxicated, and a bitter argument developed. Becoming enraged when she called him a lush, he grabbed hold of an iron on a kitchen shelf and struck her twice across the back of the head. Fatally injured, she fell to the floor.

"'Armond carried his wife into the bedroom to revive her, but his efforts proved useless. In a panic he trussed the lifeless woman, loaded her into the trunk of his car, and disposed of her body on Twin Peaks.

"'Beyond admitting he'd been in a drunken rage, Armond was evasive as to his motive for killing the woman.

"'The Captain of inspectors declared that a murder charge would be filed against Bob Armond without delay, and the coroner of the City and County of San Francisco took charge of Joanne Armond's remains.'"

Alice pushed the newspaper aside. "Poor Joanne! She was so young, so beautiful. I can't believe she's dead, a lifeless corpse. The girl was chock-full of life. Her every step bubbled with vitality. Joanne often used to say: 'Alice, I need to be active. My happiest moments are spent working in the dance studio.' That's the reason I knew it was unlike her to fail to show up Wednesday. Joanne might have missed one day at the Studio, but two days—no."

Vincent, whose conjecture pertaining to Joanne Armond's absence turned out to be incorrect, studied the headlines of the newspaper sheepishly. Striving to account for his error, he explained: "Who would have thought anything as horrible as Joanne meeting a violent death at Bob's hands was even a remote possibility. We never associate such drastic deeds with acquaintances, let alone close friends."

"I have to admit," Alice opened her mind, "apart from my womanly intuition telling me that all was not right, deep down I didn't dream that anything fatal had befallen Joanne."

"Why would Bob kill her?" questioned Bert. Before the others had an opportunity to formulate a theory on the matter, he expressed his own. "Judging from the way they were getting along, I'd surmise she was threatening to divorce him."

Bert's conjecture evoked an offhanded remark from Chandler

Corey. "Armond must have loved his wife very much to resort to such a drastic course of action to prevent her from getting a divorce."

Unwittingly the dance director had irritated a sore spot on Armstrong's psyche. "How can you say that! If a woman really is dear to a man, he couldn't bear to hurt her, and vice versa. The husband who refuses to grant his wife a divorce or the lover who beats his flame because she wants to leave him is full of prunes when he maintains he loves her.

"He is not only a liar but an egotist as well. The egotistical hog wallows in muddy self-love and is incapable of loving anybody else. And his meanness knows no bounds. Filled with hate, he is desensitized to a woman's feelings; the hog will not accept the fact that he is being rejected.

"To heal his sick pride he seeks bloody revenge. Whether or not it is justified is of no importance to him. He will stop at nothing to destroy a woman, body and spirit, solely to satisfy his selfish, stupid ego."

"It is terrifying. You would imagine he'd fear the consequences," commented Alice.

"Yes, you would." Vincent Armstrong saw her point. "Still, what are the consequences? Practically every other day in the newspapers we read of an individual who has committed a murderous act escaping the electric chair. Often he is either acquitted or given a light sentence.

"If he receives a life sentence, society pays for his room and board and allows him privileges too costly for many of us to afford. Short of execution, can any number of years in prison pay for a murdered victim's life? Allowing a killer to go free is a crime against society, not to mention the murdered victim—who could be you!"

Alice shuddered at the possibility of being a victim of a brutal murder. She asked Vincent, "Do you believe in capital punishment?"

"It is a complicated, emotional subject. Some time I'll give you my views on capital punishment. Right now, let me finish what I was trying to bring out to Chandler." After pausing to collect his thoughts, Vincent spoke his mind again: "A person truly in love will do everything in his power to make the object of his affection happy.

"Should she insist that her happiness depends upon being severed from the spouse or sweetheart she no longer loves, he would be the last person on earth to hold her against her will. That is, if he has at heart the best interests of the woman he claims to cherish."

Chandler Corey had passed his brief remark earlier in reply to Bert simply to be saying something. Not in the habit of looking into the mirror of life's ugly reflections, he did not have the slightest intention of becoming involved in a serious discussion with Vincent.

To avoid it, the dance director did a turn around the point. "By the way, speaking of ego, lowly creatures don't take a back seat to humans on holding a high opinion of themselves. The acrobatic spider when wooing the female of his species, shows off by waltzing merrily in an attempt to win her over. The execution of his movements places him in a class with conceited human dance performers.

"An expert showman, the spider beau exploits the natural lighting effect created by the sun. With his chest puffed out proudly, and a narrow waist dividing his plum-shaped body, he whirls about before his belle as the sun's rays shine brilliantly on his multicolored coat. What a splendid figure he fancies himself as he waltzes on all eight legs! His conceit is manifested in each and every wave of his palpi.

"The male cockchafer, a scarab beetle with stiff forewings, who also dances to impress his belle, is no less conceited. While dancing for her in the moonlight—beetles are notorious night owls—he moves his horny legs rhythmically as he puts on a flashy exhibition of self-adoration matched by human egotists' pompous stiff movements at a ball."

Seeing that the Craigs' and Armstrong's entrées were now being set on the table, Corey jumped at the chance to bring the conversation to an end. "Vincent, old chap, I don't mean to change the subject, but you better eat your roast pork before it gets cold. Besides, the dinner hour is dwindling away, and I haven't placed my order yet."

Chapter 38

Back in the Studio after their dinner, Vincent Armstrong and Bert Craig had gone to the Teacher's Room to use an adjoining lavatory. They needed to be neat in appearance as both were to give a dance lesson at 7:10 p.m. Bent over a basin was Bert, brushing his teeth vigorously.

Across the room, hunched in a wobbly wicker chair, Vincent sat clipping his fingernails. From a frown of discomfort on his brow it was apparent that his spirits were low. Each time he shifted his position to be more comfortable, the chair squeaked, grating more and more on his already irritated nerves.

"Cripes!" he exclaimed, "I wish I wasn't booked the next hour. I am in no mood to teach dancing tonight. Between the pork I ate—it was too fatty—and the tragic news about Joanne Armond, I'm not feeling very good. I could use a couple of Alka-Seltzers."

Not wanting to spatter his mouthful of toothpaste, Bert responded with a shrug of his shoulders. He had no container, so he cupped his hands and filled them with cold water from the basin's faucet. After rinsing his mouth, he spoke to Vincent. "I noticed you were looking sort of pale. Maybe you will feel better once you start moving around. Whom are you going to teach?"

"One of those contest winners. I have never met her. Uh-oh, there's the buzzer." Vincent rose to his feet, stretched his arms, and inhaled and exhaled breathing deeply. "I feel a little better now. It is time to shake a leg. Are you coming?"

"I have to take a leak, Vince. Go ahead without me."

"Okay, Bert. We still have ten minutes. See you downstairs in the ballroom."

Upon descending the stairs leading to the lobby, where clientele were received, Vincent was hailed by Ralph Normand. As they approached each other, Vincent saw a roly-poly woman waddling alongside the tall supervisor. If one could ignore her pudgy figure and slatternly appearance (frowzy hair, wrinkled dress, and shoes with run-down heels), he could see that she was by no means unattractive.

Observing the woman more closely, Vincent ejaculated internally, "I'll be a monkey's uncle! She is pregnant!"

"Mr. Armstrong, I would like you to meet Amy McDougal. She is your new student. The lucky lady is a winner in our Golden Opportunity Contest." Normand patted the woman on the back as he bid her farewell. "I shall leave you in Mr. Armstrong's capable hands."

The supervisor having made his departure, the teacher took control of the situation. "Congratulations on winning your free dancing lessons, Mrs. McDougal."

"Miss McDougal!" she corrected haughtily. With her chin tilted upward she looked a bit defiant.

"Oh," Vincent's mouth was agape, but he tried not to show his surprise that she was unmarried. He was apologetic "Pardon me, Miss McDougal" and careful to avoid casting an eye at her midriff, which proclaimed to the world she was enceinte. "Come this way, please," he said as he led her by a gentle touch of her elbow into the ballroom.

In order to evaluate the woman's previous experience, he queried, "Have you danced before socially?"

"Yeah, sure, lots at bars and parties," Miss McDougal replied in a matter-of-fact manner.

"Great! All we have to do is smooth out some of your rough spots." That she was an experienced social dancer pleased Vincent. He was hopeful it would make matters much easier. "The next number on the channel will probably be a fox trot. Suppose we begin by working on that dance so . . ."

The teacher's student cut him short. "I know howta fox trot. I wanna learn the samba."

Vincent was dismayed over Miss McDougal's request. He thought, "In her condition she wants to samba. Oh, my aching back!" To the woman, nevertheless, he spoke with equanimity: "A samba number ought to be coming up shortly. In the meantime, while we are waiting, let us analyze your fox-trot steps."

"N—O!" Miss McDougal spelled out an emphatic objection. "All I wanna do is samba."

"Very well, we shall work on the samba," consented the teacher, despite mental reservations that properly a student—beginner or otherwise—should master the fundamentals of fox trot and waltz before advancing to Latin-American dances.

Guiding Miss McDougal to an isolated corner of the ballroom, Vincent initiated his instruction. "First off, to give you an idea how it is done, I'll demonstrate the basic samba step. Watch closely. Once you learn it, we can go into its variations."

(Although the teacher told his student he was showing her the basic samba step, in actuality she was being taught a simple exercise designed to expose a beginner to the general principle behind sambaing. Most students are discouraged when a new step, including stylized techniques, is thrown at them all at once. And such students—who will argue?—are normally unhampered by pregnancy.)

"Now that you have a visual picture of the basic samba step, Miss McDougal, I shall break it down for you. The rhythm is 'quick-and quick-quick' or, if you prefer, the count is 1...2-3. The first count is held lengthwise as dictated by the beat of the music. The woman's directional pattern is not too complicated to follow:

> Step back with the right foot on <u>one</u>,
> step back with the left foot on <u>two</u>,
> step in place with the right foot on <u>three</u>;
>
> Step forward with the left foot on <u>one</u>,
> step forward with the right foot on <u>two</u>,
> step in place with the left foot on <u>three</u>.

"Like this." (Again Vincent Armstrong demonstrated, emphasizing the rhythm by clapping his hands.):

> HOLD...two-three; HOLD...two-three.

"The pattern is repeated as often as desired. Notice my pendulum-like motion. It is accomplished by tilting the body to and fro while bending the knees. Stand behind me and imitate my movements."

With an amazing burst of vitality, Amy McDougal attempted to carry out Vincent's instructions. Her eagerness notwithstanding, she was not successful. He had to come to her assistance. Eventually, after several trials and errors, she was able to perform the step fairly well without music.

A samba now being transmitted by the loudspeaker, Vincent adjusted Amy's arms about him in dance position and directed: "All rightie, let's try it to the music, HOLD...two-three, HOLD...two-three, RIGHT foot...two-three, LEFT foot...two-three . . . ! You are tilting back too far. Avoid bending your knees so much. Just bend them slightly. That's it! Good. Very good."

Suddenly, during their dancing, Vincent felt a strange, springy kick against his abdominal cavity. If his stomach was not upset from the fatty pork he had eaten at dinner, the strange feeling—which he readily identified—might not have affected him.

Under the circumstances, however, that fetus kicking him from within the woman's womb was sickening. He resisted an urge to vomit. Although in desperate need of a breath of fresh air, he was unable to think of a plausible way to tell Miss McDougal he needed to leave her for a few minutes. Instead of asking to be excused, Vincent loosened his tie and collar and struggled along with the lesson as best he could with a sick stomach.

Amy was enjoying herself to the hilt. She was having such fun, she became talkative. "I'm gonna love ta learn ta samba."

Vincent's cheeks were chalk white: "Of course, you realize, Miss McDougal, that you are entitled to only six free half-hour lessons, which hardly would be enough time to learn the samba, let alone other dances."

Amy's cheeks were rose red. In a devil-may-care manner she responded, "I figure on buyin' lotsa lessons."

"They are expensive," Vincent informed her. He sincerely did not want her to buy anything she could not afford.

"Shucks! I don't give a toot if they cost a barrel of dough. My boy friend, the old fart, is gonna pay for 'em. It's the least he can do after knockin' me up.

"Anyhoo, we had a whale of-ah fight last night. I smashed him in the ear, and that stinkin' skunk wacked me one in the bellybutton. I plopped to the floor on my fanny—winded like a punch-drunk boxer. It hurt. I cried. My boy friend said he was sorry.

"Ta make it up ta me, he coughed up the money for dance lessons. I've been pestern' him months to get 'em. I didn't let on I'd won any. They're extra. What he don't know won't tee him off. Ha-ha, ha-ha . . ."

As she laughed, her stomach jiggled up and down against Vincent's abdominal cavity. The fetus kicked again—harder! Vincent became sicker than a sailor suffering from *mal de mer*.

In a fraction of a knot Vincent sailed Amy across the dance floor and asked her to be seated. He quickly reeled off a fish story for the little woman, telling her he just remembered an urgent message that he should have delivered to the manager's office earlier. He promised to return shortly. With a wave of his hand he departed.

Rushing to the restroom, he got there in time to eject the contents of his stomach into a toilet bowl. After he vomited, his nausea subsided. Vincent now felt sufficiently comfortable to return to the ballroom and finish giving the samba lesson to his small but feisty student. Perhaps it would be more accurate to say "to his two small but feisty students."

The following week we find Vincent Armstrong walking in the hall upstairs with Alice and Bert Craig. The three were on their way to Ralph Normand's room to hear another narration on dance.

Bert was remarking to Vincent: "When I first entered the training program at National Dance Studios, I was under the impression the biggest part of an instructor's job was to teach dancing. How wrong I was. His main duty is taffying up students."

"I understand what you mean," Vincent replied. "Our students sure are thin-skinned. At a mere hint that their dancing could stand improvement, they crawl into a shell. Oddly enough, the worse the dancers, the less criticism they can take."

"Isn't that the truth," confirmed Craig. "I wonder why that is?"

Vincent thought about Bert's question for a few seconds before answering. "My hunch is that many of our students are lonesome women who have no confidence in themselves. Seldom dated, starved for attention and compliments, they react to a teacher's constructive criticism of their dancing as if it were a personal affront.

"Also, because of the Studio's attractive advertising, they are misled into believing that ballroom dancing is a lead-pipe cinch to learn and, at the same time, fun to do. It irks me that the mooncalves actually believe a teacher need merely wave a wand, say hocuspocus or some other magical words, and they will turn into beautiful ballroom dancers overnight.

"The students ought to see us sweating in front of mirrors during off-hours to perfect our own legwork. They'd change their tune. Anyway, sooner or later they awake to the fact that they cannot learn to dance overnight. Losing faith in their ability, they act indignantly to hide their feeling of inferiority.

"I had a lulu of an experience with one of my students several days ago. She wasn't completing her steps. I politely told the woman she needed to work harder on her follow-through. She didn't display any signs of minding my being critical. But afterward she bitched to Normand that I had been tough on her. He bawled me out, told me to be less technical and not so fault-finding. I tell you it isn't easy dealing with a bunch of frustrated females."

"Well, I like that!" admonished Alice with a loud voice. She had remained quiet all the while, content to listen to Bert and Vincent converse. But she instinctively came to the defense of her sex at his provocative statement. "Men can be just as frustrated as women. I certainly am not."

"Present company is always excluded," Vincent assured her emphatically. "I am taking about the wallflowers among our students, not about women in general."

"I know, I know," Alice acknowledged. "Yet don't kid yourself that you, and Bert, are the only ones with difficult students. I have one who must be afflicted with asthma or something. His constant heavy breathing during a lesson drives me up a wall. Another man I teach constantly wants to argue with me, no matter how agreeable I am. I demand it be put on record that males can be just as exasperating as females."

"Let it be so recorded," was Vincent's compliant reply. As he spoke, he drew out a chuckle from Alice by pretending to write her demand on the cuff of his shirt sleeve with an index finger.

Vincent now stopped being facetious. "Seriously, I wish I had some of the more advanced students who are assigned to the dance director. Shoving clumsy beginners around the ballroom hours at a stretch distorts your dancing form and is a strain on your body."

"That's no lie," Bert joined in the conversation. "There is one student of mine who can complain from morning till night if she wishes. All the same, I am going to insist she flattens her fingers and places her hand on the back of my shoulder instead of on top of it with her fingers curved, which she is in the habit of doing.

"It's beyond me how such a tiny gal—I doubt if she weighs over a hundred pounds—can grip a guy so strongly. Her thumb bores into my collarbone like a rivet. After we dance a while it seems as though I'm packing a ton of steel on my shoulder." Rubbing his collarbone, Bert to be funny let out a yelp. "Ouch! it hurts. I can still feel the sore spot where her thumb bored into me."

Bert had such a comical expression on his face that Vincent and Alice could not help but break out in hearty laughter; it did not last. As soon as the trio entered Mr. Normand's room, they switched from a mindless mood to a mindful mood proper for concentrating upon the supervisor's serious discussion about to begin.

Chapter 39

A HISTORY OF THE CLASSIC BALLROOM DANCES

Latin-American Dances

III-B. The Samba (to promote flexibility and abandon)

In the Encyclopedia Britannica, 1939 book of the year, it states: "The samba is the national dance of Brazil, much as the fox trot is in the United States. It is an intricate, graceful, and exciting dance. The samba is about 110 years old, and was invented by Don Chalasa, a courtier in the court of Dom Pedro, the first emperor of Brazil."

That the samba is danced nationally in Brazil is true. Also, though they are general, the words set forth to describe the samba are applicable. However, the encyclopedia's reference to the invention of the samba by the Brazilian courtier Don Chalasa would cause him to jingle the bells on his cap with jollity.

In Portuguese, the early language of Brazil, chalasa (written not with an s but with a c and cedilla) means 'jest.' Chalasa was indeed commonly known as The Jester. We are about to learn that while he might have contrived sallies in the 1800s to entertain the reigning family members of Brazil from the Portuguese house of Bragança, Chalasa could not possibly have invented the samba.

Among available sources pertaining to Dom Pedro I, who ruled from 1822 to 1831, no indication is given that the samba was danced by any member of royalty or his retinue. A clue to the kind of dancing that was done is to be found in Every Inch a King, a biography of the ruler, by the current Brazilian writer Sergio Correa da Costa:

"After a splendid supper had been served, Dom Pedro and the marchioness (the emperor's mistress) began the formal square dances, impeccable quadrilles performed under the watchful eye of dancing master Louis Lacomba. In the course of the evening, cooling drinks were circulated, dainty edibles, and the latest witticisms of Chalaça, the palace clown."

Because of a paucity of evidence substantiating the claim that Chalasa was the inventor of the samba, he is hereby ruled out. From a historical perspective, there does exist ample proof the dance was created by Afric Negroes.

Nonetheless, we should not lose sight of the fact that the dance under investigation is the primeval samba, which is far removed from the cultivated form danced in ballrooms around the world today. To present our case, we start by looking at the cultural heritage of the African in Brazil.

Turning the pages of history back to the sixteenth century, we see that humiliated black men and women in chains on slave ships, sailing from Africa to the New World, clung proudly to a symbol of their heritage: their time-honored tradition of dancing. Inspired either by mystic worship or magic practice, dances as well as music brought to Brazil by Africans ofttimes evolved under the spell of traditional occult ceremonials.

However, dance themes were not based solely on devotion to supernatural forces. Just about every phase of the African's life on the Dark Continent received expression through The Dance.

Among the Bantu of Angola (Portuguese West Africa) one of the most characteristic dances linked to erotic rituals was the quizomba. A nuptial dance, the quizomba climaxed with the *m'lemba*, defloration of the virgin bride.

Portuguese slave traders, journeying from Angola into nearby territory (today the Belgian Congo), witnessed a type of roundelay widely danced by Bantu tribes in that region. Since the basal rhythmic background against which the dance was performed consisted of a persistent beating of tom-toms, these white slavers are said to have applied to the natives' dancing the name batuque—a derivative of the Portuguese verb *batucar*, meaning 'to beat out rhythm,' as in drumming the fingertips, one after another.

Over the years tribesmen of the Congo introduced their roundelay to neighboring Angolans. As a consequence, a merger occurred between the quizomba's sexual choreographic components and the batuque, which came to be a generic appellation for typical African circular dances.

Throughout the Congo, during the performance of the

batuque, naked natives—standing in a circle—stamped their feet, clapped their hands, and snapped their fingers rhythmically to the accompaniment of spirit-stirring drumbeats. The circle was composed not just of dancers but of rhythm-makers and onlookers as well.

At the outset two or three pairs of dancers would go to the center of the circle. After these original pairs had performed sufficiently, they returned one by one to the ringlike formation and were replaced by others from the circle who performed different steps in the center.

In Angola, where a circle was formed by dancers and only one drummer, a variation was added to the Congoese batuque. Here male and female performers alternately occupied the center of the circle:

After doing some spontaneous solo steps, a male or a female approached the human ring, languidly deflected her body several times, and—to excited shouts of "*semba*" ('belly blow')—turned toward a member of the opposite sex whom she struck forcefully with her belly, or fruitbowl if it suits one's fancy. A *semba* upon the part of a dancer signified not only that she, or he, was making an exit but also that the recipient of the belly blow had been selected to carry on in the central spot. (Like <u>tango</u>, the term <u>semba</u> is strongly suggestive of onomatopoeia.)

Undoubtedly the Congoese-Angolan batuque had the greatest effect of all on the Brazilian-Negro folk dance. Be that as it may, the impact of other batuques cannot be ignored. Transported to Brazil by enslaved Negroes, a variety of such roundelays collectively formed a basis for the stylization of Brazilian folk dancing.

Sometime after the batuque reached Brazil, the term <u>semba</u> was mutated to <u>samba</u>, which was used interchangeably with batuque to identify Afric nonspiritual dances. Eventually these designations lost their synonymy and stood for two separate yet related dance forms.

But to create the impression that dances of the Negro in Brazil remained purely African in name and character would be a distortion of reality. Time after time, like water soaked up by a sponge, European together with Amerindian nomenclature and choreography have been absorbed into Afro-Brazilian dances.

This was well put by Sílvio Romero, authoritative Brazilian sociologist who specialized in folklore. In his Popular Songs of Brazil, issued in 1883, he stated that the bahiano, a Negroid dance common to northern Brazil, had—despite its close resemblance to the Congoese-Angolan batuque—detectable features of European and Indian dances.

[The supervisor smiled at the group of teachers he was addressing. "Should any of you ever have the occasion to visit Brazil, it would be useful to be somewhat familiar with the terminology I am referring to.

"The name bahiano was derived from the Portuguese proper noun Bahia, a coastal state in Brazil. Sometimes in English reference works Bahia is spelled B-a-i-a. An explanation is that since 1935, when changes were made in the spelling of the national language, the 'h' was dropped from Bahia and cognate words.

"Certain states in the North used bahiano instead of batuque or samba. In the Southeast it was designated jongo. In northeastern regions it was designated samba batida and batuque do jare. Whereas in the *sertoes* ('backlands') the African roundelay was named baducca."]

Take note that the bahiano was a song as well as a dance. In fact, all batuques of Brazil are song-dances. Significantly, words and steps were improvised. By the latter part of the nineteenth century, while such distinguishing features in the batuque as formation of a human ring and selection of the next dancer by a belly blow did not always occur, improvisation in either the dancing or singing was rarely omitted.

In his book Three Thousand Miles Through Brazil, published in 1886, James Wells wrote about a batuque which not only illustrates this point but also supports the contention that heterogeneous non-Negroid elements had infiltrated the batuque. The following is a description of the African roundelay as seen by the Englishman at a dance attended by laborers quartered on a farm near Porto do Gomes in the state of Minas Gerais:

> The batuque is usually danced by two couples, sometimes more, who face each other. Two tinkling wire-stringed guitars on that occasion commenced a thrum—thrum, thrum—thrum . . . . The overseer advanced and marshaled the dancers, two men and women. Thrum—thrum, thrum—three or four voices suddenly commenced a loud, high-pitched, wild, rapidly delivered impromptu refrain containing allusions to the *patrão* (their master), his merits, and incidents of the daily work mingled with the loveliness of ideal Marias.

[Turning to Alice and Bert, Vincent whispered, "What are Marias?" With a shrug of their shoulders his two friends told him they had no idea what Marias were. Ralph Normand noticed the three teachers huddled together speaking in whispers. Anticipating the trio's question, the supervisor explained Marias were lovely Brazilian girls.

"Why they were called Marias may be of interest to you. For ages expectant mothers, hoping to induce the Virgin Mary to grant them such favors as easing the dreaded travails of childbirth, or blessing newly born girls with beauty, promised in return to christen their daughters with her name. Hence girls were, and still are, commonly named Maria in Brazil, a predominantly Catholic country. This was a survival from a Portuguese consuetude steeped in superstition."]

To continue with Wells' description of the African roundelay. By the way, he is J. W. Wells, not to be confused with H. G. Wells, author of The War of the Worlds.

> The other men present joined in the chorus, each taking a second (alto) or third (tenor), a falsetto (soprano), or a bass with rhythmic songs accompanied by clapping of hands and shuffling of feet, the dance commenced . . . . A slow measure was maintained for some time; gradually it increased in rapidity, the dancers advancing and retreating, the women swaying their bodies and waving their arms, the men clapping time with their hands at every chorus. The measured tones rose and fell, then again increased in time. The songs and shuffling steps became fast and furious; hands, feet, and voices all kept time; and there was much pantomimic action between the couples.

The foregoing account is manifestly lacking in technical dance details. Wells was, after all, a civil engineer, not a choreographer. Nevertheless, he gives enough information to allow an analysis. In analyzing any Brazilian batuque, we must of necessity consider the music as well as the choreography, both being inseparable in the song-dance.

Musically the batuque is as sentimental as a fado, song form of Portugal somewhat analogous to blues in the United States or calypso in the West Indies. Though they have thrived to a certain extent among fishermen and peasants, fados seem to have prevailed mostly among urban Portuguese dwellers. Different moods are expressed in the fados of Lisbon and Coimbra. Whatever the mood, fados are so popular they frequently are sung on streets and in cafés.

In Lisbon the lyrics of a fado are down to earth, plain spoken in expressing disillusionment over romance or the hardships of life. Rarely a day passes when one does not hear fados sung with sad hearts, especially among the poor in Alfama and Mouraria, the slum sections of the seaport city. As in the Brazilian batuque of Porto do Gomes, indirect references to one's master, or boss, and everyday toil are not unusual in the fado.

In Coimbra, a university city, the fado normally is refined—idealistic in its expression of impractical, romantic illusions. Students often are heard dreamily serenading their sweethearts while they stroll arm in arm along the banks of the Mondego River. Just as singers do in the batuque, the fado singers allude to the loveliest of maidens.

Ideal lyrics of a fado are typified in the following two stanzas of an old Portuguese love song:

"Gracious, Beautiful Carolina"

The gentle Carolina was beautiful.
How beautiful was she on the flower meadow!
In her face innocence would shine,
In her breast the fire of love.

To the charms of a handsome young man
Heart, soul, and life she gave;
She was his, only his, and for him
Her breast palpitated with love.

Thus while poetic lines set to fado music bares a lover's soul with a heavy or a light heart, they also open to view the melancholy that faces a person in the day-by-day struggle to exist. Lyrics for fados have long been improvised by the Portuguese, reputed masters of coining and playing on words.

As for instruments, James Wells in his travels through Brazil, already mentioned, saw laborers at a farm dancing to the strumming of the wire-stringed guitar. In Portugal it is associated with the fado as bread is with butter. The guitar came to the Portuguese via the Spaniards who are believed to have acquired that instrument from the Moors.

Whatever the case, European guitarists passed on their skill to Brazilian Negroes. Till then they had utilized—except for a drum—

only such implements as fragments of glass, wood, and iron in order to produce dance music.

Choreographically ingredients of the fado are visible in the batuque. There are three main variations of the former; a solo dance wherein soloists alternate, a dance performed by one couple, and a dance in which many couples participate.

The last variation, most typical of Portuguese dancing, possess similarities to the Porto do Gomes batuque. During the verse the partners, with hands clasped, move sedately in a circle. But during the refrain the tempo quickens, and the dancers' movements become lively. Executing simple steps, periodically interrupted by *sapateios* ('foot-stamps') in time with the music, couples clap their hands or snap their fingers at each other.

["As teachers, your knowledge of the subject of dance would be incomplete without being informed that couple-dancing is a legacy from various peoples of Europe. Naturally members of the opposite sex among primitive black and red races mixed in the dance—however, not so frequently nor in the same mode as in neoteric Caucasoid cultures.

"A male and female, while dancing in unison, remained apart. Body-to-body contact in conjunction with pairing off of individuals throughout the course of a dance was a custom foreign to primitives. Additionally, use of callers, such as Wells referred to in his description of the batuque, was innovated by dancers in European society."]

Now let us see where the South American Indian fits into the picture. His role both in music and in dancing has been minimized on the grounds that the brutal invasion of the white man's civilization forced the Indian to flee rather early. He escaped to western Brazil where his culture was lost in the thick of the jungles.

As late as 1936 Mário de Andrade—an authority on Brazilian music and director of the Bureau of Culture at São Paulo—said: "The melodic creations of the Brazilian Indians are almost unknown. In the sixteenth century Jean de Lery (Huguenot missionary) transcribed a few of the songs of the Tupis living along the coast; but this contribution, as well as others of the same kind, we have no means of authenticating. It is very probable they (the transcriptions) are incorrect. Only during the twentieth century have accurate studies of Brazilian Indian music been made, but they are few and pertain to relatively small regions."

Yet we do know that the Brazilians are a farrago of white, black, and red blood strains. Their progenitors intermarried practically from the first day Caucasian colonist and Negro slaves set foot on *Pindorma* ('Land of the Palms'), the ancient Amerindian's appellation for Brazil.

The Brazilian coast (where the first Portuguese, French, and Dutch settlements were founded) was the habitat of the Tupis or Tupinambas, as the numerous tribes are called generically. They, more than other Indians, played a supporting part in the early stage of Brazilian national culture, including the song-dance.

That being the case, Tupian music was selected for investigation here. Music, a gift from the gods, was so highly revered among the Tupis that outstanding youthful vocalists were not under compulsion to be warriors as were their less talented peers. Moreover, during a battle, composers of merit, when captured by cannibalistic foes, were set free.

The cultural role Tupis played in the performing arts (song and dance) is not to be underestimated. Populous, powerful tribes, the Tupis inhabited a seaboard of Brazil in the 1500s. They were a subdivision of the Tupinambas, a generic designation for Indians who spoke a Tupi-Guarani tongue, which included northern Tupi and southern Guarani dialects. The Tupinambas lorded it over Brazil's shore from the mouth of the Amazon River to Cananea in the south of São Paulo state.

Like Afric Negroes, Amerindians inherited the song-dance from their aboriginal ancestors. However, the former—craftsmen in the creation of percussion instruments—dealt more with syncopated rhythms, whereas the latter—artisans in the construction of wind instruments—were primarily concerned with melodic tones.

Just the same, it should be clear that savage native song, conceived by instinct, cannot be compared with cultivated art song, inspired by training. Still, in spite of the wild nature of the Indian airs, there was an enchanting quality to their uncultivated lyrics and melodies, many motifs of which had been ingeniously begotten from legendary martial exploits and hunting feats, or from Mother Nature: sounds of birds and insects, rivers and forests.

Generalizations about the Amerindians' music is in a broad sense informative, but narrated accounts of their song-dance would be more helpful in learning about their specific attributes pertinent to the batuque. Descriptions of Tupian song-dances being unavailable, we are fortunate to have one from the Tembes who inhabited the Amazon Valley. They were an important division of the Tupis. When the Tembes' greatly relished wine *tucanayra* matured, that tribe performed a special dance at night by the light of torches.

Blowing of horns slung across the Indians' chests triggered the dancing. Their horn, called a mimê, was formed from two pieces of wood cut from a branch and joined by a resinous, milky sap. Red, black, and yellow feathers of the arara, hocco, and toucan adorned the horn. At the lower end of the instrument hung a small row of royal hawk feathers. Surprisingly, complicated as the horn looked, it could produce but a single, hollow note.

Standing beside a wine cask and ringed by a double circle of dancers—the inner circle made up of males, the outer circle made up of females—the touchau ('chief') passed around tepid tucanayra. Intoxicated by the wine, the performers stamped a side step—sometimes rightwards, sometimes leftwards—while, as a sort of prelude, they uttered repeatedly in chorus "ge-ge-ge, . . . !"

Singing was initiated by the chief who related heroic war deeds of his ancestors. Intermittently the females chanted a panegyric to souls of the departed Tembe heroes. It was believed they had found happiness in the next world, a mythical land lying somewhere toward the west. In the course of the singing and dancing great quantities of tucanayra were consumed. Amazingly despite their intoxication the dancer's movements were steady and their steps sure-footed.

In contrast to fado characteristics—which are sorrowful, solemn, or sentimental—the Tupis' song, and dance, is characterized by exhilaration, comparing to the highly spirited song-dance of the batuque. Immersed under alluvial deposits with the passing of time, golden elements in the Indian roundelay are not visible on the surface. Even experts tread on speculative ground to pan for pay dirt, often yielding bright research that turns out to be fool's gold.

A linguist and ethnographer of Bahia, Theodoro Sampaio, came up against such a situation when filing a claim in his 1928 publication, The Tupi in the National Geography, that the samba was a Tupian dance. According to Sampaio, the term samba denotes 'line.' He points out that the samba is performed in a line, with the dancers holding hands.

Sampaio's claim may contain pyrite. In Tupi-Guarani (lingua Franca of the Tupinambas), the closest term for 'line' is mussau, meaning 'cord.' Samba (a mutant of semba is African, not Indian, and means 'navel' as well as 'belly blow,' an exclusive Negro movement in the samba and batuque. Still, for the most part Sampaio's research was not de facto guesswork. He managed to pan some gold nuggets in his findings on the Tupi.

The striking thing about Tupian and African song-dances is their similarity. Tupis danced in circles; the dancers stamped their feet and accelerated their movements. Also, both the redskins and the blackamoors improvised verses.

As for African Negro elements existent in the batuque on Brazilian soil, we unearth the shuffling of feet, the swaying of bodies, the waving of arms, the quickening of pace—all of which served as substance for the modern ballroom samba. Later on, these distinguishing features, in relation to other dance forms, will be elaborated upon fully.

Just now we shall discuss a forerunner of the modern samba, the maxixe, which is an outgrowth of Brazil's annual carnival. It is an intensely interesting study, too long to go into. That is regrettable because without understanding the environment in which the samba flourished, something valuable is lost.

[The members of Ralph Normand's audience, having been fascinated in the past by his supplementary historic data, pleaded with Mr. Normand to tell them about Brazil's carnival. Their curiosity was so aroused they did not care if he digressed at length before continuing to discuss the history of the samba.

With a broad smile the supervisor acquiesced to the wishes of the teachers, not that he was easily persuaded but time happened to be no problem. Besides, he was well-prepared. He had at hand a notebook full of material on carnival.]

Chapter 40

A HISTORY OF THE CLASSIC BALLROOM DANCES

Carnival in Brazil
(stamping ground of the samba)

Popularly carnival is thought to be a derivative from Medieval Latin *carne* plus *vale*, 'O flesh, farewell.' The phrase supposedly was used in expectation of forty days of self-denial succeeding the fiesta. But some etymologists content the popular belief that *carnevale* was the derivation of carnival is erroneous. More likely, they say, carnival came from Medieval Latin *carnelevarium*, 'a release from the flesh.'

Carnival, which occurs in Roman Catholic countries during the three days preceding Lent—from Epiphany to Ash Wednesday—is a period for feasting and merrymaking. The festival is a carry-over from the Roman Saturnalia wherein demoralized slaves were uplifted by being granted delectably sweet freedom for the nonce to partake with unenslaved pagans in licentious revelry: orgies of ecstatic dancing or sex, joyous singing, and limitless wine drinking. The skylarking reached a climax upon the slaves' burning the effigy of a hated king.

Bitterness over their lot coated with hedonistic honey, pro tempore, the slaves were raised sufficiently in morale to make bondage bearable until Saturnalia time rolled around once again. As the power of Christianity spread, the Roman Catholic Church humored converts to the new faith by not suppressing their pagan observances. In sanctifying the bacchanalian debauchery, which ultimately evolved into carnival, the popes—ardent patrons and promoters of the festival—were able to regulate it and derive material benefits thereby.

To arrive at the Brazilian carnival, we begin with the year 1641 when Roman Catholic Portugal in honor of the Duke of Bragança (who was crowned king as João IV in the Cathedral of Lisbon on December 15, 1640) instituted a celebration novel to her South American colony. Rio de Janeiro broke ground for the gala first, and soon afterward, other populated areas followed suit. The celebration served a twofold purpose: to provide a loyalty-inspiring coronation festival and simultaneously to provide an opiate for Portugal's colonial subjects.

At that time the helpless Indians, flogged by Jesuit missionaries into acceptance of Christianity, were undergoing outrageous economic exploitation in the name of His Majesty. To increase the already enormous treasures of Crown as well as Church, the backs of overworked Negro slaves in mines or on plantations were bent, like beasts of burden, without mercy. Even white settlers—Dutch, English, French, Spanish—were painfully oppressed by the Portuguese whose taxes were heavy and laws harsh.

That the burdened Brazilian colonists were depressed was obvious. Such an unhappy state of mind could develop into a dangerous situation. As a precaution the royal and religious rulers deemed it wise to give the people—free and enslaved alike—an opportunity to flee temporarily from reality into frenzied fantasy. Thus they would be permitted to pour out in a harmless way the resentment bottled up in their hearts against the ruling Portuguese.

Meanwhile, facsimiles of such holidays as *Festa de Cristãos e Mouros* ('Festival of Christians and Moors') was conveyed to Brazil. The festival is a historic Portuguese commemoration of the victory in the fifteenth century of Christianity over eight-hundred-years reign of Mohammedanism on the Iberian peninsula. Bloody battles were fought between Christians and Moors before the latter eventually met defeat at Granada in 1492. Their feelings of antagonism persisted long after that date because the contempt both religious denominations had for each other was so deep-rooted it was difficult to remove.

Consequently, in the Brazilian facsimile of the festival believers in Christianity expressed their hostility toward the followers of Mohammedanism. During the festival, singing and dancing participants, costumed either as Christians or Moors, engaged in war games.

The festival ended when individuals pretending to be Moors, were submerged in water and next smeared pate to toe with starch. What this horseplay signified was that polluted black souls (Moslems) became purified white souls (Christians) upon being baptized.

Entrudo was another song-and-dance festival transported from Portugal to Brazil. Although reshaped into the ritualistic forms of the Latin Church, the festival neither originated in the rites of baptism nor in Christian-Moorish conflict.

Subsequent to Vasco da Gama's reaching Calicut in 1498, the Western World learned about Entrudo from India. That country, in fact, supplied many practices adopted by Catholicism. Entrudo was an adaptation of India's Holi, a licentious spring festival rooted in sun worship.

Traditionally the festival included four activities:

(1) Men and boys of lower castes performed grotesque dances.

(2) Songs were sung about Krishna's love affairs with herdswomen. (He is a widely worshipped deity in India.)

(3) Horns were blown, drums beaten, and scurrilities shouted mostly at women.

(4) Townsmen as well as villagers assaulted one another with tin syringes from which they squirted water; they also used bamboo blowguns from which were blown yellow, green, and red powder mixed with glistening talc.

In one form or another Holi activities appear in the Brazilian Entrudo. Brazilians celebrated it in the following way: A sack of flour was emptied over the head of anybody within reach. His face was then wet with a reddish-tinted liquid flung at him in gelatin capsules, or he was shot in the face with a silver dispenser that worked something like a water pistol. And—to give a bright luster to the poor devil's grimace—the red, pasty layer that stuck to his skin was spattered with handfuls of talc.

For some reason in Brazil the Entrudo (into which the elixir of *Fiesta de Cristãos e Mouros* was gradually absorbed) seemed to have gained most popularity among the inhabitants of the cities. In the interior of the country Entrudo was less popular.

With the annual arrival time for the festival, battling celebrators of both sexes and all ages carried on hilariously. They hurled buckets of water at one another from verandahs and windows. Noncombatant passers-by below received the worst drenchings of all.

On top of that, people were thrown into ponds and pools. Nobody was spared. In an Entrudo of 1826, His Royal Highness, Dom Pedro II—like it or not—found himself splashing about fully clothed upon being unceremoniously thrown into a tank of water.

On the streets during Entrudo pranksters would leap from concealed places to dump pounds of *farinha de mandioca* ('manioc flour') on hapless men and women. Everyone was fair game. A floured victim was sprayed with a *gamela*, a big syringe containing water. The sight of someone covered with dripping white paste brought cries of sheer jubilation from observers. Pranks often went beyond the playful point. Revelers engaged in hair-pulling and fisticuffs.

With the passing of the years, changes occurred in the rowdy merrymaking. Physical encounters became rare by comparison. While on occasion a body might be cast into a tank of water, the practice of throwing water at one another was greatly reduced. Emptying sacks of manioc flour over unwary victims ceased.

Now it was customary to toss *laranjas e limões fictícios* ('artificial oranges and lemons molded from wax') which were filled with fetid fluid. Sailing through the air, they burst like snowballs upon striking a person's head. Not only did flakes of wet wax cling to his head but a malodor also clung to his hair, for hours.

Despite tiptoes forward in improvement of human relations, the sting of the hard hand of Roman Catholic Portugal was still sorely felt by a hostile yet restrained Brazilian population. Nevertheless, Entrudo loosened the tight grip of royalty. The hostility of merrymakers was at times uncontrollable.

At Rio de Janeiro, in 1854, boisterous carousers got out of hand to the extent that they dared crash their way into the Teatro Imperial and disrupt the performance being enjoyed by no less a personage than Dom Pedro II. On the outside of the theatre, not wax but real fruits were pitched at bystanders. Consequently, an order prohibiting Entrudo was issued by the police.

All the same, the ban could not be enforced completely. Depressed over miserable living conditions, the populace needed to let off steam. Entrudo was a safety valve. Hence, Entrudo as such was eliminated; still it was retained in essence. Flower showers displaced water baths. In lieu of the smelly *laranjas e limões ficticíos*, merrymakers used the *bisnaga*, a rubber device with a tin tube designed to squirt perfumed water at close range.

Costumes, masks, serpentine, and confetti appeared along with the *corso*, a 'carriage procession,' wherein the elite—exhibiting rich regalia in phaetons pulled by thoroughbred horses—paraded before the crowds. With the change in character of Entrudo, *carnaval* or 'carnival' came into its own right.

A humorous episode had opened Rio de Janeiro's carnival in 1852. That year an unidentified Portuguese banged away skillfully on a bass drum as he paraded about the city. The drummer, a huge man, had a pear-shaped body and a widely spread black mustachio.

With his mustachio flying in the wind like the flapping wings of a bird in the sky, he was an impressive sight to behold. One by one people everywhere stopped what they were doing to parade behind him. Captivated by his bold drum beats, the gathering crowd burst into song and dance with utter abandonment.

Perhaps for want of a better name, the rotund drummer was dubbed Zé Pereira after the instrument he carried by a cord around his neck. In Portugal the bass drum, largest of the nonmusical instruments, is called *Zé Pereira*, meaning 'Joe Pear Tree.' The relation between the name and the drum is open to speculation.

Possibly its wide cylindrical shell and heavy drumsticks, with padded knobs, were once constructed from the wood of the pear tree. Struck on both vellum heads, while the wooden body is held upright in a military position, Zé Pereira booms out thunderous sounds which can be heard miles away. No carnival in Rio de Janeiro was celebrated without the presence of Zé Pereira, symbolic in spirit the time of feasting and merrymaking just before Lent.

Alterations plus additions notwithstanding, carnival as yet was not too distinguishable from Entrudo since both were informal outdoor festivals. Formalization of carnival did not commence until the establishment in 1855 of two societies: the *Sumidades Carnavaliscas* ('Carnival Celebrities') and the *Veneziana* ('Venetian'). Both societies were established, for the most part, by youthful artists and authors.

With the abolition of slavery in 1888 and the founding of the republic the next year, the Brazilian people—heretofore seeking superficial liberty in carnival—were at last on the road toward genuine freedom. Former slaves, elated over being freed, and commoners, exultant over societal reforms, rejoiced during the festal season as never before.

More and more carnival clubs were organized. Patriotic to the core, members started a policy of parading floats featuring historical episodes. Before long clubs received civic subventions to finance the costly spectacles displayed at the festival.

Carnival evolved into a national holiday taking place annually around the land in urban areas, not only in Rio de Janeiro. In other Brazilian cities, however, the festivities do not measure up in size to those of the capital city. Participation is less extensive, and they are not so well known as the *Carnaval Carioca* ('Rio Carnival'), which acquired international fame. It is of interest to note that the noun form of the word *carioca* stands for an inhabitant of Rio de Janeiro.

Still, the prominence of the *Carnaval Carioca* or the number of participants in it, is a secondary matter to us. Our primary interest lies in Rio de Janeiro mainly because it was there that the maxixe—forerunner of the samba—appeared before it caught the world's eye.

Chapter 41

A HISTORY OF THE CLASSIC BALLROOM DANCES

Latin-American Dances

III-C. The Samba: a continuation

Since the first printed mention of the maxixe is found on January 25, 1884, in an afternoon Rio bulletin, the *Gazeta da Tarde*, chances are the dance rose to popularity in Brazil that year. While the exact date of the initial appearance of the maxixe is questionable, it is a certainty that the dance was a product of the *Carnaval Carioca*. Through association of people diverse in racial background, carnival had become a melting pot in which ethnic dances and music fused.

By the late eighties *brasileiros* and *brasileiras* less frequently performed traditional batuques, fandangos, or habaneras. Also, except for impromptu combinations, dancers oftentimes did not perform foreign polkas and mazurkas, that is, not as imported from Europe. Among the impromptu combinations was a highly popular new dance, the maxixe—produced in uninhibited, impulsive merriment out of African, Latin, and European materials.

Although the word maxixe possesses a root common to such Portuguese words as *máxinho* ('small guitar') and *maxima* ('master note'), there appears to be no connective trunk showing how the name of the dance might have evolved. If a connection exists, it is not visible to the naked eye.

With tongue in cheek, Heitor Villa-Lobos, foremost composer of Brazil, tells us that the dance received its name from one Senhor Maxixe. The man, a slight-statured carioca, is said to have contrived the maxixe while lightly flitting about in an experiment with different steps of the lundú during carnival in 1882.

So much for the name of the dance, now to examine the maxixe per se. From a musical standpoint, it was composed of Afric lundú syncopation, Cuban habanera melody intermixed to a degree with Brazilian toada airs, and Czech polka beats. The lundú is a batuque-type song-dance of Angola; the habanera is a Creole country dance and melody from Havana; the toada is a Brazilian version of a Spanish song in the popular vein; and the polka is a kind of music and peasant dance from Bohemia.

In choreography the maxixe was an interesting composite. It embodied basically the plastic, unbridled figures of the lundú; the sensual, swaying motion of the habanera; and the lively, quick half-step of the polka.

Bohemians more often called the half-step a chain-step because it was repeated over and over in continuity, like links running through a chain. The half-step was executed the same way as the Czech polka except the heel was used instead of the sole when the leading foot advanced. Apparently this heel technique came from the heel-step of the Finnish polka.

Since the maxixe was a couple dance wherein the man and woman embraced, it cannot be considered authentically African. With outstretched arms raised high, the Afro-Negro danced independently of a woman, a manner of dancing still seen at carnivals today.

Despite being the dance of the hour, the maxixe was admitted into Brazilian salons only under cover. The exaggerated, difficult movements—which required the agility of an acrobat on the part of a dancer—were very fatiguing. Besides, the dance was indelicate, plebeian...shocking to polite, plutocratic society.

Even though the welcome mat was not put out for the maxixe as a dance in the salons of Brazil, it was well received musically. Ernesto Nazaré (or Nazareth), renowned Brazilian composer of popular music, was instrumental in bringing about the acceptance of the maxixe in the musical world. Paradoxically, he accomplished this in the face of the fact that his music was misnamed.

Because the music to which the maxixe was danced bore a sort of similarity to the Cuban or Spanish tango—for example, Yradier's composition La Paloma—maxixe music went under the name Tango for a number of years. Eventually, however, the practice of identifying that Brazilian music with the Argentine music was discontinued.

Although maxixes were now being referred to by their proper

name, Ernesto Nazaré persisted in captioning his piano compositions Tangos, which in actuality were maxixes. The result was that tango and maxixe music, as well as the dances, were frequently confused.

Around the turn of the century the Brazilian maxixe, along with the Argentine Tango, were exhibited in Europe. In 1905 M. Camille de Rhynal, the Frenchman who was to promote the tango two years hence, planned the choreography of a maxixe for Lady Madcap, a musical revue produced by George Edwardes, at the Prince of Wales Theater in London.

Nevertheless, some eight years were to pass before the maxixe achieved noticeable recognition. It was not recognized until the tango was accepted publicly in France and ultimately in England about 1913.

At the same time arrangers were still publishing the tango and the maxixe as one music or dance. Typically Rubé Danmark arranged Nazaré's composition Dengozo under the designation Maxixe-Tango, which was as confusing as commingling two different bank accounts. Compared to the tango the maxixe's acclaim was minimal. Yet the maxixe strongly impressed a London dancing master, W. F. Hurndall, who was inspired to create from it the maxina, a sequence dance.

[Alice Craig nudged her husband Bert to be quiet, but he was unable to restrain himself any longer. He had to have something to say. Raising his hand to attract the supervisor's attention, Bert expressed what just entered his mind:

"I know sequence is one thing coming after another. However, I don't see how that distinguishes the maxina from other dances."

Exercising patience, the supervisor explained: "As for the sequence word, your brief definition is correct. As for the sequence dance, it is one in which different step-combinations are done in a set order. And the music—composed of a twenty-four bar strain—distinguishes the maxina from other dances.

"Maxina music held great fascination for the English. Still, social dancers found it was not danceable. Consequently, the maxina met a fate that befell the maxixe: interest in Hurndall's dance did not last long in Europe."]

Although the Europeanized maxixe from Brazil was featured by such top French tango teams as Duque and Line, the popularity of the dance died away by 1915. The brisk two-four rhythm of the music—whether allegro moderato (moderately lively, that is) or simply moderate—was still too fast for inexperienced dancers.

Many learned to do the foreign-style footwork somewhat, but few could dance the maxixe and properly keep in time with the music. Moreover, the ornamental figures, with deep dips and extreme sways, were not easily executed by the average European dancer.

In the United States the story was the same. When Vernon and Irene Castle exhibited the maxixe, they stimulated in the American public a desire to learn the dance. Yet general enthusiasm over the maxixe was short-lived. Try as they might, few individuals, unless well-trained, could do the dance satisfactorily.

Besides requiring the nimbleness of the professional, the maxixe was of such a nature that much space was needed to perform it. Since social dancing was becoming more and more the vogue, ballroom floors, not as a rule spacious, were usually overcrowded. Under the circumstances, doing a dance like the maxixe proved impractical.

While Vernon and Irene spoke of the dance that they demonstrated in films and on the stage as the Maxixe Brésilienne, it was far from being the genuine article. In their book Modern Dancing they describe five steps which, according to Vernon Castle "belong to the original version of the maxixe." It is unclear whether he meant the original maxixe of Brazil, France, or the United States.

In mood, the maxixe of the Carnaval Carioca was intoxicating, the choreography lascivious, the movements acrobatic in form. Beyond the borders of Brazil the dance had been watered down.

[Addressing the group of teachers, the supervisor said: "Let us make a choreographic and historic analysis of the steps Vernon and Irene listed. We should bear in mind that the maxixe can be danced in any order, and not necessarily in the sequence to be presented now. You may take notes or ask questions after I demonstrate and explain:

    1.   The Two-Step

        Body Position: usually closed

        Two-Steps form the foundation for the Maxixe Brésilienna. They are executed on the heel of the leading foot pointed upward in the following manner:

        Leftward: step (on heel) close (on sole);

Rightward: <u>step</u> (on heel) <u>close</u> (on sole).

The closing step is glided on the sole, and the edge of the heel is placed on the floor—not with the force of a pickaxe but with the gentleness of a toothpick.

As the dancers step to the left, they start swaying their bodies from the right, side to side. Conversely, as the dancers step to the right, they start swaying their bodies from the left, side to side.

A teacher wanted to know if Two-Steps are always done to the side. The supervisor answered:

Two-Steps are not strictly side-steps since the dancers have the option of turning to a degree in different directions. That is, if choosing to go to the left, they turn counterclockwise in a semicircle. If choosing to go to the right, they semicircle clockwise.

"Except for style, The Two-Step is similar to an old-fashioned two-step that was performed in march time by chassé forward, backward, or turning. This original, obsolete two-step formed a basis for the American fox trot. More prominently The Two-Step contains features from the Brazilian maxixe: utilizing the heel is reminiscent of the Portuguese sapateio; the tendency to turn rubbed off from the Czech polka; the sway was an African bestowal.

2. <u>Les À-Côte</u> (The Single-Step)

Body Position: conversational

The man steps side-oblique onto the heel of his left foot. Then, gliding on the sole of his right foot, he brings the instep up to the left heel.

The woman's footwork is as usual opposite to that of the man's directional patterns.

Les À-Côtes are performed in the line of dance around a floor, that is, going forward. Should the dancers have the inclination, they may reverse their direction, that is, go backward.

A teacher wanted to know if the dancers also sway their bodies when doing The Single-Step. The supervisor answered:

"Swaying is used in The Single-Step, or Les À-Côte, but not as it is in The Two-Step in which dancers move essentially sideways. In doing single-steps while they navigate on a dance floor, they move their shoulders up and down like the stem and stern of a rocking ship. Whereas the motion of the waves rocks the ship, bending of the dancers' knees causes their shoulders to sway.

> As the dancers travel along executing Les À-Côtes, they change the position of their arms. The man releases the woman's right hand so she is free to draw it behind her above her waistline, where he secures her right hand in his. Simultaneously he raises her left hand from his shoulder and holds it well over their heads. Thus they assume what in modern times is suggestive of a 'window pose.'

A teacher who had a smattering of the French language volunteered some information: "In French *le seul pas* is an expression for 'the single step.' And Les À-Côte means 'the incidentals.' How come it was applied to The Single-Step?"

The supervisor answered: "That is a knotty question. I never have attempted to unravel it because Les À-Côte did not originate in France. Perhaps it is an idiomatic expression.

3.   Le Corta Jaca (The Skating Step)

Body Position: sweetheart

> The base of Le Corta Jaca is two-steps. After sweetheart position is assumed, two-steps are executed by the dancers. Since they are standing side by side and facing in the same direction, the man—who normally uses the foot opposite to the woman's—begins Le Corta Jaca on his right foot. He is thus in step with his partner. Also, since her outstretched left arm is in front of the man's chest, she stands a little ahead of him. As the pair dance, they adjust the length of their steps in order to progress together evenly.

A teacher wanted to know if sweetheart position was outmoded. He had never heard it referred to on an ice rink. The supervisor answered:

"Sweetheart is a term some dancers make use of nowadays to designate a romantic position couples assume in the ballroom. While sweetheart position bears semblance to the one ice-skating partners use, the arms are held in a different way by ballroom partners. Characteristically when dancing forward, the man passes his right leg in front of the woman just as she passes her left leg in front of the man.

> As a variation in The Skating Step, the couples execute a slow dip by kneeling on their left knees. The dip, one might say, is a finishing touch at the conclusion of a series of two-steps. In terms of music if eight measures are played, the dip occurs on the seventh measure. And the dip is held for the eighth measure.

A teacher wanted to know who created The Skating Step. The supervisor answered:

"Frenchmen created The Skating Step. They got the idea for the name Le Corta Jaca from a Portuguese or Brazilian term *corta-jaca*, a tap step of a primitive samba sung and danced in Bahia by Negro slaves. The French name gives the wrong impression. Needless to elaborate, The Skating Step (Le Corta Jaca) is entirely different from the samba step (*corta-a-jaca*). When Le Corta Jaca was introduced to New Yorkers in the U.S.A., they renamed it The Skating Step because the dance position was similar to one couples used in an ice rink.

    4.   The Back Two-Step

Body Position: reverse sweetheart

> Shifting from regular sweetheart position after doing single-steps, the man stands behind the woman instead of alongside her. He loosely embraces her folding his hands over hers below the woman's bosom.

A teacher wanted to know if the intimate body position of The Back Two-Step was something like an apache posture during a dance. She had seen a motion picture about Paris in which apache dancers at a cabaret seemed to have a similar stance as the one the supervisor had just described.

Ralph Normand replied: "Your observation is correct. The intimate body position of the dancers assumed in The Back Two-Step suggests a posture not uncommon to the apache dance.

> Once in reverse sweetheart position, the dancers start two-stepping until they are ready to go into another maxixe step. Now they . . .

A teacher impatient to ask a question interrupted Mr. Normand. The teacher wanted to know the proper pronunciation of maxixe.

The way it is spelled reminded him of Maximilian, emperor of Mexico in the 1800s.

A bit irritated over the interruption, the supervisor retorted: "I was about to say, NOW they did The Turn—one of the more attractive steps in the maxixe. But since you asked, I shall answer your question.

"Vernon Castle himself had trouble with pronouncing maxixe. He wasn't sure whether it should be pronounced maxeks, maxesse, mattcheche, or mattchsche. 'Brazilians,' he said, 'pronounce the word mashish, with a slight accent in the second syllable,' which is the way I have been pronouncing the word.

   5.   The Turn

> Body Position: open

> The dancers start The Turn from reverse sweetheart position. The man raises the woman's left hand with his left hand. (He holds on to her right hand with his.) Gently manipulating her raised hand, he turns the woman clockwise till they stand vis-à-vis. Their hands are placed palm to palm, and their arms are aligned from wrist to elbow.

A teacher told the supervisor she understood the partners stood apart face to face and had arm to arm contact. However, she did not understand the method for changing body positions while a couple danced the maxixe. She wanted to know how the change was accomplished.

The supervisor answered: "Changing from one dance position to another is usually accomplished by single-steps that serve as transitions either at the beginning or at the end of a series of steps. The number and size of single-steps needed to go into and out of dance positions depend upon which is next to be assumed. For instance, . . ." On second thought, instead of simply describing a transition, Mr. Normand requested the teacher to come to the front of the room so that she could assist him in a demonstration:

> The man starts The Turn from sweetheart position with a single-step. (While the woman is turning, he marks time in place with two-steps.) She turns by performing three single-steps to the right. Her steps are small, and she stops short to face the man.

"As you have just seen, we started in sweetheart position and ended up in open position. For clarity, I did not describe the placement of our hands while demonstrating." The supervisor thanked the teacher for assisting him. She returned to her chair at the rear of the room where other teachers were seated.

> Whenever it is timely, the dancers slowly lower their arms which were aligned in the form of an arch. Next, the man and the woman adjust their hands to assume closed position in preparation for a different series of steps.

"The Turn, I might mention, had its origin in the minuet. It was redesigned by French dancers. In tying the maxixe into their dance designs, they fashioned The Turn along the lines of Brazilian styling.

"Of course, the aforesaid five figures of the Maxixe Bresiliénne were supplemented with a number of variations in occidental societies by exhibition dancers who added elaborate steps to the dance—too elaborate for social dancers. Although the maxixe was given a cool farewell in the Western Hemisphere and in the countries of Europe, professionals retained a warm spot in their hearts for the dance. In point of fact, as late as 1919, when the world's Dancing Championships were held on the French Riviera at the Rallye Club in Nice, the maxixe was included in the competition along with the tango, one-step, fox trot and waltz."]

For quite a while it appeared the maxixe would win a place as a national dance in Brazil. That was not to be. The maxixe was edged out by the condomblé, a dance handed down to impoverished Negroes dwelling on steep slopes of Rio de Janeiro's morros, or hills, the shadowy reflections of which darken the brilliant blue bay in the harbor below. The condomblé was the earliest form of the modern-day samba.

According to a circulated story, word of mouth, late in the 1800s, a former slave called Catu came from Bahia to Rio where she introduced modified practices of the condomblé, a fetishistic dance ritual with sacred chants in which the rudimentary samba rhythm had originated. Catu was a member of Gêgo-Nagô, a mysterious cult founded by Sudanese Negroes in Africa. They used drums, bells, and rattles in their rituals. Catu induced some self-taught black musicians to form a band using ritual rhythms and instruments for the purpose of holding sessões de samba.

They are equivalent to American jam sessions. At first the samba sessions were held solely in the Negro districts. Eventually, however, the magnetism of the rhythm attracted the rest of Rio's residents, and sambas were played throughout the seaport city.

In 1897, the Brazilian government sent troops from Rio de Janeiro to stamp out a local rebellion in Bahia. After the disorder was quelled, the blacks among the soldiers, scores of whom had married *bahianas*, returned to their life of impoverishment on the morros above the seaport. The hillside dwellers existed precariously at the brink of starvation in hovels with dirt floors.

Each of the hills upon which the Negroes settled became known by a special name. Examples: Morro da Mangueira ('Mango Hill') and Morro do Salgueiro ('Willow Hill') were named after trees in their respective vicinities. A spade was called a spade when Morro da Favela ('Shantytown Hill') received its name. Another hill was named Morro do Querosene ('Kerosene Hill') because its squalid shanties had been built from discarded fuel cans. Those hills occupied by ebony-complexioned cariocas inappropriately were spoken of as the Kingdom of the Negro, for it had neither king nor queen.

On the morros the samba—reminiscent of its tribal form—was danced in circles with soloists. However, urbanization gradually altered the samba's character. The dance descended annually to an open public square (*Praca Onxe de Junho*) where on the eleventh of June the Negroes gathered to revel during carnival in Rio de Janeiro.

Taking on city ways, they organized *escolas de samba*, carnival clubs in which sambas were prepared, polished, and practiced all year long for presentation at the Carnaval Carioca. As a consequence, the Samba Carioca developed. It had been formed by combining the Samba do Morro with elements of the Samba Bahiano.

In Bahia two types generally characterized the samba. Both included the *umbigada*, Portuguese for *semba* ('belly blow'). Earlier it was explained that semba is an onomatopoetic word in the Angolese language of the Bantu tribes of Angola on the West African coast.

Samba type one in Bahia was a song-dance involving slow, sensuous, swaying body movements, offset by sprightly turns. It took the form of a competition in which the best dancer sought to emerge as the winner by a display of his skill. Whenever a break occurred in the dancing, a pair of singers, wielding small guitar-type instruments, provoked each other into a *desafio*, or poetic challenge, which is a duel of wits with improvised free verse.

A *desafio*—usually a four-line stanza in seven-syllable lines—is common to the Bahia *sertão,* the 'backland.' The stanzas we are about to lend an ear to are an interpretation of a passage from *Vaqueiros e Cantadores* ('Cowboys and Singers') by Luis da Camara Cascudo, a Brazilian writer.

Challenger:
"God is my witness, amen!
I am not jesting, you know!
The whole wide world I defy,
In singing at this grand show!"

Contender:
"In singing at this grand show!
You play with fire like a child!
At great peril do you challenge,
The might of these parts, ho, ho!"

The object of a *desafio* being to turn the laugh on the other fellow, the contender threw back the last line of verse hurled at him by his antagonist. In this way the challenge was met and fought until a singing foe ran out of improvisation.

Samba type two in Bahia also included the *umbigada.* This second type was a song-dance consisting of three fundamental figures:

1. *corta-a-jaca* ('cut the breadfruit')
2. *separa-o-visgo* ('separate the mistletoe')
3. *apanha-o-bago* ('pick up the grain')

Encircled by others, one of the dancers executed all three figures when his turn came up. He shuffled flirtatiously around a pretty girl as he chanted about *raspadura,* 'scrapings' from which brittle brown-sugar candy is made. Chorus-like, the dancers composing the circle uttered a reply after each solo part.

Soloist:
"See the ripe cane ....
It is green, it's ripe (enough) ....
To make scrapings ...."

Chorus:
"In the path (through the cane field)."

Soloist:
"There comes the priest."

Chorus:
"To marry you two."

Soloist:
"Not for me butterfly!"

Chorus:
"You can go fly!"

Donald Pierson, Sao Paulo sociologist, who cites the preceding stanzas in his book Negroes in Brazil, tells us that this song-dance has enjoyed great popularity at Mar Grande, a locality on the island of Itaparica, which faces Salvador. The names of the steps and words of the song bring to mind the work and patter of black slaves sweating under the hot sun on plantations in days bygone.

We now have adequate background to see the reason why in modern times the samba divides categorically into urban—of which the <u>Samba</u> <u>Carioca</u> is the advanced form—and rural dances. In provincial zones of such states as São Paulo, the samba is danced in a circle and in rows without the *umbigada* or, to reiterate, the 'belly blow.'

The main body of participators thus either completely surround or flank (right and left) solo performers. When the circle samba is performed, the women use their full skirts to tease the men, just as cancan dancers do. And when the row samba is performed, as in square dancing, the women face the men.

From a musical aspect, the rural samba has much greater syncopated rhythm, more variety in patterns of syncopation, and more interplay of spirited music than the urban samba. To put it bluntly, the citified samba, which ordinarily holds to a monotonous pattern (a series of even notes in rapid tempo), sounds dull compared with the backland samba.

Despite differences likenesses cannot be denied, as is always the case in Brazilian folk music, three distinctive attributes—the major key, duple meter, and brisk tempo—are invariably present in the urban as well as in the rural samba forms. Like the maxixe, the samba became impregnated with European sperms at the <u>Carnaval Carioca</u>.

Escolas de samba were responsible for the styling of the dance. Annually the carnival clubs, strictly speaking 'samba schools,' assemble in the streets of Rio de Janeiro to compete with one another for prizes offered by the city government.

When the samba schools perform in group formation on the streets during carnival, they are referred to as *ranchos*. The performances they put on call for a *côro* or 'chorus' and a *solista* or 'soloist.'

Typical of the samba styles that appear are:

a. Batucada...it is danced in the style of the batuque. The *côro* and the *solista* (ground bass) speed up their stamping and singing, which mounts to a frenzy.

b. Cancão...it is sweet, subdued in style, a sort of choral song. The *côro* and the *solista* sing softly. The latter uses expressive hand and hip movements as he takes short, unvaried steps. The melody he carries is sad with amorous, sentimental, melancholic verses.

In past carnival days the samba theme centered around laments against the infidelity of heartless females. With the samba's coming to the fore at the pre-Lenten celebration, the theme changed to loud criticism of just about every point of view and event including political and civic affairs as well as social attitudes, but quietly in criticizing religious affirmations.

There were also procedural changes involving carnival. The bisnage, the rubber device with a tin tube which squirts perfumed water, was replaced by the lançe-perfume, a hand-sized metal siphon which squirts perfumed ether. Now dancing celebrators intermittently receive squirts from lançe-perfumers whether the dancers happen to be in a *bloco* (a group sambaing in block formation) on the crowded, decorated streets or in a *cordão* (a group sambaing in line formation) at packed, masquerade balls.

The effect of the squirted ether can be as chilling as a piece of ice dropped below a man's bellybutton or between a woman's breasts. The mixing of ether and perfume with perspiration of excited dancers milling through throngs produces a fleshy odor that in a primitive way is intoxicating.

With the urbanizing of Rio de Janeiro, the rotund drummer Zé Pereira vanished as the symbolic personage of the Carnaval Carioca. In due time Rei Momo, King of Carnival, came to preside over the merriment.

[Alice Craig had a comment. "If I remember correctly, wasn't Momo a mythological god?"

"Yes. Very good!" Mr. Normand gave Alice an extended compliment. "Your memory serves you well. You are correct.

"Momo comes from Momus, in Greek mythology the son of night; he was the personification of satire and mirth. Momus delighted in mocking the gods by censuring their deeds. Because of his endless faultfinding, all-mighty Zeus, father of gods and men, exiled him from heaven."]

On the last day of carnival, which starts officially the Sunday before Ash Wednesday, a grand parade is held along Avenida Rio Branco, the main street. Above, banners from every nation are hung from buildings. Rei Momo sitting on an ornate throne atop a float leads the procession. Parading the length of serpentine-strewn Avenida Rio Branco, one also sees gigantic allegoric floats, ridiculous papier-mache figures, weird animal caricatures, uniformed military bands, men burlesquing actresses, women impersonating pages, and other colorfully costumed carnivalists.

Whereas costumes vary from carnival to carnival, a dominant idea generally is expressed in the attire of the participants. It might be any distinctive outfit worn in other lands: an English bobby's uniform, a Dutch girl's, a Japanese samurai's, a French maid's. A *brasileira* or *brasileiro*, no matter how poor, frequently goes without necessities the year round in order to scrape together enough *tostoes* ('pennies') to splurge on a costume and have a fling in this merry kaleidoscopic extravaganza.

In keeping with custom, "Momo the Magnificent" is buried on the final day of the jollity. All the carnival groups, assembling in the theaters throughout Rio de Janeiro, attend the king's funeral. The mock burial rites are performed to the musical setting of Te Deum; the obsequies less solemnized by thousands of lay singers pouring forth popular tunes proved most successful the current year.

The lifeblood of the festivities is the carnival songs traditionally circulating from the morros. There Negroes need nothing more than a cigar box to strum out a tune, the words oftentimes turn on a proverb. Many tunes are adaptations from songs arranged by popular demand in the rhythm of the samba. Of course, there are also tunes in the rhythm of the maxixe...and marcha, counterpart of the military march.

For numberless years the samba had remained confined to the Land of the Red Dyewood. Localized, it was little known outside Brazil even though the dance had been introduced to Parisians in 1923. The samba escaped public notice in 1929 when Dorothy Cropper, president of the New York Society of Dancing Teachers, exhibited the alien dance at a meeting in the Hotel Astor.

Again in France, despite a serious effort in 1931 to promote samba music by booking a Brazilian band into the Café de Paris, the samba remained unknown. After a visit to Rio de Janeiro in 1935, Virginia Gollatz, a dancing teacher from Pasadena, brought the Samba Carioca to California. Still, the dance failed to stir the American public.

Not until four years later did the United States, and in turn the rest of the world, grow conscious of the samba. Responsible for the awakening was Maria do Carmo da Cunha, born 1913 in Lisbon, Portugal. Shortly afterward, her parents moved to Rio de Janeiro where her father established a business. She meanwhile was placed in a convent at an early age, for schooling.

When she was fifteen years old, Maria embarked on a career as a radio singer over the objections of her parents. Her father had become a well-to-do produce wholesaler respected in the community. They felt it was beneath the dignity of a respectable girl to be a common *cantora* ('singer' of popular songs). Besides, how could she hope to succeed? Maria never had any singing lessons.

Although her early auditions were disappointing, years of determination proved that Senhor Cunha's little lamb had not gone astray. After recording over three hundred records, all of which were most successful, Maria began appearing at Brazilian nightclubs and theaters. Soon she received motion-picture parts. By the time she completed three films and nine tours in South America, she was applauded as one of the favorite *cantoras* below the border.

While on a South American cruise Lee Shubert, a seasoned Broadway producer, was informed about Maria by his press agent. Shubert visited Rio de Janeiro to catch Maria's act at the Casino Urca. Favorably impressed, he offered her a three-year contract, which she immediately accepted. So it was in the spring of 1939, accompanied by her six-piece band, the Latin lady shot up to the U.S.A. like a fire arrow to set Broadway ablaze with red-hot rhythm in a revue, The Streets of Paris. The amazing thing is that she appeared only for six minutes at the end of the first act.

Maria presented a flamboyant figure in her exotic, brightly colored costume—high turban, lavish jewelry, flaring skirt—styled after the *vestimenta bahiana* customarily worn by Negresses of Bahia. Small in stature but fiery in personality, she was a five-foot-two-inch package of highly inflammable materials.

[The supervisor smiled at the group of teachers he was talking to. "Before you accuse me of being hyperbolic, I shall simply say she was Carmen Miranda. She had changed part of her own name, do Carmo, to 'Carmen' and used her mother's maiden name, 'Miranda.'

"Upon the advice of President Getulio Vargas, Miss Cunha wisely had financed her personal band that traveled with her to New York. Since she spoke no English, the band leader, Aloysio Oliveira, served her in good stead as an interpreter.

"More important, musical instruments peculiar to the native band or orchestra of Brazil were needed to produce authentic samba rhythm. Drums, shakers, and scrapers comprise a large number of these instruments—which, by the way, are mostly African in origin.

"Just for fun, let me write the names of some Brazilian rhythm-makers on the blackboard. As I do so, I shall describe the instruments. See if you are familiar with any of them:

> The trocano, the jungle drum, is a burned-out tree trunk placed horizontally on a pair of wooden tripods and beaten with mallets.

> The caracaxá is made from a piece of hollow cane filled with coffee beans; the cane is shaken up and down rhythmically.

> The reco-reco consists of a length of notched bamboo; various rhythms are created by rubbing a wand over its traverse notches.

> The cuíca is a tin cylinder with a drumhead through which a resined gut string extends; when it is pulled (by sliding the hand lengthways along the string), the contrivance makes a noise that sounds like the roar or grunt of an animal.

While Ralph Normand was listing the rhythm-makers, the chalk he was using broke into pieces and fell to the floor. Oblivious to chuckles among the audience, Normand calmly brushed the powdery residue from his coat sleeve. Not bothering to pick up the pieces, he selected another piece of chalk from the blackboard's cradle so that he could continue writing.

> The chocalho often is a metal sphere or a double cone containing pellets; it must be played in strict time to the music.

> The cabaça is a large, empty gourd fitted with a handle and covered with a net of seeds; a predominating rhythm is obtained by steadily dropping the gourd on the palm of one hand so that the seeds knock against the shell.

The <u>agogó</u> consists of an anvil-like slab of iron which is struck at intervals with an iron pin.

The supervisor put the chalk he was writing with back into the cradle of the blackboard. As he turned toward his audience, he saw that Vincent Armstrong had a puzzled look hard to ignore.

"Is there anything you would like cleared up, Mr. Armstrong? Feel free to speak."

"Mr. Normand, an acquaintance of mine, who is Portuguese, happens to be a leader of a small band of musicians from Latin America. One of the instruments they use is an a-go-go. I am not sure of the pronunciation. It consists of a double bell, and each bell produces a different sound. The instrument you just described is not the same."

"That is true, Mr. Armstrong. They are not the same. The similarity is in the spelling or form of the words. But there is a difference in the diacritical and accent marks. I'll show you on the blackboard."

Normand got again a piece of chalk from the cradle and wrote: <u>agogó</u> with an accent mark. "This is the instrument I described." Next he wrote <u>agôgô</u> with diacritical marks. "That is the instrument you described."

Armstrong thanked Mr. Normand for the explanation and added: "Another instrument the band uses is a <u>cherquere</u>, which is a rattle with a net around it containing coconut beads."

"I am familiar with it." Normand squinted his eyes as if straining to read dim letters of words impressed far back in his mind. "Let me see. Oh, yes, the instrument is also called <u>piano de cuia</u>...or <u>xaque-xaque</u>. The musicians rub it to make rhythm.

"You can well imagine the plight Carmen Miranda would have been in if she had to depend on a swing band from the United States to play samba music. Undoubtedly her performances were successful because of the assistance of her *Bando da Lua*. With her band from Brazil she was able to score still bigger hits."]

In 1939 Twentieth Century-Fox Studios signed the singer for a part in Down Argentine Way, a musical comedy. As audiences sat listening in motion-picture houses across the country, she warmed their soles, which tapped energetically to her South American rhythm.

Scarcely two years later, in 1941, samba-singing and samba-dancing in That Night in Rio, her second film, Maria do Carmo da Cunha the *cantora*—now Carmen Miranda the movie star—really gave Americans a hotfoot. Her fiery style (vivacity of voice, expression of eye, and liveliness of limb) was expressed by the entertainer as *com moviemento!*—'with movement!'

The Brazilian torch singer had put a fire to Americans' wooden heels. A flaming samba craze steadily scorched polished dance floors from Manhattan to Hollywood. Foot by foot the flaming samba craze leaped higher and higher toward popularity.

This recreational conflagration soared to even greater heights in 1942 when Walt Disney produced *Saludos, Amigos*, or 'Greetings, Friends.' The purpose of the plot was to create good will between the United States and Latin America. In the animated cartoon, one of Disney's characters, a parrot named Zé Carioca, who symbolizes a Brazilian, acquaints a Yankee, Donald Duck, with cultural life in Rio de Janeiro as it exists through song and dance.

Aquarela do Brasil ('Water Color of Brazil')—the musical score of the cartoon, familiar to Americans simply as 'Brazil'—was composed by an outstanding Brazilian songwriter, Ary Barroso. In his youthful years he was inspired to compose sambas in Bahia on the *Baixa do Sapateiro*. Here, on the block-long 'Street of the Cobbler,' Negro shoemakers, pounding nails rhythmically with their hammers, are heard making samba tunes in shops at all hours of the workday.

Meanwhile, during the furor over the samba, nearly a decade was trampled away. Carmen Miranda and Zé Carioca faded from a capricious American public's mind. The samba as a heated fad gradually burned itself out, flaring up here and there like small brush fires fanned by light winds of enthusiasm.

But there is a bit more to the samba story, facts that might have some bearing on the dance's burn out. In Rio de Janeiro *brasileiros* and *brasileiras* did not approve of the way Miss Miranda exhibited the <u>Samba Carioca</u> in the United States of America.

The movement and melody of Brazil's samba are soft, subtle—not harsh or exaggerated as depicted by Carmen. It was not entirely her fault, though. Hermes Pan, the dance director of That Night in Rio, instead of portraying the true samba spirit on the screen, injected Hollywood sensationalism into the Brazilian dance routines.

In one of her numbers Carmen Miranda danced to a fast six-eight tempo. She counted 1-2-3, 1-2-3 while moving the upper part of her body circularly. At the same time she performed waltzlike turns as she did a simple polka step. Today in the standardized samba practiced in the United States is found a similar step-combination, the caixo. The name was derived from the Portuguese word *caixa*, meaning a rectangular container, literally a 'box.'

As a matter of face, the caixo is a reconstructed waltz box-step onto which the Negro shuffle was agglutinated. The caixo has two fundamental variations: the American, a closed box-step danced back and forth in place, and the Brazilian, an open box-step used in making left or right turns.

The particular styling applied to the Brazilian caixo is referred to by dancers as *rolunda* or 'circular' motion. It requires that the shoulders be rolled in a direction opposite to the turn the feet take.

Note that *rolunda* is Spanish, not Portuguese. In the language of Brazil, *rotunda* would be the word for 'circular.' While the use of rolunda in lieu of rotunda is inconsistent, there is little inconsistency in the performance of the motion.

For the most part, however, a swinging style—whereby the shoulders constantly move in the opposite direction of progress—is applied to samba steps. Such styling is called "pendulum motion." A duplication of it can be seen in the movement of a pendulum in a grandfather clock.

Pendulum motion is accomplished by swinging the body to and fro as a unit from the ankles: neither the head nor the trunk are bowed. Simply put, the body remains straight as a pendulum. Also when the feet go forward, the body swings backward; conversely, when the feet go backward, the body swings forward. To further maintain the pendulum effect, the dancers' free arms are poised straight up in the air.

In conjunction with the placement of their arms, the man, securing the woman's right hand in his left, generally holds their hands high in sambaing. However, some of the elaborate hand-and-arm positions which characterized the maxixe are also employed in the samba, especially by exhibition dancers.

An additional characteristic in conformity with samba stylization is its distinctive rhythm. Since the samba is in two-four time, the first beat is counted 1 (equal to a full quarter note), but the second beat is split and counted 2-3 (equal to two eighth notes). A slight bending of the knees on 1 emphasizes the first step. Next, transferring the weight of the body by a smooth shuffle from one foot to the other on 2-3 results in a gentle, lilting rise and fall.

Formerly, before the style was outmoded, a bounce—that is, an energetic down-up action—was associated with the samba. Knees were bent deeply on every beat of the music. The dancers counted "1 and, 2 and, 3 and, 4 and," as they bounced down up, down up, down up, down up, . . . !

Consequently, an unenergetic, inhibited public shied away from the samba. In studio interviews, people frequently complained that they went to a dance for relaxation, not to bounce around the floor like basketballs. Many heavy individuals—in particular, large bosomed women—found the samba embarrassing to do.

It is a shame to see a dance created in a salubrious environment of African-Indian-European-American folk art, waste away from neglect. Perhaps now that the samba has been rid of its exhausting bounce, the dance will recover and become popular once again. Time alone will tell.

BOOK SEVEN

Chapter 42

Some months later at National Dance Studios, Vincent Armstrong, a newspaper tucked under his arm, entered the ballroom where Bert and Alice Craig were practicing advanced dance steps. He sat down on a built-in wall bench to catch his breath, for he had been hurrying to show his two friends an article in The Examiner that he had bought from a newsstand at Stockton and Sutter Streets. In a few seconds with waves of his hand he motioned the Craigs to join him.

Attracted by his waving, they stopped halfway through a fox-trot step. As soon as they approached Vincent, he removed the paper from under his arm, folded the pages over to a predetermined section, and said: "Look. Armond, that hyena, Joanne's husband, was sentenced to nine years in prison, a mere nine years for killing his wife.

"With good behavior he will be eligible for parole in three years. Armond's shyster lawyer is going to appeal his sentence. What unmitigated gall."

Bert commented: "Joanne was such a beautiful dancer. Armond deserved to serve every one of the nine years—in solitary confinement."

Alice echoed: "She was such a lovely girl. Armond deserves to serve every one of the nine years—in sorrow."

Vincent exploded: "She was a precious human being! No number of years in prison can pay for the taking of someone's life. Armond deserves the death penalty—in the gas chamber."

Bert rationalized: "Statistics show that the death penalty does not deter people from killing. In most cases parolees do not kill again."

Vincent retorted: "But they do kill again and—in most cases— again and again. As for statistics, too often they are not collected and classified either completely or correctly. How many millions of people, at least once in their lifetime, have an unexpressed urge to kill but are deterred by fear of the death penalty? Statisticians are not mind readers."

Bert argued: "Society does not have the right to take a person's life. The gas chamber is cruel and unusual punishment."

Vincent responded: "Tell that to a victim who is cruelly murdered. Untold numbers of killers are not afraid to die. Some are even suicidal. Still they are terrified of the gas chamber...the electric chair...the hangman's noose...or any other painful way of being put to death.

"It is cruel and unusual punishment to force society to support and educate a murderer for the rest of his life in the security of a prison. Yet people for their entire lifetime are not secure indoors or outdoors from murderers. Don't overlook the fact that a victim's family and friends are members of society, too."

Bert contended: "The death penalty is capital punishment. It is an unhealthy, irreligious act of revenge."

Vincent objected: "You are using specious words. Sure, revenge is unhealthy for a murderer. And justly so. The word you should be using instead of revenge is therapy. Capital punishment inflicted on a murderer is a healthy, ethical act that is therapeutic for a victim's stricken family."

Alice intervened: "I have a problem with the death penalty, however. There is always a chance an innocent man will be executed."

Vincent conceded: "Yes. That is a possibility. One innocent man out of thousands could be executed. But how many innocent victims would be saved?

"Societies have no qualms about sending millions of innocent young men to die for their country. Societies have no qualms about ordering young men to kill millions of innocent young men from other countries. The young men who kill in wars are called heroes. Good lord! They are never called murderers."

Alice looked confused. "I don't know how to answer that, Vincent. Didn't you tell us you wanted to be a lawyer—a criminal lawyer? What would you do if you had to defend a man guilty of murder?"

Before Vincent could answer Alice, the dance director Chandler Corey came along and said: "Sorry to break in on your conversation.

I need Mr. and Mrs. Craig to put on a demonstration of the fox trot for one of my students. She is having a difficult time visualizing the way she should style some of the fox-trot figures. Come with me."

The Craigs followed the dance director across the ballroom where his student was waiting. Left to himself, Vincent, mulling over Alice's question, searched his mind for an answer, which was shelved somewhere in the past as far back as his days at the University of California.

Vincent's second semester had proved no less frustrating than the first. Faced with the incessant threat of being dropped from the rolls, he had crammed frantically in the hope of doing well on his examinations. If he believed the possibility of not passing a course existed, Vincent resorted to cheating, a desperate measure taken at times by frantic students backed to the wall, despite Cal's timeworn honor system.

Although Vincent had succeeded thus far in warding off disaster, he was still within the range of fire. He managed to obtain excellent grades, but it was a quasi-achievement. The reality was the answers in his test papers were written by rote or copied by peeks into textbooks, which was unfortunate. His problem was he was too analytical to accept questions in examinations at face value. Analysis requires limitless hours and evaluation (without the hindrance of professorial restraints).

A cause of unhappiness for Vincent, a hard blow to his pride was that he falsely acquired superior grades instead of truly acquiring superior knowledge. The collegian's confidence in his intellectual capacity began to waver. Consequently, his ambition to be a criminal lawyer, which towered in Vincent's mind above all normal proportions, wavered to the point of collapsing in utter ruin.

Like the thrust of a battering ram against a weakened wall of an undermined citadel, something Doc. Newton once said when Vincent was in high school could have been a contributing factor in partially demolishing his desire to distinguish himself in the legal profession. Several years were yet to escape the youth before he really felt the impact of Doc. Newton's powerful words.

One blue Monday morning Vincent looked in a magnifying mirror his mother left lying near the bathroom basin. He noticed a previous reddish spot at the edge of his right eyelid had enlarged and become inflamed like a boil. Painfully uncomfortable, he went into the hallway where he telephoned his family physician for an appointment later in the day.

Late that afternoon arriving at Dr. E. Robert Newton's office in the 450 Sutter Building, Vincent settled down on a leather couch in the waiting room and began to thumb through the pages of Esquire Magazine. Before long the receptionist asked Vincent to step into the examination room. Carefully and closely checking out his patient's eyelid, the doctor diagnosed the inflammatory swelling to be a sty.

In a soft-spoken low voice, Dr. Newton instructed a nurse standing by to make ready a sterile package. With efficiency, she set one on top of a metal cabinet as white and clean as her freshly laundered uniform. Unfolding the package, she nodded to the doctor indicating its contents were available for his use.

Dr. Newton, who meanwhile had exchanged brief words with Vincent, stepped over to the cabinet, reached into the package, and removed something quickly. Since the cabinet was situated at an angle to the patient's peripheral vision, he could not observe clearly what the doctor was doing. For some unexplainable reason Vincent had the impression when Dr. Newton came in line with Vincent's direct view that the man was holding a steel nail file.

"Why," Vincent inquired of himself, "is Doc. going to file his fingernails now of all times?" The high-school boy had no time to find an answer to the question.

Out of a clear sky the doctor's arms flew into the air; as he did so, his starched smock rustled. Vincent had the vision of a hovering bird suddenly flapping its wings in flight. The upward movement of the doctor's arms evidently served as a signal to the short but wiry nurse, who had sidled silently behind a chair in which Vincent was seated. She skillfully secured a grip on the patient; her fingers dug into his shoulders, rendering him helpless. A colt entangled in a barbed-wire fence could not have been more vulnerable.

Swooping down on the immobile patient like a California condor, Dr. Newton pecked sharply at Vincent's eyelid with a scalpel the youth had imagined to be a nail file. Despite the excruciating pain he was much too surprised to cry out. After a little while, his pain having subsided, Vincent smiled and jokingly said "that was a sneak attack." Laughing at his patient's remark, the doctor explained he performed the minor surgery in order to evacuate pus from a sac which had formed at the margin of Vincent's eyelid.

Dr. Newton purposely had failed to alert Vincent about the procedure to prevent him from becoming nervous or tense. In the doctor's experience, patients fared badly if they were unrelaxed in anticipation of being hurt during surgery, major as well as minor.

Afterward they seem glad not to have been given a cut-by-cut description of an operation awaiting them under the knife. The doctor was sure Vincent shared the other patient's feelings. Did he not?

Occupied throughout the explanation in thinking what an absolutely blessed relief it was that the lancing of his sty could now be referred to in the past tense, Vincent had not yet decided whether he approved or disapproved of the doctor's method. Apparently his patient's opinion did not concern the doctor, inasmuch as he listened for no reply but immediately brought up another question quite different in nature.

In a casual manner, Dr. Newton asked Vincent, "How are you getting along in school?"

"Dandy, just dandy," was the high-school boy's reply. "I shall be graduating soon. It is my expectation to continue my education at the University of California."

"Good! Wise choice. That institution is my alma mater." Dr. Newton had a far-off look as though he had a longing to relive his days on the university campus. "What do you intend to major in?"

"Prelegal, if there is such a major. I want to be a lawyer. I intend to specialize in criminal law." Vincent could not simply say <u>law</u>. He had to add the adjective <u>criminal</u> so as to describe his ambition in a grand-sounding manner. "I wish that I was through law school, and that I had already passed the bar examinations. I can hardly wait to set up a plush office, win court cases, and go skyrocketing toward the top.

"In fact, I live by uplifting words I have heard from my uncle Walter: 'Whatever a man's target is, he is much better off to be up on the mountain looking down than down in the valley looking up.'

"So my sights are aimed at being a soaring success in the legal profession, as successful as you are in the medical profession. Besides a feeling of fulfillment, I imagine you get great satisfaction from your practice.

"I mean, it must be gratifying to have status in the community, to be respected by everyone. Knowing that you at long last have achieved your life's objective in such a wonderful way should give you a marvelous sense of accomplishment.

"It is a long climb to the mountain top. I certainly would like to find a short cut."

Brushing away a fly which buzzed by one of his protruding ears and lit on his bald pate, the doctor—well along in years—simmered internally: "The nincompoop! What in the holy hell is his hurry. I would willingly trade him my profession, my position, my property for his youth...his vitality, vim, vigor...virility...his handsome head of hair."

With an expression similar to that of a circus clown contracting his painted brow to appear grim, Dr. Newton frowned: strongly marked ridges of wrinkles emerged on his high, pink-skinned forehead. Eyeing his patient somberly, the doctor spoke in a strained voice.

"Uh-uh, I have arrived at my destination, completed my life's journey."

Heavy-hearted, a tired old man, his shoulders slumped as he moped over the fact that his virile, youthful days on earth had been reduced to nothing except memories. Dr. Newton's head was bowed as if his thoughts were too weighty to bear. He began to vocalize with increased softness.

"Now, day by day, I am growing older and older waiting around to die."

Sympathizing with the aging medical man, Vincent felt sick at heart to see him in such a sad state. Despite Vincent's youth, he could read lines of deep dejection written on the man's face. It was inconceivable that somebody like Dr. Newton, who had attained an enviable lifetime goal, could be so unhappy.

"Sorry, but I'm afraid I don't understand," the youth admitted.

"You see, Vincent," the doctor heaved a sigh to regain strength to speak, "since I rose to my present position in life—a lofty standing from your point of view—I have become most conscious of a tragic thing: the fleetness of one's existence. Let me show you how limited is the gamut of life, how short is the interval between a human being's entering the world and exiting it."

Walking over to a window that was stuck at a slant between the jambs, Dr. Newton forcefully pushed it open as wide as possible. An invigorating breeze came rushing into the room. After a fast and furious struggle, he slammed the aslant window closed, shutting out the fresh air.

Chapter 43

"Vincent, open a window, it's stuffy in here," insisted one of the new teachers with whom he was practicing dance steps. She was a talented, vivacious young lady, Miss Marian Mills, who stood far above the rest at National Dance Studios. Some of the teachers would exclaim in admiration that she digested hard figures almost as fast as dance directors dished them out, while other teachers in envy said she did a great job of faking figures.

Although Miss Mills denied she had received dancing instructions elsewhere, that she had was apparent. She just turned seventeen at her last birthday. But she claimed to be nineteen, another outright fib. The motivation behind the first falsehood was not completely transparent, yet the purpose of the second was perfectly clear.

Studio policy prohibited the hiring of minors, for they could not be manacled with legal instruments, contracts which obligated personnel to remain at National Dance Studios no less than twelve months. In the event dissatisfied individuals decided to quit before the stipulated time, they had to pay a penalty of two hundred dollars. To secure the agreement, new employees (usually trainees) were required to sign a promissory note payable on demand.

Capricious, Marian thrived on flirtations; she had the lynx's wild look and furtive ways. She was either watching or stalking manly prey. Marian's tawny complexion—acquired after hours of basking in the sun at the beach—was becoming. Neatly clipped and trimmed, her reddish-brown hair went well with her small features. The same as the orbs of a cat, at night, her glaucous eyes had the reflective surface of a moonlit lake. Her dancing was animalistically uninhibited. She put every inch of her lean, lithe self into each movement.

Dreading social ostracism and disliking being obvious in their attentions to the tempting, delicious morsel of femininity, men at the studio pretended to ignore Marian, for social mores prohibit a display of the sexual appetite. When the group of teachers worked on the samba, society's enforced hypocrisy notwithstanding, every so often a hungry hunter left the pack and pursued her, like a wolf chasing the flesh of game. Should anyone happen to glance in their direction, Marian, grasped tightly by her eager partner, would be seen performing with him time and time again the *debaixo-rolunda*, a samba step danced in closed position with circular body motion.

Obviously she was in great demand as a dancing partner by the men among the group of teachers. Should she be available, Vincent enjoyed practicing with Marian on occasion in spite of the fact that there was no chemistry of sex between them. However, Bert Craig's sexual chemical reaction to her evidently was different, for he jumped at every opportunity to practice with Marian and do the *debaixo-rolunda*. Alice seemingly was not aware of her husband's fondness for that samba step. He rarely danced it with his wife.

Always anxious to perfect her dancing, Alice asked Vincent to practice with her that afternoon. He would have liked to, but he was booked the next hour; he had to rest and get in the proper frame of mind for his student. She was physically handicapped, which made her difficult to work with.

Vincent's student, Mrs. Steiner, was a fine woman. It was a pathetic picture to see her hobble as she walked, struggling to keep her balance yet retain her dignity. She suffered from partial paralysis due to an injury received at birth. Nevertheless, she had the will power to try to improve her condition by learning to dance.

At first, Vincent did his best to make the lessons easy and fun. He quickly discovered it was not easy or fun for her to dance, let alone move in all directions. After much coaxing and exhausting patience, he got her to dance little by little from side to side as well as forward and backward. Unfortunately, she stumbled several times, almost losing her balance. Discouraged, her will power weakened, she engaged in negative thinking.

It was heartrending to hear the woman say over and over: "I can't. I'll never be able to walk right."

After the first lesson, when Vincent left the studio for the day, his nerves were on edge. He stopped in at a Powell Street cocktail lounge and ordered a beer. Saddened by Mrs. Steiner's condition, he shed a tear in his beer.

Getting hold of himself, he made up his mind he was going to help her. How? He did not know, because Mrs. Steiner told him the doctors had given up on her. In the years to come, they speculated she would be lucky to be able to walk at all.

Mrs. Steiner's physical handicap continued to occupy Vincent's mind until her next lesson. As he led her into the ballroom, he said: "You know, I've been thinking about your difficulty in changing directions on the dance floor.

"From now on, I forbid you to entertain any negative thoughts such as 'I won't—I can't' or anything that even intimates you are unable to follow my instructions. In addition, we are not going to worry about your stumbling occasionally. We will go on dancing as if that never happened. Okay...follow me. Don't lean. You throw yourself off balance."

Although he had no intention of being unkind, to his regret Vincent's voice was stern; the tone of which reminded him of his basic-training days in the army. The first sergeant would bark orders to the privates with sternness as he stood straight as a flagpole. Private Armstrong disliked the sergeant's stern tone yet admired his excellent posture. Later in civilian life Vincent attempted to impose it on himself as well as others for good health.

"Mrs. Steiner, a very important thing that we must make a habit of, is proper posture. It not only will improve your appearance when you are dancing, but it also will improve your appearance when you are walking.

"Now, straighten up. Pull back your shoulders. Your head should be held high as though raised by inflated balloons attached with string to your ears. Avoid sticking out your chin. Stand a wee bit straighter."

She did what he instructed. "That's it!" He praised her: "Good. I'm proud of you;. Be sure not to stick out your rear. Just remember, whenever you feel your rear is protruding, tuck it in." To please Vincent she exerted extra effort not to protrude her buttocks while they danced.

Pleased with her efforts, Vincent said: "You are doing well. But we must not lose ground. Will you continue to take the positive approach and give me one hundred percent cooperation? I expect an affirmative answer."

"I'll try. Yes. I shall do my best." The woman's words did not match her mood. Instead of looking enthusiastic she looked forlorn.

Vincent wanted to know what was bothering the woman. Was he being too hard on her? Was she unhappy about the dancing lessons?

She replied she liked the lessons. She appreciated the exactness of his instructions. Her source of unhappiness was personal...too painful to talk about...too difficult to deal with. The hour had expired, and she left before Vincent could question Mrs. Steiner further.

The next day the Studio was bustling with excitement. An annual party for the students and their guests was in progress. The teaching staff had planned an entertainment. Most of the acts were ordinary. A few, however, are worth mentioning, which you now shall see.

Marian Mills opened the entertainment with a belly dance, or to state it in a classic manner, an abdominal dance. She was costumed in a beaded bra and a chiffon skirt supported by a satin hip-band. She had a veil draped over her head and shoulders and bangles on her wrists and ankles. Her waist was exposed and her navel bared.

She stood still yet strange as it seems every muscle in her body vibrated rhythmically to exotic background music. With each of the girl's vibrations, the men in the audience inched closer to the edge of their seats so that they would not lose sight of a single one of Marian's marvelous muscular movements.

Another entertainment presented was a pantomime performed while a concealed phonograph reproduced an aria from the opera "The Barber of Seville." Bert Craig's face was smeared with whipped cream, supposedly shaving lather. He had more whipped cream around his lips than most boys lick off theirs in a lifetime.

The barber (one of the teachers playing the part of Figaro) with a rubber razor hacked away imaginary whiskers from under Bert's chin. It is a wonder his throat was not cut from ear to ear, even though there was not a sharp edge on the razor. The audience broke out in laughter when he stuck out his tongue, licked the whipped cream from his lips and rubbed his stomach as he rolled his eyes in ecstasy.

The act that gave the audience the biggest laugh was put together by Alice Craig and Ralph Normand, the tallest individual at National Dance Studios. In his shoes he stood well over six feet tall. In her high heels she stood a little over five feet. They danced their version of the Jarabe Tapatío, national dance of Mexico.

Ralph was dressed in a colorful, flared skirt as China Pablana, a legendary princess. Alice was dressed as a *vaquero*, a Mexican cow-boy; she wore a big mustache and a huge *sombrero*; a holster on her leather belt contained a toy *pistolet* loaded with caps. Ralph got the idea for Alice's character from the Jarabe Tapatío, which was very popular with horsemen (*charros*) in the state of Jalisco, West central Mexico. Although the Jarabe Tapatío is Mexico's national dance, the true character and name of Jarabe Tapatío seems to be in question. Nevertheless, as early as 1920 it ranked high in popularity among rodeo and theatrical performers.

Characteristically the Jarabe Tapatío is a flirtatious courtship dance. The man (acted by Alice) holds his hands behind his back. And the woman (acted by Ralph) holds on to her skirt with both hands, lifting it coquettishly to reveal the lace of her petticoat.

The audience could not stop laughing as they watched Alice and Ralph do the Jarabe Tapatío. A dwarf dancing with a giant would not have been more amusing. As was rehearsed, a Chinese student, small in stature, strenuously pushed a heavy chair in front of the two dancers. Alice stepped up onto the chair and led Ralph into some underarm turns in time to the music.

While he was turning, his arm brushed by her mustache causing it to fall on a rug previously planted upon the floor. Alice nonchalantly jumped off the chair and stooped down to retrieve the mustache. Hidden behind a curtain, the Chinese student repeatedly jerked a cord attached to the rug. With each jerk of the cord the rug moved just enough to keep the mustache out of Alice's reach.

In disgust she removed her *pistolet* from her holster, pointed at the mustache and fired several caps. The mustache did not move anymore. She picked it up, replaced the mustache on her upper lip and continued dancing as if nothing had happened. The laughter of the audience turned thunderous. At the end of their act Alice and Normand received a round of applause which was more thunderous than the laughter.

On a serious note, we must not overlook Chandler Corey's wonderful exhibition of a Dynamic Tango. Assisted by Mrs. Corey, his dancing partner and choreographer, Chandler's performance was a masterpiece in motion.

There were rumors the Coreys would not be at National Dance Studios much longer. The table talk was that a producer was so impressed with the Coreys' accomplishments in the art of exhibition ballroom dances, he offered the husband-and-wife team a starring spot in a Broadway revue.

Chapter 44

The week after the entertainment, Bert Craig and Vincent Armstrong were having a conversation in the ballroom while waiting for their students to arrive. Bert asked his friend: "Tell me, Vince, how are you getting along with Mrs. Steiner? With her physical handicap, it must be tough trying to teach her to dance."

"I find it a challenge teaching her. Step by step she slowly is making progress. The woman has a stout heart. She tries very hard to follow my instructions. Considering her physical . . . Here she comes now. The hour is about to start, Bert. I'll talk to you later."

Vincent greeted his student: "Good afternoon, Mrs. Steiner. You are ten minutes early. But let's start anyway. At your last lesson we worked on posture. Today we shall work on something else."

Groping for ways to help her, he thought of something he learned in a course on philosophy at college. Plato, an ancient Greek philosopher theorized that reality in the universe is the ideal, infinite forms of perfection. And the finite forms of the world—imperfect in varying degrees—are merely transitory reflections of the universal ideal.

"Mrs. Steiner, bear in mind that none of us can do anything perfectly. Not all human beings walk perfectly, no matter how sound their legs may be. The best we can do is strive for perfection. So, in learning dance steps, that should be your goal.

"In my demonstrations I as a professional show you ideal ways to execute dance steps. It should be your goal to do the steps as perfectly as I. More important, think in terms of dancing—not walking. Learn to execute dance steps well. Your execution will improve more and more if you consistently mimic my movements. The old saying that practice makes perfect is as true today as it was yesterday."

Vincent's psychology proved practical. During the lesson Mrs. Steiner concentrated on her dancing (not on her walking). She lost her balance a bit less and missed her steps a bit less. Nevertheless, she did not appear one bit pleased with herself. Plagued by an inferiority complex, the woman insisted she was too unattractive to look good on a dance floor.

Vincent insisted she was attractive, for indeed she was. Her silvery black hair and shiny dark eyes were alluring. She had a beautiful figure; her hips and breasts were well-formed. While they were dancing chest to chest, Vincent felt the firmness of her bosom and nipples which in his mind he compared to two Bing cherries.

"Mrs. Steiner, for a woman of your years (he estimated her to be in her early thirties), you have a marvelous figure. It is the type many young girls envy. You would be surprised how many wear falsies to create the illusion that their breasts are full and lovely...as yours."

She blushed and said: "They are too big. You are making fun of me."

"Absolutely not!" Vincent replied emphatically to convince the woman. "Why should I make fun of you? You ought to know by now that I respect you very much."

Still blushing, Mrs. Steiner offered an answer which she was ashamed of. "There was a person in my life who used to torment me. He would say I am shaped like a Jersey cow. I heard him say it so often and so long, I began to wonder if it was true."

"You shouldn't have wondered about it at all. I don't mean to pry. But who could ever have said anything insulting like that to you?"

"It is really personal, Mr. Armstrong. If I tell you, promise not to repeat it to a soul." (He promised.) "Well, I am divorced. I was married about nine years. My husband was the one who said nasty things about my body."

"I have heard about men like that, Mrs. Steiner. They hate their wives for some irrational reason. They get pleasure and a feeling of superiority from tormenting and belittling their wives. Fearful of losing you, your husband did not want you to be aware of your loveliness. Your breasts must be a delightful handful."

Resisting an impulse to place her arms across her bosom, she spoke sternly because of shyness. "I wish you wouldn't refer to my body. I find it embarrassing."

Vincent was sure he had gained enough of her confidence that he could speak frankly to the woman. "Mrs. Steiner, I hope you are not a prude."

"I hope I am not either. If you knew how I was brought up, you might understand."

"Might understand." Vincent repeated her words in a questioning tone. By his repeating the woman's last two words, she was cued to offer an explanation.

"You should understand, Mr. Armstrong, my mother and father are fanatically religious. I had to wear dresses with long sleeves and long skirts. They never allowed me to go dancing or to go on picnics with boys. My parents chose my husband for me because he is of the same religion as theirs. I wasn't terribly in love with him.

"I was unhappy. I had spent a secluded childhood. If I overslept or came home late from school, my father would call me a sinner and chastise me with quotations from the bible. My life was too depressing. Marriage presented an opportunity, a means of escape to a better life. But I was sadly mistaken."

"I understand, Mrs. Steiner. You jumped from the frying pan into the fire. It is a frightful thing to be married to an abusive husband. Did he beat you often?"

"He never beat me. He said nasty things to me. He called me a slut...a female dog!" The woman started to cry.

"Please don't cry, Mrs. Steiner." Vincent tried to cheer her up. "When I was in grammar school, if a bully called me and my playmates bad names, we would say 'sticks and stones may break our bones but names will never hurt us.' Sometimes children can be less thin-skinned than adults."

Mrs. Steiner held back her tears and forced herself to smile. "When I was a little girl, I used to say 'sticks and stones,' too. After my son was born—he is eight years old now—I turned a deaf ear to my husband's name calling. It was intolerable. Still I learned to live with it. But my husband wasn't satisfied with heaping insults on me. He did much worse."

"What did he do?" (She failed to answer.) Vincent could not imagine what Mrs. Steiner's husband might be capable of. Again Vincent asked, "What did he do?"

"I can't tell you. It is too horrible to talk about." The woman's lips were trembling.

Vincent strained to control himself from pressing the woman for an answer. He feared that if he pressed her too hard, she would clam up and never confide in him again. To put her at ease, he changed the subject.

"Mrs. Steiner, next week National Dance Studios is going to have a special dance party for our students. I would like you to attend. It will be an excellent occasion for you to get some experience dancing with others."

"Mr. Armstrong, I would love to go to the party. But I am afraid. What if they play a rumba or a samba. The dances I am comfortable with are the fox trot and the waltz. The only step I do fairly well is the box."

"Don't worry, Mrs. Steiner. You are a better dancer than you realize. The box step is a basic for all ballroom dances. Regardless of which one it is, in doing the box step, pretend you are working on a square (wooden) box:

> the box step can be sawed in half and moved straight ahead or side to side;
>
> the box step can be turned in place or in circles around the perimeter of a room;
>
> the box step can be moved quickly or slowly in accordance with the time and measures;
>
> the box step can be painted with shades of color in body motions or in hand movements.

"Now, Mrs. Steiner, do a box step for me. Start in first position...feet together. Step back on your right foot; step to the side on your left foot; bring your right foot up to your left foot; step forward on your left foot; step to the side on your right foot; bring your left foot up to your right foot. Great! You have just completed a perfect square."

Having performed a box step without once losing her balance or stumbling, Mrs. Steiner was delighted in spite of her former forlorn feelings. Her eyes glistened with dew and her lips formed a big smile.

"When the music starts," Vincent instructed, "we shall perform box steps in different ways I mentioned that a square box can be worked on. In some dances, of course, a box may be rectangular. Never mind what kind of dance the music calls for. Loosen up. Let yourself perform naturally."

Mrs. Steiner relaxed and followed Vincent's instructions as best she could within the capabilities of her physical handicap. She lengthened and shortened her steps in good measure. She stepped surefootedly in the directions she was led. She turned in place and circled in the line of dance smoothly. She moved her body and hands in natural nuances indicative of her own potential style. She danced slowly and quickly in time to the music. She was in a state of euphoria.

Vincent, who could no longer curb his curiosity, decided the time was ripe to question the woman about whatever her husband might have done that horrified her. "Mrs. Steiner, isn't it wonderful to relax your body and move freely? You not only dance better, you walk better." (She nodded her head in agreement.)

"If only you could allow yourself to reveal your disturbing personal experience instead of concealing it so that it eats at your insides, I am sure you will also feel better. Wouldn't it be wonderful to relax your mind as well as your body?"

Vincent's timing turned out to be fruitful. Mrs. Steiner was in such a good mood, she was too mellow to resist confiding in him. Besides, she had no doubts he could be trusted. Seeing there were many people in the ballroom, she said: "Can we go to another place to talk? I am afraid of being overheard."

Not wasting a minute, Vincent took the woman by the arm and escorted her upstairs to the second floor. They went into one of the small studios where they could converse in private. Between her sighs and sobs, Vincent digested piecemeal bitter tidbits of the circumstances that had resulted in Mrs. Steiner divorcing her husband.

Almost eighteen months before her divorce on a bright sunny Saturday, Mary Bryant, a friend of Mrs. Steiner's, telephoned her suggesting they spend the afternoon in Golden Gate Park and also visit the Oriental Tea Garden. They had a brief conversation about the name, which sounds strange to some San Franciscans. Shamefully, because of war hysteria, in 1942 the original name was changed. They hoped before long the garden would be renamed the Japanese Tea Garden.

The two women habitually spent Saturday afternoons on shopping sprees or roaming about the city without their husbands. Since Mary had an automobile, as usual she picked up Mrs. Steiner at her home. From there Mary drove herself and her passenger toward Golden Gate Park. On their way, along Fulton Street, the automobile suddenly stopped running near Masonic Avenue. Mary could not start the motor again.

Moaning over their bad luck, the women exited the automobile.

After Mary locked the doors, they walked up a block-long hill to the campus of the University of San Francisco. In the university library Mrs. Bryant was permitted to use a telephone to call her husband.

At Mary's request he came to get Mrs. Steiner and her in his automobile. And he arranged for hers to be towed to a gas station. The two women, having lost interest in their planned afternoon outing, Mr. Bryant's wife asked her husband to drive Mrs. Steiner home.

So she arrived early, which was unusual because she always came home late on Saturday afternoon. Most of the time Mr. Steiner would be out on the weekend, usually playing golf. Mrs. Steiner's little boy would be at a movie with her next-door neighbor or playing with the neighbor's children in her backyard. Therefore, Mrs. Steiner did not expect anyone to be in the house.

As she walked through the front room, she was startled to hear her seven-year-old son screaming: "Daddy, don't do that! Please! I can't stand it! Stop it, Daddy! Stop it! You are hurting me!"

Mrs. Steiner rushed to a bathroom where the screams were coming from. She flung open the door to find her son hunched over the toilet stool. His knee breeches were lowered to his ankles. Blood was trickling down the back of his leg. The boy's father stood straddled over him unnaturally the way a bull might mount a calf.

Never had she seen a wilder, more beastly expression on caged animals at Fleischacker Zoo that she saw on her husband's face. Mrs. Steiner had a blurry picture of pulling her son away from his father and running to get her husband's hunting rifle.

Fortunately—or unfortunately, who is to judge?—it was unloaded. She dropped the rifle and ran into the kitchen. Followed by her husband, she grabbed a bread knife. Waving it wildly like a mad woman in a nightmare, she yelled at him, "Leave this house immediately, or I'll kill you!"

Now that Vincent heard the reason why she was unhappy, he was sort of sorry he asked her for an explanation. He felt as though he had trespassed on private property, personal memories of another person. But he dared not let her know how upsetting the tragic incident was to him. He reassured her it was something nobody could pry loose from him with steel tools.

Vincent praised Mrs. Steiner, saying that she was a courageous woman, very strong in character to have endured such a horrendous experience. Some other woman probably would have lost her mind. For her son's sake as well as her own she had to erase the tragedy from her thoughts. If not, her son could suffer as a consequence.

Mrs. Steiner cried a little and said: "I don't know why I told you. I shouldn't burden you with my problem."

Assuring her it was no burden, he scolded the woman for entertaining the thought. She promised not to do so again. Mrs. Steiner realized she had to defeat the monster who caused her unhappiness. The task seemed impossible.

Her husband had been granted visitation rights by the court. She was terrified every time he came to see the boy. Vincent failed to understand how her husband was granted visitation rights. Mrs. Steiner explained she tried to prevent it. But her son was too frightened to testify. Besides, Mr. Steiner hired a high-priced lawyer who was too ruthless and slick for Mrs. Steiner's lawyer, a timid soul. The judge appeared contemptuous of him.

The judge could see her son was frozen with fear. Yet he turned a blind eye to that glaring fact; he cited some legal precedent for his decision, which was over her head. What made matters worse, he smiled at her husband's lawyer and scowled at hers. After the case was dismissed, both lawyers shook hands and had a hearty laugh, at the woman's expense.

Vincent felt the woman's pain. It hurt to be wounded by the laws of the land which are supposed to protect a citizen from being harmed by injustice. To achieve justice, should not judges go beyond the letter of the law knowing that lawyers use it for status and silver regardless of right or wrong—innocence or guilt?

Some years ago when Vincent, a mere prelegal major, had the audacity to argue about jurisprudence with students from California's Boalt Hall School of Law in Berkeley, they would say, "We are a nation of laws. The law of our land is just. It must be obeyed!"

In rebuttal, Vincent would say, "Nazi Germany is a nation of laws. Are they just? Certainly they are obeyed."

His expectations crushed, he stood unsteadily on the precipice of giving up his ambition to become a lawyer, a criminal lawyer no less. World War II pushed Vincent over the edge. While still a student at the University of California, he was drafted into the United States Army.

Chapter 45

The following in certain instances is paraphrased from a unit history of the 276th Engineer Combat Battalion. On a specified date Vincent Armstrong had appeared at a local induction center. He was processed along with several other San Franciscans. The literate ones were separated from the illiterate ones into groups that were presumed to be educated (?).

Stripped to the skin, the inductees were given physical examinations not quite as rapidly as automobile parts are inspected on an assembly line. The men who passed inspection were selected for general service. That is, they were sworn in as privates in the United States Army.

One of the most important steps in processing recruits was the Army General Classification Test, abbreviated AGCT. It was erroneously called an I.Q. Test and was relied upon by too many officers as a foolproof way of determining the intelligence and ability of troops under their command.

Next the recruits received a Radio Aptitude Test in which they listened to several sounds seemingly the same. The recruits were instructed to distinguish between sounds that were the same and sounds that were not the same. Can you believe it! The men who were knowledgeable about radio code made the wrong distinctions between the sounds, whereas the men who had no knowledge about radio code made the correct distinctions between the sounds.

Each recruit was handed an unsealed envelope containing Form 20 (his test scores and statistical data). Written on the envelopes was the instruction "Keep it closed," which the recruits slyly ignored. They had yet to learn obedience.

Vincent along with the rest of the recruits were lined up in another area for oral interviews. Good talkers thought they scored points with a soft-spoken interviewer. They were misled into thinking they would be placed in soft positions. Referring to their Form 20s and guided by a number of government-issued manuals, he dutifully followed army regulations and placed the men in hard occupations that had incomprehensible relationships to their prior occupations.

What else is different? Since time immemorial the military mentality often has confused the civilian's mind. Prelegal student Vincent Armstrong—who did not know a rifle from a revolver or a shovel from a scoop—was assigned as a combat engineer somewhere in Oklahoma.

Pursuant to the authority contained in Section I, General Order Number 108, Headquarters Third Army, Fort Sam Houston, Texas, dated October 2nd, 1943, the 276th Engineer Combat Battalion was activated at 12:01 A.M. of October 25th, 1943. On that date and time the Battalion's cadre—four officers and sixty-three enlisted men—arrived in Oklahoma at Camp Gruber, unaffectionately spoken of by the ranks as "Camp Gruesome."

Vincent Armstrong and other raw recruits arrived in Oklahoma shortly after the Battalion was activated. During MTP, commonly called basic training, which had to be completed in thirteen weeks, the recruits were quick to learn the name "Camp Gruesome" whether spoken in jest or not was most appropriate.

With the swiftness of a whirlwind MTP went round and round. It involved rounds of manual of arms, close-order and extended-order drills, hikes and marches, reveille and retreat formations; classes in first aid, cleaning...care...and firing of a rifle, military courtesy, articles of war, venereal disease, tools and equipment, rigging, demolitions, map reading, interior guard, defense versus mechanized attack, aircraft recognition, bridge building, field fortifications and camouflage.

Work in the field on fortifications was at times gruesomely back breaking. Under simulated battlefield conditions the 276th Engineer Battalion man by man crawled snakelike on their bellies over rugged Oklahoma terrain. The recruits were ordered to dig foxholes in one breath and in the next breath they were ordered to refill the foxholes, which appeared to be an exercise in futility.

Eventually the recruits were ordered to stop refilling the holes; instead, they were ordered to start crawling into the holes. Almost without warning when tanks came from out of nowhere and rolled over their foxholes, the recruits wished they had dug deeper. Despite loose dirt that flew into their faces, they at last were able to see the point of field fortifications.

After completion of basic training the Battalion went to Tennessee on maneuvers, a large-scale military exercise simulating the conditions of actual combat. A deadly disaster occurred that alerted the men to the reality they were not just playing at being soldiers: maneuvers was a dangerous warlike game.

Rainy weather in northern Tennessee on the Cumberland River increased the danger of maneuvers tenfold. A raft capsized ferrying troops from another engineering unit across the rain-swelled river. Twenty-one enlisted men were drowned. A major from the 276th Engineer Combat Battalion was rushed to the area with a detail of men to drag the river for the bodies.

Although hardened by rough training, the troops were demoralized over the deaths. Still, young men—aged overnight—were so hardened that the morale of the Battalion was uplifted by light-hearted happenings. On 27 May 1944, 0900, the combat engineers were cheered up by a blessed event. Beulah, the battalion mascot, gave birth to ten puppies—five females and five males.

As soon as they were old enough to do close-order drill, the pups were to be distributed among the platoons. However, some human hound pupnapped Beulah's puppies. Heartbroken, she deserted the 276th outfit. She hid and never returned. She feared she would be court-marshaled.

On the evening of October 21st, 1944, the 276th Engineer Combat Battalion entrained for the Port of Embarkation to be processed for overseas duty. Censorship was strict. Any soldier who did not take the censorship seriously would be making a big mistake. By the way of example, two sergeants lost their stripes and were demoted to buck privates because they thoughtlessly dropped uncensored letters into a mailbox.

On the morning of October 24th, 1944, the Battalion arrived at Camp Shanks in New York. The men's expectations that they would be given passes to visit the City were not fulfilled. Telegraph or telephone communication with relatives or friends in New York or anyplace else was out of the question. The 276th Engineer Combat Battalion was about to embark on a ship bound for the European Theatre of Operations. The battalion commander heeded the warning "Loose lips can sink a ship."

On October 28th the Battalion was put on ALERT! All companies were restricted to their barracks. Neither noncoms nor commissioned officers were permitted to leave their quarters; nor were they permitted to go to the post exchange for any reason. The next night the servicemen were lined up by roster with Headquarters (H) Company in the lead. They were equipped to the man with gas masks, full field packs, duffle bags, overcoats, and rifles. Everybody's helmet was numbered with chalk to insure loading on the gangplank proceeded without a hitch.

The 276th Engineer Combat Battalion boarded a victory ship, the S. S. Exchequer. The Battalion was part of a large convoy: Task Force 0480C which consisted of twenty-three vessels. The convoy was escorted by destroyers across the Atlantic Ocean.

On November 9th the convoy started to disperse. Some ships sailed in a northerly direction. The scuttlebutt was that they were headed for the seaport of Glasgow, a royal burgh in south-central Scotland. The remainder of the convoy sailed in the direction of England. Around noon the S. S. Exchequer pulled alongside a pier in the harbor of Plymouth, city and county borough in north-west England.

At dusk the 276th Engineer Combat Battalion disembarked from the ship. A short distance from the harbor the troops boarded a train that took them to Yeovil Junction. A sign indicated their destination was four miles away. With full field packs on their backs the men marched double time in a foggy night to Yeovil, municipal borough, county of Somersetshire, in south-west England. A small town, Yeovil's population was well under twenty-four thousand.

The 276th engineers were lodged in billets. Some were billeted in halls, some in churches, some in old rooming houses scattered throughout the town. Most were billeted in a hutment, military camp where we find Vincent Armstrong and others stretched out on their bunks. Dead tired, they were prepared for a good night's sleep.

One of the men complained to Vincent that another man bunked next to him was a god-damn, loud snorer. The complainer demanded that the snorer wait until he (the complainer) was sound asleep before the snorer himself fell asleep. To keep peace, Vincent persuaded the snorer to stay awake a while longer.

The complainer mumbled thanks to Vincent and immediately went to sleep. Vincent's bold persuasive deed backfired. The complainer could have won a medal for being the world's loudest snorer. Vincent held his hands over his ears the rest of the night to deaden the eardrum-bursting noise made by the complainer as well as the snorer. At times Vincent dozed off only to be awakened by the sound of two lumberjacks cutting a log with a buzz saw.

Ultimately Vincent fell asleep from sheer exhaustion. He did not wake up until noon the next day. In the evening, at liberty to leave the hutment, he decided to investigate Yeovil. As he walked through the town, he found there were many two- and three-story houses. They were built up against one another.

He wondered if the houses shared common walls. The sidewalks and street were so narrow that the houses, which abutted on the pavement, blocked the views at the corners. Fortunately traffic was not heavy, for whenever two vehicles entered the blind intersections, there would be a loud screeching of brakes frequently followed by the crash of metal meeting metal.

Why the steering wheel on cars in America is on the driver's side at the left and the steering wheel on cars in Britain is on the driver's side at the right is an enigma. Puzzled or not, the American soldiers had to become familiar with Britain's strange customs and small change. They learned it was not impractical to drive on the left side of the road but impossible to become acquainted with the shilling and pence.

Vincent Armstrong was no exception. He had to exchange his dollars and pennies for shillings and pence, if he wanted to date a girl or buy a drink in Yeovil. In all probability he overpaid for both since he figuratively failed to fathom the difference between shilling and pence and steak and potatoes.

Not knowing there were forty-three pubs to choose from, Vincent entered the first pub he came to. It is best described as a hole in the wall where a bearded bloke assisted by a barmaid served large mugs of bitters (alcoholic liquor) to the male drinkers and small glasses of stout (dark, sweet brew) to the female drinkers.

Most of the women were too old for Vincent's taste. Spotting a woman close to his age at the bar crowded with servicemen, he politely pushed past the crowd to be within speaking distance of her. Upon reaching the bar, he ordered a mug of bitters.

As Vincent sipped his bitters, he occasionally glanced in the younger woman's direction. He could see that she was alone. By now they made eye contact. She appeared to be friendly so he ordered a glass of stout for her which she seemed pleased to accept.

After consuming a few drinks, they engaged in idle talk. Curious about her marital status, Vincent asked if the war had widowed the women in the pub. It was obvious several were unescorted. Smiling she said she was single. Most of the old dames in the pub were married. Only a couple were with their husbands. To bring home the point, she quoted an English parody:

Old father Hubbard went to the cupboard
To get himself a hankey,
But when he got there the cupboard was bare,
And so was his wife, with a Yankee.

The hot parody melted the social ice. Vincent and the young woman, her name was Judy London, drowned their inhibitions in drink. She said nothing. He said nothing. Words were not needed to express their desire for sex. It was understood. They left the pub to fulfill their desires.

Vincent was in the dark as to where to go with the woman. Coming out of the warm pub into a damp, chilly night, they were quickly chilled to the bone. Judy suggested they go to one of the air-raid shelters. Nobody would be there unless buzz bombs attacked the town.

They hurried to an air-raid shelter which was not too far away. The shelter was constructed of reinforced concrete. The open flight of stairs they descended to the bottom of the shelter was concrete. The floor was concrete. The built-in benches were concrete.

Vincent unbuckled his belt, dropped his pants, placed the young woman on a bench, lifted up her dress, and pulled down her bloomers. When their bare skin came in contact with the concrete bench, they started to shiver and shake. He was too cold to have an erection, she was too cold to spread her legs. The heatless shelter was as cold as a freezer—and drafty.

Their passion cooled, they realized sex was impossible under such freezing conditions. They dressed and deserted the air-raid shelter. Vincent walked Judy to a bus stop. She did not live in Yeovil. His mind no longer on sex, he noticed Judy was shabbily dressed. Feeling sorry for her because he imagined she was poor, he reached into his pocket and removed a handful of shillings.

Since Vincent was confused by the denomination of English coins, he stuck out his hand so she could take what she needed for bus fare. To his astonishment, she tilted his hand, pouring all his shillings onto her hand. Judy waved farewell to Vincent and boarded the bus.

Chapter 46

While at Yeovil the 276th Engineer Combat Battalion was waiting for the arrival of additional equipment. As usual, training continued. Qualified men attended nearby schools to learn how to assemble prefabricated, interchangeable, steel truss panels of Bailey bridges, designed by Sir Donald Bailey, a British engineer.

The battalion as a whole received instructions in deactivating land mines and booby traps. After a twenty-mile hike with full field packs, the men lined up in formation at the military encampment. The command "at ease" was given to the men, yet they were not dismissed.

Standing well over six feet tall, a husky lieutenant, with a huge firearm in his holster at his side, addressed the battalion. He spoke about army regulations and discipline. They were to be strictly enforced in a war zone. Anyone who did not comply with regulations or who was lax in discipline would be severely punished.

The lieutenant's admonition somewhat surprised Vincent. He always respected army regulations and adhered to military discipline. As far as he could determine, the men in the battalion did their best to be obedient and disciplined soldiers. Perhaps some needed to be reminded that was most important in a war zone.

Menacingly the lieutenant placed his hand over his holster and exclaimed in a thunderous voice: "When you are on the battlefield, if you value your life, in an offensive action, go straight forward toward the enemy. Should you retreat because of deadly fire and run in the opposite direction, you will be shot!"

Vincent stared at the lieutenant in utter disbelief. He was threatening American youths who were prepared to save the world for democracy and rid the world of the nazi-fascist scourge. Vincent had the impression only German officers threatened soldiers under their command with death should they flee for their lives against insurmountable odds on the field of battle.

He wondered if a German soldier died heroically advancing toward an enemy would the German go to heaven? Or if an American soldier was shot retreating cowardly from certain death, when engaged in battle with an enemy, would the American go to hell? Maybe it would be the other way around. It was too confusing for a mere mortal. A great God would have to sort out the confusion he created.

Vincent's thoughts were interrupted when an orderly approached the lieutenant informing the officer that Private Armstrong in B Company was wanted at battalion headquarters at once. The lieutenant singled out Vincent and ordered him to report to h.q. on the double. Dismissed, he broke ranks and rushed to the headquarters hut where he was in for the shock of his life.

Waiting for Vincent to his amazement was Judy London who greeted him with an electrifying wet kiss. She was not dressed poorly like the cockney barfly he had met in a pub. Unbelievably she was dressed richly like a queen bee—like the Queen of England! She began to chatter about how much she missed Vincent, as though they were childhood sweethearts.

His senses were benumbed. His ears numb, he did not hear a word she was saying. His tongue numb, he was unable to speak. All he could do was look at her with foolish fascination. He could not get over the fact that she was dressed like the Queen of England, the way he had seen in newsreels.

Not caring to be observed by the men at headquarters, Vincent quickly got Judy out of the hut. As they walked past the area where the battalion was in formation, Vincent's face turned crimson. From the corner of his eye he could see his buddies in B Company looking in his direction.

Vincent pretended not to notice their snickering. Facing Judy, he forced himself to utter a few words, which were meaningless. He vaguely remembered walking her off the field of the military encampment and saying good-bye to the young woman. In later years, Vincent regretted not having learned something about her. What had she expected of him? Who was she? Why in the United Kingdom was Judy London dressed like the Queen of England?

The following morning, a day before Christmas, Vincent

Armstrong put his experience in Yeovil behind him. The 276th Engineer Combat Battalion received orders to move out of billets and the hutment. The engineers departed in two groups for the port of Southampton, bordering the English Channel. One group moved by train to the port and boarded an English troop ship H.M.S. Monowai. The other group, the motor convoy, traveled by vehicle to the port and loaded their trucks aboard the S.S. Nicholas Herkheimer.

The Monowai hove anchor Christmas morning and after crossing the English Channel, dropped anchor four miles from the harbor of Le Havre, France, an hour before midnight. When landing crafts pulled alongside the ship, the 276th Battalion as well as other battalions began descending into the crafts. Hampered by their field packs and M-1 rifles, some troops shimmied down rough ropes into the crafts clumsily but carefully. Some troops slid down collapsible chutes and landed with a thud in the crafts. Fully loaded with troops, the landing crafts chugged ashore in freezing winter weather.

Back at the Southampton port of embarkation, with the motor convoy settled on board, the Herkheimer soon set sail for France also. Upon arriving at Le Havre, the motor convoy unloaded their trucks from the ship and drove to Gannesville to link up with the rest of the 276th Engineer Combat Battalion scheduled to march eighty miles to an assembly area called Red Horse, TCRP BLOCK B in military terms—in civilian terms a frozen turnip patch.

Snowbound, sleeping on snow and walking in slush, their food seasoned with snowflakes, the men of the 276th were chilled to the marrow while they waited again for additional equipment and supplies to arrive. Two weeks later, the Battalion proceeded northeast by motor column to Belgium. The winter weather was bitter cold and numerous cases of frostbite occurred. Sweet blessings were bestowed on compassionate Belgian women who rushed out of their homes with pots of hot coffee to warm the men whenever the column had to halt along the way.

On the evening of January 12, 1945, the 276th Engineer Combat Battalion was billeted in Verviers, a commune in East Belgium. A and B Companies proceeded to Spa, a Belgian town famous for its mineral springs, where the men guarded bridges on the Ambleve River. Two days later the 276th Battalion received orders to move on.

Previously on December 16, 1944, the Germans had launched a major counteroffensive against advancing American troops. The line of combat protruded forming a large, deep bulge in Allied territory, North and East Belgium. The First Army (to which the 276th Engineer Combat Battalion was assigned) steadily repulsed the German counteroffensive. With the pushing back of the Germans to their Siegfried Line, the Battle of the Bulge—fought in the Forest of Ardennes—ended January 25, 1945.

Having dutifully completed all its missions, the 276th Engineer Combat Battalion earned a battle star for the Battle of the Ardennes. Still the 276th had yet to go on to greater glory, but at a high price. Many men in the battalion were destined to die in performing their duty by a little known town (Remagen), site of an obscure bridge (The Ludendorf), captured mostly intact by advance spearheads of the 9th Armoured Division.

The Ludendorf Bridge became the most renowned in World War II, because it was the first and only bridge on which troops and supplies were able to pour across the Rhine River in pursuing the enemy. It was the beginning of the end of Nazi Germany. Thus not only were scores of lives saved, but also the world was saved sooner. The following is a copy of the citation the 276th Battalion received for hazardous work it did in maintaining the bridge at Remagen in West Germany:

GENERAL ORDERS   WAR DEPARTMENT
No. 45   Washington 25, D. C. 12 June 1945

EXTRACT

* * *   * * *   * * *

XI—BATTLE HONORS.

* * *   * * *   * * *

4.   As authorized by Executive Order 9396 (sec. I, WD Bul. 22, 1943), superseding Executive Order 9075 (sec. III, WD Bul. 11, 1942), citation of the following unit in General Orders 50, Headquarters III Corps, 26 April 1945, as approved by the Commanding General, European Theater of Operation, is confirmed under the provisions of Section IV, WD Circular 333, 1943, in the name of the President of the United States as public evidence of deserved honor and distinction. The citation reads as follows:

The 276th Engineer Combat Battalion is cited for outstanding performance of duty in action from 9 to 17 March 1945 in Germany. On 9 March 1945, the 276th Engineer Combat Battalion was ordered to repair the severely damaged Ludendorf railroad bridge at Remagen,

Germany, prepare it for two-way traffic, and maintain it in operational condition. Throughout the period, officers and men of the battalion worked continuously upon the bridge and its approaches. Because of severe enemy shelling, frequently scoring direct hits upon the bridge and working area, and numerous hostile air attacks, simple maintenance was a trying and hazardous task. Despite this intense fire, officers and men of the battalion continued their never-ending task of replacing and repairing damaged flooring and cratered approaches. Shortly after dark on 10 March 1945, the construction of a 140-foot Double Bailey Bridge was begun on the south approach to provide for two-way traffic. Despite direct hits from enemy shell fire, inflicting severe casualties, the men of the battalion labored undauntedly, completing the assignment in 2 days' time. Members of the battalion air station worked untiringly in the areas of heaviest shelling, evacuating casualties of the battalion and units using the bridge. The entire battalion was employed throughout the period 13 to 17 March 1945, in flooring both sides of the bridge and in replacing the many damaged steel members. The work of reflooring the bridge was nearly completed and the last damaged steel member was being replaced when the entire span collapsed, inflicting heavy casualties upon the working parties. The outstanding gallantry, determination, and devotion to duty displayed by every officer and man of the 276th Engineer Combat Battalion, working against time and great hazards, enabled elements of the First Army to cross the Rhine River and exploit the bridgehead upon the east bank, and exemplified the highest traditions of the military service.

* * *   * * *   * * *

By order of the Secretary of War:

Official: G. C. MARSHALL
    J. A. Ulio   Chief of Staff
    Major General
    The Adjutant General

Chapter 47

As he sat in the teachers' room at National Dance Studios checking a calendar to see how many appointments he had on March 17th, Vincent Armstrong stroked the smallish bump on his forehead to soothe a headache. He was reminded of another afternoon on March 17th some years ago during World War II when his outfit, the 276th Engineer Combat Battalion, took over maintenance of the Ludendorf Bridge, which had served to establish the First Army bridgehead across the Rhine River in Germany.

Hundreds of men in Vincent's battalion were feverishly at work placing heavy planks on the tracks of the railroad bridge and installing meter beams. All of a sudden, what seemed to Vincent to be an earthquake, the bridge started to vibrate. Dust from the planks clouded and darkened the air. Rivets popped with the rapidity of machine-gun fire. The sound of snapping steel sections was terrifying.

In the next instant, the massive steel structure collapsed into the swirling waters of the river. Only a few engineers working near the approaches were able to scramble to safety. Others farther away on the banks stood by helplessly in horror as they saw their fellow soldiers being crushed and mangled under tons of steel. Screams of pain from the injured were heart-wounding. Private Armstrong, who was working well in the center of the railroad bridge, was struck on the forehead by a loosened steel section that caused him to fall into the river below.

Previous to the collapse of the bridge, the medical detachment of the 276th Battalion had set up aid stations not far from the approaches, west and east. Both aid stations were soon packed with casualties from several outfits along with many injured men who were rescued by ambulance drivers from other units. In the confusion of the disaster, it was impossible to keep track of every company, let alone every casualty.

Private Armstrong disappeared after he was last seen floating in the river. Nowhere to be found, he eventually was listed "Missing in Action."

Unknown to his outfit he had floated a distance downstream and was fished out of the river by medics from another detachment. In a coma, he was driven by ambulance to France, where he was hospitalized. Later he was airborne to England, where he was hospitalized. Later he was transported on a hospital ship across the Atlantic Ocean to the United States, taken by train to California, and hospitalized at Dibble General in Menlo Park within a stone's throw from his home in San Francisco.

"Vince! Oh, Vince, where are you?" Bert Craig shook his friend's shoulder to bring him down to earth, as he had a far-off look in his eyes. "I have been talking to you for five minutes. You haven't heard a word I said. You look pale. Don't you feel well?"

"I have a bit of a headache. Do I really look pale? I guess I need some sunshine. I've been cooped up indoors too long." Vincent smiled a broad smile.

Untypically serious, Bert remarked: "What are you smiling about? A headache is not funny."

"I wasn't smiling about that. I was thinking about the time I was discharged from Dibble General. It used to be a military hospital in Menlo Park. Maybe it still is. I never returned there.

"The Adjutant General of the Army had informed my mother that I was missing in action. She was worried sick. At my homecoming, she was so happy she prepared all my favorite dishes, a feast fit for a king."

Bert had a thousand questions. "You were hurt in the war? What happened? How long were you in the hospital?"

"Months, mostly overseas. It's a long story. I am okay now." Vincent was not anxious to talk about the war. He was reluctant to admit that some experiences he had in the service were vague in his mind since the day he was hit by a steel member of the Ludendorf Bridge and almost drowned in the Rhine River.

As an excuse to end the discussion Vincent said: "We better go downstairs to the ballroom. Sometimes students come early for their lessons. It is more professional if we are there ahead of them."

Since Bert had an appointment to teach the next hour, he accepted Vincent's statement at face value. Before leaving the teachers' room, both cleaned their nails and combed their hair. With one last look in the mirror, they straightened their neckties. Being well-groomed was an unwritten requisite of National Dance Studios.

On the way to the ballroom, a woman caught Vincent's eye. She was a replica of a beautiful young woman he had painted from mixed colors on his mental palette: her hair was strawberry-red...her eyes were melon-green...her cheeks were pink-peach.

Mr. Buchanan, one of the interviewers whom Vincent was not fond of, walked over to the young woman and engaged her in conversation. Vincent could not resist a desire to meet her. Unfortunately he had a problem with Buchanan. Buchanan's and Armstrong's personalities clashed on occasion. He realized it would not be easy to persuade Buchanan to introduce him to the woman.

Motivated by desire, he rationalized nothing ventured nothing gained. When Buchanan left the woman momentarily to go to the office for some dance-course forms, Armstrong caught up with him to ask "Who is that gal you were talking to?"

"She is one of my guests," Buchanan replied sternly.

"I'd like to meet her," said Armstrong nonchalantly.

"Why?" questioned Buchanan with suspicion.

"Uh, she looks familiar to me," Armstrong prevaricated, hoping his answer did not sound illogical.

Dating students or guests (potential students) was against studio policy. Buchanan was hesitant to arrange an introduction. He bit his lip and hemmed and hawed but consented.

What prompted Buchanan to introduce Vincent to the woman was out of character. Perhaps it was simply a weak moment on Buchanan's part. He went with Vincent over to the woman, handed her a form, and said: "Miss Cummings, I would like you to meet Mr. Armstrong. He is one of our instructors."

Vincent wished Buchanan had mentioned her first name. Thoughts were running through his mind how he might look in the office files for her telephone number. Having accomplished more than he had expected, Vincent was thankful for small favors.

Mr. Buchanan spoke to Miss Cummings. "I have another interview now. See you tomorrow. Don't forget to fill out the form."

With the interviewer gone, Vincent tried to get Miss Cummings to speak to him. "How do you like the Studio? Do you plan to sign up for dancing lessons?"

She answered "yes" to both questions. Busy scanning the form Mr. Buchanan had handed her, the young woman seemed disinterested in carrying on a conversation.

Vincent did not believe it was prudent to become familiar at such a brief encounter. Therefore, he refrained from saying anything more except, as she started to leave, he told her that he hoped to see her again at the Studio.

Miss Cummings responded she probably would fill out the form and drop it off in the morning. Without so much as a smile, she turned on her heels and departed.

Deciding it would be unwise, Vincent resisted the temptation to follow her. He just had to take his chances he would see her again. The opportunity arose sooner than he expected.

The next day Vincent was on his way out of the Studio; he had an appointment with a chiropodist. A callus on the undersurface of Vincent's right foot had enlarged and thickened. The horny layer of skin was annoying. He needed to have it taken care of.

Just as he passed the receptionist's desk he caught sight of Miss Cummings entering the Studio. Forgetting about his callus, he retraced his steps and sat down on a sofa in the lobby. He found a discarded newspaper and pretended to read it so that he could observe her unnoticed. Not once did she look in his direction. She was too concerned with her interview. After it was over she went to the ladies' lounge to freshen up.

Vincent turned the pages of the newspaper slowly, trying to appear engrossed in what he was reading. She came out from the lounge before long and departed. Exiting the Studio, he bided his time waiting for her to go a distance away from the front of the building in which National Dance Studios was located. He was cautious about walking up to her too soon, because there was a possibility he could be seen from the upper-floor windows of the building.

He hated the no-dating rule worse than ever at this moment despite the fact that he understood familiarity between teachers and students was not considered good business practice. Miss Cummings was stopped by a red light at the intersection of Sutter and Mason Streets. Vincent hurried to the intersection before the light turned green.

"Why! Miss Cummings," he exclaimed as if he were surprised. "Fancy meeting you here. How are you today?"

"Fine, thank you, Mr. Armstrong. Are you on a coffee break?"

"No. I have an appointment at 450 Sutter Street." He omitted to say he was on his way to a foot doctor at the medical building. Bringing up such a subject sounded so unsanitary. To keep the conversation going, he asked, "Have you taken the preliminary dancing test yet?"

"Not yet. I haven't had time. I may take the test next week. I am really nervous about it. I wonder if I shall be able to pass the test. I am not a very good dancer."

Unsure of how much he could trust Miss Cummings, he failed to tell her there was no need to be nervous about the preliminary test. The studio staff was more anxious for guests to pass the tests than they were. Actually the tests, which were advertised as free, was part of a promotional program to sell guests expensive dance courses.

All the while, Vincent studied Miss Cummings to see if she showed any interest in him at all. As they crossed the intersection and walked down the block, he still could not determine how she felt about him. Her natural manner was sweet and friendly. She had the look of innocence he had seen on girls' faces years ago in high school.

Impulsively Vincent decided to lay his cards on the table, come what may. "You probably are unaware of it, but teachers at National Dance Studios are not permitted to date the students...or the guests. Although it is sometimes done on the sly, a daring teacher runs the risk of being fired. For a date with you"—he hinted—"it would be worth the risk. Besides, I don't plan to be a ballroom dancing teacher all my life."

Miss Cummings expression registered complete surprise. She was speechless. The devil must have been playing his hand. At that very instant, one of the students at the Studio happened to walk out of a jewelry store on the block. Vincent remained quiet until the student was no longer in hearing distance.

When he was sure it was safe to speak, Vincent said: "I realize you didn't expect us to become familiar. But"—he injected a bit of sweet humor—"without mincing words, would you enjoy a pitted date with me? What do you say, Miss Cummings?"

Smiling at his attempt to be humorous, she said, "I wouldn't want you to get into any kind of trouble on my account." One could anticipate a considerate thought like that from her. "I really don't know what to say."

Vincent was careful not to rush the young woman, so he replied:

"Think it over. I will phone you in a couple of days. Then we can discuss the matter more fully."

"All right," she agreed and gave Vincent her telephone number.

"By the way, what is your first name?" he asked.

"Elaine," she quickly answered. "I must be on my way." She glanced at her wrist watch and hurried down Powell Street.

Vincent watched Elaine until she disappeared from sight. Crossing over to the north side of Sutter Street, he headed for the medical building to keep his appointment with the foot doctor— unless one prefers the technical term chiropodist or podiatrist.

Two days later at the Studio, the Craigs invited Vincent to join them Saturday for an evening of dinner dancing at the Palace Hotel. Bert had an extra invitation to a social affair in the hotel's Gold Room. Single women and stags as well as couples would be in attendance.

Vincent accepted the invitation with the understanding that he might not be able to attend the social affair. Elaine Cummings was still on his mind. He had hopes of dating her. Even if she was willing to go out with him Saturday night, he had to be careful where they went. Vincent did not want to involve Alice and Bert in a violation of studio policy. Now that they were married, the Craigs could not afford to lose their jobs.

At his earliest opportunity Vincent called Elaine from a public telephone booth. The line was busy. He dialed her number again and again. The line was busy. It seems the line is always busy when a person has an urgent need to talk to someone. Impatient, Vincent jiggled the receiver several times only to lose his dime.

He listened for a dial tone, deposited another coin, and lost it, too. But he refused to give up. He tried once more. At last! he was successful. Elaine answered the telephone. He asked her whether she had decided to go out with him. She said she had. It was okay with her if there would be no problem with National Dance Studios. No need to worry he convinced her.

Since she lived in the West Portal district, he suggested they take in a movie at the Empire Cinema which was within walking distance. Saturday night, Vincent arrived at Elaine's house. Her parents were out, so she met him at the door with her coat on. They left at once for the Empire Cinema because they did not want to come in the middle of the feature film.

The following Monday morning, despite the activity at the Studio, Vincent could not stop thinking about his date with Elaine.

While watching the movie, he got a whiff of her scent, the fragrance of sweet peas. He held her hand. Her fingers felt smooth and soft as petals. He touched her fingertips gently the way one touches a flower for fear of crushing it.

For the first time in years that he escorted a girl home after date, Vincent did not try to kiss her good night at her doorstep. He felt so strongly about Elaine he wanted to wipe out the memory of his past escapades with women. His thoughts about her were clean and pure. She was somebody he could spend the rest of his life with.

Vincent set aside his pleasant plans for building a relationship with Elaine as soon as Bert and Alice entered the room (filled with other teachers). The Craigs were arguing: Bert insisted Gene Kelly—his favorite—was the best dancer on stage and screen. Alice insisted Fred Astaire—her favorite—was the best dancer on stage and screen. The Craigs turned to Vincent Armstrong to settle their argument.

He gave his opinion. Astaire's movements are aristocratic; he looks as if he was born to dance. Kelly's movements are acrobatic; he looks as if he was trained to dance. Not to create friction between his two friends, he concluded in a natural way. Both are great performers. They act great. They sing great. They are the greatest dancers Hollywood has ever produced.

Although Bert Craig was bent on arguing that his favorite dancer was the greatest, Bert held his tongue. Ralph Normand had just entered the room. The supervisor's presence commanded immediate attention. He announced to the group of teachers that he was going to discuss another one of the Latin-American dances.

Chapter 48

A HISTORY OF THE CLASSIC BALLROOM DANCES

Latin-American Dances

III-C. The Rumba (to increase coordination and self-confidence)

Contrary to consensus among some writers on Dance, the rumba is neither of Spanish nor of Cuban genesis which they have misconceived it to be. And in spite of its use as a variant the Anglicized spelling r-h-u-m-b-a is erroneous. Moreover, the word rumba is ordinarily omitted in Romance language dictionaries. Sometimes rumba is defined in a foreign dictionary simply by repeating the word rumba itself—not, as might be expected, by *baile* or *danza*, the Spanish masculine and feminine words for 'dance.'

Rumba is of an African source, as a word having no meaning and in sound rolls off the tongue onomatopoetically. That is, the vocable rumba (pronounced roomba) very likely was conceived when natives imitated the rumbling sounds made by natural forces such as cataracts, volcanoes, avalanches, hurricanes, and earthquakes.

Theoretically, rumba the dance, seeded in Africa by primitive societies, was an outgrowth of the Afro-Cuban dance la conga named after the African tribal *conga*, a telegraphic drum devised from the hollow trunk of a tree. A line dance, la conga was a form of crawl and kick patterned from the movement of the big cat in stealth, the long snake in writhe, and the nimble beast's kick in defense.

There is another view that should not be overlooked. It is believed the kick is a substitute for the regulated clang made by chains fastened around the ankles of black slaves who were privileged biennially in Cuba to dance on roads and trails.

La conga was deeply immersed in Ñañiguismo, sacrificial, black-magic practices which formed a polytheistic religion inborn in African captives abducted to Cuba in the year 1510. It is whispered that their sacred rituals (equivalent to Voodoo in nearby Haiti), though outlawed, are secretly held in the jungle and marsh of Cuba's interior even in this day and age.

Just as the great organ is an accessory of Catholicism, so the conga (large drum) is an accessory of Ñañiguismo. Emotionally energized by rapid drumbeats, fanaticized Afro-Cuban cultists have been known to dance for hours at dark rites, stopping only when overcome by sheer exhaustion. Their superstitious cavorting is also practiced on the island in the Ñañiga, a related religious ritual imbued with rhythm-dances, of ferocity and of fertility, from various tribes in Africa.

The rhythms were peculiar to the belligerent tribes on the Gold Coast. The dances were peculiar to the agricultural tribes in the Congo jungle. The strange beliefs that the spirit-fearing cavorters had, were steeped in superstition. During their rites the rhythm-dances performed were dedicated to individual gods respectively.

[The supervisor saw some self-satisfied smirks on the faces of his Caucasian audience. To clear up any misconceptions they appeared to have about their enlightenment as a race, he said: "In a 1937 issue of the Literary Digest, it was written in an article that thousands of whites—many in high places—participate in Ñañiga rituals, not only in Cuba but also in the United States."]

Generation by generation Cuban Negroes instinctively mixed rhythm-dance ingredients of their African forebears with multi-rhythmic movements produced in the Havana slums. As is usually the case, an impoverished, urban environment breeds disharmony. A rogue rumba reared its ugly head in the slum's hybrid quarter.

Illegitimate, the rumba appeared in the guise of attractive figures danced recklessly fast with hot hip swinging aided and abetted by violent abdominal contractions combined with lewd pelvis tossing. Veloz and Yolanda, unrivaled Latin-American dancers worldwide, said in 1938, "The Cuban rumba is really a suggestive sex pantomime of the half-breed quarter."

To the undernourished factually, The Oxford Companion to Music offers a spicy morsel of sarcasm about the rogue rumba. "It is not suggestive, as has been alleged—since it leaves nothing to suggest."

Undoubtedly in the slums means were often lacking to furnish appropriate orchestral accompaniment for rumba dancers. Necessity being the mother of invention, makeshift instruments were used. This was not always a disadvantage because they added spice to the urban rumba which was in pure form an exhibition dance. The instruments were made up of such household implements as ladles, pots, flasks, jugs, pans, and you name it. The syncopated music in two-four time was of course improvised, and played at extreme speeds.

Ingenuity of another sort was demonstrated on farms in the World's Sugar Bowl. The Afro-Cubans, who danced a nonoffensive rural rumba, acquired the fine art of demonstrating daily functions common to husbandry through adept performances in the dance. Cutting a row of cane...feeding the chickens...sowing a field...milking a cow...currying a horse...along with other farmlike activities were again and again cleverly exhibited in protean rumba sequences.

Cubans regard the rural rumba as well as the urban rumba to be exemplary exhibition dances. In rural areas when early black slaves rumbaed, they frequently portrayed the conduct of barnyard fowl during courtship. Their real intent was to ridicule their masters who, in breeding the slaves to increase their numbers, treated them no differently than livestock.

Over the centuries, acclimated to rumba movements that portrayed barnyard-fowl courtship, prenuptial wooing was performed after the manner of chickens, at communal gatherings. Lovers impersonated the ostentatious rooster chasing the flirtatious hen. A male was allowed to claim a female for his mate upon catching and caressing her *cara a cara* ('face to face').

As a natural result, a ruffled shirt habitually worn by agile *rumberos* became a customary display of the rooster's hackle feathers. And it follows that a ruffled train habitually worn by elusive *rumberas* became a customary display of the hen's tail feathers. White with cerulean or Congo red binding became the customary color combination dyed on the ruffles of rumba raiment.

Dr. Paul Nettle, professor of musicology, theorizes in his book The Story of Dance Music, that the rumba in some way is connected to the old rotta, a medieval dance movement. In a roundabout way he speaks of an elegiac piece of instrumental music *Lamento di*

Tristano, which, like the Dark Ages, shed no light on why it is the title of a fourteenth-century dance, a three-beat saltarello (from Italian *saltare*, 'to jump'), which in an evening of gamboling was followed by a fast two-beat rotta or rota (Italian) or rote (English) or Rotte (German), a dance which appears to have originated in an older processional dance, which in turn was followed by a pantomimic figure—The Rota.

It is difficult to see what, if anything, the rumba and the rota have in common:

first ....the rota is European in character,
second ....rota as an instrument by source is identified with a medieval lyre or a lute,
third ....musically the rota's melody and lyrics are of major importance,
fourth......in dancing movements the feet are dominate for rota style.

By contrast:

first ....the rumba is African in character,
second ....rumba in instrumental terms by source is identified with a primitive hollow trunk or a drum,
third ....musically the rumba's rhythm and syncopation are of major importance,
fourth......in dancing movements the body is dominate for rumba style.

Only if we are blinded by the glaring differences between the rota and the rumba can we fail to see there is no connection between the two dances. Unlike the rote (English), the rumba figures form small squares, not large circles. In fact, rote seems to be a generic name for 'round.' Since 1660 in the British Isles, the rote has in one form or another fascinated old and young here and abroad. Not only English children but also American children delight in singing and in dancing nursery rounds. A favorite rote is "Three Blind Mice."

In 1879 the danzón was presented to Cuba by Miguel Failde, a Negro composer. To non-Cubans it easily can be confused with the rumba because the danzón is danced to rumba rhythms. There is a difference in the rate of speed of music and movements, however. The music is played slower for the danzón, and thus it is danced slower than the rumba.

La contredanse—originally an English rustic dance—is believed to be a *parent éloigné* of the danzón. Historians claim the 'distant relation' was brought from Normandy to England by William the

Conqueror. *La contredanse* appeared without fanfare as a country dance all over Europe in the 1600s.

To put it plainly, *la contredanse* was most often performed on ordinary occasions by commoners. Performed less and less in France, after a century it disappeared into thin air. Significantly *la contredanse* ('the counter-dance') also means an 'air,' or a 'tune'.

Out of a clear sky *la contredanse* reappeared in Paris during the fifth act of an opera-ballet "Le Temple de la Gloire" produced in 1745 by Jean Philippe Rameau. The French aristocracy found the light-footed *contredanse* so glorious on the stage that it became the darling of their social affairs in the drawing-room, where it was characterized by the dancers performing in counter positions.

Around the turn of the century the danzón was at the spire of its popularity among affluent, conservative Cubans. The music was composed of a verse (sung by a soloist) and a chorus (a choral society). Dancers do the danzón during the chorus. The ladies gently roll their hips while they delicately step in time to the music, which is played more smoothly and with fewer accentuated beats than the rumba.

When the soloist starts to sing the verse, the dancing stops—a custom carried over from church ceremonies in Spain. As they wait for the chorus to begin again, *señoritas* demurely fan themselves as *señors* devilishly drip honeyed compliments in angelic ears.

Circa 1916 Cuban composers polished a dull dance-song, the son, into a bright ballroom dance. Customarily retained in the son is the verse, that is, a soloist sings introductory lyrics before the dancing starts.

Like the danzón, the son is played smoothly and with fewer accentuated beats than the rumba. But the son's rate of speed for music and movements exceeds the danzón's. Still the steps of both dances are small and slow compared to rumba steps and speed.

[Feeling that he had to give the group of teachers a more complete picture of the son, the supervisor said: "The son has two faces, so to speak. On one face it has the look of a sophisticated ballroom dance. On the other face it has the unsophisticated look of a folk dance.

"Embodied with Negro tunes and African ritual patois dating back to 1568, the dance was named Son Afro-Cubano by the folk on the island. As a ballroom dance the son succeeded the danzón to become the national social dance of an arbitrarily classified Caucasian middle class. However, with the changing political climate in Cuba, the fate of the middle-class son is not predictable.

"Somewhere along the line cultural wires were crossed in America and the son was misnamed the rumba. I shall untangle the wires before long so that you can get a straight line on the two dances."]

In 1913, Joan Sawyer and Lew Quinn, advertised as America's foremost terpsichorean artists, successfully exhibited La Rumba in the casinos at Newport and Narragansett Pier, and at Reisenweber's in New York City. Despite the success of the dance team Sawyer and Quinn, the rumba failed to titillate the American public.

[Abruptly the supervisor set aside his historical notes. Mr. Normand had an opinion about some facts he was eager to share with his audience. "Information is paragraphed in the 1946 edition of the Encyclopedia Americana that the rumba was introduced to New York again in 1914. As of that year, rumba orchestras were featured solely by nightclubs with stiff cover charges. Too often a raw rumba not well-seasoned was served to individuals in upper-income brackets, or to sorry individuals who live beyond their means, or to individuals who pay more attention to drink than to dance.

"Exhibited at late hours, the rumba seldom saw the light of day. Consequently, the general public was not exposed to a tasteful Latin-American dance. By association, the rumba's reputation was in shambles—but salvageable."]

In 1928 a noted bandleader, Don Barreto, presented Cuban rumba music and dancers to France, where they were warmly welcomed by Parisians. That year in the United States, Edward B. Marks Music Corporation copyrighted Moises Simon's *El Manisero* ('The Peanut Vendor'), a rumba from Cuba. No welcome mat was laid out for the rumba by Americans. Meanwhile, *El Manisero* became a sensational song hit in some quarters when played by Don Azpiazu's Havana casino orchestra.

Nevertheless, the rumba, music and dance, was yet to be accepted by the American public. The original Spanish text translated into English by Lewis Rittenberg and special stage version by Marion Sunshine were hard for audiences in the United States to grasp. Something must have been lost in the translation.

In 1931, Marion Sunshine, in collaboration with L. Wolfe Gilbert, rewrote the English lyrics of the Peanut Vendor so that they were meaningful to Americans. Significantly, the dance-song was arranged as a rumba fox trot.

Now the public could identify culturally with the rumba—American style. Just about every man, woman, and child, if not munching peanuts, was humming the Peanut Vendor's tune. Lady Terpsichore took advantage of the jeweled opportunity, titillating Yankee feet with the meter from the Pearl of the Antilles.

Stripped of Yankee Doodle's dressing, the rumba danced socially in the States is similar to the social son danced in Cuba. Since the son was by propinquity connected to the danzón, a few of its features sometimes are seen in the performance of the American rumba, which properly should have been named son. According to rumor, theatrically the name rumba was adapted from the Cuban's because, in spite of its risqué characteristics as an exhibition dance, it sounded like a lucrative stage name.

Essentially the son has the same rhythm as the rumba fox trot; however, the son's movement is more moderate. To a Cuban the ultimate accomplishment in soning is to be *suave* ('smooth'). Performing spontaneous side-steps (*pasos de lado*), the man leads his partner as though they were skating serenely on thin ice. She assumes the stance of a Latin Venus with a cool air of nonchalance.

[For the teachers' benefit the supervisor offered an explanation: "All the same, variations in the style and steps of Cuban dances, be they sons or rumbas or others, are determined by the tempo of the music. Musically Spanish influence on Dance is strong in Cuba.

"A Cuban guaracha can be performed to a fast, medium, or slow tempo; the dance was fashioned from Spanish clogs as well as from song-dances in lively six-eight time. A danzónette, diminutive of danzón (a strain of the Spanish contradanza) can be performed to briefer and livelier Cuban dance music. A bolero can be performed to waltz tempo, slow or fast; this Cuban dance is not far removed from the Spanish bolero performed in three-four time either by a solo dancer or by a couple."

Ralph Normand removed a hardback book from a briefcase near his desk. Contained in the book was the complete works of William Shakespeare. The supervisor thumbed through the pages to Romeo and Juliet. Finding Act II, Normand read aloud from a scene wherein Juliet asks: 'What's in a name? That which we call a rose by any other name would smell as sweet.'

"By the same token," the supervisor said, "a son by any other name would sound as sweet. Incidentally, *son* in Spanish means 'sound.'"]

Whatever the dance is called...to whatever music it is danced, traditive instruments, predominately primitive percussions, bring out the distinctive Afro-Cuban character of rumba rhythm reminiscent of the aborigines' pulse: the footpads of fauna, the fluttering of flora. As Africans felt the throb of the wilderness, they made different devices to accentuate the rhythmic beats heard in the heart of the jungle.

Here are descriptions of typical instruments that are used by rumba and son orchestras in Havana to capture the wild sounds of the jungles native to Africa and Cuba:

> Marácas (shakers) ....gourds filled with seeds, beans, or pebbles; the gourds have wooden handles; held one in each hand, like popsicles, the gourds are shaken precisely to the tempo of the music, and they maintain the dominant rhythm of the dance.

[Bert Craig could not resist asking a question, which popped out of his mouth on impulse. "Are gourds the only things used to make shakers?"

With a glint of amusement in his eye, Ralph Normand answered: "No, Mr. Craig, one that comes to mind is the Jaw Bones of a Donkey. Loose donkey's teeth in a head are rattled-rattled serving the same purpose as marácas. Now, if I may continue."]

> Claves or Palitos
> (little sticks)..............two cylindrical rosewood sticks seven inches long and an inch in diameter; the sticks produce a sharp cracking sound when they are struck against each other, in a cupped palm; they are struck at irregular but definite intervals to create counter rhythm.

[Alice Craig raised a hand indicating she had something on her mind. She was not sure whether her husband had been the butt of an asinine joke. Alice wanted to help him save face by asking a question herself. "I once saw a picture in The Musical Quarterly that showed a Haitian sitting on a boxlike instrument with wide bands of metal. I can't recall the name of it. What exactly is it for?"

"It is called a malímba in Haiti," Normand replied. "I'll describe the one played in Cuba."]

Marímbula ....spring like short metal strips fastened to a wooden box which serves
as a sounding board; plucked by the
fingers, a variety of rhythms can be
created.

Next Ralph Normand proceeded to give descriptions of other instruments utilized in accenting music by Cuban musicians or producing rhythm by cults on the island.

Bongó ....double-headed drum, carved from
solid wood, attached together by a
metal bar like Siamese twins; the
drum is held between the knees and
usually tapped with the thumbs
and index fingers to produce intricate rhythms, and a contrasting
bass.

Timbale ....smaller double-headed drum, like
the bongó, the twin heads are differ-
ent in pitch; the timbale also is held
between the knees and tapped with
the fingertips. But it is higher in
tone than the low-pitched bongó.

["The last instrument I shall describe is interesting because it is a tropical fruit, the calabash or gourd, which grows on a vine. Its hard shell is dried and used to make bottles and bowls as well as instruments."]

Güiro or Güayo ....an elongated gourd, notched for a
hand-hold on one side. With several
horizontal serrations cut on the
other side; a variety of rhythms are
created by scraping the serrations
vertically with a special wire.

A serrated cow's horn sometimes is
used instead of a gourd.

[All of a sudden the supervisor had to sneeze. He resisted the sneeze, frantically searching in his pockets for a handkerchief. Getting hold of one, he spread it open and put it over his nose and mouth just as he involuntarily expelled a blast of air and spray.

A teacher sitting in the front row of the room exclaimed, "God bless you!" In appreciation the supervisor said, "Thank you."

Vincent Armstrong quickly decided it was an opportune moment to ask a question. "Is the top of the bongó and the timbale covered with a round wooden object like the cover of a barrel, or are they covered with vellum like drums in the U.S.A.?"

Having had a good sneeze, Mr. Normand was in a good mood. He responded accordingly: "That is a good question. I forgot to cover the covers." A play on words, Normand's statement elicited laughter from his audience. "Seriously, the bongó or the timbale is covered with a piece of cowhide which is stretched tightly over the open end, and the overhanging edges are nailed to the circumference of the drum.

"Instrumentation in Cuba and the adjacent islands in the West Indies are cult works of art evolved over centuries. At the same time, the art of rumba motion, unique to the dance, cannot be mastered overnight. Yet you must master the motion before you can teach the rumba to others. Your work is cut out for you.

"I leave you with this thought—to exercise mind and body. The rumba to be correctly executed demands perpetual rotation of the hips at acute angles while simultaneously executing steps. It is something like perpetually patting your head with the right hand while simultaneously rubbing your stomach circularly as well as up and down with the left hand."

Some teachers in the group started to pat their heads and rub their stomachs. Some, on the other hand, wondered if the supervisor was pulling their legs.]

BOOK EIGHT

Chapter 49

Vincent Armstrong's enthusiasm to stay at National Dance Studios was still at a low ebb. Anyway, as far as he was concerned, activity at the Studio gave him something to do until he got his bearings. Not long ago when he was a patient at Dibble General Hospital in Menlo Park, he was permitted to leave the grounds for a few hours. Unfamiliar with the nearby city of Palo Alto, which was within walking distance, he went to the United Service Organizations (USO), a place of recreation where soldiers always were welcome.

As he entered the USO, he saw a young soldier dancing with a voluntary hostess to fox-trot music provided by a juke box. Two girls were sitting alone at a table. Armstrong asked one, a blonde in her late teens, to dance with him. Her reply was hurtful like a slap in the face. "My! you look old. I would rather not dance with you."

At that moment Armstrong realized how many years had passed since he was drafted into the army. The war had taken its toll. It had robbed him of a golden period of his youth.

Time is a great healer. He no longer felt the sting of an outspoken slap in the face by an insensitive teen-ager. The bad experiences he endured during the war were dim in his memory. There was much to live for. He had many years ahead to accomplish things. The world was his again to conquer and to change.

Now that he met Elaine Cummings, it became harder for him to spend tedious time teaching women to dance. Although he derived a certain amount of satisfaction working with women with two left feet so that they could distinguish a left foot from a right foot on the dance floor, he did not feel he had accomplished anything.

Vincent was undecided what he was going to do in life. However, by all appearances, he was convinced he wanted to court Elaine. With her at his side, he believed he could accomplish things.

At his earliest opportunity, Vincent telephoned Elaine and asked her for a date. She was agreeable. They made arrangements to go on an outing next Sunday afternoon. He knew of a quiet spot by the ocean where they could sunbathe undisturbed.

Early next Sunday afternoon, Vincent picked up Elaine in his car. As they drove along Great Highway in the direction of their destination, they were silent. Words did not seem necessary to express their feelings. After maneuvering uphill through heavy traffic past the Cliff House, Vincent turned northward stopping his car in front of a monument at Point Lobos. He got out of the car and walked around to the passenger's side to open the door for Elaine. But she had already opened the door, so all he could do was wait until she got out before he closed the door.

Intrigued by the shiplike architecture of the monument, they approached it and read the inscriptions on one of the plaques mounted on a central, triangular block:

> This memorial to rear admiral Daniel Judson Callaghan, U.S.N., and his officers and men who gave their lives for our country while fighting on board the U.S.S. "San Francisco" in the Battle of Guadalcanal on the night of 12-13 November 1942, was formed from the bridge of their ship and here mounted on the circle course to Guadalcanal by the grateful people of San Francisco on 12 November 1950.

Neither Elaine nor Vincent paused long enough to read the rest of the plaques. Stepping off the aggregate platform of the monument, he guided her a short distance away to the access above several rough-cut wooden steps leading to a cliff from which one could get an excellent view of the Pacific Ocean. They descended the steps and cautiously climbed down the cliff to a small secluded beach.

Vincent and Elaine shed their clothes; both had bathing suits on underneath. They were children again playing tag and kicking up sand as they chased each other around the beach. They waded beyond the shoreline splashing water at each other. The great body of water was in a playful spirit, too. Breaker after breaker—rollicking ridges of waves—sprayed white foam on the two frolicsome children who were up to their knees in water.

The hours melted away steadily like a burning wax candle. The sun spread a warm blanket over their bodies. The ocean lullabied them with rhythmic sounds from the tides. They were alone in a dreamland so peaceful that conflict of any form appeared powerless to disturb their harmonious state.

As they lay stretched out side by side on the beach, Vincent dozed off dreamily: He and Elaine were floating on water. Vincent took her hand and kissed it gently. "My only love," he said, "I have never before respected any woman as I respect you. I want you desperately, but I can wait until the time is right. I want you differently, not with lustful sex, but with passionate love."

Elaine looked lovingly at him. Suddenly her eyes changed colors from green to blue, deep as the ocean. She leaned over and pressed her lips smoothly against his with the firmness of a hot iron. Forcing her tongue into Vincent's mouth, she lashed at his tongue to challenge him to lash back. He did. They exchanged violent lashes with Vincent ending up the loser. He was tongue-tied.

Elaine, who was awake, spoke to Vincent (he no longer was dreaming). She asked an unexpected question. "Have you ever heard of Lesbos?"

"I haven't...no." Still sleepy, he rubbed his eyes and tried to think. "It sounds familiar. What on earth is it?"

"Lesbos is an island that belongs to Greece." She did her utmost to be explicit about the island's location: "It is in the Aegean Sea somewhere off the western coast of Turkey."

"I must admit my knowledge of geography isn't very good." He looked lost. "I would need a map to find that part of the world."

"Geography and history were my best subjects in high school," she said with pride. "Lesbos, as early as 1913, was also called Mytilene. Does that ring a bell?"

"Not one ringing sound." Confused by the academic tone of Elaine's conversation, Vincent was for the time being unable to say another word.

"Lesbos was peopled by an Aeolian race about 1000 B.C. They played a leading role in the initial stages of Greek life.

"In the seventh century, the lyric poetry of Greece attained a standard of classic excellence which flourished under Lesbians—citizens of Lesbos—notably under two, the poet Alaceus and the poetess Sappho. Because of the nature of their poetry, the name Lesbian came to symbolize eroticism. Yet without rhyme or reason, a lesbian is defined as a female—not as a male—homosexual.

"While Sappho's poetry infers she was a mentor to loving maidens, Alcaeus was also a lover of hers. It could very well be that she was bisexual, or perhaps she was more inclined to have intercourse with her own sex, for she soon rejected Alcaeus, despite the fact that he was madly in love with her.

"Whether she was a lesbian in the modern sense is a subject of speculation. Her lifestyle was mired in antiquity. The aristocratic ancients accused her of being morally dissolute.

"I read and reread her poetry and found nothing immoral about it. In the Isles of Greece the author Tennyson quotes Sappho. Let's see what you think. I shall recite a few lines of her lyrics that I remember:

> Come to me what I seek in vain
> Bring though, into my spirit send
> Peace after care, balm after pain,
>   And be my friend.

"Will you be my friend, Vincent? I am a lesbian."

Chapter 50

If Elaine Cummings could have opened the shutters over the window of Vincent's heart, she would have seen impressed deeply on a muscular wall Alcaeus' poetic words:

Ah! me forlorn! ah! doome'd to share
Every sorrow, pain, and care.

Vincent Armstrong was behind his times. He lived in a past century under the reign of romanticism. During the gaslight era man viewed womanhood in an unrealistic light. Among his possessions he had a wife whom he placed on a pedestal. The husband knelt to her like a priest with bended knee adores a Madonna.

Having sexual relations with one's saintly spouse was a necessary evil. To bear and rear her children in their sire's image...to feather his nest socially upon a lofty tree of respectability were the main functions a woman served. Howbeit, the male is by constitution a Dr. Jekyll and Mr. Hyde. Cloying his moral appetites with the sweetness of an angelic coitus-partner hardly suffices.

To satiate his fleshly cravings many a consort hid in an obscure back street where he and his paramour conducted a costly, illicit affair. Those individuals who happened to be less fortunate financially had their carnal wants fulfilled by seeking the cheap company of harlots, whose established business it is to gratify male customers' irrepressible, animalistic desires.

We would like to dismiss the foregoing remarks as calumnies, or deceive ourselves into believing they pertain to people of bygone days—not to us. Look sharply all around. Each of you can see for yourself, if you are not blind, in which way the previous pattern of human behavior matches that of life today.

Modern women, with acquisition of suffrage and other equalities, are insisting that more and more allowances be made for the vagueness society calls their "human frailties," which is subject to heated debate. Like the male, the female possesses good and bad qualities, strong as well as weak ones.

Many men—not all, though—are beginning to accept the fact that women are human, too. Despite the incompleteness of a woman's new-found independence, it has been helpful in alleviating her frigidity, which the male ever is fretting about. He forgets he contributed to the malady himself by his pious treatment of the fair sex, in particular members near and dear to him.

If the prior observation appears to be magnified beyond the truth, explain the Galahad who to make a conquest debauches a maiden whose hymen was unbroken. Yet he nobly revolts at his sister's going to bed with her sweetheart on the hard grounds they are not contemplating matrimony.

Sigmund Freud, the Columbus of sexology, over fifty years ago worked out the technique of psychoanalysis, a process based in part on the theory that certain pathological mental or physical states are produced by the repression of painful or undesirable past experiences, largely sexual, in the so-called subconscious.

Inevitably the Freudian method paved the way for freer discussion of sexual behavior than heretofore. And the eyes of women were opened wide. Ever since Freud's findings, they have been educated to the dual sides (or personality?) of man's makeup, in that—at his present stage of evolution—he desires a woman decorous within the realms of conventionality yet, by direct contrast, unrestrained within the walls of the bedchamber.

Vincent Armstrong's romantic frame of reference weakened by dry rot and shattered by Elaine, he was too sick at heart to show up at the Studio the following day. His friends, Bert and Alice Craig, called Vincent's home to inquire about his health. But he did not answer the telephone. He was in no mood to talk to anyone.

Tired of dialing his number, the Craigs stopped trying to get Vincent on the telephone. Bert said to Alice: "It's too bad Vince didn't come to work today. I just don't understand it. This is the first time he's stayed away from the Studio. I wonder what is wrong with him."

"All he said when he spoke on the phone to the girl in the office, was that he was indisposed. He probably has a cold or something. I think I have a bit of a cold myself." Her nose slightly clogged, Alice sniffled. She removed a lace handkerchief tucked under her sleeve and with a closed mouth blew her nose, making a honking sound.

The sound irritated Bert. After their honeymoon he once suggested she keep her mouth open when she blew her nose. His M.D. had told Bert that blowing one's nose with a closed mouth creates a vacuum which blocks the nasal passages and restricts the discharge. Alice seemed unable to break a habit of blowing her nose at bedtime. Should he be ready for sex, the sound and sight turned him off.

Bert rolled over on his side of the bed, feigning sleep and fantasizing about Marian Mills, the little sex pot. She looked so wholesome and smelled so good. He would get a hard-on every time she rubbed against him as they danced samba steps. For him she had a special way of moving. Bert flattered himself. Marian gave a dry run to all the men she sambaed with at National Dance Studios.

Because of her sex appeal as well as her adroitness in the performance of Latin-American dances, Marion Mills was assigned a student, Joe Johnson, who was especially interested in learning to dance the rumba. He did not have a swarthy complexion nor a slender build as one might imagine. On the contrary, he had a ruddy complexion and a thickset body, atypical of a Latin dancer.

Nonetheless, to Miss Mills' surprise, his limbs were flexible as rubber and he was light as a feather on his feet. Not surprisingly Joe was by profession a boxer. Teaching the rumba to someone with Joe's athletic ability should have been a breeze. It was not! He behaved as if he was punch-drunk.

His footwork and movements, though slow, were great on the dance floor, just like in the prizefighting ring. The problem was he suffered from so many blows on the head that he failed to remember rumba rhythm and step patterns. Still he had no problem with the fox trot, which like baseball, comes naturally to Americans.

As she observed Joe's behavior, Miss Mills soon suspected something was wrong with his memory. Possessing the patience of a saint, at each dance session she repeated his lessons all over again—from the beginning:

"Rumba music can be placed in two-four time or in four-four time. In four-four or common time there are four beats or counts to a measure. The rhythm is counted as you dance, like this: quick- (one), quick- (two), slow (three-four, combined equals a pause); to repeat, quick-quick-slow."

The teacher handed her student a crutch: "Bear in mind that most basic rumba step patterns are almost identical to fox-trot figures, except in doing the figures a dancer takes big steps and usually travels around the ballroom. And you are reminded that in doing rumba figures, the dancer takes small steps and practically dances in place, on the flat of the foot.

"Stylewise" (she used it for want of a better word) "what distinguishes the rumba from the fox trot, and other dances, is a unique movement referred to as Cuban motion. Let me show you by a simple exercise the way it is achieved."

Standing straight as a soldier in first position with her bodily weight distributed equally over both feet, she bent her left knee forward while leaving her feet—heels and soles—planted in place on the floor; a change of weight caused her hips to roll rightward. Resuming first position as before, with her bodily weight distributed equally over both feet, she bent her right knee forward while leaving her feet—heels and soles—planted in place on the floor; a change of weight caused her hips to roll leftward.

"Notice that you only bend one knee at a time. And more weight shifts to the stiff leg...fleetingly. Anyhow, do not worry about Cuban motion just yet. The movement will come to you with practice. For now it is important you learn how to apply rumba rhythm to the step patterns. Rumbas are played at different speeds or tempos. A perfect rate of speed is 36 measures or 144 beats a minute, which is far from fast."

The music being played in the ballroom was 48 to 56 measures a minute. It was too fast. Miss Mills waited until a slow rumba was played, slower than 36 measures a minute—an ideal tempo for a beginner who was struggling to learn the various figures. The teacher instructed her student to assume rumba position and start to dance with a forward-and-backward basic step pattern. (Her steps were, of course, opposite to his):

> Quick......step to the left side
>   (hips roll rightward),
> Quick......close with the right foot
>   (hips roll leftward),
> Slow........step <u>forward</u> with the left foot
>   (hips roll rightward);
>
> Quick......step to the right side
>   (hips roll leftward),
> Quick......close with the left foot
>   (hips roll rightward),
> Slow........step <u>backward</u> with the right foot
>   (hips roll leftward).

The teacher corrected her student. "You are not completing the 'close.' Be sure and bring your trailing foot directly next to your leading foot."

She was watchful of his movements as they continued to dance. They did variations of basic rumba steps including turns and rocks. He made many missteps. She pointed out his mistakes step by step. Much too soon the hourly lesson was over. Miss Mills said some encouraging words to Joe Johnson. He showed no emotion and departed for home unable to remember all that she had taught him.

As she walked out of the ballroom into the lobby, Bert Craig, who happened to be nearby, caught sight of Marian on her way to the teachers' room. He did not linger in the lobby long. No sooner had the door closed behind her when Bert changed directions: making a U-turn, he headed straight for the teachers' room, which he entered.

Smiling at Marian, he pulled out a pack of cigarettes from his inside coat pocket and offered her a cigarette. But she refused it saying she did not smoke. He made himself comfortable in a chair close to hers.

Bert was so nervous his hand trembled as he put a cigarette in his mouth and lit the cigarette, sloppily getting the tip wet. Tiny flakes of tobacco stuck to his lips. Extinguishing the cigarette in an ashtray on a stand by his chair, he removed the tobacco flakes with his fingers and wiped his lips with the back of his hand. Now that his lips were dry, to occupy his hands, Bert quickly lit another cigarette.

Just as he was on the verge of starting a conversation with Marian, his wife entered the room. Alice glared at her husband who was puffing on a cigarette and inhaling the smoky vapors. Her nose twitched as she sniffed the air around him.

"You smell like a smokestack! Why are you burning up money on cigarettes? They are nicotine-plated coffin nails. Do you want to be nailed into a coffin at an early age!"

Alice was not jealous of her husband. She was concerned that he hacked hard nights after smoking a cigarette. She had no idea he lost his sexual appetite for her. Bert wanted something different. He craved a dish like Marian Mills.

He might as well have craved beautiful wild mushrooms (the poisonous variety). In spite of his fascination with her beauty, Marian was not good for him. Besides the fact that she was still a minor, she found Bert as amusing as a clown and appealing as a clod. That fact alone, if he realized it, would have put him in his grave earlier than lung cancer.

Having scolded her husband about his smoking, Alice softened her tone. "You know I love you. It isn't the wasted money, Bert. I am worried about your health. Anyhoo, health is wealth." She tried to make light of her scolding her husband as though he were a child.

Giving her husband a kiss on his cheek, Alice exclaimed "Oh, my! I almost forgot. Mr. Normand is going to begin his lecture in a few minutes on another Latin-American dance. It may be his last lecture. Let's hurry to his studio so that we don't miss anything."

All the while his wife was talking, Bert sat sullenly in his chair. He sprang to his feet ready to leave, for he was glad to be saved from an embarrassing situation. Marian, who was embarrassed for the Craigs, also was glad Normand's lecture had come to the rescue.

Chapter 51

A HISTORY OF THE CLASSIC BALLROOM DANCES

Latin-American Dances

III-D. The Mambo (to insure solidity and musical interpretation)

Assimilation as a sociological factor has been given weighty praise by analysts for the part it played in bringing about the maturation of the mambo. Postwar (W.W.II) groups of youthful, talented dancers—from New York's poor families of Puerto Rican and other Latin-American immigrants—followed their gregarious instincts and started drifting into Harlem's dance halls and ethnic ballrooms throughout the burroughs of the big city.

There foreign children were overwhelmed, like Dorothy in the Land of Oz, by the topsy-turvy world of music and dancing they stumbled upon: swinging!...jumping jive!...jitterbugging! How to do such *loco* gymnastics? The ears of the Puerto Ricans and other Latinos were attuned to melodies with lyrics about *el amor* and *la luna*. Their feet were adapted to exotic dance movements of South and Central America, and the West Indies.

["I do not overlook the fact that the United States had a territorial relationship to Puerto Rico as far back as 1819. However, it is also true," the supervisor explained to the teachers, "that the people on the island are connected directly or indirectly with other Latin-American realms by common language, if not by cultural bonds."]

Ego and pride stepped in. The Puerto Ricans as well as other Latinos could not permit themselves to be out-stepped nor outdone. Were they not accomplished dancers in their own right? They kept pace with the swingsters and jitterbugs; and soon the immigrants excelled in their interpretation of the Lindy hop, padding it with colorful patterns from south-of-the-border dances such as the intriguing figures of the Cuban son and the exciting movements of el cammando (a short-lived dance with brisk matador's plunges at polyangles).

Thereby the new-fledged generations of Spanish-speaking immigrants expressed their endemic personalities and simultaneously accustomed themselves to the various unorthodox movements of the American rumba fox trot. Movement by movement, the Latin dancers gained recognition and respect from their Yankee counterparts. This racial mingling socially on the dance floor was the intertwining freeway on which the elementary course of the mambo choreography was laid.

Before continuing on course, we should backtrack and set our sights on two theories. One theory by the stretch of the imagination identifies the modern mambo with an ancient ritual dance named mambo. The dance which is performed in Haiti by a voodooistic cult is also the name of their high priestess.

In the ritual, Mambo the priestess dances similarly to the biblical Salome whose uncle Herod Antipas grants her the head of John the Baptist for her performing a dance of seven veils (Matthew xiv:6-11). During the voodoo ritual—it originated in Africa—the high priestess casts off her veils to a tempo as slow as the movements of the Cuban son. With all the veils removed we can see the Haitian or African ritual mambo in no way regardless of the rhythm resembles the modern mambo.

The other theory elucidates that way back in the shadows of time, the mambo was conceived near the shores of the Congo, an undefined region in central Africa on both sides of the river. Black natives clapped their hands to create rhythms or beat congos (primitive drums) to produce drumbeats and counter drumbeats to the accompaniment of a mambo.

It is defined by an African dialect, not as a dance, but as a form of musical debate in which opponents sing (sometimes shout) words expressing their differences harmoniously. Neither dancers nor dances are mentioned. Rhythmical patterns were buried alive in Africa for centuries waiting to be uncovered.

Reality frequently being stronger than fantasy, the heart of Congo rhythms was exhumed alive with strong systolic contractions long before mambo music existed. One day in 1934 Arsenio Rodriguez, a Havana musician, listened to the heartbeats of rumba rhythm (in 4/4 time, having four beats to the measure). In accordance to his ear they sounded weak. What else he heard was a melody of monotones. Seeking a new treatment, he decided to experiment with standard Afro-Cuban rhythms.

As a guinea pig he selected a Montuno, traditionally delivered at the conclusion of a song by an individual *trumpeta*. For the accompaniment he increased the *trumpeta* to three, adding a *piano* and a Cuban *tambor* or an Afric *conga* (a large drum beaten with the hands).

The musical sound that the band produced was unheard of: incredible rhythms accentuated oddly by offbeats. Thus the basis of mambo music was created. Tragically, society shuns men who are ahead of their times. Although he was a noteworthy composer, Rodriguez was given the cold shoulder and his strange composition of music and musicians icily snubbed.

Mambo music was icebound at the seaport of Havana for almost a decade. Eventually in 1943 a passage was broken through the harbor waters by Dámasco Pérez Prado from Matanzas. It is a province in west central Cuba.

[On the spur of the moment the supervisor switched subjects. He was incited by the word Matanzas to reveal, in brief, to the teachers painfully cruel history behind the Cuban province:

"In the Spanish language *matanza* means 'slaughter' or 'bloodshed.' According to etymology, the term was derived from bloody episodes in the province of Matanzas. Not long after Cuba was conquered by the explorer Diego Velásques de León in 1511, the center of Spanish activities on the continent shifted to Cuba. Slave labor was needed.

"Soon the Spaniards started to slaughter Indians, who were too stubborn to work. There were among others in the area numerous Arwaks and Caribs. They were hunters and farmers—not slaves! Mulelike resistance to bondage was an unwritten law handed down to the Indians by their gods.

"As an alternative Negroid peoples were used as workhorses. Unless they were bridled, they refused to do difficult tasks. Mercilessly, the ones who balked were slaughtered, too.

"Some analysts are of the opinion that despite their rebellious ways, if it were not for their adaptability to work as well as their ability to work, the Africans never would have been brought to the continents of South and North America. Be that as it may, the sacrifice of human flesh—whether black, brown, or red skin—was an exorbitant price to pay for terpsichorean art, which is not always authentic."]

Dámasco Pérez Prado was a black musician with a natural gift for music. With little, if any, formal training, he was accepted by the famous Orquestra de la Playa as an arranger and pianist. After receiving his first major engagement at Buenos Aires, he next toured Mexico, Panama, Puerto Rico, and Venezuela.

On completion of his engagements, he found talented Afro-Cuban musicians and formed a band of his own. In 1947 while on a traveling circuit with his band, he went to the United States where he was crowned El Rey del Mambo. Using Arsenio Rodriguez's syncopated rhythms, Prado had structured the mambo with materials from the Havana style of el cammando, the movements of the American rumba fox trot, and the interpretive capers of Harlem's immigrant youths.

Besides his strongly syncopated rhythm and powerful sounding trumpet in his arrangements, Prado's performances are trademarked by bellows like the roar of a bull. As he leads his band Prado utters in Spanish *dar, dar, dar*! beckoning his band to 'give,' 'give,' 'give!'

["Small wonder there is discord on our planet. People often see and hear the same thing at the same time. Yet they are not in accord about what they saw and heard." The supervisor chuckled as the teachers perked up their ears. "When Prado appeared at the Downbeat Club in San Francisco, his fans witnessed Prado's performance diversely.

"Some swore they heard 'grunts,' which if so was undignified to say the least. Only hogs grunt. Some were positive Prado said: *vaya, vaya, vaya*! beckoning his band to 'go,' 'go,' 'go!' Whatever the words...whatever the language, what was said was said; it cannot be diversified."]

In some ways Dámasco Pérez Prado, twenty-nine years old, seems to be an enigma. Although he is far from formal, self-taught and self-made, he is heavily highbrow in his tastes. His idols are Igor Fëdorovich Stravinsky (Russian composer) and Jean Paul Sartre (French philosopher, novelist, dramatist). Prado's masterpiece 'Mambo Number 5' is an unforgettable experience for music lovers, on all levels.

'El Mambo,' a record album by Prado, was RCA Victor's top recording in 1950. The same year, a bandleader and composer Tito Puente, also twenty-nine years old, played mambo music at Broadway's Palladium, the home of sweet jazz. It was Puente's first appearance at the Palladium. His musical performance was so popular he was called back nine times for repeat performances. The home of sweet jazz thus became home sweet home to winsome mambo music.

But the Cuban dance itself had not yet reached its full state of refinement. Unless accompanied by refined rhythm the mambo was too coarse for polite society. Mambo figures lacked etiquette and finesse. All the while professional proponents of Latin-American dances descended upon the Park Plaza Ballroom in Harlem, originally the headquarters of the ethnic order of mamboites.

The dance from Havana was the talk of the town. Dancing societies saw potential wealth in mambo figures. They were welcomed into the fold. Eager to partake of the riches, professionals—Emily Post types—rolled up their sleeves and laundered the mambo, washing away its plebeian vagaries and starching it with plutocratic mannerisms.

["From Palm Beach to Palm Springs, cash registers in dance studios ring hourly as skillful exhibition teams sensationalize the mambo. Seduced by its chic figures, Jack and Jill America spend large sums of money to get to know the mambo. Money is required, still, without the required skill, whenever somebody appears to do the dance, an abortion is performed."

The teachers howled with laughter at the supervisor's pregnant remark. "It isn't a laughing matter!" he exclaimed, forcing himself to hold back a laugh. The mambo routine is now elevated to a professional level, or to a high standard for apt amateurs.

"Most people can't do simple rumba figures, let alone complicated mambo figures. Rumba is to mambo what arithmetic is to algebra. Can you imagine trying to solve an equation in algebra without knowing addition, subtraction, multiplication, division, and fractions?

"Similarly it would be just as futile for us to attempt to dance a mambo routine if we had not mastered basics such as walking steps, rocks, breaks, spot turns, and rumba motion. Still, people who cannot rumba, or perform it poorly, insist upon being taught the mambo. And they are not deterred by costly fancy lessons. Was it Lew Lehrs who said 'Monkeys are the craziest people.'

"You should explain to your students that in the rumba, action takes place from the waist down, exclusively around the hips. Although the movement is subtle and much more in the mambo, this delicate operation is not to be neglected. Activity in the upper portion of the body is chiefly coddled by the mambo. Moreover, the mambo's necessitating greater floor space is due to its intricate and complex footwork.

"Like the rumba, the mambo is in four-four time. But the way the mambo beat is accented is the key to its performance, locking out the similarity of rumba rhythm. The dissimilar technique in the mambo is accenting the fourth beat and using staccato movements sweetly buttered with smoothness.

"Watch as I demonstrate the regular and advanced mambo rhythms that are outlined on the blackboard:

A. Regular Mambo Rhythm

Step on 1, holding the same foot for the 2 count;
step on 3, bringing the feet together; break,
that is, step and emphasize 4.

OR...Slow (L forward)—Quick (R close)—Quick (L forward).

B. Advanced Mambo Rhythm

Step on 1 with emphasis, bringing the feet together on 2 and holding that position for the 3 count; break, that is, step and emphasize 4.

OR...Quick (L forward)—Slow (R close)—Quick (L forward).

"Of course, the woman steps in opposition to the man. Also I might add that a hold, or a pause, serves as an emphasis. Simple, isn't it? Seriously, once a person masters the mambo, the rumba forfeits its fascination quite the same as casino loses its appeal to the card player who is proficient in contract bridge.

"Around 1948 when there was clamoring to enter the mambo in the social register, a type of music—bebop—had an influence on mambo music which in turn had an influence on the dance. Much is said and little is told about bebop, an ultraist subject of American jazz.

"I haven't the time now to go into it. By your expressions I can see you are disappointed. I promise at a future date to give a talk about bebop."]

Chapter 52

A week had gone by and Vincent Armstrong still failed to return to National Dance Studios. He was terribly troubled, too troubled to teach. His world was falling apart instead of falling into place. As a youth, his path in life was guided by orderly objective signs: education...marriage...career.

What had Vincent accomplished—nothing! He had yet to complete his education. He had yet to become a lawyer. He had yet to meet a woman with whom he could build a future that would lead to his objectives.

Vincent had expected Elaine Cummings to be the love of his life. His hopes were shattered into pieces, as the smashed glass of a mirror. Life had struck him a low blow. He was reeling from the hard fact that she was a lesbian. Never before had Vincent encountered someone like her. Or had he?

There was Jenny. No! She may have been bisexual. But she was not a lesbian. Vincent began to search his memory, going back in time when he was a soldier during World War II.

The Battle of the Bulge having ended victoriously for the American troops, pursuing First Army forces shifted to the north where they were able to cross the Roer River through a gap in the Siegfried Line near Aschendorff, West Germany. On the night of February 8, 1945, the 276th Engineer Combat Battalion, in convoy formation, also advanced in a northerly direction. Their trucks slithered and slid from pothole to pothole on muddy battle-ridden roads.

Suddenly the entire convoy came to a half, blocked by numerous tanks and heavy artillery mired in the mud. Finding a detour at daybreak, the 276th Battalion continued onward.

As they drove through frightening rows of concrete dragon's teeth protruding from the Siegfried Line, heavily reinforced with tank traps and huge concrete pillboxes fitted with machine guns that fired dragonlike spurts of fiery spit, the engineers swore they would have preferred engaging a real live dragon in hand-to-hand combat. They had to marvel at the efficiency of the courageous American infantry and armoured divisions who were tearing apart the dreadful line of German fortifications.

Hours later the 276th Battalion was billeted in a schoolhouse at Schleckheim and adjacent villages. The engineers immediately were put to work maintaining miserable muddy roads leading to the Roer River.

Their heavy road work was lightened—at least for a few—by a humorous event that occurred within the week. It was humorous because the event seemed so out of place in a wretched war zone. All the men in the battalion were awarded Good Conduct Medals for a year's service without a blemish on their records.

Under the circumstances, the men were less than enthusiastic about receiving such a medal, which was merely a ribbon to be worn beside their revered ribbons for service in the European Theatre of Operations (ETO). What did arouse enthusiasm, as well as envy, was the awarding of an initial series of passes to France, England, and Belgium.

To determine winners the men drew straws, long and short. Losers were disappointed. Winners were delighted. Private Vincent Armstrong was a lucky winner. He was especially delighted. He won a pass to France.

In anticipation that Vincent might have an opportunity to visit Paris, uncle Walter had sent him a package of lipsticks with which to woo French women. It seems uncle Walter heard there was a shortage of everything in Europe. While making preparations for his furlough, Vincent tossed into a small duffel bag the lipsticks, a carton of cigarettes, some chocolate bars, extra pairs of shorts and socks, and men's toiletries.

Gai Pă•rē! occasionally Vincent Armstrong heard 'gay Paris' pronounced playfully that way in San Francisco. Here he was in Paris and it looked anything but gay or playful. The war had taken its toll on the city.

There were no sounds of horns. The streets were devoid of traffic. With the exception of military vehicles, neither private cars nor public buses were anywhere in sight. Taxicabs (emergency ambulances) were allowed on the streets provided their passengers were wounded war veterans.

A splintering crash broke the silence on the streets. Vincent saw a G.I. kicking out the plate glass of revolving doors to one of the hotels. Vincent wanted to ask someone what the disturbance was about. Unfortunately Vincent could not speak French.

Pointing to the hotel, he attempted to use sign language. It did not help. He might as well have been on Mars trying to communicate with Martians. Still worse, none of the Parisians cracked a smile. Had ugly Americans spoiled things for their countrymen?

Beautiful women passed Vincent by wherever he went without as much as a glance, although he tried to make eye contact. Finally he met a handsome young Frenchman who spoke English. Vincent asked if he would direct him to a place that served good food.

The young Frenchman suggested an excellent place to dine would be Café de Rohan, one of the oldest cafés in Paris, very famous for delicious brioches. He gave the American directions to the café, but they were too complicated for him to follow. Vincent offered to treat his new acquaintance to a dinner if he could accompany him to the café. Vincent's invitation was accepted cheerfully.

On their way to the café, the Frenchman and the American boarded the Métropolitan railway, which Parisians refer to simply as the Métro. Since it was the sole means of transportation, usually the system was crowded to the hilt. The civilian paid his own fare. The soldier paid none. Métro was free to people in military uniform.

Café de Rohan was located at 1, place de Palais Royal. Upon their arrival the two young men were seated at tables on a pleasant terrace facing the world-famous Louvre as well as the Palais-Royal. The enclosure of the palace grounds forms a spacious square where among other celebrities, Victor Maria Hugo, the French author, had lived. After his demise (1885) Hugo's house was preserved as a museum.

Vincent could not help but be amazed by the marvelous architecture and size of the Louvre. Quite talkative, the guest informed his host it is one of the largest groups of buildings in the world, exactly 1,801 feet long. Constructed by King Phillip II in the twelfth century, the Louvre was originally a royal fortress and palace.

Over the century the Louvre underwent periods of remodeling. By 1793 the Louvre had been constructed, and officially converted, into a national art museum renowned for its collection of old masters: Rembrandt, Rubens, Titian, Leonardo. The museum's prize possessions are two priceless sculptures: Nike of Victory of Samothrace and Venus of Milo.

All the while the Frenchman was talking the American nibbled on a brioche; the sweet, light-textured bun truly tasted delicious. The civilian's talk was interesting except the soldier had something else on his mind...women. His pass was valid only for three days. Vincent Armstrong now had satisfied his appetite for fine food. He still needed to satisfy his appetite for fair sex.

Vincent revealed to the Frenchman that he craved the company of a woman. Where was the best place to meet one? He had lots of lipsticks to give her as a gift, if she appealed to him. The Frenchman laughed and replied, offering *une femme* a lipstick in France was the same as offering a female Eskimo an icicle in Alaska. There was no shortage of cosmetics in Paris. What was in very short supply was cigarettes and chocolates.

That was no problem, Vincent said. He removed a pack of cigarettes from his duffel bag, and handed it to the Frenchman. The guest thanked the host suggesting he visit Place Pigalle where he could meet *les femmes* of his desire.

As soon as they left the café, the Frenchman showed the American the way to a railway station where he could take the Métro to the suggested destination. They shook hands and parted company forever.

Place Pigalle, to Vincent Armstrong's displeasure, was a beehive swarming with soldiers from all branches of the armed forces. At 59, rue Pigalle, he came across Caprice Viennois. Looking inside, he found it was a nightclub with an intimate atmosphere.

Seating himself at the bar, he followed the bartender's recommendation and ordered a sidecar (1/3 lemon or lime juice, 1/3 cointreau, 1/3 brandy). Vincent preferred lemon juice. While sipping his cocktail he saw her—Jenny! They made magnetic eyeball to eyeball contact. She walked over to Vincent and without saying a word grabbed him by the crotch. She was with a girl friend, Francis, who had started to giggle in anticipation of Jenny's brazen naughtiness.

Vincent should have been shocked, but he was not. The war immunized him against shock. He had come face to face with death on the battleground; it was the shock of a lifetime. Death's frightening face had scared the hell out of him till kingdom come. Momentary mutual pleasure was nothing to fear except in peacetime under monitorship by self-righteous mortals. Perhaps he was living his last days...hours...minutes...seconds on earth. Jenny (if that was her real name) must have understood in war a soldier frequently lived on borrowed time. Why not make his unsecured, short-term life pleasurable.

Jenny spoke a little broken English and a little German. Between the two languages she and Vincent were able to communicate. Opportunely he had studied German in high school. They filled in missing words with universal body language.

The nightclub was hot and stuffy—too crowded for comfort. Jenny expressed her desire to leave and go to a comfortable hotel. She would have liked Francis to join her and Vincent. But her girl friend drifted away into the arms of another soldier. She promised to join Jenny later.

Registering at a predetermined hotel, Jenny insisted on paying for the room. In the dimly-lighted nightclub, Vincent did not get a good look at Jenny. In the bright light of the hotel room he was able to see more clearly how she looked, particularly when she disrobed.

Jenny's hair raked up in Vincent's mind the blackish plumage of a petrel. Her dark moist eyes looked as mysterious as a misty night sky. Judging by her doelike complexion, he decided she must be from the Middle East or possibly from North West Africa.

Where did she learn to speak the German language? Vincent received a quick answer, yet it was quite adequate. What little German she knew was taught to her by a Nazi officer. Jenny's birthplace was Algeria. Nazis murdered her family and abducted her.

The officer said he would release her as soon as they arrived in Paris. He was a big liar. He continued to hold her against her will. When Paris was liberated by the Allies, she managed to escape from the fleeing fascist pig.

Suddenly she was silent. Jenny's mood changed from sadness to sex. Wiping tearful moisture off her long eyelashes, she placed her salty wet fingers on his lips. Then to sweeten the man's tastebuds she drew his head onto her breasts. He suckled the woman's nipples as if he were a hummingbird extracting nectar from two flowers in full bloom.

Fingering her firm, resilient hips, he felt the emotion of a harpist stroking strings in a symphonic forest alive with glowing music of bird and beast. Vincent was on fire, overwhelmed by glowing delight. He had to clear the underbrush or be overcome by heat. As he made his way past the midst of the brush, white-hot liquid discharged from a tubular vent in his body like molten lava erupting from a volcano.

The next day some time in the afternoon, a knock on the door put an end to Vincent Armstrong's volcanic eruptions. Francis was admitted into the room. Jenny coaxed her girl friend to undress and jump into bed for a threesome. Francis said she would love to play, but her pussy was sore. The soldier she met at the nightclub was a big dick G.I.

Vincent was relieved there would be no sexual games. His mind was willing, his body unwilling. He was physically drained. The tired man invited the two young women to have a late lunch with him. They were hungry, so they accepted his invitation, and the three of them went to a nearby restaurant.

One of the dishes they ordered included baked beans. To Vincent's embarrassment Francis all of a sudden sounded off with short blasts: beans, beans, the musical fruit, the more you eat, the more you toot...toot-toot...toot-toot...TOOT!

Forcing a smile, Vincent asked from whom had she learned that? From big dick the G.I. American, she replied in a giggly manner. Glad she had stopped the unappetizing tooting, he wondered if she realized Dick was a nickname for Richard. Did Francis really understand dick was vulgar slang for penis?

Before they were ready to leave the restaurant, Vincent with the best of intentions offered Jenny some money. She promptly refused it. He also offered her lipsticks, which she refused. He also offered her cigarettes, which she refused. He also offered her chocolates, which she refused.

Jenny was not offended nor was she angry. To show her appreciation for Vincent's offerings—intended as gifts—she swung an arm around his shoulder, and gave him an unforgettable French kiss. It was her way of showing how deeply he had touched her heart. She hoped the soldier would remember her until his dying day.

Vincent had a few hours to kill before his pass expired. Now on his own, he strolled along from place to place. He came to a stop at 41, rue Pigalle, the address of the Swing Club, an American artists' and musicians' bar. Vincent was attracted to it by a feeling of nostalgia.

The Swing Club was a place where he could communicate in the English language and hear familiar American music. His expectations were fulfilled. The musicians were playing the orchestral leader Tommy Dorsey's rendition of Boogie Woogie. Vincent got a charge out of watching the piano player tickle the ivory keyboard to a boogie-woogie beat.

A soldier tapped Vincent Armstrong on the shoulder while he was engaged in conversation with artists at the bar. Speaking of coincidence, the soldier was the one who spent the night with Jenny's girl friend. The two G.I.s exchanged friendly greetings.

Without being encouraged in the least, the soldier, a paratrooper, persisted in discussing the details of his intercourse with Francis. . . . The little whore sure was a great lay. How was your whore?

Vincent was burned up. However, he held his hot temper in check. He did not want to talk about Jenny, especially in a derogatory manner. Getting no response, unaware he was antagonizing Vincent Armstrong, the insensitive chatterbox turned tell tale. On my way over here I saw her proposition some old geezer. They walked off together, and he had a hand on her behind.

Oops! the paratrooper interjected as he looked up at a wall clock. I better take off. I'm overdue at the base. I don't want to miss the next Métro train. He did an about-face and rushed out the exit of the club.

Disgusted with the paratrooper's tasteless tale, Vincent had a bad taste in his mouth, which he could not wash away with a highball. He wished the paratrooper had kept his dirty trap shut!

Rolling an ice cube around in his mouth helped cool Vincent's temper. Jenny treated him royally; he respected her for that. He soon completely cooled down, since the musicians now were playing Rum and Coca-Cola. The singers were good, but they did not compare to the Andrews sisters. They were the best.

A San Franciscan Morey Amsterdam wrote the lyrics to the song. In Vincent's reminiscing he had traveled far back in his thoughts to a foreign land at a time of war. He breathed a sigh of relief that he was home in San Francisco at a time of peace.

Chapter 53

"Welcome back to National Dance Studios, Vincent. We missed you. Didn't we?" Alice Craig said as she turned to her husband for confirmation.

Confirming his wife's statement, Bert replied: "We certainly did. The place hasn't been the same without you, Vince. Were you ill?"

Not wishing to go into a long explanation, Vincent told his friends a white lie. "I had a touch of the flu. I am over it now."

Alice expressed concern: "Are you sure you're okay. You must be feeling a bit weak."

"Not at all. I had a good rest." Vincent was ashamed of himself for lying to the Craigs. But for their sake it was best they did not know anything about his involvement with Elaine Cummings. The no-dating rule was strictly enforced. Although he parted with her in a friendly way, she was still a student at the Studio.

At that moment, after coming out of a nearby office, a studio manager and two other people were walking toward Vincent. The manager approached the teacher to introduce the two people. "Mr. Armstrong, meet Mr. Fred Burton and his wife Diana. They are your new students.

"Neither one has ever learned to dance. Divide their hourly lesson, half an hour for each." The manager's departing words to the Burtons were "I leave you in good hands."

Vincent told Alice and Bert that he would see them later. No further discussion was necessary. It was understood they would be in the teachers' room. Besides, the Craigs had no time to waste. Their own students were waiting impatiently in the lobby.

To put the Burtons at ease, Vincent smiled pleasantly while

escorting them into the ballroom. He requested they be seated. Instead of teaching them to dance separately, he decided it would be easier if they were taught together at the same time.

The teacher prepared the students with a directional analogy: "Before we get going, it will be helpful if you imagine a dance floor is a big compass indicating the four cardinal points. When two travelers take a trip, they travel in one or more of the principal directions. They go north, south, west, east comfortably at different speeds, depending on their means of transportation.

"So it is when couples dance, they move forward, backward, to either side—or combinations of the four—gracefully in time to the music: slow, medium, or fast. And, of course, dance steps can be short or long just as vacation trips can be short or long.

"I have devised a technique by which both of you will receive a full hour of instruction. It is not difficult, and you will each get two lessons for the price of one, in a manner of speaking." The Burtons were pleased but puzzled.

Vincent had the couple stand up and walk onto the dance floor. He arranged their bodies in fox-trot position and adjusted their arms so that they were properly placed. Fred faced north, Diana faced south.

Next, Vincent instructed Fred to move leftward about three feet away from his wife but still maintain the proper position, pretending she was in his arms. Vincent instructed Diana to stand in place and maintain the proper position, pretending her husband was in her arms.

Facing north, Vincent stepped between husband and wife. Vincent placed his left hand on Fred's shoulder. And Vincent placed his right hand on Diana's shoulder.

Now Vincent instructed the Burtons to move in whichever direction he moved. He would indicate where he was moving by pressure on their shoulders with his hands. He cautioned the couple not to look at their feet, which was a bad habit to get into.

Also the teacher cautioned the students not to be distracted by the tempo of the music. Their speed would be determined by the quickness or slowness of his steps. Putting an adolescent's fun into an adult's dancing lesson, the teacher quoted "one for the money, two for the show, three to get ready, and four to go":

As Vincent walked forward, Fred walked forward and Diana walked backward. They all walked in unison. As Vincent walked backward, Fred walked backward and Diana walked forward. They all walked in unison.

As Vincent moved sideward—to the left or to the right—they all moved sideward. But they did not move well in unison. They moved well in unison after the teacher instructed his students in moving sideward to step-close, step-close, and so forth.

A few numbers later, the music having stopped, Fred Burton said: "Mr. Armstrong, I operate an employment agency. From my experience in dealing with people, it is obvious to me that you are well educated as well as highly intelligent. Do not get me wrong. I, and my wife, are enjoying your unique teaching method immensely. However, I believe you are qualified for professional work on a higher plane."

"Thank you for the compliment, Mr. Burton. As a matter of fact, I intend to return to the University of California to earn more credits toward a bachelor's degree."

"Good for you, Mr. Armstrong!" exclaimed Fred. Then squeezing his wife's arm, he gloated, "You see, dear, I sensed I was right about my estimation of the man." (In between dances Fred had whispered to Diana that Mr. Armstrong was sharp—sharp as a tack.) Pleased with himself, Fred smiled broadly and asked Vincent, "What is your major?"

Vincent answered: "I shall be taking courses which will prepare me for law school. It is my ambition to become a lawyer, a criminal lawyer, but not a prosecutor."

Fred's upward curve of his mouth turned downward. No longer smiling, he spoke with a scowl. "I have no use for defense lawyers. Lawyers are liars!"

Caught off guard by the strong language, Vincent was on the defensive. "Liars? I suppose they sometimes stretch the truth. But they do that to save innocent defendants...from prison...from the gas chamber."

"Yes, and most of the time lawyers lie to save the slimy skin of criminals who are guilty as hell." By now Fred was fulminating. "How can they sleep nights knowing they have been responsible for helping criminals get away with murder? Gold dust must be a miraculous sedative."

In that he was disarmed, Vincent found himself trapped in an adverse position he really did not like to defend. "Well, they take their clients at face value. Their clients usually swear they are innocent. It cannot be assumed a lawyer is aware of his client's criminal past."

"You are mistaken, Mr. Armstrong. In most cases lawyers are not only aware of their clients' criminal past but the lawyers also cover it up." Burton swallowed hard from tension. "What is worse, they suppress incriminating evidence that could convict their clients."

"It all comes out in the trial and the criminal gets the punishment he deserves." With a wavering tone Vincent added, "He either is given the death sentence or he goes to prison for a long time to pay for his crime."

"Is that a fact," Fred Burton remarked sarcastically. He reached into his inner coat pocket and took out a narrow notebook. "You may have seen an article in the newspaper about Alden Caffery who was on trial for butchering Sarah Driskell, a beautiful model.

"Let me read a portion of the trial testimony I obtained from the court records of the Sonoma County district attorney's office:

*** September 23, 1927: Caffery was arrested in Redwood City on traffic warrants. Between April and October he was implicated in more than twenty La Honda burglaries. He pleaded guilty to burglary and was sentenced to six months in county jail and placed on probation.

*** May 10, 1929: Caffery was arrested for auto theft and possession of marijuana. He received a ten-day jail sentence.

*** July 21, 1929: Caffery's probation was revoked after he was arrested for burglary and grand theft in San Francisco. Caffery was sentenced to a term of six months to fifteen years. He was paroled from Vacaville after serving eighteen months.

*** August 23, 1930: Caffery abducted Mildred Smith, a legal secretary in her mid-twenties. After dragging her away from a Hayward bus station, he attempted to sexually assault her. She ran and hailed a passing Highway Patrol car. Informed of her ordeal, the officer, Edward Burns, searched for Caffery and arrested him.

*** November 7, 1930: Caffery was transferred to Napa State Hospital for psychiatric evaluation after he tried to hang himself in a cell at Alameda County Jail. He later admitted he faked the suicide attempt in order to be sent to a state hospital where he could more easily escape.

*** November 15, 1930: Caffery escaped from Napa State Hospital and went on a four-day crime spree in Napa. He broke into the home of Grace Forester, a nurse at the hospital, and beat her on the head with a fire poker while she slept.

Next Caffery broke into the Napa County animal shelter and stole a shotgun. He intended to use it to kidnap Betty Helfand, a bartender, when she was getting into her Cadillac parked outside the bar. Seeing that he had bindings, she rolled out of her car and at the same time grabbed a gun from under the seat. She fired six shots at Caffery as he fled.

*** November 20, 1930: Caffery broke into a home in La Honda owned by Vivian Cole, a bank employee. Caffery was arrested by a San Mateo County sheriff's deputy who had hidden in bushes behind the home to catch the burglar.

*** May 30, 1931: Caffery was sentenced to a term of one to twenty-five years in prison for the Mildred Smith abduction. A sexual assault charge against Caffery was dropped as part of a plea bargain. He later was sentenced to concurrent terms for the Napa crime spree and the breaking-and-entering into the La Honda home.

*** February 3, 1936: Caffery was paroled from Deuel Vocational Institute in Tracy.

*** February 21, 1939: Caffery with a woman accomplice, Bertha Blake, pistol-whipped Judith Patterson in her Redwood City apartment. She was dragged to the bank and forced to withdraw $6,000 from her account. Caffery and Blake made a quick getaway with the money.

*** May 26, 1947: Caffery was paroled from the California Men's colony, San Luis Obispo, after serving half of a sixteen-year sentence for the Patterson kidnapping.

"While on parole Alden Caffery stole a car and drove to Santa Barbara. Like untold numbers of hardened criminals, he was not in the least bit rehabilitated. To the contrary, he sought a wealthy community with an expensive home that was safe to burglarize. He decided to go elsewhere because the homes he was casing looked well secured and unsafe to break into.

"Just as he was about to turn on the ignition, he saw a woman pull into a driveway. She stepped out of her car, removed two pieces of luggage from the trunk, walked to the entranceway of the home, and set the luggage down on the landing so that she could open the door. After unlocking the door, she entered the home with a suitcase in each hand. Unfortunately she left the key in the lock.

"A seasoned stalker, Caffery smelled blood. She had to be the only one in the home. He jumped out of his car, ran up to the entranceway, removed the key, closed the door, unsheathed a switchblade knife, and cornered prey he lusted for.

"Caffery said he wouldn't hurt her if she offered no resistance. All he wanted was cash and jewelry. She was too terrified to resist.

With knife in hand he shoved her into the rooms making her put her valuables in pillowcases. When he was satisfied he had everything of value that was easily carried, he played a game of cat and mouse. He might release her...he might not. He might leave...he might not. He might leave after she served him some Scotch whiskey at the wet bar, which she did.

"While going through the rooms, he had suspected from photographs on the walls she was a model. Questioned, she was afraid to deny it. He motioned to her to pour him another shot glass of Scotch whiskey. She fell to her knees begging him to leave. Drunk with the power he had over her, he demanded that she take off her clothes and pose for him the way models do at fashion shows. To pacify him she posed against her will but refused to undress.

"Infuriated, Caffery slashed the counter of the wet bar with his switchblade threatening to do the same to her unless she obeyed his demands without a whimper. Praying in silence for Almighty God to save her, she removed her clothes. Her prayers were unanswered.

"Caffery forced her to place her hands on the bar stool and sodomized her mercilessly. In his depraved, criminal mind she deserved no mercy because she vomited from revulsion. Yelling at the top of his lungs that he would be the last person on earth to enjoy her beauty, he slashed her face and body until she succumbed and was no longer recognizable as a human being.

*** On October 29, 1947, Alden Caffery was arrested in Los Angeles for drunken driving—and parole violation.

"A necklace belonging to Sarah Driskell was found in the glove compartment of the car he had stolen. Bloodstains on a pillowcase hidden under newspapers in the trunk matched Sarah's blood. Caffery's fingerprints proved to be identical to the ones on the wet bar in the murdered model's home. Confronted with overwhelming incriminating evidence, Caffery confessed to the crime.

*** On September 6, 1947, Alden Caffery was formally charged with the murder of Sarah Driskell.

*** On July 14, 1950, a Los Angeles Superior Court jury recommended Caffery be sentenced from eleven years to life with the possibility of parole.

"The verdict provoked gasps throughout the courtroom crowded with the victim's family. The merciful verdict—acutely distressing to their hearts—left wounds which would never heal.

"The defense attorneys sighed with relief that the panel had opted for the more lenient of its options—the severest was the death penalty. Praise the Lord! God bless the jury for exercising mercy! Caffery's lawyer, Stern Hardin, exclaimed as he jumped with joy (and for jack).

"In a joint statement read by the jury foreman, the jurors denied being influenced by their religious beliefs or personal prejudices. The jurors said during two days of deliberations they had carefully examined the evidence and reached their unanimous verdicts accordingly.

"A reporter, who interviewed members of the jury, asked specifically what evidence they relied on for their verdict in lieu of the death penalty? They said Sarah should not have left her key in the door. She should not have served the intruder drinks. She should not have taken off her clothes. More important, she offered no resistance to the defendant's advances.

"The reporter also interviewed one of the defense attorneys who said: While they were relieved their client did not receive the death penalty, he should have been acquitted in spite of his signed confession. They will seek a new trial mainly on the grounds that one juror interpreted a document for other jurors in violation of the judge's instructions to the jury.

"The reporter asked the attorney: Isn't it a fact that the jurors—all homely women—lacked sympathy for the victim because she was beautiful? And isn't it a fact that they were sympathetic to the defendant because he is a handsome man? The attorney replied furiously, Neither question deserves an answer!

"Mr. Armstrong, I might as well tell you, the beautiful model Sarah Driskell was my sister-in-law. Well, now do you understand why I feel the way I do about lawyers?"

Vincent's heart overflowed with empathy for his student. "Mr. Burton, I understand completely. I owe you an apology. I was being the devil's advocate. The truth is, I have mixed emotions about becoming a defense attorney.

"The criminal justice system is badly flawed. Too often the punishment does not fit the crime. As an attorney, I would dedicate myself to fix the flaws. I believe trouble is brewing if the legal profession ignores the graffiti on society's protective wall of laws against criminals. If guilty defendants live to mock society, one day the wall will crack wide open...perhaps beyond repair."

Chapter 54

After they were all present and seated, Ralph Normand addressed the group of dancing teachers under his supervision. "This morning I am going to discuss bebop, music and dance, as I promised at our last session. But first I shall fill in information about boogie-woogie I omitted in my discussion on the history of the jitterbug.

"The reason boogie-woogie will be discussed first is that it preceded bebop. Both are similar species musically. Both are a kind of jazz music, which is as American as hominy grits.

"In its unhulled form jazz music had been a staple of African slaves since before Lincoln issued an Emancipation Proclamation in 1863. Afterward treatment of jazz music by American Negroes produced phenomenal soul food. However, the jazz menu lists too many things to consume. I shall simply stay with the two selected, bebop and boogie-woogie.

"Authorities claim that boogie-woogie is of indeterminate origin. Therefore, in the history of the jitterbug I stated that the origin of the word boogie is obscure and that Clarence (Pine Top) Smith used the word woogie on a label of his recording Pine Top's Boogie Woogie. Using woogie was not original yet smart show business because it rhymed with boogie and was readily remembered.

"Recently I did some research. As a result I arrived at an explanation of how boogie-woogie originated. I determined the word boogie was derived from 'bogie,' a locomotive or railroad undercarriage with a set of wheels which enables it to negotiate curves on rails.

"With the adoption of the Fourteenth Amendment (July 28, 1868) granting citizenship to Negroes, they gradually migrated to Texas and towns west of the Mississippi. To white workers who visited saloons in railroad construction camps, boogie-woogie sounded like a speeding west-bound locomotive. Thus the workers named it Fast Western. To self-taught black players who improvised as they pounded out hot jazz on a piano, the fast-moving wheels of a locomotive inspired a bogie beat and rolling rhythm, which in turn inspired the full name of boogie-woogie music.

"1940 was a year of innovation in the United States. On May 15, Vought-Sikorsky Corporation's experimental helicopter completed the first successful flight. Also that year in New York, musicians at Minton's Playhouse, a club in Harlem, were flying high with a new approach to uplifting jazz known as rebop or bebop or just plain bop. All three words were onomatopoetic, long ago formed from occasional odd sounds made inadvertently by musicians on instruments such as the trumpet and the saxophone. Rebop without doubt was a repeated bop sound popping from inside a brass instrument by a music maker, like bursting kernels in a metal popcorn maker.

"In the bebop world of musicians, two Afro-Americans are respected as royalty: John (Dizzy) Gillespie, trumpet player and bandleader; and Charles (Yardbird) Parker, alto saxophone player. Some say Gillespie, the prince of the trumpet, enriched bebop and spread it among the people. Some say Parker, the prince of the saxophone, enriched bebop and spread it among the people. The fact is they both had a hand in the enrichment of bebop, as well as anonymous musicians at the world court of jazz.

"Parker was a genius whose priceless jazz works of art were shamelessly stolen by other musicians. Gillespie was a magnificent musician with amazing agility in jazz techniques. He not only was hailed monarch of bebop but also was acclaimed top trumpeter. Parker's natural power over the saxophone was unchallenged. Unhappily he overtaxed his musical talents. Exhausted mentally, he had a nervous breakdown. For a time Parker was confined in California at Camarillo State Hospital.

"One should not be fooled by the silly sounding slang of bebop. It is a style of jazz characterized by chromatic, melodic, harmonic, and rhythmic complexities. At times they are subtly executed despite rapidity of tempo.

"To elaborate, bebop is a form of discordant jazz in which notes are played at mind-boggling speed with frequent accents on the upbeat and less frequent accents on the downbeat. The influence bebop had on jazz was to broaden patterns of harmony...loosen rigid rhythms...and permit a soloist virtually unrestricted freedom of improvisation through chord changes and transitions in music—bar after bar, for as long as a jazzman is able to improvise.

"Bebop infiltrated most jazz and almost all popular music. Consequently, scores of phrases appeared in orchestral arrangements. The black princess of jazz singing Ella Fitzgerald, winner of the Esquire Gold Award, imitating brass instruments bebopped beautifully in 1947 at a concert in Carnegie Hall.

"But bebopping by a singer was one thing, bebopping by a dancer was something else. That kind of jazz was not danceable until bop dance steps were devised on which downbeats were stressed by alternating from the flat of the toes to the edge of the heels. Such dancing is difficult if not impossible to do because of bop's breakneck tempo. In short, bebop is a fad that cannot live long...unless it will some day be miraculously resurrected."

Now that the supervisor's talk was finished, the teachers sauntered out of his room into the hallway. Some went to small studios to practice new dance steps. Some went to a technique session to sharpen their dancing skills. Some went to the ballroom to teach students with whom they had appointments. Some went to the teachers' room where we find Armstrong and the Craigs engaged in conversation.

Alice Craig was bemoaning the fact that there would be no more discussions on the history of social dancing. Bert Craig was complaining about the problems he was having with one of his students. Vincent Armstrong was expressing his regret that he had missed the lecture on the mambo.

After a while the three of them came to a conclusion: They needed a change of pace. Alice said going on a leisurely picnic would be something different. Vincent and Bert agreed a picnic was a good idea. His wife offered to pack a lunch basket. Over the Craigs' objections, Armstrong insisted upon paying his share of the lunch. The day selected for a picnic was the next Sunday. The place selected for a picnic was Sutro Heights.

Sutro Heights is a spacious public park on a bluff high above the Pacific Ocean at the western edge of San Francisco (corner of Forty-eighth and Point Lobos Avenues). At the time Adolph Sutro purchased the land, the bluff's surface was nothing but barren sand dunes, except for a small cottage. He transformed the bluff into a parklike estate. Sutro was mayor of the city in 1895. Prior to his death (July 8, 1898), he resided in the cottage, which was white as a cloud on a clear day.

Although Sutro had the cottage enlarged and designed ornately, it was a simple abode compared to the grand Victorian mansions of other wealthy land barons. In spite of the relative simplicity of his residence, he spent lavishly on formal gardens and European statuary to aggrandize the grounds of the estate.

The entrance to Sutro Heights was—and still is—guarded by two life-size concrete lions. In the mayor's era, a majestic, Gothic gateway at the entrance to the estate opened up to Palm Avenue, lined on both sides with a variety of exotic trees. They were planted in profuse groves everywhere on the bluff.

Several yards away from the cottage, steps cut into solid rock led to a lofty mound upon which Sutro built a spaced, semicircular wall of stone blocks. The mound was the summit of Mount Olympus overlooking the ocean. The stone-block wall, a circular temple, was the Greek pantheon dedicated to deities.

Assembled on Olympus were mythical gods and goddesses. From his throne on the summit, Zeus, the supreme deity, presided over the pantheon. Ruler of the sky...of the winds...of the clouds...of the rain, he poured forth words of wisdom oracularly to his underling divinities.

Prophesying to Oceanus—the god of lakes, rivers, and seas—Zeus warned him: mortal man with a diseased mind will in a century infect your healthy bodies of water. I shall use my godly powers to rain purifying torrents upon all the earthly waters. But I fear it may be too late!

Prophesying to Demeter—the goddess of fertile and cultivated soil—Zeus warned her: mortal man in his greed will in a century steal your mantle of forests—flowers will freeze...medicinal plants will die. I shall use my godly powers to renew the life of vegetation on earth. But I fear it may be too late!

In the twentieth century Sutro Heights became public land. Toppled, vandalized statues of mythological figures were moved to dark vaults elsewhere in the city. Rotted trees were cut down by the groves. (Stumps were not always removed.) Flower carpet beds were wrecked, and not replaced. The mayor's cottage fell into disrepair and was demolished.

Alice Craig set a lunch basket on a blanket spread over unmowed grass where yesteryear landscape gardeners created carpet-bed designs with flowers, trimmed grasses, hedges and moss.

Near the spot where Alice had placed her blanket, an imposing white gazebo with ten arches still stands solidly as ever despite assaults by violent storms throughout the years.

Alice opened the lunch basket and passed out neatly wrapped sandwiches to Vincent and Bert. After selecting a sandwich for herself, she put the rest of the food as well as paper plates on the blanket so that all three picnickers could help themselves to whatever they liked to eat.

It was a warm, sunny day. The ocean breezes were light and cool. Alice commented, "The weather is just perfect for a picnic." She inhaled deeply. "Isn't the fresh air invigorating."

Impulsively she removed her sandals. With the graceful form of a muse Alice danced on the grass to imaginary music. Her eyes were fixed on the gazebo almost as if she could see Terpsichore inside playing the cithara.

Delighted by Alice's spontaneous dancing, Vincent applauded her. Bert followed suit, clapping and shouting "bravo!" She made a curtsy and sat down beside her husband.

Bert expressed his feelings: "It is so peaceful here. I can't say the same for Alta Plaza. The last time I was there I heard gunshots. A prostitute was killed. The police caught the killer. He was her pimp. Do you still intend to become a criminal lawyer, Vince? What a rough profession."

"Yes, Bert, I still want to become a lawyer. I shall be leaving National Dance Studios soon to enroll in the university."

Alice looked forlorn. "The Studio won't be the same without you. I had the impression you were disillusioned with the legal system. I once asked you, Vincent, but you never answered. Do you believe in capital punishment?"

"Whether or not I believe in capital punishment is beside the point, Alice. I want to be a lawyer so that I will be in a position to reform the legal system. It not only is badly flawed but also it is not democratic."

"I don't understand. How is the legal system flawed?" questioned Alice.

Vincent paused for a second before answering. "By law, in certain murder trials, a prosecutor must show premeditation on the part of the defendant. Premeditation is the contemplation and planning of an act beforehand, showing intent to commit a crime. It may be evidenced by the fact that the defendant expressed his hatred for the victim and wished him bodily harm. Or it may be evidenced by the fact that the defendant purchased poison before the murder."

"Vincent, I understand what you are saying." Crinkling her nose, as was Alice's habit, she indicated disapproval. "I don't see any flaws."

"Let me explain. A defendant may hide his hatred for the victim. Also, the defendant may have always pretended to be the victim's best friend who wished him well. Or a defendant may have stumbled upon a bottle of poisonous liquid in a vacant lot nowhere near his home and used the poison to murder the victim."

"Vincent, you are speaking way over my head. I sense something is wrong. But I am unable to put my finger on it," Alice had to admit.

"The flaw is in the concept of intent. A defendant can secretly plot to kill somebody for...let's say five years. Without ever having told a soul about his intention, he commits the crime in five minutes. He had nothing to gain except satisfying the sadistic streak in his nature.

"If he keeps his mouth shut, it would be impossible to prove premeditation. Anyhow, would the victim be less dead if the murder was not premeditated."

Bert chimed in unharmoniously. "If a defendant is innocent, he will be acquitted. Not too many guilty defendants are acquitted of murder. The truth comes out sooner or later."

"You are right in one respect," Vincent conceded. "Guilty defendants are acquitted of murder. But if the truth comes out, it is too late. The murderer thumbs his nose at the judicial process and at the victim's heartbroken family.

"He can do so with impunity because he is protected by a senseless law: double jeopardy, which shields cold-blooded murderers by not subjecting a murderer to a second trial for the same crime he previously was tried for.

"The screams of murdered victims tormented by double jeopardy fall on society's deaf ears. Is there any reason in a sane world why an acquitted murderer cannot be retried and convicted should conclusive evidence come to light that he was indeed guilty beyond a reasonable doubt."

While Vincent was talking, Alice was thinking about something else he had said, which prompted her to ask another question. "The legal system may be flawed, but how is it undemocratic?"

"The answer to your question lies in the definition. Pure democratic doctrine pertains to and promotes the interest of the people—all the people...not just a majority...not just a minority.

"When I become a lawyer, I shall make it my goal to change criminal law so that a murdered victim—man, woman, or child—will have the constitutional power, and the right, to determine the murderer's sentence. Whether it is acquittal, life in prison, or capital punishment."

Disagreeing strenuously, Bert's face turned red as a tomato. He exclaimed: "That's impossible! Come on, Vince, the whole idea is crazy. A murdered victim couldn't possibly come back from the grave. Suppose what you are proposing was the law of the land. How the heck could a ghost communicate his will, especially a child ghost?"

"In life it is not impossible, Vincent responded with conviction. This is the way the law of the land would work: Every man and woman would be required to file a form individually with the Department of Justice stating which sentence judges are compelled to pronounce on a person who kills him or her."

Inclined to argue, Bert objected. "You lost the race. Minors are not capable of making such a decision. Do they deserve less justice?"

Vincent had anticipated his friend's argument. "Hold your horses, Bert. You are jumping the gun. Parents would be required to fill out a separate form for each child. When children reached adulthood, they would have the right to change, according to their will, the previously pronounced parental sentence.

"The prerequisite form not only will serve justice but also it will act as a deterrent. A person contemplating murder will be deterred because he will not be able to escape the judgment of his victim.

"Some men dream of conquering outer space despite the dangers and technical obstacles. I dream of conquering murderous crime here on earth despite the dangers and legal obstacles."

FINIS

FIRST INDEX
—PERSONS—

The Dance Histories'
INDEX
of persons and mythical beings

The Dance Histories'
INDEX
of persons and mythical beings

The Dance Histories'
INDEX
of persons and mythical beings

The Dance Histories'
INDEX
of persons and mythical beings

The Dance Histories'
INDEX
of persons and mythical beings

SECOND INDEX
—DANCES—

The Dance Histories'
INDEX
of dances and dance forms

The Dance Histories'
INDEX
of dances and dance forms

The Dance Histories'
INDEX
of dances and dance forms

The Dance Histories'
INDEX
of dances and dance forms